D0482579

RAY OF LIGHT

Center Point
Large Print

Also by Shelley Shepard Gray and
available from Center Point Large Print:

The Days of Redemption Series
 Daybreak

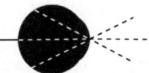

RAY OF LIGHT

The Days of Redemption Series
— Book Two —

SHELLEY SHEPARD GRAY

CENTER POINT LARGE PRINT
THORNDIKE, MAINE

This Center Point Large Print edition is published
in the year 2013 by arrangement with Avon Inspire,
an imprint of HarperCollins Publishers.

Copyright © 2013 by Shelley Shepard Gray.

The text of this Large Print edition is unabridged.
In other aspects, this book may
vary from the original edition.
Printed in the United States of America
on permanent paper.
Set in 16-point Times New Roman type.

ISBN: 978-1-61173-819-3

Library of Congress Cataloging-in-Publication Data

Gray, Shelley Shepard.
  Ray of light : the days of redemption / Shelley Shepard Gray. —
  Center Point Large Print edition.
    pages cm
  ISBN 978-1-61173-819-3 (Library binding : alk. paper)
  1. Amish—Fiction. I. Title.
PS3607.R3966R39 2013b
813'.6—dc23
                                                    2013008075

To Tom.
Because of you, I can be me.

Till at last the day begins
In the east a-breaking,
In the hedges and the whins
Sleeping birds a-waking

~from "Night and Day"
by Robert Louis Stevenson

Light shines on the godly,
and joy on those whose hearts are right.

~Psalm 97:11(KJV)

Chapter One

It hadn't been easy, but Lovina Keim had gotten her way. She was going to be the one to read her grandson's very first letter from Florida aloud.

Holding the envelope carefully on her lap, she adjusted her glasses and waited for her twin granddaughters, husband, and daughter-in-law to get settled. Actually, she was drawing out the moment. It was nice to feel like the focal point of the family once again. Too often she felt like as much of an add-on as her *dawdi haus*.

But, as usual, her granddaughter Viola was anything but patient. "Mommi, open the envelope. We're all here and sitting quietly." Under her breath, she added, "As you insisted."

Lovina heard that, of course. But she pretended not to.

Instead, she shook the envelope importantly. "Patience, Viola. I'll get to it in my own time. After all, none of us makes you rush to share Edward's letters."

"That's because she doesn't share them," Viola's twin, Elsie, said. "At least none of the good parts."

Crossing her ankles primly, Viola glared at her sister. "Ed's letters are different. He's my fiancé, you know."

"I believe we all know that, dear," Viola's mother, Marie, said behind a smile.

Standing behind her rocking chair, Aaron leaned over and pushed the kerosene lantern on the table closer to Lovina. "You'd best read Roman's letter from Florida before this whole family dissolves into another heated discussion."

Her husband had a point. Over the last few months, even the most benign topic seemed to ignite tempers. With a sigh, Lovina carefully opened the envelope, smoothed out Roman's note, and began reading. "Dear Family, Greetings from Pinecraft!"

Elsie chuckled. "He sounds like he's an advertisement."

"Indeed," Lovina said with a small smile. Clearing her throat, she continued. "Now that I've been here for three days, I'm beginning to get into a routine. Every morning, I sit with one of the cousins and drink coffee on the patio, looking out at the ocean. I never get tired of watching the waves crash along the shoreline and can only imagine what it must be like to get used to such a sight."

Marie sighed. "Being at the beach sounds *wunderbaar.*"

"You should go soon, Mamm," Viola said. "I mean, you should go when Daed gets better. . . ."

"Perhaps."

Not wanting to think about Peter's problems,

Lovina rattled the pages a bit to claim everyone's attention again. "Next door, another woman starts her morning the same way as me. She seems to be about my age. She's Amish, too, and has blond hair and blue eyes. She's quite pretty. I hear she's a mother and a widow, but I don't know if that's true or not. But whatever the reason, I can't help but be curious . . . but so far, I've had no reason to speak to her. But maybe one day soon."

Just as Lovina paused for a breath, the room erupted into excited chatter.

As Elsie and Viola discussed who this mystery woman might be, Lovina found her gaze straying to her husband and then felt her stomach drop. Aaron was looking out into the distance with such a heartbreaking expression, she knew he could only be thinking of one thing: his first wife and child.

Little by little, the other occupants noticed, too.

"Dawdi, what is wrong?" Viola asked.

Lovina was just about to tell her nosy granddaughter that not everything was her concern when Aaron slowly stood up.

"I'm all right, child. Roman's note simply made me think of something that happened long ago."

"What was that?"

Aaron looked Lovina's way, shrugged, then said, "It got me thinking about the time I buried my first wife and son."

As Marie, Viola, and Elsie watched him leave the room in shock, Lovina felt her world tilt. She and Aaron had agreed never to talk of that. Tears started to fall on her cheeks as she thought of his heartbroken expression. Even after all this time, it seemed that Aaron still carried a torch for his first, beautiful, perfect wife.

When they all heard the back door close, Viola gripped Elsie's hand. "Grandpa was married before? And had a child? Mamm, did you know about this?"

Even in the dimly lit room, Lovina saw that Marie was rattled. "*Nee.*"

Elsie shook her head in wonder, staring at Lovina with accusation in her eyes. "I assume you knew about this. First we find that Mommi was once an *Englischer*, then that Daed is secretly drinking. Now we find out that Dawdi has been married before. How many secrets does this family have?"

Thinking of her other secrets, the ones she hoped and prayed were buried so deep that they'd never be let out, Lovina shrugged. "Too many to count, it seems." Wearily, she stood up. "I better go see how your grandfather is doing."

No one seemed to notice that Roman's letter floated to the floor, only half read.

Roman Keim wasn't stalking the woman staying in the condominium next door to him at Siesta

Key. He just couldn't seem to stop watching her whenever he could.

It seemed she enjoyed the morning sunrises as much as he did. As the sun continued to rise, he sipped his coffee, wiggled his toes in the sand, and watched Amanda Yoder slip through the white wooden gate that separated the condo properties from the public beach, and walk down the path to the water.

Today she wore an apricot-colored dress that set off her blond hair, prim white *kapp*, and lightly tanned skin. As she walked along in her bare feet he was captivated. Her steps looked light and smooth. Happy. He'd heard that she was a widow. He wondered if it was true.

Actually, she looked like her own ray of sunlight, and he felt himself unable to look away when she tossed down a towel, spread it smooth, then sat right down on it, all while holding a cup of coffee in her right hand.

He was trying to think how he'd ever get the courage to talk to her when his cousin Beth stepped through the open sliding door. "May I join you, Roman? Or are you attempting to find a few moments of peace and quiet?" she asked with a wry smile. "I know we can all get to be a bit overwhelming sometimes."

"Not at all," he said, thinking what a nice change of pace his uncle Aden's family was compared to his own family's exhausting

11

problems. "Of course I'd like your company." He leaned over and pulled another chair closer. "Come sit down."

"*Danke.*" She, too, was sipping coffee and, to his delight, had brought out a thermal carafe. After topping off his cup, she sat beside him and followed his gaze. "Ah, I see you've found Amanda Yoder. Again."

He was embarrassed that his interest was so transparent. "I can't help it if she enjoys the sunrises as much as I do."

"You know, I met her yesterday when Lindy and I were out."

Surprised, he glanced her way. "You did?"

"Uh-huh. My Lindy and her daughter seemed to get along."

Roman struggled to not show his interest. "So, *is* she married?"

"No . . . No, she's not. She's widowed. It seems the rumors we heard about her were true."

"That's too bad," he murmured, trying to do the right thing and think of her loss—and not his interest. "She's a young woman."

"Indeed. Only twenty-five." Cradling her cup, Beth leaned back and closed her eyes. "I don't know the whole story, but she did say that her husband's death was a difficult thing. I guess he lingered for months in pain."

Roman inwardly winced. Her story made his family's troubles seem insignificant in comparison. "Did it happen recently?" he asked before he could remind himself that he shouldn't care.

"I don't know that answer, but I'm guessing no. She doesn't seem to be mourning." Looking at him with a new gleam in her eye, she added, "Actually, Amanda seems like one of the most restful women I've ever come across."

Restful. Now, that was an unusual descriptor. But he fancied it. "Hmm."

Before he knew what was happening, Beth stood up and grabbed his empty left hand. "Come on. Let me introduce you."

"Beth, *nee.* I was merely curious."

"If you're only curious about her, then it won't hurt you to say hello."

"But—"

"Roman Keim, didn't I hear you say that you wanted to experience something new this week?"

"*Jah,* but I was thinking about surfing. . . ."

"Meeting a new woman counts, I believe."

Because she had a point, he let himself be dragged across the gated patio, through the gate, and down the steps to the sand.

As she heard the hubbub behind her, Amanda turned and watched them approach, her eyes brightening when she recognized Beth.

Roman's mouth went dry. Amanda was even prettier up close.

With effort, he forced his expression to remain impassive.

It would never do for her to know how captivated he was by her. At least . . . not yet.

Chapter Two

Even at this distance, Roman realized, Amanda Yoder had a peaceful way about her. As she watched Roman and Beth approach, she didn't look startled or suspicious. Merely curious.

But it was more than that. She was stretched out on her beach towel as if she'd never had a thing to worry about in her life.

It was the exact opposite of the way he functioned. He got up early and usually hit the ground running. He made to-do lists and crossed off each completed task with a dark X to signal his satisfaction. He kept to himself and concentrated on working hard.

Amanda, in contrast, looked as if she never hurried through anything. She seemed like she took the time to enjoy each minute of the day, instead of worrying about plans and goals and what was up ahead.

It was completely attractive.

When she looked his way and smiled slightly, he felt his body's temperature rise another degree.

Most likely, his cheeks were flushed. With effort, Roman looked toward the sea and tried to calm his wayward thoughts.

Beside him, Beth had no such compunction. She was beaming so brightly that it was a wonder Amanda didn't look away to shield her eyes. "Amanda, hi!" she called out. "*Gut matin*! How are you?" she continued, not letting more than the briefest of seconds pass before she continued. "We saw you sitting here alone, so my cousin Roman and I wanted to say hello."

"I hope we're not disturbing you," he said, then cursed his tongue. It was barely seven in the morning, and she'd been sitting alone, obviously enjoying her own company. Of course they were disturbing her.

"You aren't disturbing me in the slightest. I was simply sitting here, enjoying the morning sun," Amanda replied. After glancing his way for a split second, she focused on Beth. "Regina enjoyed playing with Lindy yesterday."

"We should get them together again soon. It's so wonderful that our four-year-olds have found each other. And they play well together, too."

"I've been thinking the same thing."

Beth looked toward Amanda's condo. "Is Regina still asleep?"

"*Jah*. My Gina likes to sleep in, I'm afraid. She's something of a night owl."

"It would be hard to go to sleep early here,"

Roman said. "It's a beautiful area. . . . I don't want to miss a minute of daylight."

As if she was amused, she slowly smiled. "It is a beautiful place. I'm Amanda, by the way."

"Roman Keim."

"Pleased to meet you. Do you live in Indiana as well?"

"Ohio. Where are you from?"

Her smile widened. "I live in Pinecraft."

Without being invited, Beth sat down on the sand. "This is your home? I thought you were on vacation, too."

"Oh, I am on vacation, for sure. I live in town. My, uh, husband's family owns this condominium. They're encouraging me to take a week's rest." She rolled her eyes. "They seem to think I work too much."

Feeling awkward, being the only person standing, Roman sat down as well, stretching his legs as the warm sand shifted around him. "Do you?"

Her eyes widened, then she nodded after a moment's consideration. "I suppose I do. But I don't mind working. To me, it makes the days fly by."

Beth nodded. "My two kids make my days fly by, too. Well, most days."

"Mamm?" Lindy called out from the condo patio. "Mamm, I'm hungry."

Beth scrambled to her feet. "That's my cue to pour cereal," she said with a laugh. "No doubt her *daed* is standing right there, but for some reason Lindy and Cale like me to do the serving."

Amanda chuckled. "That is a mother's duty, for sure."

Backing away as Lindy called out for her again, Beth said, "Amanda, we'll knock on your door later to see if Regina can play."

"See you then," Amanda said with a smile.

With a spray of sand, Beth trotted back to the patio. In a flash, she was out of sight, leaving Roman and Amanda relatively alone.

There in the morning sun, it felt as if they were the only two people on the beach—the only two people smart enough to take time to enjoy the day's glorious start. Reluctantly, Roman realized he should probably get up as well, but he couldn't bring himself to do it. The sand was as soft as powdered sugar, the salty, faintly damp breeze coming off the water felt good on his skin, and he was enjoying the novelty of being one of only two people out on what was usually a very crowded beach.

And then there was his companion.

He thought Amanda was one of the loveliest women he'd ever met. But attracting him more than her pleasing features was the calm way about her.

"So, what is it you do?" he asked. When a line formed between her brows, he clarified. "I mean, what work do you do too much of?"

"Oh! I work at a bakery that my husband's family owns, Pinecraft Pastries. Do you know it?"

"*Nee*." Though she was talking about the bakery, he couldn't help but fixate on the way she spoke about her husband. This was the second time she'd brought him up. Obviously, his cousin had gotten her information wrong. "Does your husband work there, too?" he asked politely.

Her eyes widened. "*Nee*. Oh, no," she blurted. "I guess I need to stop doing that. I keep saying 'husband,' but he's gone. I mean, he went up to heaven two years ago. I'm a widow."

"I'm sorry for your loss." Why did he have to prod her to divulge that? Here he was, making her uncomfortable. He would've thought he could have shown a little bit more tact.

"*Danke*. I am sorry about Wesley, too." Her chin rose. "But I am thankful for my many blessings. I have a sweet daughter and a good life." Leaning back on her hands, she said, "What about you?"

"Me? I'm not married."

"And your work?"

"I work on my family's farm," he began, then realized that was about all he could say. His family was in turmoil, he'd never had a steady girlfriend to speak of, and at the moment, he couldn't seem to count very many blessings. He couldn't think of another thing he did besides work and try to stand apart from everyone else's drama.

"What kind of farming do you do?"

He shrugged, not really wanting to talk about taking care of livestock or walking behind a plow. It all sounded boring and dirty—the exact opposite of life where they were. Here on the beach, everything felt bright and new and clean.

After another second of looking at him expectantly, her warm expression cooled as she got to her feet. "I see. Well, I should probably go inside now."

"So soon?"

Bending down, she shook out the bright turquoise beach towel, then folded it in her arms. "I don't like my Regina to wake up without me being around."

"Well, it was nice to meet you, Amanda. Maybe we'll see each other around this week."

"I imagine we will," she said. "We are neighbors, after all."

Side by side, they walked back to their units, Amanda carrying her towel and empty mug of coffee, Roman empty-handed.

It was obvious to him that she was in no hurry to get to know him.

He wondered if that was because she was still mourning her husband. Or if she simply wasn't interested in him.

Well, he couldn't blame her. Roman realized that he had terribly little to offer. He was reasonably attractive, but not much more than that. He was reserved by nature, and a lifetime of standing on the sidelines and keeping to himself meant there were few bright spots in his life. In his anxiousness to remain calm and collected, he let much of life pass him by.

Back in Berlin, he'd been proud of that fact. Unlike the rest of his family, he'd had little pain, no secrets, and nothing to be embarrassed about.

But now his lack of excitement made him feel curiously flat. One-dimensional instead of three. As if he'd simply existed instead of lived.

It wasn't a good realization. Not at all.

Amanda didn't find it difficult to say goodbye to Roman Keim. Though he was lightly tanned and fit, had handsome features and attractive brown eyes, she found him to be too reserved.

She could understand a man's need for privacy, but not about such things as his occupation or his family.

Roman had reacted to her questions as if she were attempting to learn all his secrets. She definitely hadn't cared to know his secrets or his problems.

After all, she had plenty of her own to worry about.

In her twenty-five years, she'd had more than her share of hardships. She'd been scarred by her husband's failing fight with cancer, and before that, she'd married against her parents' wishes. They'd wanted her to wait to marry.

She'd insisted on marrying at nineteen.

They'd wanted her to live near them in Pennsylvania. She'd wanted to live with Wesley near his family in Florida.

And after Wesley's death, she'd gone her own way again. Instead of succumbing to her parents' demands and moving back to Intercourse to live with them, Amanda had chosen to live in the little house she and Wesley had bought with every last bit of their savings.

Now she was working hard to make the mortgage payments and take care of Regina. Her life was busy, with few moments for regret. Instead, she was surrounded by her daughter's joy. And, if, in the middle of the night, when the chores were done and Regina was asleep, she felt lonely and depressed? Well, that was her concern. Not anyone else's.

She had nothing in common with a man who had little to say for himself other than he worked on his family's farm.

Opening the refrigerator, she pulled out the quart of strawberries she'd bought at the market, and bit into the plumpest, juiciest one she could find.

The sweet taste exploded in her mouth, and she savored the flavors.

And couldn't help but contrast that zing with Roman's curiously bland manner. She wondered why he'd even agreed to walk over with his cousin to say hello.

After shaking out her towel again and hanging it on a rail on the back porch, she poured herself another cup of coffee and sat down at the kitchen table, irritated now.

She'd lied to Roman on the beach. The truth was that Regina wouldn't be up for another hour at the earliest. She just hadn't been eager to sit next to him for another moment, waiting for him to tell her something about himself.

Especially since she'd told him about Wesley being gone.

So, essentially, Roman had ruined her morning routine, her very favorite part of the day while on vacation. It was really too bad that he was staying right next door.

She couldn't very well go back outside without looking rude.

Looking around, she thought about making some jam with those strawberries. They had a refrigerator full of fruit. But that meant hours of working in the kitchen.

And that sounded like too much effort.

Amanda supposed she could read her book. Or practice on those Sudoku puzzles everyone else seemed to do with ease.

But those things didn't really appeal to her, either.

The phone rang and startled her out of her stupor. She eagerly ran to pick it up before it woke Regina.

"Hello?"

"Amanda, it's Marlene, dear. I was thinking of hopping on the bus and visiting Siesta Key today. Would you like me to bring you anything? Or have lunch together?"

Her mother-in-law was a *wonderful-gut* woman. But she was a talker. And a worrywart. And a bit controlling. Having her around today would not be relaxing.

Actually, Amanda had a feeling Marlene was worried about Regina. Marlene often watched Regina when Amanda worked at the bakery. She made no secret about how much she worried about Amanda's withdrawn little girl.

It did no good to tell Marlene that Regina was still recovering from Wesley's death. And that it didn't always make Regina feel better to be surrounded by constant talk and memories of a father she only remembered living in a hospital bed.

When she'd finally accepted her in-laws' invitation to use the condominium, Amanda had promised herself that she'd try to make this a carefree week. A happy one. She was looking forward to a few days of doing what she wanted, when she wanted to do it.

If Marlene stopped by, she would certainly comment on the unswept floors and unmade beds. The crayons strewn across the table and the sand toys in buckets by the back porch.

Worse, she would likely settle in and tell Regina a dozen stories about when her father went to the beach as a child . . . and how sad he'd been when he'd gotten too sick to see the ocean.

That wouldn't do. That didn't sound like the kind of vacation Amanda had in mind.

"*Danke*, Marlene, but I don't need a thing."

"You don't? Oh." She took a breath. "Well, how about I simply stop by for a chat? I'm worried that you're sitting by yourself day after day."

In the privacy of the kitchen, Amanda let herself smile. After all, she'd only been gone for two days. "I haven't been sitting alone."

"No?"

"Not at all. I've made friends with the family next door. Regina has, too. The Keims have a little girl named Lindy, and she's almost exactly Gina's age. They have become fast friends. We've got plans to get together with them later."

"Oh."

Amanda winced. That one sound held multiple meanings, for sure. Wesley's mother loved her very much. But she also envisioned Amanda memorializing Wesley for the rest of her days.

"Thank you for checking on me, Marlene. I'm glad you called."

"Me, too. Is Regina right there with you? Could you put her on? I'd like to say hello."

"Gosh, I'm afraid she's still asleep."

"Still? It's almost eight."

"I know." Purposely, Amanda left the conversation at that. No way did she want to try to explain their late nights to her mother-in-law.

"Oh," she said again. "Well, then . . . I suppose I'll call you later."

"I'll be talkin' with you then. Goodbye, Marlene."

After hanging up, Amanda stared at the empty spot on the beach where she'd been sitting. She wished she were still sitting outside. Then she wouldn't have heard the phone ring or picked it up.

She could've still been sitting quietly, giving thanks for the day and enjoying the antics of the seagulls as they flew in circles over the water.

Now? She was feeling guilty about rejecting her mother-in-law's invitation and about letting Regina stay up late and sleep in.

And she couldn't stop thinking about Roman Keim. The first man to tangle up her thoughts in years. For the first time in a long time, she felt a fresh slice of pain. Almost as if she was suddenly living again.

It was as if one of those rays of light from the rising sun had struck her skin and was blazing inside her.

Waking her up.

Chapter Three

"Momma?" Regina called out from her room. "Momma? You here?"

"I'm right here, dear," Amanda said with a wry smile as she walked to the hallway. "Where else would I be?"

"I don't know," her daughter said around a yawn as her bare feet padded along the white tile floor. Every few feet, she stopped and gathered up her stuffed dog in her arms. When she did that, her toes curled away from the cool surface, as if the cold tile was a little too chilly on her skin.

As she came closer, Amanda noticed Gina's white nightgown was wrinkled, and it fluttered around her ankles. It was the perfect complement to the long brown hair falling in thick waves to her shoulder blades.

As she stopped and yawned yet again, Amanda felt her heart fill with love for her little girl.

Regina always looked like an angel to her, but of course, she wasn't the quiet, peaceful sort.

Not at all!

Instead, Regina had a way about her that brought a smile to your face. Since Wesley's death, she was just a little hesitant, a little apprehensive about new things. But once she felt secure, her smile could warm anyone's heart.

Amanda didn't know how she'd been so blessed to have such a sweet little girl. "Are you hungry, sweet pea?"

"Uh-huh."

"What will it be this morning? Scrambled eggs and bacon?"

"Do we have Pop-Tarts?" Regina's eyes sparkled with mischief.

They'd played this game before. "Pop-Tarts? Here?" she asked in mock surprise.

"We might have them."

"Truly?"

Regina giggled. "*Jah*, Momma."

"Well, if you say so, I suppose I'd best go check." She made a great show of opening several cabinets and looking around in wonder, but of course, it was all in jest. In truth, strawberry Pop-Tarts were their little secret. On vacation, the two of them ate foods that were decidedly different from their usual healthy diet.

Instead of bowls of nutritious oatmeal or eggs and toast, they enjoyed box cereal with tigers and other cartoon characters on the cartons . . . and indulged in their shared love of the boxed pastries. Regina loved the strawberry ones. And Amanda? She didn't even pretend to be healthy— her favorite were the brown sugar cinnamon ones.

Regina got on her tiptoes, trying her best to peek on the counter. "Mamm, do we have any today?"

Her daughter's voice was so hopeful, Amanda

couldn't continue the ruse any longer. "Of course we do, dear."

"*Aeb-beah*?"

"*Jah*. You may have strawberry and I'll have cinnamon sugar. But you must drink your milk, too."

"I will." As Amanda was pouring milk into a sippy cup, Regina asked, "What about you?"

"What about me what?" This time, she really was confused.

"Are you going to drink healthy *millich*, too?"

"*Nee*." She held up her mug. "I'm going to stick to my *kaffi*."

"But Mommi says you don't take care of yourself."

Surprised, Amanda set the carton of milk down. "When did your grandmother say that?"

Eyes wide and innocent, Regina said, "Mommi says you don't take care of yourself like you should. 'Cause you're still missing Daed."

"I'm taking care of myself." Seeing the stress in her daughter's eyes, Amanda felt a flash of annoyance. She didn't appreciate Marlene causing Regina unnecessary worry. Regina had already had more than enough pain and worry in her short life. "Don't worry about me, child. I am fine."

"But—"

"I am perfectly fine, Regina. Please, don't worry that I'm not," she said with a bit more emphasis than she'd intended.

Just as Regina started to get that pout in her lip that signified she was going to argue, Amanda set the red plastic cup on the table and placed one strawberry Pop-Tart on a napkin beside it. "Now, what would you like to do today?"

"Go to the beach."

That was the top of Regina's list always. She loved the beach and hunting for crabs and building sand castles, and swimming, too. Never did she complain about sunscreen or getting salt or sand in her eyes. If she was outside at the beach, she was a happy girl.

"I think we can go to the beach," Amanda said with a smile. "And maybe we can go for a walk and look for shells?"

Regina nodded, as if they were discussing extremely important matters. "And maybe get some ice cream, too?"

"Perhaps. Also, Lindy might have time to play. Would you like that, too?"

"Uh-huh."

"Eat up, then." Amanda smiled, but felt her insides churning with doubts all over again. As much as she loved spending time at the beach with her daughter, something about those few moments with Roman Keim had reminded her of what it was like to have a man by her side. To be more than just a *mamm*.

Yes, she was calm and relatively content. But she was beginning to feel as if she were only half alive. Suddenly, a lazy day at the beach didn't sound as if it were the best day ever.

No, it sounded like another day to pass while she waited for something better to happen.

Was that true? Had she begun to confuse contentment with happiness . . . simply because both were far better than grieving for things that couldn't be?

"Have you heard from Roman again, Marie? Has he called, by chance?" Lovina asked from across the room where she'd been hard at work at the treadle sewing machine for two hours.

They'd been working in almost complete silence, each lost in thought. At least, that was what Marie suspected. For herself, she kept thinking about Peter . . . and wondering how he was going to react to the latest bombshell about his parents.

Marie kept waiting for Lovina to bring up the matter again. But, like always, it seemed she was content to push their problems to one side . . . almost as if they weren't happening.

"Have you heard anything?" Lovina asked again, her voice now tinged with impatience.

"Not a thing." Looking up from the pattern she was tracing for Lorene's wedding dress, she said hesitantly, "Perhaps Roman is trying to forget about us this week. If he stayed in constant touch, he'd hardly be taking a vacation from the goings-on around here." She paused, half expecting Lovina to say something caustic.

But instead, her mother-in-law chuckled. "I suppose you're right. We've had enough drama in this home for a lifetime. If I were a young man, I'd try to stay as far away as I could. At least things seem to be calming down here, I think."

"Are they?" Marie asked. "Lovina, when are you planning to explain this news about Aaron's first wife and son?"

Lovina clenched her hands on her lap. "I wasn't planning to discuss it."

"But we deserve to know more. I mean, if he lost his wife and child . . ."

"It's not my place to discuss my husband's past."

"Since he doesn't seem ready, I wish you would."

The tension in the air thickened. Marie stared at her mother-in-law, tired of playing games.

"We need to have everything out in the open," she whispered. "Only then can we begin to heal."

"Perhaps," Lovina said, but she didn't sound too convinced.

For a moment, Marie was sure Lovina was going to talk. Was finally going to share her feelings and talk about their past. Chest tight with unspent emotion, Marie waited.

And waited.

Then watched as her mother-in-law shook out

her fabric and cleared her throat. "Well, now. At least Viola is happy. That is a blessing, for sure."

So that was going to be the way of it.

With a sigh, Marie relaxed her posture and played along. "It is a blessing, to be sure. I fear the postman is going to start coming to our house with body armor on. Viola practically tackles him when he delivers the mail."

"She's in *lieb*. She can't be faulted for wanting to hear from Edward."

There was such fondness and whimsy in her mother-in-law's voice that Marie looked her way in surprise. "So, you don't think I should be worrying about Viola marrying a missionary? Moving to Belize is a big step."

"It is, but I've never known your daughter to do anything she doesn't want to do. Or to take advice." Carefully clipping some stray threads, Lovina held up the portion of the pink dress she'd just pieced together. "Elsie now has half a dress for Lorene's wedding."

Marie noticed how perfectly the sleeves were attached and again marveled at what a competent, skilled seamstress Lovina was. "Viola's dress is already done, right?"

"It is. As is mine. I only have Elsie's to finish, and yours."

Thinking about her sister-in-law Lorene, her husband's youngest sister, Marie said, "Lorene is as giddy as a schoolgirl, don't you think? I've never known her to be so full of life. It's fun to see."

"It is *gut* to see. It is time she had some giddiness, I think." Smoothing out the pink fabric in front of her, Lovina added, "I truly thought John Miller wasn't the right man for her all those years ago. I thought interfering in her life was the right thing to do."

"Maybe it was? Not everyone is ready for marriage at twenty."

"I should have let her make that choice." Lifting her chin, she gazed at Marie. "I regret my actions."

"It wasn't just your choice, Lovina. Aaron agreed, and both John and Lorene went along with your decision." Smiling slightly, she said, "But could you ever imagine Viola giving in so easily?"

Her mother-in-law chuckled. "I can't even imagine Viola eating carrots! She never was one to do something she didn't want to."

Marie smiled. "I had forgotten about that. When they were little, that was one of the ways Peter and I could tell them apart! Elsie always loved all vegetables. Viola? Not so much."

"Those were the days, weren't they? It was such a busy house, with those twin girls constantly causing mischief."

Marie felt the same spark of nostalgia. "I thought I'd never get a moment's rest when the girls were two and Roman was three. Oh, the three of them together were a handful."

"Remember when Roman announced he wanted to live in the barn, because there were no little girls there? Aaron and I couldn't stop laughing." There was more than a touch of fondness in Lovina's tone . . . and a bit wistfulness, too.

Which made Marie realize she was feeling the absence of another member of their family.

Marie hesitated, then decided to let the cat out of the bag. "I hope Peter will be able to attend Lorene's wedding. They're so close, it would be a shame if he missed it."

"So . . . I don't guess you've heard from him?"

"Only one phone call so far." Her husband had warned her that his time in the alcohol rehabilitation center would be restrictive. But somehow, she'd thought they'd talk more often. She missed him so much. Before he'd left, they'd never been apart more than two nights, when he'd sometimes go with his father to a horse auction. They'd been together so long, she felt his absence acutely, as if she were missing one of her limbs. "I sure hope he calls soon. I wonder why he isn't writing?"

"Are you worried about him, Marie?"

Once again, Lovina's voice was so kind, it almost caught her off guard. Lovina had never been one for sympathy, or understanding people's weaknesses. But ever since it came out that Lovina had grown up English, and that she'd kept it a secret all these years, there was a bit of humility in her that Marie didn't know what to do with.

Little by little, Marie had lowered the defensive wall she'd erected for self-preservation. It was time to speak the truth—even if it made her vulnerable. "Of course I'm worried. I mean, I don't want to think the worst, but hardly hearing from him for two weeks . . . my imagination takes control and I start worrying that he's sick. Or that his drinking problem has gotten worse."

"I doubt he's worse. He can't be getting into any alcohol there. And if he was sick, you would have heard from the center."

"I suppose. I'm just worried."

"Why? He is finally getting help. You should be relieved."

"I'm worried that the center won't be able to help him," she admitted, hating to even say the words out loud. "Or I fear that Peter will lie about his progress, that maybe everyone will think he's cured but he won't be. Or that it will take even longer than we thought." She worried about his faith, too. Was he clinging to it, like she was? Or was the program encouraging him to compromise —or to even set aside his beliefs in order to heal?

"I'm sorry," Marie said. "I sound hateful and selfish, don't I? I do believe in him. And I do love him. It's just, well, at night, I find myself wishing for the way things used to be."

"When he was keeping things from you?"

That was an apt question. Wryly, she said, "I want things to be like I *thought* they were, like I wanted them to be. I'm sorry, Lovina. I hate to burden you with this."

Interrupting her thoughts, her mother-in-law spoke again. "You're not burdening me, Marie. Your worries are justified." Hesitantly, she added, "I have also thought the same things a time or two."

So thankful that Lovina wasn't berating her for not being more positive, she said, "I suppose you don't know what to think of any of us."

Lovina laughed. "If you're thinking that, you would be wrong. I think you've been doing the best you can during a challenging time. Your sister-in-law is practically eloping, she's in a such a rush to get married. Your daughter is engaged and will likely move out of the country, and your husband is in a drug treatment facility. Then, Aaron lets it slip that he was married before. It's a lot to have on one's plate, I think."

The summation of their family's troubles almost made Marie smile. Almost. "And you didn't even mention Elsie." Viola's twin was the sweetest, most even-tempered daughter you could ask for, in great contrast to her twin. But she'd been diagnosed with a degenerative eye disease when she was but a child. Little by little, her dear daughter was going blind.

"That's because I'm not worried about her, Marie, and you shouldn't, either. I feel certain that Elsie will be all right, with the Lord's help. And we'll all be there for her, even if the worst happens and she does go blind."

"I'll always be there for her. As long as I'm able, that is. Thankfully, Viola and Roman have promised to always look after Elsie, too. . . ."

"What are you talking about? What are you two saying about me?" Elsie said sharply from the doorway.

"Nothing, dear," Marie replied quickly, but the look of hurt in her daughter's eyes revealed her fib wasn't appreciated.

"No, I know what I heard." Looking from Lovina to Marie, Elsie scowled. "Mamm, you two were talking about taking care of me as if I were a burden. Weren't you?"

"I was only saying that I want to make sure you always have our help. And you will, *maydel*," Marie said weakly.

"I won't always need your help, Mother. I am not a child."

Looking at Lovina in a silent request for help, Marie bit her lip. "Of course not," she said in a rush.

But Elsie wasn't buying that. "Mamm, I am not helpless."

"I never said you were." Because she didn't know what else to do, Marie found herself snapping at her dear daughter. "Don't put words in my mouth, Elsie."

"I'm not. But you need to stop treating me as if my destiny is living at home and being tended to. I will be just fine."

But how could she be, if she couldn't see? Marie felt her reply stick in her throat.

"We were only discussing your disease, Elsie," Lovina interjected smoothly. "And you are fooling yourself if you don't think your health concerns us all."

"But I am not blind. Yet," she blurted, then turned around and walked away. Two minutes later, they heard her close her bedroom door with a decidedly firm click.

Marie shook her head. "Well, I didn't handle that too well."

After a moment, Lovina spoke. "Roman has every right to enjoy a few days away from here. If I were him, I'd consider staying in Florida even longer. This family of ours has more problems than a squirrel has nuts."

Marie thought that was putting it mildly. Feeling tense, she began carefully cutting fabric. Only when the slow whir of the sewing machine started did she feel able to exhale.

When would things ever settle down?

Chapter Four

One of Roman's favorite things to do in Pinecraft was to watch the older men play shuffleboard. The numerous courts that were scattered around the boardwalks always gave a man someone to compete against, and the congenial conversation that took place around the playing was as entertaining as the game itself.

Usually, men his age played volleyball or basketball, but Roman was partial to the shuffle-board courts. Maybe it was because of his close relationship with his father and grandfather, but whatever the reason, he found he enjoyed watching the older men strategize and joke with each other. And, of course, Roman was always happy to give the men a run for their money when he could.

Walking with his cousins Evan and Jonah, and Beth's husband, Paul, Roman felt almost like his old self . . . or maybe even a better version of his old self.

The guys were an easygoing lot, and the jokes they passed back and forth made his mood lighten even more.

Especially since at the moment they were teasing Evan, who couldn't seem to make a choice between the three girls he was halfheartedly dating at the same time. Three!

"It takes a special man to manage three women, Evan," Paul commented. "I can hardly handle your sister."

Jonah snorted. "That's because she's got two *kinner* underfoot."

"That's not it," Evan countered. "It's because Beth was always difficult. Even when she was four, she was demanding."

Jonah chuckled. "Evan, you're only saying that because she constantly tattled on you."

Evan sighed, like he was the most put-upon man in Florida. "That is true. No matter what, Beth always told on us. Even when we practically begged her not to, she went running off to Mamm and Daed and told them everything."

"You mean *threatened* to tell them everything," Jonah murmured. "I happen to know of a couple of things that never reached our parents' ears."

"Oh, yeah?" A spark of interest lit Evan's expression. "Like what?"

Jonah grinned Roman's way. "I'm not telling. We don't know if we can trust Roman yet."

"Believe me, I've got my own secrets to keep," he said. Though he kind of didn't.

But maybe that was his secret? That he'd lived his life so carefully that he had nothing special to keep close to his heart? Twenty-three years of being dutiful and reserved hadn't brought him much excitement.

Now that he thought about it, it hadn't brought him a great deal of happiness, either.

"Anyway, Paul, we were mighty glad when you married Beth. You got her out of our hair," Jonah said. "The *haus* became much more peaceful when she left."

Paul grinned. "I'm right fond of Beth, even though she is a stickler for order. But as far as our falling in love? Why, I couldn't help myself. From the moment I first saw her, she claimed my heart." He paused. "But even though I'm happily married, I can't help but be interested in Evan's, uh . . . love triangle. It's fun to watch someone else's exciting love life."

"I don't think it's a triangle if there's four involved," Roman pointed out. "Three women, one man."

Jonah grinned. "It's more of a love rectangle. Evan, you're impressive, for sure."

Evan's cheeks were now bright red. "Stop; it's not like that. Well, not that bad! I simply can't choose. And Carrie, Trisha, and Sally all know about each other."

Jonah pretended to choke. "Kind of."

"You're one to talk, *bruder*," Evan retorted, his face still flaming. "You're hardly seeing any girls."

"That's only because you're dating them all. Save some women for the rest of us."

That comment, of course, brought forth a whole new round of ribbing and laughter.

Roman joined in a bit, but mainly stayed an observer. At home with his twin sisters, he was often the odd man out. Though he had many friends, it was rare that a group of them would have so much time to simply hang out. At home, chores and duty were his first priorities.

And, of course, he'd chosen to order his life that way.

Now, for the second time that day, he was regretting that. He would have liked to have fostered this kind of relationship with some of the other men in his church community.

Roman was surprised by these thoughts. Maybe it was being away from all that was familiar and his strict routine that made his heart long for more.

Here, in Pinecraft, the sun was shining on his shoulders as they walked along the boardwalk. At home? All he'd felt lately was a miserable, cold wind.

Here, the scent of sand and ocean permeated the air instead of dirt and horse and manure. Here, people were smiling and joking with each other— not complaining about the snow or the crops or the latest family drama.

Here, he felt as if anything was possible. Surrounded by short sleeves and vibrantly colored dresses and blue skies, everything seemed better.

Even the heat coming off the hot cement felt rejuvenating, like he was suddenly alive after sleeping too long in a dark room.

He envied everyone who was fortunate enough to live in such a place for months at a time.

When a group of men their fathers' ages invited them to play shuffleboard, he jumped right in, but wasn't too disappointed when he was eliminated after the first round. He enjoyed people-watching as much as anything.

Though most of the people were either Mennonite or Amish, being in Pinecraft had afforded Roman an unusual opportunity to be around men and women from all parts of the country. Many Amish came here for vacation, a way to be away from home but still among their people. The relaxed atmosphere gave him the chance to notice the differences in everything from women's *kapps* to men's hats and dialects.

Evan, Jonah, and Paul seemed to understand his preference to simply observe. When Roman took a seat on a bench and stretched out his legs, none of them seemed to care that he was sitting alone and watching the game.

And then he saw her.

Amanda was walking toward him on the sidewalk, her hand clasped around a little girl's. Amanda was wearing the same apricot-colored dress that she'd had on that morning. Her daughter's dress was a more vibrant shade of orange, and the combination of their bright dresses made Roman smile.

As did their expressions. Both were chuckling

as they sidestepped the men who were gathered around the shuffleboard courts and the older ladies who'd stopped for a quick chat.

When they moved off the sidewalk to pet someone's puppy, Roman found himself moving to one side of the bench and craning his neck to see them better.

His focus was probably obvious. Maybe bordering on rude.

But for the life of him, Roman couldn't find the will to look away. Not even when Amanda glanced in his direction, caught sight of him, and then looked a little apprehensive. Obviously she was finding his unwavering attention more than a little off-putting.

The smart thing to do would be to look away. To turn back to the men he was with. To let her have her space.

But instead, he approached her, just as if his feet had a mind of their own.

"Hi, Amanda," he said. "I thought that was you." As if he could have been mistaken.

Politely, Amanda stopped, but she didn't look all that happy about it. "*Gut matin*. Again." She reached for her daughter's hand again—an unmistakable sign of protectiveness.

He ignored it. "I'm Roman," he said to her daughter. "I met your *mamm* this morning on the beach. She said you've been playing with my niece, Lindy."

There, he was no longer a stranger, and had effectively eliminated any opportunity Amanda might have taken to keep them apart.

Looking at him with wide blue eyes, her daughter stared at him warily.

"This is Regina," Amanda said. "She's a little shy."

Roman inwardly chastised himself. He shouldn't have been so gregarious. "It's nice to meet you, Regina," he said softly.

After a few seconds of studying him, she held up the hand Amanda wasn't holding and displayed a bright blue bandage on one of her fingers. "I have a Band-Aid."

He bent down so he could examine it more closely. "Indeed you do. What happened?"

Her lips pursed. "I was stung by a bee."

"Oh my goodness, that hurts."

Patting Regina's back, Amanda said, "She was a brave girl."

After studying Roman again, Regina blurted, "I cried, but I'm okay now." Then she waved her finger as if to illustrate its good condition. "Mamm put some ice on my finger and wrapped it up."

He noticed that pink unicorns decorated the bandage. "I like those horses."

"They're unicorns, not horses. Unicorns have horns. And they're pink," she said solemnly. "They're not real, but I still like them."

"Me, too." He smiled. He liked how protective Amanda was of her daughter, and how Regina continued to carefully study him even as she schooled him on the differences between horses and unicorns.

Straightening, he faced Amanda. "You know, I was just thinking that some ice cream sounded like a good idea. Would you two like to join me?"

Regina's eyes widened. "Can we, Mamm?" she asked in a loud whisper.

Amanda gave him a chiding look that said exactly what she thought about him offering such an invitation in front of her daughter. "We may," she finally said.

Roman grinned. "Great, let me just tell these guys that I'm off. Don't go."

"We won't," Regina said.

As he walked toward his cousins, Roman noticed that his visit with Amanda and her daughter hadn't gone unnoticed. Evan and Jonah were looking at him with knowing grins.

"What's going on?" Paul asked.

"I'm going to take Amanda and her daughter out to ice cream."

All three men looked in their direction. Jonah squinted. "Ain't she our neighbor over at the condo?"

"Yep." Roman grinned.

Evan took a step forward. "What's going on? Do you like her?"

"I don't know. I mean, I just met her."

Evan brazenly looked at her again. "She's pretty."

"Don't look at her anymore. You already have three women," Roman quipped. Then couldn't believe he said such a thing.

Evan held up his hands. "Don't worry, cousin. She's all yours . . . if she'll have you."

Now he felt awkward. "I don't *have* her. Like I said, we just met. We're merely friends." And they weren't even that. Not really.

"Of course," Evan said, smirking.

Jonah and Paul exchanged knowing looks. "I think it's a fine day to go get ice cream. Enjoy yourselves. We'll see you later," Paul said. "You'll take the bus back to Siesta Key?"

"Yep, no problem." The bus ran between the two places regularly.

Roman turned back to Amanda and Regina, half expecting to find that they'd disappeared into the crowd. But there they were, waiting for him to return to their side.

He didn't want to contemplate why that made him feel so good. But it did.

Chapter Five

"I'm sorry about that," Roman said as he strode back to Amanda and Regina. "I didn't want the guys to think I abandoned them."

Amanda coolly looked at the men who were standing like a klatch of housewives, watching their departure with unabashedly amused expressions. "Is everything all right?" she asked. "They looked a little worried."

No, they'd looked amused, Roman mentally corrected. "Everything couldn't be better. They were just giving me grief," he said lightly. "You know how that is."

The look she gave him showed that she knew anything but how that was. "Are they all members of your family?"

"Yeah." Remembering how she'd seemed to like for him to talk a lot, he forced himself to keep talking. "Actually, they're my cousins. They live in Indiana. I'm vacationing with their family. Oh, and one of the men is Beth's husband. Beth's my cousin, too."

She peered at them again, then nodded. "Ah, now I remember Beth talking about them all."

"They're great, the whole family is. I am really having a good time with them. They make me laugh."

Amanda looked at him again, her blue eyes studying him seriously. But this time, he noticed that she was looking at him a little differently, as if she'd suddenly found something new about him that took her by surprise.

He was finding that this new, chatty, gregarious side of him was taking him by surprise, too. Usually, his sisters would have to prod and badger him to chat longer than five minutes.

Now, however, he couldn't seem to stop the words from coming. He seemed to be keeping her interest, though, so that was something, he supposed.

Leaning over to catch Regina's eye, who was walking on the other side of her mother, he said, "So, I can't believe you two are lucky enough to live here in Florida. You're certainly blessed to get to spend all your days in this sunshine."

Regina smiled up at him, looking happy to be included in the conversation. But she didn't say a word.

He tried again. "I love going to the beach. Do you?" When she nodded, he felt like he'd won a prize. "What do you like to do best at the beach?"

After a second's silence, Amanda started to speak. "She likes—"

"Sand castles," Regina whispered.

"I like making those, too," he said gently. "And digging for shells."

Her eyes widened. And then, she did the most

amazing thing. She circled around her mother so she was now walking between the two of them. After clasping Amanda's hand, Regina said, "I like digging for crabs."

Roman glanced at Amanda. She looked stunned. It was obvious that this wasn't Regina's usual habit.

Roman was thrilled by the little girl's acceptance but didn't want to make a big deal about it. So he continued to chat. "You like digging for crabs, do ya? Aren't you scared that one is going to snap at your fingers?"

"One did! I got a Band-Aid then, too. But it wasn't a unicorn one. It was plain old brown."

He was charmed. "I like the unicorns better."

"Me, too."

While Roman laughed, Amanda felt herself smiling, almost against her will. It was rare that people thought to include her little girl in their conversation. It was rarer still for Regina to respond like she was with Roman.

Ever since Wesley got sick, Regina had become withdrawn. More of a worrier and far less outgoing.

But now Amanda was seeing glimpses of her daughter that she'd feared would be gone forever. It was amazing, really, and made her feel flustered.

Roman, on the other hand, looked anything but flustered. Actually, he looked as if he was determined to make sure Regina didn't feel left out in the slightest.

As she watched Regina blossom under Roman's gentle, teasing banter, Amanda felt herself warming toward him. Slowly, her first impression of him was transforming. Truth be told, she was appreciating Roman's efforts to be more open about his life, too.

Instinctively, she knew he was working hard to make himself agreeable to her. He wanted her to like him. That was flattering, indeed. When was the last time someone had made her feel like an attractive woman, not only Wesley's widow?

Gosh, when was the last time she'd even felt attractive? She could barely remember such feelings.

When Wesley was battling cancer, she'd forgotten to eat, neglected to take care of herself. After he passed away, she'd had a series of illnesses—the result of being so rundown and unhealthy.

Then, of course, it had been a struggle to get through every day. She'd worn somber dresses and only focused on Regina. Only over the last eight months had her attitude shifted. She'd started to notice the blue skies again, and the kindness of other people. She'd started to find peace within herself and enjoyment from small things.

And now it looked like she'd almost come full

circle. She'd attracted a handsome man's regard . . . and she didn't hate it.

These realizations made her want to try harder, too. "So, Roman, where is your favorite place to go get ice cream?"

"I don't have a place in mind." With a wink in Regina's direction, he said, "I simply thought it sounded like a good idea."

"I love ice cream," Regina quipped.

Raising his head, he met Amanda's gaze. "Is there somewhere you two like to go? Wherever you have in mind is fine with me."

"I don't have a favorite spot."

"I do! I like the Swirl," Regina exclaimed. "They have orange swirls."

"That sounds great." He looked around. "And where is that shop?"

"Here!" Regina said, pointing to the charming whitewashed building one block away that had silly swirling ice cream pictures on the windows. It also boasted a line of at least twenty people.

"And just in time, too. I was tired of walking," Roman said with a smile. As they got in the back of the line, he looked down at Regina. "What do you think I should get?"

"Orange swirls, just like me."

"What do you usually get, Amanda?"

His voice, warm and kind, melted her more than the sun ever had. "Oh, any kind," she said, because, suddenly, for the life of her, she couldn't remember what she usually ate. Was it vanilla?

"Mamm likes vanilla swirls with rainbow sprinkles," Regina supplied.

Roman looked intrigued. "Rainbow sprinkles, hmm?"

"Ah, only on special occasions."

They continued to stand in line, slowly edging forward as person after person walked away with napkin-wrapped cones.

Amanda had stood in this line dozens of times, but it had been quite some time since she'd felt so happy or relaxed.

What was it about him that intrigued her so much?

Was it the way he was revealing himself to them bit by bit, as if he were peeling back layers of an onion?

Was it his handsome good looks, the way his dark hair, brown eyes, and muscular build looked like it could handle anything? His physique was so different from Wesley's. Wes had been slimmer, shorter. And at the end, of course, far weaker. She'd had to be strong for him.

Roman, on the other hand, looked like he could shoulder any burden easily.

All she knew was that she was terribly eager to learn more about him.

"Tell me about your family," she blurted when he and Regina had a break in their conversation. "I mean, do you have any sisters or brothers?"

"I have two younger sisters. They're twins."

"Twins?" Regina wrinkled her nose. "What does that mean?"

"He means that his sisters are like Jana and Jacob," Amanda said. "They were born at the same time."

"Except my sisters look almost exactly alike," he teased. "Somehow I don't think Jana and Jacob do."

"They don't. One's a boy and the other is a girl."

"It's good they look different then, *jah*?"

"Are you close to them?" Amanda asked.

He grinned. "If you knew them, you'd know that I had no choice but to be close to them." His expression softened. "But seriously, they're great. They're only one year younger than me, so we grew up together. My *mamm* used to say she felt like she had triplets, not twins. One of them, Viola, just got engaged to a missionary."

"And the other? Is she married yet?"

He shook his head. "*Nee*. I don't know if Elsie will ever marry."

Amanda was waiting for him to tell her more when Regina tugged on her apron.

"Mamm?" she whispered, with a pleading look in her eyes.

Offering an apologetic look Roman's way, she bent down. "What is it, dear?"

"Do they like *eis rawm*, too?"

With a soft chuckle, Amanda turned to Roman.

"I'm sorry. My Regina has something of a one-track mind."

"Regina, you didn't want to ask me about that yourself?"

"As I said, sometimes she can be a little shy."

"Oh. Well, *jah*, Regina. My sisters do like ice cream, very much," he said seriously. Just as if Regina's question meant the world to him.

Once again, Amanda felt that little, unexpected pull toward him that caught her off guard. What was it about him that made her feel so comfortable with him? That made her trust even Regina to be around him?

Luckily, she didn't have to ponder that because they had just arrived at the counter. "Ah. Here we are."

"Are you going to get vanilla with sprinkles as usual?" Roman asked with wink.

"Probably . . ."

"You're not feeling adventurous?"

"Not in my ice cream," she replied. Then realized that that had become the case with a lot of things lately. It used to be that she had loved to try new things and meet new people. But after Wesley, even deviating from her regular routine had felt daring.

As Roman leaned down to talk to Regina, Amanda realized that he wasn't merely pretending to be interested in her daughter. He actually was at ease with her. She also couldn't help noticing that Regina didn't seem to be displaying any of the typical reticence she usually did when she was around men.

Did Regina sense in Roman the same thing that she did? That there was something about him that was safe . . . and terribly attractive?

And if she *was* attracted to him, what did that say about her? She knew better than to ever put her heart in danger again. Especially not with someone with whom there was no hope of a future.

"Amanda, do you want your usual small cup of vanilla?" Cheryl, the chatty red-haired *Englischer* who owned the Swirl asked.

With a start, Amanda realized that they were holding up the line. "Sorry," she said with a blush. "I guess my mind wandered."

Cheryl's smiled broadened. "The heat must be getting to you today." Picking up a small dish, she raised her pencil-thin brows. "So, the usual?"

"You know what, I think I'm going to get a medium chocolate-and-vanilla swirl in a cone today." She paused, then added, "And I'll have it dipped in chocolate, too."

Cheryl's brows went even higher. "Well, I'll be. Wonders never cease. I'll get that for you in a jiffy."

As Regina gaped, Roman grinned widely. "Care to tell me why your order is such a big deal?"

"I've been coming here for years. Every single

time, I've always gotten the same thing. A habit, I guess you might call it."

"But today it was time for a change?"

"*Jah*. Today, it was time for a change." Of course, the ice cream was the least of it—not that he needed to know that. She shook her head in embarrassment. "That doesn't say much about me, does it? I mean a change in an ice cream order shouldn't be such a big deal."

"I disagree," he murmured. "I think it says a whole lot about you. And I think it's all good, Amanda."

After handing Amanda her chocolate-covered cone, Cheryl turned to him. "And for you?"

"It's time for me to live dangerously, too. I'll have the same," he said.

"And me, three?" Regina asked.

"*Nee*," Amanda said with a shiver. "That is far too much for you. You may have your usual."

"Oh, all right."

When Cheryl handed out Regina's cone, Roman pulled out his wallet. "I've got this."

"Roman—"

"It's my idea, my treat."

"But—"

"It's ice cream. Let me."

"*Danke*," she said, deciding to give in gracefully.

After they were all armed with more napkins, Regina having her favorite—the small orange swirl—they walked to a bench and sat down together in a row, each of them enjoying the treat and seeming to enjoy the company and the sunny day just as much.

Amanda kicked her feet out a bit, liking the way the sun heated her ankles. Liking all of it.

Until she spied her mother-in-law looking at her across the way. "Uh-oh," she murmured before realizing that she had spoken out loud.

Roman turned to her in concern. "What's wrong?"

"It's nothing wrong, but things might be a little uncomfortable," she whispered. "That's my mother-in-law, and I'm afraid she's going to be mighty surprised to see me with you."

"Just tell me what you want me to say."

"You can say whatever you want . . . just don't be surprised if she peppers you with questions."

The moment Regina spied her grandmother, she stood up and ran to her, chattering all about the beach and Pop-Tarts and Roman and the ice cream.

As Marlene listened to her, her expression became more and more concerned.

With a sinking feeling, Amanda stayed where she was. If she was going to have to explain herself in front of all of Pinecraft, she preferred to do it from where she was. She was determined to stand her ground, even if she was, well, sitting.

When Regina finally took a breath, Marlene

took Regina's free hand and walked over to them. "Hello, Amanda. You said you were going to stay at the *haus* today. And that Regina was going to be with a friend."

"Some of our plans changed, though we do still hope to see Lindy later today. Um, Marlene, please meet Roman Keim. Roman, this is Marlene Yoder. My mother-in-law."

Roman was already standing up. "Nice to meet you."

Cool blue eyes looked him over before nodding, and then deliberately ignoring him. "Amanda, what in the world is going on?"

"We're eating ice cream."

"That is not what I meant." Her lips pursed, then she continued. "Why don't you and Regina come with me to lunch?"

"*Danke*, but no. As you can see, we're eating ice cream," she protested lightly. "Plus, we have other things planned."

"We do?" Regina asked. "What are we doing?"

"We have a play date with Lindy, of course."

As she'd hoped, the news brought a bright smile to her daughter's face. "I like Lindy."

"And she likes you, dear." Turning to her mother-in-law, she said, "It was nice to see you, Marlene, but I'm afraid we're going to continue with our plans."

"Plans."

"*Jah*. We're going to be fairly busy the rest of

the day," she said firmly. Getting to her feet, she said, "Roman, let's go ahead and take that walk to the park you told me about."

Luckily, he nodded, like he had any idea what she was talking about. "Whatever you want is fine with me. It's a great walk." Bending slightly, he smiled at her daughter. "Regina, are you ready?"

"Uh-huh."

Amanda liked how he called her daughter over. Even more, she liked how Regina answered with a happy smile. For a moment, they looked like a family. And though it hurt to think that she could be in a family without Wesley, it didn't hurt quite as badly as she had thought it would.

"Amanda, I will call you this afternoon. We'll talk then."

"If I'm home, I guess we will. Good day, Marlene."

Roman blinked, then reached for Regina's hand. "Let's go to the park."

"Yay!" Regina exclaimed, just as if they did this all the time.

Amanda found herself smiling, too, as they walked down the boardwalk, the three of them a little unit. It felt nice. Almost perfect.

All she had to do was not think about how much she'd just upset her mother-in-law.

And how for just for a moment, she hadn't cared.

Chapter Six

"Viola, another letter came for you today," Nancy called out when Viola entered the staff room at Daybreak to have lunch. "I put it on the corner of my desk."

"*Danke.*" Eagerly, Viola ran to the front office and snatched up the letter that was, indeed, waiting for her on the receptionist's desk. Though her family thought it was silly, she'd begun to ask Edward to mail some of his letters to her at Daybreak. Otherwise, every letter she received was commented upon. Sometimes she just wanted to read Ed's letters in private.

Because no one was there to see, she ran her finger over her neatly printed name and address on the envelope, thinking how Edward had written it all just days ago.

Then, feeling giddy and more than a little self-conscious, she quickly walked to one of the cozy conversational areas down the hall to read his latest note from Belize.

The irony of her actions didn't escape her. For almost a year before she and Ed had met in person, she'd been practically forced to listen to every one of Ed's letters. His father, Atle, had received each one with pride, and had eagerly shared his son's news with everyone and anyone—whether they'd expressed a desire to hear about Edward's mission work or not.

But while Atle had glowed with pride about his son's work, Viola had inwardly seethed. Accustomed to managing everyone and everything around her, she'd been sure Ed should have put his father's needs first and stayed in Berlin. For some reason, everything that Ed had written about his hard work in Nicaragua had struck her as selfish.

Now, she realized that she'd taken a bunch of misconceptions about Ed and had wrapped them in a tight ball of self-righteousness.

But a funny thing had happened when she and Ed had met—sparks had flown between them, right about the time that she'd realized that she'd jumped to conclusions that weren't right at all. Before long, she'd fallen for his good looks and charming ways.

The next thing she knew, they were trading barbs and flirting with each other. And not too long after that?

They'd been falling in love.

No one had been happier about the new developments than Atle, of course. The gregarious, opinionated old man loved his son and wanted him happy. He'd thought all along that the two of them would make a good couple, and it looked as if he'd been right.

He'd loved pointing that out, too.

Now she and Ed were engaged. After much discussion, they'd agreed that, though it would be difficult, they would have to live apart for six months. That would give Ed time to concentrate on his new job as director of Christian Aid Ministries Association's mission in Belize.

It also gave her family time to plan the wedding she'd always dreamed of, and, of course, it gave her time to get used to the big changes that were happening in her life. In just a few short months, she, too, would be traveling to another country. This time, as a missionary's wife. It was thrilling and nerve-wracking, too.

Moving far away from her whole family scared her. And, in the middle of the night, when she rolled over in bed and spied her twin sister Elsie across the room on her own bed, Viola wasn't even sure if her heart would be able to stand living so far away from her sister. They were closer than close, and added to that was how much Viola worried about Elsie's illness. Elsie's sight was steadily becoming worse, and Viola knew it was just a matter of time before Elsie was going to be blind.

Sometimes Viola doubted every decision she'd recently made. She wondered how she was ever going to be able to leave her family for the brand-new love of a man who she'd really only spent a few weeks with.

But then she'd get a phone call or a letter from Ed and all her worries would fade away and she'd realize that what was happening was meant to happen. She and Edward were meant to be together, and she couldn't prioritize everyone else's happiness above her own.

Satisfied that she was completely alone, she opened the envelope and carefully unfolded the letter.

Dear Viola,
   Have I told you about the pretty sunsets over the ocean?

She'd just begun to smile when Gretta, Ed's little dachshund that was now the retirement home's unofficial mascot, trotted over. As if she read Viola's mind, she curled around Viola's feet . . . just like she, too, was anxious to hear more about her former owner.

Happy to have Gretta's quiet comfort, Viola scooped up the dog and set her next to her on the couch.

Gretta wagged her tail, obviously pleased with the special treatment.

"Just imagine, Gretta. In a week, I'll be going to visit Ed and we'll be watching the sunsets over the ocean together. Won't that be something?"

With a dreamy sigh, she continued to read.

   I've begun walking to the beach on Friday nights with two other men from the mission.

We rush to make it there just before the sun begins its descent. Once there, we take off our work boots and roll up our pant legs and walk on the sand, letting the warm grains underfoot ease our tired, sore feet. Then, we step into the warm, salty water and enjoy the sensation of complete relaxation.

When the sun starts to set, we sit on an old cement embankment. It's cracked and worn, but makes a perfect perch to watch the sun slowly glide into the sea, marking the end of another day. And another week.

Viola grinned and rubbed the dog behind her ears before continuing to read.

It's moments like that when I miss you the most, Viola. When I have time to breathe deep and count my blessings. It's then that I realize that having you here will only help me—and the people we serve, too. You've become a part of me that I miss when I'm without you.

Once the sun sets and the orange and red waves turn dark again, we hike back to the mission's compound, feeling refreshed and ready to tackle whatever comes our way again. I know when you are here, too, I'll even be feeling more at ease. I feel certain that we'll have a wonderful life here together, V. I promise I'll do everything I can to make it so.

Viola felt her eyes become damp with unshed tears as she once again contemplated what her life would have been like if she'd never given him a chance. If she'd never given herself the opportunity to learn and grow and change. If she'd only let her common sense guide her . . . instead of her heart.

But, of course, it was no secret what would have happened. She would have continued to be alone and self-centered. But most of all, she would have been fighting off the feeling that there was something more for her out there . . . if she wasn't afraid to go out and look.

"I'm so lucky and blessed, Gretta. So lucky, so blessed."

And with that, Gretta snuggled closer and closed her eyes, reminding Viola that the little dog had been abandoned and was living alone outside in the elements before Edward had brought her into his life.

Funny, though Viola had been living with her family, she too, felt as if her life had become better under Edward's care. He'd become her comfort, her own particularly vibrant ray of light.

Regina had fallen asleep while playing with her stuffed animals on the floor. Amanda lightly covered her with a thin blanket, then quietly tiptoed outside, leaving the glass sliding door ajar in case Regina woke with a start and needed her.

As was her habit, she brought out her crochet hook, intending to work on her latest project—a shawl for Wesley's grandmother's birthday. But she couldn't seem to persuade herself to pull out the yarn.

No, all she seemed to want to do was sit in the sun and spend a few moments enjoying the solitude.

"Which is what a vacation is for, you goose," she murmured to herself. "You're supposed to read and relax. Not work on your to-do list."

Hearing her own voice, Amanda winced. When had she begun to talk to herself, anyway? When she got engaged? Pregnant with Regina?

It had been when she'd been sitting by Wesley's bedside in the hospital, of course.

When he'd fallen into an uneasy slumber—on account of the many medicines he'd been given to combat the pain of the disease—she'd begun talking to him. Telling him about her day. About every little thing that Regina did.

Then, just to have something to talk about, she'd start telling him stories about her childhood. Over time, she'd begun to talk aloud just to help herself deal with all the sadness that had welled up inside her. She'd felt like she had to talk about everything; otherwise, it would get stuck inside and make her sick, too.

And she'd already been so very tired and heartsick.

Wesley's decline had lasted for months. Long enough for her chatty vigils to become a habit. After his death, she'd taken to talking to herself when she'd known she was alone. The habit felt comforting to her in a strange way. It was now something she was used to.

But living without Wesley? That was something she wasn't used to at all.

Now, she realized with a start, things had changed again. After two years, the daily emptiness that had been her constant companion had slowly abated. Oh, the pain was still there, but it wasn't as sharp or obtrusive as it used to be.

Now, missing Wesley wasn't the first thing she experienced in the morning, or the last thing she thought of before she went to sleep. She no longer thought about him every waking moment, instead thinking of him at odd times. His memory no longer brought her to tears, and she'd begun to remember their life together in a distant, almost melancholy way.

Though this transition wasn't something she was altogether comfortable with, Amanda certainly welcomed the relief. For so long she'd felt like a woman twice her age.

"Being a widow isn't for the faint of heart," she told herself. On the heels of that, she remembered an old saying of her aunt's: There is no strength where there is no struggle.

That saying had a lot of truth to it.

But sometimes, even the truth didn't bring the sort of comfort she craved.

Oh, but she hated these bouts of depression! What she needed to do was think of her blessings.

"You have Regina," she said out loud. She had Wesley's family, too. And even though Marlene was determined to keep Amanda wrapped in grief, she'd always been there for her, and that was a blessing.

Her own family was still back in Pennsylvania. And though she loved them, they'd been distant witnesses to everything she'd gone through with her husband. Never had she considered moving near them.

But now, for the first time, she wondered what she was giving up by embracing only her past with Wesley.

"You should call and write your family more often. And while you're at it, pray about your fear of moving on, Amanda," she told herself sternly. "Every time you try to give up another part of your life with Wesley, it's brought you to tears. Why, it took you six months to even take his clothes out of the house."

The memory of boxing his clothes still made her cringe. It had taken her almost three hours to pack one large box, and almost another one to carefully seal the box with packing tape.

Just when she was about to scold herself a little

more, she noticed Roman walking on the beach with a dog, of all things. The shaggy yellow dog was darting along the shoreline, sniffing the sand, scampering into the water, then rushing out with surprising speed.

Intrigued, she walked to the white picket fence and leaned her elbows along the top of it.

Roman held the dog's leash with one hand, but gave the animal enough leeway so that he could race around exuberantly. He'd run to the waves, then dart back out and shake vigorously, spraying water everywhere, like a wayward sprinkler.

Then, next thing she knew, the dog was back in the waves, dipping its nose in, darting here and there, barking happily.

He was a furry, soggy, noisy mess.

And Roman looked as if he was enjoying every minute of its company.

She was mesmerized by the dog playing in the water and by Roman's lack of concern about getting wet or sandy. Suddenly, she ached to be so carefree, so unbound by rules of propriety, or by responsibility. She yearned to be completely happy—exuberant. If only for a moment.

She realized with a start that it didn't matter if her conscience told her to be more careful with her heart—she simply wanted to be happy.

As Roman stopped almost directly in front of her, Amanda also realized she'd become attracted to Roman Keim. Why else would her heart have started beating a little bit faster . . . just because he was around?

In fact, she was so mesmerized . . . she was struck silent. Fancy that.

When the dog barked again, then darted after a crab, Roman laughed. Standing there watching, Amanda chuckled, too.

Roman looked her way, paused, and raised a hand.

Without thinking, she called out, "You've got yourself quite a dog there!"

"You don't know the half of it!" he called back with a grin, then got yanked as the shaggy dog practically galloped into an approaching wave.

"Watch out!" Amanda cried out with a laugh.

And managed to wake Regina up from her nap.

"Momma?" she asked as she sleepily sat up. "Who are you yelling at? And is that a dog barking?"

"I was yelling at Roman. He's walking a dog. Well, it's kind of walking him."

Scrambling to her feet, Regina walked to the open door and peered out to where Amanda was looking, then gazed at the pair in wonder.

"Momma, how did he get a dog? Where did it come from?"

"I have no idea." As the dog scampered back into the water, then shook himself, making the coarse-looking golden fur stand on end, Amanda said, "But it sure looks like a happy dog, doesn't it?"

"Uh-huh." With wide eyes, she added, "Mamm, do you think we could go see it?"

"If you want."

Her hand on the gate, Regina asked, "Do you think Roman will let me pet it?"

"It's all wet. Do you want to?"

"Uh-huh."

"Well, it doesn't hurt to ask if we can," Amanda said as she smoothed back her hair and shook out her teal dress. "Are you ready to go see them now? Would you rather have a snack first?"

But that was a silly question, of course. Because no sooner had she half offered the invitation than had Regina clicked open the gate and trotted toward Roman, her bright pink dress flying up around her ankles. "Roman! Roman, hi! It's me, Regina!"

Amanda was so shocked, she almost called out to Regina to come right back. But the scene that unfolded before her rendered her almost speechless.

There was her quiet Regina running to Roman, a big, bright smile on her face.

And there was Roman turning to her and greeting her with a broad grin.

And then, to Amanda's surprise, Regina held out her hand for Roman to take. Roman took it easily, then looked for Amanda. When he spied her, that warm gaze was like something out of a silly daydream. It was heated and earnest, sweet and sincere.

All directed at her.

It took everything Amanda had not to sigh. Instead, she forced herself to walk toward Roman and Regina and that rambunctious golden dog as sedately as she could.

After all, it wasn't as if anything could ever happen between the two of them. He was a farmer from Ohio. And she?

She was Wesley's widow.

Chapter Seven

For two days Marie had stewed about her conversation with Lovina. For two days, she'd contemplated keeping quiet. To allow her in-laws to keep the story about Aaron's first wife and son to themselves.

But then she realized that they could never go back to how things used to be. The proverbial cat was out of the bag and it certainly wasn't about to sneak back in.

Which was why she found herself standing outside the barn, working hard to gather her courage before confronting her father-in-law. Even though things were going to be mighty uncomfortable, it was time to really talk.

With a new resolve, she entered the barn, where Aaron was currying Chester.

"I wondered when you were going to come inside," he said over his shoulder. "What have you been stewing about out there?"

"I wanted to talk to you about your first wife and son."

After a brief pause, he set down the curry brush and turned to her. "Marie, it's really none of your concern."

"I think it is. Aaron, I've been a part of this family for over twenty years."

"Yes, but—"

"Aaron, you foisted this news on my family, then left, like we deserved no explanations."

"And you think you do deserve one?"

She forced herself to meet his gaze directly. "*Jah.*"

After guiding Chester back into his stall, he walked over to where she stood and sat down on a hay bale. "What is it you want to know?"

"I just want you to talk to me. Just tell me a little of the story." She was so tired of the way they'd been communicating lately, as if every little bit of information was something to be stingy with, and whoever revealed the most would be the loser.

His eyes narrowed, then he brushed his hands over his eyes. "I met Laura Beth when I was fourteen. She and her family had recently moved to our church district. Almost immediately, I knew she was the girl for me." He paused, then finished simply. "We married at eighteen."

"That was young."

Something flashed in his eyes. "Perhaps it was. It didn't feel that way at the time, though. You know how it is . . . when you're that age."

She nodded. "When you're eighteen, you don't feel young. You feel ready for anything." Smiling slightly, she added, "And now that I'm in my forties? Some days I feel like I don't know anything."

"The Lord gives us pride instead of experience when we're teenagers." He met her smile, then looked beyond her, as if he were peering into another time. "A year after Laura Beth and I married, we had Ben. I thought my life was perfect . . . and that it would always be that way."

"Then they died?"

He nodded. After a pause, he said haltingly, "Laura Beth was driving in the buggy in some sleet. Something happened, no one knows what. Maybe she lost control, maybe the horse got spooked? But she lost control and was hit by an oncoming car." He swallowed hard. "The doctors said she and Ben died instantly."

Marie felt tears prick her eyes. It was such a sad story, such a waste. "Aaron, why all the secrecy? It was a heartbreaking accident, for sure, and I would think you would want your new family to honor your past and your first family."

A muscle jumped in his cheek as he visibly reined in his emotions. "Not everyone thought it was an accident."

"What do you mean?" She hated to press, but Marie instinctively knew that if she didn't get the full story now, it would be a long time before Aaron would ever talk about Laura Beth and Ben again.

"Some folks thought it was my fault," he said.

"Yours?"

Abruptly, he stood up, turning his back to her. "Laura Beth was in that buggy because of me. We'd had words. I'd said some foolish things. I . . . I let my temper get the best of me."

She couldn't imagine such a thing. "Aaron, I've never seen you lose your temper."

He gazed at her, his expression soft with regret. "I was different back then, Marie. I used to be something of a loose cannon."

"Who blamed you? Her family?"

"But of course. Her brother promised he'd never forget her death . . . and that he would make sure I never forgot it, either."

"What did he mean by that?"

He blinked. And just like that, Marie knew their discussion had drawn to a close. He'd told her as much as he wanted to. "I'll see you at supper, Marie. I have a lot to do since Peter and Roman ain't here. You understand, I am sure."

She nodded as she watched him retreat from the

barn, headed toward the fields. Well, she'd gotten the answers to her questions. But instead of relieving her mind, it had only served to spark more questions and worry.

Lost in thought, she walked back to the house, and wondered if she was going to be able to ever let this new development go.

The moment Goldie spied the crab in the water, the shelter dog seemed determined to make it her own. Though Roman had tried to warn her about making friends with the creature, the dog refused to heed him.

"Have it your way, Goldie," he said. "But if your nose gets pinched, don't come crying to me."

Over and over, she'd spy the small critter, dig furiously for it, then jump away the moment she came face-to-face with an angry claw. She'd look at Roman in wonder, he'd shrug and tell her he told her so . . . then it would begin again.

"Careful, Goldie. That crab ain't going to like you disturbing it for much longer. Pretty soon it'll be the one chasing you!"

As he'd expected, the dog barked, promptly ignored his warning, and pounced.

And this time came out the loser. The crab snapped at her and its swipe stung Goldie's nose. With a yelp, she jumped back and looked at Roman in confusion.

"It's the way of it, *hund*," he said kindly. "Each

of God's creatures has ways of keeping themselves safe. That would be the crab's."

The shelter dog seemed to take the warning to heart. After a moment, she once again seemed happy to trot by his side.

Until Regina approached.

The minute Goldie saw the little girl scampering toward them, her bright pink dress pulled up to her knees, a bright smile plastered across her face, Goldie seemed mesmerized. Even the sea crab was forgotten.

"She's had the same effect on me, pup," Roman murmured. "But of course, it's her mother who makes me stop and stare even when I shouldn't. She's a pretty thing, for sure. Ain't so?"

"Roman, Roman it's me, Regina!"

"I would know you anywhere, silly," he said as he greeted her. "What brings you out to the beach?"

"Mamm and I were watching you and your *hund*. She's pretty."

Roman looked at Goldie again. The dog was wet and scruffy and covered with a good coating of sand and salt water. "She's a mess, that's what she is." After making sure Goldie wasn't about to jump or be too rough, he motioned Regina closer. "Want to say hello to her? Her name is Goldie."

"Uh-huh."

"Come on then." Carefully, he showed Regina how to let the dog smell her hand. After a few exploratory sniffs, Goldie was ready to play. She nudged Regina's hand. With a smile, Regina petted the dog.

He'd just showed Regina Goldie's dog tag when Amanda caught up. "Did you get yourself a dog, Roman?" she asked.

"*Nee.* Just borrowing one. I discovered that there's an animal shelter here that will let you take walks with the dogs for a few hours at a time. I decided to take them up on the offer."

"I've lived here all my life and never knew there was such a thing."

"Perhaps you weren't missing your own animals like I was," he said easily. Plus he had to admit to having a soft spot for an animal with no home. Every creature needed a place to live, he thought.

Amanda bent down and scratched Goldie between her ears. Goldie showed her appreciation by tilting her head just enough to give Amanda a swift, wet lick.

Amanda lifted her hand and wrinkled her nose. "Ick!"

Regina giggled. "She likes you, Mamm."

"I guess so."

To Roman's surprise, she bent a little and gave the dog a quick hug. "You're a sweet thing, for sure."

"You're going to get all wet and sandy," Roman warned.

Amanda looked fondly at her daughter. "I'm a mother. One gets used to becoming a mess."

"I can't imagine you ever being a mess," he blurted before he could stop himself.

Amanda smiled, but immediately a faint blush colored her cheeks.

"I'm sorry. Sometimes I speak without thinking. But I do, ah, think you are pretty."

"*Danke.*" She stood up and turned away.

Roman decided he had better retreat a bit and keep things light. "So, would you girls like to walk with us? We've been walking and chasing sticks and annoying crabs."

"We can for a few minutes, but then Regina has a play date with Lindy."

Roman noticed his cousin Beth and Lindy sitting on their back patio, obviously waiting for Regina. "How about we walk you over to Lindy, Regina?"

At the mention of Lindy, Regina whispered to Amanda, then after giving her a brief hug, ran toward Lindy.

He and Amanda watched as Beth and Lindy ran to meet Regina halfway, gave them a little wave, then retreated inside.

Roman was surprised at how quickly Regina had left her mother's side. "That was quick."

"She's usually not so eager to leave me, but I do believe they're going to play house. Regina loves that."

After another few moments, he gestured to Goldie. "Would you still like to stroll?"

Amanda looked doubtful. "If I do . . ."

"I promise, we'll keep things easy. I won't tell you again about how pretty I think you are."

"Roman!"

"I'm sorry. From now on, we'll only talk about what you want to talk about."

"Or not talk at all?" She smiled when she said it, so he wasn't sure if she was testing him or not.

But he didn't care. She was the first woman he'd ever not been able to stop thinking about. She was the first woman who'd intrigued him enough to want to push aside all the boundaries he'd erected in order to keep others at a distance.

With her, he didn't think he could ever get too close. Just thinking about where his mind was going made him feel even more off-kilter.

But no matter what, he was willing to pass all her tests.

"It's okay not to talk at all," he murmured. Deciding to get them going, he started walking, Goldie happily trotting by his side.

After a second's pause, Amanda followed.

Ah. He'd just gotten his way. Roman had never tried so hard to hide a smile.

Walking by Roman's side, Amanda chastised herself. She'd heard his compliment. She'd seen the look in his eyes. Wesley had once looked at her like that, as if he was smitten.

But she certainly was not. She had no business encouraging Roman's flirtations. She'd already found love. She'd already had courtship and romance and marriage. No person should expect more in a lifetime.

Especially since she had a daughter, too. Regina was almost the spitting image of her father, with her dark wavy hair. Watching Regina every day was a constant reminder of Wesley, and that was a good thing. A wonderful thing.

So why did she seem unable to ignore Roman?

Roman was being true to his word. He'd stayed silent, content to watch the dog's antics.

But now Amanda realized she was ready for something more. "So, what possesses a man to want to borrow animals?"

He shrugged. "At home, I work in the fields, of course, but my favorite chores involve the animals." He looked at her. "Perhaps you think that's strange?"

"Not at all, though I have to admit that I don't have much experience with farms. Actually, I've never had a pet."

"Not even a cat?"

"Not a one."

When she noticed his grin, she felt slightly defensive. "What do you find so amusing?"

"Only that in my experience, it's rare to find an

Amish woman who's not used to farm life. Back in Berlin, most people live on farms. Those that don't work in an offshoot of a farm—like a cheese shop. And almost all of us have a horse or raise chickens or at least have a barn cat."

"If you lived here, you'd meet a great many women and men who are the same as me. The Amish lifestyle is different down here. But it's not like I've never been around animals. I did grow up in Pennsylvania."

"I don't mean to sound critical," he replied, looking a bit contrite. "It's just unusual to me. That's all."

"Tell me about Berlin. I suppose it's much different in the winter."

He laughed. "It's about as different as night and day! Right now, it's terribly cold and snowy in Ohio, even though it's the beginning of March. We still get lots of snow into April there. Right now, you'd be hitching up your sleigh in heavy snow, and bundling up in coats and cloaks and scarves and mittens."

"And?"

"And it's hilly there." He looked out into the distance, just as if he were staring at a giant postcard in front of him. "Really hilly. The roads are winding, and there are lots of trees. In the fall, the leaves turn orange and yellow and gold. Tourists come from all over, just to look at them."

This time, she couldn't hold back a smile. "Tourists come to see leaves?"

"They come for more than that, I reckon. It's peaceful. Quiet. Out in Holmes County, the pace is slower, and not simply because we're Amish. You have to live more slowly because we're dependent on the Lord's seasons and His weather."

"The leaves are all gone now, right?"

He nodded. "Yep. The trees are bare, but that's okay, because you can see the red cardinals that much better. Or winter hares. And deer."

"You have deer?"

"We sure do. But not as pets of course . . . they just wander around. Sometimes I'll be out in the barn with our horse, cracking the film of ice that's formed on the water troughs, when I'll look up and see a pair of bucks. It's a lovely sight."

The picture he'd painted captured her interest, spurring her imagination. "Maybe one day I'll go up and see this Berlin."

"You should. You and Regina can come up on the Pioneer Trails bus and stay with us."

"Stay with you?" she blurted, taken aback.

"I live in a pretty big *haus*, my family's lived there for quite a while. Anyway, when you come, me and my family could show you around. You can visit my aunt Lorene's place of work—the cheese shop." He winked. "We'll even drive you out to Walnut Creek and Sugarcreek. There's a lot to see."

She laughed, because they were only pretending that she'd ever go up north. That she'd ever see him after he left. "You almost sound homesick."

He slowed down and looked at her more carefully. "Not at all. I like home, but I needed a break. I like it here, too. I think you're a lucky woman, to live this close to the ocean."

Amanda flinched. He was the first person in years to mention that she was lucky about anything. Most people looked at her in pity.

"Oh. I guess I stuck my foot in my mouth again, haven't I? I realize, of course, that you've lost your husband."

"Actually, I was just thinking how grateful I am that you reminded me of my blessings. Sometimes, it's very tempting to only think about what I've lost and how different my life is from how I'd hoped it would be."

He glanced at her for a long moment, his eyes serious, his gaze tender. Finally, he said, "It sounds like you had a good marriage."

"I did. The best."

Something flashed in his eyes, right before he looked forward again. "I am sorry about your loss."

"*Danke*. My Wesley, he was a good man. He would have been a wonderful husband to me forever, I think. But I have Regina and Wesley's family."

"His family?"

"Oh, yes. As I said, it's their condominium that I'm staying in." Feeling a little braver, she said, "This is the first time since my husband died that I've done something on my own."

"Doing something for the first time is always hard. Were you scared?"

"Honestly? A little bit. Before I was married, I was part of a big family. And spoiled enough to be born number six out of eight children."

He raised a brow. "I've never heard of anyone calling themselves spoiled because they were from a large family. Usually that means they are used to sharing."

"I'm used to sharing, but that's not what I was thinking of. Instead, I was thinking of the gift of privacy. And of being alone. If I had been the eldest girl, I'm sure I would have had to watch over the other *kinner*. But because I was one of the younger siblings, I didn't have to do much of that. So I developed a healthy taste for being alone. By the time I was twelve, one of my brothers and two of my sisters were already married. See, when you're always surrounded by siblings, half of who've been asked to always look out for you . . . it can be confining."

"I know what you mean, to a point. Being the only boy, I was able to get time alone." He seemed to want to say more, but instead he looked down at his feet and chuckled. "It looks like Goldie here needs a rest."

• • •

The dog was sprawled across his feet, panting heavily. Amanda pointed toward a spigot. "If you have something to hold water, we could fill it up."

Roman looked around, found someone's abandoned paper ice cream bowl wedged under a rock, and pulled it out. "This should do, if we rinse it out."

"I think so," she said, taking it from him. "I'll be right back."

"*Nee*, I'll do it," he said quickly. "This dog is my responsibility. I should be getting the water."

"I don't mind. You stay here with Goldie," she said over her shoulder as she walked briskly to the public water fountain.

As Roman looked after her, looking more than a little chagrined, she heaved a sigh of relief. That man might be thinking she was all about being helpful, but she knew the truth. At the moment, she was only thinking about herself. She needed a few seconds to catch her breath and come to terms with how she was feeling.

Though she was enjoying the conversation with Roman, she didn't like how comfortable she felt with him. The feeling was far more scary than staying at the condominium by herself.

Though she knew better, she couldn't help but feel like she was betraying Wesley.

She knew deep down that wasn't what Wesley would want. When he was ill, and she was trying so hard to be brave and stalwart, he'd told her time and again to never stop living.

Of course, at the time, she'd had no inkling of what he was talking about. All she'd been able to focus on was the fact that one day very soon her husband would be going to heaven, and she'd never be able to look into his smiling brown eyes again. The pain of watching him suffer, coupled with the knowledge that she was losing him, had prevented her from thinking of anything else.

She'd pushed aside his efforts to talk about her future, about a life spent without him. For her, it was too painful to consider. For Wesley, it had been all he wanted to think about.

"You've got to move on one day, Mandy," he'd murmured one evening when they'd been all alone and she'd been so tired she hadn't even bothered to light a candle. "One day, you're going to need to find someone else."

"I'll be fine. And Regina will, too." She'd been thankful for the dark room, hoping he wouldn't notice how she was lying. Because, really, how was she ever going to be fine without him?

"One day, you're going to be tired of being alone."

"Nee—"

"And I want you to know that I'll be watching you from heaven, smiling," he'd said, just as if she hadn't interrupted him. "I don't want you to mourn me forever."

Back then, she couldn't imagine doing anything but mourning him. He'd been her world, her daughter's father.

But perhaps he'd been right.

Because at the moment, mixing with the guilt she felt about even thinking about Roman Keim in a romantic sense was a small sliver of exhilaration, too. She'd felt his interest.

And she'd felt interested, too. Reminding her that though she was a widow and a mother, she was also a woman.

It was only lately that she'd forgotten.

Chapter Eight

Even when she didn't understand why things happened the way they did, Lovina believed with all her heart that the good Lord always had a plan. Furthermore, she believed that His plan was the right and best one. When she was tempted to despair, she simply prayed harder.

She'd grown up believing that was true faith.

Her faith had gotten her through some of the toughest moments in her life.

She'd tried to pass this on to her children. Whether she'd been successful or not, she did not know.

For the life of her, she couldn't understand why God had decided that all of their secrets needed to come tumbling out, one right after the other, all at this time in her life. It seemed to her that His timing, while always impeccable, was somehow off the mark this time. All He was doing was causing havoc in their lives and making the lot of them very unhappy indeed.

But perhaps the Lord had been giving her the chance to make changes in their lives? Maybe He was now making everything a jumbled mess so they'd all be forced to make some changes?

Thinking about the brief conversation she'd had with Marie while sewing, Lovina looked across the small living room at her husband.

Either she could avoid things a little longer . . . or finally push her husband to make things right.

Feeling as if the Lord was at her shoulder, giving her strength, she knew there was only one option. "Aaron, what should we tell the family about Laura Beth and Ben?"

Half asleep in his ancient easy chair, he didn't even bother to open his eyes. "Nothing."

"Well, why did you mention it to the family, then? You opened up a wasp's nest when you revealed you had another wife and child."

One eye opened. "Lovina, it ain't their concern. All that happened long before they were born. It doesn't affect them. Not one bit."

As Lovina smoothed out the pale yellow fabric she was making napkins out of for Lorene's wedding, she pursed her lips. She wasn't surprised by his answer. For over forty years, he'd been adamant that they only worry about the present, not the past. Time and time again he'd told her that nothing could be done to change what had already happened.

Mostly, his opinion had made sense. It certainly had kept their lives calm.

She'd done her best to abide by Aaron's wishes, to be the good and dutiful wife he'd wanted her to be. She'd even gone so far as to pretend that she wasn't curious about his first wife. Or his child.

The smart thing to do would be to say nothing and let this disagreement fade.

But it seemed she wasn't all that smart after all.

Or maybe she was just tired of being told what to think.

"Well, Elsie told me that their kitchen phone has been ringing nonstop. Our *kinner* are talking to each other. Before you know it, they're going to push us to talk about this. I know that is what Marie wants."

Both eyes were now open. Sitting straighter, Aaron hardened his voice. "Marie has more to worry about than my marriage. Her husband is in some center because he's too weak to deal with his addictions on his own."

The way he'd said "my marriage" stung. But what hurt even more was his lack of sympathy for their son. "Peter is not a weak man, Aaron. For the last twenty years, we've watched him farm this land, increase its value, be loyal to his wife, and raise three children. He is a good man who is going through a difficult time."

Aaron lumbered to his feet. "I refuse to feel sorry for him, Lovina. He brought his problems on himself, and he should be able to solve them that way, too. I did."

Her husband was as agitated as she'd ever seen him. His shoulders were stiff, and his expression was strained. And his voice . . .

His voice held a true note of sorrow in it. As if what had happened with his first wife and child was still a great source of pain for him.

Even though that accident had happened so very long ago.

Her heart went out to him. Because she loved him dearly, she pushed a little more. She knew from experience that the only way to heal a wound was to doctor it . . . not to merely cover it up. "You are being unfair to Marie, as well. She's our daughter, too, Aaron. The daughter of our hearts."

He raised a hand and made a brushing motion. "Oh, you know what I mean. And you know also that Marie shouldn't be focusing on our problems when she has so many of her own. Why, you'd think she'd be spending every free moment she has praying for Peter's health and for him to return home."

"Peter is getting help, and his well-being is in the Lord's hands now. That is why Peter left us, I am sure of it. The Lord guided him to this treatment center. I have a feeling we'll be glad he sought help."

Now his expression matched his tone. "If he gets better, it is because the Lord wanted him to get better, Lovina."

Of course the Lord had a lot to do with his improvement. But she also thought that the Lord had guided Peter to seek help, and that the Lord had given the doctors and therapists the tools to provide that help.

But Aaron would never understand her point of view. "Of course you are right," she said instead.

She waited a moment, folding the edges of one of the napkins and pinning it down. Her hands were trembling a bit and she pricked herself.

She walked to the bathroom, got out a bandage, and neatly fastened it on her finger so that she wouldn't accidently stain the cloth.

Staring at her finger, she walked back to her chair. Yes, covering up cuts was good. Necessary. But trying to cover up their past? Their memories?

Their marriages?

She was beginning to think that that was one of the biggest mistakes she and Aaron had ever made.

It was time to bring things out in the open, to force the conversation, even if it was painful. Marriage was about having the difficult conversations, wasn't it?

She vaguely recalled her mother telling her that, back when she'd been in high school.

Back when she'd had such a crush on Jack and thought she was the luckiest girl in the world.

Grabbing her courage, she pressed. "You know, you never even told me much about Laura Beth and Ben."

"We just talked about them."

"No, we talked about why you didn't want to talk about them to the rest of the family. There's a difference."

Starting to look resigned, he said, "I already gave you the chance to ask me anything you wanted."

He'd given her one evening. She'd been eighteen and knew nothing about marriage and raising children. All she'd been aware of was how different Aaron was from Jack.

"You didn't say much then, or maybe I didn't really ask the right questions. I mean, what were Laura Beth and Ben like?"

His eyes widened. "What were they like?"

"*Jah.* I mean . . . was she a kind woman? Was she young? Pretty? Silly?" A thousand more questions bubbled up inside her. Lovina wanted to know a hundred details. Had she been shy or outgoing? Had she laughed a lot or been moody? And how had they met? And Ben? What kind of boy had he been? Was he the quiet type like Jacob, gregarious like Aden? Or was he more dutiful like Peter?

More than that, she wanted to know how happy he'd been with his first wife. How happy had his life been before they'd passed away, and he'd married her? Though it had all happened more than forty years ago, she worried that his memories were still as sharp, and that after all this time, she still couldn't compare with them.

After all this time, she ached to know her competition.

Lovina stared back at Aaron, begging him silently to tell her everything she wanted to know. To give her reassurance that she'd never been a poor copy of his first wife.

She wanted Laura Beth to suddenly become a person to her instead of a woman who she could never measure up to.

"Laura Beth . . . she was . . ." His voice cracked, as if even saying her name was a difficult thing. "My Laura Beth . . . she was everything. That's what she was," he finished. He stood up.

"And Ben?" She forced the question even though she was sure she didn't want to hear the answer.

"Ben?" A line formed in between his brows. "My Ben was my first-born son, that's what he was. The three of us . . . we were a family. A perfect, happy family."

His words couldn't have been any more hurtful. Her pain couldn't have been sharper if he'd slapped her.

And the reality couldn't have been more clear.

Never had she been first in his heart. Never had he even attempted for her to be. She'd only been a substitute.

A copy of the perfect Amish woman who would always remain perfect in his heart.

She was still staring at him when he turned away and walked quietly out the back door.

Then she leaned forward and carefully folded the fabric into neat rectangles.

And realized that something else had happened. She'd never imagined she'd feel worse about herself than the night she'd come home from her homecoming dance.

But oh, she had been so terribly wrong.

Chapter Nine

Roman's time in Pinecraft and at Siesta Key had flown by. Every day, he'd spent time at the beach, going into town with his cousins, and spending time with Amanda and Regina.

On some days, they'd done little but talk briefly on the beach. Other times, though, they'd spent far longer in each other's company.

One evening Amanda and Regina had come over for a barbecue. Just that morning, he'd made sand castles with Regina while Amanda had pretended to read a book and relax.

Now, he felt as if he were as different inside as his tanned skin looked on the outside. He felt more relaxed, better prepared to deal with the pressures of home.

He was just watching the sun make its initial descent when Beth stepped out onto the patio.

Roman had been about to greet her when he noticed—with some alarm—that she had a certain "look" about her. The one that said she had much on her mind.

He stifled a groan. He'd learned from his sisters that whenever they approached with such an intent look it was time to prepare to explain himself—even if he'd done nothing wrong.

With Viola or Elsie it was usually some imagined slight. With Beth? He guessed she was preparing to talk to him about a certain neighbor.

Truth be told, he wouldn't mind discussing his feelings about Amanda. His insides knotted at the thought of never seeing her again after he got on the bus tomorrow. Those knots were warring with his usual levelheaded reasoning. He and Amanda couldn't live farther away from each other. He knew that meant they couldn't have much of a future.

But he didn't want to have to think about that right now. All he really wanted to do right now was enjoy these last precious moments of peace before they boarded the Pioneer Trails bus and headed home in the morning.

How could his vacation pass so quickly? He wasn't ready to head north. To be cold again. To say goodbye to Amanda.

Finally, Beth spoke. "Roman, you're not asleep, are you?"

"You've been hovering by my side for at least eight minutes," he said dryly. "If I had been asleep, I'd be awake by now."

"Oh."

He turned around and noticed that she looked a little dejected, as if she were carrying a great load and couldn't find the right spot to set it down.

So he decided to focus on his cousin. "What has you so spun up?"

"Oh, nothing. I mean, nothing's really wrong. . . ."

"What is on your mind, then? Is it something to do with Paul? Or the *kinner*?"

"Not at all. I mean, they're all *gut*. Paul and Lindy and Caleb are great."

"Then what is it? And don't say nothing again because I'm tired of talking in circles."

With a thump, she took the chair beside him and scooted closer. "It's just that I noticed . . . I mean, we all noticed, even Mamm and Daed, that is . . ."

Now this was even worse than dealing with his sisters. They at least didn't have a problem speaking their mind. "Beth. Noticed what?"

"That you and Amanda have spent quite a bit of time together."

Roman wasn't surprised she'd noticed. He'd done nothing to keep his feelings secret. And though he wouldn't have minded talking to Beth about his worries about a long-distance relationship, he didn't appreciate her tone with him. It sounded vaguely accusing, vaguely maternal.

And since he was twenty-three, not thirteen, he didn't appreciate it.

"And?"

"And I, um, just want to talk to you about that. If you don't mind."

"All right." After one last look at the ocean, he turned slightly, sat up a bit, and rested his palms on his knees. Looking her right in the eyes, he said, "What did you want to say?"

She looked abashed, then finally blurted, "I'm afraid you are leading her on."

"What do you mean?"

"I mean that they've already been through so much. The last thing either of them needs is to be hurt again."

"Beth, are you worried about me hurting Amanda?"

"A little. I just was thinking that you're getting ready to go back home. And she's here."

"Believe it or not, I had figured that out, too."

He knew his tone was sarcastic and harsh. But what did she expect?

Beth glared at him. "Roman, I just think you need to maybe talk to Amanda."

"We've been talking. As you pointed out. Over and over."

"No, I mean really talk."

"And say what?"

"I don't know. Maybe that you have true feelings for her?"

He was becoming embarrassed. "We are not having this conversation, Beth."

"I'm sorry if you're uncomfortable, but I know what my brothers are like. They're not always all that serious about the women they date. I mean Evan is seeing three girls at the same time . . ."

"I'm not Evan."

"I realize that. I just don't want her to get her feelings hurt. And I'm especially worried about her daughter's feelings," she said quickly, steamrolling over his protestations. "Amanda shared that Regina has only recently stopped asking about her father."

Roman sobered. He couldn't imagine what that poor girl thought was going to happen next. Four years old was too young to understand the concept of death. He'd purposely tread lightly around Regina. The last thing he wanted to do was create trouble for that little girl.

But then he remembered just how capable Amanda was, and what a good mother she was to Regina. And he remembered the smiles Regina had gifted him with. The way she'd acted around him, like their affection for each other was mutual.

"Shouldn't we be letting Amanda worry about Regina's emotions?" he said lightly. "I think she is a wonderful mother. I'm sure she can take care of her daughter without our interference."

"I agree, but . . ."

"I didn't do anything besides enjoy Amanda's company, Beth. I never tried to be more to Regina than her friend. I understand your concern, and I appreciate that. But I promise it was never my intention to hurt either of them. And I've been well aware that Amanda is a grown woman who's been through a lot in her life. I think she deserves to make her own choices about her relationships. She doesn't need our help."

Beth slumped, as a dawning look of agreement flared in her eyes. "Perhaps."

"If Amanda and I never see each other again, it's really none of your concern. And if we do continue to stay in contact, then I'll let you know how we're all doing emotionally."

She finally looked shamefaced. "I guess I should've kept out of this."

He nodded. "I know you meant well, but yes."

"Sorry."

"I have two sisters; I'm used to meddling women. But don't create problems where there aren't any, cousin. And please think, if you would, how you would feel if the shoe were on the other foot. Would you really want my unasked-for advice regarding you and Paul?"

"This is different."

"We're still talking about feelings," he said softly. "Private ones."

"I'll remember that." Just as Beth rose to give him a brief hug, Roman noticed Amanda step out onto her patio next door.

With a rush of pleasure, he watched her instantly look over her shoulder his way just as Beth closed the door behind her. And then smile when she caught sight of him.

"Hi, Roman."

"Hi." He got to his feet. "Care for some company?"

"*Jah*, if you don't mind staying close. Regina fell asleep while playing with her farm animals on the carpet inside. I need to wake her up soon."

"I don't mind. Should I come over to your patio?"

She pointed to the pair of beach chairs sitting just beyond her condominium's white picket fence. They were in the spot he'd first seen her sitting on that very first morning.

"How about there?"

With some surprise, he realized that there was still time to make new memories. Hope filled him.

"Looks good." Truthfully, she couldn't have

picked a more perfect spot. He knew he'd always remember his first sight of her sitting there, with the sun rising in the background.

Now in the glow of early evening, it felt especially fitting.

As he opened the little wooden gate for her, he felt as if every sense was heightened. Maybe it was because he was so close to returning to Ohio and his regular routine. But never had he expected that a vacation could pass by so quickly, or that he would feel as if he needed to hold each moment tightly, as if it were about to slip through his fingers like a drop of water.

He was going to miss this place.

As they walked, Amanda seemed to wilt a bit as they got closer to the chairs. Finally, she spoke. "So, you're leaving tomorrow?"

"We are. When do you go back home?"

"We'll go back sometime tomorrow or Monday. It's time, I suppose."

He noticed that she didn't seem all that enthusiastic about it. She seemed just as intent on memorizing the beauty of the moment as he did.

"What's wrong?"

Blue eyes searched his. "Are you sure you want to hear? I'm afraid it's a little bit maudlin."

"Of course." He wanted to know everything about her, to hear everything she was thinking. One day, he hoped they'd be close enough so that he could tell her that.

For now, he did his best to keep things light.

"What's on your mind?" he asked as he sat down in the bright blue Adirondack chair and relaxed.

She perched on the white chair next to his. "Well, something about getting away from my traditional routine has made me realize something. After spending the week here, away from my in-laws, I've realized how much I've been living in the past. I've been only thinking about Wesley, and my life with him."

Her hands clenched together in her lap, making her look almost as if she expected him to find fault with her statement.

But how could he ever fault a woman who had loved her husband dearly? "That seems only natural," he finally said. "Your vows were meant to last a lifetime."

"I thought so, too, but God had other plans. And Roman, even though I had promised Wesley I'd move on, I didn't."

"You were mourning his loss. There's nothing wrong with that."

"I was in mourning," she agreed. "But I must admit that I never intended to mourn for years. More importantly, I had promised myself that I wouldn't do that to Regina."

He didn't want to interrupt her, but he thought she was being a little hard on herself. Surely there was no right or wrong way to deal with a spouse's passing. What a person expects to happen and what actually does are two different things. She'd loved her husband so much that she wanted to continue to honor his memory. There wasn't anything wrong with that.

Unfolding her hands, she continued. "Lately—I mean this week—I realized that I truly do want to move forward, Roman. It's time."

"Good for you." He smiled.

"*Jah*. Good for me." She bit her lip. "Now all I have to do is find a way to get Wesley's family to agree to that."

"What are you worried about? You've told me that they can be attentive . . ."

"They are that. But they can be possessive, too." The moment she said the words, she looked horrified. "Don't get me wrong, they are wonderful people. *Wunderbaar*! They truly are! But I fear that they've forgotten that I am in my twenties. And that as much as I loved Wesley, I certainly cannot live the rest of my life as only his widow."

Roman reflected on his own community in Berlin. Because she was a widow, with a daughter to raise, in his world, some would think it was almost her duty to eventually find a husband and a father for Regina. "Do you really think they expect that?"

"I think they do. But it's not their fault. I'm afraid I've led them to think that that was what I wanted, too. But now I'm beginning to see that I'd rather look to the future than the past."

As he thought of her, and how much he was going to miss her, he realized that he was already missing her. Missing what could have been between them.

Suddenly, he realized he didn't want to let Amanda go.

Here was his chance. His chance to tell her how he felt. "Amanda, I don't want to lose you."

A flash of pleasure appeared in her eyes before she visibly tamped it down. "What do you mean?"

"I want us to stay friends," he said, though he wished he had the nerve to say more. Leaning forward, he added, "I'd like to write you. Maybe call you on the phone sometimes."

An eyebrow arched. "Why would you want to do that?"

He knew she wasn't being coy. She was nervous and unsure of herself. He felt much the same way. Like a young teen, he felt his cheeks heat with renewed bashfulness. "Because I like you." Even as he heard his words, he felt his cheeks heat so much he would have sworn they were on fire. He wished he had more poetic words to say.

But perhaps Amanda didn't need flowery language? Slowly, her lips curved upward. "Truly?"

"*Jah.* I'm sure it's no surprise. My attention has been pretty obvious."

"A woman still likes to hear the words, I think." She took a breath, then let it out. "Roman, I like you, too," she said in a rush.

"That's *gut*, then." He gave thanks that he wasn't anywhere near his sisters, because they would most certainly be laughing at him mercilessly. He couldn't seem to stop smiling.

Her cheeks bloomed with happiness, but then she looked down at her dress and fussed with a fold in the white fabric of her apron. "However, I must warn you that my daughter is everything to me. I couldn't begin anything serious without you realizing that."

"I'm glad Regina means the world to you. It's one of the reasons why I admire you so much."

Her smiled deepened.

He cleared his throat. "So, may we continue to talk to each other and write?"

"I would like that."

"*Gut.*"

"Roman, do you think anything will come of this?"

"I don't know. I suppose this friendship of ours can turn into anything we want. Maybe one day we'll decide that we fancy other people instead. Or maybe one day I'll want to move out here with you. Or you'll want to move to Ohio."

"Talk like that makes my head spin."

"It doesn't have to." Little by little, his tentativeness evaporated. He knew what he wanted. "Amanda, I want to be the person in your life who you can relax with. My needs right now are simple—at least where the two of us are concerned. See, I only want what you want."

"That's it?"

"Pretty much. Well, I want us to continue to be friends, at the very least." Yes, he certainly wanted so much more than mere friendship from her, but he was willing to wait until she was ready for more.

She gazed at him. Studied his face. "All right. Yes, let's go where this takes us."

"You sound almost sure," he teased.

She chuckled. "I'm not sure about much right now—it's all such a surprise to me. But I do happen to know one thing I'm sure of, and that's that I don't want to stop figuring out what our future holds, Roman. Getting to know you, feeling what I'm feeling? It's been like a sudden ray of light in my life. Almost an awakening. I've gone from expecting every day to be muted and gray to expecting something new."

If she hadn't been through so much he would have held her close.

But because she wasn't ready for more, he kicked his feet out in front of him, rolled up his pant legs, and leaned back in his chair. He closed his eyes as he felt the cooling breeze dance across his cheeks.

He sensed her body tense in confusion. "Roman, what are you doing?"

"Fully intending to enjoy your company, that's what." He peeked at her through one eye. "Is that a problem?"

After a moment, she shook her head. "*Nee*. Not at all."

"*Gut*. See, Amanda, all we have to do right now is take things one step at a time. The Lord will guide us from there."

To his amusement, she copied his position. "Roman, being around you makes me happy. I'm going to miss you."

Gazing over at her pretty face, seeing the vulnerability and strength that made her who she was, he said, "I'm going to miss you, too, Amanda. Very much."

Already he was missing her. And already he was wondering when they could see each other again.

Chapter Ten

Viola had just set her suitcase on her bed when her grandmother wandered into the room and sat down on the window seat. In her hands were a pair of quilted pot holders. The front of each was decorated with a beautiful star pattern. Viola recognized much of the fabric—it looked as if her grandmother had been putting the scraps of fabric from the dresses for Lorene's wedding to good use.

"Hi, Mommi," she said politely. "I was just getting ready to pack."

"Elsie told me. I thought I'd come upstairs and see for myself." Glaring at the open suitcase, she said, "Our *haus* suddenly feels like a turnstile, the way you and Roman keep coming and going. Why, practically every time I turn around, it looks like one of you has a suitcase out."

Viola shook her head. Her grandmother was either exaggerating for no reason at all . . . or she was feeling a little left out.

"Mommi, we all know that I've never left Berlin and Holmes County before. It's time, don'tcha think?"

"Maybe. Maybe not." She looked at the pot holders in her hands, but said nothing about them.

The lackluster agreement inspired Viola to now stick up for her brother. "And Roman—he is only returning from his first vacation."

But instead of sounding more understanding, Mommi scrunched her brows together, making the lines in between her eyebrows deepen. "That is true."

Viola sighed. Her grandmother could be such a stickler sometimes. "There's nothing wrong with taking days off. Even God took time to rest, *jah*?"

"I suppose."

She decided her grandmother needed a change in subject. She thought about the phone call she'd received from her cousin Beth. It seemed Roman had developed quite a friendship with the woman staying in the condominium next door. Far closer than what he'd led them to believe in his letters.

Viola couldn't wait for his bus to arrive in Berlin so that she could talk to him about it. "I'm just glad Roman enjoyed himself. Beth said he had a good time, Mommi," she said almost patiently. "We all need good times in our lives, *jah*?"

"Well, of course," her grandmother grumbled. After a pause, she said, "What did he do with all his time?"

"Beth said he played shuffleboard and walked on the beach. Slept late. Ate at restaurants."

"Hmmph." She paused, then said, "It's sure to be different where you're going. Have you thought of that?"

"*Jah.*"

"Belize sounds like a dangerous place," she said a little more softly. "I hope you'll be all right there."

Finally, Viola understood her grandmother's motivation for the visit. She was worried about her. "It sounds beautiful. I can't wait to go," she said firmly. So far, she'd pushed all of her worries about being in a strange country like Belize far out of her mind. All she was focused on was seeing Edward.

"You're the first person I've heard of to get a passport."

"Ed got one. All the folks at the mission have them, too."

Mommi folded her arms over her chest and peered at Viola through her bifocals. "Are you scared, child?" she asked at last. "Because it would be understandable if you were."

"I am scared. I mean, I am, a little bit." She wanted to pretend she wasn't worried about flying alone on an airplane, or visiting a foreign country. But she was. "I'm trying not to be. I don't want Edward to think I can't handle this."

"He seems like the kind of man who only cares about you being happy, Viola."

"He is that kind of man. But I want him to feel proud of me, too."

Her grandmother peered at her some more, then finally handed over the pair of pot holders. "I thought you might like to give these to the folks at the mission."

"They're beautiful."

"Oh, they're just from scraps I had lying around. But the folks down in Belize might like them."

"I'm sure they will, Mommi. *Danke*." Carefully, Viola set them at the bottom of her suitcase.

After a moment, her grandmother reached out a hand again. But this time, it was to enclose Viola's in hers. "There's no shame in being afraid of something that's unfamiliar. It's to be expected."

"You truly believe that?"

"I do," her grandmother said with a small smile. "After all, I've been in your shoes a time or two, you know."

Never had Viola recalled her grandmother speaking so cryptically. "Are you speaking of when you became Amish?" she asked.

After a pause, her grandmother nodded. "I suppose I am." Her eyes widened, and then, to Viola's astonishment, she chuckled. "After all these many years of keeping my past a secret, I now have the strangest urge to talk about that time. It's like I just let the genie out of the bottle."

Viola didn't know what she meant by that, but she let it pass, eager to get more information before her grandmother changed her mind. Her grandmother was one of the most private people she'd ever known. "Why did you leave your English life and become Amish, Mommi? Was it because you fell in love with Grandfather? What did you miss? What did your parents say?"

"One question at a time, Viola!"

"Well then, tell me why you became Amish."

"It was because of Aaron." She bit her lip, then added, "At least a big part of the reason was because of him."

"What were your other reasons?"

Mommi looked around the neat room, then finally smoothed a hand along the intricate quilt on Viola's bed. "Before I met your grandfather,

I made some mistakes in judgment. I, um, had gotten my heart broken."

"You did?"

"Very much so. This boy, well, he upset me." She opened her mouth, looked like she was going to continue, then pursed her lips instead. "It was a long time ago, of course."

"Was this boy an *Englischer*?"

"Don't act so surprised, Viola. *Englischers* fall in love, too." With a wince, she added, "And fall out of love, as well."

"It must have been mighty exciting."

"It didn't feel like that at the time. It, ah, was a dark time for me."

"I'm sorry. That was rude."

"*Nee*, you are only being honest. Believe me, I'd rather us be honest with each other than not. Keeping secrets and spouting lies didn't serve me well."

Seeing the faraway expression in her grandmother's eyes, Viola forgot all about her own problems. "So, who did you love, Mommi? Was he handsome?"

Mommi chuckled. "He was handsome, indeed." Her grandmother's expression softened. "At least, I thought so."

"Then how—"

"Quiet, child. This is my story, and it happened quite a long time ago. Let me tell it my way."

"Of course. I'm sorry."

Looking a bit amused, her grandmother gazed out the window, then said, "Well, it all started when I decided to help with the football players float."

"What's a float?"

"For us, it was a trailer bed that you would hook to the back of a big truck. We'd decorate it with balloons and crepe paper. Then people would stand on it during a parade. I liked one of the football players, so I made sure I was helping with their float for the parade."

"And?"

"And it was great fun. There was lots of laughter, and flirting with the boys . . . and then Jack started talking to me."

"Jack was the boy you liked."

"He was. I'd liked him for some time. Then, one day, he liked me, too." She took a breath, but just as she was about to say more, Viola's grandpa came in.

"What are you talking about, Lovina?" His voice was hard with disapproval.

With a look of warning in her direction, Mommi shrugged. "Nothing too important. Was there something you needed?"

"Supper."

"Goodness, I hadn't noticed the time." Immediately, she got to her feet. "Viola, we'll have to talk another time," she said, then quickly disappeared out the door with her husband.

Viola felt like she'd been left on the side of a hill and she didn't know whether to climb up or down. Or to hold tight where she was and hope no strong winds came along.

Frustrated, she glared at the door and wished with all her might that her grandfather had decided to enter just a few minutes later.

But then she realized that her grandmother's story had done a very good thing. Now she was no longer only thinking about how scared she was.

Instead, she was wondering how her grandparents had become the people they were, and what experiences in her life would shape her character. Make her the person she would one day be. Would moving to Belize change her for good?

Chapter Eleven

The gray skies seemed grayer in Berlin. Roman frowned in annoyance as he looked out the window of the bus. It felt as if the dreary color was draining all of the life right out of him with each passing mile.

Depression lurked on the edge of his heart as he spied the familiar landmarks.

He'd be home soon—which meant he'd be even farther from Sarasota, Florida. And though he'd made every effort to think positively about his future with Amanda, Roman knew those dreams were going to be almost impossible to turn into reality.

She had a life in Pinecraft, and he had a load of responsibilities right here in Ohio. His father was in a rehabilitation center. His mother was at her wit's end. One of his sisters was almost blind, the other was days away from visiting her fiancé in Belize. Therefore it was up to Roman to take care of the majority of the farm.

And do the majority of the work as well.

Roman didn't begrudge the work. He'd never minded working in the fields and helping to make his family's land more prosperous and profitable. But at the moment, the responsibilities weighed on him something awful.

For the first time in his life, he wanted something different from what he had.

He glanced out at the clouds again and noticed they'd darkened even more. Snow was likely on the way. He sighed in frustration. Of course it was.

The man sitting next to him noticed. "You've been on this bus ever since it left Pinecraft, haven't ya?"

"Yes." The bus had made several stops along its way north. More than a few people had boarded in Cincinnati, while others had switched buses there, some heading west toward Indianapolis like his cousins. But he'd been on it for the entire long journey.

The older man grunted in satisfaction. "I thought so. You're wearing that look."

"What look is that?"

"The one that says the beach and bright sunlight are now months away," he said with a cackle. "Don't feel bad. I was wearing that same expression three weeks ago."

"So it fades?" He didn't bother describing the feeling. The man had already pegged it perfectly.

"In my case it fades because I'm always anxious to get home. There's no place like home, you know." He flashed a smile as he paused for breath. "You married yet?"

"*Nee.*"

"Don't want to impose, but my advice is to find a woman you fancy and soon."

"Is that right?"

The man didn't catch the sarcasm. "Oh, for sure. Son, get settled down in a place of your own. Have a houseful of *kinner*. That will keep you grounded. You'll be settled and happy wherever you are, because you'll have the people who matter to you most close at hand."

"I'll keep that in mind." To his surprise, he truly meant the words. Roman wanted to dismiss the words of wisdom out of hand, but he actually thought the advice made a lot of sense. "*Danke.*"

"Glad I could help." After stretching his arms a bit, he looked around his seat with a slight grimace. "I suppose I better start getting my things in order," the man said. "Before you know it, we'll be stopping in Berlin."

Roman glanced out the window. Saw the cheese house and the row of shops that lined Market Street. They'd be arriving at the German Village shops in less than five minutes.

There, Viola or Uncle Samuel would be waiting for him in the buggy. They'd ask him about his trip, and it would be his duty to tell them just enough to assure them that his vacation had been *wonderful-gut*.

But not let on how disappointed he was to be back home. Letting them know that truth wouldn't help anyone.

Since he had nothing to organize, Roman stared out the window again and watched the automobiles pass by. Watched an Amish woman walking beside her man, both of them bundled up against the weather.

Noticed a pair of English teenagers dressed in jeans and thick coats and holding hands.

And realized for the first time that he didn't mind the idea of marriage and children anymore. Perhaps it was because when he thought of marriage now, he thought of brilliant blond hair that glinted against the bright rays of sunlight. And when he thought of children, it was in the form of a dark-haired little girl with a fondness for ice cream and animals. Who'd claimed his heart when she'd held out a soft, pudgy hand.

With a bit of regret, he realized it wasn't the lack of sunlight he minded, it was the lack of Amanda and Regina.

Unfortunately, he was far more likely to see the sun than them anytime soon.

It was always harder to pack up to go home than it was to prepare to arrive. Somehow they always left with twice the amount they arrived with.

Standing in front of a pile of sand toys, Amanda shook her head. "Regina, where did all of this . . . this stuff come from?"

"The stores, I think?" Regina said, completely serious.

Which, of course, made Amanda chuckle. That's what she got for asking rhetorical questions of her very literal daughter.

"I think you might be right about that, dear. But I sure don't know how we're going to load everything in the van when the driver gets here."

"When is he coming?" Regina plopped down on the top cement step and daintily crossed her bare feet in front of her.

"In about thirty minutes."

Regina backed away with a fierce frown. "I sure wish he wasn't."

"Why is that?"

"Because we have to go back to our regular house."

Regina spoke so dramatically, Amanda couldn't

resist teasing her a bit. "And you don't care for our house anymore? You have a lovely room at home."

"I like my room. . . ." she said slowly, then closed up her mouth tight.

There was definitely more upsetting Regina than the end of a vacation. "What will you miss here?"

"Goldie."

Ah, yes. That silly, adorable dog that had claimed all of their hearts with her happy manner and insatiable need to chase crabs. "I'll miss Goldie, too."

"She needs a home, Mamm."

"I know. But . . . I just don't think we're ready to have Goldie at our house in town."

"But I miss her." Looking petulant, she said, "I'm going to miss the beach, too."

"Ah, well, we'll visit the beach soon."

"I'm going to miss you, too."

"Me?" Amanda looked at her in surprise. "Child, you're making no sense. I'll still be with you when we get home."

"I know, Momma." Regina turned away with a little nod, and a somewhat bleak, resigned look on her face.

Amanda couldn't let that go. Brushing a wayward curl from her daughter's forehead, she said, "Regina, tell me what you mean. I promise, I won't get mad."

"Promise?"

"I promise." She sat down on the step next to her little girl, thought about grasping her hand, but decided against it when she noticed how tightly Regina had her hands fisted together. "Please talk to me. Why do you think you won't have me at home?"

"When you are home, you get sad."

With effort, she attempted to hide the shock she felt. She'd tried so hard to keep her depression hidden. But obviously, she hadn't been able to hide much. "Not so much anymore."

Regina shook her head. "It's true. You do. And you don't laugh as much."

"Well, that is to be expected. I'm working and taking care of you and our home. That's a lot to do. But we're still together a lot."

"It doesn't feel like it."

Amanda was about to argue that point, but decided to hold her tongue. After all, she knew what her daughter meant. Things were different in their "regular" lives. She did work a lot, and she was pretty much tired all the time, too. "I'll try to be better."

"Uh-huh." Her daughter squirmed a bit. Poked at a roving ant with her big toe.

Amanda watched her, wondering what else she could say that would reduce her worries but wouldn't get her hopes up too much.

Because, well, things would be different when they got home again.

Looking bored with the ant, Regina sighed as she crossed her arms over her chest. "Momma, I liked Roman."

Amanda stilled. At first it felt like that comment came out of nowhere, but she was starting to realize that Regina was finally feeling comfortable enough to speak her mind, and this was what was on her mind. "I liked Roman, too. But he had to go back to his own home in Ohio."

"I wish he was still here."

"I know, dear." Amanda drew a breath, ready to end this barrage of wistful thinking.

But Regina interrupted her thoughts. "You smiled when you were with him. A lot. And he made me smile, too."

Yes, there were lots of things to like about that man. And many things she was going to miss, too. "Roman was a *verra* nice man."

"I miss him."

"We hardly knew him." But even as she said the words, she knew she was lying. She felt like she'd known him all her life.

Regina turned away again, telling Amanda without words that she disagreed with her mother.

Well, she had raised a smart girl.

Standing up, Amanda held out a hand. "Come now, dear. Let's stop wishing for things that we can't have."

Regina ignored her hand. "Momma, are we ever going to see him again?"

"We might. It depends if he wants to come back to visit."

Regina's eyes widened, then she pursed her lips and quietly nodded. "Okay."

"Regina, Roman was just a vacation friend. At least, that's all he is now." And perhaps one day she'd even believe that.

"Are you going to talk to Mommi about him when she calls?"

"Definitely not."

"I heard her say she wanted to ask you questions." Her bottom lip puffed out in between a set of tiny white teeth. "I heard that."

"I know she did. But Gina, that doesn't mean I have to answer them. I hope you don't start telling tales about Roman to your grandmother. No good will come out of that." The moment she heard her words, heard her tone, Amanda regretted saying anything. She'd managed to frighten her daughter—all because she was confused about her life and what she wanted.

Tears filled Regina's eyes.

Quickly, Amanda sat back down and wrapped her arms around her daughter's thin frame. "I'm sorry. I didn't mean to speak to you like that. Everything will be fine, you'll see."

"You think so?"

"I do. Before you know it, we'll be settled and snug in our very own house and we'll be glad we're not here any longer. I promise, that will happen."

After a moment, Regina hugged Amanda back, then stood up. "I'm going to go check my room again."

"All right, dear."

But instead of jumping to her feet and attempting to organize all of their things one more time, Amanda stayed seated.

And gazed through the screen door at the pile of clothes neatly folded by the door . . . to an empty box of Pop-Tarts in the trash, and the open window beyond. The breeze blew in the fresh scent of salt and ocean.

Funny, it now smelled like freedom.

Chapter Twelve

"Hold still, Lorene," Lovina said. "I want to make sure your dress looks perfect."

But, just like when she was still a child, her daughter twitched and wiggled. "Mamm, the dress already looks fine. It looked perfect last time I tried it on."

"Then stop squirming! I swear, you're as jumpy as a cricket."

"And twice as chirpy," Lorene finished with a grin.

Lovina couldn't help but smile as well. "Ach. That is an old joke, daughter."

"It still makes me smile."

This joking between them was new. Lovina hadn't thought she would have embraced the bright, teasing conversation, but she was finding a lot of pleasure from their new interactions. It gave her hope for their future.

Hope where she had imagined there would be no more.

"It is nice to see you happy, *maydel*," she commented, afraid to make too much of it, in case Lorene might just pull away from her again.

But instead of turning wary, her daughter simply smiled. "It's nice to *feel* happy. I'm excited to finally marry John. And in just two weeks!"

That simple statement cut deeply into her conscience. Smoothing out fabric, then kneeling at her daughter's feet to check the hem, she said, "Lorene, do you think you'll ever be able to forgive me?"

"What?"

"You heard me. I'm only asking so that I might prepare myself," she said quickly.

"There's nothing to forgive, Mamm. While it's true that you were the one who asked me not to see John, I was the one who agreed." She shook her head. "I didn't fight your decision at all . . . and then I let years go by before I attempted to reconnect with him. Years!"

Lovina knew what kind of parent she'd been. She wouldn't have put up with any disobedience of any kind. "Things were different back then," she said hesitantly.

"Not that different." Bitterness tinged her voice and though Lovina couldn't blame her for that, Lorene's words made her heart ache.

"I know you wanted to be an obedient daughter."

"I did. But now I realize that I was afraid, too. I was afraid to go out on my own. I didn't trust my heart."

"I see." She had her daughter spin so she could ensure every part of the hem was perfect and smooth.

"And after several conversations with John about this, I don't think he was as ready for marriage as he believed, either. God's timing is always right, Mother. You were right—even though I was certainly not happy about your opinions."

"Ach," she said. Because her daughter had surprised her once again. And because she, too, knew what it felt like to not be heard.

After all, her parents had made her feel much the same way.

"All right," Viola announced as she entered the room with a pair of yellow placemats and cloth napkins. "I just finished another set for the wedding reception. What do you think?"

As Lorene oohed and aahed over Viola's handi-work, Lovina continued to kneel at her daughter's feet. As was her habit, she made a great show of concentrating on her task. But in truth, she was happy to let her mind drift back to another day, another year.

Another lifetime, really. Back when she'd gone to the Homecoming dance with Jack. The night when so much had gone so wrong. . . .

"You look real pretty, Lolly."

"Thanks." Lovina smoothed her satin gown over her knees nervously as Jack drew his car to a stop at the light. "Are you excited about the dance?"

It was a dumb question. The dance had been all her group of friends had been able to talk about for days. Who wouldn't be excited?

But he surprised her.

"I guess." He shrugged. "I was more excited to be alone with you, if you want to know the truth."

"Me?"

"Well, yeah. I mean, everyone knows your parents keep a tight rein on you. It makes seeing you a real challenge."

"I didn't think they were stricter than anyone else's."

"Maybe not. But it sure seems like it. I didn't mind though."

"You didn't?"

"Nah, I always get my way, sooner or later." His lips curved up into a devil-may-care grin. "I mean, look at us. I got you alone."

If he hadn't looked so delighted, she would have

been nervous. But he was happy and so she felt wanted. Special. So she smiled back and tried not to fuss with the curls on the ends of her hair.

Moments later, Jack pulled into a parking place far from the gymnasium's entrance. Actually, it was far from most of the other cars.

"Why are you parking way out here?" she asked. "I've got my mother's heels on, you know."

"If your feet start to hurt, I'll carry you."

She laughed, though the image made her feel all tingly—like daydreams really could come true. "Are you worried about someone hurting your car?"

"Nah, no one's going to touch my car without getting hurt." He leaned closer. "It's for privacy, of course." He grinned as he pulled the key out of the ignition. "How am I going to get a kiss if we're in the middle of a crowd?"

Her mouth went dry as her mind went blank. She'd imagined kissing him, of course. In her daydreams, he'd ask her permission, then carefully press his lips to her cheek. Maybe, just maybe, after the second or third date they'd kiss on the lips.

But what was on his face was something far different. The first tingling of nerves filtered through her. Biting her lip, she contemplated telling him that she wasn't ready for what he was talking about.

But how did a girl say such a thing to the boy

of her dreams? Too worried about her feelings and the tingling going on in the back of her neck, she chose action instead of words. With a steady breath, she opened her door and got out of the car.

He scrambled out of the car, shouting after her. "Lolly, what are you doing?"

"I don't want to be late for pictures."

"Pictures? Oh, yeah. Sure." He caught up to her, reaching for her hand when they were almost at the entrance.

Other girls hurried over when they neared. They commented on her dress, her shoes. Her hair. Lolly did the same thing, it was only polite.

Jack's friends spoke to her, too. Their expressions were different, though. Almost as if they were privy to a private joke. Jack joked around with them, then tossed an arm over her shoulders, his hand dangling around the top of her bare arm. Every so often she'd feel the warm pads of his fingers graze her skin.

After they posed for pictures, the group of ten of them strode into the decorated gym like they owned the place. Then, one of Jack's friends pulled out a flask and poured something into one of the cups for punch.

Jack shoved it at her. "Here, Lolly. Drink up."

It was liquor, the smell sharp and pungent. Wrinkling her nose, she attempted to move away. "Um, I don't think—"

"It's no biggie, Lolly," Jane interrupted. "Everyone's having some. You'll be the only one who doesn't if you refuse."

When Lolly still hesitated, Jane's voice turned urgent. "Come on."

And so she did. Because she'd felt like she had no choice. And because she didn't want to cause a scene.

Jack smiled. "Good girl."

At the moment, she felt like the opposite of a good girl. She felt wicked, and more than a little disheartened. She was with the most popular boy in her class but everything about the situation made her feel uneasy.

But it wasn't like she had a choice.

With that first sip, her spirits deflated. And she'd known that everything she'd imagined happening had been nothing but childish day-dreams of an innocent, naïve girl.

"Lolly, want to dance?"

Raising her chin, she looked into his dark eyes, saw desire and satisfaction in his expression. That was everything she'd thought she wanted. "Of course," she said, smiling as he took her hand.

And let him guide her into his arms.

And pretended she wasn't shouldering a very new, very real sense of foreboding.

As the memories spilled forth, Lovina grimaced. She'd been such a fool that night. So silly. So misguided. If she'd only been a little bit braver or a whole lot smarter, she could have saved herself a great amount of pain. Could have saved a lot of people from a great amount of pain.

"Mamm?"

Lovina started. "Hmm?"

"Mamm, I asked you a question," Lorene said. "Did you hear me?"

"I'm afraid my mind went walking. What did you ask?"

"I was asking if you thought it was wrong for John and me to want to go on a honeymoon trip to New York. I know no one else took one."

"Lorene, I think you should do whatever you want. Time passes too quickly to always worry about what others may think."

Surprise, then pleasure, lit her daughter's features. "*Danke*, Mamm. Hearing you say that means a lot."

"It's only my opinion. That's all," she said quietly.

She knew better than anyone that her judgment wasn't always good. In fact, it was sometimes very, very bad.

Chapter Thirteen

When the phone rang, Amanda practically ran across the kitchen to answer it. Before he'd left, she and Roman had made plans to speak today, just to make sure they'd both gotten home all right. All day long she'd been wavering between excitement for the upcoming call—and nervous apprehension that he would forget.

"Hello?" she asked, wincing as she heard the breathlessness in her voice.

"Amanda, it's Roman."

"Hi, Roman." She leaned against the white laminate counter, smiling from ear to ear. Not only did he call, but he sounded exactly the same as she remembered.

"Hey, I thought today would never come. I've already tried to call you several times this week. You're a difficult woman to get ahold of."

He'd been calling? "I've been working a lot," she said in a rush. "I guess I've been missing some phone calls."

"You might consider getting an answering machine."

Roman sounded so cross, she smiled, standing alone right there in her kitchen.

"That would be a *gut* idea, for sure," she agreed.

But even so, she knew she'd never get one. Even if she had known he'd called, she knew that she wouldn't have called him back. It would seem too forward. Too eager.

"I'm glad you're home now. Tell me what you've been doing. And how you are. And how Regina is. And tell me about the weather, and the beach, too."

She chuckled at his enthusiasm, loving how it mirrored her own. "That's all?"

"*Nee.* I want to know what you've been eating and reading and if you've seen our dog."

To her surprise, her eyes teared up. "You've been thinking about Goldie, too?" For some reason, that he would remember how much she had liked that shelter dog meant the world to her. It meant that he remembered what was dear to her.

"Goldie was a fine dog."

"I thought so, too," she said just as her mother-in-law wandered into the kitchen. "I miss her," she added. To her surprise, a tear escaped and she wiped it away impatiently.

Across the kitchen, Marlene noticed. "Amanda, what is wrong?"

"Nothing."

"Nonsense. You are crying." Eyeing the phone like she feared it was about to bite Amanda, she said, "Who are you speaking to?"

Covering the mouthpiece of the phone, she said, "Merely a friend."

"Who?"

"Roman."

"I don't recall a man by that name."

Just as Amanda was about to call her mother-in-law's bluff, Regina popped in. "He's the Roman from Ohio," she said helpfully as she joined them in the kitchen. "Mommi, he was our neighbor at the beach."

"Why are you speaking with him?" Marlene asked, just as if Amanda was keeping company with a dangerous man. Just as if everything in Amanda's life was her business.

And she did that probably because, Amanda realized, until this very moment, she had let Marlene have that much access. She froze, staring at Marlene, her prying mother-in-law.

Amanda felt her heartbeat quicken as she felt the gap between her former life and her future one becoming wider. Yet, at the same time she wondered what she was doing. Was a momentary infatuation with a man who lived in Ohio worth jeopardizing everything she had with Wesley's family?

Roman's concerned tone of voice filtered through her thoughts. "Amanda? Amanda, are you still there? Can you still talk to me now?"

At least she knew that answer! "*Jah!*" she chirped into the phone. "Just give me one second. . . ."

As she glanced at Marlene, who was still eyeing

her with interest, Amanda knew it was time to make some changes. Now.

There was no way she was going to be able to speak to Roman while being watched and monitored by her mother-in-law.

"Marlene, would you mind leaving the kitchen with Regina for a few moments?"

"So you can talk to a man on the phone?" Marlene raised a condemning brow. "To that stranger?"

Roman was anything but a stranger. But Amanda sure didn't feel like spending another second fending off her mother-in-law's pesky questions. "Yes, please."

"I will leave, but I don't know what to think about this, Amanda."

Oh, but she did. Amanda was sure of it! She didn't care for it one bit.

"*Danke,*" she said. Then she turned her back on any response, and took a fortifying breath when she heard Marlene take Regina from the room. "I'm sorry, Roman," she muttered. "I had to ask someone to leave the room."

"I heard you say Marlene. Isn't that your mother-in-law?"

"It is. I mean, she was." What was Marlene's relationship to her now, with her husband up in heaven?

"Is my calling causing you trouble?"

She appreciated that he cared. She appreciated that he remembered her mother-in-law's name.

But because of that, she knew she was willing to risk getting into trouble with Marlene. There was something about hearing Roman's voice that was making her feel alive again. Instinctively, she knew if she cut off her ties with Roman, a part of her would die again.

And since she'd already died once with Wesley, she wasn't willing to go through that again. Once had been enough.

"You won't cause any trouble. At least, not too much."

"All right." But he sounded doubtful.

Hoping to change the subject, she attempted to keep her own tone sounding positive. "I want to hear what you've been doing since you got home."

To her delight, he chuckled. "Then I won't make you wait another moment to hear about my exciting life."

"Do go on."

"First of all, it's been terribly cold here," he quipped, his voice thick with humor. "We've had a bit of snow, too. At least a foot."

"Snow?" Forgetting about their joking, Amanda closed her eyes and imagined a hilly Ohio landscape, covered with a thick carpet of freshly fallen snow. It sounded so lovely, and she could only imagine what Regina would have thought about such a winter wonderland! "I'm jealous. It sounds *wunderbaar*!"

/ "I don't know about that. Living with snow isn't the same as watching it fall from the warmth of a kitchen. It's been icy and cold out. Every morning I have to go to the barn and break the ice on the horses' water troughs."

"I had no idea the water in their troughs could freeze."

"The horses don't appreciate it none, that's for sure." After a pause, he continued. "I've also been keeping busy by mending fences and building a new chicken coop for my mother."

"A new chicken coop, hmm?" There in the solitude of her kitchen, Amanda allowed her smile to grow. "That sounds mighty interesting."

"You think so?"

"I do. And it sounds difficult, too."

"It's only difficult if you've never built a structure like that before."

"And you have?"

"Too many times, I'm sorry to say. And, I promise, the chickens are only interesting if you've never spent much time with them. They're nasty creatures."

"Maybe they're not so bad."

"Enough about the chickens. Now, tell me about you."

"Me? Well, I worked one day this week at the bakery, I ran errands, cleaned out two closets, and Regina lost her favorite toy dog. See, not much of interest here with me either."

"That's where you're wrong. I want to hear all about Regina losing her dog."

Amanda chuckled, sure he was teasing.

"So, did you ever find the dog?"

Her mouth went dry. "You really are interested, aren't you?"

"Yeah."

His voice was quiet. Roman wasn't joking. He really did care. Amanda realized what was happening between them was special.

More than that, really. It was rare.

Roman hadn't called just to say hello. No, he called because he really did want to hear about her life.

Even if it wasn't anything special or fancy.

He cared because it had to do with her, and that's what was important to him.

She was important.

Focusing on the novelty of her feelings, she grabbed one of the kitchen chairs, pulled it near the phone, and sat down. And carefully went about telling him all about the search for the missing stuffed animal. Felt warmth from his interest.

And then, at his urging, she talked some more.

Far too soon, she heard Roman groan. "Listen, Amanda, I had better go. I just looked at the clock and we've talked a long time. This call is surely costing a pretty penny."

"Truly?" With a touch of dismay, she realized that they'd been talking on the phone for a whole thirty minutes. "Oh, *jah*. You're right. Thank you for calling."

"Will you be home tomorrow afternoon? About the same time?"

"I should be." Although at the moment, she couldn't think about much beyond the way talking to him made her feel.

"Then I'll call. If you don't think it's too soon?"

He was giving her space. Letting her be the person to tell him no.

"It's not too soon. I'd like to hear from you."

"Amanda, we're going to have to be careful, don't you think?"

His words warred with the smile she heard in his voice. "Why do you say that?"

"If we continue this, we're going to have to plan to see each other again."

"Would you come back to Pinecraft?"

"I could try. Or, maybe you could come up here. You and Regina could see our snow in person."

"Oh, I don't know about that. . . ."

"Why not? I think you'd love Berlin. And I know Regina would love to make a snowman."

"She probably would. But I'm just not sure if she's ready for a long bus trip."

"She might be." He chuckled, the sound making her feel warm all over again,. "Don't sound so worried," he said, his voice at once comforting and slightly chiding. "It was just a thought. I'll talk to you tomorrow, Amanda."

"Bye." When she hung up, his words rang in her ears. Would she one day be brave enough to get on a bus and go see him in Ohio? Or would she only be comfortable asking him to visit her?

What would it mean if they progressed to such cross-country visits? Would it mean that they'd become serious?

She shifted in the chair, and stared across the kitchen, not seeing a thing. Not believing all the feelings coursing through her. Did it all mean that she was actually thinking about marrying again?

And if she was, what did that say about her?

Why, just a few weeks ago, she'd been sure she'd always mourn Wesley. And now . . .

Tears pricked her eyes as she felt his loss all over again. It mixed in with her confusion about herself and her future and hurt, grating on her insides, scraping her raw.

"Are you off the phone now?" Marlene asked as she walked back in.

Amanda realized it was a rhetorical question. No doubt she'd been waiting, hovering just outside the kitchen, to hear the click of the receiver. Who knows? Perhaps she even overheard some of Amanda's conversation, too.

"*Jah*," she said quietly. "I'm done."

After a moment, Marlene walked to her side and tentatively rested her hand on the back of the chair. "Amanda, may we talk?"

"Of course. Where's Regina?"

"She's coloring in the other room." After a pause, Marlene pulled out a chair and sat down across from Amanda. "My dear, what is going on?"

Marlene's gaze was direct and forthright. Amanda answered her in the same way. "As you know, when Regina and I were staying at the condominium, I met a man from Ohio. His name is Roman Keim, and he is a farmer. We spent some time together."

"He lives in Ohio?"

"*Jah*. Berlin. Holmes County."

"Do you know anything else about him?" she asked, letting Amanda know that not only did Marlene know more than she was letting on, she'd also asked Regina questions.

With effort, Amanda pushed away the burst of irritation that coursed through her. She hated when Marlene asked her things she already knew the answer to. "Well, he's New Order, just like us. But more importantly, he is a good man, a caring man. He still lives with his parents and twin sisters. His grandparents live in their *dawdi haus*."

"Do you think there is something special between the two of you?"

"I don't know." After some thought she added, "All I know is that when I'm with him I only think about the future, not the past." Amanda felt her skin heat. Her words sounded so hopeful, so earnest.

Marlene folded her hands tightly on the top of the table. "He must like you if he's calling you on the phone, Amanda."

"I guess he does, then."

"I wish you'd talk to me. I want to know what's going on in your life."

"I'm not trying to be evasive, I simply don't know what's happening between the two of us. You can be sure that I didn't go looking for another man in my life."

"It's only been two years."

Only two years. "I know." She'd been alone one hundred and four weeks—730 days. Too many hours to count. How long, she wondered, was long enough?

"And . . . and my Wesley was your husband."

My Wesley. "Yes, he was." There was nothing more to add, was there? He had been her husband, and she had certainly planned to be his wife until her last dying breath.

But he died first, when she was only twenty-three. "I still miss Wesley. I'm not trying to replace him."

"I hope not. I can't imagine that he would have wanted to replace you so quickly."

The words stung, and Amanda knew that Marlene had meant them to hurt.

Over the years, she'd been the best girlfriend and wife she'd been able to be.

She'd borne Wesley a beautiful daughter and had planned to have a whole house of *kinner*.

And then, when he'd gotten sick, she'd done nothing but stay by his side and nurse him.

And now, for two years, she'd done her best to be his good and proper widow. She'd honored his memory and cried more tears than she could ever measure.

But she was lonely . . . and she'd promised Wesley that she wouldn't spend the rest of her life grieving. Promised him more than once when she'd sat by his bedside, when she'd held a hand that was no longer strong, when she'd cared for a man who was no longer vibrant. Who slowly became almost unrecognizable except for his beautiful brown eyes that always seemed to see too much.

"Marlene, you're not being fair to me or to Wesley."

"I'm only watching over his memory."

"He didn't want me to mourn him forever."

"Yes, but it hasn't been forever, Amanda. Only two years." Her mother-in-law murmured as she stood up and turned away. But that wasn't fast enough to hide her quivering lip.

Amanda tried to remember that Marlene was

mourning her son, too. "Marlene, I am sorry if I've hurt your feelings. I don't mean to make you upset. I don't mean to be disrespectful."

With her back still to her, she said, "Amanda, I think I will go home now."

"You don't want to help me with the casseroles?" They'd volunteered to make several meals for some families in their community, and Amanda had only volunteered for the job because Marlene had wanted to do it with her.

"Not today. I'm sorry," she said over her shoulder as a bit of an afterthought.

When she heard the front door slam shut, Amanda sat back down. Heard Regina talking to herself while she colored.

And realized she'd never felt more alone. Without even meaning to, she'd finally severed the past and it couldn't be fastened back together.

Even if things returned to how they used to be, there would always be the memory of her phone call. As well as the knowledge that for thirty minutes, she'd once again been giddy and happy and flirty.

She'd once again been the woman she used to be . . . all for a man who wasn't Wesley Yoder.

Chapter Fourteen

The Keims were just leaving the Millers' home after church services and a light luncheon of sandwiches and salads when Bishop Coblentz stopped Roman as he was slipping on his black wool coat.

"It was a nice service, Bishop," Roman said politely. "Once again, I find myself uplifted from listening to the Scripture's words."

"*Jah*, the Lord always has the right words, ain't so?"

"Always." He flashed a grin. "Enjoy your nap this afternoon." It was well known that the bishop appreciated an hour's rest after church on Sunday.

"Oh, I shall." His blue eyes crinkled at the corners. "I guess my habits are no secret."

"Good ideas are always talked about. I'm thinking of taking things easy this afternoon as well. We all need a day of rest."

He started to turn away when Bishop Coblentz stopped him with a firm touch to his shoulder.

"Before you begin that rest, may I speak to you for a moment, Roman?"

"Of course." Looking around, he saw Elsie and his mother still chatting with Mrs. Miller and her newly married daughter. About a dozen other folks were either talking in small clusters, cleaning up the last remnants of the luncheon, or attempting to gather their children.

Only the back cement patio was deserted. "Why don't we head over here?" he said after motioning to his mother that he needed more time before leaving.

The bishop nodded. "That's a good spot."

Roman led the way to the Millers' back patio. In spring and summer, an iron table and chairs sat squarely in the middle, the whole arrangement framed by the sweet scent of blossoming apple trees and the beauty of more flowers than he'd ever be able to name.

Now, in the dead of winter, the area was rather desolate. Flowering plants lay dormant under the covering of snow, and the apple trees were bare, their spindly arms lifted toward the sky like misshapen scarecrows.

Without any foliage to block the wind, Roman thought the air seemed even colder. But it also felt crisp and bracing, and he gave thanks for it, since it seemed he was going to need a clear head to talk with the bishop. The older man looked like he had something important on his mind to share.

"Is everything all right?" Roman asked. "Is there something I can help you with?"

Bishop Coblentz folded his weathered hands neatly on top of one of the black wrought-iron chairs he was standing behind. "I am fine, Roman, and I thank you for asking. Actually, your well-being was one of the things I was hoping to discuss with you."

Though the bishop's words were stated, he'd lifted the end of his sentence, as if he were asking a question.

Roman started to feel uneasy. "My well-being?" he echoed.

"*Jah*." The older man cleared his throat. "How are you, Roman? I imagine you're having quite a time, what with your father in the treatment program and all."

"I am all right. Just fine." With some surprise, he realized he was speaking the truth. Just a few weeks before, he would have given almost anything to make his life easier. He'd been disturbed by his grandmother's news about her past life and had dearly wished for his father's alcohol abuse to go away. Sometimes, late at night, he'd even stayed up and worried about what was going to happen with Elsie. With Viola getting married, he'd felt that it was his duty to accept more responsibility for Elsie's future care.

Now, everything still seemed difficult, but not insurmountable.

He knew the reason, of course. Ever since he'd returned from Florida he'd been so consumed with thoughts about Amanda that all the problems in his family had ceased to keep him up at night.

After staring at him intently for a moment, the bishop nodded. "Roman, I do believe you are all right. That is *gut*. It makes this a little easier."

Roman was starting to have the feeling that he'd walked into the middle of another man's conversation. "It makes what a little easier?"

"Henry Zimmerman came to see me two weeks ago. He's in poor health and has to step down from his preaching duties. The job has become too much for him, especially what with his farming and his failing health."

"I see."

"So, we asked for suggestions for a replacement from the congregation at the last church."

"I heard. I'm sure the congregation chose several good men for the lot."

"They did." As the bishop paused for breath, a slow, sinking feeling settled deep in Roman's chest.

Suddenly, he realized why the bishop had wanted to speak to him. "Was my name mentioned?"

"*Jah*." The bishop nodded. "Your name was chosen for the lot, Roman. It got one of the most votes."

"I see." Their church district had three ministers, who took turns preaching every two weeks. Whenever it was time for a vacancy to be filled, the congregation voted, then the top vote getters would be entered into the lot. Of course, every man who had been baptized into the church was eligible. Then, a Scripture passage was slipped in a stack of hymnals. If a man picked up the hymnal with the verse inside it, he would be the congregation's new preacher.

There were precious few reasons for a man to not accept the burden. Serious illness was just about the only viable excuse that would be accepted. It was their belief that the Lord chose the next preacher.

Roman believed that completely. However, it didn't make the heavy burden any easier to bear.

If a man drew the hymnal with the chosen verse inside, he would be required to serve in the open position. For the rest of his life, or as God saw fit.

It was a good system, a fair one. And one that their community had honored for as long as he could recall. Every man he'd known who'd been chosen had approached the process with both seriousness and a heavy sense of responsibility.

But now, selfishly, Roman realized that he'd been taken by surprise. He didn't know if he was ready. He felt too young, too immature for such a large job.

And he certainly wasn't ready for the change that would take place in his life. When a man realized he'd been chosen by the Lord to be a preacher, he knew he was going to have to preach in front of their whole church district for years. In addition, he was going to have to be available to guide and counsel other men and women in their community.

But how did a man refuse? Roman had never heard of anyone not living up to his obligation. Moreover, he'd promised the bishop when he was baptized that he would be willing to accept the process, if he was ever considered a suitable candidate.

"Are we choosing a new preacher today?" he asked, mainly to buy himself another minute of time.

"*Jah*." Bishop Coblentz's gazed sharpened. "We had hoped to only announce it today, so that the men could all pray about the opportunity. But I'm afraid in two weeks many folks have plans to head south for vacation or to visit family to celebrate Easter." He shrugged. "So, we're doing it today. It's God's will anyway, ain't so?"

"*Jah*," Roman said quietly. Bishop Coblentz was right. This was all under God's control, and because of that, it made little difference when the new preacher would be named.

The bishop pressed a hand onto Roman's bicep. "*Gut*. I wanted to speak to you first, to be sure you were able to accept God's calling if He sees fit." Softly, the bishop added, "I'm sure we would all understand, Roman, if you thought that your father's troubles were weighing too heavy on you to accept His call at this time." He shrugged. "Life has a way of taking twists and turns for everyone. If you don't feel ready for the responsibility, I'm sure there will be another opportunity to serve."

Roman sighed in relief.

He didn't have to say yes. Bishop Coblentz would understand. Perhaps the other men in his community would, too. But forevermore Roman knew that he would feel guilty if he refused the calling. It wasn't the Amish way to push things aside because they felt too hard or scary. More important, it wasn't his way. "If God wants to use me, I am willing and able to try my best."

"You are sure?"

Now, Roman didn't even hesitate. It was as if the Lord was behind him, prodding him forward. Helping him be the man he wanted to be. "I am sure."

Slowly, the bishop's lips curved above his long, graying beard. "Roman, I am happy to hear you say that. I promise, a willingness to be used by the Lord is all that anyone can ask for." He clapped a work-weathered hand on his shoulder. "*Jah*, I am most pleased. Well now, the four other men are already gathering in the barn. Let's get on with it then."

He turned and walked back toward the barn. Strode forward with steady, even steps, never pausing or looking over his shoulder to see if Roman was following.

But of course, there wasn't any need for that. Roman had given his promise.

Silently, Roman followed, nodding to John Miller and another couple of men who were standing around, watching to see who would be part of the lot. A few women looked up as he passed, then turned back to their conversations after giving him encouraging smiles. It was obvious word had already spread that a new preacher was about to be selected.

As he entered the dark barn and met the gazes of the other men assembled, Roman secretly told himself that his chances to be chosen were slim. He was the youngest man by a good eight years.

Surely God would choose a better, more experienced man than him? Someone who wasn't so confused about his life and his family? Who wasn't half in love with a lady in Florida?

That made him pause. Was he already "half in love"?

Was he *already* in love? Did he love Amanda Yoder?

Yes.

The answer came to him as clearly as if the Lord himself had just whispered into his ear.

He loved Amanda Yoder.

His mind spun as Bishop Coblentz walked to the front of the barn and gestured toward the neat stack of hymnals. "The Lord speaks to each of us in His own way," he began to the group of them. "It is up to each of us to open his heart to God's will."

Levi, the man on his right, murmured his agreement.

As Bishop Coblentz spoke, talking about responsibility and commitment, Roman let his mind drift to the one person he couldn't stop thinking about. He wondered when he could get away to see Amanda again. Perhaps he could go see her in three or four weeks, even if just for a few days. It would be a hard trip, of course, and his family would probably be displeased about him going away again so soon.

But Roman knew he could ask the other men in the family to watch over things . . . and after all, it wasn't like he had always shirked his duties.

No, he'd never shirked his duties. . . .

"Roman? It's your turn," Levi muttered.

"Huh?" With a start, he realized that the other men held hymnals in their hands. "Oh. Sorry," he muttered, as he walked up to the stack and picked the next one. He held the book with both hands.

Silence settled over them as each man seemed to tense slightly in anticipation.

"It is time," Bishop Coblentz said. "Open your hymnals. Inside one is a verse from First Corinthians."

In unison, the five men did as the bishop directed. Some flipped through their hymnals quickly. Others were like him, letting their nervous fingers flip through the paper-thin pages carefully, trying not to rip the pages.

As men found nothing, they shut their books with firm hands. And Roman's heart began to beat a little faster. Realizing he was borrowing trouble, he mentally berated himself. There was no way he would have the Scripture verse. In just a few seconds, he would be closing his hymnal, too. Then he could go back to thinking about Amanda, and making plans to see her again.

Visions of their reunion calmed him. Before he knew it, he was imagining her in a blue dress on their wedding day.

Yes, it was fanciful to imagine her as his wife, but the daydream was doing what his reality hadn't been able to do. He was feeling calmer, more at peace.

More slowly, he thumbed through his hymnal, looking for a loose slip of paper. Little by little, he realized that the other men were now sitting quietly.

And that everyone's eyes were focused on him.

Then he saw what he'd been dreading—and what he'd thought he wouldn't actually see. Beside him, Levi nodded.

Swallowing hard, he felt his options for the future slip away. With a heavy hand, he lifted the paper. "It is I," he said.

Bishop Coblentz stared at him intently. "Roman Keim, will you accept God's will?"

"I will accept," Roman said solemnly, not daring to look at John Miller or his uncle Sam or his grandfather. He didn't want to see the sympathy in their eyes. Not even the warm glow of pride.

Instead, he looked straight ahead and kept his back stiff.

And tried not to think at all.

Bishop Coblentz nodded. "His will is done."

He'd managed to avoid most of the family until supper time on Monday night.

But as Roman sat down across from Viola, felt Elsie's gaze on him, and saw the knowing glance of his grandfather, he realized he had no choice but to talk about his new responsibilities in the church. It was obvious they'd all heard. And just as obvious that they were trying their best to let him be the leader of the discussion.

He knew they were curious. But for the life of him, he couldn't bear to talk as if he was ready to be one of their district's preachers.

Even though he'd already told all the men that he'd accepted God's will.

Which, of course, made him feel even more confused and upset.

Tucking his chin, he forked another bite of green bean casserole and chewed. Anything to delay the inevitable.

For the last twenty-four hours, the feeling of following God's will warred with his own selfish wishes. In the middle of the night, he'd felt so torn, he wasn't able to fall back to sleep and had lain there, restlessly struggling with the news.

"Please pass the sweet potato casserole,

Roman," his mother said. "And while you're doing that, perhaps you could at last speak to us about what's happened."

Feeling like the glass dish weighed three tons, he lifted it and passed it clumsily to Elsie. "Here."

She took it without a word, but he could almost feel her frustration with him. And he saw clearly that she'd had to shift her hands quickly in order to not drop the dish on the table.

Which made him feel worse than he already did.

"Yesterday after church, Bishop Coblentz told me that I was one of the men who had received the most votes from the congregation for the open preaching position. The five men who were nominated drew hymnals. Mine was the chosen one," he said matter-of-factly. Because after all, those were the facts.

As he'd expected, no one burst into praise. Or shouted a congratulation. All knew it was a heavy burden to carry, especially in a man his age. Preachers were expected to carry out all sorts of pastoral duties, the same as in any other Christian denomination. However, in the Amish community, the preachers were not supported by the church.

Therefore, men kept their regular jobs, then added the new duties. For some men, it could be too much, especially over a long period of time.

"Well, what do you think about it?" Viola asked.

Roman met his grandfather's gaze. Roman had seen him sit quietly in the back of the barn when the hymnals had been drawn. To his credit, he hadn't said a single word about what had happened, either.

Instead, he'd let Roman have the time he needed to come to terms with what lay ahead.

"There is nothing to think about," Roman declared. "What's done is done. Besides, it's the Lord's decision."

"*Jah*, that is true," his grandfather said with a nod. But he didn't look entirely in agreement with his words. "Accepting God's calling is not always easy to do, but it is necessary. A man who accepts God's will without complaint is a man to be respected."

Just as his grandmother nodded, Viola shook her head. "Hold on. I understand that you had no choice but to be in the lot, and that you've accepted the Lord's calling."

He raised a brow. "But?"

"But you must have some opinion about it. Are you excited? Nervous? Upset? Confident?"

"It doesn't matter what I think." Roman shifted uncomfortably, wishing he could ease out of the room and sit and stew in private.

"Of course it matters what you think," Elsie blurted. "As a matter of fact, I think it might matter a lot."

Elsie's comment drew more than one startled glance. "How so?" their *mamm* asked quietly.

"Well, the Lord's will may be final, but that

doesn't mean we have to agree with His decisions."

"Elsie, you can't mean that," their grandmother exclaimed.

"Sure I do," Elsie countered. "I mean, I've accepted that one day I won't see . . . that one day I will no longer enjoy the sunrise or spring pansies or the sight of your faces. I've accepted that will be my future, but I'm not happy about it."

Around the table, everyone lowered their heads, anxious to change the subject as almost always happened when Elsie mentioned her disease.

But instead of remaining quiet like she usually did, she glared. "Ignoring things doesn't make them better. But sometimes talking about how we feel can make our burdens easier to bear."

To Roman's surprise, it was their grandmother who spoke up. "That is true, Elsie. You are right. We should all be talking about things that are on our mind. Roman, I know your father isn't here to advise you. Have you found someone to talk things through with?"

There was no way he was going to share his private thoughts around the dinner table. He could hardly imagine what they might say about his love for Amanda Yoder and his fear about preaching in front of the whole church.

"There's no need to discuss anything, Mommi," he said sharply. "I gave my consent to be considered to the Bishop, I drew that hymnal, and I've accepted the Lord's choice."

His grandmother didn't look cowed in the slightest. "But what about the girl in Florida?"

He set his fork down. "Amanda?"

She looked impatient. "Of course I mean Amanda. I've seen you on the phone in the kitchen, Roman. Hasn't she been the girl you've been talking to?"

"I've been calling her. And writing," he admitted somewhat grudgingly. Because, well, his phone calls weren't his grandmother's business.

"Well, then? What are you going to do about her?"

His temper broke. "Well, then?" he echoed. "Well, I have no idea. I hadn't planned on being a preacher, and especially not anytime soon."

Now that he'd begun, he could hardly stop; it was like another person had taken ahold of his tongue. "Actually, I'd been hoping to see her again, but now it looks like the Lord has made other plans for me."

Standing up, he pushed the chair out behind him with a noisy scrape. "I'm sorry, Mamm. I'll clean up my plate in a moment. But for now, I need to get out of here."

Like a sulking child, he tore out of the room, pulled open the back door, and raced outside.

Only when the cold wind whipped against his cheeks did he realize he was crying.

And only then did he speak the awful, awful question that had been brewing in his stomach from the first moment Bishop Coblentz had asked him to chat. "Why me, Gott? Why me? Why now?"

Chapter Fifteen

While the rest of the family sat stunned, staring at the closed door, Viola stood up. She couldn't simply sit and worry, and she certainly didn't feel ready to debate Roman's behavior with her mother and grandparents. "I'm going to start clearing the table, Mamm."

Her mother looked at her in surprise. "Oh. Well, all right . . ."

"I'll help," Elsie said just as quickly.

More than ever, Viola was thankful for her twin. Elsie was the one person she never needed to hide her feelings from. It was usually because she was feeling the same way. After picking up both her plate and Roman's, she walked to the kitchen. Elsie followed with her own plate in her hands.

Once they were together in the privacy of the kitchen, they put down the plates on the counter and stared at each other in wonder as they began to fill the sink to drown out their voices.

Elsie broke the silence. "Have you ever seen Roman like this before?"

"You know I haven't," Viola answered, adding soap to the water. "Gosh, Elsie, I didn't even think Roman knew *how* to be angry. All he's ever done is hold his temper and calmly discuss things."

"He's always been the one to remind us to be patient."

"And to pray and follow the Lord's way," Viola added. When they were younger, Roman's patient, preachy ways had driven her crazy. He'd never understood her need to act on things impulsively, and had made no bones about sharing his opinions.

Elsie lowered her voice. "I think he really is missing that woman. I know he misses Daed, too. And now he's been given this new responsibility. I can't even imagine what he's feeling. I bet he's worried and frustrated and hurting."

Elsie always did have a way of reading other people clearly. "I bet you're right."

"I sure don't know how to help him, though."

"Elsie, there's got to be a way to make things better. He's a *gut* man, and a *gut bruder*. I want him to be happy."

"I know, but he's got to come to terms with the reality. He's pining for a woman who lives over a thousand miles away. Sometimes it doesn't matter how much you want something. Sometimes you have to understand that there are things you simply can't change."

Viola felt her heart clench, knowing that Elsie

was referencing her disease. "I agree, but maybe Amanda could come here? Then Roman could see Amanda without leaving the farm and his new church responsibilities."

"I don't know if Roman will feel comfortable asking that. A woman likes to be pursued. Plus she has a daughter. Roman said she had a nice life out there in Florida."

"We could ask."

Elsie's eyebrows rose. "You mean *Roman* could ask her."

"No, I mean *we* could give her a call and ask her if she'd be interested in visiting. If she says yes, then we can let Roman know."

"He won't like that."

"That's true, but that's also what sisters are for, I think. To meddle in places where their brothers don't want them involved." As Elsie shook her head slowly, Viola couldn't help but grin. "Oh, come on, twin. It will be like we're *kinner* again."

"No, following him around on the playground at school would be like we were *kinner* again. This is interfering with his life, Viola."

"It's in his best interests." She pushed away Elsie's protests by gesturing to the dining room. "We better finish clearing the table before Mamm asks what we are doing."

"I know what you're doing, you know," Elsie said. "You're hatching a plot that I'm going to have to put into play—and have to deal with the consequences of."

"What do you mean?"

"While you're in Belize, I'll be here, dealing with the repercussions."

Viola felt slightly guilty. But not guilty enough to back down. "You're always telling us you're stronger than we think, sister. Now you can prove it."

And with that, she strode back into the dining room and picked up her grandparents' plates. They were deep in discussion with their mother. Not one of them even looked Elsie's and Viola's way as they finished clearing the table.

And just like that, Viola felt every bit of her exuberance fade away. Her family was feeling the burden of change more than ever.

When they returned to the kitchen, she noticed that Elsie's playful manner had faded as well.

After scraping the plates, Elsie walked to her side, a dishcloth in her hand. As Viola washed each plate, Elsie silently dried it and put it in the cupboard. It was a task they'd easily done a hundred times before, and the familiar comfort of the chore brought a peace that an hour-long conversation never could have done.

When their stack of dirty dishes was gone and the leftovers neatly put away, Elsie turned to her. "Viola, you are exactly right. Something needs to be done for Roman. It's not in his nature to push for something he wants. He's always been the member of the family to stand aside while the rest of us get our way." She paused. "Roman deserves happiness. We all do." Taking a deep breath, Elsie added, "If you don't have time to call Amanda, I will."

"Are you sure? Tomorrow I can get Amanda's phone number from Beth."

"I can do that, too, Viola. Actually, calling Amanda will make me feel good inside. Useful."

"*Danke*, Elsie," she said quietly, feeling her sister's resolve.

More than a week had passed since Amanda and Regina had returned to their regular schedule. But even though they were now settled only a few minutes away from the beach, everything felt different. Gone were the Pop-Tarts and beach towels. In their places were eggs and oatmeal and rain boots.

For some reason, the sun had decided to begin a vacation when they left the beach. Their usual sunny days were now filled with rain clouds.

"Mamm, when will it ever stop raining?" Regina asked from her spot at the window.

"When the time is right, I suppose," Amanda said to her daughter as she finished packing Regina's lunch.

She slumped. "I'm tired of the rain."

"I know."

"It's ruining our day."

"Well, it will make us wet," Amanda corrected. "But I'm not so sure if it's been ruining our day." As she watched her daughter continue to stare at the rain out the window with disappointment, she brightened her voice. "You know, it's a good thing we aren't too sweet, Regina. Otherwise we'd melt in the rain."

"I don't want to melt."

Of course, Regina had taken her statement seriously—she took all her statements seriously. And there was no reason she would have ever heard her grandfather's saying about melting in the rain before. Living in Pennsylvania, Amanda's parents hadn't had the opportunity to spend much time with Regina. "I was only joking, dear. I meant that a little rain never hurt anyone. It's not a terrible thing."

"I still feel sad."

"And why is that? Does the rain make you feel gloomy?"

"*Nee*. On rainy days, Mommi only wants to look out the window and talk about Daed."

Amanda winced. Soon she was going to have to find a different situation for Regina. Her mother-in-law's perpetual state of mourning wasn't healthy.

"I am sorry about that. We could pack you some books to look at while you're with your grand-mother."

"All right." Regina scampered off to her room to retrieve the thick canvas book bag that held her dozen library books.

Fighting off the feeling of guilt that was nagging at her, Amanda carefully closed up Regina's lunch bag, smiling as she did so. About four months ago, while grocery shopping at the store, Regina had seen a bright purple nylon lunch sack with Velcro on the ends of it. Decorating the sturdy fabric were yellow and orange starfish and red polka-dotted seals. Amanda had privately thought it was an ugly, garish design, but Regina?—she'd fallen in love.

For weeks she'd complained about the sturdy basket lined with pretty cloth napkins that Amanda used for her lunch. It was too heavy. It didn't keep the food cold. Amanda had tried to hold firm, but then didn't see the harm in a new lunch bag for her daughter. They'd gone to the store and bought it together. Ever since, Regina had carried it with pride.

Funny how something so small could matter so much to a little girl.

She was still thinking about that when the phone rang, jarring her thoughts. "Hello?"

"Is this Amanda Yoder?"

"It is," she said hesitantly. She didn't get many telemarketers, but this woman didn't sound like she was selling anything.

"My name is Elsie Keim. I'm Roman's sister."

Her heart leapt to her chest. "Is Roman hurt? Is something wrong?"

"Hurt? Oh goodness, no. He's fine. Well, kind of fine. He could be better."

Well, if that wasn't the strangest comment! "I'm afraid I don't understand."

"I'm, uh, calling to invite you and your daughter to Ohio. To Berlin. Would you like to visit us?"

Instantly the pictures Roman had created in her mind tumbled forth. She started thinking of snowmen and crisp, cold air. Pine trees and scarves and mittens. "Thank you for the invitation. But why are you asking me instead of Roman?" And furthermore, she chided herself, why was she even considering such a thing?

"Well," Elsie began, "my brother has recently been called to be our district's newest preacher. It's a heavy responsibility, you know."

"Yes?"

"Anyway, we all know that he wants to see you, and was hoping to plan another trip to Florida, but now he canna get away."

"I see." That told her many things, but not why Roman wasn't the one asking her to visit.

"No, I don't think you do," Elsie replied, just as if she could read Amanda's mind. "See, my brother is the type of man who doesn't care to make waves for anyone. When he learned of this new responsibility, he decided to work hard to honor it."

"I still don't understand why you are calling and not him."

"Because he is stubborn. We all know you and your daughter mean a lot to him, but we also know that he's the type of man to put everyone else's wishes and needs before his own. He wants to see you, but doesn't want to let that interfere with his duties at the farm."

"Elsie, do you mean to tell me that you are inviting me without his knowledge?"

"Actually . . . that would be true."

Amanda could tell that Elsie was getting impatient with all her questions. But while Amanda knew that she longed to drop everything for a surprise visit to see Roman, she certainly could never do that with Regina's heart on the line. Never could she risk taking Regina to a place where she wasn't wanted. Her little girl had already been through so much.

"I appreciate the invitation, but I cannot accept. It wouldn't be right."

"No, it would be right. Roman will love that you're here. I promise you that."

"I'm not thinking of him, I'm thinking of my daughter. She is who I must concentrate on."

After a pause, Elsie spoke again. "Yes, I suppose so. Well, I'm sorry for the phone call. I hope I haven't offended you."

"Not at all. I can only imagine what it must be like to have a *shveshtah* who loved me so much."

When she hung up, she noticed Regina lurking at the edge of the kitchen.

"Who was on the phone, Mamm?"

"Roman's sister Elsie."

"Why did she call?"

"Merely to ask me something."

"What did you say?"

"I said I didn't know the answer," she said quickly. Clearing her throat, which seemed suspiciously tight all of the sudden, she said, "Now, daughter, it is time to get on our way." She held up the lunch tote. "You need to get to your grandparents' house and I need to go to work."

"Even in the rain?"

"Yes, dear. Even in the rain we must do what we are supposed to do."

Always. Even when she wished to do otherwise. Even then.

Chapter Sixteen

It was raining. "Could there be anything worse than rain in March?" Roman asked his horse as he double-checked the lines on the buggy that he'd just attached. "Our journey to the store is going to make us both a wet, soggy mess."

Chester tossed his head as if in agreement . . . or maybe it was annoyance. Roman figured the old horse was probably as irritated by the bit in his teeth as the cold rain soaking his coat. Of late, Chester had become quarrelsome. "Sorry, *gaul*," he murmured, rubbing the horse's neck. "We've all got our jobs to do. Pulling me in the rain is yours today."

Chester looked away and pawed the ground with a hoof.

He was still smiling at his horse's strong personality as he strode into the barn and saw Elsie standing next to one of the stalls. "*Gut matin*," he said. "What are you doing out here so early?"

"I have something to tell you."

Elsie was wearing a look he knew well, one that said she was ready to chat for hours. Well, the horse wasn't the only one in the barn impatient to get on his way. "Can it wait? I've got to get into town before the weather gets worse."

She shook her head. "I don't think so."

"Go ahead, then. What is it?" he asked as he shrugged into his coat.

"I called Amanda this morning."

Roman froze. He wanted to ask a million questions. Ask if she was talking about *his* Amanda. Ask how she'd even gotten Amanda's telephone number.

But instead, he asked the question that mattered the most. "Why would you do that?"

She tugged on the edge of her apron. Crinkled it into her fist. "Well, Viola and I got to talking . . ."

"And?"

"And, we were discussin' how you've been mooning over her . . ."

"Lord, save me from twin sisters! Elsie, you and Viola had no business talking about me like that."

Releasing the apron, her chin rose. "You're our brother. Of course we're going to talk about you." She pressed on, her words tumbling out of her mouth in a rush. "It was easy enough to get her number. Cousin Beth had it."

He breathed a sigh of relief. He supposed it was good that the pair of them hadn't gone through his room, looking for the small scrap of paper in his desk drawer that held the precious information. "What did you say to Amanda?"

"Oh, not much. I introduced myself. Told her about me and Viola . . ."

"Elsie, get to the point."

"Well, actually, after we talked for a bit . . . I invited her and her daughter to come visit."

He could hardly believe his ears. She'd picked up the phone. Called up Amanda. And asked her to come to Ohio. That's all. "It's Regina," he said.

She blinked in confusion. "Hmm?"

"Her daughter's name is Regina," he repeated, mainly to buy himself some time to rein in his growing temper.

"So, what do you think?"

He thought he had the two most interfering sisters on the planet. That's what he thought.

"I'm not sure why you care what I think, Elsie," he snapped. "Seein' as how you've taken it upon yourself to get involved in my life and all."

"It wasn't just me."

"You. And Viola."

"So you're mad at us?"

"You could say that," he bit out. "Honestly, did you two really think I'd be grateful for your interference?"

After a moment, she nodded. "*Jah*."

"You two are more trouble than a pair of goats in love."

She blushed. "I think not." Stepping a little closer, she said, "It's been my experience that family members usually meddle with the best of intentions."

"Just because someone doesn't mean to cause damage, when they do, things still need to be repaired. You should have minded your own business." He could only imagine how horrified Amanda must have been, receiving a call from his sister.

"Nothing is hurt, Roman. Nothing needs to be repaired."

"Oh, really? What am I supposed to do now?"

"Call her and say you want her to come."

"Is that right?" He snapped his fingers. "I'm sure it's just that easy."

"It sounded to me like it was."

He stared at her, forgetting about the rain, about

his ornery horse, about his irritating younger sisters. "Did . . . Did Amanda sound like she wanted to come north? To see Ohio?"

"Well, she sounded like she wanted to see *you*, Roman."

"She said that?" With effort, he tried to keep his body and expression cool and detached. Inside, however, he was raising his fist in the air in triumph.

"More or less." Amusement lit her voice. "Amanda said she would look forward to speaking to you about it. So that sounded positive to me. But then again, I don't know her like you do."

Roman couldn't help but smile. He liked the thought that he knew Amanda, that he understood her. But then he gathered his resolve again. He had a sister who couldn't see him softening. "Elsie, you don't know her at all."

"But I'd like to. She sounded really nice. She sounded fond of you, Roman. Which, of course, makes me like her a whole lot more. I do want to meet this Amanda in person. Viola and I both do."

His sister was so earnest, so sincere, he couldn't stay mad at her for long. "Have I ever told you that you're my favorite twin?"

"Last month, just days after you told Viola the same thing. Right before you said we were going to be the death of you."

"I didn't mean that."

"But this time?" She raised a brow.

"This time I think it's true."

She chuckled. "Call Amanda sometime today, Roman. What can it hurt?"

"I might just do that," he said grudgingly. "*Danke*, Elsie. I owe you."

"Don't worry, one day you can help me when I'm being courted. Viola's going to be of no use, since she'll be in a foreign country and all."

"Of course I'll help you," he called out as he watched her carefully make her way back to the house.

But as he watched her stumble on the edge of a stone step and straighten her glasses, Roman wondered when Elsie was ever going to come to terms that she would most likely never have a husband.

As he trudged out to the buggy, he couldn't help but shake his head. It truly was a shame, he realized. Because in many ways, she was the best of the three of them. Continually happy, eternally poised. A hard worker and patient.

She would have made some man a wonderful wife.

A wonderful wife.

Pushing off thoughts of his sister, he let his mind drift back to Amanda and the upcoming phone conversation. And to his surprise, he wasn't dreading it at all.

Turning back to Chester, he said, "Well, boy,

let's get this trip to town over with. It looks like I have much to do today. So much, I might not even mind the rain."

The disdainful look Chester gave him in response was priceless.

And pretty much made him grin most of the way into town.

It seemed everyone wanted to go to the airport with her. "I told ya, Mr. Cross said he'd be happy to take me and make sure I got on the plane just fine," Viola said to her siblings, her grandparents, her mother, and—unbelievably— Mr. Swartz. "He took Edward."

"I'm sure Mr. Cross is a *verra* nice man. But he ain't family," her mother said briskly. "And he is most definitely not your *muddah*."

"That is true," Atle said with a gleam in his eye. "It's been my experience that no one can take a mother's place when it comes to fussin'."

As they piled in the van that her grandfather had hired for the day, Viola held her purse tightly on her lap, and double-checked her papers and plane itinerary again. And then slowly opened her passport and glanced at the photograph of herself.

Not for the first time, her grandfather held out his hand and examined the blue booklet carefully, running his finger over her signature.

Though he'd never actually said so, Viola felt that of everyone in the family, he'd been the one who was most unhappy about her choices. "Are you terribly upset, Grandfather?"

"With what?"

"With me, because I'm getting on an airplane and going to Belize."

"To see your man? *Nee*. I'm not upset."

"Then you understand?"

"I understand what it's like to miss someone you love. And I understand what it's like to take a chance on something new, too. You forget, when your *mommi* and I moved to Ohio, we didn't know anyone at all. It was a scary adventure." He glanced to his right. "Wouldn't you say that, Lovina?"

She chuckled softly. "Well, I would have to admit that that time is all a blur to me now. I was newly married, and had just become Amish."

This was the first time her grandmother had ever mentioned her transformation in such a casual way. Viola wished Elsie was sitting nearby so she could give her a nudge.

But perhaps Elsie had already read her mind. "Mommi, what was it like, moving with Dawdi?"

"Scary. I didn't want to let him down."

That seemed like a strange comment. Viola looked at her grandmother in surprise. "Why would you have been worried about that?"

"Because I was always doing things wrong." She shook her head in a guilty manner. "I could hardly speak Deutsch."

"I didn't expect you to know everything." Her

177

grandfather looked at Viola then and grinned—a very cheeky, very male grin. "It didn't matter so much to me, anyway. She was the prettiest woman I'd ever seen."

This time it was her mother who spoke up. "Is that right, Aaron? You were taken in by a pair of pretty brown eyes?"

"Yes, I was." He cleared his throat in a gruff way as he handed the passport back to Viola. "And that will be the end of this talk."

They all laughed. The mood in the van was light and comfortable, bringing back memories of times when things weren't so confusing and hard at home.

Viola gave thanks to God for reminding her that while things weren't perfect in the Keim family, it wasn't completely broken, either. It was the first glimmer of hope she'd felt in weeks—just as she was leaving town.

"Everyone is going to have to tell me how Roman looks at Amanda," she said just to keep the conversation light. "Because we all know Roman won't tell me about the visit."

"I'm sure there will be nothing to tell," Roman said.

"I'm sure there will be lots to tell," Elsie teased. "After all, you called her just days ago, and now she's on the bus to Ohio. That was quick."

"She got a special price on the tickets, that's all," Roman said.

"I'm putting my money on the girls, Roman," his grandfather said with a wry look.

Roman scowled. "When she gets here, no one better be looking at the two of us."

Viola raised her brows at Elsie, conveying silently that Elsie better plan to give her a full report.

Her mother and grandmother chuckled.

As did Atle. "Come now, Roman. Are you really so backward that you don't think everyone's going to be watching you together?" he asked. "I'm counting on getting as many reports as possible at Daybreak."

To their amusement, Roman's cheeks turned red. "I don't want Amanda to feel awkward," he sputtered. "Plus, she will have her daughter with her, you know. Everyone needs to take care around her."

"Whose name is Regina, I believe," Elsie said. "Isn't that right, Roman?"

Roman groaned.

Viola bit her lip to refrain from commenting on that. Around her, she felt the rest of the group's efforts to hold their tongues. Roman was a private man. If they teased him too much, there was no way he'd ever say another word about Amanda again.

Luckily for her brother, their driver soon announced they were approaching the Cleveland Hopkins International Airport. Now she had no thoughts except for her worries about traveling alone to a foreign country . . . and an almost breathless anticipation about finally seeing Ed again. Their six-week separation had felt at times like an eternity.

She only hoped when they were together again that their reunion would be as sweet as she'd imagined. What would she do if Ed acted differently toward her in Belize?

What would she do if she hated Belize? If she found that no matter how hard she tried she couldn't live in a foreign country?

Or if she realized she didn't want to be a missionary's wife?

Or, worst of all, if she didn't think she could work with the people that Edward served? She would be so embarrassed.

And Edward would be so disappointed!

As they stopped in front of the terminal, she felt a calm hand on her shoulder. "Don't," her grandfather murmured, just for her ears.

"Don't what?" she whispered right back.

"Don't start fretting and worrying." When her eyes widened, he said, "Your thoughts are written as plain as day, all over your face." Moving his hand from her shoulder to her chin, he raised it slightly. "Have faith, Viola. Have faith in yourself and in Edward, and in the Lord. I feel certain that he isn't leading you down this path just to feel pain."

Her grandfather's words were just the boost she needed. Feeling better and more confident than she had in days, she led the procession out of the van and inside the airport.

The moment they were in the brightly lit, noisy building, no less than three airport personnel rushed to their side. Viola guessed their Amish clothing stuck out like sore thumbs.

When she told them what airline she was flying on, and to where, they guided her—and the whole family—to a check-in booth.

Ten minutes later, her suitcase was on a conveyer belt, she had her travel documents in hand, and another person was offering to walk her to the airport security station.

"But your family can't come with you, miss."

Though she was trying to be brave, tears pricked at her eyes as she glanced at Elsie. "I guess I better go. All by myself."

One by one, everyone hugged her. In between hugs, her mother asked her about money and snacks and if she had her new Karen Kingsbury novel to help pass the time.

Her grandparents reminded her to pray.

Roman teased her about being such an independent woman.

Last of all, she was in Elsie's arms. "I'm going to miss you so much," she whispered into her twin's neck. "I don't know what I'm going to do without you."

This time, it was Elsie who was the strong one. "Of course you do, twin. You're going to be yourself and enjoy every minute of your adventure."

Finally, she admitted her greatest fear. "And if I decide it's all not for me?"

"Then you will know that it isn't," Elsie said with her usual patient manner. "You need to know for sure, Viola."

A lady in a security uniform cleared her throat. "Miss, it's time to go. You're holding up the line."

"*Jah*. Okay." Biting her lip, she waved to them all, then turned and walked toward the many people in their blue uniforms.

And tried not to listen for her family as they walked away.

"You've got a great family, miss," her escort commented. "It's been a long time since I've seen someone get such a sendoff."

"Yes. They're *wunderbaar*, for sure." Had she ever truly realized that?

Still dwelling on her family, she handed the security person her passport and plane ticket, then walked toward the screening station.

Before she started putting her things on the conveyer belt, she turned, trying to catch one last glimpse of her family.

But they were already out of sight. She was completely on her own now. Completely on her own, for better or worse.

Chapter Seventeen

The Pioneer Trails bus had traveled through the night, with frequent stops along the way. Through it all, the rest breaks and the naps and the snippets of conversation, Amanda had felt as if she were in a daze. Well, she would have been if Regina had not kept her on her toes.

While others slept through the stops, Regina had insisted on getting out and exploring the truck stops, waffle houses, and McDonald's. Each one was a new experience for her, and Regina seemed determined to enjoy every locale to the fullest.

While others complained about greasy food or uncomfortable seats, Regina asked for seconds and cuddled close. When some men grumbled about the colder temperatures, little Regina had beamed when Amanda placed her new pink cardigan over her dress, saying that the cooler weather necessitated it.

Yes, Regina Yoder was a champion traveler, happy and excited. Her mother, on the other hand, was tired.

Mighty tired! Only Regina's obvious excitement kept Amanda from turning cranky. But sometime around two in the morning, when Regina was cuddled next to her, sleeping deeply, and most of the other folks on the bus were sleeping, too,

Amanda realized that she was just as excited as her daughter.

And thankful to have something new to look forward to.

After all, it wasn't every day that a woman took a fifteen-hour bus ride north to see a man she'd only spent five days with. And to bring her daughter along, too?

She was a little embarrassed about the trip. Well, not embarrassed as much as hesitant to tell the strangers on the bus about her private business. So she kept to herself more than usual, and was thankful no one pushed her for information when she answered their questions in a vague way.

Sure enough, dawn had come, the rising sun bringing with it yet another chance for a quick breakfast, and an excellent way to see the country-side. She and Regina had passed the last two hours looking for different state license plates.

Now they were only twenty miles away from the Berlin German Village Market, where Roman had said he would be waiting for them in his buggy. Nervous flutters had begun to dance in her stomach as soon as they'd entered the state of Ohio. Now that they were so close, she wondered how she was going to appear calm and relaxed when she and Roman came face to face again.

Or when she met his whole family!

What would they think of her? she wondered. Would they be eager to meet her? Or instead wish that Roman was interested in someone a little younger, or at least a woman who hadn't been married before?

Or maybe even they wished he was seeing someone who didn't have a child.

Knotting her fists, Amanda frowned. One would have thought she would have outgrown such nervousness. After all, she'd already been married and had buried a husband. It's not like she was an anxious teenager.

Regina tapped her on her arm. "Mamm, did you see all the snow outside?"

Craning her neck over her sweet daughter's white *kapp* and black bonnet covering a pair of braids that had long since started to fray, Amanda gazed at the huge expanse of hills and valleys covered with a thick blanket of snow. "It's pretty, indeed. Why, it looks just like the clouds have come to visit us."

As Amanda hoped, Regina giggled. "Do you think we're going to get to play in the snow?"

"Of course. I'm sure Roman will let you play in it as much as you want."

"I can't wait to roll around in it. And make a snow angel."

Her daughter had been fascinated by snow angels ever since she'd seen a picture book of Amish children playing in the winter. "I'm sure you will make a mighty fine snow angel."

"And then I want to see Roman's horses."

"You will. He's coming with a van and driver. We'll get to his farm quickly."

"I want to see his cows, and the chickens. Oh! And the pigs, too."

The older couple they were traveling next to laughed. "Just wait until you smell the farm animals, Regina. That's when you might change your mind. And snow is cold. You might not like that much at first. It takes some getting used to."

"I'm going to like it all," Regina stated confidently. "I'm sure of it."

Amanda felt Regina would like it. She had always been a happy girl, and eager to try new experiences—or at least she had until Wesley had died. Her father had been like that, Amanda recalled. He'd been an easygoing man. The very best of husbands.

"Look," Anna, the Mennonite lady next to them said, pointing out the window, "we're almost there."

Once again, Amanda craned her neck. Then gulped as she saw the green sign stating that they were now in Berlin.

"You're going to love it here," Anna said.

"We're only here for a short visit," Amanda replied quickly. Though she wasn't quite sure if she was assuring Anna or herself.

Regina started bouncing up and down in her seat. "Settle, child," Amanda cautioned.

Then, all too soon, they had arrived at the

German Village Market. For the next few minutes, Amanda busied herself with gathering all their belongings and making sure Regina was bundled in her scarf, black bonnet, and thick wool coat.

"Let's go," she finally said. Leading the way down the aisle, into the sunny day that beckoned through the doorway of the bus, they were met with a burst of cold air.

"Brrr!" Regina said.

"Indeed, child," Amanda replied with a tight smile. "It is cold and snowy and sunny. All at the same time."

"Amanda? Regina?"

She turned to find Roman striding toward them, an intriguing combination of smiles and confidence.

Her pulse started racing as Regina pulled away from her hand and scampered to Roman. She told herself it was simply because she was no longer holding on to her daughter.

Roman picked up Regina and spun her around. Regina squealed happily.

And then Amanda felt short of breath. Surely that was due to the fact that it was so cold her breath was a puff of vapor in front of her lips.

But when he settled Regina on the ground again, then started forward, looking at no one else but her, Amanda knew she couldn't fool herself any longer.

She was foolish and delighted and excited and

happy—all things that had been absent from her life for much too long.

She held the feeling tight and hoped it would stay deep in her heart for a very long time.

Or at least for a few hours.

"Peter, I need you home again," Marie said into the phone, wishing—not for the first time—that they had to go to a phone shanty like the Old Order Amish. Though she was grateful not to be out in the cold, she privately thought that having a phone in the kitchen sometimes created more problems than it helped. It was a struggle to have a private conversation in the busiest room in the house.

"I know my being gone is hard on you, but the therapists say I need to stay here a little while longer. No one wants me to have a relapse."

She was so frustrated she felt tears prick her eyes. "So you're sure you have to stay?"

He sighed. "You know coming here wasn't an easy decision for me. I don't want to leave until they say I'm ready."

"I know you don't," she said around a cough.

"Marie, are you sick?"

"It's just a little cough. It's nothing."

He paused. "Marie, you have to know I wouldn't wish this on you. I know you're having a difficult time. But I have faith in you. You are a strong woman, and I have a feeling that you are doing a *gut* job keeping everything together—even with a cough," he teased.

She smiled in spite of herself. "I'm doing my best. I don't know if it's good or not."

"I'm sure you are doing great."

His confidence in her felt good, but Marie ached to lean on him. Usually, they'd end each day going over things, rehashing discussions they'd had with the kids or with friends or other family members. She'd grown to rely on that time to reflect on the way she or he handled things. "I hate complaining to you."

"Complain all you want," he murmured. "You've earned that right."

Just because she was strong didn't mean she wanted to be strong all the time. And just because she knew it was all right to complain and whine, well it didn't make her feel any better. If anything, it made her feel like she was living a lie. Here, everyone in the family thought she was being supportive and kind. . . .

But inside, she was harboring a multitude of secret complaints. The worst of which was that she resented Peter for leaving her to deal with everything.

His voice as smooth as silk, Peter prodded her to open up more, "Why don't you tell me what's going on?"

"Roman is picking up the woman he met in Florida right now. And Viola left for Belize."

189

"How was she when you dropped her off?"

"Excited, but nervous."

"That sounds like our Viola."

She smiled, enjoying his comment. Then, she steeled herself. "And, ah, it turns out your father was married before and had a child."

"What?"

"Oh, yes. He only met your mother after they passed away. Peter, did you know about any of this?"

"*Nee*! Not at all."

"Well, it was news to all of us, too," she said.

"What happened? Did he say?"

"He didn't tell us much, but I went and asked him for more information. And," she added proudly, "after a bit of hemming and hawing, he told me a bit more." Briefly, she told him about how Aaron had met Laura Beth and Ben, how they died . . . and about how Laura Beth's family blamed him for her death.

"Maybe that's why he married Mamm and moved away."

"Maybe so."

After a pause, he said, "What else is going on?"

"Nothing besides preparing for Lorene's wedding."

He whistled low. "That's enough, I think."

"Indeed." She twirled the telephone cord around her finger and chuckled, enjoying their conversation.

"How are the livestock? Have the seeds come in that I ordered for spring planting?"

"I don't know."

"What do you mean? Marie, that's our livelihood."

Sometimes men were so dense. "Come now, Peter. You know I haven't had time to think about plants. You'll have to ask Roman or John or Sam about that."

"Please ask them and let me know next time I call."

"I'll try. But please, try to come home soon." Closing her eyes, she felt full of regret. She didn't want to be this kind of person. But it was as if the devil had gotten ahold of her and was making her say things where before she'd only thought them.

A clatter jangled outside the kitchen window, followed by Elsie's happy cry. "They're here!"

"I must go, Peter."

"Oh. Well, all right . . . I'll try to call you again soon."

"Don't worry about calling. Just get better," she snapped, then immediately felt contrite. "I'm sorry. I don't mean to sound so terrible. I'm just feeling overwhelmed."

"I know. Hey, Marie?"

"Yes?"

"*Ich liebe dich.*"

Her heart softened. "I love you, too."

"Soon, this will all be in the past. Try to remember that."

"I'll do my best," she said wearily. She knew he was right. But she feared she was just about at the end of her rope.

She needed her husband. She needed her partner, her helpmate back. Quickly.

Lord, what was happening to her? Opening her eyes, she looked across the room and spied Lovina lurking in the doorway. It was obvious that she'd been eavesdropping.

Marie wished she would have been surprised. "I guess you heard me talking about Aaron and Laura Beth and Ben?"

Twin spots of color lit her cheeks. "I . . . I did."

"Peter needed to know," she said in a rush.

"I agree. If I've learned anything over the last few weeks, it's that some secrets come back to haunt us. It's better to talk about things."

As they heard the van doors close, Marie pointed to the door. "I better go out there."

"*Jah.* I . . . I think I'll wait here. No sense in us all descending on poor Amanda."

Feeling wearier than ever, Marie turned away and started walking outside. Ready to greet their houseguests . . . and to pretend that everything was as wonderful as it ever was.

Chapter Eighteen

As Lovina stood in the shadows of the hallway, listening to Roman introduce his mother and Elsie to his guests, she knew she'd made the right decision.

It really was best to wait to say her hellos.

To her ears, Amanda and Roman sounded a little reserved, a little nervous around each other. Marie sounded hesitant but friendly.

Elsie, on the other hand, seemed especially exuberant and excited.

Lovina smiled at that. Elsie's happy, honest personality helped just about every situation.

As the stilted conversation continued, Lovina leaned her head against the hall wall and smiled softly. It all sounded so ordinary. So right. So like what a "normal" family should sound like.

Lovina heard the kitchen chairs scraping against the wood floor as they were pulled out. She heard the clinking of Marie's good china as she poured coffee and served blueberry coffee cake. Every so often, she heard the high-pitched voice of Amanda's daughter. Questions about the bus trip floated her way, as well as gentle teasing about the daughter's fondness for junk food.

When she heard Amanda chuckle, and then the

deep voice of Roman combine with hers, Lovina smiled fondly.

Ah! Young love. There was nothing like that first bit of excited nervousness, she mused. Even when she was ninety, she didn't think she'd forget how giddy she'd been around Jack.

Or how nervous she'd been when she'd first met his parents. She'd probably sounded much like Amanda did now, Lovina decided.

But, of course, she'd been nervous for far different reasons.

She hadn't met Mr. and Mrs. Kilgore in their kitchen. Instead, she'd been drunk and on the side of the road. Ambulances and fire trucks had lit up the street, decorating the dark, narrow road with shades of flashing red and orange.

The garish colors had matched the blood on her hands, the blood that stemmed from the gash on her head. And the blood that had covered Jack. The windshield had cut them both when he'd lost control of his car, then slammed it into a fence on the side of the road.

It was a night of horrors. First had been the alcohol that she'd never wanted to drink. Then, she and Jack had gone way too far in a corner of an empty classroom, which had led her to dissolving into near uncontrollable tears and demanding he take her home.

Jack had agreed, but then Billy Thompson had asked for a ride, too. If she'd just said no to

Jack's advances, she wouldn't have needed to leave. And if Jack had just said no, Billy wouldn't have been in the backseat of the car.

Then Billy wouldn't have been thrown from the car. He wouldn't have been . . . dead.

She flinched at the memory, of seeing Billy broken and bleeding.

When Jack's parents had arrived, she'd looked at them groggily, in a daze. Fear and grief and disbelief had mixed with the last bit of alcohol in her system and had caused her to be rendered mute. When they'd leaned over her, she'd only stared back at them through foggy vision.

They'd glared at her as if she'd caused the accident. Then they'd surrounded Jack, comforting him as the paramedics loaded him into an ambulance.

She'd gone in the other ambulance to the hospital for X-rays and fifteen stitches.

Her parents had met her at the hospital. But they'd looked confused by the police reports, not sympathetic. No, far from it.

They'd been disgusted by the smell of alcohol on her breath. And bothered by the stunned look of guilt and sadness she couldn't quite hide.

And, of course, shocked and upset by Billy's death.

She'd been released right away, but her parents had refused to let her go see Jack. "He's in surgery, and his parents said he's in no condition to talk to anyone. He's very upset about Billy. Billy was Jack's best friend, you know."

"I know," she said weakly. She'd ached to tell them that of course she'd known that Jack was upset. She'd ached to remind everyone that she wasn't just some girl. After all, she'd been Jack's date for the dance. She'd almost been his girlfriend.

But she'd been too upset to argue. So she'd gone home, carefully unzipped the pretty dress she'd been so proud of, and stepped into the shower.

There, in the privacy of the small space, she'd cried hot tears under a cold spray of water, keeping the water cold on purpose, almost feeling the need to torture herself some more. She'd welcomed how its sting felt like needles on her skin.

Shame and sickness had warred in her stomach, making her realize that it actually was possible to hate herself.

No, she hadn't been able to stop Jack from agreeing to take Billy home. And no, she didn't try to take the blame for Billy's death.

But she had been there. She'd done things she wished she hadn't. She'd learned the difference between the sharp, anxious strike of infatuation and the slow, warm flow of contentment that came with compatibility and love.

When she was dry, she wrapped herself up in a long flannel nightgown, brushed out her hair, and curled into bed.

Then promised herself then and there that she would become someone different. Someone everyone would admire.

And if not admire? At least respect.

A few weeks later, she'd gone out to the country for a day at the farmers' market, and started visiting with a few of the Amish. Later, she'd gotten a job as a teller at the bank. Then, one day Aaron Keim had come to her window and he'd struck her fancy.

Jack's life had changed, too. Because there were rumors that Mr. and Mrs. Thompson were thinking about pressing charges against him, Jack's parents encouraged him to volunteer for the army.

The army had been anxious for volunteers for the conflict in Vietnam.

Stunned that she could still cry about those days after all this time, Lovina wiped the tears from her cheeks and forced herself to concentrate on the Lord instead. How He directed them always to the right place, even when it didn't seem like it at the time. Looking back on all that had happened forty years before, Lovina wondered how she could ever have been so naïve.

She'd been a bright girl—but for a brief moment in time, she'd had her head turned by the smile of a too-handsome man. She'd let her usual common sense get turned on its side for the chance of excitement.

Then she'd realized that it hadn't been excitement that she'd craved.

Instead, it had been the need to feel wanted. Maybe even special.

Never wanting to be in such a position again, she'd given up that craving, just like an alcoholic gave up the taste for liquor.

But, perhaps like the alcoholic, that craving had never completely left her. It had only been tamped down.

Ignored.

"Mommi? Mommi, where are you?" Elsie called out.

Pushing away from the wall, Lovina pinched her cheeks, then smoothed a wrinkle from her dress. Then she stepped forward with smile, just as if she'd only just entered the main house. "I am here, Elsie. What is wrong?"

"Not a thing. Not a single thing," she replied, all smiles. "I was wondering where you were, that's all."

"I haven't been far. I never am."

"I'm glad about that. Oh, Mommi, come on," she encouraged, grabbing her hand. "You've got to come meet Amanda and Regina."

Lovina curved her hand around Elsie's but didn't let herself be dragged down the hall. "Before we go, tell me what you think. How are they?"

"Pretty and sweet," Elsie said immediately. "You're going to like them." Then she lowered her voice. "But the best part is Roman. Oh, Mommi, you should see how he acts around them," she commented, her voice bright with amusement. "He is smitten!"

"You think so?"

"He's completely head over heels! He can hardly take his eyes off Amanda. I bet he hardly even realizes that we're in the room."

Remembering those feelings, of aching for just a few moments of privacy, Lovina chuckled, "I bet he realizes that."

"Barely." Elsie tugged. "Come on, Mommi. I promise, you've never seen anything like it."

Lovina laughed. "Yes, I must see this smitten boy."

Two minutes later when she saw his face, Lovina knew Elsie had hit the nail on the head. Roman Keim was completely smitten.

In love.

But her favorite granddaughter was wrong—she *had* seen the like. It had been how she'd looked when she'd been taken in by foolish wishes and wants, only to pay the price for it in spades.

And after all that?

Why, she'd made sure she never dreamed about such things ever again.

Belize was beautiful, perched right on the Caribbean Sea. Viola spied turquoise blue waters and white sandy beaches as the plane made its approach to Belize City. It looked like nothing she'd ever seen before.

Definitely very, very different from snowy Berlin, Ohio.

Only as the plane was about to land did Viola see an assortment of shacks. Pressing her nose to the window, she saw more disturbing sights. Dirty, cramped narrow streets. Worn-out vehicles and skinny children.

She knew Edward was there because there were people in need. But now, for the first time, she wondered if she was ready to be faced with people whose lives were filled with such hardship.

When she stepped off the plane and followed the rest of the passengers along the tarmac and into the main airport, she felt as if all her senses had come alive. Belize felt hot and humid and smelled of sand and salt and humanity. She noticed both smiling faces and the wary, watchful eyes of men.

She felt small and insignificant. For twenty-two years, she'd been content to manage herself and her family in her small town. She'd felt brave and independent when she'd taken a job at Daybreak. She'd felt vaguely maternal toward her twin, always ready to step in and help her life run smoothly.

But this? It put everything in her past into a new perspective.

A little shiver snaked its way up her spine as her unease grew. What if she wasn't ready to live here? What if it was too big of a change from what she was used to?

How was she going to be able to tell Edward that? And how was she going to live with the knowledge that she wasn't nearly as strong as she'd thought she was?

She kept her head down and followed the officials' directions as best she could. As she walked through the airport, she felt as if her black stockings and heavy winter dress were slowly suffocating her.

Already her neck was sweating, what with both her *kapp* and black bonnet covering her hair.

She felt like such a fool. Ed had reminded her that it was warm and muggy in Belize. But for some reason she hadn't put that information to good use. Instead of packing lots of lighter dresses, she'd merely packed the three that were hanging in her closet . . . each one warmer than the next.

"You okay, Viola?" Karen asked.

Karen had sat beside her on the plane, along with Karen's husband of one day, Bob. Karen and Bob had flown down to Belize for their honeymoon and seemed as intrigued by Viola's reasons for traveling as she was about the *Englischers'* fancy wedding stories.

Karen, especially, had acted delighted when Viola told her about her recent engagement, and Edward's mission. They'd chatted the whole way to Belize, and Viola had been so thankful for their company.

But they weren't friends, of course. There was no way Viola could mention any of the doubts she was experiencing.

"I'm okay."

"Nervous?" Karen asked.

"I am, but excited, too," she admitted.

"We'll stay with you until you find your guy," Bob said as they continued through the customs area.

"Oh, that's not necessary . . . but thank you." She really didn't want to be by herself in the unfamiliar country.

At last, the three of them were walking toward the main part of the terminal.

"We're almost out of here," Karen teased. "I bet you can hardly stand the butterflies in your stomach."

Viola smiled, but was too nervous to acknowledge just how correct Karen's words were.

What if Edward wasn't outside waiting for her? What would she do then?

But then she didn't have to worry any longer because Ed was right there, waiting for her with a broad smile on his face. "Viola! Over here!" he called out.

"Is that him?" Karen asked.

"Oh, yes." For a moment, all she could do was

stare at Edward. Yes, he was still as handsome as she'd remembered.

Bob laughed. "I think you're in good hands now. Enjoy your reunion, Viola."

"*Danke*. And God bless," she said quickly before practically racing away from the couple.

She only faintly heard their soft laughs as she skirted around a number of people, then finally got to his side.

"Edward, I made it!" she said with a smile.

"You did. Oh, Viola, I'm so happy you're really here."

He was beaming. Everything inside her wanted to launch herself into his arms, to raise her chin for a kiss. But of course it wasn't seemly. She made do with smiling into his eyes, mentally comparing his appearance with the one in her memory. Thank goodness, he still seemed exactly the same.

As if Ed couldn't stand not touching her, he reached out and squeezed her hand. "I'm so glad to see you. How was your trip?"

"It was fine." In truth, her first plane flight wasn't nearly as scary as she'd anticipated. "A nice lady was sitting next to me on the first flight. She helped me switch planes in Miami. And then I was seated next to a honeymoon couple on the way here."

Scanning the area, she saw Bob hail a taxi. "That's them there."

"They look nice."

"Oh, they were. I heard all about their wedding. And then Karen wanted to know all about Amish ones. It made the time go fast."

He squeezed her hand again. "Viola, I knew you would be okay traveling. You're a strong woman."

She beamed. Maybe he was right. Maybe she was stronger than she'd thought, than she'd ever imagined. "You know what? Roman said the same thing. Of course, I thought he was teasing."

"I don't know if he was teasing or not. But I am proud of you." He reached down and grabbed the handle of her suitcase. "Let's get on our way, I can hardly wait to show you around."

As they walked to the crowded curb, the noises and foreign smells assaulted her again. "It's mighty different here. Different than what I imagined."

"That's because we're in the city. The mission is in the country, on the outskirts of the area. And I promise, the beach is beautiful. You're going to love going to the beach."

"I saw the ocean when we flew in," she admitted. "The water looked like the color of one of my teal dresses. Do you think one day we can go look at it?"

He scoffed. "Viola, we're going to go to the beach right now."

"What?"

"I made plans for us, for your first day here in

Belize," he said with a broad grin. "The folks at the mission helped. Here's what's going to happen. Manuel is going to take your suitcase directly to the mission while we go do something else."

"That is possible?"

"Of course it is, silly. We're a family here. We help each other out. Everyone understands that I want some time with you all to myself. After all, it's been six weeks."

"It has been a long time. . . ."

"See? That's why we're going to play lazy tourists for a little bit. I'm going to take you to the beach. And after you get your toes sandy, I'm going to take you to a nice little restaurant and have lunch. After that, we're going to go out to the edge of the rain forest, so you can see what I was talking about when I wrote that the rain forest was the most beautiful place, ever." He winked. "Maybe we'll even see a parrot."

She was taken aback. "I didn't think we'd ever have days like this."

"No?"

"I thought we'd be working." She shook her head, irritated by her word choice. "I mean, serving."

"Viola, we do lots of good works here, and we work hard, truly we do. But even missionaries need to enjoy life, and you're only here for a few days. I want you to see how pretty it is here— Belize is a beautiful country. So, what do you say? Would you like to go walk on the beach, barefoot?"

"Um, all right." Wearily, she glanced at her stocking-covered legs. She was going to have to visit the ladies' room and take them off soon. Oh, why hadn't she thought about the heat when she'd been packing?

At her rather unenthusiastic reply, Ed's grin faltered. "Is that okay with you? Did you have something else in mind?"

Now she felt stupid. Here Edward was attempting to make her first hours in Belize wonderful, and all she was doing was acting upset because she was dressed wrong.

"I didn't have anything in mind," she said weakly. "You caught me off guard. For some reason I assumed we'd go straight to the mission first. I mean, I want to see it. I want to see the work you're doing. . . ." What *they'd* be doing.

"I'm anxious for you to see it, too. Of course I am. But once we get there, it will be all work, and we'll be surrounded by a dozen people at all times."

His gaze flickered over her lightly, almost like a caress, warming her insides and making her even more aware of the fact that there was much more between them than just friendship. "I want to spend a little bit of time with you first, Viola," he said, his voice hinting of love and desire. "I've missed you."

"I've missed you, too." She noticed that her

voice had turned slightly breathless. Embarrassingly so.

Grinning, he took her hand again. Squeezed it gently. "I can't wait for you to fall in love with this place, Viola. I promise, I'm going to do everything I possibly can to make you fall in love with life here."

"Is that right?"

He nodded. "See, the alternative can't be considered."

"And what is the alternative?"

"That you never want to come back," he said simply. "That you decide that no matter how much you might love me, you don't love me enough. That I couldn't bear."

Don't love me enough. The phrase wasn't something she'd ever heard before, but it made sense. With all that had been going on with her family, she now understood that such a thing could happen. Relationships were all about balance. Balancing the good and the bad. What was easy and what couldn't be borne. What was worth everything . . . and what was worth nothing at all.

"I understand," she said.

Some of the hope fled from his eyes. She turned away, feeling slightly guilty. She knew she hadn't given him the unconditional approval he needed.

But she now knew better than to promise things she couldn't be sure of.

Chapter Nineteen

It had been years since Amanda had been a true guest in another person's home. Of late, life hadn't given her any time for things like that. First, she and Wesley had had Regina, and all the time constraints that came with a new baby. Not a year after that, Wesley had been diagnosed with cancer.

Her days had become a matter of survival instead of enjoyment. Each morning, she'd wake up with only thoughts about Wesley's health and Regina's needs filling her head. She'd jump out of bed and attempt to help them both as much as she could.

The only time she'd made for herself was for sleep . . . and some days, she'd only given in to that grudgingly.

She'd had no time for visiting friends or sipping tea or planting a garden or simply enjoying a good book.

After Wesley went to heaven, she'd been too overcome with grief to do anything but attempt to get through each day the best that she could. On some days, her main goal, besides caring for Regina, was to try to last until bedtime before dissolving into tears.

When the dark cloud of grief began to lift, she'd

focused on Regina's needs. Her sweet little girl had been as traumatized by her father's death as Wesley's parents and Amanda had been. She'd become withdrawn and nervous. Amanda had soon realized that only a steady, reliable schedule would help her. Regina had needed structure like most other small children needed naps or a favorite toy. She'd craved the same foods, the same activities, the same schedule day after day. A way of life that had no surprises, nothing to catch her off guard or make her worry.

Amanda had been happy to oblige her. After all, that reliability had eased her grief, as well. Concentrating on filling a day hour by hour was far easier than contemplating a life without her husband.

Which was why she couldn't help but smile as she followed Roman's mother down the hall. Even eight months ago, Amanda would have doubted that they'd be able to travel to a far-off state, visit with strangers, or sleep in an unfamiliar bed.

To do all this because another man had caught her eye would've been unthinkable.

God was amazing in His glory. Of that, she had no doubt.

"This is your room," Marie said as she opened the second door on the left. "I hope you will find it comfortable."

Amanda walked inside, finding a wide queen-sized bed covered with a thick ivory quilt in a double shoofly pattern. A small little trundle bed covered in a pink, white, and yellow fan pattern stood right beside it.

Beneath her feet, wood floors glowed from years of care. And not a speck of dust could be found on the dresser or bedside table. Starched white curtains covered the window, and a pair of thick well-washed, soft-looking quilts lay over a rocking chair. The room smelled like lemon oil and Windex.

It smelled like someone had gone to a great deal of trouble to make things nice for them.

"This is a lovely bedroom. *Danke*," she said politely.

Her daughter, however, was far more exuberant. "Ooh!" Regina scampered to the small bed and clambered on top of it. "This bed is just right for you, Momma."

While Marie gasped, Amanda chuckled. "That is a *gut* joke, but I'll take the bigger bed, if you do not mind." Turning to Marie, she said, "We do appreciate your hospitality. I guess you can tell that staying here is a special treat for us."

"It's our pleasure," Marie said. "We were looking forward to meeting you."

She looked like she wanted to add something more—a whole lot more—when Roman appeared at the door. "Here are your suitcases."

"*Danke*, Roman."

After setting Amanda's in front of her, he

comically crossed the room toward Regina, acting as if her little suitcase weighed a ton. "What did you put in your bag, Regina? Rocks?"

Her eyes widened. "*Nee*. Only my dresses and my nightgown. And my toothbrush, too."

"I was only teasin' ya, Regina," he said with a smile. Holding out his hand, he said, "Would you care to go to the barn with me?"

She stilled. "Can I see the *pikk*?"

"Of course. Sam the pig has been asking where you were."

"He has?"

Roman looked at Amanda and smiled. "He's been counting the minutes. Let's go put on your cloak and go see him. And Chester, too."

"Who's Chester?"

"You'll see. If you're ready."

In answer, Regina slid off the quilt and reached for his hand. "Bye, Momma," she said before walking with him down the hall.

"Bye," Amanda replied, feeling both relieved and somewhat at a loss. For so long, Regina had clung to her. It was a bit disconcerting to watch her daughter take another healing step forward into the world without her by her side.

Marie watched the pair of them depart with something that looked very much like the shock Amanda was feeling. "I've never seen Roman like this, Amanda. He's usually much more reserved."

"My Regina is, too."

"I'm glad they're getting along."

"Me, too. Regina is mighty fond of Roman, and has been ever since he asked her if she liked ice cream, too."

Marie laughed. "My son always did have a sweet tooth."

"So does my daughter." After sharing a smile with Marie, she added seriously, "I have to admit that I'm grateful for their friendship. Regina's needed someone in her life who makes her laugh and smile."

"I believe we all do," Marie murmured before sitting on the edge of the bed. "She is an adorable girl, Amanda. You must be so proud of her."

"She's my pride and joy," Amanda said, taking a seat on the padded chair next to the window. "With Wesley gone, I've kept asking God to help me raise her. I think He heard my prayers. I couldn't have done much without His help."

"I've raised children, too. And, though I've often given our Lord the glory, I sometimes selfishly like to think we mothers have to take some of the credit for wonderful children."

Regina smiled. "Perhaps. But truthfully, she is an easy child. She has Wesley's temperament. I got lucky in that regard."

At the mention of Wesley, Marie's easy expression sobered. "I imagine the two of you have had a time of it. Both of you were too young to lose a husband and a father."

"We have had a time of it," Amanda agreed. Softly, she added, "Losing Wesley so young was nothing any of us could have anticipated." However, she refused to dwell on it. Not any longer. "But we are doing better."

Marie stood up. "I'll let you have some privacy, but I did want to take this moment and ask that you please consider our home yours. Feel free to help yourself to whatever you or Regina might need, whether it be more towels or a late-night snack."

"That is kind of you."

"It's our pleasure. Roman is happy you are here, so of course we are happy, too."

"*Danke,*" she said as Marie walked out of the room. When she was alone, she closed her eyes and gave thanks to the Lord for bringing her on the journey, then lay down and rested her eyes for a few moments. Traveling with a four-year-old was not always easy, no matter how agreeable the child was.

And leaving her in-laws hadn't been easy, either. Marlene had tried her best to understand Amanda's need to visit Roman and his family in Ohio, but Amanda knew she hadn't understood Amanda's feelings at all.

Plus, Amanda had her own nerves to contend with. Over and over she second-guessed herself, and questioned her reasons for the trip.

Then, once she felt like she had gotten her head

on straight, she'd find herself worrying about Roman's family. What if they didn't like her? What if Regina acted up and they thought she was a naughty girl and, therefore, Amanda a bad mother? Would they think she presumptuous to come visit a man she barely knew?

And then, just when she set her mind at ease about that, she'd start fretting about Roman. It had taken a huge leap of faith to take this journey all on the basis of a brief interlude and a series of long-distance phone calls and letters.

It felt almost foolish to let such a short relationship dictate such a big step.

Then, too, she'd feared Roman would seem different in his home surroundings than he had on vacation. She'd been afraid that he'd be cool to her. Distant.

But he wasn't acting distant, she reminded herself. *He's been warm and attentive and loving.*

Yawning, she let her mind drift back to their first sight of each other at the German Village Market. From the first moment their eyes met, all of her doubts drifted away. Right then and there, she'd felt his warm regard for her. And she'd felt drawn to his side, felt that ache inside her, the kind that she'd first felt with Wesley but had later pretended had been childish infatuation.

But now she knew better.

No, none of what she had feared had happened. Instead, everything was as good as it could possibly get. Surely nothing could go wrong now.

With that in mind, she drifted off to her first easy slumber in five days.

It was fun, seeing the farm through Regina's eyes. She was fascinated with everything in the barn, from the scent of hay to the plow and other farm implements to the pile of horse manure.

"That's stinky," she said, wrinkling her nose.

"I agree," Roman said.

"I'm glad we ride bikes or walk where I live."

"So even your grandparents don't keep a buggy and horses?"

"*Nee.*" Gazing at Chester, she said, "I like your horses, though."

"This is Chester, and I do believe he likes you, too."

Her little face brightened. "You think so?"

"I know so. Why, look at him watching you."

She lifted a hand about a foot, obviously wanting to touch the horse, but then thrust it back down to her side. "Is Chester soft?"

"His coat is. Do you want to pet him?"

"Will he mind?"

"Not at all. Chester is a sturdy horse. And, like I said, he wants to be your friend." Knowing that she'd like to pet his velvety nose best, Roman said, "Okay if I pick you up?"

"Uh-huh."

"Here you go, then," he said as he picked her up

by the waist and held her securely against his hip. "Lean forward and give Chester a pat on his forehead." When he saw that she was being gentle, with his other hand, he gently rubbed the horse's muzzle. "See how I'm being careful here? Do you think you can rub him softly, too?"

She nodded.

"All right then. You try petting his nose."

Tentatively, she followed his example. He was rewarded with a beaming smile. "Roman, his nose is soft."

"It is indeed." Just then, Chester shook his head as if he were nodding. "Look at that, Regina. He's agreeing with ya, too."

She giggled, and the exuberant happiness warmed his heart, as did the realization that he was actually enjoying every minute in her company. He liked holding her and introducing her to his life.

"Ready to get down and see the pig?"

"*Jah!*"

He'd just put her down when his grandfather appeared at the door.

"I heard we had a guest, so I came to say hello," his grandfather said softly.

"Hi, Dawdi. This is Regina, Grandfather. Regina, this is . . ." What should she call him? Mr. Keim?

"Regina, you may call me Dawdi Aaron, if you'd like."

"But I already have a grandpa." Regina looked worried, like she was about to do something wrong.

"Lots of *kinner* have more than one grandfather," he said easily. "Or, you could call me Aaron. I'm fine with that."

Roman tensed as he waited for Regina to make up her mind about his usually stern grandfather.

"Do you know where the pig is, Dawdi Aaron?" she asked.

His grandfather's answering smile could have lit up the entire barn. "I know more about that pig than most anyone else. You want to see it?"

"Uh-huh. Roman says he's smelly, though."

"That's only because Roman needs to give him a bath."

Regina's eyes widened, then to Roman's astonishment, she left his side and scampered to his grandfather's. And to his greater amazement, his grandfather held out his hand to the little girl, and she took it like they'd been friends forever.

Then, away they went, Regina asking him questions and his grandfather answering each one carefully. Roman followed slowly behind, trying to remember if he'd ever been so comfortable around either of his grandparents. He couldn't remember a time, but surely there had been?

When they reached Sam's pen, Roman watched Regina grip Aaron's hand tighter. "He's a mighty big *pikk*."

"Yep."

"And he does smell."

"He does, but he can't help that, I'm sorry to say. It's a pig's way to smell. They're smelly by nature."

"My *mamm* makes me take baths. Sam needs one, too."

With a wink in his direction, his grandfather said, "You hear that Roman?"

"I hear you, Dawdi."

Sam, not used to so much attention, lifted his head and stared at Regina, his beady dark eyes looking like he was sizing her up for his next meal.

Sam was an enormous Yorkshire pig, and Roman prepared himself for Regina to back off quickly, maybe even be a little scared of him. As he walked to Regina's other side, he pressed a comforting hand between her shoulder blades. "Sam is big and smells, but he's not mean, Regina. He won't hurt you."

"Can I pet him?"

Aaron laughed. "I think not. He's not one for companionship, unless it's with the lady pigs. Would you like to see the hens now? I do believe we might find us an egg."

"Uh-huh."

"Roman, I'll take good care of her, if you want to see if your grandmother could make us some hot chocolate." Comically, he paused. "Do you even know what hot chocolate is, Regina, living down in the sun and sand like you do?"

"I know what hot chocolate is."

"Would you like to have a *cuppa* with my wife and me?"

"*Jah*."

Roman backed up a step. "I'll go talk to Mommi. Oh, and Grandfather?"

"*Jah?*"

"*Danke*."

"*Nee*, Roman. I am the one who should be giving thanks. This little visitor of yours has brightened up my day."

As Roman noticed how Regina was beaming at Aaron, he said, "I think the feeling is mutual."

Chapter Twenty

Edward opened a thick, heavy wooden door with a flourish. "And this, Viola, is our main office and meeting area."

As she stepped into the cool, large room with the cement floor, Viola took care to keep a smile on her face. It took effort because inside she was feeling slightly dismayed.

Though she'd loved their visit to the beach and the rain forest, somehow, she'd hoped the exquisite sights would make her feel more comfortable and at ease . . . even though she was in a foreign country.

Oh, she had found a number of things awe-inspiring. Her first view of the ocean had been mesmerizing, and she'd been intrigued by the beautiful trees and flowers that had surrounded them.

But it had also been a bit overwhelming.

Actually, more than a bit. She was realizing that she'd been terribly sheltered, living her whole life in rural Ohio. Experiencing a new place was far different from reading about it.

What she really needed was a few minutes to cool off and rest her head. It had been so long since she'd seen Edward—part of her just wanted a moment to give thanks that they were together again.

But Edward, on the other hand, seemed more intent on showing her everything about Belize and the mission as quickly as possible.

She hadn't wanted to disappoint him, so she'd listened attentively and followed him as quickly as she could.

But the tour was starting to take its toll. She was overheated, and feeling a little nauseous—surely the result of a nervous stomach, mixed with the sights and smells of unfamiliar food.

Now, this room smelled of a curious combination of disinfectant and mildew. In the middle of it were two old couches and a pair of older looking metal desks. Against the far wall was a pair of doors with heavy locks on them. And though it was cooler, and they were blessed with two ceiling fans, it didn't feel cool enough. Under her apron, her dress was sticking to her skin. She ached to rip off her hot dress and stand underneath an ice-cold shower.

"Come over and meet everyone, Viola," Ed said.

She walked to where he was pointing. Several men and women were gathered near a table loaded with strange-looking food. Some of the people gathered were obviously Amish or Mennonite. Others were locals.

All of them were smiling at her.

She tried her best to smile back, but all she could think about were the trays of unfamiliar food. And of the skinned animals she'd seen in the street market.

And of how she was going to be expected to eat so as not to appear rude.

Her stomach gurgled. In an effort to keep her composure, she looked away from the food, toward the side of the room. There, a somewhat scrawny-looking orange cat was chasing a mouse. A lizard was climbing one of the walls.

All of a sudden, she felt a surge of resentment toward Edward.

Why had her fiancé never mentioned just how primitive things were in any of his letters? All he'd talked about were sunsets and smiling, grateful believers. Never had he mentioned the dirt and the mice.

Or the lizards.

Or that the mission was surrounded by sharp, ominous-looking barbed wire. And that he'd had to hire guards to stand at the mission's entrance.

When he'd talked about his living arrangements, he'd mentioned the thick walls that kept the rooms cool. He'd told her all about the way he could smell the ocean breeze while lying down in bed.

Viola felt like her feet were glued to the floor. Each step forward felt like she was inching toward oblivion.

Everything inside her screamed to turn around. To rush back home, where she could be in control of things. Where she knew the language, and knew the rules.

Where she was comfortable and felt safe.

Where she wasn't so, so terribly hot.

Edward moved closer to her side, nudged her a bit farther forward. Then grasped her shoulders. "Viola, I'd like you to meet our team."

"Hello," she said, wishing that he would remove his heavy, hot hands. They felt like brands on her shoulders, pinning her in place.

"This is Viola."

She kept a smile pasted on her face like a porcelain doll as people introduced themselves. She muttered her thanks when they pushed a plate into her hands, full of food she didn't recognize.

As she stared at it in wonder, Ed's easy expression turned determined. "They made this in your honor," he whispered. "You've got to eat."

"I have no silverware."

Picking up a tortilla from his plate, he scooped up some of the strange-looking meat into it and brought it to his mouth. "Like this," he said, demonstrating easily.

Feeling sick to her stomach, she dutifully followed his lead, knowing she was being watched the whole time. But the food was spicy and she was exhausted and shaky. Nervous about making a good impression. And still full from their lunch.

And then, just as if she were right in the middle of an awful nightmare, her stomach began to churn and clench. In a panic, she thrust the plate at him and looked frantically for the bathroom.

But of course there wasn't one.

Standing up, she covered her mouth with a hand. Looking left and right, she searched for an exit. For anywhere to go.

"Here," a lady said, grabbing her wrist. In no time at all, she dragged Viola out back into the scorching sun, across a dirt yard, to a dilapidated outhouse. Once there, she yanked open the door.

Viola ran in and promptly threw up just as the door slammed behind her.

Tears stung her eyes as she heaved, then as she tried to regain some self-control.

And though it was dark and hot and the stench was terrible, she stayed inside. At least here she had some privacy.

At least here she could admit to herself that she wasn't okay.

Slowly, tears traipsed down her cheeks, dropping to the front of her dress.

She hated herself right at that moment. This wasn't the type of person she wanted to be.

Shame mixed with the heat. She'd just completely embarrassed Ed in front of everyone. She'd just been unforgivably rude and disrespectful to her hosts. Their first impression of her had been that of a flighty girl who couldn't take the slightest bit of discomfort.

And now she had to go out and face them all, without even being able to wash her hands or rinse out her mouth.

There in the tiny structure, she attempted to gather her courage. She needed to go out and apologize to everyone. To make amends.

And she was going to do that. She was. Just as soon as she was able.

But two knocks interrupted her plans. Yet again, she was causing trouble.

"Viola? Viola, are you all right?"

It was Edward. And he sounded concerned, not angry.

And, no, she wasn't okay. But how could she tell him that?

Taking a deep breath, she opened the door and walked out into the blinding sunlight. And tried to look anywhere but at him.

"Did you have a nice nap?" Marie asked when Amanda walked into the front parlor of the Keim house.

"I did. That bed was so comfortable, the moment I lay down and closed my eyes, I fell fast asleep. I didn't mean to sleep so long, though."

Roman's mother smiled kindly. "Please don't apologize. Traveling is hard work, especially with a child in tow."

"I think you're right, though Regina wasn't any trouble," she said, glancing around the quiet room. There were no signs of either Roman or her daughter. A mild undercurrent of panic bubbled in her stomach. "Marie, do you know where Regina is?" Hopefully, she added, "Did she fall asleep, too?"

"Oh no. She's been up the whole time. I believe she's currently having hot chocolate with my husband's parents."

"But she left my room with Roman." Had Roman already passed Regina off onto someone else? If so, her timid little girl was probably feeling lost and alone.

"Regina met my father-in-law when she was exploring the barn. Aaron invited her for hot chocolate. Aaron and Lovina live in the *dawdi haus*. You met Lovina in the kitchen earlier, remember?"

"*Jah*. But I didn't expect Regina to be with anyone but Roman." Of course, as soon as she said that, Amanda realized that she couldn't sound any less gracious.

"I promise, Regina's in good hands," Marie said, not appearing to be offended in the slightest. "If she wasn't happy, they would have brought her to Roman or you."

Thinking about how Marlene both enjoyed Regina's chatty personality but sometimes yearned for frequent breaks from the girl's exuberance, she frowned. "I hope she's not bothering them. Regina can sometimes be a chatterbox." That is, if she felt comfortable.

Marie waved off her concerns. "If she is a chatterbox, I'm sure they are enjoying every minute of it. It's been too long since we've had a four-year-old keeping us company. She's a sweet child, Amanda."

"*Danke*."

"Now, please sit down and relax. I'm eager to get to know you."

Hesitantly, Amanda sat down. She was used to being in charge of Regina, and it felt odd to accept a stranger's help. Even more peculiar was coming to terms with the fact that Regina was happy with them.

That she didn't need her mother there to hold her hand.

But Amanda knew she should take the opportunity to get to know Roman's family as well. As she settled into an easy chair by the window, she wasn't sure what to say. She was used to people only asking about Wesley, or about being a single mother and widow.

Marie, of course, wouldn't be likely to ask her about Wesley. Not when she was here to see Roman. Which in some ways was a nice change.

So, what was she now, if not just a widow? It was disheartening to not be quite sure of that answer.

Marie gestured to a teapot wrapped in a bright green quilted tea cozy. "I brought an extra cup out in the hopes that you'd be able to share some tea with me," she murmured, her voice as soothing as Amanda was sure the hot tea would be. "Would you care for a cup of spiced orange tea?"

"That sounds heavenly," she said, relaxing. "*Danke.*"

"You're welcome." After filling two cups with fragrant tea, she added a splash of milk and a spoonful of sugar to her cup. Then Marie sat back against her chair. "Before I forget to tell you, please let us know if you need to borrow some sweaters or stockings or anything. I imagine this cold weather is something of a shock to your body."

"It is chilly, but I think I'm all right."

"*Gut. Gut*, I'm glad. So, Roman tells me that you're not originally from Florida."

"No, I'm not. I was born in Lancaster County. So, I do have a little bit of experience with winter weather."

"I should say you do! Well, now, that is a pretty area. Are your parents still there?"

"They are. I moved to Florida when Wesley and I married. After he passed away, I found I wasn't eager to leave the sunny weather behind."

"I can only imagine. Roman seemed to enjoy the beach tremendously, and I know my husband's brother and his family do as well." Marie frowned slightly, as if she'd just said something awkward, but Amanda couldn't imagine what she'd said that was out of the ordinary.

"I like Florida," she murmured. Feeling a bit uneasy, she sipped her tea. "And Pinecraft is a wonderful community."

"I'd love to visit one day. So . . . is that where you intend to live? Always?"

Marie's questions were hardly subtle. But Amanda didn't mind. "I don't know," she said simply. She really didn't. Amanda was learning that life was filled with unexpected circumstances, and it did no good to make lots of plans, at least the forever type of plans.

"Ah," Marie said. Obviously she was waiting for Amanda to expand on her answer.

But what could she say? Instead of talking, she sipped her tea again.

Luckily, before the conversation got more stilted, the door opened and Roman came in. The moment their eyes met, she felt something inside her relax. His gaze was warm and loving.

"Hi," he said.

"Hi." Was she smiling as brightly as she thought she was? She felt her cheeks heat when she realized that she must look like a love-struck schoolgirl.

"Would you like to go find Regina with me?"

"I would like that very much." She practically jumped to her feet. "Thank you for the tea, Marie."

"I enjoyed our visit." Roman's mother smiled as she crossed her legs and made no secret that she was pleased by her son's new relationship.

When they walked out the kitchen door and stepped onto the chilly path that led to the *dawdi haus*, Roman's grin broadened. "So, was my mother grilling you? When I walked in, you looked like you would rather be anywhere but sitting in that room."

No way was she going to discuss *that* conversation. "Your mother couldn't have been more gracious. I . . . uh, I think I was still waking up."

"Ah, yes. That must have been it." Taking her hand, he folded both of his around it. "Are you feeling better now that you got some rest?"

"I am. I think I just needed a nap." Looking down at her hand in his, she once again felt a little burst of warmth flow through her. She'd missed Roman.

Running a finger along the back of her hand, gently tracing a line of veins, he said, "Don't worry, all right? No one has any expectations, least of all me. I want you to enjoy a few days in Ohio and for Regina to get a taste of the snow. If you two enjoy a few days off, then that's enough for me."

"Truly? Because, Roman, I don't know what I'm doing." There, that was as honest as she'd dared to be for the last few years.

"I'm glad you don't know. What is happening between us is something new for me, too. I want to enjoy every second of it."

And then, before she could think of anything else to say, he gave her hand a gentle tug and pulled her into the *dawdi haus.*

Any thoughts of quiet contemplation evaporated the moment she heard Regina's chatter.

"Mamm, I saw the *pikk*," she called out, looking so grown-up from where she sat at the oak table she shared with Roman's grandparents. "His name is Sam and he smells. And I petted a horse's nose, and now I'm having hot chocolate."

Amanda smiled shyly at Mr. and Mrs. Keim. "It sounds like a *wonderful-gut* afternoon."

"It was *wunderbaar!*" Regina said. "I liked

everything. I like it here, Mamm." Her daughter's eyes were shining, and for once, she didn't look stressed or worried or like she was trying to be happy when she wasn't.

After all this time, in a place that wasn't even home to them, it seemed Regina had become herself again.

Right there and then, Amanda felt all her doubts about the trip to Ohio fall away. This was what she cared about; this was where her heart lay . . . with Regina.

And having a happy daughter made everything worth it. It gave her hope, too. Hope for a future that was going to be better than she'd imagined. "I'm so glad," she murmured.

Roman glanced her way, making her realize that her voice was hoarser than she'd intended; thick with emotion. She shook her head slightly. "What I meant was, that if today was one of your best days ever, then I am mighty happy," she said lightly, moving closer to pat her daughter gently on the back.

Mrs. Keim didn't look fooled for a moment. She was gazing at Regina steadfastly. As if she knew exactly what it was like to feel pain. "Amanda, won't you join us for some hot chocolate?"

She wasn't really thirsty; she'd just had that cup of tea with Marie. But the offer was kind, and she couldn't pass up an opportunity to sit with Regina and share the treat.

"Danke," she said. When Roman sat down, too, and started chatting with Regina, Amanda realized that it wasn't just her daughter who'd had a wonderful day. Something special was happening with her, as well.

At the moment, she was happy. Happy almost like she used to be.

Chapter Twenty-one

Opening the door of the outhouse and stepping into the sun was one of the hardest things Viola had ever done.

Actually, as Ed stared at her in concern, his handsome face expressing no disdain, only worry, Viola realized that she'd never been more miserable in her life.

Well, perhaps she'd been more miserable when she'd been twelve and had been besieged by chicken pox and strep throat at the same time.

But this certainly came in at a close second.

"Edward, I'm so sorry," she murmured yet again as they started walking back into the main building of the mission house. "I don't know what happened to me."

"There's no need to apologize, Viola," he said as he waved to a few of the local children sitting under the shade of a tree. When they waved back, he smiled, then continued to lead the way across the compound.

As she followed, Viola knew it wasn't okay. Everything in Edward's body language told her that he was upset with her. With the children, his smile was easy, genuine.

But now, every time he looked at her, he looked upset.

She didn't blame him. Of course he had to be upset about the first impression she'd made with all his coworkers. Embarrassed about the way she'd gotten sick, practically in front of everyone.

No, she didn't resent his disappointment. She felt the same way. She'd reacted in the worst possible way and now it was going to take everything she had to start over on the right foot.

If that was even possible.

So, though she still felt queasy and lightheaded, she grabbed his hand and tried her best to infuse some life into her voice. "Edward, we could continue our tour now, if you'd like."

He stopped and looked down at his feet. The brim of his straw hat shielded his face from the sun . . . and effectively blocked her from seeing the expression in his eyes. "I think it would be best if we stopped the tour. At least until tomorrow."

"I don't want to stop."

"Viola—"

"Ed, I promise, I do feel better." Distressed, she

pointed to one of the crudely built buildings. "Would you like to show me what those buildings are?" she asked quickly, her words practically tripping over themselves. "They look like barns to me."

"They are barns." Finally, he lifted his chin. "Viola, I think it might be a good idea if I took you to your room and let you lie down for a while."

"But—"

He interrupted her and started moving back toward the main building. "It's getting late, anyway. I bet you are anxious to get some sleep."

"I'm not that tired." But even to her ears, her voice sounded shrill. Like an exhausted child's.

"I've got a lot of work to do anyway, since I've been away all day. It would be best for both of us if you got some rest."

Though she knew all of this was her fault, she felt rejected. Quietly, she nodded, then let him lead the way into the main building, down a narrow hall, and back into the central gathering room.

Unlike before, when it had been teeming with energy and excitement, it was now empty. Only the faint scents of the meal they'd prepared in her honor remained. "Um, where is everyone?"

Ed looked around the room, then shrugged. "Oh, they, ah, decided to give us some privacy."

She knew she'd made a fool of herself, but for them to put away the celebration? They must have felt that she hadn't liked them. "I really do feel horrible about this, Ed. I want to make amends."

"You shouldn't feel bad, and you certainly don't need to make amends. No one can help getting sick."

She hadn't been able to help herself, that was true. But she also realized that her illness had been triggered not only by the heat, but also by her nerves. She was scared to live somewhere so different from Berlin.

But she was also just as afraid to lose Edward.

But if she corrected him, it would only make things worse.

After they crossed the large, empty room, he led her down another narrow hallway. Only a bare lightbulb illuminated their way. Finally, they stopped at a door. To her surprise, he pulled a key out of his pocket and unlocked the door. "Here we are," he said.

She stepped inside and almost gasped. Inside was a double bed, neatly made with a pair of quilts and what looked like ironed, white sheets. Pegs lined the wall, and hanging on them were Edward's clothes. "This is your room, isn't it?"

"*Jah.* I thought you might like to use it while you're here. It's clean, and will give you some privacy and quiet."

It was obvious that he'd very carefully cleaned what was clearly the nicest room in the mission complex.

Seeing how much trouble he'd gone to, how much preparation he'd made for her arrival, she felt even worse.

Oh, he must be so disappointed in her.

"Where are you going to sleep?"

"I'll bunk with some of the other men in one of the dormitory rooms."

"I can't take your room, Edward." As she glanced around, at his shirt hanging, at the pile of notes and loose change on his chest of drawers, she was certain that every little thing was going to remind her of him. Even his scent filled the room. But then again that helped her finally feel a little more relaxed, as if she really wasn't so far from home.

And that new glimmer of well-being was so wonderful, she wanted to hug him close and promise that she'd never embarrass him ever again.

But she wasn't sure that she could promise him that.

"Viola, this is really the only appropriate place for you to sleep." He stepped away. "Plus, I, ah, I had imagined you'd want to see where you'd be sleeping when we married."

"Had imagined?"

"Yes." He shrugged. "But perhaps this isn't the best place for you."

"What do you mean? Where else would I go?" All the hotels that they passed coming in from the airport looked too far away and too expensive.

"Perhaps you'll want to stay home."

She heard what he was saying, but it didn't want to register. "You mean Berlin?"

"*Jah*." His face looked expressionless. Stoic.

"Where would you be? You wouldn't quit, would you?"

"No, I told you, I have a commitment to the mission. My chance to withdraw was back in February, when I came out here the first time. I can't leave now, it's my job." He cleared his throat. "But, like I told you, some wives stayed behind."

"I thought perhaps that was out of necessity. That they were raising *kinner* and wanted them to be at their schools and such."

"It's also by choice." He shrugged. "There's no need to make any sudden decisions, but I want to assure you that if staying in America is something you need to do, I'll understand."

"But you said—"

He cut her off. "I said a lot of things, Viola. We both know that just because I want something to happen, doesn't mean it will. I think it was wrong of me to push you so. I didn't want to be away from you. I wanted to marry you quickly. I wanted you here, by my side. But I should have asked what you wanted to do."

It almost sounded as if he were trying to find a way to break things off. "Edward, I love you."

"And I love you, too, Viola. Of course I do."

"Then give things some time. Give me some time. I mean, I only got here a few hours ago, Edward. Surely you don't expect us to make decisions about the rest of our lives in just a few hours? Do you?"

"You're right, of course." Gently, he reached out and caressed the side of her cheek. She looked into his eyes and realized that he looked sad. "Get some rest. We'll talk more in the morning."

"All right," she murmured, waiting for him to caress her cheek again, and then hold her close.

Instead, he turned and closed the door tightly behind him.

Dismayed and yet again on the verge of tears, she took off her shoes and sat on his bed. She lay down and curled on her side, inhaling the comforting scent of him on the sheets.

He was right. They could talk more later. Who knew what that conversation would be like, anyway?

She could only hope it went better than the one they'd just had.

"I don't know the last time I laughed so much," Lovina said with a smile as she sat with Aaron at the kitchen table the morning after Amanda and Regina's arrival. "That little Regina has already drawn a ring around my heart."

Aaron smiled at her over the rim of his coffee

cup. "I have to agree that the child is a delight. I hope her mother and Roman can come to some kind of agreement and soon."

"They must be feeling something if she's bringing her daughter up here to see Roman."

"And us," Aaron corrected. "I recall Roman saying that he wanted her to meet his whole family."

"Sam and Lorene are coming over tonight. We'll either scare her off, or scare Roman," Lovina joked. "The Keims all together can be overwhelming."

"I suppose so." Her husband looked to add something more, then kept his tongue.

"What is it?"

"Oh, I was just wondering how you first felt when you met my family."

"I was overwhelmed, too," she said with a burst of laughter. "I wanted to please you." Almost shyly, she gazed at him through lowered lashes. "Of course, I was afraid your family would shun you for even thinking about dating an *Englischer*."

He scratched his beard, as if he was trying to remember. "They were surprised I fancied you, for sure. But they were happy I was smiling again."

Leaning back, he rested one foot over the opposite knee—the way he used to sit all the time. "After Laura Beth, I didn't smile so much. You changed that."

She was touched. So rarely did they speak to each other like this. To cover up her deep feelings, she said, "I was always doing something wrong. I'm sure everyone had a lot to laugh about."

She looked at her husband fondly, not seeing his unruly, thinning gray head of hair. Instead, she recalled how his hair had once been thick and the color of dark caramel. His eyes had held a tired expression . . . like they'd seen too much.

Except when he gazed at her.

Years ago, it had felt as if she were the only person in the world.

"To be honest, I'm not really sure what I thought about when I met your relatives. All I remember was that I wanted to change," she murmured. "And that I wanted you." To her surprise, she felt her cheeks heat. Even after forty years, he could make her blush.

"We were two souls in need of fresh starts. I had lost Laura Beth and Ben. You had lost your boyfriend."

"We were both in need, for sure," she agreed.

"Well, the chores aren't going to do themselves. Best go see if Roman needs a hand." Aaron was always the practical one. Meanwhile, her head was still in the clouds, remembering Jack, when Aaron closed the back door with a thud.

Thinking about how she'd sneaked out of her house the day after the accident and took the bus to the hospital to see Jack.

When she'd gotten there, his parents had barely acknowledged her existence.

Even worse was when one of the nurses had told her that Jack didn't want to see her. Right in front of a bunch of his friends.

She'd realized that she had never really meant all that much to him. Not even after all the things they'd done. Especially not after Billy's death.

But after he'd left for basic training, Jack had written her a carefully penned note that had revealed more than he'd ever told her in person.

In it, he'd told her that after he'd left for boot camp, he'd thought about her more and more. She'd made an impression on him, for the better. And because of that, he wanted to change. He wanted to be a better person, and he hoped she'd give him another chance. He'd asked her to write him back.

And so she had. They'd exchanged a few brief, hesitant letters. Each filled with grief and regrets about Billy.

Then, of course, things had changed again.

And Lovina had realized that the pain she had been feeling, while bad, had only been a taste of what was about to come.

Chapter Twenty-two

The day had been wonderful. Now, as he and Amanda sat on the couch in the front parlor, Roman finally understood what Viola had felt with Edward.

Now he understood why his sister was willing to pledge herself to a man who was determined to live all over the world. Feeling the way he did about Amanda, Roman knew he was willing to change his idea of his life, of who he was, of who he wanted to be.

That's what happened when a person was in love, he realized. Love made everything in life worthwhile . . . and much in life seem hardly significant at all.

As he turned to the beautiful woman he was falling in love with, he noticed that she'd become increasingly withdrawn over the last few minutes.

"You're pretty quiet," Roman said after he brought them fresh cups of coffee. "Is something wrong?"

She shrugged in that winsome way he noticed she did when she was at a loss for words. "Not a thing. I'm simply content." After taking a sip of her coffee, she added, "I guess I've been quiet because I'm so used to Regina constantly chattering in my ear. Perhaps I've forgotten how to have a real conversation."

"My grandparents have become smitten with her and her chatter."

"I think she feels the same way. She is enjoying being around a big, gregarious family."

Her comment surprised him. "I would have thought she would be used to being around so many people, living close to Wesley's family the way you do."

"We live close to them, but it isn't the same as what you have here."

Her words seemed a bit evasive. "Why not? Did Wesley not have a lot of siblings?"

"No, he only had one sister and they were never terribly close. But the main reason is that the Yoder family isn't loud by nature. They're fairly quiet people, I guess," she said after some reflection. "Then, of course, Wesley's sickness and death cast quite a dark cloud over us all. It was hard to concentrate on anything but the cancer, and that he was fading from us in spite of our prayers and the doctors' drugs and treatments. We all became quieter after his death."

Roman was again reminded of their different life experiences. His naiveté embarrassed him. Until he'd met Amanda, he'd thought of himself as someone who was strong because he'd shouldered many of the farm's responsibilities. Now, he realized that his strength couldn't hold a candle to hers. "Sorry, I didn't mean to be so thoughtless."

Resting a slim hand on his arm, she shook her head. "Oh, Roman, don't think that. You're not being thoughtless. Truthfully, I never thought about why we are the way we are. I just always accepted it . . . for better or worse."

She smiled at him, her smile turning the dark night a little brighter. "Though Marlene and Micah have been good grandparents to Regina, I think their grief for Wesley dominated their actions. They've been kind, but a little stand-offish." She wrinkled her nose. "*Nee*, that's not quite right. Anyway, they haven't spoiled her near as much as she would like them to. Not like your family is doing, anyway."

"I never would have imagined anyone saying that my grandparents were the spoiling kind."

"They pay attention to her. That's what counts. Roman, haven't you seen how she practically glows around your mother and grandparents? She eats up their attention like a hungry caterpillar! In a lot of ways, Regina is just a little girl aching to fill the gap of all that she's lost."

Something about the way she said that made Roman realize that Regina wasn't the only one who was trying to fill the gaps in her life. Amanda had been so focused on taking care of her husband and now her daughter that she'd put her own needs aside. Now, she seemed just as eager as

Regina to try new things, to have some fresh experiences.

Now, that was something he could help with.

"Hey, I thought I could take you for a ride in our sleigh. What do you think about that?"

"I think it's freezing out!"

"I know, but we could bundle up under some wool blankets." He waggled his eyebrows. "We could sit really close to keep warm that way." Just to tease her, he added a little bit of a challenge. "Unless you think your Florida blood can't take the Ohio cold?"

"I was born in Pennsylvania. I can handle the cold and snow."

He raised his brows. "Are you sure about that?"

"Perfectly sure," she countered, then chuckled. "Boy, you got my dander up, didn't you? You are incorrigible, Roman."

"Sometimes being incorrigible has its advantages."

"And what are those?"

"It lets me get my way." Taking a chance, he slid closer to her on the couch, wrapped his arm around her shoulders. "Take a chance, Amanda. Come for a sleigh ride with me."

"Just the two of us?"

"Of course." He would be happy to take Regina for a sleigh ride one day. But at the moment, all he wanted to do was tease and cajole Regina's mother. And maybe, kiss her in the moonlight.

He was, after all, incorrigible.

"Come on, Amanda," he whispered. "What can it hurt?"

Amanda felt a burst of alarm flash through her. His words were igniting all sorts of feelings she'd long ago resigned herself to that she'd never experience again. But here they were, alive and well inside her.

Realizing how eager she was for Roman's attention was more disconcerting than the feel of his arm around her shoulders. Was she even ready for this?

Wesley hadn't been demonstrative with his love for her. Even when they were alone, he hadn't been one to touch or hug her. He was far too reserved for that. But she was finding herself to be much like her precious daughter. She, too, was enjoying the sensation of being around someone who was so open and affectionate.

In her own way, she was soaking up the warmth as much as her daughter was.

But of course, she knew what getting so close to Roman could do. It could hurt her very much. She could get her heart broken.

His arm fell away, making her skin feel chilled.

"Amanda?" he murmured, his gaze searching. "Have I upset you? Did I push too hard? Talk to me."

She was still focused on her arm. The way it felt

so cold with his hand gone. Who knew an arm could be so sensitive, anyway?

But that feeling cemented her decision. If she stayed away from him, if she stayed safe and wary, then chances were very good that she wouldn't be hurt. She could get used to being a little bit cold. Soon, she would forget what it felt like to be warm. She would forget how much she'd ever craved another person's touch.

She could go back to her life, and go back to work. She could find comfort in strangers' smiles.

But she was so tired of being cold.

"That sleigh ride sounds like a good idea," she finally replied, making her decision. "It sounds *wunderbaar*."

Roman gazed at her like she'd made his day. "That's great. I promise, I'll bring extra blankets. And I'll heat some bricks for our feet. I won't let you get cold, Amanda."

She was staring at him, her lips slightly parted, thinking about everything he wasn't saying, when they heard footsteps approaching.

"Mamm?" Regina called out.

Pushing all those thoughts of romance to one side, she turned to find Regina and Elsie. "Hi, you two. Were you looking for me?"

"Regina here was wondering where you two were," Elsie said. With a meaningful look directed at Roman, she added, "I thought it might be a good idea to find you."

Regina scampered forward. "Mamm, Mrs. Keim said we could start making cupcakes for the wedding."

"Truly?"

"My aunt Lorene and aunt Mary Beth are coming over tomorrow," Elsie explained. "Lorene thought pretty cupcakes iced in different pastel colors would be a nice change from the traditional wedding cake. We need to bake over two hundred. Three hundred if possible. We're going to refrigerate them until Monday or Tuesday when it's time to add icing. We'd love your help."

"And I would love to help you. Regina, you will like making the cupcakes very much."

"Are you going to make them, too, Roman?"

"Definitely not. Baking and icing cupcakes is a woman's project."

"What will you do?"

Looking terribly put upon, he sighed. "I suppose I'll have to work."

"Where?" She wrinkled her nose. "In the smelly barn?"

"That very place. But wait a minute, weren't you just telling me a few hours ago about how much you liked the barn and all the animals?"

"Oh, I like them."

"Even smelly Sam?"

Her lips curved up. "Especially smelly Sam."

He chuckled, then to Amanda's surprise, he scooped Regina up and twirled her around.

Regina grabbed hold of his arms, squealed in delight, then said, "Again!"

Amanda felt her insides turn to mush as she realized what was happening. She was falling in love.

Just as she was pretty sure Regina was, too.

With every tug and hug of her daughter, Amanda felt the last of her resistance slip away.

Later that night, Roman ignored the knowing glances of his mother and sister as he prepared the sleigh for their ride. While Amanda and Regina were helping with the dishes, he'd gathered a pile of fluffy quilts and a sheepskin cover for the cold leather seat.

Then he'd buckled up the horse to the sleigh. As Roman expected, Chester was excited about being out in the snow. He was shaking his head impatiently as Roman fastened his reins. "Settle, boy," he said soothingly. "I know you're excited. I am, too, but we need to bide our time. Amanda will be out when she's ready. That's a woman's prerogative, I guess." And something, he realized, that he might have to get used to.

And though his sisters' dawdling had always annoyed him, now he was finding that he wouldn't mind waiting for Amanda whenever she needed him to.

Chester, obviously not in the same frame of mind, snorted and pawed the ground with a hoof.

"Sorry, horse, she'll be coming along soon. She said she was only five minutes behind."

In the distance, he heard a familiar laugh. "Are you speaking to the horse about me?"

"Guilty," he replied with a laugh. "Talking to the animals is a longtime habit of mine, I fear." As he watched Amanda approach, he added, "I see I'm going to have to watch my mouth in the future. You have ears like a hawk."

"I believe it's ears like an elephant, and eyes like a hawk."

"Whatever the case, your hearing is good enough for me to learn to be a bit more circum-spect in the future." Simply thinking about a future of watching for her made him happy. "I'd sure hate for you to hear something best kept secret."

"Animals do keep the best secrets."

He held out a hand to help her into the sleigh. "I'm glad you're dressed warmly. You look pretty. I like your violet sweater."

"Elsie let me borrow it, and the scarf, too." She tilted her head up at him as he climbed in the sleigh beside her. "I'm surprised you didn't recognize it."

He wanted to tell her that he rarely noticed much about what his sisters were wearing, but thought that might sound mean. So he concentrated on rearranging the quilts around her more carefully. "Are you warm enough?"

She snuggled a bit closer. "I think so. Where are we going?"

He slipped on his gloves. "Nowhere special. Only down a few roads."

"Do you use your sleigh much?"

"Hardly ever, if you want to know the truth. I think my father or grandfather bought it in a romantic moment. Or a moment of weakness," he added after some thought. Actually, he only remembered his parents taking him, Viola, and Elsie out on Christmas mornings. "Right now I can only remember them using it once a year."

"Whatever the reason, I'm glad you are taking me out."

"Me, too." He jiggled the reins and Chester trotted forward, pulling the old sleigh with an eager jerk.

Amanda laughed as they got on their way, then laughed some more as they increased their pace. "I didn't think we could go so fast!"

"Chester is feeling frisky. I hope you're not frightened."

"Not at all, Roman. I think this is *wunderbaar*!"

Feeling like he was the king of the world—or at least someone terribly special—he clicked the reins, giving Chester permission to continue his brisk pace.

In answer, the horse almost pranced down the road, kicking up bits of snow in his path. The breeze kissed their cheeks and made his eyes water.

But all he seemed to be able to concentrate on was the feeling of her beside him. She felt warm and comfortable. Perfect.

He curved an arm around her shoulders, and after only the slightest hesitation, she snuggled closer. Close enough for him to drop his hand to her waist and give in to temptation by pressing his lips to her cold cheek.

She smiled in return.

He felt euphoric. Lifted. So blessed. He'd found his soul mate, and she felt the same way about him. Before long, they could start discussing weddings and house sites.

After another twenty minutes, Chester finally grew weary and slowed. Roman let the horse set the pace, only gently guiding him to follow the well-worn path back to their home.

As Chester quietly clip-clopped along the snow-covered path, and the white fields and bare trees glimmered in the snow's reflection, Roman felt as if the whole world was at peace. "I love this," he whispered. "I love right now. I love this very moment."

"I love it, too," Amanda said after a moment. "I don't know how to tell you this, but this, this right now? It's one of the best moments of my life."

"It's one of my best moments, too, Amanda. Being with you like this—it almost surpasses my dreams."

Her eyes widened at his flowery words.

Then, to his astonishment, she started crying.

Roman froze, not knowing what to do, not understanding why she was crying.

Not understanding anything except that for some reason all this happiness made her sad.

And he had no idea about what he was supposed to do next.

Chapter Twenty-three

After a good night's sleep, Viola felt better. Oh, she still felt awkward and out of sorts, but the haziness of travel and the uneasiness she'd felt being in a foreign country had lifted. She was starting to feel more like her usual self.

Thank the Lord, her mood had improved as well. Even though she was still unsure about Belize and still unsure about her ability to do God's work as a missionary's wife, she couldn't have felt more sure about her relationship with Edward. From the moment she spied him waiting for her at the airport, she'd felt the same strong feelings of happiness and love that she'd experienced when they'd been courting in Berlin. They were meant to be together. She was sure of it.

Now, all she had to do was find a way to make it work.

Late last night, one of the women handed her a thin cotton dress, telling Viola that she might find it more comfortable in the heat and humidity.

Viola had accepted it gratefully.

Now, as soon as she put on her borrowed light blue dress with its short sleeves, white apron, and *kapp*, she felt a thousand times cooler than when she'd arrived.

With a feeling of hope, she gathered up the pot holders her grandmother had made, left Edward's room, and ventured out to the kitchen area. The kitchen was a unique combination of her mother's kitchen at home and the commercial kitchen at Daybreak. Though it had an oversized oven, outdated refrigerator, and large range, somewhere along the way, people had added some lovely hand-stitched hand towels, and a collection of brightly painted ceramic jars.

And though the spices that permeated the room smelled unfamiliar, she also saw two loaves of bread, glass jars of homemade jams and preserves, and a stoneware pitcher.

Two women about her mother's age looked up when she tiptoed through the doorway. "*Gut matin*," one said, her smile as bright as her blue dress and matching apron.

"*Gut matin*." Feeling awkward, Viola smiled slightly.

"Would you care for *kaffi*?"

That definitely sounded like heaven. "*Jah. Danke.*" When one of the women went to reach into one of the top cupboards to grab her a cup,

Viola waved her away. "Please, I can help myself. Just show me where everything is."

"I can do that," the slim brunette offered. "The cups are here, and you'll find milk and sugar on the table."

Viola opened the designated door, found a large collection of white and blue mugs, and gratefully poured herself a cup of the fragrant brew. "This smells heavenly."

"The *kaffi* is wonderful here, for sure," the brunette said as she lifted her own mug. "Especially after a day of travel. I'm Amy, by the way."

"I'm Viola. Did we meet last night?" she asked hesitantly. "I'm afraid my mind is a blur."

"Only for a moment." With a look of concern she asked, "Are you feeling better?"

"Much." She bit her lip, then decided to plunge forward. "I know I got off on the wrong foot with all of you. I promise, I don't intend to act like that in the future." Presenting the pot holders, she added, "My grandmother made these. I thought you all might be able to put them to good use."

The other woman came forward and patted Viola on the back. She took the quilted pot holders with a pleased smile. "These are lovely. We will, indeed, put them to good use."

She then leaned over and looked Viola straight in the eye. "Don't fret, dear. There's nothing to say, or to apologize for. We felt bad for ya."

The lady's words were kind, but how could they be true? Viola had a feeling no one had ever made as poor of a first impression as she had.

"And I'm Rachel." After playfully winking at Amy, Rachel added, "If you want to know the truth, we all enjoyed our director fussing over you a bit."

"You did?"

"Ah, yes. Your man? He is a bit of a whirlwind, Viola. Our young director always seems to be working on two projects at a time."

"At least," Amy added.

With a chuckle, Rachel continued. "Edward has a real gift for connecting with people. Truly, I've never seen him flustered. So, it was kind of nice to see him at such a loss."

"It was obvious Ed was worried about you something awful," Amy added.

"I feel bad about that."

"Ach. Like I said, not a one of us thought you were being difficult or unseemly."

Viola took another bracing sip of coffee. "Truly?"

"Definitely. See, all of us have been through the same thing a time or two."

"Or five," Rachel added with a grin. "We've got a few years on you, Viola. I promise, I've had my share of embarrassing moments."

The women's frank talk did more to ease her nerves than Ed's gentle reassurances ever had. "I can't tell you how relieved I am to hear you say that. I was thinking that I was the worst sort of woman."

"I promise, you're in good company," Amy said after pulling a tray of biscuits from the oven. "A woman's first taste of this life can be overwhelming, and that's a fact. Our families enjoy sheltering us, and we enjoy being sheltered. That's *wonderful-gut* when we don't have to do anything out of the ordinary. But going to work as a missionary in a foreign country is anything but that."

"How do you like mission work now?"

"I enjoy it."

Amy looked at the clock, then motioned to Viola. "I'll tell you more, if you come with me," she said, then walked straight toward the food pantry. She looked over her shoulder. "Care to help me get the rest of our breakfast together?"

"I'd be happy to." Reaching out her hands, she grabbed the basket Amy held out to her while Amy began putting little boxes of cereal, jars of canned fruit, crackers, and nuts into the basket.

She said, "I've been with CAMA seven years. I have three months to go before I return to Missouri."

Viola put the filled basket down, picked up the next one, and followed Amy toward where the shelves were filled with paper goods. "Do you ever miss home?"

"Before I started, I thought I would. I was sure I would. But it hasn't been bad."

"Why is that?"

"Viola, have you ever been away from home before?"

For the first time in her life, she was embarrassed to have been so content to stay in Berlin. "*Nee*."

"Ah. You're much like I was. Being away from home can be hard. Well, you might think differently, but I've noticed that when I first leave, I always think of home. I find myself comparing where I am to where I've been. But then, as the days pass and I begin to feel more comfortable, I begin to see my new place more clearly."

She still wasn't sure she understood. "More clearly?"

Amy shrugged. "I guess I stop seeing only generalities. Little by little, I don't just notice that people or places are different. I start to think of them by name."

Finally, she understood what Amy was talking about. It comforted her to think that her perception about the mission might change with time, too.

But then she remembered the look of dismay on her fiancé's face. "I hope Ed will try to understand and give me time to get settled."

"He will. If he seemed disappointed to you, it

may be because he's forgotten that sometimes a person's first impression isn't always the clearest. Especially for a man like him, who seems more suited to this life than most."

"I hope you're right. I want to be able to fit in here. I think I was so nervous and warm that I made myself sick."

Amy chuckled. "Like I said, I understood your reaction." Taking the basket from Viola's hands, she said, "I think we have enough paper cups, napkins, and plates. Let's go put them on the tables."

As they headed toward the main room, Viola followed Amy's sure strides, carrying the basket filled with cereal. They set the table and arranged the food.

She was just picking up the empty baskets to return them to the pantry when Edward walked in.

"Viola? What are you doing in here?"

"I'm helping. I mean, I'm trying to help," she corrected sheepishly.

A line formed between his brows. "Are you sure you're up to that? You were so sick last night. Viola, you should have asked someone to find me when you woke up."

"I didn't want to bother you and I wanted to be of use."

"You are doing okay?"

Remembering the other women's reassuring words, she nodded, "I think that maybe last night

I was a little overwhelmed. I feel better now." Fingering her dress, she said, "I'm much cooler, too. That helps, I think."

He fell into step beside her. "How did you sleep?"

Feeling more like herself, she risked teasing him. "I slept very well in your bed, Edward."

To her great amusement, his cheeks heated. "You shouldn't say such things," he said under his breath. Just as if a dozen people were actively listening to their every word.

Finally, she felt as if they were on more even ground. She didn't know how to live as a missionary. She found Belize scary and the idea of living here as his wife more than a bit overwhelming.

But his embarrassment and sudden awkward-ness merely made her feel a little bolder. Here, at least, she felt comfortable. She was used to teasing Roman . . . and after bantering back and forth with his father for months, she felt she was pretty capable of holding her own with Ed.

"If you don't want to know how I slept in your bed, then you mustn't ask such things," she teased. "Now, I must put these baskets away. Would you like to help me carry them?"

"Of course." As he took both from her, he cast her a sideways glance. "Viola, this is what life is going to be like with you, isn't it?"

"Like what?"

"You're going to flirt and tease and laugh and cry." He looked her over like she was the most unique of persons. "You are going to be such a girl."

"I am a girl, and a far from perfect one at that, Ed," she said, all traces of humor gone from her voice. "I'll try my best for you, but I fear there are sometimes going to be moments like last evening, when we both are at a loss for what to do or say."

Still staring at her intently, he exhaled a heavy breath. "That's *gut*. Because I, too, am far from perfect."

Unable to help herself, she rubbed the smooth skin of his cheek. The smooth skin that would one day soon be covered with a beard, signifying their marriage. "I don't want perfect, either."

"If we're in agreement on that, then I suppose we will be all right," he said before leading the way to the pantry.

With a lighter heart, Viola followed.

Maybe, just maybe, everything was going to be fine after all.

It was beautiful out. The air was brisk and still. Tiny snowflakes dotted their skin and clothes, feeling like cold kisses on her face.

Roman beside her was everything she could have hoped for—a man who understood that she'd loved before but was willing to love her all the same. A man who understood how much Regina needed someone in her life who could bring light and happiness into her dark days.

He was offering her a future again. It was *wonderful-gut*. It felt almost perfect.

So why couldn't she seem to stop crying?

Amanda covered her face and inhaled deeply, hoping the cold shot of frigid air would clear her head and calm her nerves.

Or at least temper her tears.

But it was useless. The tears just kept coming of their own accord.

"Amanda?"

She waved off his concern. "It's nothing. Don't mind me."

"Don't mind you?" With a light chuckle, Roman pulled back on Chester's reins, then guided the horse to the side of the road. When they were stopped and not another noise could be heard—beyond her sniffling tears—he turned to her. "Amanda, right at this very moment, I can think of nothing but you."

Ah, the romance of it. His words were the stuff of a girl's dreams. The kind of dreamy words that Wesley had never even said.

Which, of course, made the tears fall harder. She swiped at them in frustration, then stilled as she felt his thumbs gently catch the tears on her cheeks and brush them away. "Amanda, cry if you want to, but I'd rather you tell me what you're feeling. If something is wrong, I could maybe try to help."

"Ah, Roman." She took a deep breath, then turned to him. When she looked into his brown eyes, she noticed they were gazing at her steadily. There was compassion there. And affection. And complete confusion, too.

She didn't blame him; she was feeling pretty confused herself. "I'm sorry," she said. "When we were riding down the road, I suddenly felt so happy, it caught me off guard. Before I knew it, everything kind of came tumbling down around me." Hopefully, she glanced at him. Perhaps he knew what she meant?

He didn't. Instead of nodding in agreement, he continued to stare at her in confusion. "You don't seem happy, Amanda. In fact, you sound pretty sad."

"Oh, I am sad, too. I'm happy and confused, sad and hopeful. I'm everything."

"What are you talking about? Did I do something wrong? What did I say?" His hand clenched the edge of the leather seat, like he was striving for control. "Did I push you too much? I know when we talked about you coming out here, we promised not to have too many expectations."

"But did you mean that?"

"Yes," he said quickly, then, slowly, he shook his head. "*Nee*, that's not the full truth. I had hopes that you would see that there was something special between us. I wanted that to happen."

This was why she was falling in love with him. He was so kind to her, so eager to be the man she needed him to be. "You didn't do anything wrong, Roman."

"Then why the tears?"

Even though she didn't think she had the words to try to explain herself, she knew she had to give it a try. "For so long I've been missing Wesley that I didn't think I could feel anything but dead inside. At first, I was sad. Then, I felt empty. Then, little by little, I began to look around at other men in my life. But not a one interested me. I started to think that I was destined to spend the rest of my life alone."

"But now?"

"Now I feel hope." She smiled. "For the first time in a long time, I feel like I have something to look forward to. It's, ah, overwhelming. That's why I was crying. I can hardly believe that I really am going to be able to say goodbye to my past."

He took off his stocking cap and tossed it on the bench beside them and ran his hand through his hair. "So, even though you're crying, it's for a good reason."

"I think so."

He brushed a finger under her eye, catching her tears as delicately as if he were trying to catch a butterfly. "I wish you weren't crying."

"I do, too. But all in all? These tears aren't a bad

thing. I'm starting to realize that my future can be special because of you."

"I like the sound of that . . . we need to string special and future and you all together more often."

She chuckled, as she knew he'd hoped she would.

Yes, she still felt guilty about Wesley, but she was also starting to realize that he'd been right when she'd sat by his bedside and he made her talk about a future without him in it.

"If that's the reason for your tears, then you can cry all you want," he said with a smile as he leaned forward and lightly brushed his lips against her cheek. "You make me happy. Both you and Regina make me happy. I can hardly wait for us all to be together one day."

It was almost a proposal, Amanda realized. He wasn't going to push her, but his intent was clear. Wiping away the last of her tears with a swipe of her mitten, she said, "Roman, I can hardly wait for you to return to Pinecraft. I'll take you all around, and we'll start to make plans."

"That sounds great. You know, Sam and Lorene have been talking to my uncle Aden. I think my family might even buy a cottage there. That way we'll have a house to go to when we visit."

"Visit?"

"Yes," he said with a smile. "I know we're jumping ahead of ourselves, but I didn't want you to ever think that I mean to take you away from everything in Florida."

"Roman, I've never considered living anywhere else."

"Not even here?"

"No. I need to stay in Florida." That was where Regina's grandparents were. That was where Wesley was buried. Where all their memories were. Even though she might be ready to move forward, she certainly wasn't ready to forget about everything she'd had with him.

He pulled away from her. The two-inch gap that now lay between them chilled her skin. Just as his words froze her heart.

"Amanda, I can't move to Florida." He ran a hand through his hair again. "I thought you understood that."

"*Nee.*" With a sense of dismay, she felt their future slipping away as fast as Roman said the snow melted in spring. As fast as she knew the water receded from the shoreline during low tide.

"Amanda, my life is here."

"In Florida, you told me you weren't happy here."

"My family is going through a rough patch, for sure. That was what I needed to get away from."

"But you said you loved Pinecraft."

"That was true. Of course I love Pinecraft. What's not to like? It's warm and sunny. Everyone there is more relaxed. People are smiling. The beach is there."

"Then what has changed? Why do you sound like you now could never make a home there?"

"Now that I've been home, and things have settled down, I realize that I had only needed a vacation. And though I do like Florida, I realized I loved Pinecraft because you were there. I realized I was unhappy because I didn't have you in my life. That's changed."

He scooted closer again, obviously eager to press his point. "If you move here, we can still have each other. I know right now all this cold and snow feels strange, but in time you'll get used to it. And summer does come." He smiled slightly. "It always does."

He was missing the point. She wasn't worried about the weather. She was thinking about her life! She couldn't just up and leave it. She couldn't plan for a future where she had to give up practically everything she had.

After all, she'd already given up so much already. She'd already lost Wesley. Did she need to lose everything else, too? "Roman, I don't think you're seeing things from my side."

Though he looked in her eyes, he wasn't seeing her. "We can figure this out, Amanda. Don't worry. You'll like it here, and I feel certain everyone's going to love you."

"But—"

He spoke again, effectively stopping anything she had to say. "Amanda, I'm a farmer, and this is where the farm is. And I just accepted the preaching position in our church district. I'm a leader in our church community now. That's a serious commitment."

"But wouldn't a marriage to me be a serious commitment, too? I mean, that is what we are discussing, right? Marriage."

"Of course."

But he hadn't actually asked, had he?

And he hadn't actually mentioned love, had he?

The shine of happiness faded as the realities of what they were discussing came to light. "I think it would be best if we went back."

"I'd rather we stayed here and talked things out."

"Please, it's time to go back."

"Amanda, we don't have much time."

"Of course we do," she said impatiently. "You've waited your whole life for some woman to be just 'right' for you."

"And you are." He reached for her hand. "You're perfect for me."

She snatched her hand right back. "There's more to a relationship than that. I can't only be the woman who fits in with your plan. I need to be the woman in your life who you want to move heaven and earth to have."

Even in the evening night, she could see his bemused expression. "Move heaven and earth? I would have thought you would have been long past spouting such fanciful phrases, Amanda."

"And I would have thought you'd be more than ready to spout them," she replied sharply, trying to cover up her embarrassment. "Please take me back. Now."

He clicked the reins and motioned Chester forward. The bells on the side of the sleigh jangled as they glided forward. They sounded merry and bright.

Snow was still gently falling, but whereas before it had felt magical and special . . . now it only felt cold and wet.

Amanda scooted farther away from Roman. Needing space as her future evaporated and became what it had been all along . . . just spun dreams that dissolved with the night.

So quickly grasped . . . too easily gone.

Chapter Twenty-four

"You, brother, are a fool," Elsie declared when she entered the barn just as the sun began to rise the following morning.

Glancing over his shoulder, seeing her bundled up in her thick black cape and bright pink mittens, he almost smiled. But nothing, not even Elsie's pink mittens, could lighten his mood. "*Gut matin*, to you, sister," he said sarcastically. "What brings you here on a Sunday morning?"

"Oh for heaven's sake, Roman. Is that really all you have to say? I heard Amanda crying last night."

"I feel bad for her but I don't see how her tears are any concern of yours."

"I know why she was crying."

"And you know this because . . ."

"Because I went and knocked on her door, of course."

"Last night?"

"Yes, Roman. Last night," she replied matching his sarcastic tone. "She told me about not wanting to leave Pinecraft and you not wanting to leave here."

"I'm glad you're caught up to speed. Do you have anything else to report? Maybe you went and listened outside Mamm's door, too?"

She stopped him with a hand. "Don't be like that."

"Elsie, I don't want to talk to you about my personal life right now. No, make that ever."

"Well, I'm not going to let you settle back into your old ways. I'm not going to let you hold everything inside. Not this time."

"There's nothing to talk about, sister. Amanda and I are at an impasse."

"Not necessarily. People can change their

minds. Maybe she'll come around. Or, maybe you will."

He was so frustrated with the situation, with his life, he jerked his arm away from her touch. "Elsie, there is no coming around for me. I have responsibilities here." Bitterly, he said, "Haven't you heard that Daed is gone and Viola is too?"

"Daed will be back soon. And the rest of the family can help you farm. Lorene's John said he'd help in a heartbeat. You only have to ask."

"It's not just the farm that I'm concerned with. There's my new position with the church. I'm taking my responsibilities as preacher seriously, Elsie."

"I'm sure people will understand if you say you have to move. People do move, Roman."

He was annoyed that she seemed to have all the answers. Life couldn't be manipulated as easily as she seemed to think. Sometimes certain things were more important than a single person's selfish wants. He truly believed that.

He wasn't happy about it, but he believed it.

"Roman, you're making things too difficult. You need to put yourself first sometimes. I promise, there are many able men who will make a good preacher. And we will find a way to work the farm."

Oh, her confidence grated on him. "It's not just the land or the church I'm worried about, Elsie." He didn't want to say it. Didn't want her to know how much they worried. But how else would she understand? "To be honest, I'm thinking about you. I promised Viola I'd look after you if she left."

She stepped backward. "Me? Wh-what do you mean, you promised Viola?"

"Since Viola is going to be living far away, it's up to me to stay here. We talked about it, and it's fair."

"I don't need you to stay with me. Why on earth would you think that?"

Her expression was incredulous, and he knew she was completely baffled. So, even though he didn't want to hurt her feelings, he realized he had little choice. He had to be honest, there was no other way. "Because you're going to need help," he said quietly. "One day, a lot of help."

"Because of my eyesight, you mean?" She adjusted her eyeglasses over her eyes, maybe in another attempt to see better. But Roman knew those thick lenses could never fix her eyesight. Elsie was going blind . . . and she seemed to be the only person who was in denial about that.

"Of course, because of your eyesight, Els. Even though it's hard, you've got to realize that you have special needs. You're going blind, and you're going to need help. It's inevitable." Lowering his voice, he said, "And I don't mind, Elsie."

"But I'm not blind. I can see."

"Not well. And it's going to get worse. And

Mamm and Daed won't be able to take care of you forever." He looked down at his boots, hating the way she was staring at him, full of hurt.

But just like their father had to own up to his problems, and their grandparents had to admit their pasts, Elsie needed to finally face her future.

"I know you hate to talk about this, but it will be easier if we both face the facts."

"Which is that you're planning to give up everything in order to take care of me, your poor, blind sister."

"I don't mind," he repeated. "I really don't."

She flinched. "Roman, do you really think I'm going to be sitting around the house, expecting to be waited on hand and foot?"

"You are twisting my words, Elsie." He shook his head in frustration. This conversation was hard for him, she had to see that. "You know what, never mind. We'll talk about this another day. When there isn't so much going on."

"Oh, really? You're going to make that decision, too?"

"Elsie—"

"Roman, you might be shocked to hear this, but listen to me well. I *am* going to be married one day. I'm sure of it! I'll be taking care of my own *kinner* and husband and *haus*. I won't be needing you to be hovering around me. I can promise you that."

"I hope that's what happens. I really do." But of

course, what he wasn't saying was what they both heard, clear as day: That he didn't really believe it would ever happen.

"Until that day comes, I advise you to make some plans of your own. Hasn't everything that's happened in our family given you a wake-up call? Bad things happen. But the Lord never promised us an easy life, only that he would be there for us. Let Him shoulder some of your burdens, Roman. And take a chance with your heart while you're at it."

Too tired to argue with her anymore, he didn't reply, only stood stoically until she turned with a grunt of contempt.

Wearily, he followed her back to the house, hoping to make things better between them. But by the time he'd removed his muddy boots and hung his coat on a peg, she was nowhere to be found.

Needing something to warm his insides, he poured a cup of coffee and sat down.

He was still staring at his filled coffee cup when Regina came in.

"Hi, Roman!" she said, pattering over to him still in her nightgown.

"And hello to you. How are you this morning?"

"I'm *gut*." She smiled. "We're gonna make some cupcakes today, 'cause there's gonna be a wedding soon and Elsie says we need tons of 'em."

He'd been so focused on Amanda's visit, and his new duty at the church, he'd completely forgotten. "That is true," he said gently. "Aunt Lorene's wedding day is coming up on Wednesday. That's sure to be a special day. Have you been to a wedding before?"

"Uh-huh."

"Then you know it's going to be busy around here for the next few days. I bet all the women are going to be cooking."

She nodded. "Mamm said a wedding takes a lot of hands. Marie said lots of ladies were coming over to set things up."

"I think tonight when everyone's cooking, we'll have to go out for pie and then go for a walk in the snow."

Her eyes lit up. "We can do that?"

"We can if you want to."

She clapped her hands. "Can I go see Sam now?"

"Sam only likes to have visitors who are dressed in warm clothes. I'll take you to the barn when you're bundled up."

With a little cheer, she scampered off.

He smiled at the sight . . . and wished all his problems could be solved by a visit to a cold barn and an irritable pig.

Moments later, he was brushing down Chester, when the barn door opened. He turned, prepared to greet Regina.

But was faced with Amanda instead.

"Did you come out here to see Sam, too?"

"*Nee*. I came to tell you that I got a reservation on the Pioneer Trails bus today. Regina and I are going to leave."

"Today?"

"I think it's best."

He was so stunned, so hurt, he blurted the first thing that came to his mind. "But what about the cupcake making? Regina just told me that you two planned to help all the ladies bake today. She's excited about it."

"I'm sorry, but I can't do that. I can't bear to think about another wedding right now."

"Because it will only remind you of Wesley?"

She blinked, as if he'd surprised her, then nodded. "Yes. Because of that."

Well, that was that, then. No matter what he did, he was never going to measure up to Wesley Yoder. He turned away to hide his hurt. "I guess you better pack then."

He felt her presence, then breathed a sigh of relief when she turned and walked back out of the barn.

She was only a few steps away, but it felt as if she'd already walked out of his life.

Chapter Twenty-five

Marie gripped the phone a little harder as she finally heard her husband say the words she'd been praying for.

". . . so I should be home before you know it. As long as the weather stays clear and we don't get any snow."

Doing her best to stifle the annoying cough that she couldn't seem to wish away, she said, "Peter, I'm so happy about this."

"I am, too, Marie." His voice sounded hoarse, a little choked. "It's been a difficult couple of weeks, but good ones, too. I'm a better, stronger person now. And I'm done trying to hide behind a bottle of alcohol."

"I'm so proud of you. Going to the clinic was the right decision."

"I think so. I'm only sorry that this right decision has made your life so difficult."

Now that she knew he was coming back, her whole world felt brighter. Even all the things she'd been so worried about didn't seem that overwhelming. She had a feeling his return would even make her body feel better, too. Of late, she'd been so tired it hurt to move. "I'm okay," she said lightly.

"Are you sure? You sound a little off."

"Oh, I've still got this little cold I told you about. It's nothing to worry about." Brightening her voice, she said, "Peter, we're all going to be just fine now."

"All right, if you're sure." He paused. "So, tell me what's been going on. How is Roman's young lady?"

Thinking of what had been happening with their son, Marie frowned. "She is a lovely woman, but they're having some trouble, I fear."

"I'll look forward to meeting her."

"I don't think that's going to happen," Marie murmured as she glanced at Amanda's suitcase standing by the door. "She's leaving today."

"What?"

Rubbing the lines that had formed between her brows, she said, "That is a story better told in person. I'll let you know everything when we see each other again."

"All right. I suppose I should get off the phone anyway. Goodbye, Marie. I'll see you soon."

After speaking to him for a few more precious seconds, she hung up the phone and stared hard at that suitcase.

So many people had been coming and going lately. She didn't know why they all had to travel so much to find their way, but she certainly hoped that everyone would elect to stay in one place very soon.

Otherwise, she was going to be the one who needed a vacation from the drama in their lives.

Roman was as stubborn as a mule. From the moment he'd come into the kitchen, he'd glared at her with his hands stiffly folded across his chest.

But instead of changing her mind, it only made her more eager to get out of his house.

"This isn't easy for me, Roman. I wish you wouldn't make it more difficult," Amanda said as she prepared another peanut butter and jelly sandwich for the long bus trip home.

"I haven't tried to stop you. I'm merely offering my opinion. I think you're running away."

"I guess it's good that I've discovered your true colors," she retorted. "You're not nearly as easygoing as you were in Florida."

"I was on vacation then. And that has nothing to do with you refusing to see my side of things."

"That is not what is happening," she said sharply. Wearily, she neatly sliced through the center of the sandwich and wrapped waxed paper around it.

"Well, something is. Amanda, I think there's more going on here than just my desire not to move. What is it? Is it that you've changed your mind about me?" He paused, then raised an eyebrow. "Or is it more likely that you changed your mind about yourself?"

She flinched, hating his words. Hating that he

was right. She wanted to hold her irritation with him close to her heart. It was so much easier to blame someone else than to face her demons all over again.

At the very least, she owed him her honesty. "I don't know."

"Why not?"

"You came into my life unexpectedly, Roman. I didn't plan to meet you on vacation. I didn't plan to start waiting for your phone calls. I didn't plan on Regina liking you so much." Though all that was the truth, it wasn't the full truth. What she wasn't brave enough to say was that she didn't plan on liking him so much.

He gazed at her, his expression a combination of dismay and anger. That made her realize that he, too, knew she still wasn't telling him the whole truth. She still wasn't sharing everything in her heart.

Which was a problem.

"All right," he finally said. "I'll go take your suitcase out to the front porch. The driver should be here soon."

"A driver is picking us up?" She'd thought he'd take her to the German Village in his buggy.

"Yes. I think that's for the best."

"Yes. Yes, I imagine it is." Carefully, she screwed on the peanut butter cap and set the last sandwich on the top of her lunch sack. "I'll go get Regina and meet you on the front porch."

When he walked away, she washed her hands, pressed a damp paper towel to her cheeks and forehead, hoping to cool her flushed face, then strode to the *dawdi haus*, where Regina had been from the moment Amanda had told her that they wouldn't be making cupcakes today. Instead, they would be going home.

Her knock was quickly answered by Lovina. "Is it time already?" she asked as she led Amanda to her tidy kitchen. There, Regina was sitting at the table with Aaron. A small puzzle with large pieces was spread out in front of them.

The older lady looked as distressed as Amanda felt. But it would do no one any good to see how she really was feeling. "It is. Uh, Roman was able to hire a driver to take Regina and me to the shopping center to wait for the bus."

"But Momma, we're not done with the puzzle."

Amanda was familiar with what Regina was doing. She was concentrating on things she could control instead of what she couldn't.

She'd done that often while Wesley was sick, arguing over what dress to wear, or what food she would eat.

To see that the painful habit had returned broke Amanda's heart but it didn't change the way things were. "I'm sorry about the puzzle, but we're on the bus's schedule, dear. We must go now."

"But I don't want to." This was a comment

Regina had made often before. Usually it came out as a babyish whine. This time, though, was different. Regina looked genuinely distressed. She spoke in a soft whisper. Yet again, Amanda felt that rush of guilt.

But she had to be strong enough for the both of them. Already they were too involved with the Keims. Already she could imagine living in their midst, attending church in their district. Watching Roman preach, encouraging him, being by his side.

But if she did all these things, she'd be saying goodbye to her life in Pinecraft, and that would be wrong. She might be thinking about moving on without Wesley, but she had never intended to leave her life with him completely behind.

"It is time, Regina," she said with iron in her voice. "Maybe we'll meet some nice people on the bus," she added brightly. Just as if they were on the way to the county fair.

But no one was fooled for a minute. Both Mr. and Mrs. Keim looked glum, and Regina was on the verge of tears.

She had to get out of there. Had to move on. Stepping forward, she reached for her daughter's hand. "Let's go, now."

Regina jerked back her hand. *"Nee."*

"You have no choice." Through clenched teeth, she turned to Lovina and Aaron. "Thank you for being so nice to Regina."

"It was no trouble. We enjoyed being with her," Aaron said.

"She's a *wonderful-gut* girl, Amanda," Lovina added. "*Wonderful-gut.*"

"*Danke.*" Amanda didn't know what to do with her hands. She ached to hug Lovina and Aaron goodbye, but it didn't seem right. "Well, goodbye."

The couple exchanged looks. Then Lovina nodded. "Goodbye, Amanda. Safe travels."

Just as she started to turn away, Regina rushed over to Aaron and hugged him tight.

While Amanda simply stood and watched, Lovina went to her husband's side and hugged Regina, too. Then, when Regina started crying, the woman bent down and whispered to her, carefully calming her.

As seconds passed, Amanda felt like the worst mother ever. Especially when Regina turned from the security of the couple's embrace and calmly announced she was ready.

"Let's go then," Amanda answered. Surprised she could even speak around the lump in her throat.

The next five minutes were excruciating. They said goodbye to Marie and Elsie. To Lorene, who was over making cupcakes for the upcoming wedding.

The wedding that Amanda had promised Regina that they'd get to attend. Through it all, Roman remained to one side while Regina stayed silent.

Only the beep from the van's horn offered any relief.

"We must go," she said, after double- and triple-checking that she had her purse and their lunches and Regina's stuffed dog. After getting Regina settled in the van, Amanda looked at Roman. "Thank you for inviting us to Berlin. I'll never forget it."

"You're welcome. Goodbye, Amanda."

She halfheartedly waited for him to ask her to call him when they got home. Waited for him to say that he understood, that he would change his mind about where he wanted to live.

But he did none of that. Instead, he stood stoically while she turned away and got into the van. While she fastened her seatbelt, he closed the van's door. Then he turned away as they drove off.

Beside her, Regina was hugging her stuffed dog tightly, looking for comfort there instead of from her mother.

And that was when Amanda realized that she'd been terribly wrong. It certainly was possible to feel that all-encompassing pain again.

But unlike Wesley's cancer, she'd been the one in charge of this loss.

Yes, it turned out that she was perfectly capable of causing pain and heartache and loss, all by herself.

Walking back to their house, Lovina blinked back the tears that she hadn't been able to will away but luckily had held back until no one else saw them. "I'm going to miss that little girl," she said.

"Me, too," Aaron said. "I don't think I'm going to be able to finish that puzzle without her. Half the fun was cheering with her whenever she got a piece in the right spot."

"We'll put it away so you won't have to be reminded of it." Uncertainly, she glanced at Aaron's stoic profile. "Do you think, perhaps, we'll need it for another day? For when she comes back?"

"Hope so." He stuffed his hands in his coat pockets. "It's a real shame Amanda and Regina had to leave. That grandson of ours shouldn't have let that happen. He won't do better than that pair."

"Sometimes our grandchildren can be so stubborn and silly."

"That is a fact." Slowly, the sides of his mouth turned up. "I wish I could say I've never been that way, but I can't."

"Truly?"

"Oh, *jah*. Lovina, I've certainly done my fair share of stubborn things. For sure, I have."

Rarely had Aaron ever admitted a mistake. Never could she remember him pointing out his own faults. "Like what?"

"Like . . . making you keep your past a secret. I know now that was a foolish idea."

"Not so much. I kept it secret for forty years," she reminded him.

"But at what cost?"

Just a few weeks ago, when the secret had first come out, she'd been sure that their relationships with their children and grandchildren were lost. But as each day passed, things had seemed to ease. Time really did heal all wounds. "Maybe that secret didn't cost as much as we feared," she said. "We still have our family."

"Things are strained."

She stopped at their front door. "That's because everyone is now focused on your first family."

"My first family?" he echoed sarcastically.

She ignored his tone, choosing instead to focus on what was important. "You need to talk about Laura Beth and Ben, Aaron."

"I can't." He opened the door and stepped inside.

She followed on his heels all the way to their sitting room. "Why are their deaths so difficult for you to talk about? It's not like you caused the accident."

Gripping the back of his chair, he looked at her directly. "Some thought I did."

"Who did?"

"Laura Beth's brother." After a pause, he added, "Every year on the anniversary of Laura Beth's death, he sends me a letter. Inside are always the same two things—a photocopy of the news article, and a letter from him. In it, he says he still hasn't forgotten his sister's death or forgiven me for my part in it."

Lovina was stunned. "I never knew about the letters."

"That's because I didn't want you to know about them."

"But you don't take the notes seriously, do you? I mean, for someone to continually send you the same thing, year after year? That's ridiculous!"

Aaron shrugged.

Feeling assured that her husband clearly needed some sense talked into him, Lovina continued, her tone stronger. "Laura Beth died forty years ago. Her *bruder* must be mentally imbalanced or something." She walked toward him, ready to grasp his hand. To show him that even though she didn't understand all the secrets, she believed in him.

Believed the best of him.

But instead of curving his palm around hers, he stiffened. "Lovina, there's something else I never told you."

"And what is that?"

"I was driving that buggy. Her death really was my fault."

Once again, Lovina felt her world tilt. "I don't understand. You said she was driving."

"I never wanted to tell you the truth."

She was beyond dismayed. "Aaron?"

He rushed on with his explanation. "The police deemed it an accident, but we all knew better. She and I were fighting, arguing. I was yelling at her while I was driving the buggy in the rain."

"But—"

"After it was all over, I couldn't take the guilt," he whispered. "I knew I needed to get away, to start over again. . . ."

His voice drifted off, but now Lovina realized she could fill in the gaps.

Now she understood why he'd courted her, even though she wasn't Amish. Now she understood why they'd moved to Ohio and never went back to Pennsylvania.

All this time, she'd imagined it was because of her painful memories, but it had been for his.

"I killed my wife and son, Lovina," Aaron said, his voice flat. "Then I married you on top of a pile of lies and moved you far away so I could pretend it never happened."

She felt like all the air had been forced out of her. "For forty years, you did a good job of it."

"Possibly." He shrugged. After a few seconds, he added, "Lovina, I don't know what else to say."

"I think I do." Abruptly, she made a decision. "We need to go back. Aaron, we need to go back to Pennsylvania and face our pasts."

Even from her position across the room, she

could see every muscle in his body tense. Then, with a sigh, the fight left him. "Lord help me, but I think you are right."

Meeting his gaze, she saw everything she was feeling reflected in his eyes. He looked terrified, and pained. Weary.

But a new resolve was present, too.

"Please, Lord, help us both," she murmured.

With her words still echoing in the air, she walked to the kitchen and filled up her kettle with water.

At long last, there was nothing more to be said.

Chapter Twenty-six

"I can't believe it's already time to leave," Viola said on Monday afternoon as she stood outside the airport's entrance. "I'm not ready."

Under his straw brim, she saw Ed's blue eyes twinkle. "That's quite a change of heart from when you first got here."

Even under the hot sun, her cheeks were able to hold a fierce blush. "Are you going to remind me of my behavior for the rest of our lives?"

"I hope not . . . but maybe." His tender gaze, mixed with the way he held her hand between his two lessened the sting of his words. "Everything's fine now, though. Ain't so?"

"Everything is more than fine," she agreed. It

was amazing the way the Lord had worked through her during the last few days. She'd gone from being nervous and insecure to feeling braver than she thought possible.

And the best thing of all . . . she'd come to look at the mission as her home, and the people there as potential friends. Not just her future husband's coworkers or people who were in need of help. She'd been transformed and made stronger . . . and none of it would have been possible without Edward in her life.

Now she couldn't imagine merely living her life in Berlin. Now she couldn't imagine getting as much satisfaction at her job at Daybreak. Here in Belize, by Edward's side, she felt needed and valued and worthwhile.

A car horn blared behind Edward, making them both jump.

He let go of her hand. "Don't forget to call me when you get back. I know phone calls here are expensive, but I'll worry otherwise."

"I'll call."

He gently touched the end of her nose. "Promise?"

"I promise."

"*Gut*. And I promise that I'll be back soon, and we'll get married."

"That's another three months." Right now it felt like a lifetime. A very long, very lonely lifetime.

"But then we'll always be together." Wrapping

his arms around her, he hugged her close. "I miss you already. And I love you, Viola. Don't forget," he whispered before stepping away.

"I won't forget." She swiped away a tear.

"Please don't cry. Now, off you go." He raised a hand. "Bye."

Slowly, she raised her hand, too. "Goodbye, Edward. I love you, too."

And with that, she turned and walked inside, right to the ticket counter.

"Going home, miss?" the lady said as she examined Viola's plane ticket and passport.

"Yes. I'm going home for now," she replied.

And found herself already counting down the days until she was coming back to Belize. As Mrs. Edward Swartz.

"Do you think your wedding will be like this?" Elsie whispered to Viola ninety minutes into Aunt Lorene's wedding service on Wednesday morning.

They were sitting about four rows from the center on the women's side in the barn. The barn was packed with at least two hundred people, and overly warm, because the cold weather prevented too many doors from being opened. Because of that, the three-hour wedding ceremony felt longer than usual, especially for the Keim women, who'd had next to no sleep for the past twenty-four hours.

They'd been cooking and cooking and cooking.

Even at that moment, a group of women were in the portable kitchen they'd rented, putting the finishing touches on all the dishes. Four women who worked with Lorene at the cheese shop were setting out paper napkins, placemats, and plastic silverware on the long tables under the white tent Roman and their uncle Sam had put up the day before.

"I imagine my wedding will be much like this," Viola answered. "But hopefully it will be a little cooler in this barn. I'd be *verra* grateful to have fresh air to breathe."

Elsie shifted yet again and pulled the collar of her dress out from her neck. "Fresh air would be a blessing," she murmured.

"I'm *verra* glad that Edward and I are getting married in May."

"It will be here before we know it."

Viola glanced at her with worry. This wasn't the first time Elsie had made a comment like that. Viola feared Elsie was dreading their separation as much as she was. Of course, their circumstances were different. Viola would miss Elsie terribly, but she had a new life with Ed in Belize to look forward to.

And Elsie? All she could look forward to was a series of adjustments at home. She was going to have to pick up some of Viola's chores . . . and also learn to do without Viola's help.

As Viola thought about Elsie being home

without her, a fresh new wave of guilt slammed into her.

It was likely Roman was going to move out soon, too. Either he and Amanda would have their own home in Berlin, or he would move to Florida. That is, if they ever decided to stop being so stubborn and learned to compromise.

But Elsie? Elsie was destined to live with their parents. Poor Elsie.

"Viola, you all right?" Elsie whispered.

Viola realized she'd been clenching her hands together. "I'm fine."

One of the elderly ladies turned to them and frowned. "Shh."

"Sorry," Viola mouthed, then returned to the service again.

At the center of the barn, in between where the rows of men and women on benches faced each other, Viola watched Lorene sit primly in her lovely navy blue dress and black *kapp*.

Directly across from her, John Miller sat primly as well. His matching blue shirt drew all their eyes, though he probably had no idea. It looked as if he was hardly aware of what the ministers were saying.

No, it looked like he only had eyes and ears for Lorene.

Viola shifted as two girls scooted past their row, purses in hand. Two rows back, a young boy left his mother's arms and walked directly across to the other side of the barn, quickly locating his *daed*.

And still the minister talked.

"I wish Daed could've been here," Elsie whispered after another ten minutes. "It don't seem right that he'd miss his sister's wedding."

"Mamm said she expects him home any day."

Elsie grunted, a terribly untypical response. "She told me that, too. It was kind of her to be so nice and vague."

Viola treaded carefully. After all, usually she was the one who was impatient while Elsie was the one who kept things positive. "I'm sure he wishes he were here, twin."

Elsie opened her mouth, then shook her head in a gesture filled with regret. "I'm sorry. I sound awful, don't I?"

"Is something wrong with you?"

"Other than I seem to be the only one out of the three of us who hasn't fallen in love?"

Viola pursed her lips. There was nothing that she could say to make things better. Poor Elsie was not likely to ever fall in love.

But Elsie took her silence as another offense. "You don't think I ever will have a husband, do you?"

"I didn't say that."

"Viola, how do you think I feel, knowing that no one in the family believes that I have a future?"

"You're putting words into our mouths. We all think you have a future," she said.

Another lady turned around and shushed them again.

Thankfully, further conversation was prevented by the minister raising his hands and calling them all to stand.

A thick silence settled over the congregation as the bishop gestured for Lorene and John to stand up. And then, after reading several verses from First Corinthians, Lorene and John began to recite the vows that everyone had heard a dozen times, and that many of the assembled girls had even practiced saying late at night, in the privacy of their rooms.

Viola felt a thrill go through her as she realized that her wedding might very well be the next one the community attended. Most likely she, too, would only have thoughts and eyes for her beloved.

Across the room, she met Roman's eyes and wondered what was going to happen with him and Amanda. She felt certain that he, too, had found his perfect match. All he and Amanda needed to do now was figure out a way to live together.

Obviously, she knew that wasn't always an easy task, but it could be done . . . if they wanted a life together.

Moments later, the vows were completed, and only the ending prayers needed to be said. It was the family's cue to leave and prepare for the arrival of the wedding guests and the bride and groom in the celebration tent.

Picking up her own purse, Viola led the way for her and Elsie to exit the barn. Behind her, Elsie stumbled but quickly righted herself. It took everything Viola had not to reach for her, to hold her hand.

But she couldn't refrain from looking her way.

"I am fine," Elsie said irritably. "I am fine."

Viola nodded. Even though they both knew Elsie wasn't fine. Not at all.

Late that night, after Lorene and John Miller had driven away, after the party had continued into the night, and most of the chairs and tables and trash had been put away, Roman came to a decision.

He wanted what Lorene had. He wanted what his parents and grandparents had. What Viola was looking forward to. He wanted marriage. He wanted vows. He wanted his family and friends around him, encouraging him, teasing him.

Being there.

He wanted it all. Most important, he wanted it all with Amanda and Regina. Only that lady and that little girl would make him feel happy, and would give him the life he'd been dreaming of. A fulfilled life, one with laughter and tears. With excitement and contentment.

He realized that he'd been letting everything else get in the way of his happiness. Yes, he had responsibilities to his family and their farm, but he instinctively knew that he would only grow to resent those responsibilities if he gave up his happiness for them. And that wasn't how he wanted to be. He wanted to joyfully give of himself, not do things begrudgingly.

And though he hated the thought of going to Bishop Coblentz and telling him that he couldn't be a preacher, Roman had to think that the Lord wouldn't be too disappointed in him. After all, He had been the one who had put Roman and Amanda next to each other in Pinecraft. Surely He hadn't intended for them to meet and fall in love . . . only to be apart because of a church job?

And so he was going to have to reach out to Amanda. To call her and make some changes.

Suddenly, he realized that he didn't want to simply call her on the phone. He needed to see her face when he told her that he wanted to move to Florida, if that was the only place she could live and be happy.

But as he thought of the countless hours he'd have to wait on the bus down to Florida, with its many stops along the way, he made a decision. Yes, if Viola could go gallivanting about on planes for love, he could, too.

After a lifetime of being restrained and dutiful, he was ready to throw all those traits out the window.

Being in love really did make a man different, he decided. It made him impulsive and excited.

Actually, it made him better.

Chapter Twenty-seven

Just when she thought it would never come, Marie got the phone call she'd been waiting for. "Peter, where are you?" she asked the moment she heard his voice.

"I'm at the bus station in Berlin."

"Where have you been? I thought you were going to be here two days ago?"

"I tried to get there, dear, but my counselor's child got sick, so we couldn't meet on time, then I missed my first bus, then the second one broke down. It's been quite the adventure."

"I guess it has." She felt bad for him, but she wished she could turn back time, too. He'd missed Lorene's wedding, Amanda's visit, and now Roman was back in Florida.

"But I'm here now. Do you think you can come pick me up?"

Her smile was so wide, she could hardly speak. "Of course. I'll be there as soon as Chester and I can make it."

"There's no reason to rush, Marie." He paused. "Marie, you sound much worse. How sick are you now?"

She did feel dizzy and short of breath. But that was nothing compared to the happiness she was feeling. "It's nothing. I'm still just a little under the weather."

"Why don't I call for a driver?"

"Don't be silly. It's only a cough. I'll be better when you're home, I'm sure of it."

"All right, then. Well, I'll be here waiting, so take your time. I don't care how long it takes you and Chester to get here."

His romantic words melted her heart, and renewed her spirit. Maybe things would be better between them. Maybe their troubles were over. They'd been through their difficult patch but things were better already. "I can't wait to see you."

When she hung up, she turned to her mother-in-law, who was cutting up vegetables for the evening's planned supper of chicken and dumplings. "Peter's come back."

Lovina paused in her cutting. "I figured as much. That is *gut* news."

"I'm so glad he's home."

"Me, too." She smiled.

Marie's mind was spinning as she looked from her dirty apron to the dust rag that she was somehow still holding. "I feel light-headed, I'm so excited."

Her mother-in-law laughed. "Reunions have a way of turning us all into young girls. My advice is to wait until you get your bearings, then hitch up the buggy and go find your husband."

"Yes. Yes, that's what I'll do." After switching her apron, she ran outside toward the barn, fastening her cloak and tying the strings on her bonnet as she did so. When her cough forced her to stop to catch her breath, she told herself that she'd sit down to rest later.

In no time, she'd hitched up Chester and guided him out toward the main road. As she drove the horse, her mind was filled with dreams and questions. She wondered what it would be like, to see her husband again after his month's absence.

Wondered if things really would be the same like she hoped . . . or if they would be different like Peter said they would.

And then there were all the other things to consider. Like how his relationship with his parents would be now. Better, hopefully?

And how would Roman treat him after his absence? Though her son had never confided in her about this, she feared that Roman resented his father for forcing him to accept so much responsibility around the house.

By the time she pulled the buggy up to the front of the German Village Market, she felt dizzy and feverish.

"Marie!" Peter called out. But then his happy smile turned to worry. "Marie? Marie, you're sick."

Vaguely, she was aware of him holding her, then calling out to a pair of men walking by.

"Marie, we're calling a driver. I'm taking you to the hospital."

"There's no need. And Chester—"

"They're going to help me with Chester. I'm back now. Trust me, Marie. I'll take care of you now."

As his words sank in, she let herself lose control. Gave in to the fever and the cough. Gave in to the headache and the ache in her chest.

And was hardly aware when her husband and another woman helped her into a van.

The beach had never looked so empty. Or so depressing. Devoid of people, only the rhythmic churning of waves broke the silence of the evening.

Over and over again they crashed to the shore, spitting water and debris onto the packed sand, reminding Amanda that much of her life had been spent like that. She'd been stuck in a rut, doing the same things, even when it only dredged up more hurt and painful memories.

Beside her, Regina walked stalwartly like a small soldier, silently staying by her side, though whether it was by choice or habit, Amanda didn't know.

Ever since they'd left Roman's grandparents' house, Regina had been depressed. She'd laughed rarely, smiled even less.

Feeling desperate, Amanda went to the shelter

and signed the papers to make Goldie theirs. Now, only the silly dog's antics made Regina smile.

And only Regina's smiles were able to lift Amanda's broken heart.

It had been a difficult two days, trying to be strong, attempting to resign herself to being without Roman. Doing her best to pretend that she'd made the right decision, and that sometimes, it was a mother's lot to give up her wants. To put her daughter's needs first.

But this time, a small, needling voice whispered, *Wasn't it your wants that took precedence?*

"Momma, watch this!" Regina exclaimed as she threw a stick and Goldie ran to the edge of the water to retrieve it. "Look at her go."

"She does love those sticks, that is true," Amanda said, glad to concentrate on anything else besides her drab thoughts.

When the current lapped against her paws, the dog scampered away, then trotted out into the water a little farther. Then, tongue hanging out of her mouth, she began dog-paddling in the shallow current. Standing back on the beach, Amanda crossed her arms over her chest and chuckled. "She is getting mighty wet."

"Goldie loves swimming!"

"She does."

Goldie leapt out of the water, gave a good shake, then trotted back to Regina, the stick in her mouth. Tail wagging, she stopped right in front of her and dropped the stick on the ground. Regina dutifully picked it up and tossed it again.

With a happy bark, Goldie ran off to retrieve it . . . and then went for another swim.

"I'm glad we got Goldie."

"I am, too," Amanda said. Now this, at least, was something she could be completely truthful about. This dog was sure to be a perfect pet. Already housebroken and, at four years old, already out of the precocious puppy stage, Goldie wanted to play with Regina, but so far seemed just as content to spend much of her days on her soft dog bed while Amanda went to work and Regina went to her grandparents' house.

Last night, Goldie had seemed to know exactly what each of them needed the most. She sat between them on the couch and snuggled, seeming to enjoy their petting as much as they enjoyed the dog's unspoken love and comfort.

"Goldie needed a home, Momma."

"Yes, she did."

"Being at the dog shelter was no fun," Regina added seriously. "Remember how noisy it was there? Poor Goldie!"

Amanda struggled to hold off her smile. They'd had this conversation several times already. Her daughter was intrigued by the idea of animals needing homes.

"It was no fun for Goldie, for sure. Now she's

happy, though, wouldn't you say?" she asked as they watched the half golden retriever, half who-knew-what dog come trotting back to them with that same stick secured in her mouth. "Now she lives in a nice, cozy home. And has a fluffy dog bed, too." Tickling Regina's back, she added, "Plus, now that she's in an Amish home, it's mighty quiet."

But instead of nodding in agreement, Regina shook her head. "*Nee*, Mamm. That's not it."

"No?"

"Mamm, Goldie is happy because she's around people who love her," Regina said. "That's why."

"Ah, yes. I suppose that is what matters the most," Amanda murmured, then felt a lump form in her throat as the meaning shone through.

It was being loved that mattered, Amanda realized. That had been what everyone, from Roman to Regina to Wesley had been trying to tell her all along.

A person couldn't live a life on memories. Not a good life, anyway.

No, the past was in the past, and the future was in God's hands. All she had was the present. What she did now was what counted . . . not what she'd done years ago . . . or what she hoped to do one day.

And what really mattered, when all was said and done, was love.

And she'd had that. She'd been loved. Deeply. She'd been blessed to be loved not once but twice. Both by good, upstanding men.

But what had she done?

She'd clung to her grief and ignored the precious gift she'd been given. She'd pushed Roman away, pushed the future she could have with him away. For some reason, she'd decided that it would be easier to live in the past. Had it been fear that had driven her? Perhaps.

But even knowing it was fear that had driven her, it didn't make her consequences any easier to bear. She'd hugged her misplaced sense of loyalty to Wesley like a badge of honor. But now she realized that she hadn't done it for him.

When he'd known his time was coming, he'd told her time and again not to mourn for him. He'd told her over and over that life was for living, not simply for wishing.

And definitely not for grieving.

She'd promised him she wouldn't do that. But she hadn't even tried to keep that promise.

She'd fallen into an uneasy habit of living alone, and never imagining that her life could be better or different.

And worse, she'd made her dear daughter live that way, too.

It was time, Amanda decided. It was finally time to live, to grasp happiness, even if it was as shimmery as a hazy ray of light.

Even if it meant moving and changing and giving up some of her security.

Just like that silly dog, who had a past no one knew about but had happily found love again, she could, too.

It was time, time to go home and make that call. Call Roman and tell him she'd been wrong. That she'd been afraid to want more, to ask for happiness, but she wasn't any longer.

"Momma, look!" Regina called out, pointing just behind her.

"I will. In one second. But first I want to talk to you about something."

"But—"

Amanda knelt down. "Regina, just for a second, listen."

"But, Mamm—"

"Please, Regina."

Blue eyes widened. "Yes?"

"Regina, what would you say if I thought we should move to Berlin, Ohio, after all? To live with Roman and his family? What would you say if I told you that I know I was wrong? That I now know I was wrong to leave?"

Regina's eyes widened, but then they crinkled at the edges as she beamed at her. "I'd like that."

"Sure?"

"I'm sure." Her smile widened. Almost as if she had a secret.

Amanda hugged her tight. "*Gut*. Then that's

what we'll do. We'll gather up Goldie and walk to the condo and—"

"Mommy!"

"What?"

"This time, you need to listen."

"All right. What is it that you need to tell me?" Panic coursed through her. Maybe Regina was changing her mind? Maybe she was upset? Maybe . . .

Regina pointed behind Amanda again. "Mommy, just look over there, will ya?"

"All right." Amanda turned around and gaped.

There was Roman, standing tall and handsome, his gaze warm and loving. Just as if she'd conjured him from a daydream. "Roman, look at you," she whispered.

After giving Regina a little wink, Roman walked forward. He was carrying a pair of brown work boots, thick socks tucked into the tops of them. "You look surprised," he said after hugging Regina.

"I am."

"Are you upset?" His gaze studied her face, obviously looking for clues about what she was thinking.

"I was just telling Regina that we needed to call you."

He got to his feet. "Were you, now?"

"Yes. I . . . I wanted to tell you that I'm sorry,

Roman. You were right about everything. We can be happy everywhere. Anywhere."

"Listen, I wasn't right about everything. I was too impatient. But," he added boyishly, "I am younger than you, remember. We young men sometimes need a little bit of guidance."

"I'm only two years older."

He laughed. "Two years still counts."

Regina beamed up at him. "Momma said we're going to call you about Berlin."

"Really? Are you going to come for another visit?"

"No. We're going to live there," Amanda said softly.

He stared in shock, then closed his mouth. "Amanda, I appreciate that, but, ah, you don't have to. I mean, I know you want to be here, where your life with Wesley was. It was wrong of me to expect you to leave everything. If this is where you need to be, then I can be here, too."

Amanda felt so loved. Roman said so much with those words. "I loved Wesley, but he's gone. I'll always love his memory. And I'll always be grateful that he gave me Regina. And I'll treasure the memories of our brief time together. But you're my future, Roman. I know you are."

"If you want to stay here . . . I decided that you were more important to me than even my church obligations."

"That much?"

"Amanda, I don't want to lose you."

"You haven't lost me. I'm ready. I'm ready to start over. Both Regina and I are. Right, Gina?"

"Yes. But Goldie needs to come to Ohio, too."

Roman grinned at the dog, who was currently digging in the sand. "Do you think Goldie will mind the cold weather?"

"I think she's a pretty resilient dog," Amanda said as she rubbed the dog's shaggy head. "I think she'll be happy as long as we're there."

"Then that's settled," Roman said with a grin. "As soon as possible, we're all going to go to Ohio."

"We're getting married, Roman?" Regina asked hopefully.

"Yep. We're all getting married as soon as possible."

There were so many more things to say. And so many things that would probably forevermore be left unsaid. But all that mattered was that moment.

Where they were all together. The three of them plus one shaggy dog.

And this moment would one day rest in her memories, tangled in a hundred, a thousand moments of her life. She'd remember the time Roman had appeared on the beach, loving her enough to give up everything.

At almost the same moment that she'd decided the same thing.

She'd remember the way the sand had felt under her feet, the way she spied the sun sinking low over the horizon. She'd remember the sharp smell of the ocean and the faint scent of Regina's faded sunscreen.

She'd remember feeling exhilarated and awake and so, so very alive. She'd remember feeling in love and happy.

She'd remember it all for the rest of her life.

Forever.

Roman had just leaned close to kiss her when the condominium manager called her name.

Surprised, Amanda turned to him. "Yes, Mr. Conway?"

"Amanda, we just got an urgent message for your beau," he said as he came rushing out to greet them, seemingly oblivious to the way the sand he was kicking up was sticking to his dark slacks. "Son, are you Roman Keim?"

Roman strode forward. "I am. Is something wrong?"

"I'm afraid so. We just got a call from your grandmother. Your mother has just been admitted to the hospital."

"What?"

"That's all I know." He thrust a piece of paper into his hands. "But here's the phone number of the hospital. Your grandmother asked you to call as soon as you can."

Turning to her, Roman's face was a study of

disbelief and grief. "Amanda, Regina, I don't know what to say."

"I do," she said simply. "We had better see if Pioneer Trails has room for us on the next run to Ohio."

"You're sure you want to go back right away?"

"I'm positive. I want to be there for you. I want us to be together."

"What about Goldie?" Regina asked.

"We can put her in an animal carrier and she can ride the bus, too," Roman said. "She won't like it, but she'll do all right."

"I don't deserve you," Amanda whispered.

"Of course you do. We all deserve each other," Roman said with a smile. "We're a team now, you, Regina and I. Together, we'll be able to get through anything."

Roman reached out for both of their hands. Then, the three of them started the long walk back, Goldie for once walking sedately at their heels.

Though so much in life could hurt and go so wrong . . . at the moment nothing felt more right.

Epilogue

This is how life goes, Lovina decided as she took a turn by Marie's bedside in the intensive care unit at the hospital. Some days it was wonderful. And other times? Not so much. Life was truly a series of hills and valleys.

Sometimes it was also downright scary.

The doctors said that Marie was going to be better soon, and Lovina hoped and prayed that was true. Currently, Marie had a number of tubes and cords attached to her, as well as a noisy machine that helped her breathe.

She'd woken in fits and spurts, but had been so drowsy and feverish Lovina didn't think she understood where she was.

The rest of the family was coping with her sickness the best they could. Aden and his family had come in from Indiana. Lorene and John had cut short their wedding trip and were back in Berlin, too. The house was as full as it had ever been, and the noise and commotion brought back memories of when their five children were still small.

As the machines beeped and blipped and Marie's slumber continued, Lovina stretched out her legs and let her mind drift.

First, she thought of happier times, such as

when Roman and Amanda had returned to Berlin together and announced their engagement. Or how radiant Lorene had looked on her wedding day.

Oh, indeed, her daughter had looked so happy. So, so different from the last few years, when Lorene's demeanor had seemed so bleak.

Remembering that, of course, took Lovina to another time, back when she was simply Lolly.

When everything about her life had felt bleak and dark, too.

She remembered going to the market, her arms full of miscellaneous items for her mother. Near the checkout counter she'd seen Jack's parents, their steps faltering when they caught sight of her.

She'd ached to dart back down an aisle, but experience had shown her that hiding solved nothing.

Lifting her chin, she strode forward to meet them. "Hi, Mr. and Mrs. Kilgore."

Almost reluctantly, they stopped. "Hello, Lolly," Mrs. Kilgore said.

With a start, she noticed that Mrs. Kilgore's eyes were red-rimmed, and the lines around Mr. Kilgore's eyes looked deeper than she remembered. They both looked haggard. Exhausted, really. They also were staring at her. Glaring, really. Almost as if they were daring for her to challenge them.

Or maybe they were daring her to speak?

She felt thoroughly confused. "How are you both?" she asked reluctantly, feeling as inane as her words sounded.

Mr. Kilgore blinked, just like she'd managed to surprise him. "Lolly, have you not heard?"

"I don't know what you're talking about. Have I not heard what?" But of course, the moment she said the words, a curious buzzing started to ring in her ears.

And she knew.

"Jack is gone," Mrs. Kilgore said through clenched teeth. "His helicopter went down over Saigon."

Lovina blinked, hearing the words, but not fully comprehending them. "Went down, you say?"

"The helicopter crashed," Mr. Kilgore said flatly. "Our boy died in Vietnam."

Jack was gone. Gone, just like Billy. Just like their innocence. Just like all her dreams, and all the silly, too sweet dreams she'd had about her future.

Gone.

Her world began to spin.

"Lolly? Lolly!" Mrs. Kilgore exclaimed. "Jim, I think she's about to faint."

Vaguely, she was aware of being helped to the ground. Next thing she knew, she was sitting on the cold linoleum of the grocery store floor, leaning up against a shelf full of canned tomatoes.

When her vision cleared, she looked up at Jack's parents. The couple she'd imagined would one day be her in-laws. "I'm so sorry," she murmured, just as tears started falling down her cheeks.

The couple, now looking like all the fight had filtered out of them, hovered ineffectually over her. Mrs. Kilgore was wringing her hands. "Lolly, dear. I am sorry we told you like this. I guess we should have thought to have given you a call. Or called your mother. . . ." She continued to talk, with Mr. Kilgore adding something every now and then.

But it all sounded garbled to Lovina. She hardly understood what they were saying.

Well, perhaps she didn't remember it now, Lovina reflected as she returned back to the present.

Somehow she'd made it home. A couple of weeks later, she'd moved on and got a job working as a clerk at the local bank.

And then, one day, in had come Aaron. Looking so healthy and proud and Amish.

Looking so different from any man she'd ever known.

Then, of course, everything had changed. They'd started talking, one thing led to another . . . and she'd left all the pain behind.

Well, she'd thought she had.

"Lovina, I hope you're not worrying too

315

much," Aaron stated from the doorway. "Peter just spoke with the *doktah*. He said Marie's health is improving."

"That's *gut* news."

"It is *gut*, indeed. Marie will get better. She has to. Why, all of us are praying for her recovery."

Once again, she looked at her husband. Thought about the trip they were planning to take to Pennsylvania in an attempt to finally put their pasts behind them. If they could find the strength to do that, why, she was sure that Marie could find the strength to regain her health.

Slowly, she got to her feet and met him at the door. "I was just sitting here, thinking about how time marches on."

To her surprise, he took her hand and gave it a little squeeze. "One day this, too, shall pass. Just like everything else." In an obvious effort to cheer her, he said, "Why, it seems like not so long ago that we were corralling our *kinner* at the grocery store."

The memory made her smile. It had been exhausting, trying to get five children anywhere on time. It had been fun though, too. "It was more like they corralled us," she said. "Some days, I fell into bed feeling like I was the tiredest woman on earth."

"They did have a way about them," Aaron agreed, his eyes bright. "They were busy and rambunctious and loud."

"So loud!" she agreed, remembering all the arguments and joking and giggles.

"But they turned out okay."

"Better than okay," Lovina said fondly. "I'm proud of them. They're *gut* people."

"Soon, we'll be marrying off more grand-children. Viola next."

"And maybe Roman . . ."

"Yes, and maybe Roman sooner than we realize." He yawned. "Peter is outside, waiting for his turn with Marie. I think we should let him come in. Are you ready to leave?"

"Almost. I'll be there in a moment."

He paused, almost looking as if he was going to say something else. But then simply nodded. "All right."

Quietly, Lovina walked back to Marie's bedside and opened the blinds a bit. Let the sun shine into the darkened room, brightening things up.

And though Aaron was waiting for her and Peter was anxious to sit with Marie, Lovina sat down and watched the rays of sunlight stream across the sheets and blankets that covered Marie.

Little by little, the constant noise from the squeaks and pings of the machines drifted over her and faded into the background. Until she hardly heard them anymore.

When she was sitting in silence again, she felt peace settle over her. One that was as calming and sustaining as it was unexpected.

Here in the hospital room, when everything seemed so dark, she recognized the feeling for what it was . . . a glimmer of hope.

A chance for happiness that she'd almost forgotten existed.

Until recently, hope was something that she'd long ago given up on. Something that, over time, she'd twisted and turned and damaged . . . so much so that she'd even started to imagine that the emotion had never existed.

Or at least had passed her by.

But now she saw what it was. Hope was a ray of light in a life filled with regret and disappointment. It had always been there, lurking in the background. As perfect and as endearing as God's love.

"Light shines on the godly, and joy on those whose hearts are right," she whispered.

Yes, all she'd had to do was open the blinds covering her heart a bit. Let in the light.

"I believe," she whispered to the Lord. "I believe," she repeated to Marie.

And then, carefully, she reached out and grasped Marie's hand and gently moved it to rest in one of the rays of light shining on the bed.

And felt the warmth of the sun cover both of their hands.

She closed her eyes and gave thanks.

And basked in its glow.

Questions for Discussion

1. Roman Keim has spent much of his life trying to stand apart from his family—even going on vacation while his father is away. Ironically, going away enabled him to become closer to them all. Have you ever felt the need to "step away"?

2. Amanda struggles to move on after her husband's death. Do you think there's an appropriate timeline for grief? What has helped you during the grieving process? How does one know when it's time to move on?

3. New Order Amish are allowed to have a phone line in their home. Do you think this makes their lives much different from the Old Order Amish?

4. Little by little, Aaron reveals more about how his first marriage ended. What do you think was harder for Lovina to hear—that he never told her about his brother-in-law's letters, or that he was, in fact, driving Laura Beth and Ben in their buggy?

5. Viola's first impression of Belize is different from what she expected. She's deeply embarrassed about her behavior and worries about disappointing Ed. Have you ever gotten off on the wrong foot in a new town or with a new

group of people? How did you make amends?

6. How does Regina grow and change during the novel? Is it surprising that she has an easier time adjusting to life with the Keim family than Amanda does?

7. Amanda is Roman's Ray of Light. Who is yours? Why?

8. What do you think will happen when Lovina and Aaron go back to Pennsylvania to visit?

9. I used the following Scripture verse to guide me while I wrote this book. What does this verse mean to you? *Light shines on the godly, and joy on those whose hearts are right.*
—Psalm 97:11

Center Point Large Print
600 Brooks Road / PO Box 1
Thorndike ME 04986-0001 USA

(207) 568-3717

US & Canada:
1 800 929-9108
www.centerpointlargeprint.com

HARD TIMES

LEADERSHIP IN AMERICA

BARBARA KELLERMAN

STANFORD BUSINESS BOOKS

An Imprint of Stanford University Press • Stanford, California

Stanford University Press
Stanford, California

Special discounts for bulk quantities of Stanford Business Books are available to corporations, professional associations, and other organizations. For details and discount information, contact the special sales department of Stanford University Press. Tel: (650) 736-1782, Fax: (650) 736-1784

Printed in the United States of America on acid-free, archival-quality paper

Library of Congress Cataloging-in-Publication Data

Kellerman, Barbara, author.
  Hard times : leadership in America / Barbara Kellerman.
    pages cm
  Includes bibliographical references and index.
  ISBN 978-0-8047-9235-6 (cloth : alk. paper)
  1. Leadership—United States. 2. Political leadership—United States. I. Title.
  HD57.7.K4478 2014
  303.3'40973—dc23
                                                              2014021439

ISBN 978-0-8047-9301-8 (electronic)

Typeset by Classic Typography in 11/15 Minion Pro

For Ellen Greenwald and Cathy Utz . . .
Forever Family

"To see what is in front of one's nose needs a constant struggle."

George Orwell

CONTENTS

Acknowledgments   ix

Prologue: What's Been Lost?   1

PART I: FOUNDATIONS

1 History   13

2 Ideology   25

PART II: EVOLUTIONS

3 Religion   39

4 Politics   50

5 Economics   62

6 Institutions   74

7 Organizations   84

8 Law   93

9 Business   105

PART III: REVOLUTIONS

10 Technology   119

11 Media   130

12 Money   142

13 Innovation   154

14 Competition   163

PART IV: POPULATIONS

15 Class   177

16 Culture   187

17 Divisions   199

18 Interests   210

PART V: FUTURES

19 Environment   223

20 Risks   233

21 Trends   244

PART VI: INVERSIONS

22 Leaders   257

23 Followers   270

24 Outsiders   283

Epilogue: What's Been Found?   295

The Author   309

Notes   311

Index   351

ACKNOWLEDGMENTS

My thanks to Laura Aguilar, Margo Beth Fleming, Kenneth Greenwald, Sasanka Jinadasa, Klara Kabadian, Mike Leveriza, Thomas Patterson, Todd Pittinsky, and Thomas Wren.

DILBERT

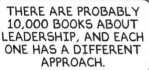

HARD TIMES

PROLOGUE
What's Been Lost?

WHAT'S BEEN LOST in the discussions on leadership—in the infinite number of discussions on leadership—is context. I refer not to context that is proximate, such as a particular group or organization, but to context that is distal, to the larger context within which leadership and yes, also followership, necessarily are situated.

This book will fill in that all-important missing piece. It is not a "how-to" book—a book about how to be a leader. Instead it is a how-to-think-like-a-leader workbook that provides a clear, cogent corrective to the thousands of other instructions already available.[1] *Hard Times* is a checklist of what you need to know about context if you want to lead in the United States of America in the second decade of the twenty-first century. It is not a handy-dandy manual on what to do and how to do it, for the specifics of the situation determine the particulars. What it does do is make meaning of leadership in America in a wholly new and different way. What it does do is provide every American leader with a framework for seeing the setting within which work gets done.

Anyone who knows my work knows that sometimes I am a contrarian. I have written extensively about leadership, but deviated from the norm in at least four ways. First, I focus as much on bad leadership as on good leadership. Second, I think followers every bit as important as leaders. Third, I am skeptical of what I call the "leadership industry"—my catchall term for the "now countless leadership centers, institutes, programs, courses, seminars, workshops, experiences, trainers, books, blogs, articles, websites, webinars, videos, conferences, consultants, and coaches" claiming to teach people, usually for money, much money, how to lead.[2]

Finally, frankly, I take issue with America's relentless leader-centrism, with America's obsessive fixation on leaders at the expense of followers and at the expense of the context within which both necessarily are situated. Instead I argue for a more complete conception of how change is created. I have come to see leadership as a *system* consisting of three moving parts, each of which is equally important and each of which impinges equally on the other two. The first is the *Leader*. The second is the *Follower*. And the third is the *Context*—the focus of this book.

If we accept the proposition that leadership is a system, the leadership industry should be as invested in followers as it is in leaders, and as focused on context as on only some of the leading actors. But it is not. Instead it is fixated, still, laser-like, on leaders. This explains why leadership learning is biased toward self-improvement, skill development, and self-awareness—toward instilling competence and, possibly, character in a single individual. We attempt to develop individual capacities such as communicating and negotiating, and we attempt to develop individual characteristics such as authenticity and integrity. The relentless implication is that what matters most is internal, individual change, not external, collective change. Put another way, our study, practice, and promotion of leadership are inner-directed, not outer- or other-directed.[3] They are leader-centric and solipsistic.

It's not that we ignore context altogether. Quite the contrary: leaders are taught to take context into account. But the context they are taught to take into account is circumscribed. It is context as proximate—context of interest and importance to the leader, not context of interest and importance more generally. Some prominent leadership experts have, for example, properly and pointedly stressed the value of diagnosing the situation, of stepping back to gain perspective. But still, they keep close. Their eyes are trained on the context that immediately pertains—which is "your company's structures, culture and defaults"—rather than on the more expansive context within which the organization (the "company") itself is located.[4]

Followers, when they even enter the picture at all, are drawn similarly narrowly, as opposed to more broadly. Wharton School professor

Michael Useem has written smartly and sensibly about what he calls "the leadership template."[5] The principles of his template include fostering teamwork, building interdependence, and coaching individuals to reach the next level. However his principles are drawn from his particular population—large companies, financial institutions, and his classroom at the Wharton School. They are not drawn from the larger context within which people in the private sector also are situated.

Let me be clear: I have no quarrel with this sort of proximate approach. The question I raise is not whether it is necessary, but whether it is sufficient. The leadership industry has a problem—a screamingly obvious one. It has failed over its roughly forty-year history to in any major, meaningful, measurable way improve the human condition. In fact, the rise of leadership as an object of our collective fascination has coincided precisely with the decline of leadership in our collective estimation. Private sector leaders are widely viewed as greedy to the point of being corrupt. Public sector leaders are seen as hapless to the point of being inept. And leaders previously regarded as virtually sacrosanct—religious leaders, for example, and military leaders—have been diminished and even demeaned.[6] The numbers tell the tale. In 1964, 74 percent of Americans thought that their government could be depended on "to do what is right just about always or most of the time." By the late 1970s this number had dropped to under 50 percent; in another thirty years it would fall to an alarmingly low 19 percent.[7]

What is to be done? Can the leadership industry improve? Can it do a better job of teaching leadership, of educating, training, and developing leaders so that they are prepared to lead wisely and well? And how can leaders themselves—or those who aspire to be leaders—become autodidacts?

The answers, of course, must be preliminary. But in this book I provide a response that should be integral to leadership education and development at every level. I keep it simple. I focus here on a single corrective: *contextual expertise*. Up to now I too have concentrated mainly on leaders and, later, on followers, and on the changing balance of power between them. I too have paid less attention to the third component of the leadership system—context.[8] Here this will change and context will get its due. Here I will remedy what social psychologists call the "fundamental attribution error," which consists on the one hand of an "inflated belief in the importance of personality traits and dispositions," and on the other of a "failure to recognize the importance of situational factors in affecting behavior."[9]

Again, the context I consider is not proximate. It is not specific to any single individual or institution, any group or organization. Rather it is distal, it is general. It is the larger circumstance within which all Americans are situated in the second decade of the twenty-first century. Think of context as a series of concentric circles. The inner ones are your own immediate, proximate, context. The outer ones, the ones that constitute the core of this book, speak to questions such as, What are the larger forces that impinge on us all? And what are the overweening circumstances with which leaders across the board—American leaders—need be familiar if they are to be effective? When leaders come to understand this more expansive environment, they will similarly come to understand those other, less accessible components of context—ideological, political, economic, cultural, technological, and financial, among others—with which, inevitably, they have also to contend.

I use the term *contextual expertise*—as opposed to *contextual intelligence*—to distinguish what I provide in this book from what has come before.[10] My focus is not on how well leaders are able to address whatever it is the situation requires. My focus is on what they need to know first, on what they need to know before they can even begin to act. My interest in this book is not, in other words, in developing a leadership trait. Rather it is in developing a body of knowledge, in pointing to a part of the leadership system that up to now has been entirely ignored.

The impact of context is something that I learned, finally viscerally as well as intellectually, from becoming a regular blogger. It became easy to see that the so-called crisis of American leadership is much less about leaders themselves and much more about the complex context within which they are expected to operate.[11] Let me give an example—John Boehner. Boehner, a Republican, became speaker of the House of

WHAT'S BEEN LOST   5

Representatives in January 2011. Beginning on day one he found it difficult to do what he was elected and expected to do—to lead. He found it difficult if not impossible to collaborate with both the Senate and the president. More to the point, he found it difficult if not impossible to lead even House Republicans, his own putative followers in his own chamber. Was this because Boehner was himself so woefully inept, so utterly clueless that he lacked the capacity to get his House in order? Was this because his putative followers refused under any circumstance to follow? Or was there another reason? Was it due instead, or at least in addition, to the circumstance within which Boehner found himself? Was it due instead, or at least in addition, to Washington's inordinately discordant political culture?

This raises the hypothetical question of whether Boehner would have been more effective if he had had a deeper and richer understanding of the context within which he was embedded—if he had had contextual expertise. I don't honestly know—there is no proving the point. But this I do know. Boehner was not new to the House when he became speaker.[12] To the contrary; he had previously served as congressman from the state of Ohio for twenty years. Yet right around the time he was elected speaker the context changed. The emergence of the Tea Party, seemingly out of nowhere, altered the Republican Party in ways that Boehner was not prepared for or equipped to contend with. In other words, by 2010 Washington had changed and the House had changed right along with it. What seems clear, certainly in retrospect, is that neither Boehner nor for that matter hardly anyone else grasped just how profoundly these changes would diminish his capacity to lead. The old ways of doing business no longer sufficed—and he, speaker of the House, had no real conception of what other ways of leading might look like.[13] Had he better understood how America was changing, better understood the populist anger that made Tea Partiers so formidable a congressional foe, he would have, or at least he could have, adjusted accordingly. He could have, for example, been far less accommodating than he was for so long, and far more initially resistant to the extremism that was consuming both his party and his speakership.

I hasten to add that this lamentable lack of contextual expertise is shared equally, by Democrats as well as Republicans. Not only was Barack Obama comparatively new to leading when he was elected president, he was comparatively new to Washington. Notwithstanding his naiveté, his obvious lack of sophistication about the ways of the nation's capital, there is ample evidence that he did not care to familiarize himself with the larger political and social contexts within which the White House itself was embedded. By and large Obama remained cocooned in the Oval Office, reluctant to leave it either to socialize or to wheel and deal in ways that near certainly would have been politically advantageous. In fact, he was reluctant even to invite the outside in, to bring into the Oval Office, to the White House, members of Congress, say, who could have helped grease the wheels of the political process beginning day one.

The context that constitutes the stuff of this book is no less than, and no more than, the *United States of America in the second decade of the twenty-first century.* To be sure, the American context is in many ways similar to contexts in other countries. Everywhere leaders are finding it difficult to lead without using or threatening to use force because everywhere followers are making their lives difficult—and because everywhere context is both a cause and an effect of this power dynamic. Still, to say that there are overarching similarities, worldwide trends, is not to say that what is happening in one country is the same as what is happening in another. There are differences, from one place to the next, and from one decade to the next, which is why here I confine context to the U.S. at this particular moment in time.

What I provide is a checklist of what you need to know about context if you want to lead. In his recent bestseller, *The Checklist Manifesto*, Atul Gawande argues that the deceptively simple strategy of employing a checklist improves performance. It's a way of managing the unmanageable—of taming information and decoding context. Gawande is a physician whose initial interest was in managing information and complexity in hospitals. However, quickly he realized that checklists have far broader applications, across different industries and institutions. And

WHAT'S BEEN LOST   7

quickly he realized that there were bad checklists and good ones, the former being long and imprecise, the latter efficient and easy to use. Gawande also found that checklists are limited in their uses. They can remind whoever is in charge of how to cope with a complex process, and what particularly to watch out for. But they cannot compel anyone to use them to maximum advantage, or to adapt. Still, on the basis of his research, Gawande became a convert, arguing passionately and persuasively for "the simplicity and power of using a checklist" whatever the specifics of the situation.[14]

Gawande's checklist is action-oriented. Mine is not, not directly. It is a compilation of information, an iteration of items that constitute context. My checklist is more detailed than Gawande's. Still, each of the sections is brief and to the point, and each is efficient and easy to access. This being said, the checklist is neither all-inclusive nor engraved in stone. To the contrary: it is intentionally fungible. It can be tailored by anyone, anywhere to whatever the circumstance. Nevertheless the items themselves—such as history and ideology, media and money, class and culture, risks and trends, leaders and followers—are transferable and transportable. They pertain to the United Kingdom and to the United Arab Emirates, as they do to the United States.

The content that this book comprises is what leaders need to know to develop contextual expertise. I do not, however, claim that leaders need to know everything there is to know about, say, the law. What I do claim is that leaders in twenty-first-century America—political leaders, corporate leaders, nonprofit leaders, educational leaders, religious leaders, all leaders—are situated in a litigious, regulatory context that likely as not will have an impact on how they lead and manage. While it might seem to some that the law is an abstraction, something in the distance that has little or nothing to do with how leadership ordinarily is exercised, it is not. In fact, it is a stark example of what I mean by the importance of distal as opposed to proximate context. And it is a vivid example of the sorts of things that you need to know to lead smarter and better.

Consider this. In the old days, principals of elementary schools were primarily concerned with how to lead and manage their particular teachers and students in their particular schools. Now these same principals are situated in a larger context that mandates, among other things, that their schools follow relatively new rules and adhere to relatively new regulations. The Americans with Disabilities Act (ADA), for example, is a major piece of federal legislation, enacted in 1990, intended to protect the civil rights of individuals with disabilities. As parents and other advocates for children with disabilities have come to understand the ADA, and appreciate what it can do for their children, school principals have been required to respond to requests for services to which disabled students are now legally entitled.

The ADA is obviously well-intentioned. Still, it has enormously complicated the task of leading and managing the nation's public schools. As various websites make clear, school leaders nationwide struggle to comply with the federal law: "In responding to requests for technical assistance, the Office for Civil Rights (OCR) has determined that school officials would benefit from additional guidance concerning the effects of the Americans with Disabilities Act Amendments Act of 2008 (Amendments Act) on public elementary and secondary programs."[15]

Of course, public school leaders are scarcely alone in having to cope with the law in new and different ways. The threat of being sued for malpractice has changed the way hospitals are administered and medicine is practiced across the U.S. And, as the explosive growth in the numbers of legal compliance officers testifies, leaders of all sorts of groups and organizations have been similarly tasked with warding off the threat of litigation. So while the law does not and should not, in and of itself, dictate how leaders lead, it is nearly impossible to lead wisely and well in twenty-first-century America without being aware of the law as a component of context. And I might say the same about every other component of context, each of which similarly impinges.

As suggested, the checklist itself is simple, and so is the brief discussion of each of the items. Though I do not explicitly connect all of the dots—this book is intended to be short and to the point; it's a checklist, after all—the ways in which the components of context complicate the exercise of leadership in twenty-first-century America nevertheless will be immediately apparent.

To delineate the various relationships I divide the book into six parts. The first, "Foundations," is a discussion of the basics, of history and ideology and of their impact on how leadership in America is exercised, to this day. The second, "Evolutions," paints a picture of how times change, which implies obviously that leadership and followership change as well. It looks at components of context including religion, politics, economics, institutions, organizations, the law, and business, and suggests how they constrain the capacity to lead. The third part of the book, "Revolutions" also paints a picture of how times change. But in some areas— technology, media, money, innovation, and competition—change has been and continues to be so swift that leaders who fail to keep pace risk being undone by the very context within which they are doing their leadership work. Part Four—"Populations"—is about us, the American people. The question is how who we are shapes the American leadership experience. How, more specifically, do class and culture, divisions and interests, have an impact on the capacity of leaders to lead? Part Five, "Futures," peers into the distance. I anticipate how the environment, risks, and trends will in time affect agents of change. Finally, in Part Six, "Inversions," I return to the role reversal to which I regularly allude: how leaders in democracies increasingly are demeaned and diminished and followers increasingly are emboldened and empowered. I conclude the checklist on context with*in* America by pivoting to context with*out*. I place the U.S. itself in the larger international system within which U.S. leaders necessarily are located.

Finally, a few words about the title of the book: *Hard Times*. It signals my bias, my strong bias. Leadership in America has always been difficult to exercise. But, for reasons that will become clear, *leadership in America is more difficult to exercise now than it has ever been before.* Context changes over time—and so do leaders and followers. All three are different now from what they were five hundred years ago, fifty years ago, even five years ago. So while leadership in the U.S. has been problematical since the beginning of the republic—there is an inherent tension between leadership and democracy—changing times, hard times, continue to complicate the task. In fact, the contemporaneous context makes leading and managing so challenging that I would argue they should be looked at in an entirely new way.

The contextual checklist that follows is, then, a series of signposts. Each is an indicator of why leadership in twenty-first-century America is so fraught with frustration. Each is an indicator of why leadership in twenty-first-century America will continue so complicated a charge. And each is an indicator of why leadership in twenty-first-century America is more likely to be mastered if it is better understood. This book is not by any stretch a theoretical exercise. It is instead as indicated—a how-to-think-like-a-leader workbook intended to instill the importance of time and place.

PART I   FOUNDATIONS

1 HISTORY

EVERY NATION has its founding myths, myths about its genesis that not only endure but that set the stage for whatever is subsequent. In the case of leadership in America, it matters that our founders were revolutionists, leaders who first were followers, subjects of the British Crown, until they successfully seized power and ultimately authority by force. It matters to leadership in America that many of these founders, including General George Washington, were ready and willing to put their lives at risk for the principles they held dear. And it matters to leadership in America that they refused to suffer a system that they had come to detest, to deem not only tyrannical but illegitimate. War wrenched the American colonies from the British Empire and secured the United States of America. To this day this war, the American Revolution, has an impact on how leadership in America is exercised.

History matters. It matters that American history is different from, say, Canadian or Mexican history, or for that matter from British history. The United States is singular in that it was the first to boast a band of revolutionists that declared the old authoritarian order dead, and a new democratic order begun. It was the first among nations to put into practice or, better, to try to, the humanistic ideas that distinguished the ideals of the Western Enlightenment.

The American Revolution was not the first of the American rebellions. By the time independence was declared in 1776, the colonies had a history of resistance, a history in which those who ostensibly were powerless took on those who obviously were powerful. In 1676 in Virginia, for example, there was Bacon's Rebellion, an uprising of white frontiersmen joined by slaves and servants that so threatened the British governor he was forced to flee the capital, Jamestown. England's response was to send a thousand British soldiers to pacify the forty thousand American colonists and, after order was restored, to hang the leader of the insurrectionists, Nathanial Bacon. But Bacon's Rebellion was just one among many revolts against the English, all up and down the eastern seaboard, in colonies from Massachusetts to Virginia. In New York there were strikes of coopers, butchers, bakers, and porters. In New Jersey there were demonstrations by farmers against landowners. And years before the Boston Tea Party, in Massachusetts there were protests and petitions and pamphlets, all signs and symbols of growing hostility to the English Crown.[1] In truth, while the colonists lived in a monarchy and were monarchical subjects, they never did much respect royalty. From the beginning they were "the most republican of people in the English-speaking world. Every visitor to the New World sensed it."[2]

In the decade or so before 1776, resistance against the British came to a head, especially, again, in Massachusetts. In 1767, riots in Boston broke out, against the Stamp Act. Three years later came a fight since known as the Boston Massacre. (Ten thousand Bostonians, over two-thirds the total population, took part in the funerals.) And in 1773 there was the Boston Tea Party—a protest against the English government and the English-owned East India Company—that led to the imposition by the British of martial law.

As historian Edmund Morgan has vividly detailed, there was from the start a striking inconsistency, a stunning hypocrisy. Here is a case in point: two Virginians, both leaders, George Washington and Thomas Jefferson. On the one hand both led the fight for freedom. On the other hand both owned slaves. It was not that every single white man was a slave owner. Rather, it was that the men who came together to found the

United States of America, which was dedicated to the proposition that all men are created equal, either did own slaves or were "willing to join hands with those who did."[3] This striking contradiction characterized American history not merely briefly, but for nearly two hundred years, from before the revolution straight through to emancipation. Still, it never precluded a conglomeration of republican ideas and ideals from dominating politics. In colonial America a slave labor force was isolated from the rest of society, while the rest of society—a body of large planters and a larger body of small planters—was increasingly committed to freedom and equality. In fact, (white) Virginians remained throughout the colonial period at the forefront of opposition to England, and took leading roles in creating the American republic.[4]

The American Revolution was, then, the culmination of decades of resistance and rebellion, which in time hardened to righteous rage at royalty thousands of miles and an ocean away. As Thomas Paine put it in his iconic, incendiary booklet *Common Sense*, intended to persuade the public to support independence from Great Britain, "This new World hath been the asylum for the persecuted lovers of civil and religious liberty from every part of Europe. Hither have they fled, not from the tender embraces of the mother [country], but from the cruelty of the monster; and it is so far true of England, that the same tyranny which drove the first emigrants from home pursues their descendents still."[5]

Above all, the freshly minted governors of the United States of America determined to protect against tyranny. The Constitution was to be crafted with this in mind, structured to preclude the possibility of too much power held by a single individual or institution. Put on notice by yet another revolt—Shays' Rebellion, in 1786, again in Massachusetts—the framers viewed their task as a balancing act. They wanted a system of representation that would respond to the legitimate needs of the people, but they also wanted to curb the peoples' passions and greed. Similarly, they thought to gain safety and security by creating a stronger and broader union, but they did not intend for this union to be so broad or so strong as to tip toward tyranny. It was James Madison who proposed the solution that ultimately prevailed—the Constitution of the United

States. It was he who perhaps best understood that in order to preclude populism and factionalism from destroying the Revolution's hard-won gains, it was necessary to secure the new nation, in its entirety. It "alone could be thought to stand superior to the people of any single state."[6]

It is difficult to exaggerate the importance of the Constitutional Convention. For if the intention of the revolution was utopian, no less than the destruction of the old monarchical society, the reality the morning after was different. It is, as we have seen even in our own time, one thing to destroy the old, and quite another to build the new. "To form a new Government requires infinite care and unbounded attention," George Washington warned in 1776, "for if the foundation is badly laid, the superstructure must be bad." A "matter of such moment," he continued, "cannot be the Work of a day."[7]

And it was not. It took over a decade, until 1787, for the founders to agree to and sign off on the United States Constitution. Above all their intent was to fragment political power while, simultaneously, providing sufficient political power to make possible good governance. The Constitution included a federal system, which gave some powers to the federal government and others to the states; staggered elections for the president, the House and the Senate, so that no majority could seize power in a single swoop; and a separation of powers among the executive, legislative, and judicial branches.[8] Whatever the deficiencies of this fragmented political system, it did over time accomplish what the framers wanted and intended. It precluded tyranny, even by the executive, while providing a system of governance that, whatever the mood of the moment, over more than 225 years of American history has served the United States of America relatively well. (The Constitution is not beyond reproach, however, especially not now, when the federal government is so obviously dysfunctional.[9])

But so far as leadership is concerned, leadership of any kind, America's fractured political system has complicated the task. Democracy is, under the best of circumstances, a messy business. Leading democratically is far harder and less efficient than leading autocratically. (As Winston Churchill famously put it, "Democracy is the worst form of government, except for all those others that have been tried.") And when the history of a country leaves a legacy that renders its citizens virtually allergic to authority, leadership is the more difficult.

America is unlike other modern democracies—say, those in Western Europe—not only because of its revolutionary genesis, but also because Americans have never known another form of government. There never was a king on American soil. Nor did the papacy ever rule here, in contrast to England, for example, where the Anglican Church was in the grip of the crown. Nor was there ever a despot or autocrat to rival those in other lands. Nor was the colonial aristocracy ever as well established, as wealthy, or as dominant as its British counterpart.

Democratic political leadership is the only sort of political leadership ever enshrined in America, which is precisely why effective leadership has always been relatively difficult to exercise, and why effective followership has always been relatively easy. Put differently, historically it has been comparatively hard to create change from the top down, and comparatively easy to create change from the bottom up.[10] Again, this is in consequence of history. "In the end the disintegration of the traditional eighteenth-century monarchical society of paternal and dependent relationships prepared the way for the emergence of the liberal, democratic, capitalist world of the early nineteenth century."[11]

Until the mid-eighteenth century, most Americans, if they were white, assumed that life in the "new world" would continue to mirror the life they left behind in the old world, in Europe. It would be hierarchically ordered, with some rich and others poor, some honored and others obscure, some powerful and others weak. The assumption was that authority would continue to exist without challenge. But the Revolution changed all that, permanently. There was no clinging to the past once *defiance* of power "poured from the colonial presses and was hurled from half the pulpits of the land." There was no clinging to the past once "the right, the need, the absolute obligation to *disobey* legally constituted authority had become the universal cry" (italics mine). And there was no clinging to the past once, instead of obedience, it was *resistance* that was a "doctrine according to godliness."[12]

After the United States of America became hard fact as opposed to imagined figment, after the Constitution was finally and fully ratified (1790), the anti-authority fever that had fueled the Revolutionary War hardened into an anti-authority attitude that has marked America's political culture ever since. In an earlier book, I wrote that so far as leadership in America is concerned, it has three key characteristics: a general antagonism toward governmental authority; a particular ambivalence toward those in positions of power; and an uncertainty about what constitutes effective leadership and management in a democratic society.[13] And no wonder, for in the half century that followed the Revolution, what little did remain of the traditional social hierarchy virtually collapsed. In its place was a quest for independence that historically was unprecedented: first was independence from Great Britain, then independence of the states from each other, then independence of the people from the government, and "lastly, the members of society be equally independent of each other."[14]

Some fifty years after the conclusion of the Revolution, the Frenchman Alexis de Tocqueville, in his classic treatise, *Democracy in America*, marveled at how independent and idiosyncratic were ordinary Americans. "Since they do not recognize any signs of incontestable greatness or superiority in any of their fellows, are continually brought back to their own judgment as the most apparent and accessible test of truth. . . . There is a general distaste for accepting any man's word as proof of anything."[15] The implications of this for leadership in America—*for leadership in general, not just for political leadership*—are easy enough to see. I will follow your lead if it is in my interest to do so, for whatever reason, such as the promise of reward or the fear of punishment. But if I am to follow your lead of my own free will, you will have to persuade me that it is what *I* want to do, not merely what *you* want me to do. If you cannot, or will not, I will chart my own course as I see fit.

There are alternative views of American history, "spirited controversies about the underlying dynamics."[16] Some historians are persuaded that the founders were not much better than their predecessors, the English, the earlier entitled class that sought to control profits and power.[17]

They see the nation's progress as more fundamentally marked by economic fights than shared values, and they are persuaded that early patterns of power persist to this day. (These patterns presumably explain why to this day the haves remain strongly advantaged over the have-nots.[18]) In addition, as earlier suggested, it has become almost impossible in the past several decades to comment on the American experiment without referencing the large swaths of people originally excluded from the promise of the process—particularly women and people of color.

Still, as I will further explore in the next section, ideas have an impact. They affect how and what we think, and what we do and why. In this case they explain why, with the benefit of hindsight, it seems obvious that the odious legal inconsistencies that had stained the republic since its inception would eventually, inevitably, be eradicated. Eighteenth-century America was, then, about promises made on paper: "We hold these truths to be self-evident: that all men are created equal, that they are endowed by their creator with certain unalienable rights, that among these are Life, Liberty, and the pursuit of Happiness." And nineteenth-century America was about promises realized—about extending these "inalienable rights" to all men and, finally, early in the twentieth century, to women.

Change took time, change spilled blood. That most wretched of all American wars, the Civil War, is still widely regarded as a necessary evil, necessary to preserve the Union and emancipate the slaves, necessary to put into democratic practice democratic theory.[19] But notwithstanding our lionizing, our veritable worship of President Abraham Lincoln, he did not initially intend to upend the system by freeing the slaves. At the start of the war his goals were to restore the Union and bar slavery from spreading further. In fact, in order to keep Kentucky in the Union (to use as a military base), Lincoln deliberately muffled any talk of abolition, changing course only when he realized the South was so strong that the Civil War would likely not end until slavery did. Not by accident was the ex-slave turned abolitionist orator, Frederick Douglass, more prescient than his president. It was Douglass who foresaw even in 1861 that "the Negro is the key of the situation—the pivot upon which the whole rebellion turns."[20] He could see in a way that Lincoln could not that the inexorable logic of events would eventually oblige the American president to make eradication of slavery the spear point of the war.[21]

The trajectory of American history suggests that change of great magnitude—such as the abolition of slavery—nearly never happens of its own. Nor is it typically initiated by leaders, people in positions of authority, who generally are invested in the status quo.[22] Rather, change of great magnitude requires pressure from below, populist pressure exerted by those in the middle or even at the bottom. The reason is, as Martin Luther King pointedly put it in "Letter from Birmingham Jail," those *with* power nearly never surrender to those *without*—unless they are compelled to do so. "We know through painful experience," King wrote, "that freedom is never voluntarily given by the oppressor; it must be demanded by the oppressed."[23]

To understand this particular truism is to understand why even the most liberal of American leaders do not generally get elected by promising or, as some would have it, by threatening to overturn the system, to initiate radical change. To be sure, there are moments of crisis—Franklin Delano Roosevelt elected to the White House at the height of the Great Depression—moments when the American people want major change and the president provides major change. It was under Roosevelt that the American welfare state—federal programs to help the old, the poor, the unemployed, and, more recently, the sick—was initially created. But such a shift initiated and implemented from on high is the historical exception, not the historical rule.

Clearly, then, notwithstanding America's original revolutionary rhetoric, the pursuit of rights in America has been a messy business. Neither emancipation, nor universal suffrage, nor any other single step forward has meant that rights, the rights of all Americans, were finally fully and formally secured. In his second inaugural address, President Barack Obama acknowledged as much, describing Americans as being on a "journey" that even now is incomplete. "Our journey is not complete until [women] can earn a living equal to their efforts. Our journey is not complete until our gay brothers and sisters are treated like anyone else under the law. . . . Our journey is not complete until no citizen is forced to wait for hours to exercise the right to vote. . . . "[24]

Even in the second decade of the twenty-first century, then, Americans remain engaged in an ongoing and generally ragtag process, in which leaders are pressed by followers, to different degrees at different times, to surrender something, usually power or money. It's not always apparent what sets the process in motion, what gets it to going faster, or what brings it, eventually, to a temporary halt. What is evident is that the process continues—and that its most recent apogee was reached in the late 1960s and early 1970s, a time of great change when those without came knocking on the door, hard, of those with.

In part, certainly, the 1960s and 1970s were so febrile and fertile a period in American history because of the war in Vietnam. The energies that went into the antiwar movement seemed then and still seem now to have spilled easily and effortlessly into other vaguely related causes, the one fueling the other in a fireball of anti-authority activity.

The various rights revolutions—civil rights, women's rights, gay and lesbian rights, children's rights, people with disabilities rights, animal rights—in the middle years of the twentieth century were in the event little short of revolutionary. America *after* was strikingly different from America *before*.

Yet even so careful a student of these rights revolutions as Steven Pinker admits to being unable to explain exactly why they started when they did, and what made them so successful in so relatively short a period of time. Pinker finally concludes it is impossible to pinpoint "an exogenous factor that would explain" why these particular rights revolutions bunched up as they did, in the 1960s and 1970s.[25]

What we do know though is this: that even these most recent of the recurring rights revolutions had the same ideological origins as their predecessors, in the liberal ideas and democratic ideals of the Enlightenment. Ideas and ideals like these inevitably debunk ignorance and superstition, and they necessarily, if sometimes only slowly, sow change.

I hasten to add that by no means is the United States of America invariably on the cutting edge of liberalism, or even of sociopolitical change. For example, in the nineteenth century the British beat the Americans to the banishment of slavery—the Slavery Abolition Act was passed in 1833, though it was easier for England to end a system not so deeply entrenched. And in the twenty-first century, some countries are by some measures well ahead of the United States: they are better, for example, at narrowing the gap between rich and poor and at narrowing the gap between women and men. Similarly, while same-sex marriage is still prohibited in many American states, it is entirely legal elsewhere, for instance, in Britain and Belgium, and in Sweden and Spain.[26]

Still my overarching point is this. So far as leadership and follow-ership are concerned, the United States of America is singular. First, because of its revolutionary inception it has always been characterized by a political culture that is anti-authority, that ensures and even en-courages conflict between, and also among, leaders and led. Second, because of its revolutionary inception it has always been characterized by a political structure that makes it difficult for anyone at any level politically to lead—up to and including the chief executive. Third, be-cause of its revolutionary inception it has always been characterized by a national character that is independent and idiosyncratic, by men and women who as soon follow their own path as anyone else's. Fourth, because of its revolutionary inception it has always been characterized by an ideology that, however idealized, advantages the have-nots at the expense of the haves. And, finally, because of its revolutionary incep-tion it has always been characterized by a set of documents—by laws, if you will—that codify, sanctify, the fulfillments of followers as well as of leaders.

Anti-authoritarian attitudes and practices are, then, part of the American political system and national character in a way that they are not, or at least have not always been, of other political systems and na-tional characters.[27] Obviously, this advantage in theory was not then, in the late eighteenth century, and is not now, in the early twenty-first, necessarily always an advantage in practice. Even this cursory chronicle demonstrates how hard it has been for those without power, authority, and influence to get what rightfully, literally, is theirs. Still, when the weak are furious enough and fierce enough to take on the strong, history suggests that the former will get what they want, or at least some of what they want, if not today, then tomorrow.

Precisely because political leadership in America has always been difficult to exercise, other types of leadership have been difficult to exercise as well—there is a relationship, a corollary or parallel, between them. So, for example, private sector leaders obviously do not have the same kinds of constraints as do public sector leaders, but they suffer, so to speak, other kinds of constraints. Business leaders are not, in other words, exempt from the importance of culture and character. And they are not exempt from the ideological, intellectual foundations on which this country was built. As a result—because leadership in America has never been other than democratic, at least in theory, and because, as Tocqueville put it, there is a general "distaste for accepting any man's word as proof of anything"—leadership in America, including corporate leadership, has always depended at least somewhat on the capacity to personally persuade, as opposed to only on the capacity to control.

In general, historically, leaders in other countries—say in Germany, Russia, China, and Japan—have been able more easily than leaders in the United States to command and control, to tell their followers what to do and when and how. Because they have had more power and greater authority they have not had to rely as much, if at all, on influence. But in the United States influence—my ability to get you to do what I want you to do, *of your own volition*—has always been relatively important, precisely because power and authority have always been relatively *un*important.[28] There is, in other words, along these general lines a difference between Americans and people from other places.[29] It's one of the reasons why the leadership industry is, largely, certainly originally, an American industry. And it's one of the reasons why the leadership literature—again, largely American—emphasizes soft skills, including communication, ingratiation, and emotional intelligence, even over hard ones relating to the particulars of the position.

In his second annual message to Congress, Abraham Lincoln said, "Fellow-citizens, we cannot escape history."[30] To this general rule, patterns of dominance and deference are no exceptions. The anti-authority fever that fueled the Revolutionary War, and that hardened over time into an anti-authority attitude, left a legacy that endures to this day. Americans remain by national nature and political culture relatively recalcitrant—one of the reasons why exercising leadership in twenty-first-century America is relatively hard.

2 IDEOLOGY

THERE IS A DISTINCTION between an ideology imagined and an ideology realized. Government "requires make-believe"—which explains why the Declaration of Independence claimed that "all men are created equal" while, simultaneously, slavery in America flourished.[1] Still, what Americans believe to be right and good and true constitutes their collective conscience, and it constrains the governing few as it does the governed many. The American ideology represents what we aspire to be—even if it is not, at least not necessarily, what we really are.

This book is a contextual checklist—primarily though not exclusively for leaders. So it matters, matters a great deal, that the American ideology is about nothing so much as leadership and followership. It is about how leaders—particularly political leaders, but leaders more generally as well—should rightfully exercise power and authority. As important, it is about what followers, the American people, should rightfully claim as intrinsically and irrevocably theirs, for example, freedom. More precisely, the American ideology is about *constraints* on leaders and *liberties* for followers. Again, this does not mean that American theory is tantamount to American practice. What it does mean is that the American ideology on leadership and followership informed the American experiment at its inception—and informs it still.

As historian Bernard Bailyn detailed in his influential book *The Ideological Origins of the American Revolution*, the ideals of the European Enlightenment heavily influenced and deeply informed the ideas of the Revolutionists. Europe's leading secular thinkers, reformers and social critics, were quoted nearly everywhere in the colonies by nearly everyone who was anyone. In "pamphlet after pamphlet" the Americans cited European *philosophes* such as Locke, Voltaire, and Montesquieu, repeatedly grappling with the question of how power in America should be exercised.[2] (In the end, of course, radical changes in social relations were not confined to the United States. They spread throughout the Western world.[3])

Above all the founders were realists. They focused on leadership and followership precisely because they had no illusions about the human condition. They believed that man was above all self-interested. That he was as likely to be rapacious, ambitious, and contentious as generous or beneficent. They fixated on people's proclivity to pursue power; on lessons of history which taught that some men dominated other men; and on power as essentially aggressive, as serially seeking to expand beyond its legitimate boundaries. Bailyn lists a litany of metaphors, similes, and analogies all used by the founders, the Revolutionists, to register their fear of power. Power, it was always said, trespasses, encroaches, and creeps by degrees. "The hand of power" clutches and seizes, and whatever it can grasp it will seek to keep. It is "restless, aspiring, and insatiable."[4]

Given their deep belief that man was easily, even essentially, corruptible—James Madison wrote that "[i]f men were angels, no government would be necessary"—the founders were bound and determined to constrain man's capacity to control. From the beginning of the republic, leaders were leashed so as to preclude or at least reduce an excess of authority; any amount of power redolent of the royal regimes was left willfully behind. The American ideology explains why the American government was intentionally fragmented, and why the Constitution was written to compel competing interests to check and control one another.[5] Similarly, it is why even the supreme leader, the chief executive, the president of the United States, was tethered at every turn by legal and political forces that were difficult and often impossible for him to override or overturn.

The American president is the single most powerful leader in the American political system. He is chief of state, and chief executive, and commander in chief. As well, he plays a host of lesser roles, described variously as chief diplomat, chief legislator, and chief of his political party—in addition to his part, especially in the twentieth and twenty-first centuries, as world leader. Still, I would argue that what is most striking about the American presidency is not how capacious the powers associated with the office, but rather how limited.

Presidential power is contained by constitutional (legal, structural) constraints, including institutional checks and balances and the limit on presidential tenure. Presidential power is further contained by political constraints. We know from everyday evidence how hard it is for presidents to convert their particular policy preferences into public policy more generally. And we know from everyday evidence how hard it is for presidents to persuade other people to support their positions, whether members of the political elite (Congress, interest groups) or of the body politic (public opinion). We know, in short, how hard it is for presidents to lead. We know how, although both in theory and practice presidents have more power, authority, and influence than does any other American political leader, it is not necessarily sufficient to create change, certainly not in the politically fractious second decade of the twenty-first century.[6]

The American ideology led logically to constraints on leaders, and it led, equally logically, to liberties for followers. Three of England's greatest political philosophers provide us with touchstones for thinking not only about leadership but, as important, about its inevitable counterpart, followership. Of themselves they trace the trajectory from a single individual right under an authoritarian leader to the full panoply of rights, under a democratic or even libertarian leader.

Thomas Hobbes (1588–1679) was early to consider not only the rights of the high and mighty but also the rights—or more precisely, the sole right—of ordinary people, the right to life. It was Hobbes who in his classic *Leviathan* proposed, in effect, a trade-off. We, we followers, we ordinary people, submit to the state (the leviathan of the title) in the form of an absolute (authoritarian) ruler. But we have the right to expect, to demand, something in return. No longer was this a one-way street in which leaders had a claim to everything and followers to nothing. For, in exchange for our submission, we the people had the right to protection—to a guarantee of safety and security in a world otherwise unsafe and insecure. (It was of course Hobbes who famously declared life, "solitary, poor, nasty, brutish, and short.")

John Locke (1632–7204) was the most direct and dominant intellectual influence on the American colonists. He was so powerful an influence that he was cited as a sage by both sides—by royalists and revolutionists. His seminal *Second Treatise of Government* had the greatest impact and, yes, it was all about leaders and followers, with an increasingly sympathetic eye toward the latter at the expense of the former. First, Locke argued that the social contract—the contract between leaders and led—should preserve as much individual freedom as possible under a government that is responsive and responsible. Second, Locke favored decision making by majority rule, a sea change from previous systems of governance, in which decisions were made either by a single leader or by an all-powerful political elite (which was often but not always royal or ecclesiastical). Third, though he was not alone in developing the doctrine of separation of powers (Montesquieu did the same), the fact that Locke made a case for "balancing the power of government by placing several parts of it in different hands," made him the right man for the right time, especially for what would become, one hundred years later, the United States of America. Finally, Locke claimed the ultimate constraint—the right of those without power or authority to unseat those with, if necessary by force.[7]

John Stuart Mill's extended essay *On Liberty* was published in 1859, some seventy years subsequent to the ratification of the American Constitution. It does not, at least not directly, speak either to leadership or to followership. It is instead an ode to liberty and individuality—which is why, implicitly at least, it near obviates the need for anyone to exercise any power or authority over anyone else. "Neither one person, nor any number of persons, is warranted in saying to another human creature of ripe years, that he shall not do with his life for his own benefit what he chooses to do with it."[8]

Philosophers such as Hobbes, Locke, and Mill laid the foundation. But it was up to the Revolutionists, the founders, to build on it, to erect an ideological edifice that would be persuasive to begin and then stand the test of time. This ideology—the ideas and ideals that have been identified with the American people over the course of the past two hundred plus years—has been called the American Creed.[9]

Given the ideological origins of the American Revolution, and given that the United States of America was the product of this revolution, it comes as no surprise that the content of the Creed is concerned primarily not with leaders but with followers. But what more precisely does this content consist of? What are the core components of the American Creed? Political scientist Samuel Huntington has argued that there are five, that they appear in nearly all studies of the subject, and that they were already in evidence in the Declaration of Independence. They are (1) liberty, (2) equality, (3) individualism, (4) democracy, and (5) the rule of law under a constitution.[10]

To deconstruct the essence of each of the five is to buttress my argument—the American ideology is *im*plicitly about constraints on leaders, and it is *ex*plicitly about liberties for followers. They are of course related: constraints on leaders are a necessary consequence, even a byproduct, of liberties for followers.

Liberty is primarily about freedom from governmental control. It is about the rights of the led taking precedence over the preferences of the leader. *Equality* is a leveler. It denies leaders any rights other than those shared by their followers. It further implies that leaders, no matter how vaulted their station or position, are not, either by their nature or by any right, superior to their followers. The former differ from the latter only in rank. *Individualism* reached its apotheosis in Mill, who, as we just saw, argued that I have the right to be what I want, and to do what I want how I want when I want, without interference, so long as I do not intrude on the rights of anyone else. *Democracy* is governance by representation. It is, as Lincoln famously put it, "government of the people, by the people, for the people." It presumes that the body politic will control the government—not the other way around. It further presumes that the task of the governors is to secure for the governed the right to life, liberty, and the pursuit of happiness. Finally, there is the *rule of law*, the Constitution. Its overarching purpose is to restrain the government or, more precisely, to restrain the governors from unwarranted and illegal intrusions on the governed.[11]

These five components of the American Creed do not, of themselves, constitute a consistent or coherent whole. For example, liberty and equality can clash, and individualism can counter constitutionalism. But the ideas and ideals of the American Creed, the American ideology, do have a single common thrust: they unite in imposing limits on power and on the institutions of government.[12] In fact, Huntington went so far as to claim the distinctive aspect of the American Creed is its antigovernment character. "Opposition to power, and suspicion of government as the most dangerous embodiment of power, are the central themes of American political thought."[13]

It is impossible to overestimate the impact of the American ideology on the American national character. It is equally impossible to overestimate the impact of this ideology not only on *political* leadership and followership, but on leadership and followership more generally. To take the most obvious example, the literature on leading and following in the private sector echoes, reflects, to some degree the literature on leading and following in the public one.

The conventional wisdom is that in decades past the literature on leadership in business was all about commanding and controlling. The idea was that CEOs, especially of large corporations, were, ideally, take-charge guys, who ran their companies with something considerably closer to an iron hand than a velvet glove. Employees, in turn, were thought mere cogs in whatever the organizational machine, their needs, wants, and wishes attended to but only minimally, as something of an afterthought. In other words, the conventional wisdom is that the literature on leading in business is actually the antithesis of leading in government. The latter is, purportedly, of, by, and for the people, while the former is not. The former is, purportedly, all about shareholders, whose interests are represented and protected by leaders such as high-ranking executives and members of corporate boards.

But, in fact, the literature on leading and managing in corporate America, even the early literature, is replete with references to followers, that is, to the well-being not only of employers but of employees. This is not to say that theory on leading in business was practice on leading in business—any more than theory on leading in government was practice on leading in government. As we have seen, the gap between the two can be and often is cavernous. But it is to say that there is an American ideology of leadership and followership in business, just as there is an American ideology of leadership and followership in government. And it is further to say that this ideology—the American ideology writ broad—has had an impact on how they are exercised not only in the public sector but in the private sector as well.

As far back as 1933, when the literature on leadership in corporate America was still in its infancy, Mary Parker Follett, a pioneer in the study of leadership, made it a point also to address followership. In an essay titled "The Essentials of Leadership," she wrote, "And now let me speak to you for a moment of something which seems to me of the utmost importance, but which has been far too little considered, and that is the part of the followers in the leadership situation." Followers, she continued, were far more significant than people generally understood. "Let us not think that we are either leaders or—nothing of much importance. As one of those led we have a part in leadership. In no aspect of our subject do we see a greater discrepancy between theory and practice than here."[14]

In the main, however, as expected—this literature was, after all, based on research conducted by faculty in schools of business—the focus was on the employee in service of the employer, on followers only in so far as they mattered to leaders (and managers). This is not to say that this literature, this research and writing, was inhumane. Rather, it is to point out that most of the time, the implicit or explicit question was how leaders might extract from their followers maximum productivity. For example, in an important book published in 1960, *The Human Side of Enterprise*, MIT Sloan Professor Douglas McGregor distinguished between "Theory X" and "Theory Y."[15] The former, management by being authoritarian, presumed that ordinary people (employees, followers) inherently disliked work and would avoid it if they could. It therefore further presumed that good work would get done only if superiors closely and carefully monitored their subordinates. Theory Y in contrast, management by being (relatively) libertarian, presumed that ordinary people (employees, followers) actually wanted to work and wanted to work well. Ergo, they could generally be relied on to be self-motivated and self-directed. Theory Y, in other words, presumed that subordinates would be happier and perform better if their superiors led with a light rather than a heavy hand. The primary purpose of McGregor's work was, then, to explore which management style best served the manager and, in turn, the employer, the organization. But the net effect of his work was that the well-being of the leader (the manager) was inextricably tied to the well-being of the follower.

Similarly, though his eye was trained on the leader, Peter Drucker, the so-called father of modern management, was equally, if implicitly rather than explicitly, focused on the follower. In fact, according to Drucker, it was the follower who held the key to the leader's success. "The leaders who work most effectively, it seems to me, never say 'I.' . . . They think 'we,' they think 'team.' They understand their job to be to make the team function."[16] Drucker believed that unless there was trust, leaders would lack followers or, at least, they would lack followers who followed freely. This was critical to Drucker—his idea of a good superior was someone who elicited from his or her subordinates compliance that was other than compulsory. It was voluntary.

In the past several decades the focus on followers has, for various reasons, intensified. Efforts have been made, are being made, again, at least in theory, to close the gap between those at the top and those in the middle and at the bottom. Come to think of it, my imagery is wrong, for hierarchies are not now what they were—they are flatter. *Flattened hierarchies*—a term that at least seems to lessen the distance between leaders and led—has become a mantra, along with other, related words such as *empowerment, engagement, collaboration, cooperation, participation, networks,* and *teams.* So not only has the political culture imprinted the corporate culture—think, for example, of inclusiveness, diversity, and equal pay for equal work—but the corporate culture has of its own evolved toward greater equity. Among other reasons, the changing technologies, the plethora of information and ease of communication, explain why the traditional organizational pyramid has been turned on its head, again, at least in theory, if not necessarily always or even mostly in practice.

I do not want to inflate the point. I myself argue that the leadership industry—which is supported largely by the private sector, not the public one—is testimony to our fixation on the leader at the expense of the other, of the led. Still, the theory of leadership in business is not entirely unlike the theory of leadership in government. Both the former and the latter assume a kind of collective, in which the well-being of everyone, from those with obvious sources of power, authority, and influence to those without, is at issue.

Corporate concern over followers—over those who are other than the leader, other than the CEO—is in evidence in other ways as well. Just as twenty-first-century political leaders are being urged to take into account public opinion—think polls, surveys, and focus groups—so twenty-first-century business leaders are being urged to take into account "stakeholders." Stakeholders run the gamut: they are board members and stockholders and clients and customers and the public at large and, yes, employees, subordinates, in addition to employers, superiors. Leaders are regularly reminded that they should attend to individuals and groups who are stakeholders, to watch them and to watch out *for* them. Similarly, they are regularly reminded that the exercise of leadership is not exercise taken alone. It's a team effort that necessarily implies, or it should, the engagement and participation of others.

Some of the recent leadership literature goes even a step further. It recommends that leaders in American business emulate leaders in American government—they should be democrats exercising democratic leadership. In *Primal Leadership* (written mainly for a corporate audience), author and psychologist Daniel Goleman writes, "The democratic style builds on a triad of emotional intelligence abilities: teamwork and collaboration, conflict management, and influence. The best communicators are superb listeners—and listening is the key strength of the democratic leader. Such leaders create the sense that they truly want to hear employee's thoughts and concerns and that they are available to listen. They're also true collaborators, working as team members rather than top-down leaders."[17] Similarly, the Ken Blanchard Companies, seeking to identify the "best boss," claim that the most important common characteristic is the "relationship aspect." People say that their best boss "cared about them, gave them opportunities, created a great working environment, made work fun, and was flexible and supportive."[18]

Arguably then, ideally, twenty-first-century corporate leaders are supposed to be no more dominant or directive than twenty-first-century political leaders. Rather than the traditionally or conventionally imagined titan of business and industry, an employer who barks out orders at cowed employees, Goleman's democratic leader and Blanchard's best boss is more a friendly and interested parent, or a kind and considerate coach, than he or she is anything else.

This returns us to the ideological origins of the American Revolution—and four final, related, points. The first is that so far as leadership and followership are concerned, democracy—the idea that people should govern themselves—is of overarching importance. It supersedes or, perhaps better, integrates or synthesizes all the other components of the American Creed. Second, the idea of democracy dominates our collective thinking to this day. Not only has it lost none of its original intellectual heft, it has become over time more persuasive and pervasive. This holds true abroad—many more countries are democracies now than even twenty-five years ago—and it holds true at home. As a result of the most recent rights revolutions (in the 1960s and 1970s), virtually every American group, even those previously marginalized, has by now staked a claim to participate fully in American life. Third, the American ideology permeates leadership and followership across the board. No sector or segment of American society is exempt from the ideas and ideals that we are taught when we are young. Finally, though good leaders are essential for a well-functioning democracy, they of themselves challenge democracy's core animating principle: government not only of the people but by the people. There is, in other words, an inherent tension between democratic leaders on the one hand and their legitimacy on the other.[19]

For some time I have maintained that the leadership industry is a response—primarily but by no means exclusively by American business and American business schools—to a perceived leadership crisis.[20] I have suggested that while leadership in America has always been difficult to exercise, for reasons that will become clear, beginning in the last half of the twentieth century the difficulties have been exacerbated and exaggerated. The industry then is a manifestation of our determination to overcome the difficulties associated with leading in a country that is, in theory, in opposition to power and authority. And it is a manifestation of our determination to overcome the difficulties associated with leading in a country that is, in practice, replete with roadblocks to deter any but the most dedicated agents of change.

Edmund Morgan pointed out that while the word *leader* is old, the word *leadership* is relatively new, part of our parlance only since the late eighteenth century.[21] This change in our rhetoric reflected a change in our social relationships, a decline in deference. No longer was there a presumption that social rank, or for that matter any other kind of rank, automatically conveyed political authority. Instead there was *leadership*, the beginning of a new way of deciding who should stand among the few to govern the many, and the beginning of a new way of ensuring that the many would have a say. No wonder the industry, the leadership industry, took root in American soil. Perhaps nowhere on earth have relations between leaders and followers been so fraught with frustration from inception.

PART II EVOLUTIONS

3 RELIGION

WE GENERALLY KNOW that since the beginning of the republic religion played a prominent part in American life. We generally do not know that it played a prominent part in American life even before the republic was born. Not only was it a source of friction among Christians struggling with whether or not religion should be politicized, it was a source of friction between Native Americans and European settlers. The former practiced a religion rooted in geography—they thought their relationship to the land sacred—while the latter thought it was conquest that had been divinely ordained.[1]

The American Revolution was itself about religion. It was not, of course, only about religion; it was also about politics. But if political freedom was an impulse animating rebellion, so was religious freedom. The earliest colonies were settled by groups, such as the Puritans, who fled England to avoid persecution on account of their religious beliefs. Similarly, the War of Independence was as much about freedom from tyranny of the church as it was about freedom from tyranny of the state.

To understand the role of religion at the inception of the American experiment is to grasp two truths that seem on the surface to be contradictory. On the one hand the founders were intent on separating church and state, and on securing for individuals the right to worship as they saw fit. But on the other hand the nation they envisioned was a Christian one, albeit one in which Christianity was to be embraced freely and voluntarily, rather than imposed by any individual or institution.

Religion soon was ritually practiced in public, as well as in private. Never in American history has religion not played a role in our collective, political, life. In fact, from the beginning, America's political leaders understood the importance of religion to the body politic and they embraced it, publicly, and used it to their advantage. To put it directly, America's leaders have always used religion as a resource, one as well employed for professional or political gain as for private purpose. Similarly, notwithstanding the insistence in theory on religious freedom, in practice Americans had a national religion all along. For most of the nation's history it was widely understood and generally agreed that the United States of America was tantamount to Christian America. More specifically, until the twentieth century, it was tantamount to Protestant America.

Recently, however, things changed. The refrains now are diversity and inclusiveness; they are embracing, not exclusive. Americans are told regularly that whatever their religion, or no religion, they too are part of the national tapestry. Declared President Barack Obama in his first inaugural address, "We are a nation of Christians and Muslims, Jews and Hindus, and nonbelievers." (He was also the first president to hold at the White House an Easter prayer breakfast—and the first to hold at the White House a Passover Seder.) Increasingly, in other words, religion is defined rather broadly: belief in a transcendent God of some sort, generally expressed through the performance of certain rituals and adherence to a moral code.[2]

Religion, then, always did play and still does a prominent part in American life. In general, it implies an ordered universe, with a powerful being somehow presiding. And, in general, it further implies that the natural world mirrors or reflects the supernatural one, and the secular the religious. So when George Washington, Abraham Lincoln, Ronald Reagan, and Barack Obama invoked God, as chief executives invariably did and still do, as in "God Bless America," they implied that they, in their capacity as president of the United States, were carrying out (or trying to) God's will. They implied some sort of connection, communication between them and God—the natural leader beseeching the supernatural one to bestow on America (his) blessings.[3]

In 2008 the United States had six major religious traditions: three were Protestant (Evangelical, black, and mainline), comprising some 58 percent of the total population; another 20 percent were Catholic; 1 percent Jewish; and 21 percent "secular."[4] Sometimes these religious differences reflect political ones, for example, in the 1930s when Jews, Catholics, and African American Protestants were likely to be liberal Democrats. Similarly, beginning in the 1970s Evangelicals were likely to be conservative Republicans. And in 2012, 81 percent of Republicans agreed with statements such as "I never doubt God's existence," whereas among Democrats the number was only 61 percent.[5] Those who have no religious affiliation tend similarly to cluster. In the 2008 presidential election, the religiously unaffiliated voted as heavily for Barack Obama as did white Evangelical Protestants for John McCain. As well, they, the religiously unaffiliated, are much more likely to be Democrats than Republicans, and much more likely to be liberal than conservative. In fact, if current trends continue—if the number of unaffiliated continues to grow in the next few years as it did in the past few, especially among the young, and if the Republican Party continues to be as conservative in the near future as it has been in the recent past—it likely will lose support and the Democratic Party will gain.

What's more striking, though, than the differences among the different faiths are the similarities: how remarkably successful has been the American experiment in keeping to a minimum religious tension. General agreement on and adherence to the Judeo-Christian tradition has enabled political leaders throughout American history to convey to the whole a sense of religious unity, even in times of political disunity. George Washington—as perfect a leader in the realm of religion as in virtually very other—was the original exemplar of the American ideal, of a national leader demonstrably tolerant of different faith-based traditions. He told a meeting of Quakers that he believed "the conscientious scruples of all men should be treated with great delicacy and tenderness." And he wrote to a Jewish community in Newport, Rhode Island, of his belief that freedom, including religious freedom, was a "natural right." It was not merely an "indulgence" of toleration that the majority was free to withdraw at will.[6]

After Washington and before the second inauguration of Abraham Lincoln there were some eighteen inaugural addresses, delivered by fourteen presidents. Each contained the same prevailing themes: tolerance and the idea that the United States of America was somehow special, providentially selected to be one nation under God. Every president referred to God in his inaugural address at least once, and in his *Second Inaugural Address* Abraham Lincoln went a step further, freely and frequently invoking the Bible.

In fact, some of the most memorable of Lincoln's phrases from this most memorable of his speeches reworked a psalm, or drew on a gospel, or quoted Jesus, as in "but let us judge not, that we not be judged."[7] Moreover, references to God ripple through Lincoln's text on the occasion as a stream through a wood—so much so that his address is as religious as political. "The Almighty has His own purposes," said Lincoln, even if these cannot be divined by ordinary men. It is God who will decide when and how "to bind up the nation's wounds," for his judgments, "the judgments of the Lord are true and righteous altogether." While to this day there is question about what in private was the nature of Lincoln's faith, there is no question that to recover from the trauma that was the Civil War, Lincoln thought it wise publicly to invoke the Almighty.[8]

The civil rights movement is the most vivid recent example of how religion and leadership in America intersect. Though on the surface it was a political process, religion was the inspiration and justification, at the heart of the movement from beginning to end. Lines were blurred: between private life and public life, between leadership and followership, and between the religious and the secular. Ordinary people became public figures and political players. People in positions of power and authority had no choice but to bend to the popular will. And gospel and grass roots entwined. The civil rights movement was, in other words, a social and political upheaval informed by, driven by, Christianity and the Judeo-Christian tradition.

In his book on religion in American politics, historian Frank Lambert wrote that "Martin Luther King, Jr., was a Baptist preacher, and many other [civil rights] leaders, including Ralph Abernathy, Andrew Young, and Jesse Jackson, were ordained ministers as well. King's organization bore a distinctive religious title: the Southern Christian Leadership Conference. Civil rights meetings and rallies often took place in black churches, which had long constituted the one organization that blacks controlled—a community's social and political center as well as its religious heart. Blacks envisioned the struggle for equal rights to be a Christian mission akin to that of the Apostle Paul to spread the gospel to the gentile world."[9]

Martin Luther King's single greatest contribution to the leadership literature, "Letter from Birmingham Jail"—which was addressed, not incidentally, to eight white clergy—bears resemblance to Lincoln's *Second Inaugural Address*. It too is laced with the Lord, the Bible, and the Christian tradition. "I am in Birmingham," King wrote, "because injustice is here. Just as . . . the Apostle Paul left his village of Tarsus and carried the gospel of Jesus Christ to the far corners of the Greco-Roman world, so I am compelled to carry the gospel of freedom beyond my own home town. Like Paul, I must constantly respond to the Macedonian call for aid."[10]

Of course, just as religion has by and large united the American people, it has on occasion divided them. The United States is not immune to the sort of religious extremism that engenders conflict as opposed to cooperation. Some issues broadly defined as religious, for example abortion, do not lend themselves easily to compromise. And some beliefs, especially when they are strongly held, pit one group against another. Religious fundamentalists of every sort tend to play rather a divisive role, their certain conviction that they in particular claim God's truth inclining to injure a nation that ideologically is pluralistic.

This said, so far as leadership is concerned, religion in America has had an effect more positive than pernicious. Leaders of different faiths have been able, sometimes explicitly, sometimes implicitly, to draw on religious values, indeed on the Almighty, to convey community as the occasion required. In fact, the aforementioned Samuel Huntington argued that seventeenth-century Protestantism was central to the development of democracy in America. Protestantism "stressed the primacy of the individual conscience [and] the close connection between the spirit of liberty and the spirit of religion." Protestantism "provided the underlying ethical and moral basis for American ideas on politics and society."[11]

Others elaborated on the theme, asserting that it was Protestantism that upheld beliefs and espoused values that were compatible with the development of democracy. They claimed that the rights that we demand and have come to expect, including human rights, are integral to this tradition: they are "mandated by the equality of human beings before God." There is, in other words, a long list of American religious beliefs (again, originally Protestant) that support American political beliefs—including those on leadership and office holding. Both are ideally regarded as public trusts, inspired by "the example and teachings of religious prophets, such as Jesus, who accepted such a service 'to the death.'"[12]

This is not to say that as religion in America becomes more inclusive and diverse, and less powerful and pervasive, leadership in America will necessarily suffer. But it is to say that the Judeo-Christian tradition has contributed generously to the American liberal tradition. It is also to say that political leaders in particular have used religion to further whatever their policies and preferences. I am suggesting, in other words, that in several different ways—conscious and unconscious, explicit and implicit, public and private—leadership and religion in America have proved mutually reinforcing. In fact, overwhelmingly, the leadership class has itself been Christian, leaders in American business following the demographic trajectory of leaders in American politics. The overwhelming majority of such leaders have been white. And they have been male. And they have been Protestant. Moreover, most still report that they regularly attend church.[13]

To be sure, in recent years American leaders like Americans more generally have become somewhat more diverse. For example, since 2006, the CEO of PepsiCo has been Indra Nooyi. Regularly acclaimed by *Fortune* and *Forbes* as "one of the world's most powerful women," she is also described as a "devout Hindu." More striking, numerically at least, is the more than thirty CEOs of *Fortune* 500 companies who have been Jewish, though some number, such as Laurence Tisch of Loews, were CEOs of companies that they themselves (or their forbears) founded.[14] Still, notwithstanding the greater religious diversity, no high-ranking corporate leader of any faith is likely for the indefinite future to deviate from the American tradition: public performance reflective of the nation's Judeo-Christian heritage. Put differently, all corporate leaders, like all other leaders, may be presumed to have been properly socialized. They will continue to push the prevailing norm—divergence (diversity) on the one hand and convergence (in the Judeo-Christian tradition) on the other.

Of course, given that the context is changing, sustaining religious convergence will be more difficult in the future than it was in the past. As Harvard professor Diana Eck has pointed out, the Immigration and Nationalities Act of 1965 had a profound impact on religion in American life. She makes clear that twenty-first-century America is no longer Judeo-Christian—it is multi-religious. "The new immigrants who have come to America have brought not only their economic ambition and their dreams of freedom, but their Bhagavad-Gitas and their Qur'ans, their Buddhas and Bodhisattvas, their images of the Goddess Durga and the Virgin of Guadalupe. They have built mosques and Islamic centers; Hindu, Jain, and Buddhist temples; Sikh gurdwaras; Hispanic and Vietnamese churches all over this land, in cities large and small."[15] Nevertheless, as indicated, and as Eck herself concedes, Americans are still nearly 80 percent Christian, with Christianity remaining disproportionately highly represented among members of America's leadership class.

American religion has, by and large, served this class well. Members have, in general, practiced it privately; simultaneously they have, in general, used it to public advantage. America's leaders have used religion to engage their followers and to sell them (us) on the idea, first, that the United States of America is the most blessed of all nations, and second, that God has always been and remains to this day on America's side. American leaders have, in short, used American religion to bind us—to the nation, and to them, and to each other. To be sure, there are some exceptions to the general rule. Sometimes God, religion, has been invoked to point to our shortcomings. Martin Luther King was expert at this; for example, in his iconic speech, "I Have a Dream," he reminded that God still waits for the day when we will all join hands as equals. "When we allow freedom to ring . . . all of God's children, black men and white men, Jews and Gentiles, Protestants and Catholics, will be able to join hands and sing in the words of the old Negro spiritual, 'Free at last, Free at last, Great God a-mighty, We are free at last.'"

But, again, American religion is not now what once it was. It is not only more diverse, it has, of itself, been weakened. Therefore, whatever resources religion provided in the past, provided to leaders in particular, in the present have been somewhat depleted. To be sure, we remain significantly more religious than our most obvious counterparts, people in places with similar Western values and at similar levels of economic development. For example, while only 58 percent of Americans still say that religion is very important in their lives, in Germany that number is much smaller, only 21 percent, in Britain it is only 17 percent, and in France merely 13 percent. Still, however the numbers read now, they are changing fast. Polling results make clear that so far as religion is concerned, Americans are becoming more like Europeans.

Pew Research confirms that "the number of Americans who do not identify with any religion continues to grow at a rapid pace."[16] In fact, among Americans ages 18–29, one in four now say that they are not currently affiliated with any particular religion, and more than one-quarter of American adults have left the faith in which they were raised, either for another religion or for no religion at all.[17] The ranks of the unaffiliated now include more than thirteen million self-described atheists and agnostics (nearly 6 percent of Americans), as well as nearly thirty-three million people who say that they have no particular religious affiliation

(14 percent).[18] In particular, Protestantism, once dominant, is waning, to the degree that the United States is on the verge of becoming a minority Protestant country. In short, religion in America is in flux. As the Pew Research Center puts it, "religious affiliation in the U.S. is both very diverse and extremely fluid."[19] Every major religious group is simultaneously gaining and losing adherents. This diversity and fluidity extends, incidentally, to the nation's highest office. In 1960, Americans finally elected as president a Catholic, John Kennedy, and in 2012, Americans finally selected as candidate of one of the two major parties a Mormon, Mitt Romney.

Social scientists Robert Putnam and David Campbell have argued that the growing secularization is "the most noticeable shift in how Americans have become polarized along religious lines." Though they do not prognosticate serious strife, they do point out that Americans increasingly are concentrated at opposite ends of the religious spectrum— "the highly religious at one pole, and the avowedly secular at the other." They also confirm that there are political consequences to this polarization. The "coalition of the religious," which includes voters of different faiths, tends to vote one way (conservative), while Americans who are not religious or who are secular tend to vote another (liberal).[20]

Still, many of the country's forty-six million unaffiliated adults "are religious or spiritual in some way." A large number say that they believe in God, and a large number say that they feel a deep connection with nature and the earth. So what the unaffiliated appear to be disenchanted with is not God. Instead "overwhelmingly" they "think that religious organizations are too concerned with money and power, too focused on rules and too involved in politics."[21] Put directly, twenty-first-century Americans tend increasingly to suspect that organized religion—religious institutions and individuals in formal positions of religious authority—is associated in some nefarious way with "money and power." They tend increasingly to distrust the religious leadership class.

Of course there is a range of reasons why the number of Americans with no religious affiliation has increased, including the impact of science on the American psyche, political backlash (religion and conservatism are equated), social disengagement, and the spate of scandals associated with organized religion, most visibly but certainly not exclusively in the Catholic Church. Though older Catholics are, for example, much more likely than younger ones to say that they are "proud to be Catholic," even among this more devout demographic attendance at mass has fallen off, from 64 percent in 1999 to just over 50 percent in 2011. "Catholics in the past 25 years have become more autonomous when making decisions about important moral issues; less reliant on official teaching in reaching those decisions; and less deferential to the authority of the Vatican and individual bishops."[22]

Of course, Pope Francis (elected in 2013) has proven immensely popular. His benign countenance, charitable nature, and avowedly, refreshingly simple lifestyle have provided a welcome contrast to the "money and power" with which so much of organized religion has come to be associated. Still, given that by an overwhelming majority (78 percent) American Catholics report that they would follow the dictates of their conscience before the dictates of any pope, a radical reversal of existing trends in American Catholicism is unlikely.[23]

In 2013 only 54 percent of American adults said that they planned to attend Christmas religious services. While this number remains relatively high, it is low in comparison with the 69 percent that reported traditionally attending church when they were young—yet another sign of the times.[24] What we can reasonably conclude then, is that leaders in twenty-first-century America are less able to use religion—to draw on the Judeo-Christian tradition—to engage, motivate, or inspire their followers than were their predecessors. Religion has obviously not vanished as a component of our collective life. But it has been diminished in its importance. It has been degraded as a source of authority, including moral authority. And it has dwindled as a resource on which leaders can draw to further whatever their purpose.

The fact that more of us consider ourselves now to be religiously unaffiliated—or to be affiliated less strongly—inevitably has consequences for how leadership and followership in America are exercised. Not only are leaders weaker and followers stronger in general, leaders in religion specifically have been deprived of at least some of the moral authority previously associated with clergy.

The overarching consequence of the decline in religious affiliation, and of the weakened nature of this affiliation, is, then, the further feeding of the follower. The writer Christopher Hitchens, who in the last years of his life was famous, or infamous, for being a militant atheist, was especially contemptuous of people in positions of religious authority who referred to themselves as shepherds and to the faithful as their flock. "Jesus is Santa Claus for adults," he wrote.[25] Well, however sheeplike were the faithful in the past, in the present they are no longer—or, at least, not so much. In American religion, as in every other realm of American life, followers are less inclined to follow and more inclined to act as independent agents. This means that whatever American leaders might or might not believe in private, in public they are less able to use religion in order to enlist followers in their personal, professional, and political crusades.

4 POLITICS

THE AMERICAN POLITICAL SYSTEM seems to some of us—maybe to most of us—to be broken. But it's not. At the most fundamental level, state and local governments, and the federal government, do what needs to be done. Basic services are generally delivered, schools are open, highways are more or less maintained, there is access to medical care, and every attempt is made, usually successfully, to protect our national security. (Of course there are exceptions to this general rule; for example, in 2014, in Charleston, West Virginia, Governor Earl Ray Tomblin had to inform some three hundred thousand people that their tap water was not safe for "drinking, cooking, washing, or bathing."[1]) Moreover, some political leaders have done most everything right. Former New York City mayor Michael Bloomberg could be said to fall into this category—he was honest, smart, and, mostly, exceedingly competent. (This did not preclude his successor, Democrat Bill de Blasio, from having run for mayor by denigrating Bloomberg at every turn, in particular for cultivating "two cities," one rich, the other poor.)

Notwithstanding, as a whole our leadership class, in this case our political leadership class, is held in disdain if not distrust. Outside observer and Oxford scholar Stein Ringen puts the American predicament this way: "The very idea of government as an instrument of good is challenged, perhaps even abandoned. Being a politician is disreputable and contempt for politics a free-for all."[2] Arguably this particular disillusionment is the single most important explanation for why so many of us are convinced that the United States is on the way down as opposed to on the way up. In 2013 Pew Research Center reported that Americans' "trust in the federal government remains mired near a historical low and frustration with government remains high."[3] Similarly, in response to this question posed by Gallup in 2014, "In general, are you satisfied or dissatisfied with the way things are going in the United States?" only 23 percent of Americans reported being satisfied.[4] Figures like these, figures that relate to the ethics and effectiveness of government, have over the past fifty years declined sharply. The demographics, moreover, are similarly disheartening. Those under thirty are especially disposed to feeling politically alienated—they "seem to feel that politics and voting simply is not for them."[5]

To an extent then, there is a disjuncture between what's real and what's imagined. It's not completely clear, in other words, that such widespread disenchantment with government in the abstract, and with political leaders, is deserved. In fact, when Americans are asked about their own congressional representatives, they tend to have a more favorable view of them than of Congress as a whole. Moreover, for all of President Barack Obama's political problems, his approval ratings remained reasonably high, at least until the second half of 2013, in part because he did in fact get some things done. To take the most famous, or infamous, example, whatever you may think of the Patient Protection and Affordable Care Act, "Obamacare" is a major piece of federal legislation and a significant expansion of big government. In addition, by the end of 2013 many Americans were better off than they were four years earlier: over two hundred thousand jobs a month were being created (in 2008, seven hundred thousand jobs a month were being lost); unemployment dropped in November 2013 to 7 percent (the lowest level since November 2008); and the wars in Iraq and Afghanistan were, successively, wound down, at least so far as the U.S. was concerned.

Still, there is a pervasive sense, largely justified, that even if things are working, they are not working nearly as well as they should, or nearly as well as they did. This matters of itself—and it matters because our opinion of leaders in government affects our opinion of leaders more broadly. Disappointment in the former tends to contaminate our view of the latter. It's one of the reasons why leadership in twenty-first-century America is so difficult to exercise: the political culture generally, and political leaders specifically, have poisoned the well.

What's happened? What's gone wrong? More particularly, what's gone wrong during the past half century when Americans' trust in government and in those who people it, particularly at the federal level, have plummeted? The reasons fall into two categories: exogenous, external to politics; and endogenous, internal to politics, that is, to politicians and the political system.

Given that this book is a contextual checklist, I will simply name some examples in each of the two categories. The list is not intended to be complete. Rather it is to provide an indication of why the political environment has become so hostile, particularly to political leaders. Each of the following has one thing in common: each has made it difficult and sometimes impossible for even the most powerful of America's political leaders to get what they want when they want it. They are powerful reminders of why and of how vulnerable leaders are to the vagaries of context.

Exogenous Problems

ASSASSINS: Three assassins who murdered in relatively quick succession three legendary leaders—John F. Kennedy (1963), Martin Luther King Jr. (1968), and Robert F. Kennedy (1968)—traumatized the national psyche and changed American politics forever. In consequence it took some fifteen years before Ronald Reagan was able to steady the ship of state. Lyndon Johnson was, in effect, hounded out of office. Richard Nixon was the first president ever forced to resign. Gerald Ford turned out unable to win a presidential term in his own right. And after what is widely seen as a weak or even failed presidency, Jimmy Carter suffered an ignominious defeat in his bid for a second term. By committing acts of murder, Lee Harvey Oswald, James Earl Ray, and Sirhan Sirhan robbed us of our innocence and set us on a path toward something new and different—self-doubt.

SEPTEMBER 11, 2001:   The attacks on American soil by Al Qaeda, on 9/11, deprived Americans of what had been up to then a magnificent illusion: that they, we, were impervious to attack by outsiders. Unlike other countries with which Americans were most familiar, especially some in Europe such as England, France, and Germany, the United States had generally been spared the devastation of invasion. And so we thought ourselves immune. But on 9/11 that immunity came in an instant to a mind-bending halt. No longer did we feel exempted from the evils of the twenty-first century; no longer did we feel protected by being exceptional, a shining city on a hill. Instead we had become ordinary—a nation like other nations, vulnerable to, among other things, terrorism in the homeland.

TECHNOLOGY: The revolution in information and communications technologies has changed relations between leaders and led in ways we have not yet begun fully to appreciate. Suffice it here to say that social media especially empower followers—ordinary people—at the expense of leaders. In part due to technology, America's political leaders have lost their capacity to control their followers or, at least, their capacity to control their followers to the extent they did previously. This change is by no means confined to the United States; it is worldwide, certainly in systems that are democracies. Moreover, while this shift in the balance of power and influence is especially in evidence in politics, it applies across the board, to every institution and organization in every sector—including the private sector, the nonprofit sector, the military, and, as we have seen, even religious organizations and institutions. Ever wondered why it was only relatively recently, early in the twenty-first century, that long-standing and widespread sexual abuse in the Catholic Church came finally to light? Ever noticed how it affected the relationship between the Catholic hierarchy and the Catholic laity? Ever considered why the story broke in the United States (in Boston), as opposed to anywhere else in the world, where the situation was equally bad or worse—for example, in Ireland?

CULTURE: It has always been good sport for American followers to tear at American leaders, for subordinates to mock their superiors, and for the powerless to undermine and sometimes even to overturn the powerful. But in the past there were greater distinctions between what was said and done in public and what was said and done in private.[6] The former was typically more decorous, more careful and cautious than the latter—for several reasons. Open subversion used to be less socially acceptable and more risky. Open subversion did not in the past as it does in the present allow for anonymity. And open subversion was not so synchronous with the larger culture, which has in the past twenty, thirty years become coarser (think Rush Limbaugh and Howard Stern), more confessional (think Eliot Spitzer and Anthony Wiener), more intrusive (think Monica Lewinsky and Paula Broadwell), more aggressive, and more virulently anti-leader than previously. Leaders of all kinds have become fair game for followers who are less cowed now than they used to be. It is not, in other words, that leaders now are different from before—for example a number of presidents have had relationships with women other than their wives. But the changing technologies and the changing culture have twinned in ways that make even the nation's highest elected official grist for the gossip mill.

MEDIA: The still relatively new news cycle (24/7), and the still relatively new news media (cable television, the Internet), chew up content. They oblige (or seem to) news providers to be hyperbolic and hysterical even in situations when neither is called for. And they encourage extremism in an environment in which centrism would seem not only more benign but more beneficial. In addition, they personalize the properties of whatever it is that happens. Talking heads don't deal in nuances—in the complex mix of contextual components that fully and accurately explain what transpires and how. Instead, if anything goes wrong, they, so-called experts, or "strategists," blame those they perceive the perpetrators. But to what extent should the president of the United States be faulted for an American economy that still provides too few jobs? Are there other reasons that might pertain? And to what extent should any chief executive officer be held personally responsible for a falling stock price? It depends, of course, but in any event, are there other reasons that might pertain?

GLOBALIZATION: Even a couple of decades ago, say when Bill Clinton was president, the United States controlled, or seemed to, its own destiny. Now, though America remains a major world power, many of its most intractable problems are beyond its capacity to contain, at least single-handedly. Climate change? Terrorism? Cheap labor? Nuclear proliferation and arms transfers? Currency fluctuations? Violations of international norms? These are only some of the challenges the U.S. cannot even begin to address on its own. More than before, protection from harm demands multinational, transnational cooperation—yet even the most well-intentioned of such efforts tend to fall miserably short. There is, for instance, not the slightest chance that the United States can avoid altogether some of the dire consequences of climate change—evidence for this is already in. So whatever the president does or does not do in this general regard, and whatever the captains of business and industry do to support his environmental efforts, they are unlikely to make much of a dent in what is, obviously, a complex, multinational problem, not, at least not exclusively, a simple, national one.

Endogenous Problems

DECLINE OF POLITICAL PARTIES: The number of political independents has continued to grow in recent decades, with both Democrats and Republicans losing ground among the general public. In 2012, 38 percent of Americans described themselves as independents, up eight points from only eight years earlier. In fact, independents are more numerous now than at any point in the past seventy years.[7] On the surface this would not seem a particular problem—what's wrong with having more independents and fewer party affiliates? It happens though that the corollary effects of this shift tend more to be pernicious than anything else.

They include an electorate that is increasingly alienated and angry; a primary system favoring those at the extremes rather than those in the middle; a candidate-centric system that makes it difficult for aspirants to raise the money now needed effectively to challenge incumbents; and a congressional cadre more likely to go it alone than to hue to any party line. They also include candidates for the American presidency and vice presidency—think Herman Cain, Sarah Palin, even Rick Santorum—who would never have made the cut had political parties remained more prominent and powerful.

IDEOLOGICAL CONTENTIOUSNESS: In the second decade of the twenty-first century, Americans tend to divide into two factions: left and right, liberals and conservatives. In general, liberals believe that because many Americans do not get the benefit of equal opportunity, the proper role of government is to play the part, in so far as possible, of equalizer. Thus liberals tend to support public policies that redistribute income from the rich to the poor, for example, extended unemployment insurance, and to support services such as strong public schools, expecting that to some extent at least they will level the playing field. Conservatives, conversely, question the moral imperative and political capacity of government to remediate whatever our collective problems. Instead they believe that "private citizens, operating without the encumbrances of government constraints, are more effective in motivating growth, innovation, and opportunity."[8]

IDEOLOGICAL EXTREMISM: The most striking recent example of extremism in American politics is the emergence, seemingly out of nowhere, of the Tea Party. The Tea Party is the product of a split among Republicans, between those on the right and those closer to the center. It is also the product of a genuine (largely white) grassroots movement that tapped into anti-government populism to become a major force in American politics, especially congressional politics.[9] Moreover, just when its heyday was said to be over, the Tea Party proved itself resilient, continuing to complicate the lives of traditional party leaders, whether Republicans or Democrats, or in the House or the Senate, or in the

White House. The essentially leaderless Tea Partiers, or, if you prefer, the multi-leader Tea Partiers, have scant interest in playing politics by the usual rules of the game. They are, quite literally, independents, free agents, content often as not to sidestep their ostensible leaders and to gum up the system that they profess to support. Of course, though the effects of extremism have been more visible on the one side (Republican) than on the other (Democratic), they are systemwide. Voter anger and alienation have bipartisan effects. On the right the populist pandering encourages Republicans to provide simplistic solutions; on the left it encourages Democrats to bend to their base.

LACK OF COMITY: Politicians are not only more likely than before to engage in acrimony, they are less likely than before to engage in comity, in simple social niceties. Much has been made of the lack of cordiality, of friendly and fruitful interpersonal relations, in the nation's capitol—both within Congress and between Congress and the White House. The reasons include a shorter DC work week; families remaining in their home districts rather than making the move to Washington; the humungous and pernicious role of big money in politics; and a two-term president, Barack Obama, who is not exactly big on small talk. The result in any case is a political culture in which politicians are less disposed to civility than they were before—and this in a political system in which civility is of paramount importance. As we have seen, Americans are cursed, or blessed, with a political system in which it's hard to get anything done. This puts a premium not so much on political power, or on political authority, as it does on political influence. And political influence, in turn, depends to some considerable extent on feelings of friendliness and on a modicum of good will.

GREAT DIVIDES: In addition to the aforementioned ideological divide are two others that bedevil Washington and preclude good governance at the federal level. The first is the mismatch between the two fiercely ideological political parties on the one side and our system of governance on the other—a system heavily dependent on the capacity to compromise.[10] Specifically, it has been difficult recently if not impossible to get anything much through Congress without a "supermajority," without the sixty votes required in the Senate to overcome a filibuster. In 2013 Senate Democrats did finally take the significant step of eliminating filibusters for most presidential nominations; still they remain an option for legislation, which is why the fix was necessary but insufficient. The second of these divides is between the government and the people, that is, between the people and those who represent them. To be sure, Americans are divided. But they are not nearly as divided as the conventional wisdom would seem to suggest. For instance, some 72 percent of Americans support immigration reform, at least to the extent that they support giving undocumented workers either a green card or citizenship. Similarly, more than 80 percent of Americans favor gun control measures such as universal background checks and prohibiting the mentally ill from purchasing arms. And seven out of ten Americans favor higher emissions and pollution standards, while 69 percent support more funding for wind and solar energy. These are impressive numbers—they constitute substantial, highly persuasive majorities—especially in a large, diverse democracy such as ours.[11] Still, the chances that majority political preferences will translate into public policy remain slim. Why? Because there is a significant disconnect between the American people and the elected officials who people the nation's capital.

AMERICAN PEOPLE: It is said that we get the leaders we deserve. What exactly does this mean, in this case? It means that our dysfunctional political system is not only the fault of bad leadership, it is also the fault of bad followership. It means that we share the blame for what's gone wrong. For instance, while we, the American people, have been much better at cutting down our household debt, we have not been much better at cutting down our national debt. At the current pace, by 2025 entitlement spending and debt payments will suck up all federal revenue, leaving not a dime to spend on anything else. Among other things, this is an issue of generational justice. Legendarily successful money manager Stanley Druckenmiller has spoken out (including on college campuses) against what he calls "generational theft."[12] He judges existing entitlement programs to be not only unaffordable, but profoundly unfair, demonstrably benefiting the old at the expense of the young. *New York Times* columnist David Brooks makes the same point: "The average Medicare couple pays $109,000 into the program and gets $343,000 in benefits out. . . . This is $234,000 in free money. Many voters have decided they like spending a lot on themselves and shifting costs onto their children and grandchildren. . . . And they have made it clear that they will destroy any politician who tries to stop them from cost-shifting."[13] A large number of Democratic voters reject out of hand decreases in entitlements; a large number of Republican voters reject out of hand increases in taxes. By failing to reach reasonable compromise on this issue, by failing to resolve reasonably the problem of the national debt, leaders in Washington are doing no more than, and no less than, responding to the popular will. Of course the problem extends far beyond any single issue or institution. By insisting at every turn that everyone has a voice whenever they decide they want to have a voice, we may, counterintuitively, be doing democracy a disservice.

COMPLEX CONTEXT: There have been times when it was worse—when the United States was in a situation more vexing than it is now. Still, the multiplicity and complexity of current concerns can be nearly overwhelming. Moreover, our political capacity to address the plethora of problems is more meager in the present than it was in the past. This does not hold true every time and everywhere. In fact, a strong case can be made that precisely because Washington will not or cannot take on the big issues, some cities and some states have gone ahead and done just that.[14] Nevertheless, what happens or does not in Washington dominates the conversation, as it should. Washington is the nexus of our national government, and the repository of the bureaucracy that affects the lives of every American man, woman, and child. Even setting aside the array of foreign policy problems, the array of domestic policy problems itself is long. These include but are by no means limited to still relatively high unemployment and underemployment;

banks still too big to fail; national debt still too high; entitlements still too costly; health care still too unwieldy and expensive; a decaying national infrastructure; immigration; gun violence; an arcane, outmoded tax code; a shrinking middle class; and the growing disparity between the rich and the rest. The issue of the national debt is especially instructive, for the solution would seem, on the surface, to be relatively simple. As the long-praised and highly touted but nevertheless widely ignored Simpson-Bowles plan would have seemed to attest, a centrist compromise, a "grand bargain" consisting of some combination of higher taxes and lower spending is, in theory, in reach. But in practice it is not. This is not because it or something similar is bad, but because it has proven impossible in the current political climate to strike a serious deal of significant consequence.

·   ·   ·

To return to the point I made earlier is to be reminded that although the United States is widely perceived, both at home and abroad, to be in a period of political dysfunction, all is not lost. Both the captain and the crew have kept the ship afloat—there is no risk, at least not for the moment, at least not so far as we can tell, of any imminent American disaster. Moreover, it's important not to lose sight of America's strengths. This country remains a political, economic, and military powerhouse, and there is no real, conclusive evidence that it has entered a period of irrevocable decline.

Still, the truth is that American politics in the second decade of the twenty-first century does not present a pretty picture. Political leaders are held to constant account by the chattering classes—with the chattering classes themselves to blame for at least some of the incessant contentiousness. Certain individuals, some political leaders, do manage in the morass to stand out, to persuade and even prove to their followers that they are both effective and ethical. But the overweening impression is that political leaders in the present are less excellent than were those in the past. The overweening impression is that our political system is distressed to the point of dysfunction. The overweening impression is that democracy is falling short of its promise. And the overweening impression is that the contextual complexities are now so great that they are difficult if not ultimately impossible for political leaders collectively, effectively, to address. *Wall Street Journal* columnist Gerald Seib captured the malaise: "America and its political leaders, after two decades of failing to come together to solve big problems, seems to have lost faith in their ability to do so. A political system that expects failure doesn't try hard to produce anything else."[15]

Again, the pollution is not confined to the political arena. As pollution is wont to do, it seeps out, spills out, and contaminates nearly every aspect of American life in the second decade of the twenty-first century. It's a critical component of the context within which all American leaders conduct their business and comport themselves—it's one of the reasons times are hard.

5 ECONOMICS

AMERICANS TEND TO UNDERSTAND rather well the ideas and ideals that support their political system—freedom, for example, and democracy, and independence. Americans tend to understand rather less well the ideas and ideals that support their economic system. We have scant sense of what exactly economics is—not for nothing is it called "the dismal science," a "weak field."[1] We have scant sense of when exactly economics and politics intersect. And we have scant sense of how the theory and practice of our economic system—of capitalism—impinge on every aspect of everyday life. We worship at the altar of the almighty dollar, but we don't know much about how the dollar came to be almighty or even if, in this day and age, it still is.

The idea of property as a "right" that we could reasonably claim was ours was propagated most famously by John Locke in *Two Treatises of Government*. Though the Declaration of Independence did not identify property as something to which the American people were entitled, it was understood nevertheless that property was included in its intention. The claim that all men are "endowed by their creator with certain inalienable Rights" meant not only the right to life, liberty, and the pursuit of happiness, but also the right to own property, broadly defined.

Americans always have, then, thought private property was in effect untouchable, inviolable. Individuals have the right to invest in and accumulate property, and money, and other financial assets, and then to dispose of them as they see fit. In addition, they have the right to assert their economic self-interest, and to assume that the government has an obligation to protect what rightfully is theirs. As historian Richard Hofstadter put it, the "business" of American politics is to "protect this competitive world, to foster it on occasion, to patch up its incidental abuses, but not to cripple it with a plan for common collective action."[2] In fact, it is not too much to say that the history of the United States of America has coincided, not coincidentally, with the history of capitalism.

What exactly is "capitalism"? Even now we oppose it to communism, associating capitalism with individualism, independence, and free enterprise, and communism with collectivity, control, and government involvement. Better though is this: capitalism is a system of political and economic relations characterized by private ownership; the free exchange of goods and services, for profit; and the use of free markets for the purposes of production and distribution.[3] Capitalism is also a system with certain implications, especially inequity. In a capitalist system, those who start in life well advantaged are likely to stay in life well advantaged. (The converse is, of course, also true.) It's what Warren Buffett refers to as "winning the ovarian lottery."

Almost from the start Americans seemed cut out to be capitalists. As sociologist Max Weber pointed out in his classic *The Protestant Ethic and the Spirit of Capitalism* (1905), Protestantism and capitalism seemed perfectly to complement each other, each with a set of values that encouraged individual responsibility, personal progress, and economic self-fulfillment. (Weber's contention was that capitalism was rooted in religion, specifically in the "Protestant ethic."[4]) To be sure, during the first few decades of the American experiment there were no significant breakthroughs, nor was there much industrialization or urbanization, certainly not in comparison with England.[5] But by the 1820s the number of American patents awarded was averaging three times that in Britain and, while the U.S. remained still largely rural and agrarian, beneath the surface it was increasingly commercialized.[6] In fact, while the hallmark of the United States has always been growth, this first applied in full in the first half of the nineteenth century, "when an unparalleled rate of growth took place in three dimensions: population, territory, and economy." The population of the United States doubled and then doubled again. Americans in addition quadrupled the size of their country by "settling, conquering, annexing or purchasing territory that had been occupied for millennia by Indians and claimed by France, Spain, Britain and Mexico." Finally, the gross national product increased sevenfold. "No other nation in that era could match even a single component of this explosive growth."[7]

By the late 1860s the United States had positioned itself to be "world leader in the production of timber and steel, meat packing, the mining of coal, iron, gold, and silver." Not that this upward trajectory was nonstop. Cycles of boom and bust, panic and depression—all were intermittent intrusions on the growing prosperity. But for reasons already suggested and two in addition—changing technologies and the unusually strong American work ethic—the U.S. continued throughout the nineteenth century to make remarkably rapid economic and technological progress. By the early twentieth century, "celebrated American firms and their famous inventors were becoming the talk of the business world, even of industrial exhibitions abroad." In short, American capitalism had asserted itself worldwide not only economically but politically and culturally as well.[8]

By the early twentieth century investing, entrepreneurship, urbanization, large corporations, and the accumulation by a few of great private wealth were becoming the norm. Men such as Jay Gould, Andrew Carnegie, and John D. Rockefeller personified the limitless possibilities of capitalism—as well as its obvious, in some cases onerous, excesses. For Americans had divided in time into three different classes: a small number who were famously rich; a large number who were infamously poor; and some number, a growing number, who were members of an emerging middle class.

None of this was without divisiveness. As industrialism increased and the classes cleaved there was a growing awareness of class differences—an awareness that while capitalism worked stunningly well for some, for others it provided nothing so much as a life of hard work, or of no work, with at best meager reward. But for reasons that are debated to this day, capitalism's obvious counterparts, communism and socialism, did not ever in any enduring way impress themselves on the American imagination.

The hardest test of American capitalism was of course the Great Depression. Ironically, the decade preceding was for many, not for all but for many, a heady, even frothy time. Real national income had soared and millionaires multiplied. "From its cornucopia the huge American workshop showered goods onto eager buyers. Industrial production almost doubled . . . and spending skyrocketed—on cars, telephones, cigarette lighters, oil furnaces, fresh fruit and vegetables from distant parts. The smell of money hung in the air."[9] It was the age of Ballyhoo. It was the Jazz Age. It was the Roaring Twenties.

But by 1929 the speculative fever had morphed into a speculative frenzy—which brought it all to a sharp, shocking end. The stock market crash was not a single event on a single day. Instead it was several collapses, each followed by brief rallies, until, finally, "Black Thursday." October 24, 1929, was the day on which stocks started their geometric slide.

President Franklin Roosevelt is widely credited with lifting the nation out of the Great Depression—and with doing so in a way that was in keeping with capitalism. To be sure, the New Deal signaled a somewhat modified, less pure, if you will, form of capitalism, one in which the United States government would play a larger role in America's economic future than it had in the past. But it was capitalism nevertheless. The New Deal was not socialism, and certainly it was not communism. Rather, the New Deal was a series of economic programs, enacted between 1933 and 1936, that were implemented either through a presidential directive (executive order) or through a law enacted by the congress.

They focused on what historians refer to as the "3 Rs"—relief for the poor and unemployed; recovery of the economy; and reform of the system so as to preclude in so far as possible the recurrence of a depression.

I reference Franklin Roosevelt because he was the last American leader to exert single-handedly such great power over the American economy. This is not to say that other leaders—other presidents, for example, or chairpersons of the Federal Reserve, or even private sector innovators and entrepreneurs such as Bill Gates and Steve Jobs—were unimportant. Rather, it is to say that in the past half century the American economy has been influenced less by single individuals and more by components of an increasingly complex context, some of which are endogenous and many others of which are exogenous. In recent decades especially, the impact of globalization on the American economy— think increased competition, expanded markets, and cheap labor—has been the most obvious of these changes, impossible to overestimate or to calculate precisely. In the 1970s, for instance, economic growth was stagnating and inflation was skyrocketing. But the doomsters were done in by three trends, all unanticipated and all independent of any single individual: the decline of inflation, the information revolution, and globalization.

Economic policy at the national level has actually been quite consistent. Notwithstanding the ideological differences personified by two famed economists—Friedrich Hayek on the one hand, an avowed non-interventionist, and John Maynard Keynes on the other, a proponent of government spending as necessary to stimulate the economy—for at least thirty years both Republicans and Democrats have generally gone along with, followed rather than led, the American people. And where exactly did they, we, lead? Most obviously we led in the direction of more government services and lower taxes—simultaneously. The result has been deficit spending, a ballooning national debt, and a general refusal to lead to repair the imbalance. In fact, since the presidency of Ronald Reagan, with the exception of a brief period in the late 1990s, the federal deficit has stayed above 3 percent. In 2013 it was an untenable 7 percent.

For various reasons the United States has more room to maneuver than other developed countries, such as those in Europe (Germany excepted). Still, it remains burdened by a litany of problems that impinge on the nation's economy, including, in addition to those already mentioned, burdensome regulatory systems and a messy patchwork of federal, state, and local laws. But the issue that particularly bedevils America's economic system is America's political system, to wit fiscal cliffs, debt ceilings, government shutdowns, and repeated refusals to reach budget agreements. The bottom line: too many leaders too much of the time, especially members of Congress, are refusing to be constructive because they judge it not to be to their personal political advantage either to repair the broken budget process or to exercise strict financial oversight. Reform requires leaders to assert the national interest over self-interest, "something increasingly difficult to do in a democracy."[10]

The past several years have been difficult because the problems that now plague the American economy are so complex that they challenge good leaders, not to speak of bad ones. Here are three of the most obvious. The first is increasing income inequality. Contrary to America's meritocratic ideal, many of us are now stuck low on the economic ladder, seemingly permanently. Moreover, at the same time (in 2012) the top 1 percent of income earners took home 93 percent of the growth in income, wage growth more generally remained sluggish, with middle class households having lower incomes (adjusted for inflation) than they did a decade and a half before. In fact, the compensation received by chief executives of companies in the S&P 500 index was fully 354 times that of rank-and-file staff.[11] This figure is enormously higher than comparable ratios for most other developed countries.

The middle class has, in other words, been shrinking, while households have been added both to the lowest income bracket and to the highest one. Worse, fully one-fifth of American children now live in poverty, not only an aberration among rich nations but another chronic problem without an obvious solution.[12] (Recent research seems to support the liberal contention that government programs such as food stamps and unemployment insurance preclude these figures from being even worse.[13])

American capitalism has become, in other words, a system that increasingly is unequal and that, except for the wealthiest among us, is chancier and less secure. Notwithstanding our earlier illusions, it seems clear that not only are capitalism and inequality indivisible—but that inequality does not ebb as economies mature. French economist Thomas Piketty, whose recent book *Capital in the Twenty-First Century* has received a great deal of attention and mostly extraordinarily high praise, makes precisely this point. His own longitudinal data seem to suggest that only a progressive global tax on wealth would rectify, to some degree, the growing worldwide inequities.[14]

Republicans have tended to ignore the problem, hoping it will go away of itself, through free market forces (per Hayek). Democrats, in turn, have been disposed to throw money at it (per Keynes), despite the fact that, as mentioned, at their current levels social programs including entitlements are unsustainable. In any case, whatever the dispositions of politicians, it turns out that income inequality tethers our economic system to our political one: polarization in Congress maps on to economic inequality better than to any other measure: "The smaller the gap between rich and poor, the more moderate our politicians; the greater the gap, the greater the disagreement between liberals and conservatives."[15]

The second obvious problem is the still relatively high level of unemployment and underemployment, some significant percentage of it long term. This is by no means only an American problem—it's global, with simply too few jobs, especially decent jobs, for too many people—but the American people continue to consider gainful, reasonable employment a right. Still, changes over time—shifts from an economy based on agriculture (eighteenth century) to an economy based on manufacturing (nineteenth century) to an economy based on the delivery of services in addition to goods (twentieth century) to an economy based on changing technologies (twenty-first century)—suggest that there will be less of a need for workers who are skilled and semi-skilled indefinitely, and more of a need for workers who, at the one end have low skills and get low pay, and at the other are well educated, technologically sophisticated, and (relatively) highly paid.

Among its other effects, globalization has reduced America's manufacturing base, simply by moving jobs from country to country, wherever labor is cheapest. Though in 2013 and certainly early 2014 the unemployment rate went down, the overall picture remains sobering. A backlog of 12.3 million workers remains idle, and the average worker who is unemployed and looking for a job has been hunting for thirty-five weeks. Christine Owens, executive director of a labor research and advocacy group, says that the "decline in the unemployment rate masks how protracted the crisis really is."[16] Dean of the Columbia Business School Glenn Hubbard echoes the point, noting that only 63.2 percent of all Americans sixteen or older participate in the labor force. He makes clear that what hasn't recovered since the end of Great Recession "is the labor force participation rate, which today stands roughly where it did in 1977."[17]

Put slightly differently, the unemployment figures are improving in part for the wrong reason, "because people are dropping out of the labor market or not entering it." The bottom line: millions of Americans have exhausted their unemployment benefits with no other income in sight.[18] In nearly every way then, many of America's skilled and semi-skilled workers have become disempowered. Organized labor has been particularly hard hit, with union membership in near steady decline for over a half century, to the point where now, excluding public sector unions, only 7 percent of American workers are union members.

What we have here then is a paradox: on the one hand, leaders—whether political or corporate—unable, unwilling, or both to fix what's broken, especially increasingly extreme inequities and chronically high levels of unemployment, underemployment, and numbers of those not even looking for employment; and on the other hand, leaders to at least an extent responsible for the situation in which Americans find themselves. Nowhere has this contradiction been more apparent than during the recent financial crisis, the worst since the Great Depression, which brings us to the third obvious problem.

The American financial system is so complex no one can determine precisely who is responsible or accountable for what. As economist Alan Blinder points out, several years after the worst of the financial crisis was over Americans still had only a limited understanding of what business did to trigger the crisis, and of what the U.S. government did in response. It gets worse: the government itself contributed to the crisis by deregulation, by, for example, repealing (in 1999) the Glass-Steagall Act, which had restricted affiliations between banks and securities firms. Blinder writes that one of his own "biggest frustrations was how little explanation the American people ever heard from their leaders, whether in or out of government . . . which remains true right up to the present day."[19]

During the waning months of his administration, President George W. Bush virtually dropped out of sight. And though President Barack Obama was vastly more visible, he never provided the American people with the explanation they deserved. By default then, the job of explaining the financial crisis, which nearly led to financial catastrophe, was outsourced to private sector leaders who, not surprisingly, failed to take it on. "While our financial industry is allegedly teaming with brilliant people who understand all this stuff," writes Blinder, "hardly any industry leaders have stepped up to explain what happened, much less to apologize." One might reasonably conclude, then, that the reason for the failure to detail what happened is that no single individual—no person with either positional or expert authority—was both clever enough to understand it and intrepid enough to explain it so that ordinary people could understand.

What we do know, of course, is that to some extent, in some way, people—public sector leaders, private sector leaders—are responsible. This raises, however, another problem: the "problem of many hands." The problem of many hands is when a policy failure is so complex, so multifaceted, and with so many different players in so many different places that no single individual, or even group of individuals, is ultimately held to account.

The financial crisis was just such a case. Who should bear the blame for what happened? President George W. Bush? After all, things unraveled on his watch. Congress? Clearly it failed, among other things, to play the part of watchdog, to sustain or enact legislation that would have precluded the calamity. Cabinet officers—most obviously Secretary of the Treasury Henry Paulson, his successor, Secretary of the Treasury Timothy Geithner, or both? Chairmen of the Federal Reserve—Alan Greenspan or his successor, Ben Bernanke? Or maybe key government regulators? Or ratings agencies? Or bankers—any bankers, commercial bankers, investment bankers? Or traders, all those experts on derivatives and credit default swaps, terms most of us cannot even begin to understand? Chief executive officers—at least those in the financial services industry? Or maybe the media, for blowing big the various bubbles—the tech bubble, the stock bubble, the bond bubble, the housing bubble? There's blame enough to go around—which is why no one, no single individual or institution, has ultimately been held responsible for what turned out to be the nation's worst financial crisis in eighty years.

Interestingly, similarly, no single individual or institution has been credited with saving the nation from financial disaster, with enabling it since 2008 to slowly but certainly dig itself out, at least to a modest degree. (The most recent economic recovery has been weak, in contrast with earlier such recoveries. The economy has grown at an average annual rate of just 2.3 percent since the recession ended, versus a 4.1 percent average for the first four years of other expansions since World War II.) Maybe history will ultimately render a judgment. But for the moment, twenty-first-century America seems saddled with a capitalist system so complex that when things are bad we have no idea who ultimately to hold to account—and when things are good we have no idea who properly to credit.

This is not to say that we don't try to lay blame. In the immediate aftermath of the recent crisis there was a backlash—a tide of anger by followers against leaders and a tide of anger by some leaders against other leaders. In the 2010 midterm elections, the American electorate turned hard against the Democratic president and Democratic congress, leaving the House with the most Republican members since 1946. Congress, in turn, attacked the Federal Reserve, questioning its political and fiduciary powers, even its constitutionality. And there was a general backlash against the idea that government is good, even that it should intervene to save the system from its own worse excesses. The rise of the Tea Party was perhaps the most visible and consequential manifestation of the backlash, its various anti-tax, anti-spending, anti-deficit, and anti-government positions testimony to anger in the heartland.[20]

Tellingly, leaders in the private sector, most obviously in the financial services industry, by and large got away with whatever it was they did, or did not do. They were not held to adequate account because (1) what they did was too complicated, too obscure for ordinary Americans to understand; (2) there was no easy, obvious way for ordinary Americans to hold their feet to the fire; (3) they left few fingerprints; (4) the investigative role of the press, especially of old media, has been diminished; (5) the institutions that some of them head are designated, if only sotto voce, "too big to fail"; and (6) political leaders are loathe to go after corporate leaders because they depend on them. Too much money in the political system necessarily implies too heavy a reliance by public sector leaders on their private sector counterparts. Where else to get the big bucks it now takes to run even the most modest of political campaigns?

Not long before the 2012 presidential election, more Americans thought Mitt Romney would do a better job of handling the nation's economy than Barack Obama.[21] Of course, in the end Romney lost and Obama won. Still, the poll was a measure of what Americans thought of Obama as an economic leader—not much. Though he and his team might reasonably be credited with pulling the nation back from the precipice in the immediate aftermath of the financial crisis, there was widespread dissatisfaction with the president's performance. It turns out that this is typical: though we expect our public officials, presidents in particular, to effectively manage the nation's economy, they tend, typically, to disappoint. They tend, typically, to disappoint because, among other reasons, the degree of control they have over the economy is, at most, modest.

So why does it seem that *economic* leadership in twenty-first-century America is in a class by itself—*that* difficult for leaders in general to exercise? First are the complexities of modern capitalism. On a theoretical level they are difficult if not impossible to master; on a practical level they are difficult if not impossible to tame.

Second, even the experts, such as the president's economic advisors, cannot compensate for whatever the executive's deficiencies. When Obama was elected, neither he nor his vice president, Joe Biden, had any demonstrable economic experience or expertise. Worse, economic experts tend themselves to disagree, both ideologically and intellectually, and they practice a trade that remains in the end opaque. Precisely because economics is "the dismal science," it's not uncommon for experts in the field to differ radically, for example, when long-time *New York Times* columnist Floyd Norris wrote that the economic forecasts of the generally respected Congressional Budget Office were "almost certainly wrong."[22]

Third, economic leadership is difficult to exercise because power is diffused, divided between, among others, the president and the Congress, the White House and the Federal Reserve, the Federal Reserve and the financial services industry, and the public sector and the private one. There is no single lever of power.

Fourth, the economy has gone global. What happens in the United States affects what happens elsewhere in the world. And what happens elsewhere in the world affects what happens in the United States.[23]

Finally, economic leadership is so difficult to exercise because of democratic followership—because the "grave problems of American public finance will not yield to the populist solutions that command political and public support."[24] The United States is not a planned, socialist economy but, for better and worse, a capitalist, democratic one. What this implies is an inevitable tension between capitalism on the one hand and democracy on the other. Capitalism promises property and the pursuit of happiness—but it does not necessarily deliver. When it does not, when it disappoints, democratic discontents simmer. The Tea Party, and the Occupy Movement, and the elections of progressives such as Massachusetts senator Elizabeth Warren and New York City mayor Bill de Blasio are only the most visible manifestations of these democratic discontents—of the frequently yawning gap between what we want and what we get.

6 INSTITUTIONS

AS I USE IT HERE, the word *institution* has, perhaps, gone out of fashion. It has something of an antiquated ring, a word seemingly reserved for use by academics, pollsters, and, occasionally, the press. So what do we mean when we speak of American *institutions*?

One way to respond to the question is to turn to a well-known article on the subject, written some thirty years ago by two prominent social scientists, titled "The Decline of Confidence in American Institutions."[1] The piece was prompted by the finding that by the early 1980s one public opinion poll after another registered a steady decline in trust of government, and of business, and of other institutions as well, including the press, the military, and the various professions. In other words, "American institutions" was in this case defined as it usually is, as organizations, or establishments, or regularized relationships that constitute core components of American life.

Given the perceived importance of institutions, declines in institutional trust are nearly invariably taken seriously as emblematic of decline overall. American institutions were in the past and are in the present considered the bedrock of the American experiment, the foundation of everything else. If our faith in institutions erodes, so, it is presumed, does our faith in the United States of America and, indeed, in democracy more generally.

In truth, it's not completely clear that trust in American institutions is the powerful indicator it is widely presumed to be. What is clear is that this measure has been considered for three-quarters of a century to be of significance, replete with political, economic, social, and cultural implications. What is equally clear is that our confidence in American institutions has waxed and waned over the past seventy-five years, being relatively low during the 1930s, the years of the Great Depression, ascending thereafter considerably higher "until by 1965 the great majority of those interviewed by various pollsters were giving consistently positive evaluations" of institutions in every area of American life.[2] It turned out though that the mid-1960s were the high point—not since then have Americans been so positively disposed. In fact, by every measure our overarching confidence in American institutions has continued to decline, and continues to do so even now. The numbers are relentlessly grim, the long-term trend being "down, down, down," with new lows recorded only recently for Americans' level of confidence in public schools, churches, banks, and television news.[3]

Obviously these new lows ensnare not only the various institutions but also those who lead and manage them. *Institutions* are something of an abstraction; *individuals*, in contrast, are not. They are clearly identifiable, by name and by face, which is why in the second decade of the twenty-first century all leaders of all major American institutions are under constant scrutiny, for both their ethics and their efficacy. To quote from the article mentioned above, "The decline of confidence appears to be general in nature but not fundamental or systemic. The system is good, but it is not performing well because the people in charge are inept and untrustworthy."[4] So when the Internal Revenue Service runs into trouble for singling out conservative groups, no one seriously proposes abolishing the agency itself. Instead we chew up and spit out those who lead and manage it—it is they who are held personally and professionally responsible for what went wrong. One could go so far as to say that when trust in American institutions declines, what is really declining is trust not in the institutions per se—again, they are abstractions—but trust in the individuals who head them. As developmental psychologist Howard Gardner similarly has argued, we are nearly devoid now of "societal trustees," leading men and women who are widely renowned, esteemed, and valued for their intelligence, impartiality, and integrity.[5] Of course, on one level this is nothing new. As indicated earlier in this book, Americans have never been disposed to being, exactly, deferential. However, on another level this growing disrespect across the board, this declining appreciation for what is peculiarly American—American institutions—is an indicator.

For some years (beginning in 2005 and ending in 2012) the Harvard Kennedy School's Center for Public Leadership (with which I am affiliated) compiled a report titled *National Leadership Index*. Unlike the earlier study to which I referred, and unlike so many other studies of "American institutions," this one was a metric not of the institutions themselves but of those who lead them. In fact, the word *institution* was not even mentioned in the *National Leadership Index*—suggesting again how vague is the word, how fungible its applications. Rather, the *Index* was a "multidimensional measure of the public's confidence in leadership within different sectors of [American] society."[6] In other words, the *Index* employed the word *sector* the way that other similar surveys employed the word *institution*. Once again, these sectors, or institutions, were presumed the bedrock of American life. The assumption, even if unwritten, was that if our faith in them erodes, so would our faith in the American Dream.

The *Index* provided polling results on leaders in thirteen different sectors: military, medical, nonprofit and charity, local government, religion, Supreme Court, business, state government, education, Executive Branch, news media, Wall Street, and Congress. Clearly the distinctions were somewhat arbitrary; just as clearly, taken together they provided an overview of levels of confidence in leaders and in institutions in twenty-first-century America. As we would anticipate, the news on leaders of institutions was virtually identical to the news on institutions themselves. In both there have been upticks and downticks. (For example, business leaders did better in 2012 than they did a year earlier.) In both, some institutions or leaders fared better than others. (For example, our levels of confidence in the military, and in military leaders, have been far higher than our levels of confidence in the Congress and in our Congressional representatives.) And in both, the overarching trend has been relentlessly down, not up.

The 2012 *National Leadership Index* survey found that fully 69 percent of Americans believed that we are in a leadership crisis. Moreover, "confidence in sectors [institutions] that are critical to the nation's strength and strategic direction remains abysmally low." Worth noting is that these grim polling results pertained not only to the usual bogeymen of American institutions, such as large corporations (Wall Street). They pertained as well to institutions of which Americans remained rather proud until rather recently, such as the nation's schools.

The *Index* pointed out that "educational leadership, so important to the country's future competitive strength, continues to languish in fifth place from the bottom, among the sectors for whom Americans have 'not much' confidence."[7] Gallup polls confirm the results: in 2012 only 29 percent of Americans expressed a "great deal" or "quite a lot" of confidence in the nation's public schools. These figures are down from just a few years earlier, and they are dramatically down from 1973, which was the first year that Gallup included public schools in its "Confidence in Institutions" polls. Then the figure was 58 percent of Americans giving their strong approval, which suggests that over the past forty years confidence in the nation's schools has dropped by roughly one-half.[8] I might add that this lack of confidence is well founded. U.S. fifteen-year-olds have made no progress on international achievement exams; in fact they continue to fall further behind in comparative rankings in math, science, and reading.[9] Similarly, I might repeat an earlier point, which is that another previously widely admired institution, organized religion, has suffered some of the same setbacks. Again, along with banks and television news, Gallup's 2012 "Confidence in Institutions" survey found that America's religious institutions were saddled with levels of trust that were at record lows.

Even this brief overview yields several findings. First, levels of trust in American institutions have declined across the board, in some cases precipitously. No institutions and no leaders of institutions have escaped being tarnished by this brush. Second, levels of trust in some institutions are depressingly, arguably dangerously, low. Again, this applies not only to the usual culprits, such as banks, but also to previously widely admired institutions including Congress and the presidency. By every measure, according to every poll, Congress is in the pits—our level of confidence in our national legislature is lower even than in Wall Street. The presidency, not incidentally, does not fare all that much better. Twenty-three percent fewer Americans have confidence in the executive branch than did just a decade ago.[10]

Finally, the loss of confidence in American institutions—in the American Dream—is widespread, not confined to any single group or demographic. Americans of every stripe, ordinary people, followers, are fed up. They are angry or at least totally turned off by what has become of their beloved country. Says journalist Andrew Sullivan, "People have stopped trusting institutions. We live in a society in which *The New York Times* feeds us government lies, the United States government presides over the systematic torture of prisoners, and the Vatican presides over a global conspiracy of child rape. Do you really expect anyone under 30 to trust institutions anymore?"[11] (Sullivan's tirade roughly coincided with the resignation of Pope Benedict.) And says sociologist Laura Hansen: "We have lost our gods. We lost faith in the media. Remember Walter Cronkite? We lost it in our culture: You can't point to a movie star who might inspire us, because we know too much about them. We lost it in politics, because we know too much about politicians' lives. We've lost it—that basic sense of trust and confidence—in *everything.*"[12]

Why such a decline in confidence in American institutions? Is it justified? And what are the implications? Of course, there are several different reasons, each of which is related to the specifics of the situation, and each of which is also related to the times in which we live. The reasons for the decline in confidence in Wall Street stem in good part from the recent financial crisis, while the reasons for the decline in confidence in religious institutions do not. What then are the overarching explanations for the overarching deterioration?

First, as earlier indicated, changing culture and technologies have twinned to entitle and empower followers to take on their leaders, to challenge them openly, and freely, publicly, to criticize them. We know more. We are less intimidated by people in positions of authority. And we feel no particular compunction about humbling or even humiliating them. Leaders are convenient scapegoats for whatever is going wrong. As Stein Ringen concludes about the U.S., simply, depressingly, the "foundations of good government are eroding, or have eroded."[13]

Second, things have changed so much so fast that we feel adrift, unmoored, not fully in control even of our own destinies. Once we lived where we were born and stayed put. No more. Once we had jobs that lasted a lifetime. No more. Once we could depend on our elected officials to collaborate and compromise, no matter their partisan preferences. No more. Once the United States of America was the unchallenged leader of the so-called Free World and China was a backwater. No more.

Third, Americans can see with their own eyes how their country is failing to measure up—not only in comparison to its own previously high standards, but in comparison to other countries. Anyone who travels knows that relative to many nations in other parts of the world, America's infrastructure is antiquated. (It ranks twenty-fifth, behind countries that include Oman and Barbados.[14]) Anyone who follows such statistics knows that relative to many other nations around the world, Americans' life expectancy has fallen behind. And anyone who has an interest in schools knows that relative to many other nations around the world America's system of education is as indicated, considerably less than first rate. I could go on.

It's hard to argue against the obvious. It's hard to argue that the decline in confidence in American institutions is without foundation. Above all, perhaps, as has been clear for years, the profound partisan differences between the two major parties, Republicans and Democrats, and even within them, have hampered and finally hamstrung the political process. The extreme distinctions and differences have led to an "us versus them" mentality, which, in turn, has precluded the collaborations and compromises critical to a separated system. Even politicians who once were friends or at least consistently cordial, "seem now barely able to countenance each other's presence." One hot summer's day in 2013, for example, Senate Republican leader Mitch McConnell suggested that his Democratic counterpart, Senator Harry Reid, would be remembered as "the worst leader of the Senate ever."[15]

No wonder we suffer such high levels of public mistrust in the federal government. They are predictable, understandable responses to a political process as obviously dysfunctional, as dyspeptic, as ours and to politicians as obviously ineffectual as ours. In his memoir, the widely esteemed former secretary of defense, Robert Gates, is nothing short of scathing about the U.S. Congress: "I saw Congress as uncivil, incompetent at fulfilling their basic constitutional responsibilities (such as timely appropriations), micromanagerial, parochial, hypocritical, egotistical, thin-skinned and prone to put self (and re-election) before country."[16]

Of course, other institutions are not exempt from blame. For example, the press plays a role in degrading our political culture, in part because it recently experienced nothing less than an institutional transformation. Traditional journalism has been under siege by new technologies that gave rise to changing organizations and methods of information distribution. One of the several different consequences of these changes is that media new and old tend now to exacerbate extremism rather than to support centrism. Moreover, the concentration of ownership in big conglomerates has "exaggerated the pursuit of economic success at the cost of sacrificing journalistic values."[17]

But, lest I myself fall into the trap of condemning those at the top while exempting from responsibility everyone else, let me hasten again to add that we ourselves, the American people, are also to blame for what's gone wrong. In addition to the problem of our overweening apathy—for example, the level of our participation in elections other than for president is appallingly low—is the problem of our collective ignorance. Great swaths of the American people cannot identify any of the three branches of government, and know little or nothing about how the political process is supposed to work. In a 2011 *Newsweek* survey, 29 percent of Americans could not name the vice president; 73 percent could not say why we fought the Cold War; 44 percent were unable to define the Bill of Rights; and 6 percent could not locate Independence Day on a calendar. Again, comparisons between the United States and other countries are, at the least, unsettling. In 2009, 75 percent of the British people were able to identify the Taliban, whereas only 58 percent of Americans could do the same.[18]

In the event, whatever the constellation of explanations, there is no evidence that the decline in confidence in American institutions will revert anytime soon. As suggested, it's not completely clear that this much matters and, if it does, precisely how. In other, more elegant, words, "the costs of lost trust are not amenable to precise calculation."[19]

Still, some are persuaded that if only we somehow became again more trusting, believed again both in our institutions and in our leaders, America would be healthier, better, and so would the American people. How, though, might this be done? How to restore trust when so many forces seem to preclude such a reversal? Social scientists have, in fact, done some work on "trust repair," though up to now most studies have been conducted in the laboratory, not in the so-called real world. In addition, "trust repair" generally refers to overcoming the deleterious effects of wrongdoing by a particular (identifiable) someone(s) that requires an apology or compensation of some sort. This is in contrast to trust repair that, in theory at least, would need to be systemwide, and applied to both institutions and their leaders. This second is far larger and vaguer a task, more difficult obviously even to begin to take on.

Several professors of management did tackle a somewhat analogous problem by asking how, subsequent to the recent financial crisis, trust in financial institutions might reasonably be restored. First, they demonstrated that trust, in fact, had been violated, concluding that the crisis constituted a "massive trust failure at the systems level."[20] Next they explored what, more precisely, it means to say that trust was violated, arguing that in this case at least it implied a lack of ability (risk management failed), a lack of benevolence (rules of fairness and concern for stakeholders were violated), and a lack of integrity (ample evidence of deception and dishonesty). Finally, they applied the literature on trust repair to the global financial crisis.

By and large this literature is based on examinations of single organizations, as opposed to the many organizations that, together, constitute an institution (or "sector"). Therefore, extrapolating from these findings, applying them to systems considerably more complex than those on which the research was based, is problematical. Still, the researchers suggested several "institutional trust-repair strategies" that themselves are indicative. They include changes in governance that hold management to greater account, changes in mission and strategy that require increasing liquidity and decreasing risk, changes in culture that emphasize core values, and changes in leadership and management that range from the more substantial to the purely cosmetic.

When I say that these institutional trust-repair strategies are themselves "indicative," what I mean to suggest is how feeble, even unrealistic they are when measured against the magnitude of the task at hand, This is not to say that the strategies are stupid or wrongheaded. Rather, it is to point out that however persuasive they appear on paper, they would be so difficult to implement, and subsequently to sustain, that they are unlikely over time to reverse a long-term trend—to stop or even slow the decline of confidence in American institutions. There is no evidence whatsoever that any of these strategies would work vis-à-vis the Congress, or the presidency, or the press, or for that matter educational institutions, religious institutions, or any other sort of institutions. The overweening issue is the size of the problem of mistrust. It transcends any single institution and any single individual. It is endemic to life in twenty-first-century America, endemic to the context within which we live, within which leaders lead.

Differences among and between generations confirm, not disconfirm, that what I am describing is a phenomenon much more likely to be enduring than evanescent. The fact is that young people are even less disposed than their elders to trust people in positions of authority—leaders of institutions. "Many youths withhold trust from distant targets such as political leaders and other figures in public life. Furthermore, their withholding tends to be passive, which indicates a lack of motivation to even consider extending trust."[21] Similarly, young people are less inclined than older ones to trust those they don't know. Whereas older people generally express a willingness "to extend at least thin trust" to those with whom they're unfamiliar, younger people are more cautious. They're more skeptical—at least until they have evidence it's safe for them to be otherwise.[22] It's possible of course that people change over time—become more trusting as they age. It's equally possible, even probable, that succeeding generations will have even less confidence in American institutions than do their immediate predecessors.

American institutions are not now what once they were. Or, at least, they seem to us in the present not to be what they were in the past. Perhaps we romanticize what's long gone and demonize what's here and now. However, from the perspective of a leader trying to get others to follow, to go along, it does not much matter. The bottom line is that even the best and the brightest of the leadership class are now saddled with a reputational problem. Both they and the institutions for which they are responsible carry an albatross—skepticism, even suspicion—that cumulates to a considerable, cumbersome burden.

7 ORGANIZATIONS

THE TOP-DOWN MANAGEMENT structure with which most of us are most familiar first proliferated in the U.S. in the second half of the nineteenth century. Corporate barons discovered that the easiest way to "govern hundreds of thousands of miles of railroad" was to set up a chain of command, which extended from central offices in New York or Chicago to field offices on the frontier.[1] Once this same system proved effective in leading and managing organizations more generally, it was extended to large banks and telephone companies and, in time, to PC manufacturers and multinational data-processing firms. It's no surprise: hierarchy is prominent in all species and across all cultures for good reason. It "reduces conflict, helps with role differentiation, and vastly increases coordination."[2]

Hierarchy in organizations was codified early in the twentieth century by the German sociologist Max Weber, who among his other contributions is widely considered the most influential thinker on organizations ever. In his classic *The Theory of Social and Economic Organization*, Weber explored the nature of organizational authority, concluding that there were three major types: rational-legal, traditional, and charismatic. The first of these applied to, and in time came to define, organizational life in the twentieth century.

Rational-legal authority was objective, impersonal, and logical. It implied certain rules and regulations that applied to everyone within the organization's "sphere of competence," including the leader. The leader was, however, separate and distinct, responsible for the organization as a whole. It was he—yes he—who was at the apex of the organizational pyramid.[3] However, the leader also had important subordinates, who while on the one hand were under an immediate superior, on the other hand were authority figures themselves. They, the "administrative staff," exercised authority over other members of the organization, who were lower on the pyramidal hierarchy than they. Ultimately, if the organization was a workplace, every employee, up the organizational ladder and down, was under a manager. And every employee, up the organizational ladder and down, was subject to the organization's rules and regulations, at least while at work.[4]

Another seminal figure in organization theory was another early twentieth-century German sociologist, Robert Michels. Michels developed the "iron law of oligarchy." The law declared first that organizations (oligarchies) were inevitable in the twentieth century, if only because those at the top were willing to take on, in exchange for rewards that included money and power, whatever the collective work. The law declared second that as organizations became larger and more complex, superiors were likely to be better educated, more expert at the task at hand than their subordinates, or both.

Finally, the iron law of oligarchy declared that even in groups and organizations that purportedly were democratic, as these organizations increased in size, members at the bottom could not possibly control those at the top. "The members have to give up the idea of themselves as conducting or even supervising the whole administration," Michels wrote, for they will be compelled in the end to turn over to "salaried officials" most of the important tasks. The rank and file will ultimately have to "content themselves" with limited information and "summary reports," which is why the law of oligarchy is ironclad.[5] It dictates that all organizations inevitably become hierarchies (bureaucracies), led inevitably by a small group of leaders who inevitably are self-serving.

All this was theory for what in practice became the single most important way people in the twentieth century grouped: the hierarchically structured organization. Of course, hierarchies did not everywhere apply; in general, only industrialized or industrializing countries had organizations as we conceive of them. Nevertheless, they were so dominant a model that by and large working outside the home, certainly in the U.S., came to be equated with working in organizations, working in places that structurally were pyramids. While not all organizations were large, even those that were small usually adopted and adapted in some general way the hierarchical model that Weber and Michels had earlier described.

The bottom line is that for over one hundred years the idea of the organization—as first evidenced in practice in the late nineteenth century and as first evidenced in theory in the early twentieth—dominated American thinking about how those of us in the modern world should and did order ourselves. From the beginning and for decades to come the model that prevailed and persisted had the leader at the top, with everyone else arrayed and arranged somewhere below. In the middle were those who in time were called mid-level managers, and at the base were most of the members, and the lowliest of members.

Though it applies equally to all organizations, historically the organizational model in which the leader clearly is dominant has been studied most closely by those who focus on the private sector. This explains why American business schools and the literature on business in America have long paid more attention, much more attention, to leaders and managers, to executives and elites, than to anyone else.

This is not to say that organizational theory has been focused always and only on leaders, on those at the pinnacle of the corporate hierarchy. As we have seen, even early on there were some references to followers—there was some research and writing on employees as well as employers, which was, not incidentally, vaguely in keeping with democratic theory. An example of a relevant researcher is the aforementioned Douglas McGregor, who in the 1960s developed his "Theory X" and "Theory Y," with implications both in theory and practice for relations between superiors and subordinates. Further, in the private sector there were some (proximate) contextual components considered important, such as product cycles and market shares. And in the public sector there was public administration, an area of study centered not on organizations in business but on those in government, such as, say, the U.S. Department of Defense or the Office of the Mayor in Little Rock, Arkansas.

Still, it's safe to say that in the past half century the study of organizations usually though by no means always meant the study of leaders and managers, and it's similarly safe to say that usually though by no means always these leaders and managers were in the private sector, not in the public or nonprofit one. As management professor Sydney Finkelstein and his colleagues have noted, "hundreds of academic and applied articles, books, and monographs on top executives and their organizations have been written in the past twenty-some years. It is now rare to pick up any issue of a major management or strategy journal and not find at least one article dealing with top executives."[6]

Even the study of corporate governance—of heightened interest since the recent financial crisis and the subsequent demand for greater accountability—has the leader at the center. To be sure, one of the reasons for the emphasis on corporate governance is to remind corporate governors to take into account not only those within an organization, but also those without, stakeholders such as customers and communities. Still, most experts on corporate governance continue to focus and even fixate on the corporate elite: members of boards and, more pointedly and prominently, chief executive officers who have "responsibility for the running of the company's business." What this suggests is that even in those cases in which the board chair plays a relatively powerful role, it still is the CEO around whom everything and everyone continues to pivot.[7]

Obviously then, followers, subordinates, and employees have been tangential to the study of organizational behavior, while leaders, superiors, and employers have been central. Recent changes in conventional thinking are, then, a shift away from the traditional hierarchical model of organizational life that held sway for so long. Put directly, it took until the twenty-first century for the twentieth-century model finally to give way, not radically or dramatically, but perceptibly. Weber's conception of "rational-legal authority" is still everywhere in evidence, as is Michels's "iron law of oligarchy." But by now both have been tempered by time, softened and changed in ways that have implications not only for those on high but for those in the middle and at the bottom as well.

There was evidence of change as early as twenty, thirty years ago—not incidentally or coincidentally in the wake of the rights revolutions of the late 1960s and early 1970s—when questions began to be raised about the purported virtues of the traditional hierarchical model. These questions centered on how many layers of management really were needed, and on whether too many managers and too much management interfered with, rather than contributed to, invention and innovation. The organizational changes that ultimately ensued were further in consequence of the changing technologies, which eventually mandated decreasing reliance on physical capital and increasing reliance on human capital. There was, in other words, a growing sense that the *knowledge worker*—a term first coined by Peter Drucker—so essential to the burgeoning knowledge economy, might not exactly thrive on hierarchy.

From the beginning the verb *flatten*, as in "to flatten," was used to describe what should happen. But early on "the flattened firm" suggested something somewhat different from what it does today. A decade ago the discussion centered on eliminating "layers of intervening management," on eliminating unnecessary or redundant largely mid-level managers in the interest of efficiency, productivity, and innovation. But, as it turned out, this change actually expanded rather than contracted the authority of the CEO, the chief executive officer. For as a result of the fewer managerial layers, the CEO, the leader, ended up with more direct reports, not fewer. A 2003 survey of three hundred U.S. companies found that during the fifteen years immediately previous, the number of division heads who reported directly to their CEOs went up by 300 percent, while the number of levels in the managerial hierarchy, between division heads and CEOS, went down by 25 percent.[8] A study that came out in 2012 similarly found that the flattened firm was "not as advertised." Instead of pushing decisions down to lower-level managers, as was the original intention, the flattened firm actually had more CEO involvement with direct reports, not less, "suggesting a more hands-on CEO at the pinnacle of the hierarchy."[9]

In spite of unanticipated consequences such as these, and in spite of unending debates about the various virtues and deficits of the flattened hierarchy, in the past several decades the conviction that at least somewhat flatter is at least somewhat better gradually took hold. In 1980, fewer than 20 percent of companies on the *Fortune* 1000 list claimed at least some sort of team management structure. By 1990 it was 50 percent, and by 2000 it was 80 percent.[10] Obviously, not every organization adapted in ways that ultimately were meaningful. Moreover, even now many and maybe even most organizations retain rather a rigidly hierarchical governance structure—not so distant from Weber's original conception. Gradually, however, there evolved the conventional wisdom that even the most hidebound organizations would do well to be somewhat flatter in the future than they had been in the past. Even the most hidebound organizations were advised "to flatten their informal channels of communication and influence, which all management theory admits are as important . . . as an organization's formal structures."[11]

But at its most extreme, the flattened firm was something else altogether: it was so flat as to eliminate virtually entirely the pyramidal hierarchy. In fact, taken to its logical conclusion, the flat organization was a leaderless organization. Ori Brafman and Rod Beckstrom's influential book, *The Starfish and the Spider*, exemplified the ideology. Spider organizations were old organizations, dated fixtures ill-suited to life in the twenty-first century. They were coercive and hierarchical, they depended on maintaining order inside a certain (physical) space, and someone was always in charge. Starfish organizations, in contrast, were decentralized. People could make suggestions, but they could not give orders. No one could give orders because no one was in any obvious way expected or supposed to lead. Moreover, the group, or the organization, or whatever the nomenclature, did not have a single, central physical plant. Instead it was distributed. The work was done in more than one location so that if, for some reason, work had to stop in one place it could go on in another. In short, everything that spider organizations were, starfish organizations were not. Above all, the former were centralized, while the latter were decentralized.[12]

What began then as something of a tentative experiment not much more than a decade ago has since become, at least in some cases, a radical restructuring if not the elimination altogether of the pyramidal organizational structure. In 2012, the *Wall Street Journal* featured an article about a company called Valve Corporation, based in Washington, D.C. Here was a real-world example of a firm flattened in the extreme. There were no bosses. Instead, decisions on pay, on hiring and firing, and on determining which projects to take on were decided by employees.[13] In 2013, *New York* magazine carried a similar piece about a company called Menlo Innovations, based in Ann Arbor, Michigan. Here was another example of a firm as apparently flat as flat can be. Again, there were no bosses in any traditional sense, and no middle managers. Virtually everything was open and transparent, and virtually everything of any consequence was decided on not by a single leader, or even by a leadership team, but by the collective.[14]

Examples like these notwithstanding, the important point is that even in those cases that are the great majority, where the organization of today bears considerable resemblance to the organization of yesterday, the hierarchy is notably less rigid now than it was. What this inevitably suggests is not the elimination of the leader, but the diminishment of the leader. Put directly, leaders of twenty-first-century organizations are likely to have less power, authority, and influence than leaders of twentieth-century organizations. For even in those organizations that continue much more closely to resemble spiders than starfishes, some devolution of power and authority has got to the point not only of being considered best practice, but of being considered inevitable.

One of the ways in which the trend toward shared responsibility has manifested itself is the relatively recent preoccupation with the team. There is a shift away from the individual (leader) alone at the top and toward the small group—namely the by now ubiquitous team. Of course, in those cases in which the leader is more autocratic than democratic, teams matter less, or even not at all. But more than before, the leader is seen as one among several members of several groups—as one member of an executive team that, in tandem with other teams, shares responsibility for the whole. In fact, the immense popularity of the "team" (in theory and practice) is itself indicative. For the executive team is, in any case, a compromise. It is a compromise between the old Weberian model in which the organizational leader stands alone astride a pyramidal hierarchy, and the new model, the starfish model, in which the organizational leader is all but obliterated. The team occupies the middle ground. On the one hand the leader is no longer a solitary figure, singly responsible for organizational outcomes. But on the other hand the leader has not abdicated; executive team notwithstanding, the leader is where the action is.

Executive teams, or top management teams as they are also known, can be analyzed in several different ways, from the perspective of their composition, say, or their structure, or their process.[15] For example, a recent study found that not only has the size of the average executive team changed dramatically in recent years—it has doubled, grown from an average of five members to an average of ten—its composition has changed dramatically was well. The number of members of executive teams has gone up because many CEOs along with their boards have decided it is to their advantage to include among them functional managers. Unlike general managers, functional managers have the experience and expertise to assume responsibility for single, specialized areas, such as information (technology), finance, or marketing, with which CEOs, especially in this day and age, might well not be sufficiently familiar.[16]

Generally left unsaid, though necessarily implied, is that more than before, leaders of all stripes, not just CEOs of large corporations, are obliged to defer to those who know more than do they about a particular project or area—especially technology. In other words, Weber's model of rational legal authority, which was so obviously applicable to twentieth-century organizations, is not so obviously applicable to twenty-first-century organizations. The complexities of the context within which organizations currently are located, the complexities of organizations themselves, and the complexities of the challenges that organizations face, mandate against an organizational structure that is rigidly hierarchical and therefore, by definition, leader-centric.

Business school professor Amy Edmondson has gone so far as to transform the noun *team* into the verb *teaming*. She notes that while "many organizations still rely on the top-down, command and control approaches that fueled growth and profitability in the industrial era," twenty-first-century problems mandate twenty-first-century solutions.[17] Such solutions require the collaborative work—across disciplines, companies, sectors, and nations—that the word *teaming* necessarily implies.

Two final notes: first, to repeat, while most of the literature on organizations is about organizations in business, the points I make here apply across the board, to government organizations, nonprofit organizations, educational organizations, religious organizations, military organizations, and so on. Every one of them has been affected by the changing times, by the idea of the flatter hierarchy, by the idea that leaders should lead in teams as opposed to leading alone, and by the idea that followers, subordinates, should, for various reasons, have a voice.

Second, a comment on the connection between what happens within organizations and what happens without, even far without. In particular, what happens in the public sector, in politics, relates to and has an impact on what happens in the private sector, in business. Attitudes toward corporate leaders are not independent of attitudes toward political leaders, or for that matter toward any other kinds of leaders. Moreover, they connect to the temper of the times, to the zeitgeist that in the twenty-first century is not only, not merely, national. It is also international. Put directly, the push to democratize organizational life is connected to, even in consequence of, the push to democratize political life. In neither circumstance is the leader history. But in neither circumstance do leaders now have as much power, authority, or influence as they did even a generation ago. In democracies at least, the voice of the people, of ordinary people, has never been louder or more ubiquitous. This is not to say that the people speak in one voice, or that the many (followers) control the few (leaders). Rather it is to say that, increasingly, plain people are insisting on participating—which is one of the reasons why flat is in fashion.

8 LAW

THAT THE UNITED STATES of America is governed by the rule of law has long been judged one of its greatest strengths. Americans depend on the law to protect them from arbitrary justice, and to regulate their economic system, which otherwise would be freewheeling to the point of self-destruction. More particularly, the U.S. Constitution always has been and still is considered the highest law in the land, and the bedrock on which all other U.S. laws are based.

In the beginning of the nineteenth century the United States was small and agrarian. By the end of that century the United States was urbanized, industrialized, and capitalist. During the intervening decades American law matured and came into its own, especially business law (to regulate such newfangled phenomena as corporations and commercial transactions), family law, and criminal law. But because the federal government was still rather modest in size, most legal activity was at the level of the state, not the nation.

In the twentieth century this changed. The government in Washington grew exponentially—it became what legal historian Lawrence Friedman has called an "administrative-welfare state"—and along with it the federal bureaucracy.[1] What followed, likely inevitably, was a similarly exponential expansion in the numbers of laws required to monitor the now large, in time very large, policymaking apparatus. A slew of new laws was passed even early in the twentieth century to regulate the various tasks for which the federal government was increasingly responsible—such as the first income tax law, the Sherman Anti-Trust Act (to protect consumers and small businesses), and the Food and Drugs Act.

The growing role of the law in America—and its growing impact on the exercise of leadership—was the result of great change, both political and economic. Franklin Roosevelt's New Deal was of itself a significant contributor to the explosive growth in the numbers of statutes, rules and regulations, and ordinances. "The Securities and Exchange Commission (SEC) was meant to be a watchdog for Wall Street. Federal insurance guaranteed bank accounts. The National Labor Relations Board regulated union elections and collective bargaining. The Social Security Act established a system of old-age pensions, among other programs. All were popular and durable innovations." And all required a spate of new laws first to enact them, and then to regulate them.[2]

Later in the twentieth century came other major changes, which further expanded the legal system. These included the various rights revolutions, which on the one hand were (to a degree) supported by the courts (as in *Brown v. Board of Education*) and on the other hand were themselves responsible for major new legislation that included the Civil Rights Act (1964), the Voting Rights Act (1965), the Age Discrimination in Employment Act (1967), and the Americans with Disabilities Act (1990). Predictably, laws such as these led each year to thousands of complaints to the various civil rights agencies, suggesting to some that Americans had become overly dependent on litigation as a cure for whatever it was that ailed them. Claims like these did not necessarily succeed, of course, but over time there were so many in number that civil rights law necessarily grew to the point at which it became a prominent part of American jurisprudence.[3]

For a constellation of reasons—including the complexity of contemporary society, modern technology, the heterogeneity of the American people, and the size of the social safety net—the most striking aspect of American law is how much there now is of it.[4] Not for nothing is the

U.S. known as a litigious society: nearly no aspect of American life is untouched by the law, exempt from its enveloping, some would say suffocating, embrace.

Obviously, this has demanded an enormous expansion of the legal profession. In fact, though in the past few years this growth has come to a halt—by 2013 at least half of American law schools had cut the size of their classes—the United States still has by far the largest legal profession in the world. In 2006, more than one million men and women were practicing law, a number that for many years grew far faster then the population overall. Which raises the question of what it is that all these lawyers actually do.

We know from our own experience that American lawyers help people obtain divorces, and sell their homes, and draft everyday legal documents such as wills. We also know, if only from watching television, that lawyers prosecute and defend criminals. Similarly, as indicated, we know that they get embroiled in various rights cases, going to court to protect individuals who for one or another reason have a claim or feel aggrieved. What we tend not to know, or to know only dimly, is that most lawyers in twenty-first-century America are in one or another way occupied with the nation's business. Small law firms generally work for small businesses; large law firms generally work for large businesses. The point is that a giant economy such as ours, which is counted in the trillions, not billions, is, again to quote Friedman, "an economy that generates deals, mergers, incorporations, buyouts; it is an economy with huge antitrust suits, huge tort actions, class action cases that last for years and call for whole armies of attorneys, patent and copyright matters on which the fates of industries rest. . . . It is an economy that floats on a sea of lawyers."[5]

Though it is little noted and even less understood, it seems obvious that the ubiquity of the law in twenty-first-century America must have an impact, does have an impact, on leadership in twenty-first-century America. It is not too much to say that the long arm of the law reaches leaders in government, and in business, and in nonprofits such as schools and hospitals, and in virtually every conceivable area of American life. Even religious leaders, who until relatively recently were generally immune to prosecution in the nation's courts, are now vulnerable.

This emphasis on, dependence on, the legal system as, so to speak, the court of last resort is a peculiarly American phenomenon. Americans have more adversarial legalism; we depend more than people in other countries on lawyers and lawsuits, on tort actions, and on actions against administrative agencies. This explains why only Americans feel that they are in a litigation crisis, and why so many American leaders think that they have no choice but to "lawyer up," to make certain that they have their own legal experts to protect them and the institutions for which they are responsible against legal liability.

America's uniquely litigious culture is directly responsible for complicating and constraining the lives of leaders—if only because it takes time and consumes resources. "Who benefits from the growth of complex and cumbersome regulation?" asks one critic. "The answer is lawyers. . . ."[6] He might have added *not* leaders, for attending to litigation, to the possibility thereof, or both is an important part of what leaders are paid now to do. Put directly, because of our litigious culture, our litigious policies, the threat of a lawsuit always looms, even if it turns out no lawsuit is actually filed.[7] This atypical, aggressive litigiousness is, I might point out, completely in keeping with American history and ideology. It is of a piece with our decentralized form of government, with our congenital distrust of authority, and with our proclivity to challenge whoever the authority figures, in this case turning to the courts to take on those who have more power, authority, and influence than do we.

The enormous proliferation in recent years of compliance officers opens a window on how the law impinges on leaders. Say you're the chief executive officer of an organization of some size, a business, or a hospital, or a school. How to protect yourself against a lawsuit, frivolous or otherwise? And, if you cannot protect against a lawsuit, how to protect yourself against the possibility that the lawsuit will do real damage? Bring on a compliance officer.

Not long ago compliance officers were hardly heard of and few in number. Now they're all over the place, charged with ensuring that companies, organizations of all kinds, comply with internal policies and, more important, with outside rules and regulations, especially regulatory requirements. "A compliance officer may review and set standards for outside communications by requiring disclaimers . . . or may examine facilities to ensure that they are accessible and safe. Compliance officers may also design or update internal policies to mitigate the risk of the company breaking laws and regulations, as well as lead internal audits of procedures."[8] Compliance officers are, in short, shock troops, intended to protect leaders and managers and other stakeholders against the unpleasant if predictable surprise of litigation.

Compliance officers are relatively well paid, especially in certain industries, such as biotech and pharmaceutical. Still, their services are in high demand, so how more specifically do they protect their superiors? By knowing whatever the relevant regulatory issues, and whatever the relevant federal and state laws and regulations. By developing, implementing, and maintaining an appropriate compliance program. By providing others in the organization with the necessary legal compliance training. And by properly responding if a violation is uncovered, either by someone on the inside (by management or an employee), or by someone on the outside (by government or the media).

Here is an example of how the law complicates leaders' lives. In the old days, running a restaurant was, if not easy, at least straightforward. One hundred years ago the idea that the owner or manager of a restaurant would have to worry about arcane legal niceties was unimaginable. But now everyone who runs a restaurant or who is responsible for providing any kind of food service must pay attention to, among other rules and regulations, the Americans with Disabilities Act (ADA). The ADA is a federal civil rights law that applies to people with disabilities and protects them against discrimination. The Equal Employment Opportunity Commission, a federal government agency, enforces the sections of the ADA that prohibit discrimination in employment. So far as the food services industry in particular is concerned, employees and, even more, employers, are well advised then to understand the relevant ADA mandates in order to comply in full. In fact, the food services industry has developed a guide specifically for leaders and managers in this particular line of work, cautioning them that "food service employers must avoid discriminating against people with disabilities while obeying strict public health rules. Food service workers with disabilities have rights under the ADA when applying for jobs or when working for a restaurant, cafeteria, or other food service employer."[9]

Arguably, though, it is leaders in education—superintendents, principals, teachers—who have been most affected by legislation such as the ADA. Consider the impact of the Americans with Disabilities Act Amendments Act, and Section 504 of the Rehabilitation Act, on the lives of such leaders in North Royalton, Ohio.

In a case involving a nine-year-old with an anxiety disorder, the Midwestern Division of the Office for Civil Rights (OCR), located in Cleveland, found several areas in which the North Royalton City School District had "failed to comport with the requirements of Section 504." As a result of the OCR's finding, it and the district reached a resolution in which North Royalton agreed to meet all requirements specified by the federal government. This meant that the district had to notify students, parents, faculty, and staff of all the revised procedures. It also meant that the district had to send a letter to the parents or guardians of all students currently receiving services under emergency allergy plans. The letter was to inform them of the revised Section 504 procedures, and of their right to request an evaluation under Section 504, at no cost to themselves, if they believed that their "child's medical impairment substantially limits one or more major life activity."[10]

I make no value judgment about this particular case or about the many thousands of others like it. But by providing some level of detail, I am pointing to how far now extends the reach of the law in America—how the law in America now affects leaders in America. School administrators nationwide are being obliged, legally as well as morally, to comply with a whole raft of federal enactments that, while well intended, nevertheless consume vast amounts of time, energy, and human and fiscal resources in ways that were not originally anticipated. (Recall the "law of unanticipated consequences.")

This drift toward a system of education dominated by legalisms and litigiousness, and by the bureaucracy required to sustain them, has not gone unnoticed. Reformers such as lawyer Philip Howard have wondered aloud about the harm done by the law both to school leaders and to the students to whom they ultimately are responsible. "How many rules are there in American schools?" Howard asks. No one really knows, but here is an indicator. In 2004 an inventory was made of all of the legal rules imposed on a particular New York City high school. "It found thousands of discrete legal requirements, imposed by every level of government. There was no act or decision—how to be fair, how to provide feedback, how to arrange the classroom, how to clean a window, how to keep files, how to order copier paper—that wasn't covered by a rule."[11] Again, the point is not that the law is bad, but that too much law in too many places might well be doing more harm than good, especially, arguably, to the leader's capacity to lead. In fact, in his book titled *The Rule of Nobody*, Howard takes his own argument to its logical extreme. He writes that federal, state, and local laws so completely hamstring all leaders of both parties that they have little leeway to exercise their own judgment.[12]

In yet another example of their enduring impact, Howard has found that the laws that distort schools—as well as bureaucracies more generally—are primarily a product of the rights revolutions of the 1960s and 1970s. Parents have come to believe that their children have a right to full-service primary and secondary schools. Parents have similarly come to believe that if such schools have not been provided, they have a legal right to challenge the system, to challenge in court those in charge with what is, in effect, malfeasance. The question is, have we gone too far? "The new rights are amorphous, a kind of catchall for protections against unfair authority. People assume that there's a right to due process on almost any decision that affects anyone, in the classroom, on the playing fields, in the workplace, you name it. Students regularly accuse teachers of violating their rights. This belief in legal rights, mainly unfounded, has become its own reality. Rights are everywhere."[13]

Product liability law, while in obvious ways very different, is nevertheless in one obvious way similar. It too has pervaded the system, and it too is a way for followers to get at leaders—for those without power, authority, or influence to hold responsible those with. In this case ordinary people have the right to hold legally liable a business that manufactures or sells a product that incurs injury to a buyer or to a user, even to a bystander, as a result of a defect or malfunction. In general, management is vulnerable to lawsuits based on the claim of a flaw in production, or of a defect in design, or of a failure to properly instruct or warn. (Sometimes federal regulators step in before the question of product liability even comes up. In 2013, in light of growing evidence that some of America's top-selling diabetes medicines could lead to pancreatic disease, regulators made the decision to review diabetes drugs produced by, among others, Merck and Bristol-Myers Squibb.[14])

But again, it's not so simple. There is serious debate about whether or not product liability law is in the general interest. While in principle such law would seem a social good—a way for Little People to hold Big Business accountable—there are downsides. The cost of product liability insurance (for which consumers ultimately pay) is high; when there's a well-publicized suit, business is hurt, sometimes unfairly; and it has not been proven that product liability laws necessarily have their intended deterrent effect.[15] What we do know though is this. Product liability law is like other bodies of law that were enacted only relatively recently: a complicated mix that has some obvious benefits and some obvious costs. What we also know is that whatever the social good, leaders typically consider them a drag. They limit leaders, whose preference is to be unfettered—by the law or, for that matter, by anything or anyone else.

Finally, a comment about the role of the law in the recent financial crisis or, more precisely, about the role of the law in the wake of the Great Recession—an issue about which there seem to be two, mutually exclusive, truths. On the one side is the general public, which to this day believes that in this instance crime paid, that by and large the distorters of truths and perpetrators of deception—that is, mostly leaders in financial services—got off scot-free. On the other side are many if not most leaders, certainly in financial services, who likely feel quite differently. While only a handful have been taken to court, in general executives in financial services are under far greater legal scrutiny today than they were before the crisis hit.

Everywhere there is evidence that the law is interceding more aggressively in the nation's financial system now than it did in the recent past.

NEW LAWS: It will take years to determine the ultimate impact of major new legislation, such as the Wall Street Reform and Consumer Protection Act, commonly known as Dodd-Frank. But its impact is already in evidence, legions of lawyers and compliance officers having been hired by banks, for example, to help them navigate the new regulatory landscape of a bill that is no fewer than 848 pages long.[16] In consequence of Dodd-Frank, new rules were established, such as the so-called Volcker Rule, intended to curb banks from proprietary trading in securities, derivatives, or futures, for their own gain. (The Volcker Rule is supposed to replace the aforementioned Glass-Steagall Act, which had separated commercial and investment banking.) There were new requirements as well, such as those that now mandate that big banks keep on hand enough cash, government bonds, and other high-quality assets to fund their operations for thirty days in the event of a severe economic turndown.

NEW TARGETS: The U.S. government is casting a wider legal net. For example, the Justice Department filed a claim against Standard & Poor's, a rating agency, alleging that it ignored its own standards by rating mortgage bonds so as to cause them to implode during the financial crisis—costing investors billions. Similarly, after a multiyear effort, federal authorities (primarily the Securities and Exchange Commission) finally secured from the giant hedge fund SAC Capital Advisors an agreement to plead guilty to insider trading violations and to pay a record penalty ultimately totaling $1.8 billion. (SAC was the first large Wall Street firm in a generation to confess to criminal conduct.) Said the U.S. attorney in Manhattan, Preet Bharara, after the settlement was reached, insider trading at SAC was "substantial, pervasive, and on a scale without precedent in the history of hedge funds."[17]

NEW CLAIMANTS: Because they smell blood, players not previously known for being litigious are going to court. (Sometimes they're incentivized by whistleblower laws, some of which were recently enacted under Dodd-Frank.) For example, two pension funds, the Laborers'

Local 265 Pension Fund of Cincinnati, Ohio, and the Plumbers and Pipefitters Local 572 Pension Fund of Nashville, Tennessee, filed a claim against BlackRock, the world's largest asset manager. They charged BlackRock with having systematically "looted" securities lending revenues from investors.

NEW DOCUMENTS: Somehow, some of the time, records are coming to light that previously were hidden. The means of disclosure vary, but e-mails, instant messages, tapes of phone conversations, and even plain old files are, for various reasons, including leaks, somewhat easier to come by and certainly easier (due to technology) to disseminate. Here is an example from the *Wall Street Journal*: "In one potentially ominous sign for banks, an internal report by a U.S. government watchdog says federally backed mortgage companies . . . may have lost more than $3 billion as a result of banks' alleged rate manipulations." The report was reviewed by the *Journal* even though it was described as "unpublished."[18] This is not even to speak of the likes of Julian Assange, Bradley/Chelsea Manning, and Edward Snowden, who are responsible for government leaks of unprecedented size and consequence. And it is not even to speak of politicians such as New Jersey's Governor Chris Christie, unwittingly ensnared by documents, initially in this case e-mails, in a mortifying and debilitating political scandal.

NEW HUMILIATIONS: None have died from being openly shamed. Nevertheless, financial services executives recently paraded before the American people cannot have found the experience exhilarating. When in March 2013 Senator Carl Levin took on JPMorgan Chase chief financial officer Douglas Braunstein, to quiz him about statements he had earlier made to investors, Braunstein was manifestly discomforted and Levin manifestly exasperated. "I'm going to read this to you," Levin said, waving Braunstein's past statements in the air. "I'm going to keep reading it to you until you give me the answer."[19]

NEW RISKS: The financial services industry faces a range of punishing fines and lawsuits. One measure of the litigation risk facing banks, for example, was in a 2012 quarterly report, again from JPMorgan Chase.

At the time, it estimated that the bank faced "possible losses" of as high as $6 billion. Its litigation expenses alone were hair-raising—$3.8 billion during the first nine months of 2012, and $4.3 billion during the same period a year earlier. Predictably, in 2013 the bank's litigation costs escalated still further. JPMorgan's legal tab for the third quarter alone was $7.2 billion after taxes—it led to the bank's first loss since Jamie Dimon took over as CEO in 2004. (One banking executive reported spending fully half of his time dealing with regulatory and legal issues, instead of meeting clients or running the business.[20]) Nor is this a short-term issue for extreme cases like Dimon's. By 2013 at least eight federal agencies were investigating his bank, including the Federal Deposit Insurance Corporation, the U.S. Commodity Futures Trading Commission, and the Securities and Exchange Commission.[21]

NEW ZEALOTS: Several major players, lawyers all, have made it their mission to chase down leaders in financial services. In the summer of 2011, when the Obama administration was crafting a settlement with the banking industry to resolve claims resulting from dubious foreclosure practices, the deal needed the support of the fifty state attorneys general. However, New York State attorney general Eric Schneiderman balked, calling it a giveaway to Wall Street. Several months later, the White House compromised, agreeing, among other concessions, to increase the industry's payment to homeowners by billions. Another such "zealot" was Gary Gensler, former chairman of the Commodity Futures Trading Commission, who was described as "one of Wall Street's toughest cops."[22] He played a pivotal role in exposing the biggest banking scandal since the start of the financial crisis: the manipulation of LIBOR interest rates. And then there's New York City Comptroller John Liu, who broke new ground by getting banks such as Citigroup and Capital One Financial Corp. to broaden their clawback policies. Clawbacks—which take back pay from executives found responsible for acts of wrongdoing or negligence—do not usually do real financial harm. Mostly such executives already are rich, and after whatever the clawbacks they remain rich. But clawbacks do mortify, publicly humiliate, which is, of course, precisely what they are intended to do.

None of this is to say that either the financial services industry, or those responsible for leading it, are about to be brought down. To the contrary: there is evidence that, if anything, banks are bigger than ever and that bankers remain "too big to jail." Attorney General Eric Holder admitted as much when he said that he was worried that the size of some institutions had become so large they made it difficult if not impossible "to prosecute them when we are hit with indications that if we do . . . it will have a negative impact on the national economy, perhaps even the world economy." He acknowledged, in other words, that for all the government's attempts to rein in big banks, they had, if anything, grown larger, to the point of having an "inhibiting influence."[23]

But this does not mean that the law is impotent, nor does reform, in particular tort reform, to reduce litigation and damages seem imminent.[24] Whatever its imperfections and inadequacies, then, the law is likely to continue to have a significant impact on nearly every aspect of twenty-first-century American life. Inevitably, this implies an impact of similar magnitude on twenty-first-century American leaders—in ways that make their lives more complex and complicated rather than simpler and easier.

9 BUSINESS

IN SPITE OF ITS IMPORTANCE to the national interest, the study of American business lags behind the study of American politics. Of course some fields, notably economics and obviously business, explore the subject in depth.[1] In addition, we all have easy access to old and new media that cover, sometimes in great detail, a range of relevant topics from business cycles to market trajectories to the latest on corporate leadership and management. But not much has been written about some of the larger questions. What is the relationship between business and a free society? What do we know about business as a social and cultural institution?[2] How does corporate life impinge on political life, and vice versa? What are the implications of the expanding size of corporations? What is the impact of the declining role of America's corporate elite in addressing many of America's most pressing problems? And what are the implications of government relying so heavily on corporate profits, on taxes generated by high levels of economic activity?[3]

Notwithstanding this presumably benign neglect, the role of business in twenty-first-century America is near equal to—some would say bigger than—the role of government. Not that this is altogether new. We know that corporate America has played an important part in American life, certainly since the late 1800s, since the rise of industrial capitalism.

We similarly know that, spurred by the expansion of the railroads and the development of the telegraph, the United States experienced rapid growth—along with the rise, in time, of the large corporation. Finally we know that along with the ascent of big business was the ascent of the big business leader, corporate titans in railroads and steel, in oil and finance, and later in automobiles. All stood for the importance of private power alongside public power. And all signaled that the business elite was taking its place right alongside the political elite.

In contrast to Americans now, Americans then, early Americans, had little interest in chartering businesses for the sake of private profit. In 1787, a Connecticut newspaper warned against creating "little aristocracies"—corporations whose sole motive was money.[4] Even a half century later, around the time of Andrew Jackson, anticorporatism was still strong, large businesses reminding people of nothing so much as the British-controlled East India Company, against which they only rather recently had railed and rebelled. But by the late nineteenth century things were different: modern corporations were no longer organizations chartered by the government in the interest of the common good. Instead, because big businesses such as railroads required big investments—large amounts of private capital in addition to whatever available public capital—corporations became "an instrument of private purpose, organized mainly for shareholder profit." At the same time it became clear that if Americans were to enjoy the benefits of mass transport, they would, for the first time, be employed in large numbers by large corporations. Working for the railroads meant that they were obliged to obey the dictates not of the free market, but of corporate superiors.[5]

Whatever were the downsides of industrialization, it soon became obvious that Americans' embrace of capitalism was full-throated, all-out. Historian Gordon Wood wrote, "In the end, no banks, no government, no institutions could have created the American economic miracle." Rather, it "suddenly emerged a prosperous, scrambling, enterprising society not because the Constitution was created or because a few leaders formed a national bank, but because ordinary people, hundreds of thousands of them, began working harder to make money and 'get ahead.' Americans seemed to be a people totally absorbed in the individual pursuit of money. 'Enterprise,' 'improvement,' and 'energy' were everywhere extolled in the press." One contemporaneous witness put it this way: "The voice of the people and their government is loud and unanimous for commerce. Their inclination and habits are adapted to trade and traffic. From one end of the continent to the other, the universal roar is Commerce! Commerce! At all events, Commerce!"[6]

However, a half century later it became apparent that between private interests and the public good there was an inevitable, inexorable tension. "Protecting private property and minority rights from the interests of the enhanced public power of the new republican governments eventually became, as Madison had foreseen, the great problem of American democratic politics."[7] Government began regularly to regulate private enterprise, starting in the late 1800s; the Sherman Antitrust Act was passed by Congress in 1890. However, on account of the magnitude of the crisis of the Great Depression, constant, considerable involvement by the American government in American business began only in the 1930s. The passage of Franklin Delano Roosevelt's New Deal signaled a significant quantitative shift in the level of public sector involvement in the private sector and, therefore, a significant qualitative shift as well.

The most important development of the 1930s was not government's involvement in business per se, "but rather the conception of the state's proper role, as protector of both the economy and the citizenry."[8] Since it was government, not business, that enabled ordinary Americans to survive and ultimately to surmount the Great Depression, it was assumed from that point on that the public sector was responsible for protecting plain people from the excesses of the private sector—an inversion, if you will, of what Madison had foreseen as the "great problem" of American democracy. But, whatever the origin or explanation of the tension between government and business, between political leaders and corporate leaders, the point is it persists. This is not to say that there has not always also been between them a symbiotic relationship, a mutual dependence. In fact, as we will later see, political leaders have become, in recent years, excessively dependent on their corporate counterparts. Still, they are not natural allies—not natural bedfellows.

Our perception of corporate America in the second decade of the twenty-first century is in large part in consequence of what happened in and to corporate America in the first decade of the twenty-first century. Beginning with the ignominious collapse of Enron in 2001, American business has seemed ever since somehow, somewhat tarnished. One could, in other words, make the argument that it never fully recovered from this particular debacle, from the failure of a famously high-flying energy company previously thought virtually impervious, or from the criminal convictions of corporate officers previously thought virtually invincible. Or, one could make the argument instead that Enron was simply the first in a series of corporate failures and embarrassments that set the stage for what was subsequent. Up to 2001 Enron was the largest bankruptcy in history. But it was closely followed by the collapse of other companies with big names, companies such as WorldCom, Tyco, Adelphia, Qwest, and Global Crossing, each of which fell victim to bad leadership, and each of which ingloriously bit the dust. While most Americans most certainly did not closely track these various corporate collapses, they did catch the whiff of failure, of greed, of corruption. They did understand that like some of their most vaulted political leaders—whose overreach, wrongdoings, miscalculations, and ineptitudes had already been exposed (think Lyndon Johnson, Richard Nixon, and Jimmy Carter)—some of their most vaulted business leaders were other than what they were cracked up to be. Most were mere mortals and many had been, were still, overpaid and overpraised.

The recent financial crisis did not change our opinion or help the situation. Corporate debacles "scorched" the global economy, with the IMF calculating that they resulted in total bank losses of about $2 trillion. They also led to a "collapse of trust in business." A 2013 survey of trust in the professions found that businesspersons and bankers ranked last, along with politicians.[9] Even now, some years after the worst of the crisis has passed, the bad odor lingers, especially around Wall Street.

The sense persists, and it is pervasive, that "the financializion of the American economy, a process by which we've become inexorably embedded in Wall Street, just keeps rolling on. The biggest banks in the country are larger and more powerful than they were before the crisis, and finance is a greater percentage of our economy than ever."[10]

Sometimes our anger is directed at institutions—such as Wall Street, banks, and businesses—and sometimes at individuals, at CEOs in particular. No wonder. We know that leading up to the crisis some number of executives were guilty of incompetence, mendacity, and fraud.[11] We similarly know that they generally continue to earn astronomically high sums—in 2012 America's CEOs enjoyed a median pay package of over $15 million. And, finally, we know that large numbers of leaders in corporate America have been sitting on piles of cash while thinning their payrolls and refusing to hire new workers.

In 2008, more than a million homes were foreclosed, and unemployment soared from under 5 percent in 2007 to nearly 10 percent a year later. By 2008 the number of American children living in poverty had reached 21 percent, and the number of Americans receiving food stamps was over forty million.[12] True, by 2014 the numbers were better; the rate of unemployment, for example, had dropped. Nevertheless, when people compared even these improved numbers with the enormously generous increases in executive pay—in one year alone, from 2011 to 2012, executive pay went up 16 percent—the disparity between those at the top and those in the middle and at the bottom was disheartening.[13]

Among liberals the conventional wisdom is that in the 1980s the balance between the private and public sectors tipped in favor of the former over the latter. "It was in this decade that an aggressive embrace of the private sector, a diminishing role for government regulation of the economy, and the widening chasm between rich and poor, all began to seem the most striking aspects of American capitalism."[14] Liberals further contend that, notwithstanding recent legislation intended to have the opposite effect, such as Sarbanes-Oxley and Dodd-Frank, the trend continues, maybe even accelerates. Of course, conservatives argue the opposite, that in part because of excessive legislation that simultaneously is excessively complex, it is getting more difficult to do business in America. In any event, there is no disagreement that corporate interest groups have at the least become a significant part of the American landscape, especially the political landscape. Wealthy donors play major roles in presidential and congressional elections, and benefits ranging from tax breaks to direct subsidies increasingly benefit the private sector over the public one.

So far as leaders in corporate America are concerned then, what we have in this second decade of the twenty-first century is something of a paradox. On the one hand CEOs and other top executives are generally held legally blameless for whatever it was that triggered the financial crisis, and they have considerable political clout. Moreover, on average they are earning record sums, corporate profits are at or near record highs, and certainly in 2013 the markets in equities had a remarkable run, more or less straight up. In addition, housing and other key sectors of the American economy are showing clear signs of improvement, growth is up (though still somewhat sluggish), and America's energy sector is astonishingly promising, with what now are said to be larger reserves of oil, gas, and coal than in any other country in the world.

But on the other hand are challenges that complicate in unprecedented ways the lives of those at the top. Yes, business leaders are being supremely well compensated for whatever their travails. This is not, however, to say that they are riding high, that their lives as leaders are trouble free. Slings and arrows come at them from every direction, and at every turn are constraints that hinder their capacity to lead.

Let me count at least some of the ways. First among them is a level of anger against big business that, while not generally in evidence in the streets, is nevertheless palpable. The signs are everywhere, even in addition to the low poll numbers, from many more registered Democrats (who tend to trust Big Government more than Big Business) than Republicans (who tend to favor Big Business over Big Government); to the Occupy movement that, notwithstanding its rapid demise, nevertheless had real resonance (99 percent versus the 1 percent); to the out and out rage registered by some of the country's most considered observers. How's this for the title of a book—Charles Ferguson, *Preda-tor Nation: Corporate Criminals, Political Corruption, and the Hijack-ing of America*?[15] Or this one by David Rothkopf, *Power, Inc.: The Epic Rivalry Between Big Business and Government—and the Reckoning That Lies Ahead*? Rothkopf asks why we measure success by a gross metric of wealth creation rather than by citizens' well being. And he wonders why, although during the financial crisis big banks caused "great damage to society—often as a direct result of misrepresentation, concealment, and rapacious pursuit of their narrow self-interests—they were able to wield their power both to be rewarded for their wrongdoing in the form of bailouts and, for the most part, to avoid prosecution."[16]

Second is the way leaders are being contained. CEOs are being watched as never before—ask even some of the survivors of the financial crisis (not to speak of those pushed from their perch), such as Goldman Sachs's Lloyd Blankfein and of course, famously, infamously, JPMorgan's Jamie Dimon. CEOs are being monitored as never before—ask erst-while chiefs such as Duke's Jim Rogers, Procter & Gamble's Robert Mc-Donald, and Mozilla's Brendan Eich. And CEOs are being leashed as never before. Example 1: in 2013, in response to a fierce backlash from followers (users), Instagram's leaders were forced to reverse their new policies on terms and conditions. Example 2: at its annual meeting in 2012, executives at Chesapeake Energy were confronted by angry insti-tutional investors shouting for a shakeup. Example 3: in 2012, activist investors had a "banner year," forcing companies to shift strategies and improve governance.[17] In 2013, the numbers were even higher. As leg-endary activist and one of the richest men on Wall Street, Carl Icahn, put it, "You've got to have people that own the companies sitting on the boards to hold them accountable."[18] In fact, the trend is so strong that companies, corporate leaders, "now view the threat of shareholder ac-tivism similarly to how they viewed the threat of hostile takeovers in the 1980s."[19] Example 4: in 2013, even though under his leadership Walt Dis-ney Co. has performed well, CEO Robert Iger nevertheless came under fire for his expanded power and pay, testifying to the vulnerability of even the squeaky clean. Example 5: increasing numbers of companies are splitting the roles of chief executive and chairman. In 2012, more than 20 percent of companies in the S&P 500 Index appointed an independent outsider as chairman, up from 12 percent in 2007. "The development is gradually creating a second seat of power at the top of big companies and easing CEOs' grip on the one institution charged with overseeing their performance and decisions."[20]

This development is particularly significant. For various reasons boards have been roused from their long years of slumber, now to assert themselves in unaccustomed ways. A book tellingly titled *Boards That Lead* documents how important boards have become to corporate governance—obviously, necessarily to the detriment of the power, authority, and influence of the chief executive officer.[21] By 2014, nine out of ten governing boards of S&P 500 companies had a lead or presiding director, and 43 percent had a board chair separate and distinct from the chief executive. To be sure, only about half of these chairs were genuinely independent. Still, the trajectory is clear: in a growing number of cases CEOs are having their wings clipped by their boards, to whom, after all, they are ultimately accountable.

The third reason leaders increasingly are limited is the larger global picture that I described in *The End of Leadership*.[22] In his similar subsequent book, *The End of Power*, Moises Naim argues as did I that, notwithstanding its still considerable clout, corporate dominance is "under siege." Companies themselves are under attack, and so are those who lead and manage them. Naim points to figures that confirm CEOs' jobs have become considerably less secure, their average tenure having been halved from about ten years in the last decade of the twentieth century to about five-and-a-half in the first decade of the twenty-first. In addition, nearly 80 percent of CEOs of S&P 500 companies were ousted before retirement.[23] Executive search firm Spencer Stuart confirms the trend, reporting that by early December 2013, fifty companies in the S&P 500 had announced CEO changes, up from 37 in all of 2012.[24] In short, like their political counterparts, business leaders have become fat targets. They are vulnerable to an array of forces, some of which are beyond their capacity even to begin to control.

The siege mentality—CEOs playing defense—is so great that it has given rise to a trend, which is, literally, to list the most obvious of the various "challenges." One such, published by The Miles Group, a consulting company, is called "10 Key Challenges for CEOs in 2013." They include, among others, coping with stakeholder overload (stakeholders include governments, regulators, special interest groups, industry watchdogs, consumer groups, the public at large), managing involved and even intrusive boards, maintaining control of the brand, and bracing for disruptive technologies.[25] Another such list—this one by Thomas Donohue, CEO of the United States Chamber of Commerce—itemizes various goals for corporate leaders, many of which would require precisely the kind of collaboration, even of collective action, that in twenty-first-century America has been in such lamentably short supply. They include, for example, greater growth, reforming the regulatory system, and addressing the fiscal crisis.[26]

And still another is "Seven Surprises for New CEOs." This particular litany was assembled by three professors at the Harvard Business School, who cautioned those recently risen to the top that although they would be held responsible for what happened on their watch, they were likely to find that they were unable to "control most of what will determine" their companies' performances.[27] Surprise number one is "You Can't Run the Company." Surprise number two is "Giving Orders Is Very Costly." And surprise number three is "It Is Hard to Know What Is Really Going On."[28] Get it? The message to corporate leaders is that, notwithstanding your high position, your power and influence and even your authority have waned. Times have changed, and so have leadership and followership, and so has the context within which you are embedded—all conspiring to complicate the task of corporate leaders who would create change. This likely explains at least in part why a 2012 survey of Harvard Business School alumni yielded results that were nearly relentlessly gloomy. Seventy-one percent expected that America's competitiveness would decline. Sixty-four percent predicted that American firms will find it harder to pay high wages and benefits. And a puny nine percent thought it likely that America would pull ahead of other industrialized nations.[29]

I want to be clear here. Again, times are not terrible: it's not exactly torture to be a leader in corporate America. Markets have generally been strong, and by every measure executives in the private sector are continuing to be exceedingly well, excessively well, compensated. Moreover there is no evidence that any of this will change any time soon. In fact, the "say on pay" experiment mandated by Dodd-Frank is already being judged "a bust."[30]

In addition, corporate leaders and managers continue to benefit from inordinate amounts of attention and significant investments in their professional development. Specifically, the leadership industry, which in the main serves them, continues to thrive, with huge sums of money spent on honing the skills of private sector leaders and managers. (In 2010 the investment in leadership development programs was reportedly $171.5 billion.[31]) Of course, I would argue, have argued, that the industry itself is evidence of executive anxiety. Notwithstanding the scant evidence that leadership training and development make the world a better place, they continue to be a big business. Coaching alone—which includes both leadership coaching and life coaching—has grown into a huge $2 billion industry worldwide.[32] And it is supplemented at every turn by a host of other supports for corporate leaders and managers, not least including rosters of readings regularly targeted at business executives who feel they need or want help. In December 2013, the *New York Times* Business Best-Seller list included, among similar others, Cheryl Sandberg's blockbuster *Lean In* (targeted at women leaders); Liane Davey's *You First* ("a plan for transforming your team into a happier, more productive group"); and Tom Rath and Barry Concie's *Strengths-Based Leadership* (speaks for itself).

Finally, for all my own emphasis on the empowerment of followers, the fact is that leaders in American business have little immediately to fear from their own most obvious followers, their employees, in spite of the fact that labor's share of national income manifestly has gone down.[33] This is the result not only of the near decimation of American unions but of American labor having to compete with foreign labor, cheaper labor in, say, China, Peru, or Bangladesh, or even better labor.

The fact is that "the skill level of the American labor force is not merely slipping in comparison to that of its peers around the world, it has fallen dangerously behind."[34] Of themselves these reasons explain at least in part why the American worker has so far been generally quiescent, in spite of increased unemployment and wages that are, at best, flat.

Withal, the context for leaders in American business is complex to the point of being daunting. Among the many reasons is the larger global context within which they, like other American leaders, necessarily are situated. In the second half of the twentieth century the United States was the dominant power. But who will dominate in the twenty-first century is not yet known. India likely will be the largest in population and China the largest in output. Where will this leave the U.S.? How should business leaders lead in this brave new world characterized not only by contextual complexity but by "complex companies"? Complex companies—companies with different products, companies with outposts the world over—are creating "unprecedented challenges," not only for the executives who lead them but for the boards that oversee them.[35]

One of the many consequences of the many recent changes is that America's corporate elite nearly never acts as a collective, either in the interest of the common good or even in its own self-interest. Though there are some exceptions to this general rule—business leaders did make it clear to political leaders that they were not happy with the apparent willingness of many lawmakers to risk defaulting on the national debt—by and large today's corporate elite is fractured, and ineffectual therefore as an agent of the public good.[36] This explains in part the persistence of government dysfunction at the national level. And it explains in part why tasks that must be done if America is to remain competitive—such as investing heavily in infrastructure—remain undone. So long as private sector leaders do not invest some of their time and energy in addressing, in tandem, the most pressing of our public sector problems, so long must they share blame for whatever it is that ails us.

PART III   REVOLUTIONS

10 TECHNOLOGY

ONE OF THE PROBLEMS raised by the furious pace of technological change is generational. In general, leaders are in their forties, fifties, and sixties. And in general, people in middle age did not grow up digital. In fact, the first cohort to get the Internet, viscerally to get it, was the "Net Generation," Americans born between 1977 and 1997, who even now, in the second decade of the twenty-first century, are just beginning in significant numbers to assume leadership roles.

What we have had, then, beginning with the information revolution in the 1990s, is a role reversal. Younger people understood better than did their elders how to master the new technologies, how to adapt to an age in which digital was destined to dominate. Business author Don Tapscott captured the curious circumstance: "For the first time in history," he wrote early on, "children are more comfortable, knowledgeable, and literate than their parents with an innovation central to society." The Net Generation, he correctly predicted, would "develop and superimpose its culture on the rest of society." It would become a "force for social transformation."[1]

Let me state this as plainly as I can: leaders in the second decade of the twenty-first century are by and large disadvantaged by having been born before the information revolution. The revolution changed so much of such importance—how information is collected, disseminated, and stored; how plain people communicate from one to the next; how followers expect leaders to lead; how followers respond when leaders do something they don't like; the nature of work and of the workplace—leaders across the board seem forever to be playing catch-up, trying to control a context that to them is as unknowable as it is uncontrollable. One might reasonably argue, in fact, that one of the reasons the leadership industry has exploded in the past few decades, in the United States in particular, has been a free-floating feeling that those responsible for leading and managing are, in at least one critical area, ill-equipped to do so.

The changes to which I allude—those better understood by younger generations than older ones—are by no means confined to technology per se. As Tapscott and others since have pointed out, technologies themselves are transformative. They change how we think and what we do— and what we expect from others in return. Above all, the Net Generation and the generation that has already succeeded it are demanding in ways that their predecessors were not. They want freedom of choice and expression; they want to customize and personalize; they want openness and transparency; they want connection and collaboration; they want innovation and entrepreneurialism; and they want speed. Their attention spans are shorter and getting shorter still, which means they get a charge from rapid change. What we are talking about, then, when we talk about technology as a component of context, is a gap between older Americans and younger ones that in some ways advantages the latter over the former, but that also distinguishes between them in ways that transcend technology. It is no accident that at their early stages technology companies themselves are nearly always led by leaders who are younger rather than older.

The challenges posed by changing technologies are, then, complex, multifaceted, of near unprecedented magnitude. Here some additional ways in which leaders are being tested by change faster than most can master. This is not, I hasten to add, to say that followers—those with few sources of power, authority, and influence—are necessarily getting the better of the deal. Rather it is to point out that the changing technologies challenge leaders nonstop.

In addition to the size of change is the speed of change, the lightning alacrity to which I just referred. Leaders have always had to cope with game-changing technologies, with innovations that, in turn, changed the context within which they sought to keep control. The printing press, the cotton gin, the atom bomb—these are just three of the more dramatic examples of how new technologies obliged those in charge to change with the changing times. But never before have the shifts been so swift. "By now, the presence and reach of the Internet is felt in ways unimaginable twenty-five or ten or even five years ago: in education with 'massive open online courses,' in publishing with electronic books, in journalism with the migration from print to digital, in medicine with electronic record-keeping, in political organizing and political protest, in transportation, in music, in real estate, in the dissemination of ideas, in pornography, in romance, in friendship, in criticism, in much else as well, with consequences beyond calculation."[2]

In a single decade arrived Facebook, Twitter, FourSquare, Instagram, iPhones, iPads, high-speed broadband, wireless that was ubiquitous, the cloud, big data, cell phone apps, and Skype. In a single decade technology provided people without technical knowledge the capacity to easily share information, ideas, emotions, convictions. In a single decade the Internet was recast as a network, as a social and political platform that was tantamount to a global forum.

Never in the past have leaders had to learn to manage one sort of technology only to discover a year or two later it had been supplanted by another sort of technology, one that only the most advanced technophiles could even begin to master. The fact is, "unlike the steam engine, which was physical and doubled in performance every 70 years, computers 'get better, faster than anything else, ever.'"[3] This combination—size of change plus speed of change—has been dizzying, making it as good as impossible for most leaders in most circumstances to keep up. As one observer, a chief technology officer at a business software company put it, "Technology is far outpacing managers' ability to use it to their business advantage."[4]

Now add to size and speed, level of complexity. It was one thing for leaders, gradually, to come to grips with the power of the printing press.

It is quite another for them to master—if they ever do—the power of, say, cloud computing. In 2011 appeared an article in the *Harvard Business Review* titled, "What Every CEO Needs to Know About the Cloud." It convincingly conveyed the dread that many leaders—again, by and large non-experts of a certain age—continue to feel when coping with technological change. First, it published the results of a survey of more than fifteen hundred CEOs worldwide, which found that fewer than half thought their companies were adequately equipped to cope with changing technologies. Second, the article suggested the technologies already existing at many large companies "actually impeded their ability to sense change and respond quickly." Third, it argued that cloud computing was a "sea change" that was as "inevitable and irreversible as the shift from steam to electric power in manufacturing." Finally, most ominously, the piece concluded that any CEO who would delegate the task of cloud computing, who would leave it to the experts, was, in effect, derelict in his or her duty. "The cloud is a topic CEOs must engage on, because many of the executives they typically delegate technology decisions to are precisely the wrong people to offer unbiased guidance."[5]

There is another sort of complexity as well, which has less to do with the technologies per se and more to do with the abundance they provide—the abundance of information. Considered by some to be a new asset class, big data have grown at an astonishing rate.[6] In 2000, only one-quarter of the world's stored information was digital; the rest was stored in traditional ways, such as on paper or film. By 2005 there were thirty billion gigabytes of video, e-mails, Web transactions, and business-to-business analytics. And by 2013 that number was some twenty times larger, with exponential increases expected to follow in the years ahead. How much data is that? Cisco has estimated that in 2013, some two trillion minutes of video alone traversed the Internet every month.[7]

The term *big data* means different things to different people. Not only does it signify an ocean of information, it further implies a bundle of technologies, a potential revolution in measurement, even a philosophy or point of view about how decisions should be made and control should be exercised.[8] Of course, it's too early to know how exactly all this will play out. Some would argue, as do Kenneth Cukier and Viktor Mayer-Schoenberger, that the implications of big data are huge, that big data are transformative.[9] Big data, they write, are "poised to reshape the way we live, work, and think. . . . They will become integral to address-ing many of the world's pressing problems."[10] Others wonder whether big data really are going to be a big deal, or whether instead they're going to be a big bust.[11] No matter—at least not for the moment. For the moment, leaders and managers are, again, being urged to keep up lest they be left behind. One expert warns, "You can't manage what you can't measure."[12]

Of course, in some of the most important ways information remains as it has always been: a valuable resource harbored by leaders and sought by followers. But the debate over who controls what data has intensified, in part because there's so much of it, in part because it's more porous, and in part because plain people now agitate for it in ways that are new and different. Activist groups such as Anonymous and activist individu-als such as Julian Assange and Edward Snowden believe deeply that far too much information has resided for far too long "in the clutches and control of governments, business, and religious institutions which have manipulated, restricted, and withheld truth from the public."[13] No one could argue that the man from nowhere, Snowden, has not in any case changed the national debate on security versus privacy. "There is a far cry between legal programs, legitimate spying, legitimate law enforce-ment," Snowden has argued, "and the sort of dragnet mass surveillance that puts entire populations under a sort of an eye and sees everything, even when it is not needed."[14]

Nor is government the only institution intruding on our private lives; so is business. According to author Sue Halpern, an investigation by the *Wall Street Journal* found that fifty of the most popular websites, representing 40 percent of all web pages viewed by Americans, placed more than three thousand tracking devices on the *Journal*'s test com-puter, most of which "were unknown to the user."[15]

What we have then is a tension, again, between leaders on the one side and followers on the other. We know by now that government leaders have intruded on the privacy of ordinary people to a degree earlier thought unimaginable, and that they have hoarded secrets to a degree earlier thought indefensible. What we do not know, or have come to know only slowly and reluctantly, is that business leaders have been similarly intrusive and similarly secretive. For example, Facebook's Mark Zuckerberg has presided over an empire that used peoples' pictures to shill for their clients without permission.[16] And Amazon's Jeff Bezos has boasted a "culture of metrics" that kept close track not only of his customers but of his employees.[17] In fact, leaders in technology, leaders who only five minutes ago were cultural icons—the result of their youth, inventive entrepreneurialism, and apparent lack of materialism (picture Zuckerberg in his hoodie)—are morphing into cultural goats, some of the most ruthless capitalists around. "So far they have succeeded in protecting themselves from the tax authorities and shareholders alike. Mark Zuckerberg owns 29.3% of Facebook. Larry Ellison owns 24% of Oracle. By contrast the largest single investor in Exxon Mobil controls only 0.004% of the stock."[18] In other words, while firms such as Apple appear new age in their imagery, the reality now is that many if not most are old school in their practices.[19]

The challenge to leaders in government and business and, for that matter, near everywhere else is obvious. On the one hand they get a gift: big data that yield information and insights previously unimaginable and certainly unavailable. But on the other hand is a sneaking suspicion that technology threatens our way of life in ways that no single leader or even consortium of leaders can significantly slow. To be sure, every one of the changes suggests opportunities as well as impositions. But leaders as well as followers can, and typically do, experience them as daunting, if only because they foretell a future not only unforeseen but unprecedented. This applies, not incidentally, at the international level as well. The furious pace of technological change risks leaving global governance in the dust. "The growing gap between what technological advances permit and what the international system is prepared to regulate can be seen in multiple areas, from drones and synthetic biology to nanotechnology and geoengineering."[20]

Emblematic of the changing times is the rise of robots or, more precisely, of the software that runs computers and other machines and devices that accomplish more efficiently tasks that until recently were done by humans. Every month the American economy gets more automated. The increase in manufacturing jobs during the last half of 2012 was exactly zero. Yet, in an apparent paradox, manufacturing activity rose at relatively a rapid clip. How to explain the discrepancy? Robots—the difference is robots. Robots are on the march, especially on assembly lines, building cars; making electronic devices; and processing food, drugs, and chemicals. Robots are also beginning to spread beyond the factory, from manufacturing jobs to service jobs; sales of service robots are expected to grow by 25 to 30 percent a year for the next few years.[21]

To be clear, I am talking here about more, much more, than robots taking on only those tasks done by rote. MIT's Erik Brynjolfsson and Andrew McAfee put it nicely when they write that the "second machine age" is unfolding "right now." It is an age in which we will be automating not only routine or manual tasks, but cognitive ones. It is an age that constitutes no less than "an inflection point in the history of our economies and societies because of digitization," because many technologies that used to be found "only in science fiction are becoming everyday reality."[22]

The more robots, the better it generally is for growth, and for leaders, since technology boosts productivity. However, the more robots, the worse for many in the middle class: technology costs them in particular jobs, large numbers of which, once vanished, will never return. Employment now is polarized: job growth is concentrated in the highest- and lowest-paid occupations, while jobs in the middle continue to decline. More precisely, employment rates are going up, but only in high-wage, managerial, professional, and technical occupations, and in low-wage, in-person service occupations. (This is not, obviously, exclusively an American phenomenon. In the Euro Zone alone are nearly eight million young people who neither have a job nor are in school or in training.[23])

This suggests that America's leaders—its political leaders, business leaders, union leaders, educational leaders, to take obvious examples—must address a whole host of issues threatening to become major long-term problems: (1) advances in technology that suggest a dramatic, permanent reduction in the number of jobs in manufacturing, in office buildings, in retail establishments, and in large and small businesses; (2) advances in technology that eliminate workers at the lower levels of the middle class (especially those performing repetitive tasks); and (3) advances in technology that lead to a decline in total U.S. employment while, simultaneously, companies in the Standard & Poor's 500 stock index enjoy record-breaking profits.[24] Even now, almost 15 percent of Americans between the ages of sixteen and twenty-four are neither in school nor employed—confirmation that the supplanting of human labor by robotic labor has political, economic, and social implications that leaders in America have yet to come to grips with.[25]

Here is another disruptive technology, this one in education, particularly higher education, where MOOCs—massive open online courses— have already swept through the system. Coursera is a company founded in 2012 by two Stanford University computer scientists. It offers hundreds of online, brand-name college courses, has more than thirty institutional partners, and has attracted $85 million in venture capital as well as nearly seven million customers. In the fall of 2013 Coursera reported earning its first $1 million, and in the spring of 2014 it appointed the former president of Yale University, Rick Levin, as its chief executive officer.[26] Udacity is a similar for-profit enterprise, this one specializing in computer programming and software design, whose mission is to bring "accessible, affordable, engaging, and highly effective higher education to the world." And MIT and Harvard each invested $30 million in edX, a nonprofit similarly founded in 2012, and similarly intended to "create a new online-learning experience with online courses that reflect their disciplinary breadth."[27]

No one yet knows where exactly online learning will lead—scenarios range from the demise of higher education as we know it to, merely, the transformation of executive education—and it remains controversial, especially in the humanities.[28] Moreover, some high hurdles remain, such as assessing, credentialing, and developing financial models that work over the long term. But there is little doubt it is a game changer, the Internet providing access to education to anyone with a laptop, not only abroad but at home, where colleges and universities are figuring out how to fit their own individual situations to the new technologies. For leaders in education this has at least one obvious implication: those who fail to appreciate the changing times, who fail to make smart decisions financially and technologically, will be left back.

The sneaking sense that the new technologies disrupt or even threaten the American way of life is, in short, palpable. While the thing to do publicly is to embrace them, those who look more closely will see that fear if not loathing is widespread. Those charged with leading and managing in this brave new world in which technology rules are being challenged at every turn, deprived of the luxury of standing even briefly in place. A frenetic, even frantic quality is in evidence in the leadership literature or, more precisely, in the leadership literature that actually addresses the relentless change.

One writer warns that a "chaotic approach to technology investment fatally wounds projects, products, and entire businesses."[29] Other writers compare the shift from old media to new (especially to social media) to a "groundswell" that cannot be "tamed"—it "comes from a thousand sources and washes over traditional business like a flood."[30] Another expert invokes the "R" word, "revolution," cautioning that the old models of organizational behavior essentially have "fallen apart."[31] And still another describes the incessant pressures on leaders and managers as being driven not only by outside factors such as size and speed of change but by inside ones as well: "Demands for digitalisation are coming from every corner of the company. The marketing department would like to run digital campaigns. Sales teams want seamless connections to customers as well as to each other. Everyone wants the latest mobile device and to try out the cleverest new app. And they all want it now."[32]

Experts on politics are similarly disposed to foreshadow scenarios in which technology seems to threaten as much as promise. This applies to dictatorial, even authoritarian leaders who one day not far into the future will be able to access powerful new technologies enabling them to suppress dissent entirely.[33] And it similarly applies to democratic leaders, compelled to contend with an Internet culture unfamiliar to the point of being alien. There are "unconferences" and "hackerspaces" and "pirate parties," and hardly any leader anywhere who is confidently in control. Not even the American defense and foreign policy establishments are immune. They are told to "ensure the Internet remains an open, global, secure, and resilient environment for users." They are told to "do more to prevent a potential catastrophic cyberattack."[34] And they themselves issue regular warnings ranging from those bluntly accusing the Chinese military of cyber espionage to those cautioning that cyber security is an issue no longer confined to traditional nation states. Organized criminal gangs that are only loosely associated with nation states, or even not at all, "constitute an entirely new category of threat to our cyber security.[35]

In addition, the Internet facilitates social movements that would be difficult or impossible without it. In his book titled, tellingly, *Networks of Outrage and Hope: Social Movements in the Internet Age*, sociologist Manuel Castells writes about the years immediately following the recent recession: "Suddenly dictatorships could be overthrown with the bare hands of the people. . . . Financial magicians went from being the objects of public envy to the targets of universal contempt. Politicians became exposed as corrupt and as liars. Governments were denounced. Media were suspect. Trust vanished."[36] Why? What explained upheavals like these, that cut across sectors and borders with equal ferocity? It was the Internet—or, put another way, in some cases anyway, it was inmates taking over the asylum, large numbers of followers humbling small numbers of leaders. This is not to say that the Internet, a revolutionary technology, necessarily has revolutionary consequences. Rather it is to say that so far as leaders are concerned, attention must be paid.

The Internet culture—which putatively is leaderless—defies our conception of how change is created. *New York Times* columnist Thomas Friedman worries that the lack of leadership is getting out of hand, transcending the technology that spawned it in the first place. "Popularism," he writes, is the "uber-ideology of our day. Read the polls, track the blogs, tally the Twitter feeds and Facebook postings and go precisely where the people are, not where you think they need to go." But then he asks, "If every one is 'following,' who is leading?"[37] Here are some more questions: How to exercise leadership in a context within which the technologies themselves are transformative?[38] How to exercise leadership in a context within which technologies themselves change relations between leaders and led? How to exercise leadership in a context within which communication and connectivity, horizontally, not vertically, have become the coin of the realm? How to exercise leadership in a context within which followers are free to communicate, to connect, without a leader as central, critical node?

In *The End of Leadership* and here I argue that technology and culture have twinned to change forever the balance of power between leaders and followers. Only repression can stop or slow the trend, which otherwise renders leaders weaker and followers stronger.[39] As younger generations become politicized, professionalized, or both, they bring with them tech savvy that, however, carries a price: the "expectation that peers and authority figures alike will communicate with them in a dynamic, two-way fashion."[40] Moreover, because younger generations, "digital natives," are adroit and confident users of technology, leaders are obliged to depend on those who, on paper anyway, have less power, authority, and influence. "These are the active social network users, with smart-phones, tablets and laptops an arm's length away. It's not a leap for them to understand how hardware and software can improve business processes and customer relationships."[41] Small wonder that superiors are more disposed now than before to give subordinates some leeway. What good does it do to nominally control the technology if you have no clue how to use it?

For leaders across the board, then, twenty-first-century technology presents two overweening challenges. First, it is difficult to tame, not to speak of master. Second, the Internet culture to which the technology itself gave rise has transformed the context within which leadership is expected to be exercised. Recall this seemingly simple shift. In the past, most companies were organized in ways that had chief information officers reporting to chief financial officers. No more. Chief executive officers are now so acutely aware of the importance of technology that more than 60 percent of CEOs have their chief information officers reporting directly to them.[42]

11 MEDIA

AMERICAN MEDIA is like American everything else—American history, say, or American ideology. It is distinctive. Since the beginning of the republic, the American press was different from the European press, just as the United States of America was different from England and France. American politics never was as consumed as Europe by class conflict— so American media were never other than mass media, catering in the main to popular taste.

The press was a reflection of the nation. Our revolutionary heritage and anti-authority mentality are why American journalists historically have tended toward exposing and denouncing America's political leaders. And they explain why American journalists historically have tended—at least since the late nineteenth and early twentieth centuries—to see themselves more as watchdogs than as agents of change.[1] Put differently, whereas in Europe the press was either an object or an instrument of state control, in the United States it generally has been a *check* on state control. The founders got what they wanted and intended: a free and largely independent press that has been the hallmark of American journalism since newspapers first circulated in the British colonies.[2]

In the first half of the twentieth century there were two kinds of journalism: the tabloid press and press based on information as opposed to entertainment. Both were, in the main, consensus builders; they brought Americans together as opposed to driving them apart. However, once radio and then television entered the media mainstream—by 1940, four out of five American households owned a radio; television became gradually ubiquitous roughly a decade later—the media landscape began to change. In time television altered the nature of the collective conversation, which became more extreme, discouraging rather than encouraging civil discourse. In fact, journalism, especially broadcast journalism, heightened and exacerbated the tensions that characterized the 1960s and 1970s, especially the war at home over the war in Vietnam, and the fight for civil rights.[3] Journalism, television journalism in particular, also heightened and exacerbated our criticisms of Washington. By putting political theater front and center—domestic dramas such as the Watergate scandal, the Iran-Contra hearings, coverage of Robert Bork's nomination to the Supreme Court, the Monica Lewinsky Show, even the various presidential campaigns—television led us slowly but certainly to conclude that America's leadership class was less admirable in the present than it had been in the past. The more familiar American followers were with American leaders, the less likely were the former to hold the latter in high regard.

So what does the media landscape look like in this second decade of the twenty-first century? So far as leaders are concerned—all leaders—the situation can be seen in two quite different ways: that they are both advantaged and disadvantaged. They are advantaged because new media have joined with old in ways that enable a rich and powerful few potentially to control large swaths of the entire media environment. There are proposals for huge new media mergers—Comcast and Time Warner Cable, for example. And new media companies such as Google, Facebook, and, more recently, Twitter have book values wildly beyond anyone's early imaginings: their largest shareholders, usually their founders, are wealthier than Croesus. Moreover, it's hard to believe that some day these quintessential American capitalists—to wit, Amazon's Jeff Bezos, who has already gobbled up the *Washington Post*—will not more aggressively seek to have their newfound economic power translate into newfound political power.[4]

Leaders continue also to dominate the conversation and, in some cases, quite literally, to control it. When Hillary Clinton decided to make "a politically crucial pivot toward a long-awaited endorsement of gay marriage," she did so "in a meticulously composed video on the web." It allowed her to dodge the not insignificant question of why on this particular issue she had waited so long (in comparison to other leading Democrats) to change course.[5] The fact is, media still rely much more heavily on information supplied by people in positions of power—most obviously but by no means exclusively in business and government—than they do on any other source. Moreover, the national news is fixated on what happens in America's major power center, Washington, D.C. What happens everywhere else—in, say, Bangor or Bakersfield, Tallahassee or Boise—is largely ignored. Even during as critical a period as the run-up to the U.S. invasion of Iraq, the most sophisticated of news-gathering services, including the *New York Times*, depended largely, often entirely, on what they were told by a single, central source: members of the administration of President George W. Bush.

Finally, to the advantage of leaders, there is, for the moment at least less investigatory journalism, less watchdog journalism, less journalism that monitors leaders on behalf of followers.[6] Press expert Alex Jones refers to this as "losing the news." He points out as do a number of others that the serious news, the news that most matters, is being sacrificed at the altar of media expediency.

The main reason is the decline of the newspaper business, the miserable economics of the newspaper business, which have jeopardized the sorts of serious reporting required first for gathering and then for reporting whatever constitutes hard news. To be sure, the number of digital paywalls is gradually growing. But so far they cannot begin to compensate for the losses in newspaper advertising revenues, which have dropped more than half since their 2005 peak.[7] Jones estimates that at least 85 percent of news that is professionally reported by reputable sources still comes from newspapers. "While people may *think* they get their news from television or the Web, when it comes to this kind

of news, it is almost always newspapers that have done the actual reporting. Everything else is usually just a delivery system"—which is why
hard news has been hard hit by the "economic ravaging of newspapers."[8]

To be sure, newspapers never were disposed to invest heavily in investigative journalism; it always was expensive and it always risked alien-
ating various audiences, especially coveted advertisers. But the situation
now is far worse. Save for a very few exceptions, the resources required
to aggressively undertake explanatory journalism, or investigative journalism, or what media expert Thomas Patterson calls "knowledge-based
journalism," journalism based on reflection as well as information and
analysis, have virtually vanished.[9] Estimates for newspaper room cut-
backs in 2014 put the industry down by one-third since 2003, and below
forty thousand full-time professional employees for the first time since
1978. While, as the Pew Research Center points out, this does not detract from the astonishing improvements in the *distribution* of news, it
does detract from *obtaining the information* that constitutes the news.[10]
What this adds up to is "a news industry that is more undermanned and
unprepared to uncover stories, dig deep into emerging ones or to question information put into its hands."[11]

Explanatory journalism requires reporting that is careful and complete, that tells the whole truth and nothing but. Investigative journalism
demands even more dedication and persistence because, by definition,
it is done in the face of resistance, in the face of someone(s)' attempt
to keep information secret. And knowledge-based journalism implies
considerable intellectual rigor that, while never much in evidence, has
become harder still to come by. All three types of journalism clearly
pose at least a potential threat to those in positions of power and authority. Explanatory journalism poses a threat if only because it reveals,
presumably with intelligence and insight, who did what to whom, and
when and why. Investigative journalism poses a threat because inherent
in the concept is news that someone with power, authority, or influence
does not want the public to know.[12] And knowledge-based journalism
poses a threat because its intrinsically high standards make the reporting difficult or even impossible ultimately to refute.

There are, I might point out, some occasions on which journalists themselves are agents of change—they are leaders. Bob Woodward and Carl Bernstein of Watergate fame fall into this category, as do others from earlier in the twentieth century, including Ida Tarbell, Ray Standard Baker, and Lincoln Steffens, whose explanatory, investigative, and knowledge-based reporting was so persuasive it played an important part in the passage of major reform legislation. In the event, to get an idea of how threatening are these sorts of journalists, is this sort of journalism, to leaders with something to hide, and how important is the press to sustaining such reporting, one has only to turn to the *New York Times*. Especially now, in this second decade of the twenty-first century, the *Times* remains essential. It is, as critic Frank Rich writes, one of the last news organizations still "fielding ambitious correspondents in most places where news is made, and still investing untold man-hours, serious investigative talent, and acres of paragraphs to enterprise reportage that spans the globe and nearly every field of human endeavor."[13]

Just imagine how thrilled were the powers that be at Walmart that the *Times* investigated the company's growth in Mexico, only to unearth widespread corruption. (The *Times* series led to investigations by the Justice Department, the Securities and Exchange Commission, and the Mexican authorities.[14] And at least eight senior Walmart executives have since lost their jobs.) Just imagine how thrilled were the powers that be at Apple that the *Times* investigated its production practices in Asia, only to find that the company was exploiting its workers. (The *Times* series, which focused on Apple, but was not confined to it, led to apologies from Apple CEO Tim Cook, and to significantly improved conditions, especially for workers in China who produced Apple products.[15]) Just imagine how thrilled were the powers that be in China that the *Times* revealed some of their most sensitive secrets, for example, that relatives of Prime Minister Wen Jiabao had accumulated vast personal fortunes through businesses with ties to the state. (Changes resulting from this particular *Times* series are more difficult to gauge but, at a minimum, the paper revealed the convergence in China between public influence and private wealth.[16])

So, although there never was a golden age of investigative reporting but rather a few shining exceptions, such reporting is more seriously in peril now than before.[17] This is a shame—for to the degree that it is diminished, leaders get a pass. Democracy and everything that it implies—liberty, equality, and a reasonably equitable distribution of power and money—depends not only on a free press to sustain it but on a strong press as well. If it is at risk, the powerless sustain a loss and the powerful chalk up a win.

But to the story about the media in twenty-first-century America there is another side, for if on the one hand leaders are advantaged and followers disadvantaged, on the other hand the reverse also holds true—leaders disadvantaged and followers advantaged. People with power, authority, and influence have more economic control over media than those without—but in some other significant ways they have less control, less control now than before. For new media—those increasingly sophisticated technologies that bestow on those without power, authority, or influence previously unimagined access to information, communication, and connection—have changed the ways in which news is produced and processed. Put directly, new media make it harder than before for leaders and even experts to control the news—both its production and dissemination.

Thus the classic functions of journalism are being undermined not only by polarizing argumentation, by the continuous news cycle, by lower standards, and by news in bits and bites, but by online journalism that is well beyond the capacity of any single individual or even small group, no matter how wealthy, politically powerful, or otherwise authoritative, to control. Moreover, those *not* highly positioned—ordinary people, followers—now have a voice that is, in effect, unchecked. This does not mean necessarily, importantly, that anyone is listening, that anyone is paying attention to what it is we have to say. In fact, for all the talk about how blogging is empowering even the ignorant and uninitiated, it turns out that the blogosphere is a hierarchy: "a small group of A-list bloggers actually gets more political blog traffic than the rest of the citizenry combined."[18] Still, in the past no one was listening to you and me; in the present someone is listening to you and me, or they could be, they might be.

It's not that new media have rendered old media obsolete. Rather it is that old media, traditional media, now operate in a much more competitive environment. Some one billion people worldwide are on Facebook (around only since 2004), and Twitter (around only since 2006) has more than two hundred million monthly users. Completely controlling or censoring technologies like these is impossible or, more accurately, it is impossible save in regimes that either are totalitarian or authoritarian in the extreme. Put another way, in the second decade of the twenty-first century only a people totally in thrall to, or under the yoke of, either a single leader or a small leadership cadre, are vulnerable to complete media control. Though countries such as Iran and China regularly control or constrain access to the Internet, anything short of absolute oppression, of absolute repression, will fail to be 100 percent effective.

New media have been called "mass self-communication." They are *mass* communication because they have the capacity to attract a global audience. And they are *self* communication because we are free to produce our own content, select our own audience, and decide what communications to consume. Put directly, we the people—people without any obvious sources of power, authority, or influence—have a level of control over new media that until only recently was inconceivable. Again, while new media have not entirely supplanted old media, and while the level of passive consumption remains high, the media world has changed, irrevocably. Information has become porous. And people all over the world, of every station, use their capacity to communicate to advance their own interests and ideas, to further their own particular programs and projects, and to discover what they in particular need or want to know.[19]

The implications of this for leadership and followership are impossible to overestimate, for they are not only at the level of the individual, they are also at the level of the group. Until around 2006 the name

Barack Obama was virtually unknown.[20] His executive experience was as good as zero, and he had only recently come to Washington (in 2005) as a freshman senator from the state of Illinois. Moreover, those Americans who paid close attention had every reason to assume, and did, that the next Democratic nominee for president would be the highly esteemed and extensively experienced candidate of the Democratic establishment, Hillary Clinton. But, thanks in part at least to new media, to mass self-communication, it was not to be. Obama's team was early to the new media party, earlier than Clinton's; the former understood in a way that the latter did not the context of the Internet. Put directly, in the 2008 presidential campaign Obama's supporters were far more active and resourceful in harnessing the web to their political purposes than were the supporters of any other presidential candidate, Democratic or Republican.[21]

This is not to denigrate the importance of old media during the 2008 campaign for president; it remained then, as it still does, of considerable importance. Rather, it is to point out that the high level of grassroots activism enabled by the Internet explains in good part how a relatively young and widely unknown black man was able to come out of nearly nowhere to triumph over his opponents and become, against all odds, president of the United States. In fact, Obama's tech savvy, that is, the savvy of his team, gave him a similar advantage four years later. During the 2012 presidential campaign, Obama posted nearly four times as much content as did Mitt Romney, and he was active on nearly twice as many platforms.[22]

I should add that this new media savvy has been in evidence not only on the left, among Democrats, but also on the right, among Republicans. The Tea Party, which was established only in 2009, is the product of a libertarian eruption that was, in effect, leaderless. Not unlike Barack Obama, the Tea Party came out of nowhere; and, not unlike Barack Obama, in order to come out of nowhere it depended on the Internet. It was and remains, implicitly if not explicitly, grassroots and anti-establishment—most strikingly, anti-mainstream Republican. To be sure, some of America's richest and most powerful have contributed handsomely to the Tea Party's cause—it's one of the reasons the party has been able to sustain itself so well for so long. But it is not, as some would have it, simply an artifact of conservative and corporate interests. Moreover, Tea Partiers themselves tend not to belong to the leadership class. Fewer than half are college graduates, and only a quarter earn more than $100,000. Instead, rather like Team Obama in 2007, the Tea Party is the product of a genuine sociopolitical movement that tapped into both antigovernment populism and widespread distrust of establishment institutions that Americans not so long ago had widely admired. The effects of all this have been, as we know, considerable. Mainstream Republicans have been vulnerable to the effects of this anti-leadership, anti-authority mentality, with Tea Partiers making life nearly as hard for their own putative leaders (to wit, Speaker of the House John Boehner) as they have for the Democratic opposition.[23]

The fact that American politics have been so obviously upended in recent years—by those on the left and those on the right—suggests that something fundamental has changed in the nature of how we participate in collective life. Elsewhere I have argued that these changes are cultural, in part the legacy of the rights revolutions of the 1960s and 1970s. And I have equally argued that they are technological—the changing technologies having major implications for leadership and followership.[24] Perhaps the best way of looking at the role of new media in all this is by entertaining the idea that followers have in some fundamental way been changed, emboldened, by the relatively rudimentary act of participating in the collective conversation, online. The inability of the other—whether subordinate, peer, or even superior—to turn us off and shut us up is not only new, it is different. It could be that the right to be heard, coupled with the capacity to be heard is, of itself, transforming.

Manifestations of people participating are everywhere in evidence, such as with WikiLeaks, which brought to our collective attention the issue of radical transparency. Wikileaks was the brainchild of Julian Assange, an Australian anarchist who, so far as disclosure and dissemination of information were concerned, broke every rule in the book.

Assange not only believes in radical transparency but manifestly relishes what happens in consequence—the hoisting of leaders, particularly political leaders, by their own petard. Thanks to Assange and his enablers (including Bradley/Chelsea Manning, now sentenced to long years in an American prison), we learned, among many other things, that the war in Afghanistan all along went much less well than the administrations of presidents George W. Bush and Barack Obama were willing publicly to admit; that the war in Iraq was fought to an unprecedented degree by private contractors; and that, contrary to their public posturing, Iran had long been the object of fear and loathing not only by Israel, but by most of its other neighbors as well. And then there is Edward Snowden. Whether whistleblower or traitor, it is impossible to deny that by using old media and new to leak enormous quantities of information the government previously had deemed secret, this man single-handedly turned the American national security establishment on its head. As earlier indicated, there is no question that Snowden started an important conversation about balancing our security interests on the one hand with our privacy interests on the other.

Similarly, consider the impact of new media on leaders in business. In the past companies could control the messages that went out and came in. Now times are different—now it's a free for all. The main point of contact between the customer and the company used to be customer service. This meant communication nearly always was one-way: from the company to the customer with hardly any opportunity for the customer to shape the experience. Now corporate leaders and managers are unable any longer to control the conversation. Now they have no choice but to listen, to learn from their customers and whichever other stakeholders choose to weigh in. This lack of corporate control is especially in evidence in customer complaints. In this brave new world, the world of "spreadable media," what once were solely "customer service" issues increasingly are, in addition, "public relations" issues. Customers spread their own information about, and experience with, brands and businesses virally, which is why corporate America now has to use its online presence not only to send its own messages and to present its own content, but to respond as rapidly as possible to the demands of disgruntled customers.[25]

Finally, there is the Steubenville rape case, which is similarly emblematic of the new media environment. It's the case of an apparently local story that grew to the point of attracting widespread national attention only because of new, online media, and only because of those who used new media to force a political point. For weeks the case was big news only in Ohio, mainly in the town in which the rape, by two sixteen-year-old high school football players, was said to have taken place. But persistent bloggers, documentation on Instagram and Twitter, and the eventual involvement of Anonymous—a decentralized group of hacktivists dedicated to promoting radical transparency, especially in cases it considers good causes—changed the course of the case. The Steubenville story was gradually transformed, from one of small town justice into a national cause célèbre in which the "rape culture" itself was on trial, and in which the rights of the victim finally claimed center stage.[26] The story was transformed, in other words, by ordinary people who took it on themselves to target with a vengeance the issue of rape—and the local authorities.

So far as relations between leaders and followers is concerned then, the new media environment has several implications, including the far freer flow of ideas, the far more expansive distribution of information, and the far greater degree of sharing. But most important of the implications is as suggested above—the expanded possibilities for, and the different manifestations of, public participation. One of the inevitable effects of this enhanced and invigorated participation by ordinary people—by followers, not leaders—is that the ostensibly powerless are increasingly ready, willing, and able to take on the ostensibly powerful. Put differently, a grassroots mentality pervades the twenty-first-century media environment. It suggests—though it does not confirm—that anyone, anywhere positioned, can take on anyone, anywhere positioned.[27]

The new media environment is, then, threatening to leaders in at least three ways. It places them under a new kind of scrutiny, their public lives and their private lives. It subjects them to more and coarser attacks. And it inflicts on them the inability to completely control even the contexts that ostensibly they dominate.

But again, there is an irony here, for media are under attack by the very participatory culture that they (new media in particular) created. By every measure the American people hold media, the press, in lower esteem than they did even a decade or two ago.[28] In 2012, 60 percent of Americans said "they have little or no trust" in any mass media "to report the news fully, accurately, and fairly."[29] Even newspapers, once considered generally respectable purveyors of the nation's news, are no longer so widely trusted. Newspaper believability dropped some thirty points, from 84 percent in 1984 to 54 percent in 2005.[30] Moreover, a survey conducted by Harvard University's Center for Public Leadership confirmed that more than three-quarters of the American people have hardly any confidence or even no confidence at all in media leaders. They rank third from the bottom, just above leaders in Congress and on Wall Street, who fare even worse.[31]

Part of the problem is that nearly no one in the media was prescient to the point of imagining just how radical would be the changes to which they themselves, the media, were vulnerable. Frank Rich noted that this is typical, that in the modern history of media even "the reigning giants have nearly always been caught napping by transformative change." This holds true in music, in the movie industry, in the newspaper business, in radio and television, and in the overarching media environment that has recently been transformed by the encroachment of new media on old.[32]

The bottom line is that no leader, anywhere, of any kind, without exception, now gets a pass. Even media moguls, old media and new, though plenty powerful, are vulnerable to being victimized by changes they are too blinkered to foretell.

12 MONEY

I WAS NOT ORIGINALLY PERSUADED that "money" should be an item on this checklist, separate unto itself. After all, money as a component of context comes up elsewhere in this book, implicitly and explicitly, for example, in the sections on economics, business, and interests. Among the many issues regularly raised by money—too much of it, too little of it—is the growing gap between the rich and the poor, and the dwindling middle class, themselves exacerbations of life in twenty-first-century America.

But the more I thought about it, the more I was persuaded that "money" was of its own so key a component of context it merited a discrete discussion. In particular, the impact of so much money in the hands of so few, poured into so small a subsection of people and places, is as powerful as it is pervasive. Money as power, money as influence, is an inescapable fact of contemporary American life. It's become as American as motherhood and apple pie—though with implications more malignant than benign.

A single, unobtrusive item in the *New York Times* makes my case. "Koch Group Has Ambitions in Small Races," reads the headline, the story going on to say how a group called "Americans for Prosperity," backed by the immensely wealthy and extremely conservative Koch brothers, Charles and David, had inserted itself in local elections in states that included Iowa, Kansas, Ohio, and Texas.[1] Who knew? The point is not that people with money try to influence political outcomes—there's nothing new in that. Rather, it is that the audaciousness of such people, on the left as well as the right, enabled and enhanced by the new technologies and their collective incentive to intrude themselves into the political process, is historically unprecedented. By nearly every account private money plays a more important role in America's public life than it has at least since the Gilded Age. Great or at least considerable wealth, concentrated in a relatively small number of hands, coupled with the culture of money, has resulted in Washington itself awash in cash, peopled by politicians who themselves are wealthy—or depend on the wealth of others just to stay in office. As one insider summarized the situation, "The rest of the country may be divided into red and blue, but D.C. is green."[2]

I will return to the role of money in politics later in this section. But first, quick mention of the pervasive importance of money in twenty-first-century America—of how big bucks play a part even in places not usually considered tainted by the color of money. Here are two examples: the role of money in schools and the role of money in sports.

Americans are regularly assured, by presidents among others, that we as a nation are committed to nothing so much as a good education—for everyone. In signing the No Child Left Behind Act, President George W. Bush said that our biggest national challenge was to ensure that "every single child, regardless of where they live, how they're raised, the income level of their family, every child receive a first class education in America." Similarly, his successor, President Barack Obama, told students at the State University of New York in Buffalo, "There aren't many things that are more important to that idea of economic mobility—the idea that you can make it if you try—than a good education."[3] As *New York Times* columnist Eduardo Porter has observed, it's a comforting consensus. "It provides a solution everyone can believe in, whether the problem is income inequality, racial marginalization or the stagnation of the middle class." But, he goes on to add, at the same time it raises a difficult question. "If education is a poor child's best shot at rising up the ladder of prosperity, why do public resources devoted to education lean so decisively in favor of the better off?"[4] Notice how Porter frames the question. He asks about "public resources," not private ones. But, of course, inevitably, there is a link between the two.

The most obvious of the several problems that contribute to the divide to which Porter alludes is that the federal government provides only about 14 percent of funding for all public school districts, from elementary school through high school. This means that more than half the funding for schools K–12 comes from local sources, in the main property taxes, which are dependent obviously on the value of the properties. The axiom is simple enough: in general, the greater the value of the properties, the higher the tax revenues, and the more money to invest in local public schools.

Some state governments attempt to address the imbalance that is the inevitable consequence of public policies such as these. But there are other states, for example, Illinois, Texas, New York, and North Carolina, in which "children attending school in higher poverty districts still have substantially less access to state and local revenue than children attending school in lower-poverty districts." Put another way, states such as these could distribute their resources more equitably if public policies were in place that mandated distributions be based on student need.[5]

Again, not every state is regressive. Some seventeen states provide more money to students in high-poverty districts than to those in low-poverty ones. But in most states the differences in funding are jarring, leaving an observer such as Porter to wonder, "As income and wealth continue to flow to the richest families in the richest neighborhoods, public education appears to be more of a force contributing to inequality of income and opportunity, rather than helping to relieve it." (I might add that the U.S. is an outlier here. Most developed countries either invest equally in every student, or they invest more in disadvantaged students. The United States is one of only a small number of countries that does just the opposite.[6])

Some of the major education reform proposals have had, counterintuitively, a similar effect, channeling big money into only a small number of specially selected schools and students. One idea has been to turn some parts of public education over to private hands, under the theory that privatization will make education more equitable, in part by injecting innovation and competition into otherwise stifled government bureaucracies. However, most studies show that in spite of the huge investments, privatization has failed so far to live up to its early promise—it has had "no visible effects." First, there is evidence that under charter school programs government officials "preferentially grant charters to organizations with connections to the political establishment," which, in turn, leads at least some of the time to corruption. Second, only a fraction of students get to share in the benefits provided by, for example, charter schools, which tend to screen out those deemed undesirable or to base their selection of students on vouchers, which benefit only the small number who luck out in a lottery.[7]

Even the most well-intentioned efforts of some of the most well-intentioned individuals—author and researcher Sarah Reckhow calls them "boardroom progressives"—sometimes fall short. Well-known players in the education reform movement such as Bill and Melinda Gates, Mark Zuckerberg, Geoffrey Canada (of the Harlem Children's Zone), Michelle Rhee, and Joel Klein (former school district leaders) have all been known to make mistakes, including falling victim to the easy assumption that throwing money at a problem will fix it. Reckhow argues persuasively that we need to more rigorously assess the role of philanthropy in urban education, which is not, obviously, to say that foundations should get out of the school reform business. It is, however, to argue that they might be more mindful of their own power and influence. And it is also to argue that they might be more mindful that their power and influence are not necessarily, by definition, salutary.[8] Again, among the obvious problems is that whatever the monies being invested in the nation's schools, from wherever or whoever is the source, they are being invested unequally. This accounts to some considerable degree for the measurable decline in American education, and the measurable decline in trust in America's educational leaders.

Sports are like schools—both are examples of how big money injects itself into American life. Dave Zirin, the "gutsiest sportswriter in America," zeros in on the connection between sports on the one hand and money and politics on the other.[9] "If you really want to talk about corporate greed pile-driving the interests of 'the 99 percent,'" Zirin writes, "look no further than the NBA [National Basketball Association]. The league's billionaire owners locked their doors and threatened to cancel the 2011–12 season following the most lucrative year in league history. They locked out not only the players' union but thousands of low-wage workers—the people cleaning the arenas, parking the cars, and selling the overpriced, foamy swill the league calls beer. It's the 1 percent version of the high pick-and-roll, their go-to-play: magically spinning our tax dollars into their profits. While workers are laid off and the infrastructure of our cities rots . . . $2 billion has gone into building eight new NBA facilities. Of that amount, $1.75 billion has come out of our pockets."[10]

The National Football League (NFL) is, predictably, similar to or even worse than the National Basketball Association. It too fleeces taxpayers for, among other things, upgrades in facilities. For example, taxpayers in Hamilton County, Ohio, were hit with a bill for $26 million in debt service for stadiums for the NFL's Bengals and Major League Baseball's Reds, plus another $7 million in operating costs. Subsidies like these exceeded the $23.6 million that were cut during the same fiscal period from Hamilton County's health and human services budget, and they represented a good chunk of the $119 million that were cut from funding for local public schools. One estimate is that league-wide some 70 percent of the capital costs of NFL stadiums have been provided by taxpayers, not by NFL owners.[11]

Charges of money grubbing have been leveled in recent years not only at pro football but also at college football. In 1950, Oklahoma's football coach earned $15,000. By 1971 the figure had climbed to $35,000 and in 1988 to $88,000. In 2013 Oklahoma's coach earned $4.45 million to perform miracles in a stadium that by then had undergone a $125 million renovation in order to seat more than eighty-two thousand fans. (Seats on StubHub near the forty-yard line, and about thirty rows up, cost $650.)[12] In 2010, when Alabama's Auburn University won the national championship, its net football income was $37 million, not all that much less than the $43 million of that same season's NFL champion, the Green Bay Packers.[13]

Here is author Joe Nocera, writing in the *New York Times*: "The hypocrisy that permeates big-money college sports takes your breath away. College football and men's basketball have become such huge commercial enterprises that together they generate more than $6 billion in annual revenue, more than the National Basketball Association. . . . The glaring, and increasingly untenable, discrepancy between what football and basketball players get and what everyone else in their food chain reaps" has led to "deep cynicism" among the athletes themselves and to "increasingly loud calls for reform."[14]

Case in point: Texas A&M quarterback Johnny Manziel. It is estimated that Johnny Football, as he is known to his fans, cost the school about $120,000 in scholarships during the three years that he attended. It is similarly estimated that in 2012 and 2013 Manziel contributed so significantly to raising the profile of his university, that donations to Texas A&M rose by some $300 million in one year, to a record $740 million. It's no wonder the National Labor Relations Board finally issued a ruling (likely though to be challenged in court) that football players, in particular those at Northwestern University, may have the right to form a union and bargain collectively.[15]

Finally, there is this. In 2013 the NFL agreed to pay $765 million to settle a lawsuit brought by more than forty-five hundred athletes and their families who had sued for compensation after dozens of former players were diagnosed as having a degenerative brain disease. A settlement was reached only because both sides had a short-term interest in doing so. The NFL was eager to close the case for what amounted to peanuts—its annual revenues are nearly $10 billion—because it "faced the possibility of billions of dollars in liability payments and a discovery

phrase that could have proved damaging if the case had moved forward."
And lawyers for the plaintiffs were anxious to reach a settlement—arguably too anxious—because many of their clients had debilitating symp-
toms that needed prompt medical attention.[16]

Though the NFL was obliged to pay, it was widely seen as having
scored a legal victory. Michael Le Roy, an expert on labor law, faulted
the settlement for being much too low, "considering the number of
claimants and the severity of their conditions." Former NFL player
Aaron Curry (who was not part of the suit) concurred: "Settlement on
concussions not gonna make up for early death, forgetting kids name
and rest of stuff that come w/ brain trauma," said Curry on Twitter.[17]
And, it was later revealed that only those players who had the most severe brain injuries could even hope to be compensated. Moreover, the
estates of retirees who died earlier than 2006 were excluded from the
settlement altogether.[18]

A well-documented book published in 2013, *League of Denial*,
charged that the NFL has all along willfully ignored or stonewalled
the mounting evidence that football threatens the brains of the three-
hundred-pound men who now play the game.[19] It has, in other words,
become almost impossible to believe that those most closely associated
with the sport—from commissioners to team doctors—all of whom
stood to profit enormously from its riches, have been for the duration
oblivious to the costs incurred by at least some of the players. Ironically,
tellingly, none of this precludes the National Football League, widely
considered the most profitable sports league in the world, from enjoying
tax-exempt status. The NFL is still considered, at least for U.S. tax purposes, the charitable or nonprofit organization it has been since 1966.
While critics charge that it, along with other professional sports leagues,
is getting a free pass, so far any attempts to change the existing legislation have been thwarted.

This enormous infusion of cash into sports ultimately has had a cor-
rosive effect, not only on those directly involved, but on the American
people more generally. It contributes to the escalation in American cyn-
icism, and to the impression that American sport is like everything else

now in America—dominated by the rich and powerful, by, if you will, leaders, not followers.

But for all the evidence of the impact of big money on American life, in areas ranging not only from schools to sports but from medicine to media to munitions, it is perhaps nowhere as blatantly obvious as it is in politics.[20] Again, I allude to this elsewhere in this book, for example in the discussion on lobbying. But all the other references together cannot fully capture the extent of the involvement, the extent to which concentrated wealth has infiltrated, had an impact on, the nation's political system. There is a modest literature on this, books written by authors who tend left, which is another way of saying that they tend to be dismayed by this trend, which so far has proved unstoppable. But it's hard now for anyone who pays any attention at all to politics not to be at least dimly aware of the preternatural relationship between the political system and the big money that has come to riddle it.

Sometimes we focus on too little money, on individuals and institutions, cities and states, even the federal government, in desperate need of cash. I am thinking, for example, of the city of Detroit, which was forced finally to file for bankruptcy, the largest such filing in American history. Why did this come to pass? Because Detroit, like many other governments across America—another big city example is Chicago—made promises to its people it was unable ultimately to keep. It's an insidious kind of corruption, really, all centered on the intersection between money and politics, on the tension between self-interest and the public interest. Governors and mayors from East to West have "long offered fat pensions to public servants, thus buying votes today and sending the bill to future taxpayers. They have also allowed some startling abuses. Some bureaucrats are promoted just before retirement or allowed to rack up lots of overtime, raising their final-salary pension for the rest of their lives. Or their unions win annual cost-of-living adjustments far above inflation. A watchdog in Rhode Island calculated that if a retired local fire chief lived to 100, he would collect pension payments totaling $800,000 a year. Somewhat similarly, more than 20,000 retired public servants in California receive pensions of over $100,000."[21] All this because of pandering—all this because in order to win public office and then hold on to public office politicians refrain from telling the truth. Instead they pay people off, buying votes with promissory notes.[22]

At other times we focus on too much money, too much money sloshing through the political system, the rich on the inside running the government and the rich on the outside peddling influence. Here are just two quick salient points: first, the ever-widening gap between the wealth of members of Congress and the wealth (or lack of it) of their constituents. In 2012 the median net worth of the 112th Congress was $442,007, while the median net worth of the American household was $68,828.[23] Second, how in the wake of the 2012 elections, Democratic Party leaders gave a PowerPoint presentation that urged freshman legislators to spend up to four hours a day making fund-raising calls. These same freshmen were similarly encouraged to tack on to every working day another hour of "strategic outreach," holding breakfasts or other sorts of "meet and greets" with potential financial supporters. Put directly, seasoned Congressional hands were advising their unseasoned counterparts to spend as much or even more time each day on raising money than on tending to the nation's business.[24]

Of course, there are some exceptions to the general rule. Republican House Majority Leader Eric Cantor was, to everyone's astonishment, upset in a primary by an underfunded unknown, Dave Brat. But, in the main, money plays a major part in politics at two different points in the electoral process: during the election campaigns and after the elections are over. First is the electoral process and the role that money plays in the wake of the 2010 Supreme Court decision, *Citizens United v. Federal Election Commission*. Nearly no one has claimed that *Citizen United*— which ruled that corporations and unions had a constitutional right to spend unlimited amounts on elections—was a bolt out of the blue. To the contrary: the decision is widely considered the product of a decades-long drive to rethink legal doctrine in ways that favor moneyed elites.[25] In fact, even before *Citizens United* the average amount it took to run for reelection to the House went from $56,000 in 1974 to more than $1.3 million in 2008.[26] As Lawrence Lessig put it, "The day before *Citizens*

United was decided, our democracy was already broken. *Citizens United* may have shot the body, but the body was already cold."[27]

Still, even to the experts, this particular legal finding came as something approximating a thunderclap. One wrote that it arrived "like a long-anticipated earthquake, leveling precedents and generating ongoing aftershocks."[28] Another, former Senator Russ Feingold, said that the decision did no less than alter "our system of government." And there was more. In a subsequent decision handed down in 2014, the Supreme Court "continued its abolition of limits on election spending, striking down a decades-old cap on the total amount any individual can contribute to federal candidates in a two-year election cycle."[29] I hardly need add that while conservatives generally supported this latest decision removing constraints on campaign spending, liberals generally condemned it, lamenting what was nearly certain to be the declining number of people motivated even to try to influence the political process.

Citizens United, in any case, by nearly all accounts, contributed to making the 2012 presidential election by far the most expensive in American history—at a cost of somewhere between $6 and $10 billion. Political operatives of all types spent money in ways that they did not dare to do before, including creating nonprofit "social welfare" groups that were allowed to raise and spend money on campaigns without disclosing their sources.[30] (One such group, "Crossroads GPS," which was "advised" by prominent Republican Karl Rove, received 80 percent of its money in 2012 in donations of $1 million or more—including a single gift of $22.5 million.[31]) The most famous, or infamous, of the single big spenders was multimillionaire Sheldon Adelson, who shelled out some $150 million on just this one presidential (2012) campaign, much of it to loser Newt Gingrich.

But, arguably, the real story was the degree to which ordinary people simply stayed on the sidelines. Tens of millions of Americans were mere spectators, sitting out the election altogether, aware that their votes did not much count, and that their money counted even less. In the 2012 election, some 87 percent of Americans contributed not one dime to either federal or state election campaigns.[32] Conversely, the historically high spending was dominated by "a small number of individuals and organizations making exceptional contributions."[33] Let me be clear here: there is a link between feeling politically impotent and feeling inclined to participate. One of the main reasons Americans have scant interest in elections is because they have come to believe that the candidates are beholden not to their constituents, but to their financiers.[34]

About the culture of cash that now infuses the nation's capital, it suffices here to provide just three quick facts. Fact number one: the Washington, D.C., area recently overtook the Silicon Valley area as that with the highest income per head. Seven of the ten counties with the highest household incomes in the nation are in the D.C. region. Fact number two: in 2012, Bill Clinton earned $17 million just for giving speeches, including one to a company in Lagos for $700,000. Harry Truman, I might add, did things differently. "I could never lend myself to any transaction, however respectable," he said, "that would commercialize on the prestige and dignity of the office of the presidency."[35] Fact number three: in 1974, only 3 percent of retiring members of Congress became lobbyists. This number is now 50 percent of senators and 42 percent of House members.[36]

Disapproval of Washington is not only because it is dysfunctional, it also is because it is peopled by political elites tied inextricably to corporate elites—who, I might remind, are paid more than their equivalents anywhere else in the world.[37] In 2012, chief executives in America were paid 273 times more than their average employee.[38] And in 2013, the three highest-paid CEOs—Oracle's Larry Ellison, CBS's Leslie Moonves, and Liberty Global's Michael Fries—made a total of $188 million.[39] In the meantime, as we of course know by now, wages for 70 percent of the nation's workforce remain stagnant, unemployment and underemployment remain relatively high, and millions of Americans, even many with jobs, feel financially insecure.

Still, as we have seen, notwithstanding small signs of change, so far the 99 percent have not in any significant way taken on the 1 percent. So the U.S. in important ways stagnates, and in important ways even deteriorates. Despite its being among the richest countries in the world, the United States is one of the worst performers among industrialized nations according to some of the most important measures, including income inequality, literacy inequality, infant mortality, and child poverty.[40] No wonder large numbers of us now believe that America has seen its better days, "that a distinctly American feeling of inevitability of greatness—culturally, economically, politically—is gone."[41]

The smell of money lingers. It permeates life in twenty-first-century America to the degree that not even the arts are exempt. The market for fine art is sky high, way higher than ever before, with paintings by artists you've never heard of selling for millions, and paintings by artists you have heard of selling for mega millions.[42] (A large untitled painting by Mark Rothko sold in 1998 for just $2.8 million. In 2010 it was sold at Sotheby's, this time for $31.4 million. When, if, it is sold again, it will almost certainly be for much, much more.[43]) It's insidious—it's insidious if only because the widespread inequity undermines the most fundamental assumptions of American capitalism.[44] We know perfectly well that capitalism is never fully fair; it is virtually by definition a system in which some stand to gain more than others. But in the main we have assumed for about three-quarters of a century that capitalism was fair enough—that within the American system most could and would prosper sufficiently. And in the main, we have further assumed that within the American system the divide between those at the top and those in the middle and at the bottom would be short of shocking. Now these assumptions have been called into question. "Morning in America" has come to ring hollow—not least because America itself seems to be up for sale to anyone rich enough to pay in cold hard cash or, for that matter, powerful or persuasive enough to borrow big on credit.

13   INNOVATION

INNOVATION USED TO BE our mother's milk. Americans once prided themselves on living in a country that manifestly was more innovative than any other, that for many decades, more than a century really, was on the cutting edge of everything new and different. That was then. In recent years, beginning in the last quarter of the past century, the tide turned. Americans are aware that they are no longer necessarily on the cutting edge. They are aware that certainly in some areas other countries have surpassed their own, which is why mere mention of innovation is fraught with implicit if not explicit anxiety. Leaders worry that even if they're ahead, they're in danger of falling behind. They worry because innovation has become a battleground on which they vie with each other—with other leaders both at home and abroad—in the race to stay out front.

Of course, not everyone sees the U.S. as vulnerable. Some consider Americans paranoid without good reason, citing certain benefits that other countries might well envy, including entrepreneurial dynamism, size, and heterogeneity.[1] But most of those who understand innovation, and many Americans who actually are in positions of leadership and management, are worried—worried about a world in which everything changes so fast that mere mention of innovation easily is experienced as more perilous than promising.

An article titled "Why Isn't America Innovating Like It Used To?" asks why the new technologies do not increase productivity in the present the way they did in the past.[2] Another article, "America the Innovative?" questions the long-held assumption that Americans have an advantage because "democracy is central to innovation." This is not necessarily so, argues the author, presenting evidence to the contrary, for example, data on international patent filings that indicate that in 2011 the world's single most prolific innovator was not an American company, but rather ZTE, a Chinese telecommunications organization.[3] Still another piece, "The Future of Innovation: Can America Keep Pace?" claims that "everyone wants innovation and agrees that it is the key to America's future," but then goes on to cite the "growing signs the U.S. no longer has the commanding lead it once did."[4] Then there is this one. "When It Comes to Innovation, Is America Becoming a Third World Power?" is, as its title suggests, a clarion call. It warns that the U.S. now competes with many other countries around the world that "are much more serious about innovation than we are." The evidence to support the claim includes, again, the number of patents issued to American applicants—that number has been decreasing while the number issued to foreign-based applicants has been increasing. (In 2013 the American company that posted the most patents was IBM.) Data gathered by the Information Technology and Innovation Foundation support the concern over America as innovator, which is still further reinforced in a study on innovation conducted by the Boston Consulting Group. It concludes that America is "disadvantaged in several key areas, including work force quality and economic, immigration, and infrastructure policies."[5]

It is difficult to exaggerate the degree to which in the past few years Americans have been fixated on the importance of innovation, and on the question of how to spur the U.S. to, depending on your point of view, stay ahead or get ahead. Leaders in each of the different sectors—especially but not exclusively the public and private —have been inundated with facts and figures, with reports and commissions, all dedicated to "securing our economic growth and prosperity" through innovation.[6]

The Brookings Institution produced a working paper titled "A Dozen Economic Facts About Innovation," which argued that the pace of innovation in the U.S. has "slowed during the past four decades" and that "reinvigorating the momentum of innovation that benefits all Americans is imperative."[7] Another report, this one produced by several high-level government agencies, including the Council for Economic Advisers, cautioned that "America's future economic growth and international competitiveness depend on our capacity to innovate."[8] And still another, this one drafted in part by the Department of Commerce, sent a similar message, warning that whatever the advantages the U.S. enjoyed in the past, they are in danger of eroding, with dire consequences. Other countries have become "better educated," the report points out, and "our manufacturing sector lost ground to foreign competitors." How to combat the decline? Again, through innovation: "Innovation is the key driver of competitiveness, wage and job growth, and long-term income growth."[9]

Not to be left behind, the National Governors Association got on the innovation bandwagon by, among other things, drafting a document titled "Innovation America: A Final Report." It similarly insisted that innovation is "the hallmark of a successful economy." It claimed that innovation introduces new ideas, ultimately determines what is produced, and finally affects how production itself is organized. Given that the report was sponsored by a governors' group, it was more specific, at least somewhat more specific, on how exactly some of these ideas on innovation might actually be implemented. It argued that each of the fifty governors was "uniquely suited to create a unified vision for innovation in education and the economy." And it suggested that each of the fifty governors use their bully pulpits to enlist both the private sector and the federal government in joining with them to reach their own innovation goals.[10]

Because the National Governors Association is dedicated to the successes of governors specifically, it has a political agenda and also an economic one. So far as innovation is concerned, governors are motivated by the vigor and success of the United States in general, and of their states in particular. They know full well that their own political fortunes depend on their capacity to keep the U.S. broadly competitive, and to keep the states for which they directly are responsible strongly positioned relative to other states.

What we can say then is that whatever the particulars of their position, America's political leaders, legislators as well as executives, have an overarching challenge: to encourage innovation to keep the United States at a comparative advantage relative to other countries around the world. The literature I just cited speaks to this issue. It is a cautionary literature, intended to incentivize, even to intimidate America's political leaders into doing whatever it takes to keep America innovative. The message to these public sector leaders is clear: unless you support public policies that support innovation, the U.S. is finished. Well, not finished exactly, but doomed to fall behind in this dog-eat-dog world, in which dozens of other countries around the world are doing whatever they can to get a leg up.

Nor is the focus on innovation in government confined to the national and state levels. In fact, one of the Centers at the Harvard Kennedy School, the Ash Center for Democratic Governance and Innovation, recently focused on innovation in three American cities, Boston, Denver, and New York. "Today's fiscal, social, and technological context is making *innovative governance* increasingly important for city officials and the agencies and jurisdictions they lead. Cities are reframing innovation from a value-based concept to a concrete goal with specific targets in the same manner they have transformed their approach to values such as efficiency and transparency. And . . . cities are beginning to tackle the challenges of measuring their effort and results in supporting and promoting innovation" (italics mine).[11]

The Ash Center's overarching message is, obviously, that innovation is mandatory, and that it is doable. Of course it is doable only under certain circumstances. For example, New York City's Center for Economic Opportunity (CEO) has innovation "at the core of its mission." To realize its mission, CEO has developed strategies—such as a "culture of innovation"—that support new ideas and creative thinking at every stage of the process.[12] The work of the Ash Center makes clear in any case that innovation is not only about competition, not only about staying one step ahead. It is also about the need to innovate in order to survive—and to thrive in the second decade of the twenty-first century.

Naturally, the competitive environment at home and abroad applies to business leaders as to political leaders, and indeed to leaders across the board, to American leaders everywhere, all of whom are being relentlessly pressed and pressured to be innovative. For instance, America's educational leaders are being pushed to be more innovative pedagogically and also technologically, in the so far frustrating quest to make America's learning systems as obviously contemporaneously effective as those in, say, Singapore or Shanghai. Similarly, America's military leaders are being pushed, also tirelessly, to be more innovative, especially since the old ways of war, of boots on the ground, increasingly are less viable, less politically supportable and sustainable. Inevitably this means turning to technology to develop new hardware (such as drones), lest the United States take second place militarily to anyone else.

Corporate leaders certainly are being tirelessly driven, harangued even, by shareholder activists, by boards, by the media, even by government to innovate if they want to have even a prayer of becoming or remaining competitive. A study confirms the anxiety. Senior executives in every major industry and on every continent were asked two key questions about innovation. The first: On a scale of one to ten, how important is innovation to the success of your firm? The second: On a scale of one to ten, how satisfied are you with the level of innovation in your firm? Not surprisingly, "the executives rate the importance of innovation very high: usually a nine or 10. None disputes that innovation is the No. 1 source of growth. Without fail, however, most senior executives give a low rating—below five—to their level of satisfaction with innovation."[13]

The literature on innovation in business tends to fall into two categories: easy and hard. Easy is advisory: this is what you, the CEO, can do to get your company to be innovative. A random sample includes develop core capabilities, remember the consumer is boss, be nimble, learn from your mistakes, cut your losses, be externally focused, discover opportunities, test and assess new ideas.[14] Of course, each of the experts takes a slightly different approach, some concluding, for example, that creativity is more likely when people are encouraged to think not outside the proverbial box, but inside it. Drew Boyd and Jacob Goldenberg write, "People are at the most creative when they focus on the internal aspects of a situation or problem—and when they constrain their options rather than broaden them. By defining and then closing the boundaries of a particular creative challenge, most of us can be more consistently creative—and certainly more productive."[15] The implication, in any case, in every case in which a leader is being told "how to," is that you too can be a leader who encourages innovation, who supports followers (employees) in an effort to develop the new and different.

The literature on innovation that makes it all seem hard is similarly replete with advice, with suggestions and words of wisdom. But this more ominous literature mirrors that on innovation more generally. Danger is always lurking, which means that if you do not heed the advice (which is hard to follow) and pay attention to the instruction (which is hard to implement), you'll fail and fall behind. This applies perhaps particularly to innovations in technologies, which on the one hand are opaque to many of the leaders and managers who are responsible for them, and on the other hand have the potential at least to have great impact. Thus there is this question: How does a firm respond, what does a leader do, when faced with an altogether new technology that threatens the firm's survival?[16]

At the head of the pack of experts on innovation in business is business school professor Clayton Christensen. He is the author of one of the seminal books on leadership and management in recent years, *The Innovator's Dilemma*.[17] Christensen describes two types of innovations specifically in technology. The first are sustaining technologies. These are incremental improvements targeted at current customers of companies dominant in a particular sector. The second and more threatening (at least to the status quo) are disruptive technologies. At first, disruptive technologies tend to result in inferior products, certainly in comparison to the original ones. But once the technologies improve, so do the products to which they're applied. In time the process results in products that serve new, typically unanticipated markets, at which point the companies that previously were dominant are vulnerable to falling victim to their more innovative competition.[18]

Christensen used the history of disk drives to illustrate his primary point, which is that changes in an industry can be so "pervasive, rapid, and unrelenting," that they cause leaders to have "nightmares." He describes the problem as an innovator's "dilemma," but it might more aptly be described as a paradox. For when the best firms succeed they do so because they listen carefully to their customers, and invest aggressively in the technologies and capacities necessary to anticipate their customers' future needs. However, when these same best firms subsequently fail, they do so for precisely the same reasons—they listen carefully to their customers and invest aggressively accordingly. Hence this caution: "Blindly following the maxim that good managers should keep close to their customers can sometimes be a fatal mistake."[19] Of course, the trick is to know when to keep close and when not, since failing to distinguish the difference between them can be "fatal."

In a subsequent volume optimistically titled *The Innovator's Solution*, Christensen tries to becalm his constituency—corporate leaders pushed to take risks who then are threatened by the very risks they were pushed to take—by suggesting ways of dealing with the inherent dilemma.[20] Specifically, he talks about how "senior executives" have three main tasks: first, to determine "through judgment" which of the corporation's resources should be invested in mainstream businesses and which in (disruptive) growth businesses; second, to "shepherd" the creation of the "disruptive growth engine," and third, to "sense" when circumstances are changing.[21]

One could argue that these rather general nostrums are small beer, given the ominous tone on page one of the book. "There is powerful evidence that once a company's core business has matured, the pursuit of new platforms for growth entails daunting risk. Roughly one company in ten is able to sustain the kind of growth that translates into an above-average increase in shareholder returns over more than a few years. Too often the very attempt to grow causes the entire corporation to crash. Consequently, most executives are in a no-win situation." Of course, it's possible if not probable that general nostrums are all that anyone, no matter how much of an expert, can, under the daunting circumstances, reasonably muster.

If Christensen's work was inadequate to the task of warning "most executives" that they could well be in a "no-win situation," a more recent piece in the *Harvard Business Review* might finally get their attention. In an article again with an ominous title, "Big-Bang Disruption," and in a subsequent book of the same name, authors Larry Downes and Paul Nunes suggest that Christensen's cautions are actually obsolete, replaced by innovation so fast and so unpredictable that no leader, no matter how clever or alert to the danger, can adequately protect against it.[22] Big-bang disrupters, they argue, change the rules. Entire product lines can get created or destroyed "overnight," disrupters coming at breakneck speed, out of nowhere and everywhere, making dislocation difficult if not impossible to contain or contest. In other words, even the best and brightest of the nation's leaders, here specifically corporate leaders, are at risk.

Again, speed is the demon. Technologies change lightning fast— which means that nearly anything and everything can be built quickly and cheaply. This allows even startups to come out of the gate with products that are disruptive and, at least some of the time, superior to anything previous, including the market leader. Moreover, the culture has changed, permitting, even encouraging failure. This means that innovators get to test many different ideas relatively quickly and easily, throwing out the bad ones while focusing on the good ones. Downes and Nunes argue that many of the apparent failures are not really failures at all. Instead they prime the demand pump by teaching the market what's possible. As they put it, "in today's hyperinformed world, each epic failure feeds consumer expectations for the potential of something dramatically better."[23]

Innovation is, of course, a good thing, not a bad one. But so far as leaders are concerned, it can seem a threat. Why? Because, as we have seen, in the second decade of the twenty-first century it often *is* a threat, something new and different lobbed at high speed in their general direction. This applies equally to different leaders in different sectors, though broadly speaking we can say that political leaders are especially threatened by innovations in other *countries*, while business leaders are especially threatened by innovations in other *companies*.

The pressure to innovate is in any case extreme. In Washington, any mention of innovation receives rare bipartisan support. Companies including Citigroup, Coca Cola, and DuPont have chief innovation officers. Venture capitalists are more attracted to something that smacks of innovation than they are to anything else. Management consultants such as McKinsey have entire practice groups dedicated to innovation.[24] And management experts such as London Business School professor Gary Hamel swear by it, claiming that we owe our "existence" to innovation, and our "prosperity" to innovation, and our "happiness" to innovation, and our very "future" to innovation.[25]

There is however an irony here: innovation requires risk, and Americans are becoming more risk averse, not less. Companies are adding jobs more slowly; investors are putting less money into new ventures; and Americans are starting fewer businesses. In 1982, new companies made up roughly half of all U.S. businesses. By 2011, this figure had dropped to just over a third.[26]

So what's a leader to do? One could argue that it's best to play both sides—to maximize the upside by making innovation a strategic priority, and to minimize the downside by managing the here and now with insight and intelligence. What is in any case clear is that leaders reluctant to risk, risk being left behind. Innovation requires not only the willingness to be "misunderstood for long periods of time," but the willingness in the short term to fail in order in the long term to succeed.[27]

14 COMPETITION

CONVERSATIONS ABOUT COMPETITION generally fall into two categories: those on how to compete, and those on the context within which competition is taking place. Over time the conversations about how to compete tend generally to remain the same. People always have been and always will be competitive. There always have been and always will be leaders charged with improving their group's, their organization's, competitive advantage. And there always have been and always will be certain leadership tactics and strategies that tend more or less to repeat themselves. But the second, the context within which competition takes place, is radically different now from what it was even a decade ago.

What exactly is meant by competition? That depends, of course, on the nature of the situation and on the task at hand. The struggle to get to the top and then to stay there, to be a winner, not a loser, not even second best, can be about who makes the best widgets, or about whose military is strong enough to withstand any threat, or about who educates their young more efficiently and effectively than does anyone else.

So far as Americans are concerned, in any case, the biggest competitive change, the biggest competitive challenge, is contextual. It is the degree with which we now compete not only with each other, within the U.S., but also with people from other countries. Global competition is not altogether new, of course—all along, some things were better made, or perceived to be better made, in countries other than our own. We long have coveted watches made in Switzerland and continue to even now. But as the literature on competition makes plain, the world in which we live at this moment in time is one in which the United States of America is only one among a number of potentially rival nation states, any one of which could stand out, surpass the U.S., in any given area. Most American children who were born in the late twentieth century or early in the twenty-first will come to understand, viscerally as well as intellectually, that they are citizens of a country that in many ways excels, but that matching, not to speak of surpassing, the global competition is a gain hard fought, not a God-given right.

As good a place as any to start the discussion on competition is with the literature on leadership in business, specifically with two books widely considered classics of the business literature: Michael Porter's *Competitive Strategy* (1980) and *Competitive Advantage* (1985). Both have dominated the discourse on what it takes to gain and maintain a competitive advantage in the private sector—within an industry. Porter sees competition as pervasive and, in general, as a force for good. Competition, he writes, makes "things better in many fields of human endeavor."[1] However, his long-standing preoccupation with the subject suggests, implicitly if not explicitly, how difficult, how stressful, is the competitive context within which private sector leaders necessarily now operate. The quest to get out front has become even in the past decade or two a never-ending struggle which, if lost, can rapidly reduce a leader to a has-been. Put directly, to be a leader in Porter-world is to be, by definition, intensely competitive.[2] *On Competition* is, then, a manual of sorts, which implies that leaders who fail to understand the complex context, domestic and foreign, within which they operate, and then to act accordingly, are destined to fail. Why? Because if you fail to be fiercely competitive, and if you fail to compete smart, the competition will eat your lunch.

According to Porter, of paramount importance to gaining competitive advantage is strategic analysis. But analysis of this sort is not simple. For competition is a concept at least somewhat elastic. Competition could be with established industry rivals, with potential entrants, for good customers, even for reliable suppliers. In other words, within any given industry there is competition at every turn, which explains why strategic analysis is as critical as it is complicated. Porter identifies some of the steps necessary to such analysis, including (1) defining the relevant industry, (2) identifying the participants and distinguishing among them, (3) assessing the motivation of the competition, (4) determining the overall industry structure, and (5) analyzing change in the past, in the present, and in the projected future. But if for the sake of brevity Porter's complex work on competition were to be simplified, his suggested strategies would look something like this: work hard, think ahead, expend your energy in looking outside not in, and use common sense.

By implying that leaders in business would be better off looking out than in, it's clear that Porter is more interested in context—the context within which the business is situated—than he is in anything else. His interest, in other words, is in the development of what I am calling contextual expertise, though he refers in the main to context that is proximate—that is, industry-wide, whether national or international—not distal. Not for him the virtues of leaders' self-awareness or the benefits to them of leading a balanced life. This is not to suggest that Porter by definition disdains individual, internal work, such as, for instance, skill building and developing self-awareness. Rather, it is to say that individual, internal work is not what Porter does. What he does is promulgate the critical importance to competitive advantage of contextual expertise, of looking beyond the personal to the organizational and to the larger environment within which the organization itself is situated—looking to the "relevant industry."

Porter points out that most corporate leaders think of threats to their organizations as emanating only from the outside, from changes in, say, technology, or in the nature of the competition. He goes on to correct, in a way, the misperception: "The greater threat to strategy often comes from within. A sound strategy is undermined by a misguided view of competition, by organizational failures, and, especially, by the desire to grow."[3] In keeping with his argument, Porter is not even especially impressed with the radical changes in technology. He is decidedly not caught up in what he calls the "general fervor" brought on by the assumption that the Internet changes everything, that it renders the old rules about companies and competition obsolete. Not so, he argues. In fact, common sense about context dictates that the Internet is no more than, though no less than, a "powerful set of tools that can be used, wisely or unwisely, in almost any industry and as part of almost any strategy."[4]

I use Porter as a lodestar on the subject of corporate competition because in this particular area he himself is a star—he has his own competitive advantage. It's not that other voices on the subject are invalid or unimportant. But books are based on Porter's work, and when he speaks, elites, both in business and government, are likely to listen.[5] Given his own competitive advantage in this general area, it's important we be clear about his target audience: primarily, though not exclusively, chief executive officers of major American companies. In fact, he concludes his most recent tome on competition with a short chapter titled "Seven Surprises for New CEOs." (I refer to this material also in the section on business.) Notwithstanding the breezy language, the message is seriously sobering. The "seven surprises" are in fact cautionary notes to newly minted CEOs, certain to find that in this dog-eat-dog world leadership is exceedingly difficult to exercise:

- You can't run the company.
- Giving orders is very costly. (Notice the "very.")
- It is hard to know what is really going on.
- You are always sending a message.
- You are not the boss.
- Pleasing shareholders is not the goal.
- You are still only human.[6]

Porter is hardly oblivious to the issue of global competition—in 1990 he wrote a book titled *The Competitive Advantage of Nations*—and in recent years his ideas in this regard have of course evolved further.[7] But given that his first major work on competition was published some thirty years ago, and given that his base is business, not politics, his context remains, first and foremost, the "relevant industry," again, whether only within the U.S. or also without. Times have changed, however, which is why included among contemporary experts on competition are experts on international relations.

In the twenty-first century our conception of the context within which competition takes place has expanded exponentially. In nearly no area of human endeavor is the subject of competition confined any longer to context conceived of as national. Almost without exception, competition is conceived of now as being, also, international, trans-national, and even trans-sectoral. So, for example, on the question of how competitive is the U.S. with other countries, say with China, competition is not confined to any particular area, to any single sector or "relevant industry." Rather, competition is conceived of as being in every sphere, across the board: in politics and business, in markets and the military, in education and health, in technology and biotechnology, you name it.

Of course, individual business leaders still focus primarily on their own businesses, and on their relevant industries. However, nearly no corporate executive is exempt any longer from the more overarching concern over how well the United States is doing relative to other countries. For example, in one key area to which every leader can or at least should relate, Internet services, there are regular warnings that the United States is in danger of falling behind, far behind, our global competitors. Lawyer and tech expert Susan Crawford insists that because the U.S. lacks an industrial policy that includes long-term planning, America will in the not distant future "be a Third World Country when it comes to communications."[8]

Foreign affairs expert Fareed Zakaria makes a slightly different point. He emphasizes "the rise of the rest"—the rise of countries that only recently enjoyed unprecedented rates of growth. He goes on to add that this remarkable, robust growth has been in nearly every "sphere of life . . . industrial, financial, educational, social, cultural," and military.[9] What this means obviously is that our conception of competition, our notion of what competition consists of, must be expanded and extended, far further than what we have been used to up to now. Just like American cars, American schools and American singers compete in the global marketplace—which suggests that competition overall, across the board has gotten stiffer. American cars compete against other American cars; American schools and singers compete against other American schools and singers. However, American "products" compete now not only against each other but, in addition, against products from places on the planet that until recently were not even on our radar.

It all begins, Zakaria writes, with economics, with rates of growth. But discussions of global competitiveness necessarily involve politics as well. Several years ago the Harvard Business School launched a project it titled "Competitiveness at a Crossroads" in order "to help U.S. leaders understand, assess, and improve U.S. competitiveness." The results were sobering, in part precisely because it was obvious that the problem—and yes, there was ample evidence of a "deepening U.S. competitiveness problem"—extended beyond the private sector to the public one. Survey results revealed a high degree of pessimism among business leaders, with a large majority anticipating a continuing decline in America's competitive position. They did not, however, fault themselves for their predicament. Rather, they placed the blame, albeit indirectly, on other leaders, that is, on leaders responsible for other components of the American context, such as the political system, the legal system, K–12 education, economic policy, and the regulatory environment.[10]

"Competitiveness at a Crossroads" is a remarkable document for two reasons. First, it is targeted primarily at private sector leaders who implicitly if not explicitly blame public sector leaders (and other leaders as well) for their own managerial travails. Second, at the most obvious level the focus of the report is not on leaders per se, but, interestingly, tellingly, on components of the context within which they do their leadership work. For example, one of the charts, titled "Elements of the National Business Environment," is divided into two parts: "Macro Elements" and "Micro Elements." Macro elements include macroeconomic policy, the political system, the educational system, the legal system, and the tax code; micro elements include infrastructures, availability of skilled labor, availability of top-flight higher education, and the quality of capital markets.

So far as leaders per se are concerned, the report concludes with a few specifics. Somewhat counterintuitively, though certainly not surprisingly, it suggests that policymakers, political leaders, are not the only ones who should be doing what they can to restore U.S. competitiveness. "Business leaders can and should play an equal or greater role." The report goes on to name eleven different things that CEOs can do to enhance competitiveness, ranging from improving the general business environment "in your firm's region" to "increasing sourcing from local suppliers."[11] While the various recommendations are well taken, they seem again perhaps to be somewhat lame. At least they seem lame when stacked up against the "deepening U.S. competitiveness problem" to which the report draws attention, and which motivated it in the first place.

I might make note here that the problem of the problem keeps repeating itself. Here's what I mean. The analysis of the problem, whatever the problem, is, typically, not only well intentioned but well executed. But the solutions to the problem, equally typically, are lame, not up to the magnitude of the challenge at hand. What I am suggesting is that by always implying that there are remedies for what ails us might be misleading. Maybe some problems have no solutions. Maybe some problems cannot be fixed, or, at least, they cannot be fixed in any way that in the current climate, the current context, is politically, economically, and socially feasible.

In the event, a report somewhat similar to "Competitiveness at a Crossroads" was prepared by the World Economic Forum (known to those in the know simply as "Davos"). It is titled, aptly, "The Global Competitiveness Report." It defines competitiveness as the "set of institutions, policies, and factors that determine the level of productivity of a country" which, in turn, determines the level of prosperity. After studying 144 countries around the world, the authors of the report conclude that there are twelve "pillars of competitiveness"—or, as I would put it, twelve components of context that pertain to achieving a competitive advantage at the national level: (1) institutions, (2) infrastructure, (3) microeconomic environment, (4) health and primary education, (5) higher education and training, (6) goods market efficiency, (7) labor market efficiency, (8) financial market development, (9) technological readiness, (10) market size, (11) business sophistication, and (12) innovation.[12]

Competition at the global level is, then, a theme that now dominates. To be sure, concern about American competitiveness is not universally shared; there are occasionally experts who remain entirely sanguine about America's future. For example, an article in the *Harvard Business Review* suggests that the American fixation on competition with China is misplaced, that the U.S. retains fundamental strengths "that China, for all its recent success, can only envy."[13] However, the titles of many other recent articles confirm that, by and large, Americans are quite concerned. Here is a sampling: "The Surprising Reasons Why America Lost Its Ability to Compete" and "What's Killing America's Global Competitiveness?" and "U.S. Slips Down the Ranks of Global Competitiveness" and "U.S. Productivity Growth Lags Behind That of Foreign Competitors."[14] Most everywhere is the impression that America is falling behind what it was. Most everywhere is the impression that America is falling behind in comparison with other countries. And most everywhere is the impression that leaders are falling down on the job.

Nearly invariably now it is China that looms in the distance. China is the challenger, the country that more than any other seems to threaten American supremacy. It is huge. Only recently it lifted hundreds of millions out of poverty. Its growth rate (over 9 percent a year for almost thirty years) has been the fastest of any major economy in recorded history. It is the world's largest holder of money. It has an ancient history, culture, and system of governance, each of which is unfamiliar to the point of being alien. And it poses a potential military threat.[15] China is perceived as particularly competitive in certain areas, such as technology, which is why rhetoric on the subject is urgent to the point of being combative: "For many U.S. firms, the first battleground will be within China. . . . Numerous companies now complain about a host of issues, from intellectual property theft to nontariff barriers to aspects of China's regulatory regime. . . . But the next battleground will be the global marketplace for sophisticated technologies," where China is already competitive in, for instance, high speed rail and solar energy.[16]

Finally, China poses an existential challenge, for its stunning successes in the recent past raise a fundamental question: Is the American experience necessarily everywhere the experience to emulate? If getting on top and staying on top is the ultimate goal, is it anywhere written that capitalism in tandem with liberalism, with democracy, necessarily is the best path, the only path that is right and good and true? Or are there alternatives to Western ways that other countries in other circumstances, especially developing countries, can and should carefully consider? Foreign policy expert Charles Kupchan has pointed out that China's brand of one-party rule, of autocracy, has had strong advantages. Above all, it has, largely though not entirely, spared Chinese leaders from dealing with Chinese followers, or, as Kupchan put it, "Chinese leaders are able to make policy decisions absent the pulling and hauling of the democratic process."[17]

What is giving ground in any case is the idea that the only way is the American way, that the United States not only did dominate in the past but that it will continue to dominate in the future. Now the global discourse is at least somewhat different. Now many of the experts no longer believe that the optimal model for a just society, for a competitive society, is necessarily, by definition, the American model. And now many of the experts no longer believe that the alternative to liberal hegemony, dominated by the United States of America, necessarily is chaos. "The rules and norms of that order are subject to much more extensive and intensive debate than ever before." Put differently, competition nowadays is not only about goods and services. It is about ideas—there is a global competition of ideas.[18]

Given that competition is such a preoccupation, it makes sense that it extends to education. If Americans are to compete successfully both with each other and in the global marketplace, American students must have the benefit not only of a world-class education, but of an education that is best in class.

Yet, as earlier mentioned, the evidence suggests that also in this all-important area America is falling short. We have known for some time that America's educational system is in trouble, that by different measures, including proficiency tests and graduation rates, it falls short of where it was even a generation ago. What we have learned more recently is that it also does poorly in comparison with other countries; some number of them do a notably better job of educating their young than does the United States. Though the U.S. invests more in K–12 public education than many other developed nations, its achievements lag behind. According to one previously referenced international assessment, which measures the performance of fifteen-year-olds in reading, mathematics, and science, U.S. students rank fourteenth in reading, twenty-fifth in math, and seventeenth in science, compared to students in other industrialized countries.[19] Similarly, another recent report found that students in Latvia, Chile, and Brazil make gains in academics at rates three times faster than American students, while those in Portugal, Hong Kong, Germany, Poland, Lichtenstein, Slovenia, Colombia, and Lithuania improve at twice the rate.[20]

Clearly, American students are on average increasingly ill-prepared to compete with their global peers. In fact, a document prepared by the Council on Foreign Relations frames the problem in precisely this way, in terms of America's competitive advantage—or, more precisely, America's competitive *dis*advantage. "The United States' failure to educate its students leaves them unprepared to compete and threatens the country's ability to thrive in a global economy and maintain its leadership role," warns the Council's task force. "Educational failure puts the United States' future economic prosperity, global position, and physical safety at risk." It will not be able to "keep pace," that is, to compete highly successfully in the global marketplace unless it moves to "fix the problems it has allowed to fester for too long."[21]

Of course, the key word in the preceding sentence is the adverb *highly*. One might reasonably ask, in other words, where it is written that the United States of America must always be first, first in every-thing that is anything of consequence. The answer to the question lies in American history and culture. Suffice it to suggest that competitive-ness has historically been part of America's DNA, with competition imprinted on our collective, capitalist consciousness. At every age and at every level—from the individual to the institutional—we are taught that first is best and that second is, merely, second best. This means that American leaders who fall short of this imagined ideal are destined, doomed, if you will, to disappoint.

PART IV   POPULATIONS

15 CLASS

WE IMAGINE SOMETIMES that we live in a classless society. Classlessness is, after all, the American ideal, in keeping with the American ideology. But in truth, Americans have never been equal. The United States of America never was a classless society, not at its inception in the late eighteenth century and not now, early in the twenty-first. The key questions then are, What are the current class differences? and What is their impact on leadership and followership?

Class implies distinctions that are, among others, economic, social, and cultural. For the purpose of this discussion I define class as conventionally conceived—as a division or stratification based primarily on income. It is by this measure that in the late nineteenth century the United States divided more obviously into upper and lower classes and, in time, into a middle class as well. Driven by industrialization, the distinctions among different people based on how much money they earned and how much wealth they accumulated—and everything that this implied, including level of education—grew sharply. The select few, those few who were members of the upper class, ranked even then according to how many millions they had. Up to the 1880s, wrote one contemporary observer, "for one to be worth a million of dollars was to be rated as a man of fortune, but now . . . New York's ideas as to values, when fortune was named, leaped boldly up to ten millions, fifty millions, one hundred millions, and the necessities and luxuries followed suit."[1] Around the same time, America began also to boast a burgeoning middle class, characterized by, among other things, the growing number of women free to stay at home, free to be domestic rather than to have to go into field or factory to bring home food or earn a day's wage.

In the late nineteenth century the working classes, and the even the lower classes, lived, famously, infamously, in Dickensian squalor. Cities such as New York, Chicago, and Pittsburgh were home to men, women, and children living in utterly abject conditions. The data are imprecise, but they give an idea of how great was the American divide, between those in the upper class and those in the lower. While Phillip Armour was earning in excess of $1 million, and John D. Rockefeller in excess of $3 million, and Andrew Carnegie some $25 million, the wages of factory workers rose from slightly more than a dollar a day in 1860 to slightly more than a dollar and a half in 1890. In Pittsburgh the working poor lived in "rickety shanties, ramshackle cottages, and filthy overcrowded tenements with primitive sanitation and toilet facilities." And in New York the tenements were so bad that social reformer Jacob Riis described them as made "for evil." They were hotbeds of "epidemics that carried death to rich and poor alike" and "nurseries of pauperism and crime" that filled the jails and the courts.[2]

So, by the end of the nineteenth century the distribution of income, wealth, and political power was more unequal than it had been at any time since the start of the Civil War, making the U.S. far from a classless society. According to James MacGregor Burns, "something insidious and ominous" had taken place in the "vaunted land of liberty and equality— the continuation or creation of sets of social outcasts who comprised virtually an array of castes, who could not break out of their castes, and hence could hardly hope to rise through the class hierarchy. . . . At the bottom of the caste system lay, as usual, black workers and their families." It was not until the twentieth century that the caste system, as Burns called it, began to give way, somewhat.[3]

For a constellation of reasons—including the natural affinity between Protestantism and capitalism, huge tracts of land, a single language, enforceable laws, and a "rough social contract" that could accommodate the expansion of capitalism without excessive social tension—Americans never turned to the great working-class movements that emerged in Europe during the industrial revolution, communism and socialism.[4] They did, however, develop a strong trade-union movement, which played a consequential role in transforming the lives of American workers. And they did develop another, more middle-class impulse that rivaled working-class ideology in its intellectual and moral power and, ultimately, in its social impact. This was the social reform movement that had its origins in the three Western religious traditions, Protestantism, Catholicism, and Judaism.[5] In addition, by the time Franklin Roosevelt became president, he was in a position as a result of changing American attitudes and the Great Depression to enact legislation that greatly improved the position of American labor. Together with the social reform movement, new laws such as the Wagner Act, which legally protected the right of unions to organize, enabled America's middle class to grow and to thrive as it never had before.

The task of adapting capitalism or, better, restraining it in ways that protected it from its own excesses, fell then to the government. The government became the "instrument for counterbalancing the inequalities of unregulated capitalism." Social Security protected against poverty in old age. Unemployment insurance and workers' compensation saved, at least for a time, those who suffered job loss or work-related accidents. And the right to join a union mitigated the imbalance of power between employer and employee.[6] Of course, the New Deal did not eliminate altogether gross income inequities, or class conflicts between those whom Karl Marx referred to as the proletariat on the one hand, and the bourgeoisie on the other. But the New Deal and the government programs that were the result did give millions of working-class Americans access to the middle class. Moreover, they created the impression, the expectation, of a meritocracy. Ostensibly at least, nothing now stood in the way of Americans getting the good life if only they, we, worked hard enough and well enough.

The decades subsequent to World War II were characterized by increased government spending and the economy thriving in ways that provided the middle class with jobs, pay raises, and opportunities for their children. In addition, Lyndon Johnson's Great Society was a remarkable expansion of the sorts of programs initially introduced by the New Deal: government was considered an instrument to be used for the greater good. Medicare and the War on Poverty were to be financed by the government, largely though not entirely the federal government, which in turn would secure the necessary revenues from the strong economic growth that, it was presumed, would continue indefinitely. Author Jeff Faux captures the mood of the moment, the optimism that suggested that everything was possible in this best of all possible worlds—including a top-notch education: "As legal racial discrimination was abolished and the poor were helped out of poverty, full employment and a massive expansion of higher education would provide new opportunities for all Americans. . . . State universities became avenues of upward mobility for millions. In California, the top 12.5 percent of high school students were eligible to go to college. The top 30 percent could go to the next level of state universities. And everyone who could do the work could go to a community college. Tuition was free."[7]

Between 1947 and 1973 about 80 percent of the American workforce enjoyed an increase of about 75 percent in their average overall compensation. During the same period, the average household median income more than doubled, and unemployment dropped to 4.6 percent. Moreover, the U.S. was not only increasingly egalitarian, it was increasingly rich. The poorest 20 percent of Americans had an income rise of fully 117 percent, while the income for the middle fifth rose on average 104 percent. In other words, notwithstanding the several political traumas that Americans only recently had endured—assassinations, the war in Vietnam, Watergate—in the early 1970s economically the country was on a high. "Virtually all Americans looked toward a personal future that was brighter and more promising that at any other time in our history."[8]

By the mid- and late 1970s this optimism had started to wane—the tide had started to turn. The decades of growing prosperity had slowed or even stopped. After 1973, average real wages for non-managers fell for several years, then inched back up, and then more or less stagnated for the next three decades. Though the decline was gradual, prices over-all were rising (notwithstanding little or sometimes even no inflation), while income and wages stayed stuck. By 2005, "people were not earn-ing any more than their counterparts in age and education had earned a quarter century" earlier.[9] There is, of course, endless debate about why the decline. Some blame exogenous forces, globalization, for example; others blame endogenous forces, such as poor political leadership. Clearly the best explanation is the usual one: a complex mix of contex-tual components that together put the United States on a trajectory of decline which it has yet fully to reverse. Put differently, it's not clear at this point that the high level of class equity that Americans enjoyed in the late 1960s and early 1970s will ever again be repeated. Since then the distinctions, the divides between and among the different classes, have not decreased, they have increased.

This brings us to the present—to the current context within which leadership and followership are being exercised. It is not too much to say that one of the recurring refrains in recent years, certainly since the financial crisis and yes, since the Occupy Movement, is America's grow-ing inequality. There is a drumbeat of criticism about the rich being too rich and getting always richer, about the poor being too poor and getting always poorer, and about the shrinking middle class. The class divide is exacerbated by the divide between the races in income and, especially, in wealth. For about three decades the income gap between white Americans and nonwhite Americans has stayed more or less the same. But when it comes to wealth—as measured by assets including cash, homes, and retirement accounts, minus debts such as mortgages and balances owed on credit cards—white families have far outpaced black and Hispanic families. "Before the recession, non-Hispanic white families, on average, were about four times as wealthy as nonwhite fami-lies. . . . By 2010, whites were about six times as wealthy."[10]

The debate about what exactly is happening and why is raucous in part because people disagree even about the fundamentals. What, for example, or who exactly constitutes the middle class? During the 2012 presidential campaign, Republican candidate Mitt Romney said that he considered "middle income is $200,000 to $250,000 and less." Others have argued that a much more appropriate approximate figure is $100,000, with those earning more upper middle class, and those earning far less lower class. I might add that in 2011 the median U.S. household income was $42,000—an income that as we know goes much further in some parts of the country (say in Akron) than it does in others (say in Seattle). The bottom line is that about half of American adults describe themselves as being in the middle class, including almost half of those earning more than $100,000.[11]

However, in 2012 the Pew Research Center found that the share of people who self-identify as lower or lower middle class rose substantially in recent years, from 25 percent in 2008 to 32 percent in 2012.[12] Moreover, the greatest growth in this category has been among younger Americans, who feel squeezed in a way that their parents generally did not.[13] Other survey results are similarly bleak, revealing that an "overwhelming majority" of self-described middle-class adults feel that it is harder today than it was a decade ago to maintain their standard of living, and that most middle-class adults blame leaders, political and corporate, for their straightened financial circumstances.[14]

Other data similarly confirm that the middle class is shrinking and that people are feeling squeezed. In 2011, the U.S. Census Bureau reported that the middle class had lost some of the "income pie," while the share that went to the affluent grew. "The 60 percent of households earning between roughly $20,000 and $101,000 collectively earned 46.6 percent of all income, a 1.5 percent drop from a year earlier. In 1990 they shared over 50 percent of income." As one expert put it in response to the tightened "vise on the middle class," their "pay rate has gone down, the number of hours that everyone in the household works has gone down, their homes have lost value. These are the people really ravaged by the recession."[15] However you look at it then, the size of the middle class—defined by the Census Bureau as anyone living in a household with two-thirds to double the national median income—has dropped. In 1970, 61 percent of all Americans lived in households considered middle class. In 2012, the figure was 51 percent.[16]

An obvious by-product of the contracted middle class is an expanded, impoverished lower class—and an expanded, enriched upper class. In 1980, 23 percent of U.S. lower-income households lived in majority low-income neighborhoods. By 2010 the figure had climbed to 28 percent. According to a 2014 article in the *New York Times*, notwithstanding Lyndon Johnson's War on Poverty, large numbers of poor people have remained "a remarkably persistent feature of American society." About four in ten black children live in poverty, and about three in ten Hispanic children. Moreover, some 1.7 million households are living on cash incomes of less than $2 a person a day, "with the prevalence of the kind of deep poverty commonly associated with developing nations increasing since the mid-1990s."[17] At the other end of the economic scale, the share of upper-income households living in majority upper-income neighborhoods doubled, to 18 percent in 2012 from 9 percent in 1980.[18]

Growing inequality has become particularly pronounced at the extremes. A study published by the Brookings Institution concludes that the "growing gulf between the rich and the poor is the result of remarkable gains at the very top of the income distribution and little advance at the bottom." In fact, the income of the top 1 percent of earners has "soared" so high that the current degree of income concentration is greater than at any time since before the Great Depression.[19] Nobel Prize–winner Joseph Stiglitz summarized the growing disparity with a single statistic: the upper 1 percent of Americans brings in nearly a quarter of the nation's income each year. It is from Stiglitz that the short-lived but nevertheless in some ways effective Occupy Wall Street movement got its slogan, "We are the 99 percent."[20]

So what is the impact of this growing income disparity, the growing sense that the United States of America is not only not classless, but riddled with class divides that rankle? The implications are considerable, if only because the message of inequity is being driven home, pounded into our heads now, with relentless regularity. Our minds are stuffed with big data, so crammed with information ceaselessly provided that it's almost impossible not to be repeatedly reminded of how much America has changed in recent years, how much more elusive now is the American Dream. Here's a *Huffington Post* headline from July 2012: "Average Student Loan Debt for Borrowers Under Age 30 Is Nearly \$21,000, Study Finds." The story went on to say that the average student loan debt among young borrowers had more than doubled since 2005, and that student loan debt overall had "skyrocketed," up 248 percent. This, moreover, "in a weak job market" that does not give young college graduates a clear path toward paying off their debt.[21] Whither the days of free tuition? I might add that by 2014 the number had climbed still higher: the average 2014 graduate with student-loan debt owes \$33,000.

Arguably the greatest impact of the increased class cleavage is the sense that America's future is unlikely to replicate its golden, relatively recent past. This is not to say that things won't get better; since 2009 the economy has improved and it continues by many measures still to improve. But it is to say that what the United States looks like tomorrow is not likely to differ greatly from what it looks like today. Economist Lawrence Katz articulates the widely held view that America is becoming a place where the top tier will remain wealthy beyond most of our imagining and the rest will work in jobs that make the lives of the elites not only more comfortable, but more plush. In Katz's view, America is "starting to belie [its] promise as a land of equal opportunity in which the place that you were born was not as important as the talents that you were born with."[22]

Again, the data, both objective and subjective, confirm Katz's conclusion. A 2007 study, the Economic Mobility Project, estimated that 40 percent of children born to parents in the bottom quintile of the income distribution will remain there—and 60 percent of the children will move up. Not bad at first glance. But the data further suggest that this 60 percent is unlikely ever to move far, ever to move up the economic ladder in any meaningful way. Put differently, children born into families with low income (in the bottom 20 percent) have only a 1 percent chance of reaching the top, while children born into families with high income (top 5 percent) have a 22 percent chance of remaining at the top.[23] The subjective findings support the objective ones. Americans now have less faith in their long-held beliefs about the efficacy of hard work. And while they remain optimistic about the long term, they are pessimistic about the short term. Of those who suffered substantially during the Great Recession, about half said it would take them at least five years to recover.[24]

The impact of growing class divisions on leadership and follower-ship in America is, of course, impossible to assess precisely. But some surmising is in order. First, it seems reasonable to suppose that there is at least some correlation between the two. I, in any case, am hardly surprised that decades of increasing class distinctions (1970–2010) and a shrinking middle class coincide with decades of decreasing trust in leaders nearly across the board. Again, however unreasonable or un-fair—for followers matter and so does context—we hold leaders, people in positions of power and authority, responsible for what happens. Not only do fully 69 percent of all Americans believe that the U.S. is in a leadership crisis. And not only is confidence in sectors critical to the nation's strength and strategic direction "abysmally low." It now happens that even leaders in sectors of which Americans historically have been proud—such as education—have a bad reputation. Again, when Americans were asked if they had confidence in their educational lead-ers, most replied, "not much."[25]

Second, it seems that not only are we critical of our leaders, we tend ourselves more to withdraw. In a short essay titled "America Discon-nected," Theda Skocpol summarizes the situation. "Our civic life," she writes, "has changed fundamentally in recent decades. Popular mem-bership groups have faded while professionally managed groups have proliferated. Ordinary citizens today have fewer opportunities for active civic participation and big-money donors have gained new sway. Not coincidentally, public agendas are skewed toward issues and values that matter most to the highly educated and the wealthy."[26]

Our comparative, collective withdrawal from civic life and civic responsibility is itself related to leadership and followership. When membership groups were run by ordinary people, as opposed to by professional leaders and managers, the opportunities to exercise lead-ership were considerably greater. Skocpol estimates that in 1955 3 to 5 percent of the adult population was serving in one or another leadership role, and that more recruits were needed each year. Opportunities like these—to lead and to manage and to learn how democracy works—simply don't exist anymore or, more precisely, they do not exist nearly to the extent that they did.

Instead, as we will see in the section on Interests, beginning in the 1960s old-line membership organizations were replaced by professionally led advocacy groups, with their own particular agendas. So, not only have we, we ordinary Americans, we followers, lost opportunities to become leaders in the interest of the common good, we have been replaced by professionals whose interests are, in contrast, narrow and sectarian. Again, compounding the problem is that professionally led advocacy groups tend to exacerbate the class divide: they are more inclined to support issues of interest and importance to the upper and middle classes, and less inclined to support issues of interest and importance to the lower one.

So, far from being a classless society, the United States of America is a society in which distinctions among the different classes are obvious, sometimes even egregious. What's most striking about class in the second decade of the twenty-first century is how our perceptions of it have changed, even in the recent past. Until relatively recently, most of us believed in the American Dream. But for many of us the American Dream has become the Impossible Dream—a dream so elusive as to seem unreal. Has this change gone unnoticed? Obviously not. Will this change have an enduring impact? Who knows? But I venture to say this. If the idea of equity turns out permanently to have morphed into the ideal of equity, the leadership class, which by and large is upper class, will some day somehow pay a price.

16 CULTURE

WHAT CONSTITUTES CULTURE? And how does culture affect how leadership and followership are exercised? We talk about popular culture, political culture, and corporate culture, about high culture and low, about cultural trends and culture as art, and about culture as habits of the heart. Given the mixed meanings and messages, and the competing definitions, I'll simply say that this discussion touches on American culture in two ways: first, as it pertains to power, authority, and influence; second, as a reflection on and of the American way of life. Culture is, then, as I use the term here, a component of our collective context. It is about things learned, shared, and transmitted.[1]

It's a cliche I've already invoked, but the fact is that a half century later we still live in the world the 1960s made. The various rights revolutions reached their apogee only recently—with increasingly widespread acceptance and legalization of gay marriage. The sexual revolution changed our sexual mores, apparently forever. (Between 1969 and 1973 the percentage of Americans who believed that premarital sex was "not wrong" doubled, from 24 percent to 47 percent. By 1982 the number had climbed to 62 percent.[2]) The long hair on men and blue jeans on women that were what hippies wore bespoke anti-authority attitudes that persist to this day. And in the 1960s shock art went mainstream, adopted by artists from Frank Zappa and the Velvet Underground to Andy Warhol and Yoko Ono, and was soon to become the "motto of every would-be punk rocker, gangsta rapper, indie filmmaker, and stand-up comedian."[3] Moreover, in the 1970s and 1980s, when telecommunications were dramatically deregulated, previous restrictions on self-expression were nearly entirely eliminated. This lack of legal constraint—this testing of the limits of public propriety—was virtually unprecedented. It was part of the anti-authority euphoria—sex, drugs, and rock 'n' roll in full throttle—that gained speed in the 1960s and has not since been reversed. (It took a while, but now even marijuana is being legalized for other than medicinal purposes.)

The upheavals of the 1960s were triggered by turmoil wrung from tragedy: a series of assassinations; rebellions, the product of repressions; and the Vietnam War. What's remarkable is how deep and widespread was the cultural change, how full-throated was the assault on the status quo, and how enduring its legacy. Hardly any institution or sector of society was immune from attack, especially youthful attack, and virtually every major controversy divided Americans not only for the remainder of the twentieth century, but into the twenty-first. It was the beginning, but not the end, of what now we call the culture wars.[4] "The existence of a basic shift of mood rooted in deep social and institutional dislocations was anything but ephemeral. . . . [It] was perfectly clear to any reasonably observant American that the postwar revival of the Eisenhower years had completely sputtered out, and that the nation was experiencing a *crise de conscience* of unprecedented depth."[5]

The legacy of this "basic shift" remains everywhere in evidence. Reinforced now by the changing technologies, our anti-authority disposition is as highly honed as it ever has been. No leader or follower is exempt from this general, generational shift. None of us is immune to the effects of this popular intrusion on the leadership class.

Until relatively recently someone like me—a professor in an institution of higher education—was addressed as "Professor" or "Doctor." Now, sometimes I'm still called "Professor Kellerman." But I'm likely as not to be called "Barbara," even by students I've never met before.

Similarly, we used to defer to experts, for instance to physicians. We'd take their word as gospel and do what they told us to do. Now we pocket their instructions and then we second guess them. We get another opinion—or maybe another ten thousand opinions, by checking out the Internet. More generally, once upon a time we simply obeyed orders issued by superiors—by whoever were the relevant authority figures, whether priests or rabbis, police or politicians, leaders or managers. Now, though, we incline not to unless we really need to or we really want to. In the workplace, of course, we generally risk punishment if we refuse to go along and, conversely, we generally anticipate reward for good behavior.

Now we have a different habit: we challenge people in positions of authority, all of us emboldened by the spread of democracy, by flattened hierarchies, by the rhetoric of empowerment, and by the practice of participation. "The evidence of the decline in respect for authority is everywhere—and everywhere are leaders who labor to lead. The change is cultural, contextual. Norms are now such that followers demand more—and leaders succumb more often."[6] When the most famous and most admired of American generals—David Petraeus—is reduced to apologizing publicly for a sexual indiscretion, you know that something dramatic has changed. In his first speech after resigning as head of the CIA, Petraeus felt obliged to address the issue openly, to, in effect, beg for public forgiveness: "Please allow me to [reiterate] how deeply I regret—and apologize for—the circumstances that led to my resignation . . . and caused such pain for my family, friends, and supporters."[7]

A leader abject in apology has become, not incidentally, commonplace, so routine we scarcely even notice anymore.[8] Here is just one of countless examples: when Target (in 2013) had a massive security breach at thousands of its stores, endangering or at least inconveniencing millions of its customers, Target president and CEO Gregg Steinhafel did what he could to make nice. Among other things, he wrote an open, personal letter of apology that was published in most of the nation's major newspapers. It read in part, "Our top priority is taking care of you and helping you feel confident about shopping at Target, and it is our responsibility to protect your information when you shop with us. We didn't live up to that responsibility, and I am truly sorry."[9]

Evidence of this leveling—between leaders and followers—is abundant, including in the popular culture. In times past no one much cared what you thought or what I thought, about anything. The ones who counted were the experts on, say, food or film, while our opinions languished—no one could care less. Now, seemingly suddenly, we're the ones that matter most. Life is one big participatory democracy. Everyone wants to hear what we have to say—about everything and anything, about everyone and anyone. Whether a hotel or a restaurant, a book or a movie, a politician or a performer or an area of public policy, it's our views and our votes, in person or online, that most matter. Technologies transmit our preferences, and these preferences—not those of experts or other authority figures—hold sway. We have final say on what's good, what's bad, and what's simply irrelevant or indifferent. Polls prevail. Focus groups rule. 360-degree feedback serves as jury and sometimes judge. We tweet and we text and we expect and demand to be heard—and guess what? We *are* heard—sometimes. Of course we are hardly heard all of the time, in every area and on every issue, on gun control, for example, where our views seem not in the least to matter. As noted, background checks are supported by more than 80 percent of the American people; still Congress has been unable to pass the requisite legislation. But we are heard most of the time, and when we are not, sometimes at least we don't let up, we keep pushing our point.

Further, our leaders are being denigrated as never before—in person, in the blogosphere, on new media and old. Once again culture and technology twin; the result is an invasion of privacy and a dissemination of information that until recently was culturally inconceivable and technologically impossible. "When did the culture become so coarse?" asks one observer.[10] A turning point was during the presidency of Bill Clinton, in his second term, his relationship with Monica Lewinsky. Clinton was president when he was caught, so to speak, red-handed. He was caught in a trap of his own making, in an inappropriate affair with a twenty-one-year-old White House intern, Ms. Lewinsky.

I make no judgment here about what the president did, or about the outcry and upheaval that were the result. Rather, I take note of the toxic mix: an intemperate president, an available young woman, a plethora of politicians excited by the smell of blood, a press corps with apparent license to invade the most private parts of a president's personal life, and an insatiable public that felt no evident compunction about peeping at an unzipped president.[11] In the end, the scandal cost Bill Clinton dearly. And it cost us, the American people, dearly as well. The price we paid for prying was one year of a president way too distracted to lead effectively.

This Oprah-ization, if you will, of American life, this intrusiveness and relentless debasement of our national discourse, is as telling as it is astonishing. Leaders in every sector are vulnerable now to new levels of exposure and ridicule. You too can name some of the targets (in addition to Petraeus and Clinton) of our collective fixation, leaders such as Mark Hurd, former CEO of Hewlett-Packard; Mark Sanford, former governor of South Carolina; Anthony Wiener, former congressman from New York; and Cardinal Roger Mahony, former head of the Los Angeles diocese. Thus the culture—the context, the zeitgeist—is conducive to diminishing leaders and concomitantly, relatively, to elevating followers. The change is dramatic. Suffice it here to say that when Woodrow Wilson was in the White House the American people had no idea that he had been felled by a stroke and was utterly incapable of conducting the nation's business. Similarly, most Americans had no clue that for the duration of his presidency Franklin Roosevelt was essentially crippled, paralyzed by polio and confined to a wheelchair. And we had no hint that Camelot featured a president, John F. Kennedy, who was a bounder so relentless it was reckless. Who knew then? Who would *not* know now?

While what happened in the late 1960s and early 1970s changed American culture forever, what it did more precisely was exacerbate and accelerate an already existing trend. Critic Paul Cantor has written about the enduring tension in American culture between individual liberty on the one hand and the authority of the collective (usually the government) on the other. So, yes, the 1960s were a time of great change. But they were also no more than a variation on, an exaggeration of, a theme that has been threaded through American culture since the beginning of the republic. Again, it's the tension between liberty and authority or, if you prefer, between those who are powerless (followers) and those who are powerful (leaders). Cantor writes about the difference in American life between two models of order: the "top-down" (leader) model and "bottom-up" (follower) model. And he poses the perennial question, "Are Americans better off running their own lives or submitting to the guidance and rule of various kinds of elites and experts?"[12]

Film, for example, frequently asks the question, at least implicitly, whether freedom and order are compatible—a theme of that most quintessential of all American art forms, the Hollywood Western. Nearly invariably, Westerns celebrate freedom—individual freedom. But freedom in film is nearly always problematic. On the one hand is the frontier, the open, empty spaces to which people from the East move to be released from the shackles of society. But on the other hand is the need to tame, to bring some semblance of order to the very frontier that, from a distance, is alluringly free of nearly any constraint. The paradox is obvious: as soon as the frontier is settled by those seeking to escape civilization and its discontents, some sort of order (leadership) is imposed, lest the fledgling society deteriorate, disintegrate, into anarchy.

Because the tension between liberty and leadership has been so powerful a running theme in Hollywood Westerns—of course this mirrors a running theme in American culture, especially American political culture more generally—they tend to have heroes who neither are leaders or followers. (Check out John Wayne's character, in John Ford's great film *The Searchers*.) Rather they are outsiders, not apparently part of any identifiable social system, not apparently situated on any identifiable political or economic hierarchy. They are not typically powerful—even though usually they get their way—nor are they typically powerless. Rather, as Cantor writes, "The heroes of American popular culture often do not seem to be orderly in any conventional sense. They are more inclined to break rules than to obey them. They are frequently mavericks, creative individuals who go against the crowd and chart their own course. But these seemingly disorderly characters often create the new orders that a country needs to keep making progress."[13] So liberty trumps authority—but only for a time. In the end liberty is not cost free, nor is authority dispensed with for the duration. The hero has been an agent of change, but to describe him as a leader in the usual sense, one who wants and intends to solicit and sustain followers, is simply incorrect.

I might add that the American archetype as alone but resolute in facing down a threat of some sort—think Gary Cooper in *High Noon*—reappeared at least three times over in American film in 2013, albeit in somewhat different guises. Again the examples of this were men, and in one case a woman, outside the system, removed from society as we generally understand it. And, again, they were on some level apparently ordinary people caught in an extraordinary circumstance, in this case an existential nightmare that compelled them to display near superhuman feats of endurance. Tom Hanks in *Captain Phillips*, Robert Redford in *All Is Lost*, and Sandra Bullock in *Gravity*—all were exemplars of the American ideal in which the lone individual, not the collective, emerges in some way that in the end is triumphant.

Here three more points on Americans as loners, as independent agents (neither leaders nor followers) who are other than part of a crowd: the first pertains to language; the second to being alone, even living alone; and the third to the loneliness of the long-distance leader. To begin, there is the English language as it reflects the American national character in the twenty-first century. Put simply, communal words such as *community* and *share* and *united* are being used less, while individualistic words such as *personalized* and *self* and *standout* are being used more.[14] This change in our language, confirmed in studies conducted with search engines, is not happenstance. It suggests that our contemporaneous disposition increasingly is to individualism as opposed to collectivism.

Similarly, we have over time inclined more to being alone—as opposed to being in the world of other people. In 1971 Philip Slater published an important book, *The Pursuit of Loneliness*, in which he argued that even within families Americans were seeking ever greater privacy. Americans were unique, he wrote, in that each member wanted a separate room, and a separate telephone and television, and even their own cars.[15] Some thirty years later, Robert Putnam's book *Bowling Alone* described a syndrome somewhat similar: fewer Americans were participating in the groups and organizations that previously had engaged them regularly in civic life, in collective life.[16] And a decade after that, in 2013, came *Going Solo*, by Eric Klinenberg, which reported that more and more Americans were now actually living alone, not sharing their daily lives on a regular basis with any other human being.[17] (Apparently Americans do, however, enjoy sharing their lives with nonhuman animals. In 2013 pet ownership in American households reached an all-time high.) Men and women marry later than they used to, they divorce more easily, and large numbers of them seem actually to prefer living "solo." In this second decade of the twenty-first century, more than half of all American adults are single, and roughly one in seven lives by him- or herself.

Not incidentally, there is a literature that suggests that modern technologies—especially social media—are not bringing us together but driving us apart. We are smitten these days not so much with each other as with our devices, to which we are tirelessly tethered.[18] This leads me to conclude that at least some number of those who are choosing to be alone, especially to live alone, are choosing implicitly if not explicitly liberty over authority. To be alone is to be autonomous—no accommodation is required, and there is no having to manage up or, for that matter, manage down. Moreover, to live alone is to be free to imagine even the humblest of homes a castle, a kingdom to rule as we see fit. Put differently, being alone, living alone, obviates the need for leadership, and for followership, at least in the domestic sphere.

Finally, I would point out that leading is itself rather a lonely business. Not always—it is not necessarily solitary, and some leaders do make a special effort to preclude isolation. But in general the higher up you go, the more difficult it is to stay connected to ordinary people in any ordinary way. Robert Crandall, former chair and CEO of American Airlines, put it this way: "For all the years that I was working, I was trying to achieve a particular goal. So I wasn't interested in balance. . . . I ran American Airlines and it pretty much took up my whole life."[19]

The all-consuming life of nearly all leaders explains why recent American presidents have tended to lean heavily for support on their wives or on other family members—for example, John Kennedy on his brother Robert; Richard Nixon on his daughter Julie; Jimmy Carter on his wife, Rosalynn; Ronald Reagan also on his wife, Nancy; and Barack Obama on his nuclear family, wife Michele and daughters Sasha and Malia. And it explains why Harry Truman purportedly said, "If you want a friend in Washington, get a dog." The most elevated of our leaders can easily be cocooned, cut off by their own exalted levels of power, authority, and influence, and by those around them, advisors and hangers-on bent on hoarding their privileged proximity. And the most elevated of our leaders can easily be cocooned by their own fixations, a vision that persuades them that they are exempt from the rules that govern everyone else.[20]

To imagine twenty-first-century American culture is to imagine something resembling a pie, a pie that can be sliced several different ways. On the one hand it is a pie, a whole pie, in which every piece looks much like every other piece. But on the other hand are a number of different pieces that are, each of them, distinct. Put directly, American culture is, simultaneously, homogeneous and heterogeneous. To a degree our national culture is variable, distinguished by, among other things, region, ethnicity, race, gender, and generation. Similarly, our culture is expressed in different ways, through multiple mediums and mechanisms, everything from art to advertisements, from literature to entertainments, from preaching to politics, from social media to sports to food to sex. In addition, our national culture is reflected in the world of ideas, in the so-called culture wars that pit left against right, liberal against conservative, white against black, poor against rich, men against women, big-government enthusiasts against small and against libertarians who, if they had their druthers, would opt for nearly no government at all.

Withal, in all, American culture has been and remains sufficiently uniform to constitute an important export. People the world over habitually adopt American preferences and proclivities, a sign that while in the second decade of the twenty-first-century Americans might hesitate to use hard power, soft power continues to be a signal resource. Music is an obvious example—in addition to film and television, it is one of the clearest expressions of American culture, particularly popular music for popular audiences. Jazz, country, rock 'n' roll, rap, hip hop—they are as much of an American idiom as any other component of culture, highbrow or low. A review of the top-selling albums of all time confirms the persistent preeminence of American music worldwide. Taking into account only certified sales—counting illegal downloads has become almost impossible—American performers dominate now as they have for decades. As of November 2011, twenty-seven albums had sold more than fifteen million copies worldwide. Sixteen of the twenty-seven were stamped "Made in America," featuring performers such as Michael Jackson, Billy Joel, Garth Brooks, and the Eagles.[21]

Music is as important at home as it is abroad and, since this is a book about the context within which leadership and, yes, followership, are exercised, I should make this point: American protest songs have an especially long and respected, even esteemed lineage that can be traced back to the Revolution and to the anti-authority culture within which it originally was incubated. By definition, protest songs imply rebellion—tension between those with power and authority and those without. In the nineteenth century were such songs about abolition, slavery, and poverty. And in the twentieth century were such songs about, yes, again poverty and injustice, and, later, civil rights, women's rights, and peace not war. Some protest songs themselves had a galvanizing effect. In the early twentieth century Joe Hill, a socialist activist, traveled widely, organized workers he believed were being exploited, and coined the phrase "pie in the sky." In the 1920s and 1930s there were protest songs about the class divide and, yes, also of course about the racial divide. One such had anti-lynching lyrics, with the legendary Billie Holiday singing, "Southern trees bear strange fruit/Blood on the leaves and blood at the root/Black bodies swinging in the southern breeze." And in the 1940s, 1950s, and 1960s, protest songs were associated with icons that included Woody Guthrie, Paul Robeson, and Pete Seeger, each an outlier, not unlike the heroes of Hollywood Westerns. Indeed, like them they paid a price, especially the great Robeson, a powerful black man before black power was in. He was investigated by the FBI, called before the House Un-American Activities Committee, and denied a passport, all for his left-leaning views, which he did not hesitate to tout.

The 1960s and 1970s were, of course, ripe for, rife with protest music—protest against whatever was the establishment, against whoever were those in positions of power. The Civil Rights movement and the women's movement and the anti–Vietnam War movement each incited rebellion through song. Of the troubadours of trouble, Bob Dylan was and remains the most influential and enduring—a protester who was an artist, a pied piper who led legions. The songs for which Dylan is most famous were written in a burst, from January 1962 to November 1963. "Influenced by American radical traditions . . . and above all by the political ferment touched off among young people by the civil rights and ban the bomb movements, he engaged in his songs with the terror of the nuclear arms race, with poverty, racism and prison, jingoism and war."[22]

Arguably the single most famous of all American protest songs—of songs pitting followers against leaders—is associated with the Civil Rights movement. "We Shall Overcome" was adapted from a gospel song and became, in effect, the anthem of the movement, sung repeatedly by individuals and groups, maybe most memorably by Joan Baez standing before the Lincoln Memorial during the historic 1963 March on Washington. The song has since been sung by protesters worldwide—its symbolic status forever enshrined. "We shall overcome. We shall overcome. Deep in my heart I do believe that we shall overcome some day."

Notwithstanding the obvious degradation of the American political culture, and notwithstanding the conspicuous consumption of the American corporate culture, the twenty-first century has not so far had any significant protest movement. The Occupy movement fizzled fast, and no single protest artist has captured the American imagination. The music and lyrics of country, punk, rap, hip-hop, and hard rock reflect rebelliousness, and they are not to be trivialized. But they have not been transcendent, nor have they instigated the widespread disquiet that is the hallmark of any social movement. But let us not be misled, lulled into thinking that the American culture has been dulled. American history suggests otherwise. It suggests that the American culture will mirror forever the tension between liberty and authority; that disrespect for authority will endure in the future as did in the past; and that leaders will continue to find it hard to lead followers who will, from time to time, resist them. American culture is now what it always has been—a reflection of the American experience and of the ideology that explains and sustains it.

17 DIVISIONS

CONTRARY TO POPULAR OPINION, not everyone is persuaded that Americans are divided—that they are "polarized." Political scientist Morris Fiorina has found that while Americans are "closely divided," they are not "deeply divided." His research suggests that the reason we split in elections, or sit them out, is because we, the majority of the American people, "instinctively seek the center." It's the base—the base of the Republican Party and the base of the Democratic Party—that "hangs out at the extremes." Even on an issue as contentious as abortion, Fiorina asserts that most Americans are not militants; they are not implacably and irrevocably committed to one of the two opposing camps, one pro-choice and the other pro-life. Rather they are somewhere in the middle, likely to be "content with compromise laws" whenever such laws can actually be passed.[1]

But, Fiorina is in the minority. The overwhelming majority of researchers, reporters, pollsters, and ordinary Americans believe that the American people are deeply divided: ideologically, demographically, economically, regionally and religiously, and divided as well on many of the most important issues of the day. The number of recent books (and articles) with titles conveying divisiveness is daunting. Here is a sample: Desmond King and Rogers Smith, *Still a House Divided: Race and Politics in Obama's America*; Thomas Mann and Norman Ornstein, *It's Even Worse Than it Looks: How the American Constitutional System Collided with the New Politics of Extremism*; Timothy Noah, *The Great Divergence: America's Growing Inequality Crisis and What We Can Do About It*; Douglas Schoen, *Hopelessly Divided: The New Crisis in American Politics and What It Means for 2012 and Beyond*; and E. J. Dionne Jr., *Our Divided Political Heart: The Battle for the American Idea in an Age of Discontent*.[2] To be sure, the United States of America was more divided in the past than in the present. We are talking here about class and "culture war"—not civil war. Still, the sense that the nation is fractured is pervasive, contributing to leaders feeling hapless and followers frustrated. This is, I hasten again to add, an issue facing not only political leaders but, in addition, corporate leaders, educational leaders, military leaders, religious leaders, and leaders in the various professions—all having to grapple with leading in a nation increasingly more heterogeneous than homogeneous.

For the purposes of this discussion I divide the divides into two groups—general and specific. My purpose here is not to deconstruct the various schisms or even completely to catalogue them. It is simply to point to a component of context—divisiveness—that complicates the exercise of leadership.

General Divides

Divided by Income

We have seen that Americans now split roughly into the extremely prosperous 1 percent and the far less prosperous, or not at all prosperous, 99 percent. The 1 percent benefit, handsomely, from U.S. income growth; the 99 percent do not. As mentioned, 99 percent of Americans are actually worse off today than they were a decade or two ago. There is, moreover, little or even no upward mobility. "Whether because of blatant nepotism or a privileged head start in life that nurtures talent and ambition, opportunities for the children of the top 1 percent are not the same as they are for the 99 percent."[3] In other words, the pretty picture of America as a land of opportunity is dated—the fantasy not seeming any longer a reality. What we have instead, Nobel economist Joseph Stiglitz has concluded, is disillusionment, distrust, disempowerment, and disenfranchisement—the "evisceration" of American democracy.[4]

Stiglitz is hardly alone in his pessimistic perceptions, especially as they relate to "the hollowed out" middle class. Journalist Timothy Noah similarly found that in the past several decades the difference between being a rich American and being a middle-class American has become more pronounced, *much* more pronounced. Noah notes that "the democratization of incomes that Americans had long taken for granted as a happy fact of modern life" has been reversed. We have even got to the point of significant differences between those at the top and those at the tippy top—between those whom Noah calls the "really rich" and the "stinking rich." In other words, even within the top tier, the top 1 percent, there are useful if perhaps galling distinctions to be made, between those earning, say, over a million dollars a year, and those earning over nine or ten million.[5] After another jump in 2013, executive pay is drawing particular scorn as "an engine of income inequality." After pointing out that in 2013 the median compensation of a chief executive was $13.9, up 9 percent from 2012, *New York Times* writer Peter Eavis writes, "In some ways, the corporate meritocrat has become a new class of aristocrat."[6]

To be sure, even skeptics such as Stiglitz and Noah do not argue for socialism over capitalism. Noah explicitly acknowledges that *some* degree of income inequality is necessary to a capitalist system, in order to reward both effort and skill. His objection is to the *excessive* degree of income inequality, which is why the figures he provides are of interest not only of themselves but because they have consequences. These include depression and dystopia, especially among those "toiling in the economy's lower tiers."[7] I might add that the widely (though not universally) praised, and wildly popular tome by French economist Thomas Piketty, *Capital in the Twenty-First Century*, revisits the debate about the merits of capitalism in the light of new longitudinal data. His conclusions about the inevitable, systemic inequities are rather dire.[8]

Divided by Ideology

I could as well have titled this section "Divided by Politics"—for whatever our ideological differences, they play out in political life. In fact, nothing is so indicative of our sharp ideological divide, especially during Barack Obama's two terms in the White House, as the Tea Party, which of course appeared rather recently out of nowhere to take on not only the Democratic political establishment but the Republican establishment as well. This is not to say that right-wing populists—the ultra-conservative Republicans who constitute the Tea Party—are a wholly new political phenomenon. Nor is it to say that the Tea Party is, single-handedly, responsible for the might of the Republican right, which more accurately is traced back to former Speaker of the House Newt Gingrich. It was Gingrich, after all, who, both before and during his time as speaker (in the 1990s), first steered his party in an increasingly conservative direction, while assuming an increasing assertive style. Nevertheless, since 2009–2010 the Tea Party has become emblematic of hard-right Republican politics. In the meantime it has been tail to the mainstream Republican Party dog.

"Scholars have amply measured and established the sharp increase in political polarization over the last three decades."[9] As well, during this same time, the level of vitriol between the opposing camps has intensified. What this means in the corridors of Congress is that the overlap between partisans on the one side and partisans on the other is near zero. Of course, the professional politicians are not alone, are not the only ones who politically are polarized. Thomas Mann and Norman Ornstein point out similar dispositions among party activists more generally, among members of the so-called base, including delegates to national party conventions, local opinion leaders, issue advocates, donors, and even some members of the general public—many of whom engage on a regular basis in polarized, partisan conversation.[10]

What, more precisely, is everyone in such fierce disagreement about? Hot-button social issues provide the most obvious grist for this mill, issues such as abortion and gay marriage. But the more significant divide is between those who lean to the right more generally and insist on low taxes and small government, and those who lean to the left more generally and insist on increased revenues to support those they think need government help. By galvanizing the right wing, and by reconnecting the Republican Party to some of its traditional principles such as deficit reduction and constitutional conservatism, the Tea Party has become the "crucial player" in the right-wing political spectrum.[11] It's possible, of course, that the Tea Party will significantly weaken and even fade gradually from the American scene. Still, its rise to political prominence in such short order has been, for lack of a better word, "stunning."[12]

Divided by Demographic

Again, imagine a pie that can be sliced several different ways. Here is a quick cut at us, divided in three: by race, by gender, and by geography.

Just when we thought America was "post-racial," something comes along to remind us that America is no such thing. In 2013, the trial of George Zimmerman for the killing of Trayvon Martin proved if proof were needed that the old, deep scars had by no means healed—that Americans remain divided by race. Our perceptions of the past are different, our experiences in the present are different, our attitudes and opinions are different. A poll taken shortly after Zimmerman was declared not guilty in the shooting of Martin (a seventeen-year-old black man, or child, depending on your point of view) revealed a "vast racial divide between blacks and whites," not only as it pertained to this case but as it pertained to the American system of justice more generally. Roughly 86 percent of blacks and 60 percent of Hispanics believe that the system fails them, that it does not fairly treat members of minorities. In stark contrast, only 41 percent of whites believe the same.[13] America's first black president chose to discuss the distinction. In remarks he made several days after the Zimmerman verdict, Obama said he thought it "important to recognize that the African American community is looking at this issue through a set of experiences and a history that doesn't go away."[14]

Of course, the Zimmerman trial was only emblematic, a symptom of the divides between, among, the races that are so deep and enduring, so stark, they of themselves belie the American Dream. King and Smith summarize the situation: "Entering 2010, blacks were more than twice as likely to be poor and nearly two times more likely to be unemployed than whites, with Latinos in the middle. The median incomes of black households barely exceeded . . . three-fifths of that of whites, and Latino households were only slightly higher. Homeownership for blacks and Latinos was roughly two-thirds that of whites. In terms of infant mortality, cancer, heart disease, and stroke, health statistics were substantially worse for blacks than for whites. For both blacks and Latinos, school segregation was on the rise, in fact even if not by law. Perhaps most grimly, in a nation that was still roughly three-quarters white and only 12 percent black, the nation's inmate population included only slightly fewer blacks than whites, and Latinos were also greatly overrepresented. In the early twenty-first century, the stark reality is that the United States remains a house divided, on race and by race."[15]

The divide by gender is less vivid, but no less real. What it is, in any case, is a paradox. For in some ways women have made great strides—either ahead of or rapidly gaining ground on men—but in other ways they remain behind, well behind. Women have pulled ahead in education: they earn almost 60 percent of all bachelor's degrees; 60 percent of all master's degrees, half of all law and medical degrees, and 44 percent of all business degrees. Moreover, in 2009, for the first time women earned more PhDs than did men, with the rate accelerating even in male-dominated fields such as math and computer science. In addition, women have pulled ahead or nearly even in the world of work. About half the total workforce is now made up of women: they hold over half of all managerial and professional jobs, make up over 60 percent of the nation's accountants, and hold about half of all positions in banking and insurance.[16]

Withal, the gender gap, particularly the divide between men and women that advantages the former over the latter, is by no means closed. There is a wage gap: in 2013, women in the United Sates were paid about 80 cents for every dollar paid men—and the gap was worse for African American and Latina women. This wage gap exists in every state, and in every one of the country's fifty largest metropolitan areas.[17] Similarly, there is a leadership gap: in 2013, women led only about 3 percent of *Fortune* 500 companies; they held only about 17 percent of board seats; and they constituted only about 18 percent of elected congressional officials. For women of color the gap was greater. They held only about 3 percent of board seats, and 5 percent of congressional seats. Finally, there is a gender gap in public policy. Women are more interested than men in certain issues—for example, in child care and health care—and their opinions are likely to be different as well. In fact, "on virtually all the hot-button issues that bedevil Washington today—guns, health, how to fix the economy, the state of the Obama presidency—the differences between men and women is striking."[18] Here is just one example of an "extreme gender difference" on just one issue: drone strikes. In 2013, 61 percent of American adults approved of such strikes. But within the 61 percent was a striking distinction. Fully 70 percent of men approved of drone strikes, while only 53 percent of women did the same.

Then there is the divide by geography, which though not so widely appreciated, is no less real. There are significant differences between living in one area of the country and living in another; between living in one state and living in another; between living in one community, a particular city, say, and living in another. In California the cost of owning a home is nearly twice the national average. In some states, such as Texas and North Dakota, there are "right to work" laws; in other states, such as Washington and New York, there are no such laws.[19] And, though this is changing fast, for years in some states, such as Iowa and Connecticut, same-sex couples were free legally to marry, whereas in other states, the majority, they were not.

While Atlanta is one of the most affluent cities in the U.S., it is also one of the most physically—geographically—divided by income. This division, rich and richer in some parts of the city, poor and poorer in other parts, is one of the reasons why Atlanta is one of the hardest cities in the country in which to achieve upward mobility. It turns out that where you grow up, literally, specifically, has an impact on the likelihood of your climbing the socioeconomic ladder. As a result, there is less upward mobility in the southeastern United States, and in the industrial Midwest, with the odds against you if you are from cities that, in addition to Atlanta, include Charlotte, Memphis, Raleigh, Indianapolis, Cincinnati, and Columbus. In contrast, there is measurably greater upward mobility in other areas of the country such as the Northeast, the Great Plains, and the West, and in cities including New York, Boston, Salt Lake City, Pittsburgh, and Seattle.[20]

Similarly, there is a big difference between the communities of, say, Menlo Park, California, and Visalia, California—even though driving from one to the other takes only about three hours. Menlo Park is in the heart of Silicon Valley, which for three decades has thrived as it has grown into one of the most important centers of innovation in the world. In Menlo Park jobs abound, wages are high, the crime rate is low, schools are among the best in the state, and the air quality is excellent. In Visalia things are different, worse, significantly worse. It has the second-lowest percentage of college-educated workers in the country, its crime rate is high, schools are among the lowest ranking in the state of California, and Visalia "consistently ranks among American cities with the worst pollution, especially in the summer, when the heat, traffic, and fumes from farm machines create the third highest level of ozone in the nation."[21]

There are other geographical divides, geographical differences, as well. One is between urban America and rural America, the first generally trumping the second. "In the most basic sense, there is an urban/suburban/exurban America that is headed in a relatively positive direction . . . and another, more rural America that is falling behind."[22] In the thirty-year period between 1980 and 2010, the more urbanized areas tended to see their (inflation-adjusted) incomes rise, while the more rural areas tended to see theirs fall. But perhaps most striking are the lingering differences between the American North and the American South. While some major Northern cities are hotspots of inequality, on a par with some of those in the Deep South, the Deep South nevertheless remains one of the poorest regions in the United States, and still the most unequal, even into the second decade of the twenty-first century.[23]

Specific Divides

America is not only divided in some general, overarching ways, it is divided on a whole host of specific issues. What follows is no more than an indicator of how considerable the differences of opinion on a range of public policies.

• A decade after the U.S.—led invasion of Iraq, the public remained split on the question of whether or not the war had succeeded, and on whether or not the U.S. should have invaded in the first place. Forty-six percent of Americans said that the U.S. had mostly achieved its goals in Iraq; 43 percent of Americans said it had not. Similarly, there was a nearly even split on our entering the war to begin with: 44 percent said it was the wrong decision militarily to intervene (with boots on the ground); 41 percent said the U.S. government's decision to go into Iraq was the right one.[24] (Of course now that the situation in Iraq has badly deteriorated, these numbers will almost certainly change.)

• Support for same-sex marriage among the public has been growing, especially among the young (18–29) who favor same-sex marriage by a large majority. Still, the country remains divided. Forty-nine percent of Americans said they favor allowing gays and lesbians to marry legally; 40 percent are opposed.[25] Even after the June 2013 Supreme Court decision that struck down the 1996 Defense of Marriage Act, about one-third of Americans opposed the decision.[26] Moreover, while more states have been legalizing same-sex marriage, almost all of the red (Republican, conservative) states continue to ban it. (The courts have, however, started to overturn such bans, declaring them unconstitutional.) Red states are, not incidentally, also "competing to impose the tightest restrictions on abortion since the Supreme Court established the national right to it" in 1973, in Roe v. Wade.[27]

• Notwithstanding the tragic, traumatic elementary school shooting in Newtown, Connecticut (2012), and notwithstanding agreement on implementing mainstream gun control laws, Americans remain closely divided over whether it is more important to control gun ownership or to protect gun rights. The differences of opinion tend to be along the typical fault lines, including between Democrats and Republicans, blacks and whites, rural dwellers and urban ones. For instance, 79 percent of Democrats believe that stricter gun control laws would reduce the number of deaths caused by mass shootings. However, only 29 percent of Republicans believe the same.[28] Similarly, no fewer than 78 percent of blacks support stricter gun control laws, while only 48 percent of whites do the same.[29]

• About four in ten Americans say that the level of U.S. government support for Israel has been about right. However, on this issue as on most others there is a partisan divide. The majority of Democrats (55 percent) favor current U.S. policy on Israel, but the majority of Republicans (34 percent) do not. Curiously, though, "conservative Republicans stand out for their belief that the U.S. has not been supportive enough of Israel"—fully 57 percent of this particular demographic believes that the U.S. should be doing more.[30] (Right-of-center Republicans have a history of strong support for Israel.)

• The divide in the debate over immigration is between those who believe that the border must be secured first, before doing anything else, and those who believe that illegal immigrants should be allowed to remain in the U.S. *while* security improvements are being made. Republicans and Democrats are on opposite sides of the fence on this issue, so to speak, but within each of the major parties there are substantial differences as well. For example, Tea Partiers favor a "border security first" approach by a margin of more than two to one.[31]

• The divide over affirmative action continues to run "deep." In 2013, 62 percent of blacks and 59 percent of Hispanics agreed with this statement: "We should make every possible effort to improve the position of blacks and other minorities, even if it means giving them preferential treatment." But only 22 percent of whites did the same.[32]

We have seen that some of the experts emphasize American centrism. They conclude that compromise is possible if only our elected officials, our political leaders, would do the necessary compromising, collaborating, and cooperating. Still, 61 percent of the American people themselves have come to believe that they, that we, are far more divided now than we were even ten years ago. However far-fetched this might seem to some, fully one in five Americans doubts that the United States will remain over the long term united, will remain over the long term "one nation, indivisible."[33]

This brings us finally to the implications of all this—these divides, differences, and disagreements—for leaders. What are the implications not only for political leaders but for leaders of other groups and organizations as well? It's obvious that divisiveness makes leading that much harder. It's difficult to lead any group or organization that lacks cohesion, a sense of community—which is exactly why *diversity* has become such a buzzword. (The idea is to have diversity work for the group or organization, not against it.) It's similarly obvious that divisiveness makes following with even a semblance of enthusiasm less likely. Why should I bother to follow, say, a political leader, or a school leader, or a religious leader, if he or she does not represent me? Similarly, why should I bother to follow if the opposition is so obstructionist nothing will likely ever get done? These are the sorts of questions that are driven by divisiveness—which means that these are the sorts of questions with which leaders must wrestle.

18 INTERESTS

IT WAS JAMES MADISON who first observed that to pursue their special interests, Americans would inevitably group, coalesce, into "factions." And while he knew that factions would threaten the democracy he held so dear, he believed nevertheless that our inclination to align was innate. The "causes of faction," he wrote in *The Federalist Papers*, are "sown in the nature of man."[1]

What Madison did not anticipate, however, was that certain factions would evolve over time, harden into interest groups that would become, of themselves, permanent players in American politics. What he further did not anticipate was that by the second decade of the twenty-first century interest groups across the board—business firms, trade associations, professional associations, church organizations, foreign governments, labor unions, citizens groups, political action groups—would become, in their own right, powerful political players.

For the purpose of this discussion, "interest group" will be defined as any non-party organization whose primary purpose is to engage in political activity.[2] Why would anyone invest heavily in political activity? Because what the government does do, or does not do, has an impact, sometimes a major impact. The AARP, for example, formerly the American Association of Retired Persons, has tens of millions of members.

American retirees receive federal government assistance, most obviously in the form of Social Security and Medicare benefits. So when anyone of any consequence in Washington starts even to think about tampering with these humungous government programs, the AARP goes into full lobbying mode, targeting any and all politicians even remotely involved in the relevant policy debate.[3]

The line between an organization and an organization that is for the primary purpose of exercising political influence is difficult precisely to pinpoint. Is the AARP, for instance, more of a lobbying group than it is anything else? Or does it provide its members with so many other services that "interest group" does not precisely apply? It's not clear. Suffice it here to say first that interest groups are influence groups; second, that interest groups are narrowly focused and carefully targeted; and third, that interest groups are located outside the government that they are trying to engage. Interest group members attempt to influence policymakers by lobbying, which can be done directly, by targeting public officials themselves, or can be done indirectly, by trying to sway public opinion, which, in turn, is presumed to sway public officials.[4]

Over time factions have become fixtures affecting the lives of leaders. Interest groups used to be few in number and insignificant. They were players, but only at the margins of political life. Now they are not—now they are central. Now there are many interest groups—many, many interest groups. And now, a good number of these interest groups are large, powerful, well-financed, and unregulated. What's new, in other words, is the extent of their reach and the degree of their political clout. By every account, the number of interest groups has exploded in recent decades, beginning in the 1960s and 1970s, when Washington became the epicenter of interest group activity.

Exactly why interest groups proliferated only relatively recently remains something of an open question. The United States has always been hospitable to special interests and to special interest groups. The right of free speech, the right to associate, and the right to petition the government to redress grievances—assurances like these have supported special interests for over two hundred years of American history.[5] It's likely then that the various rights revolutions to which I earlier referred account at least in part for the relatively recent explosion in the number of advocacy groups.[6] The rights revolutions of the 1960s and 1970s—again, civil rights, women's rights, children's rights, gay and lesbian rights, the rights of the mentally and physically challenged— were turning points, each a series of demands made by the powerless on the powerful. It was the beginning of a new age of entitlement in which Americans across the board demanded to be heard, in which Americans on even the lowest rungs of the socioeconomic ladder insisted they had a claim. It was, in other words, a time during which followers pressed leaders for rights and privileges to which they, followers, previously had little or no access.

Interest groups are in some sense similar. They lack political power and authority. So they try to exercise influence: they press people who have political power and authority to give them something that they believe rightfully is theirs. In this limited sense, the expansion in the number of interest groups, and in the level of influence they exercise, is an expansion of free speech, of democratic participation. But interest groups have other effects as well. They complicate, even constrain the lives of leaders; they pit leaders against each other; and they make compromise more difficult, not less. By every measure there is more lobbying in Washington in the present than there was in the past—and the political and financial stakes are far higher. In the second decade of the twenty-first century there are somewhere between fifteen and twenty thousand interest groups in the Washington area alone; outside the nation's capital there are two hundred thousand more.[7] So what is it that these tens of thousands of groups and organizations actually do?

If all public officials are in some sense "leaders," one can say simply that interest groups, that is, the lobbyists who staff them, spend whatever their resources, including money and time, targeting these leaders in particular. Interest groups are leader oriented. It is the leader—here the person in the position of political authority—who is the target of the influence attempt. Of course, the nature of that attempt depends on variables such as what is the issue, who are the players, and what is the context within which the issue is located. Good advocates, smart lobby-ists, choose issues that appear to be at least somewhat amenable to influ-ence attempts. They locate policymakers who might be receptive, open to persuasion. And they select from an array of tactics and strategies to develop something resembling an action plan. Of course, none of this is necessarily easy or straightforward. In fact, lobbyists often have "little control over the policy process and many of their actions are reactive rather than proactive, forced upon them by the actions of other policy-makers and advocates."[8]

Lobbyists try in any case to be as clever and persuasive as they possi-bly can, marshalling an array of different arguments based, for example, on the public interest, or on feasibility, or on cost, or on the expertise that they provide, which can be important. But making an argument, presenting a persuasive case, is only one of the many different direct lobbying techniques. Others include meeting personally with the per-son who is the target of the influence attempt; meeting personally with a member of the person's staff; helping to draft legislation, rules and regu-lations, or both; testifying at legislative hearings; engaging in informal contacts; and doing favors for key players, even giving gifts.[9] The bottom line is this. While the status quo is always advantaged—change is dif-ficult to sell—the jockeying for position between buyer and seller, be-tween (political) leader and lobbyist, can be a drain, on both individuals and institutions. On the one side are leaders of, say, businesses, non-profits, foundations, or educational institutions, typically represented by lobbyists making their case, trying to sell their wares. And on the other side are political leaders, pushed and pulled and prodded by lobbyists coming at them from every direction. (Political scientists refer to the re-lationship among congressional committees, government agencies, and interest groups as the "iron triangle." The implication is slightly insidi-ous: the public is not well served when these ties become too close.)

The preceding paragraph references direct lobbying only. Indirect lobbying techniques include, among others, use of the Internet. Tens of thousands of interest groups now have their own websites, which are inexpensive, easy to update and to access worldwide. The Christian

Coalition's website, for example, provides information on what it stands for, on what it does, and on how it operates. It also tells how to join, and donate, and lobby leaders on the Coalition's behalf.[10] Multiply this plethora of information a thousand times and you have some conception of how cluttered is the context within which government leaders necessarily now operate.

This is not to say that political leaders are equally responsive to every interest group, or to every leader for whom these groups are lobbying. Some interest groups are more powerful and persuasive than other interest groups, and some lobbyists are more powerful and persuasive than other lobbyists. (Former members of congress and of the government bureaucracy are particularly well positioned to lobby anyone who previously was a peer, a colleague.[11]) Of course, the sector of American society now best represented by interest groups is the private sector—especially big business—a fact of political life that for good and obvious reason is controversial. As Jeffrey Berry and Clyde Wilcox point out, the controversy is not inconsequential, for it implies a major mismatch, between big business on the one side and every other interest, including the public interest, on the other. They cite one expert who believes that the increasing intrusion of big business on big government is nothing short of "the centerpiece in the breakdown of contemporary democracy."[12]

At the heart of the matter is, of course, money. Over the past ten, fifteen years, "corporate America (much of it Wall Street) has tripled the amount of money it has spent on lobbying and public affairs consulting in D.C."[13] This is not necessarily to suggest that big money necessarily equates always to political power. But it is impossible now to believe that money is irrelevant to political power, independent of it, especially given the amounts available to big business, which typically dwarf the amounts available to other groups that represent other interests.

Here is an example: Microsoft has an in-house staff of some sixteen full-time lobbyists, it retains more than twenty different lobbying firms, and it belongs to different trade associations that themselves have clout. In addition, the company backstops the Washington office with help from headquarters whenever such help is needed. Having headquarters in Washington State supporting lobbyists in Washington, D.C., enables Microsoft to use technical experts to shape the debate in the nation's capital. Executives can speak to legislators, or to their staffers, or to administrators, with great authority—which is buttressed of course by the roughly $10.5 million dollars Microsoft spends on its overall lobbying effort.[14] And here is another example: when Comcast, the largest U.S. cable company, wanted to grease the wheels in Washington, to win approval to buy the second largest U.S. cable company, Time Warner, it spared no expense lobbying, including wining and dining our political leaders. Comcast, in fact, spends more money on lobbying than any other American company save Northrop Grumman. It famously lobbies at the highest levels not so much by arm-twisting as by ingratiating, by "making itself a familiar and welcome fixture inside official Washington's transactional culture."[15]

The growing role of money in politics is one of the major reasons for the greater concern over the expansive impact of interest groups. Large sums of money feed large and powerful interests, which in turn contribute to "the breakdown of contemporary democracy"—to a playing field much less level than it was just a generation or two ago. As was noted in the section on money, the concern was exacerbated by the Supreme Court decision handed down in 2010, *Citizens United v. Federal Election Commission*, which was that interest groups such as corporations and labor unions could spend their own money directly to support, or directly to oppose, candidates for federal office. The argument that won the case was essentially one of free speech, with the majority of judges concluding that stopping special interests from intervening in elections was using "censorship to control thought."[16]

Some have concluded, not unreasonably, that this particular Supreme Court decision was a game changer: it handed to interest groups, especially those that were already rich and powerful, a new tool to manipulate the American political system. This is not to say that interest group intervention in federal elections is new altogether; rather it is to point out that for most of American history interest groups including corporations could not and did not use their own funds directly to support or oppose candidates who were running for federal office.

By the 1970s and 1980s, most interest groups of any size already had in place policies to address the level and nature of their electoral involvement. Many formed political action committees (PACs) for the precise purpose of targeting their political activities. But during the decades subsequent, the polarization of politics, in tandem with heightened competition for control of Congress and the White House, led many interest groups to increase their electoral involvement still further, and also to be involved in entirely new ways. By 2010, interest groups were engaging in "record-breaking levels of activity in congressional elections."[17] Since then, argue a number of experts, interest groups have been unleashed—their power and influence in American electoral politics nearly entirely unrestrained and unregulated.

To be sure, precisely assessing the political impact of corporations in particular is not easy. Among other reasons, the lack of disclosure laws makes transparency on this issue, as on so many others, elusive. Still, there is circumstantial evidence to support the claim that their impact is now outsized, far greater than it should be given other, competing, interests. We can assume, for example, that the U.S. Chamber of Commerce had $33 million to spend on the 2010 election because its coffers were full of cash from corporate contributors. Similarly, we can assume that the many wealthy individuals who contribute large sums to particular political candidates or to particular political causes do so to support public policies that further their financial interests. Therefore, "any discussion that ignores large contributions from individuals to interest groups likely underestimates corporate influence."[18]

When Barack Obama first ran for president he, like so many others before him, promised to be different. In the speech he gave declaring his intention to run for the White House, delivered in Springfield, Illinois, in February 2007, he zeroed in on "the cynics, and the lobbyists, and the special interests who have turned our government into a game." This game, Obama insisted, would end. "They think they own this government, but we are here today to take it back." It was a theme he would repeat frequently during his first presidential campaign. More specifically, as Edward Luce has pointed out, Obama tended to blame Washington's decline on two kinds of players. First were politicians, who, Obama claimed, were lame as they were tired; second were lobbyists, whose "money and influence drown out people's voices."[19]

But notwithstanding Obama's righteous rhetoric, during neither one of his two terms did the situation improve. In fact, his first year in office "was the best year ever for the special interests industry, which earned $3.47 billion lobbying the federal government."[20] Obama made what ended up a specious distinction between lobbyists and their clients. No one, he maintained, who had recently worked as a lobbyist would be allowed to work in his administration; and no one who had previously worked in his administration would be allowed to lobby it. However, as things turned out, there were many exceptions to the president's rule. Quite a number of former lobbyists did in fact assume senior positions in the Obama administration. And any number of lobbyists simply re-registered themselves as lawyers, in order to circumvent the administration's ostensibly new rules.

One senior official excused the lapses, saying, "We didn't want to hamstring the new administration or turn the town upside down." Luce in any case concluded that whatever the initial intent of Obama's ostensible reforms, so far as special interests are concerned, they failed. They "rested largely on a technicality, which hinged on whether or not you self-identified as a lobbyist." So, if Obama was really serious about limiting the influence of money in American politics, he would have had to take measures that were considerably more aggressive.[21]

This brief discussion of the Obama administration is not intended as partisan. It is simply a description of a system that is resistant to change. This then is the bottom line. In spite of the now dwindling pool of lobbyists who formally are registered, the amount of money spent by special interests on official lobbying rose by almost one-fifth in 2009, and then again in 2010. This makes lobbying Washington's third largest industry—immediately after government and tourism.[22]

I earlier suggested that factions, special interests, lobbyists, are in some ways good. They are in keeping with democracy by connecting followers to leaders, citizens to public officials. Moreover, interest groups are easily formed. In theory at least, they provide Americans across the board with an easy way to participate in political life. However, even this cursory glance makes clear that interest groups are also in some ways bad. It is not that factions per se are bad. Rather, it is that their impact has turned out skewed, unbalanced and unfair.

First, the interests of business, of business leaders, are "disproportionally represented." Second, advocacy groups tend to represent not so much the interests of ordinary people but rather those of a "narrow stratum" of the relatively wealthy and privileged.[23] In his book, pointedly titled *So Damn Much Money: The Triumph of Lobbying and the Corrosion of American Government*, journalist Robert Kaiser summarizes the sentiment: "Washington was thriving. It was the center of a vast industry devoted to influencing the American government on behalf of big business, small business, foreign governments and the multitude of interests and interest groups comprised by the modern United States. The captains of this industry . . . were all doing well. Their fat paychecks and big bonuses helped make the Washington region one of the country's two richest. Also doing well, curiously, were the members of the House and Senate whom the influence-peddling industry sought to influence. For years, incumbent senators and congressmen had been reelected at unprecedented rates—more than 95 percent by the early twenty-first century."[24]

Of course, my own focus is not directly either on interests or on interest groups. Rather, it is on their impact on leaders in twenty-first-century America. It is best to address the leaders in turn: first, those who are the influence agents, primarily through interest groups and the lobbyists who staff them; second, those who are the influence targets, primarily political leaders, public officials.

Leaders of groups and organizations that are in any way beholden to the government generally have no choice but to play the lobbying game. (This applies at the federal level and at the level of the state as well.) This necessitates they invest considerable resources in advocacy activities— their own personal, professional, and political resources, and their organizational resources in addition. The nature of their investment depends obviously on the nature of their situation; time and money in any case enter into the equation. In fact, it has got to the point at which the salesmanship that constitutes lobbying is part of the job description. Leaders leading organizations of any size—no matter their domain, say health care, or education, or business, or the military, or religion, or even public interest groups such as Common Cause—must think of lobbying as an important part of the job they are expected now to do. Sometimes they pitch their client, whichever public official, directly; more often they delegate the task to others, to lobbyists, to make the pitch for them.

For their part, political leaders, government officials, or for that matter candidates for political office, have no choice but to respond in some way to the numberless influence attempts. Sometimes, of course, they respond by doing nothing, by simply turning off and tuning out the clamor and clutter that constitute whatever the special interest. But given the nature of American politics in the second decade of the twenty-first century, politicians cannot survive for long if they pay no attention at all. Part of what political leaders are obliged now to do is to sort the wheat from the chaff, to separate those interest groups to which for some reason they think they should pay attention from those they conclude they can afford to ignore.

Recent experience suggests that the system is stuck. Special interests have increased exponentially in recent years—in size and in number, in the amount of money they spend, and in the power and influence they wield. Still, there is no evidence that this trajectory is slowing, that they will dwindle in importance, not to speak of quit center stage. So whatever the good they do, their influence has by now become skewed, outsized. In aggregate they suck up too many individual and institutional resources, and too much individual and institutional time. Withal, they constitute yet another component of context with which leaders across the board necessarily have to contend.

PART V FUTURES

19 ENVIRONMENT

WHEN RACHEL CARSON published her pioneering book on the environment, *Silent Spring*, in 1962, Americans were mostly ignorant of everything relevant. While to this general rule there were some exceptions, degradation of the environment was hardly discussed. Instead, we assumed that what planet earth was it would continue to be, indefinitely.

Carson's book is widely credited with changing the conversation, though only gradually. Only gradually did we become aware that the ecosystem was evolving. And only gradually did we become aware that to protect it from harm would require us to do something, as opposed to doing nothing. In fact, only in the past few years—characterized by excessive heat, drought, and flood; natural disasters including hurricanes, tornadoes, and wildfires; and increasingly incontrovertible scientific data—has there been a growing sense of urgency, an understanding that unless something is done, soon, environmental change, especially global warming, likely will become as unmanageable as inevitable. With ice caps melting and ice in the Arctic collapsing, sea levels are expected to rise and storms to become more intense, threatening coastal communities worldwide. In the meantime, local climates are shifting drastically, with heat waves and heavy rains intensifying while fish and many other creatures migrate toward the poles or in some cases become extinct.[1]

But climate change is a fiendishly complex issue, and controlling climate change is difficult beyond imagining. It's a hydra-headed monster, theoretically involving every person and place on the planet, and phenomena that include but are not limited to greenhouse gases, severe weather, land conversion, water availability, water and air pollution, biodiversity, exposure to chemicals, and managing waste. The *Oxford Handbook of Climate Change and Society* presses the point, particularly the chasm between the complexity of the problem and our limited capacity to address it. "Climate change presents perhaps the most profound challenge ever to have confronted human social, political, and economic systems. The stakes are massive, the risks and uncertainties severe, the economics controversial, the science besieged, the politics bitter and complicated, the psychology puzzling, the impacts devastating, the interactions with other environmental and non-environmental issues running in many directions. The social problem-solving mechanisms we currently possess were not designed, and have not evolved, to cope with anything like an interlinked set of problems of this severity, scale, and complexity. There are no precedents."[2]

The challenge of climate change is so great that responsibility for meeting it ought, ideally, to be equally shared, by Americans and by everyone else, by leaders and by followers. In fact, such progress as historically has been made on, say, water pollution, often as not has been the result of pressure exerted from the bottom up, not leadership exercised from the top down. Social activists have been dedicated to the issue of climate change since the 1960s and in a few cases earlier, even while leaders across the board were silent on the subject or paid it little more than lip service. It was followers—particularly activist groups such as, for example, Sierra Club, Greenpeace, and Hudson River Sloop Clearwater (brainchild of Pete Seeger and his wife, Toshi)—who drew our attention to a problem of growing dimension.

Of course by now, more than a half century after *Silent Spring*, the problems posed by climate change are so obvious, and so obviously large and complex, we understand that solutions to scale will have to be implemented if not initiated by people in positions of power and authority. No leader is or ought to be exempt from involvement. Educational leaders, media leaders, religious leaders, community leaders, nonprofit sector leaders—all have a role to play, not least raising public awareness.[3] But, as the magnitude of the challenge of "the coming climate" has become clear, responsibility for managing it has been assumed—or not—by two kinds of leaders in particular: leaders in government and leaders in business.[4]

What, more precisely, do these leaders have to contend with? Why, more precisely, is this particular problem so "profound"? First is the level of its complexity: climate is "a system that is characterized by multiple driving forces, strong feedback loops, long time lags, and abrupt change behavior."[5] Second, climate entails concepts, even language, with which most lay people, including leaders in government and business, are not familiar. To wit, "the current observed warming trend is driven primarily by a suite of greenhouse gases, including methane, nitrous oxide, and tropospheric ozone in addition to carbon dioxide."[6] Third, climate change is not a national problem, but an international, multinational, transnational one. However, no international, multinational, transnational body is in a position to develop a plan that is scientifically sensible and, simultaneously, politically feasible.[7] Fourth, the time horizon on climate change is close to meaningless, especially to leaders, who tend to think short term, not long term. Fifth, the problem of climate change entails equity or, better, inequity. For example, although China recently overtook the U.S. as the largest single national emitter of carbon dioxide, the figures per capita tell a different story. The average American emits over twenty tons of carbon dioxide per year, compared to less than four for the average Chinese. Finally, the problem of climate change is so "profound" because of possible "tipping points"—the collapse of large polar ice sheets, for instance, or large-scale changes in ocean circulation—that could trigger an "unexpectedly large and rapid or irreversible change."[8] In sum, the problems presented by climate change seem so overwhelming that leaders have inclined to nothing so much as to ignore them.[9]

It's unfortunate but apparently unavoidable that the issue of climate change has, in addition to everything else, become politicized. It seems that everything about climate change is contested: Is it really a problem, or is it merely hype? If yes to the former, are there any solutions? If yes, what are they? Moreover, while within the scientific community there has been growing consensus on the evidence and significance of climate change, outside this community there has been a decline in support for the proposition that global warming is of paramount importance. According to a poll taken in 2013, while 69 percent of Americans agree that there is solid evidence that the earth is warming, only 33 percent consider it a problem that is "very" serious. Moreover, when Americans were asked subsequent to the 2012 election what ought to be a top presidential and congressional priority, the issue of global warming ranked dead last, with only 28 percent of Americans ranking it first.[10]

The reasons why there is a discrepancy—between what the American people at least recognize is a problem and what they are willing actually to do about it—include politics.[11] In particular, there are schisms on climate change, between Democrats and liberals on the one side and Republicans and conservatives on the other. In general, Democrats are more disposed to support substantial environmental controls than are Republicans. And, in general, Republicans vote no on climate change legislation while Democrats vote yes. Underlying many of these differences are conflicting interests and ideologies, including between those who at the one extreme believe absolutely in the scientific method (even when it yields findings that are conflicting) and those who at the other are ill-disposed to science, especially if its findings conflict with otherwise preferred policy choices.

In 2013, President Barack Obama delivered a major speech that was billed as a "coordinated assault on a changing climate." While he promised to deploy every weapon in his arsenal, the fact was his arsenal was meager. In the main he was going to have to rely on authority already granted him by Congress—he could, for example, direct the Environmental Protection Agency (EPA) to limit further the legal emissions of carbon dioxide by power plants—because Republican lawmakers were highly unlikely to approve additional measures. Some House Republicans continue to wonder aloud if the planet is heating up at all, while other House Republicans are, in principle, opposed to government intervention. Moreover, even the rules the EPA does try to enforce are vulnerable to legal challenge, to lawsuits by, for example, large corporations ready to shell out big bucks to protect what they profess is rightfully theirs. Of course this did not stop Obama from announcing in June 2014 new rules to cut carbon emissions at power plants: the goal is to reduce such emissions 30 percent by 2030. (During Obama's two terms in office the most strident fight involving the environment was, however, over the proposed expansion of the Keystone Pipeline. Supporters of expansion touted virtues such as more oil at lower prices; opponents warned of dangers to the environment, to land and to water. Environmentalists, in any case, consider Keystone to be Obama's signature environmental issue, especially given that "there are few opportunities to influence the politics of climate change and to leave a legacy."[12])

The issue of climate change is typical in that compromise was more easily reached in the past than in the present. As Thomas Friedman and Michael Mandelbaum point out, conservatism on, say, conservation "did not used to be us." Republican president Richard Nixon signed into law major environmental legislation. Under the leadership of both Presidents Gerald Ford and Jimmy Carter, the United States responded to the 1973–1974 Arab Oil Embargo by demanding higher fuel-economy standards for cars and trucks. And in 1975, with broad bipartisan support, Congress passed the Energy Policy and Conservation Act. In turn, Ronald Reagan's secretary of state, George Shultz, oversaw the successful conclusion of a landmark international agreement intended to protect the ozone layer from damaging UVB radiation. And President George H. W. Bush introduced the idea of "cap and trade," a financial incentive to polluters to limit emissions.[13]

Now, though, times are different: the political climate is different, the political parties are different, and even some political processes are different. As a result, now even simple solutions to cutting energy consumption—such as putting a price on carbon, or setting stronger energy-efficiency standards—remain difficult if not impossible to implement. Our political leaders are so hellbent on getting reelected that they tend to refrain from even trying to convince their constituents to bear short-term pain in exchange for long-term gain. Obama has spent some political capital on climate change. However, the political reality in Washington is such that the passage of any major climate change law that requires Republican support remains unlikely.[14]

Some would argue that states and cities are out front on this issue, governors and mayors trying against long odds to stem climate change, and to prepare for what is considered by many if not most to be inevitable. Cities are actually critical to the conversation, because for the first time in history most humans live and work in urban environments. Moreover, cities are "warming at a substantially higher rate than the planet as a whole," which puts considerable onus on city managers, who have a considerable stake in an issue typically thought beyond their capacity to control.[15] They are not, however, without resources. Big-city mayors, for instance, usually control hundreds of square miles, which means they can usually influence, if only to a very modest degree, components of climate such as temperature, humidity, and wind speed. City officials need not, in other words, be mere bystanders to climate change. They can take on a problem—an inconvenient truth, to use climate change proselytizer Al Gore's apt phrase—that should be addressed, not avoided.[16]

Toward the end of his time in office, New York City's three-term mayor Michael Bloomberg, moved to do so by the devastating effects of Hurricane Sandy, went into action. (Sandy, which struck in October 2012, took the lives of forty-three New Yorkers, displaced countless others, and cost the city at least $65 billion in damage and economic losses.[17]) In 2013, Bloomberg called for a sweeping, near $20 billion initiative, including new coastal protections and zoning codes, and new standards for telecommunications and fuel provision. "I strongly believe we have to prepare for what scientists say is a likely scenario," he said at a press briefing. "As bad as Sandy was, future storms could be even worse." The mayor backed his call to arms with a four-hundred-page report titled "A Stronger, More Resilient New York." It was prepared by his "Special Initiative for Rebuilding and Resiliency," which, in turn, was established in Sandy's wake to assess the anticipated impact of climate change on the nation's largest city.

Bloomberg's response to the calamity that struck New York City was emblematic of the problem—which is as political and psychological as much as it is anything else. Before Sandy, neither New Yorkers nor their mayor were oblivious to the threat of climate change. In fact, to its credit, the Bloomberg administration was looking at sustainability issues as far back as 2007. But it was only after disaster struck—a disaster that almost certainly was in consequence of climate change—that New Yorkers and their mayor ramped up their efforts to mitigate the effects of global warming on a city that was, after all, surrounded on all sides by water. I should add that it is one thing for an outgoing mayor to propose a $20 billion climate change initiative; it is quite another for his successor, in this case Bill de Blasio, to find the funds, not to speak of the political will, necessary actually to implement it.

The challenges of climate change, the tasks related to climate change, are, obviously, different for leaders in the private sector. Here are three. The first is to assess and address the ways in which climate change might have an impact on their business. The second is to manage individuals, groups, and organizations that pressure them to stop degrading the environment. The third is to plan for the future, particularly to provide sustainable, renewable energy. In all three cases there is no shortage of advice or paucity of information. So for leaders in business the issues are knowing which experts to trust, deciding what information needs seriously to be considered, and determining how many resources to allot to an issue that, however important, is unlikely in the short term to be to their obvious advantage. How many Americans give a hoot or even know anything about whether or not Ford or Oracle or Proctor & Gamble has switched to sustainable lighting?   What's apparent is that individuals and institutions with a dedicated commitment to the environment—for example, the Center for Climate and Energy Solutions (C2ES), an "independent, nonprofit, nonpartisan organization working to advance strong policy and action to address the twin challenges of energy and climate change"—have a major hurdle to start.[18] They must persuade leaders, here corporate leaders, that threats related to the environment, to climate change, are real; that they loom in the near future, not only in the distant one; that they could damage them and the businesses for which they are responsible; and that to address them is not only in the general interest but in their self-interest.

How can this be done? Step one is to marshal facts and figures frightening enough to give pause to even the most hardened of skeptics. In a lengthy 2013 report titled "Weathering the Storm: Building Business Resilience to Climate Change," C2ES warned that the "recent increase in costly extreme weather events has provided a clear signal to many companies of the near-term risks associated with climate change." The authors of the report cited extreme droughts, severe heat waves, damaging floods, and destructive storms as examples of extraordinary events, all of which were recent, and all of which were nearly certain to be repeated sooner rather than later. Step two is to hit members of the corporate elite where it matters most—in the bottom line. The intention is to cow them by citing potentially huge losses both at home and abroad, and by invoking "stakeholders" who are "increasingly concerned" about costs associated with more frequent and intense weather events.

Finally, step three, persuading leaders in business to invest precious resources into something as unfamiliar and uncertain as mitigating climate change must take into account how formidable is the psychological hurdle. "Understanding the likelihood or severity of impacts remains a significant barrier for companies deciding how and when to invest in resilience beyond 'business as usual.' As a result business activities to build resilience are largely a continuation of existing practices and policies that are based on a historical picture of past risks." What is the inevitable outcome? Companies are by and large underprepared to weather the future—to withstand what most of the experts consider the inevitable, considerable future costs of climate change.[19]

The discrepancy between the facts on the ground and what business executives are ready and willing to acknowledge openly is a theme regularly repeated. On the one hand is corporate concern over how, for example, the changing climate could raise costs, reduce demand, and disrupt operations such as supply chains and production capacities. But on the other hand corporations overall have been sluggish in their response, tardy in undertaking comprehensive climate vulnerability assessments. Most leaders are, to put it simply, in denial, at least publicly. Just like leaders in government, leaders in business are, to all appearances, disposed to judge the risks to them, to their followers, to their businesses, as "relatively minimal, too distant in time to be of concern, too difficult to quantify, or too uncertain to support business decisions directed specifically at improving their resilience."[20]

There are, to be sure, some exceptions to this general rule, some signs that corporate America is starting to be cognizant of the problem and to act accordingly. Jeffrey Seabright for example, Coca-Cola's vice-president for environment and water resources, has gone on record as listing "increased droughts" and "100-year floods every two years" as endangering his company's capacity to produce its soda.[21] Still, change is slow or, at least, much slower than it should be, given the magnitude and relative immediacy of the impending threat.

Again, there is no shortage of specifics—of facts, figures, analyses, commentaries, recommendations.[22] One report assesses the operational, market, reputational, and policy implications of environmental trends on ten different types of businesses, including building and construction, chemicals, electric power, finance, tourism, and transportation.[23] Another focuses on the virtues of renewable energy, and on how companies can and should set renewable energy targets to cut their operating costs, diversify their energy supply, hedge against market volatility in traditional fuel markets and, above all, "achieve greenhouse gas emissions reduction goals and demonstrate leadership on broader corporate sustainability and climate commitments."[24] In addition, there is a raft of material available on, say, the *Harvard Business Review Blog Network* that reiterates the importance of encouraging companies to exemplify and indeed proselytize for action on climate change.[25] Finally, there are countless groups and organizations across the country that tirelessly urge all of us to take climate change seriously. Among the more prominent is the Clinton Climate Initiative (CCI), part of the Clinton Foundation that builds on President Bill Clinton's "longstanding commitment to the environment." CCI prides itself on working with both business and government to reduce carbon emissions, increase energy efficiency, and improve access to clean energy technology.[26]

For leaders in government and in business and just about everywhere else, it's fair to say then that there is good news and there is bad news. The good news, if you can call it that, is that slowly but certainly there is recognition of a problem. It will be less hard in the future than it was in the past to lead on climate change, simply because the dangers of doing nothing are more widely appreciated now than they were even five years ago. The bad news is as earlier indicated: the magnitude and complexity of the problem, the magnitude and complexity of the threat. As one expert put it, mincing no words, "We face a real risk of the collapse of human institutions that we take for granted—agricultural systems, water-distribution systems, health-care systems, national borders, and international peace, to name a few."[27]

Some leaders in some places will never accept the idea that climate change is a challenge we must meet. Other leaders in other places will never accept the idea that there are some circumstances in which the costs of environmental damage could be outweighed by the benefits.[28] For once, such divisiveness is somewhat defensible. For as the title of a significant book on climate makes clear—William Nordhaus's *The Climate Casino: Risk, Uncertainty, and Economics for a Warming World*—the issue remains engulfed by uncertainties and strong differences of opinion.[29] Yet "decisions must be made taking the future—and sometimes the very long-term future—into account."[30] Leaders have an obligation then to engage the issue. They have an obligation not to avoid it, whatever their personal, professional, or political preferences, and whatever their multiple, inevitable, lingering doubts.

20 RISKS

LEADERS HAVE ALWAYS BEEN RESPONSIBLE for managing risk, especially downside risk. Managing risk is part of the job, part of why we need leaders, want leaders in the present as we did in the past. Part of the leader's job description is to protect followers from danger, to keep them from harm. Followers, in turn, expect their leaders to provide them with safety and security—this in a world that frequently is experienced as being unsafe and insecure.

If leaders have been responsible for managing risk since the time of, in Freud's memorable phrase, the "primal horde," what now is different? How are the challenges of managing risk in twenty-first-century America different from what they were before? Of course, in some ways they are not—some of the fundamentals of risk management never change. Now as before leaders are supposed to assess risk, and now as before if there is a threat of some sort, anticipated or unanticipated, leaders are supposed to cope, to address whatever the threat expeditiously and effectively. But for a variety of reasons, the world is, or at least so it seems, riskier now than it was, at least in the recent past.

For the purposes of this checklist, twenty-first-century risks can be categorized as either internal or external. Internal risks are those that leaders face, in effect, alone, for example because they make an egregious personal mistake, as did Larry Summers, who, when he was president of Harvard University, stated publicly that it was possible women were less innately suited to science and math than men. (Summers finally felt obliged to resign.) Or because they make egregious professional mistakes—as when under the leadership of Ron Johnson, J.C. Penney lost over $4 billion in sales in 2012 alone. (Johnson was finally fired.) These sorts of risks are greater now than they were because of changes in context—specifically changes in technology that disseminate embarrassing information in the proverbial heartbeat, and changes in culture that make us more critical. If, for one or another reason, a leader makes a bad mistake, or engages in wrongdoing, we are more likely than before to know about it, and we are more likely than before to insist either on public penance or on summary dismissal.

External risks are those over which the overwhelming majority of leaders have little or even no control. These too seem to us to be more menacing than they were in, say, the last quarter of the twentieth century, if only because of two so-called "black swan" events, both of which were relatively recent. The first is 9/11, the catastrophic attack on the World Trade Center. And the second is the recent financial crisis, the most severe since the Great Depression.

Of course, there are other reasons for leaders to fear unanticipated events as well. As Nassim Taleb and colleagues wrote in the *Harvard Business Review*, "because of the internet and globalization, the world has become a complex system, made up of a tangled web of relationships and other interdependent factors. Complexity not only increases the incidence of Black Swan events, but also makes forecasting even ordinary events impossible."[1] Black swan events (the term was coined by Taleb) do not, by definition, have negative outcomes; sometimes the outcomes are positive. But the term has come to be associated with downside risk because by definition a black swan event (1) is a surprise, (2) has a significant impact, and (3) is rationalized in hindsight. Suffice it here to say that whether or not the world really is riskier now than it was in the past, or whether we only imagine it to be so, American leaders are as conscious of risk now as they have ever been. A constellation

of changes—the information revolution, easy exposure to embarrassment, two recent shocks to the system, globalization and its discontents,
modern urbanization, even the leadership industry—all have combined
relentlessly to remind of risk.

Here, for example, is a headline that would, or at least should, give
any leader pause: "By 2047, Coldest Years May Be Warmer Than Hottest in the Past, Scientists Say."[2] My point is not, of course, that climate
change is, will be, a black swan event. With some possible exceptions,
such changes in climate as do take place will not, as we have seen, come
as a surprise. Rather, it is to indicate that the conversation about risk
is constant, to the point at which managing risk is ranked among the
most important of all leadership skills. In fact, teaching leaders how
to manage risk, both internal and external, has become integral to the
leadership industry, the implication being that a leader bad at risk management is a bad leader period.

For at least the past thirty years the leadership industry has, in fact,
prided itself on teaching leaders skills. These include communicating,
mobilizing, negotiating, decision making, and, now, managing risk,
both general and specific. In fact, the leadership literature has come to
convey the idea that while leaders cannot control risk per se, they can
control, to at least a degree, the consequences of risks realized. So, for
example, the aforementioned article by Taleb and others says that leaders should not delude themselves—they should not engage in futile attempts to manage risk by trying to foretell the future. What they should
do instead is to avoid making stupid mistakes, such as assuming that
hindsight will lead to foresight, focusing their attention only on a few
extreme scenarios, and failing to inject risk management into mainstream management.

To be sure, some general risk management measures are, again,
little more than nostrums, such as "take a moment to figure out what's
going on," "act promptly, not hurriedly," and "manage expectations."
But others are more serious attempts to provide leaders with a template
for coping with risk in a world in which stress over risk is more typical than not. Another article in the *Harvard Business Review*, this one

titled "Managing Risks: A New Framework," falls into this category. Though it applies equally to leaders of all organizations, it is primarily targeted at corporate leaders who want to get smart about risk management.[3] "Managing Risks" explores (1) preventable risks that arise from inside the organization, (2) strategic risks that are deliberately assumed for potentially big gains, and (3) outside risks that are beyond the company's capacity to contain or control. Each of these risks has different mitigation objectives, each entails different ways of controlling the consequences, and each is associated with different tasks. Of course, the overarching message is—risk management is hard. It runs counter to the "can do" culture that leaders try to foster. And it runs counter to the idea that leaders should be investing resources in building the business—not in preparing for problems that might or might not arise at some point down the line.

Whatever the merits or deficits of risk management strategies in general, they seem somehow dwarfed the minute the risk, especially external (outside) risk is specific. This is not to diminish the more general efforts to control risk, to contend with risk. Rather it is to point out that these can seem puny when stacked up against the real thing—against real-world risks such as terrorist attacks, natural disasters, and financial crises.

Terrorist Attacks

It is impossible of course to precisely calculate these things. But it is not too much to say that the attack on American soil that took place on September 11, 2001, was among the most traumatic single events in American history. The nearly entirely unanticipated horror in the homeland changed the national mind-set—never again were Americans likely to feel as strong, as invulnerable, as impervious to external risk as we did up to then.[4] New York and Washington, D.C., were directly in the line of fire, so it's a given that the attacks were especially hard on those who lived or worked in one of these cities as opposed to those in, say, Portland, Oregon, or Portland, Maine. But we all knew then what we all know now. From "sea to shining sea" the nation would never again be the same—nor was anyone anywhere in America safe altogether from terrorist attack.

This is not to say that until the World Trade Center disaster Americans had never been in fear of the other. Not at all—in fact, for years during the Cold War Americans were warned about the possibility of a nuclear attack by the Soviet Union. But there are important differences between then and now. Then, disaster preparedness was entirely in the hands of a handful of experts. Managing risk was their job, not ours. Historian Scott Knowles writes, "Disaster knowledge of the Civil Defense Era was created under secrecy and funneled from Washington. . . . From the civil defender's point of view, the control of nuclear risk was too wrapped up in national security to be left to states and municipalities."[5] Now, though, there is terrorism—a threat generally assumed to be less cataclysmic than a nuclear conflagration, but more directly injected into everyday life. Terrorism is a risk faced by every American, and every American is expected to participate in protecting against it. Recent episodes of domestic gun violence have had, I might add, a similarly chilling, rippling effect. To take a glaring example, after Columbine, after Newtown, which educational leader, which school principal anywhere in the United States, can afford to ignore the issue of school safety?

This is the definition of terrorism used by the U.S. military: "The calculated use of unlawful violence or the threat of unlawful violence to inculcate fear, intended to coerce or to intimidate governments or societies in the pursuit of goals that are generally political, religious, or ideological."[6] Defending against violence on American soil is, of course, a task primarily in the hands of leaders in the public sector. It is leaders in government—or, better, leaders in governments at the federal, state, and local levels—who are charged with protecting Americans against a terrorist attack. In fact, it is expected that they engage in external risk management every minute of every day.

Managing external risk entails managing people, processes, and information. It requires robustness and flexibility, and the capacity to respond effectively, even, or especially, to events that are unanticipated.[7] Risk management can be said, therefore, to involve five basic steps: analysis, planning, mitigation, response, and recovery.[8] These, in turn, assume the involvement of public officials (leaders and managers) in the executive and legislative branches of government(s), and in the military. These further assume experts (sometimes but not always leaders and managers) in gathering information and intelligence, and in law enforcement, and in emergency services. Finally, as suggested, these assume the engagement of civil society (followers), the engagement of nearly every American in the task of keeping America safe. Terrorism expert Paul Shemella put it this way: "Civil society organizations can be a powerful tool against terrorism. The list of such groups is long, including nongovernmental organizations [and] private volunteer organizations. . . . Civil society (and the individuals who constitute it) can assist government with identifying terrorist threats [and also with] alleviating poverty, reducing unemployment, and building programs that strengthen social cohesion."[9] The point is that while those on the front lines are leaders and managers in the public sector, neither other leaders and managers nor, for that matter, followers are exempt from responsibility for guarding against terrorism.[10] In fact, at every turn leaders try to engage followers in the collective task, such as by repeating this slogan, now adopted (from New York's Metropolitan Transit Authority) by the Department of Homeland Security: "If you see something, say something."

Finally, a note on cyber terrorism, or cyber warfare, or cyber crime, all risks that until recently seemed remote and therefore easy to ignore, even to dismiss because they were, in effect, invisible. Such blissed-out ignorance has, however, already given way. The public at large is increasingly aware of cyber threats to virtually the entire American system, including the financial system, the telecommunications system, and the transportation system, as well as to electric power grids, government agencies, companies, institutions, and individuals.[11] Of course, controlling the risk of cyber attack is a task necessarily left to the experts. But in this second decade of the twenty-first century, no leader anywhere in America is exempt from such an attack, and from managing the consequences in the event it occurs. The warnings in any case inevitably are chilling. To wit: cyber attack could at any moment be so severe as to have "an immediate and debilitating impact on national security, economy, public health, and safety."[12]

Natural Disasters

Single events such as the attacks on 9/11 focus the mind. So it was with Hurricane Katrina, which struck New Orleans and other areas along the Gulf Coast in 2005. This was not, obviously, the first hurricane to hit America hard. But there was something about Katrina that seared our national consciousness—the widespread destruction in New Orleans, one of America's greatest, most idiosyncratic cities; the dreadful damage that targeted the poor (many of whom lived then and still do now in low-lying areas) in particular; and the mismanagement in the wake of the disaster, which quickly morphed into a monumental national embarrassment.

The hurricane was not unanticipated. The New Orleans area was well-known to be vulnerable to a storm such as this one; moreover, this particular weather event, a Category 3 hurricane, was widely predicted. Still, it was a disaster; not only a natural one, but a bureaucratic and political one that left more than thirteen hundred people dead and hundreds of thousands in Louisiana and in four other states displaced. In the end, Katrina was the most costly natural calamity in American history.[13] Why? Why this sad, bad outcome when so much about hurricanes in general and Katrina in particular was known in advance? Among the reasons was the lamentable lack of coordination among leaders at the federal, state, and local levels. In other words, despite all the foreshadowing, "government officials were woefully underprepared."[14] What was learned, or should have been once and forevermore, was that disasters do not respect boundaries, not among the different governments, not among the various organizations that constitute them. "Almost by definition, these disasters fall outside normal routines."[15]

Given that a storm such as Katrina was anticipated, and given the resistance to managing risk, especially when it necessitates significant investment, the question is, What do we do with the information we have? How, in other words, do leaders get followers to pay the price for protection? The problem clearly is not a lack of information. Rather it is our psychological predisposition to avoid considering the unhappy consequences of what we know to be true. Individuals are prone to ignore disaster until they are forced by circumstances to face it, and so are institutions inclined to postpone action, especially expensive action, until a crisis actually hits.

Public policies can considerably mitigate the consequences of natural disaster. For example, public sector leaders can develop better housing policies, and better insurance procedures, and better emergency services. But what they cannot easily do is fly in the face of human nature. In an essay on why we "under-prepare for hazards," Robert Meyer addresses how ill-equipped we are to engage in risk management effectively. We are ill-equipped psychologically and, it turns out, cognitively as well. "As human decision makers we are not well equipped to [decide] in settings where feedback is rare, ambiguous in its meaning, and where optimal decisions require astute skills in foresight. In particular we are overly prone to succumb to three classes of decision bias: an excessive tendency to learn by focusing on recent outcomes, a tendency to see the future as a simple extrapolation of the present, and an inability to see the value of long-term benefits when compared to short-term costs."[16]

Hurricanes are not, of course, the only natural disasters that risk managers, leaders, need to worry about. Tornados and earthquakes can be even more devastating—and wildfires are near certain to be more extensive and destructive in the future than they were in the past. In 2013 there was a huge fire in one of America's most beloved national parks, Yosemite, which actually rained ash on San Francisco's water supply. It was a sign of the times—times in which increasing incursions by humans into forests (including dwelling there), altered forest ecology, and the changing climate (hotter, dryer), inevitably combine to make fires more frequent and furious. Between 2000 and 2006 alone, the United States broke five records for acreage burned in wildfires. Again, as with other natural disasters, the problem with fires is not the lack of information, nor is it the lack of good public policy on disaster mitigation.

Rather it is that in the second decade of the twenty-first century we live in a "nation of hazards"—which leaves us with two big problems.[17] The first is different hazards competing for whatever the available resources, including money and time. The second is leaders and followers alike simply preferring, if at all possible, not to make significant investments in risk management.

Financial Crises

It seems we're barely recovered from the recent financial crisis and already we're being warned about the next one. Some of this risk is generic, systemic, related to capitalism itself. The authors of a book titled *Capitalism at Risk* point out that the last half of the twentieth century was a period of unprecedented prosperity, driven by the "widespread adoption of market capitalism." But, they wonder, can this pattern, such sustained growth, continue? "What are the long term prospects for the global economy and the market system that drives it?"[18] Various threats to the capitalist system are identified, including growing complexity; lack of transparency; environmental degradation; failure of the rule of law; and inequality along with the inevitable, eventual consequences thereof, including populism, radicalism, and even terrorism. The authors conclude on a cautionary note, suggesting that unless leaders in twenty-first-century America take threats like these seriously, and try in some serious way to address them, capitalism itself will be at risk.

Another sort of risk is American decline, a gradual descent from where we were to where we are now, and from where we are in the present to a future of more scarcity and less security. Economist Robert Gordon predicts that for at least the next fifteen years, the American economy will grow at less than half the rate it did on average in the past hundred years. His reasons for the projected slowdown include the aging population, lower levels of educational achievement, fiscal tightening, and the pressures of globalization. The result, Gordon predicts, is an inexorable, inevitable, slide—a generation of Americans now in their twenties destined to be the first not to be significantly better off than their parents, and a standard of living that will, at best, be stagnant.[19]

The financial system is at risk in other, more narrowly defined ways as well, for instance the lack of financing to enable home ownership, economic recoveries that increasingly are "jobless," too great a dependence on easy monetary policy, pressures on bankers to do nothing so much as increase profits, and a relatively weak social safety net.[20] (A case in point: unemployment benefits, which are lower in the U.S. than in other developed countries, and briefer in duration.)

Invariably, the leadership industry and others similarly disposed give advice, provide counsel, and make recommendations, in this case recommendations for reinforcing the financial system so it is as resistant as possible to crisis. Some call on leaders in business to guide "governments toward policies and programs that will strengthen the market system" and to participate more actively in discussions on public policy.[21] Others look to leaders in government, to "guardians of finance," to protect us from harm. Who exactly are these "guardians of finance"? They are the ones responsible for "financial policies, rules, enforcement procedures, and official supervisory practices associated with shaping financial market activities."[22] Of course it is precisely these "guardians," these leaders, who failed us the last time around, who enabled "the colossal failure" that was the financial crisis.[23] No wonder at least some of the experts insist that not a single one of our existing institutions can ultimately be relied on to do what's right. "The only institutions capable of assessing the financial regulatory institutions are the financial regulatory institutions themselves, and they are not effectively designed to act in the public's long term interest."[24] Now *that's* a problem—a problem to which there is no obvious solution or, at least, no obvious solution that politically is feasible.[25]

Finally, it is suggested that we protect against the risk of another financial crisis by getting business and government to cooperate, to act in tandem.[26] This seems a good plan—and sometimes there is, in fact, collaboration between the two. But just as often they conflict, not cooperate, with leaders in government wanting more control over business and leaders in business straining to be free of government constraint. The bottom line is that notwithstanding the grim reality of the last financial crisis, the grim possibility of another financial crisis has not exactly been precluded.

So what if anything has been learned? It is true that in the aftermath of 9/11 and Hurricane Katrina grew a cottage industry: risk management. And it is equally true that some kinds of risks are better managed now than they were. To take an example, Boston's response to the explosions of two pressure cooker bombs at the 2013 Boston Marathon received high marks for disaster planning and preparedness. "While certainly not perfect, only a massively collaborative effort could have orchestrated the skills, databases, intelligence, technology, operational capabilities, and personnel needed to accomplish the many law enforcement tasks involved."[27]

However, in a nation of risks, in which leaders are made regularly, relentlessly aware of how vulnerable they are to crisis, the trick is not only to manage risks that are more or less predictable, such as, sad to say, a bomb going off in some city center. It is, in addition, to manage risks that are black swans. It is risk management based not on what we know, or think we know, but on what we do not know. It is risks like these—not knowing, being done in by our biases, refusing to invest in risk preparedness—that are riskiest of all.[28]

21 TRENDS

IT TOOK LONGER than five decades for her to be properly appreciated. But now it is widely agreed that the previously mentioned Mary Parker Follett, who wrote about leadership and management in the 1920s and 1930s, was a seminal figure. Among her many contributions was the suggestion that leaders think holistically—that they pull "the unifying thread" from a "welter of facts, experiences, desires and aims." Similarly, they should see their circumstance as being fluid. Their "wisdom" and "judgment" should be based "not on a situation that is stationary, but on one that is changing all the time." Ultimately, she wrote, leaders should see "all the future trends and unite them"—decisions made today must anticipate tomorrow.[1]

But who knew then what we know now? Who knew in 1933, when Follett put these words to paper, that the election the same year of Adolph Hitler as chancellor of Germany would foreshadow World War II? As vexing is the context that constitutes the second decade of the twenty-first century—it compounds the complexity of prognosticating. For a range of reasons that include globalization, the speed of change and, counterintuitively, information overload, discerning trends and distinguishing those that matter from those that do not has been difficult if not impossible.

Nevertheless, predicting the future is an impulse apparently irresistible. Since the beginning of recorded history and, famously, since apothecary and seer Nostradamus in the early sixteenth century, prophecy and prognostication have become part of our collective discourse. So it is no surprise there is a plethora of materials on prediction—much of it targeted directly at people in positions of leadership and management.

Some forecasts are highly speculative, not much more than guesswork. Others, however, are the products of serious people doing serious work, people who presume it in our interest to anticipate what lies ahead—sometimes even far ahead. In 2012, the National Intelligence Council published *Global Trends 2030: Alternative Worlds*, which distinguished between "megatrends" (likely) and "game-changers" (less likely). Though the document acknowledged that foretelling the future was "an impossible feat," it claimed nevertheless to provide "a framework for thinking about the possible futures and their implications."[2] Who was the audience? Of course, it was "decision-makers"—that is, leaders "within government or without."[3]

So what did this particular crystal ball foresee? There were four megatrends. The first two—"individual empowerment" and the "diffusion of power"—are similar to one of my own running themes, changing relations between leaders and followers.[4] The third megatrend is changing demographics. And the fourth is growing demands for food, water, and energy. (These are in consequence of climate change; an expanded middle class, worldwide; and an increase in population, worldwide.)

Game-changers are more speculative—we cannot ultimately foretell how the pendulum will swing. What, for instance, should leaders do with the idea of a "crisis-prone global economy," given they cannot know if the future holds a "global breakdown and collapse or whether the development of multiple growth centers will lead to resiliency"? Similarly, what exactly should leaders do with "black swans," events that, as we have seen, are by definition out of the box and that conceivably range from a severe pandemic aggravated by more antibiotic-resistant drugs to more rapid than predicted climate change to solar storms that knock out satellites, electric grids, and sensitive electronic devices?[5]

The editors of *The Economist* decided similarly to peer far into the distance, to identify "the great trends that are transforming the world" and to explore how "these developments might shape the world in 2050."[6]

They took a sweeping view, covering everything from culture and technology to health care and warfare to science and space to the state of the economy and the state of the state. Not surprisingly, what they ended up with was more of a fun frolic into the distant future than a carefully reasoned defense of the virtues, to leaders, of looking so far ahead. "Prediction is a mug's game," admitted Matt Ridley, one of the contributors. "Everybody who has ever done it has proved to be terrible at it."[7] Indeed, when psychologist Philip Tetlock conducted a comprehensive study of forecasting, he found that although a given expert might foretell one extreme event, "doing so consistently was next to impossible." This would explain why the history of forecasting is "littered with examples of experts who were acclaimed as visionaries, only to disappoint."[8]

But when there is an already existing trend that seems strong and likely as not to last for some time, leaders might do well to take it seriously. Such projections are not a "mug's game." Rather, they are measured attempts to, among other things, provide people with power, authority, or influence with information that might better equip them to lead wisely and well. I refer, for example, to the work of Paul Taylor, of the Pew Research Center. In his recent book, *The Next Generation*, Taylor undertakes a comprehensive and well-documented analysis of a whole host of trends, especially those that differentiate Baby Boomers (soon certifiably old) from Millennials (twenty-somethings). The differences apply nearly across the board—in values, attitudes, and opinions; in financial circumstances; in affiliations, the lack thereof, or both; in life-style choices and constraints; and in preferences and proclivities.[9]

The trends referenced in the following sections could well be of interest and importance to leaders across the board, to all leaders in the United States of America in the second decade of the twenty-first century. It is, however, also the case that those in the business of naming trends typically target one or both of these two audiences: leaders in the public sector and leaders in the private one.

For the purpose of this discussion I am putting different trends—several of which have been touched on elsewhere in this book—into four broad groups. They are demographics, economics, technology, and ideology.

Demographics

Aging is one of the most important of all demographic trends.[10] Between 1950 and 2010, the average American life expectancy went up ten years.[11] More than forty million Americans are now sixty-five or older—and the number continues to climb. Similarly, although the "oldest old" (ages eighty-five and older) now constitute only about 15 percent of the population over sixty-five, this number will also grow. By 2050, the oldest old will constitute fully one-fifth of Americans over sixty-five. This, in turn, will have significant social and economic consequences: on marital status and living arrangements; on health and well-being; on work, retirement, and pensions; and on all costs, public and private, associated with caring for the old and oldest old.[12] In addition, our aging population will—it already has—raised questions about intergenerational equity. In time, as a result of financial and political pressures, the resources allocated to older Americans will almost certainly diminish.[13]

Another demographic trend is diversity of population. For various reasons including increased immigration, America is rapidly becoming more racially and ethnically diverse. In 2000, about 81 percent of the population was white; by 2050, this number is projected to drop to 74 percent with non-Hispanic whites constituting only about 47 percent of the total population. The increase in the numbers of non-whites will be most dramatic for Asians and persons of "some other race," such as American Indians, Native Hawaiians, and those who identify as being of more than one race. Similarly striking is the growth in the numbers of Hispanics. Early in the twenty-first century Hispanics became the nation's largest minority; by 2050 they are projected to constitute nearly one-third the total American population.[14]

A third trend is changes in patterns of population. Non-marital childbearing is at an all time high—41 percent of births.[15] However, teen pregnancy rates have declined. Birth rates have declined. (The birthrate in the U.S. is the lowest in recorded history, so low that one expert argues the "root cause of most of our problems is our declining fertility rate."[16]) Divorce rates have declined. Marriage rates have declined. Mobility rates have declined. (The percentage of Americans moving across state lines has fallen by about half since the 1990s.[17]) Crime rates have declined. Voting rates have declined. Confidence in leaders has declined. SAT scores have declined. Health status has declined. Home ownership rate has declined. Household income has declined. Net worth has declined. Labor force participation has declined. Job tenure has declined. Average household spending has declined. And death rates have declined. Since 1950, overall educational attainment has, however, "soared." By 2010, 87 percent of all Americans aged twenty-five or older were high school graduates; thirty percent were college graduates. Women in college now outnumber men. Women's incomes have risen more than men's. Four in ten American households with children under eighteen now include a mother who is either the sole or primary earner for her family.[18] The young are more dependent. The old are more worried about retirement. Nuclear families—married couples with children under age eighteen—now account for only about 20 percent of households.[19] One in every seven American adults lives alone. And the turnover in our intimate partnerships is "creating complex families on a scale we've not seen before."[20]

Economics

Earlier I discussed growing inequality in America. The United States is singular among all developed nations in that, since 1970, the bottom 90 percent of earners have had in effect no increase in their average income. At the same time, the U.S. has the highest income share for the top 1 percent of earners. This slow growth at the bottom and rapid growth at the top "have polarized the extremes of income distribution more in the United States than in any other advanced country."[21] Further, it has generated at least three disturbing trends: increased poverty (in 2012, the official U.S. poverty rate, 15.1 percent, was at its highest level since 1993); macroeconomic instability (there is a link between high levels of inequality and macroeconomic instability); and cascading expenditures for "positional goods," goods we consume for the sole purpose of improving our positions relative to those of others.[22]

The recent recession; the widening gap between those at the bottom and those at the top; the squeezed, dwindling middle class; and the rise of the postindustrial economy all raise questions about the future of the American Dream—and they have more immediate effects as well. One is a change in relations, in economic relations, between men and women. In preindustrial and industrial economies men's physical strength gave them a relative advantage over women; now one-fifth of men in their prime working ages are out of the labor force. Women, in contrast, appear to have skills and capacities "more important in an economy more oriented to human services than to the production of material objects." (Men on average still earn more than women, but the gap between them has narrowed.) The result is that men's labor has become less valuable and women's labor more valuable—which explains in part why two-income households have increasingly replaced those with a male breadwinner and a female homemaker.[23]

Gender and class intersect in other ways as well. Changing patterns in marriage and family structure contribute to the growing inequality, and they pose fresh barriers to upward mobility. Specifically, the United States is becoming a society in which marriage and its various benefits, social as well as economic, are accruing to the benefit of those that already have, as opposed to those that do not. As sociologist Andrew Cherlin put it. "It is the privileged Americans who are marrying, and marrying helps them stay privileged." Equally sharp is the educational divide. Less than 10 percent of the births to college-educated women occur outside marriage, while for women with high school degrees or less the figure is nearly 60 percent. Since a large body of research supports the finding that children of single mothers are significantly more likely than children with married parents to experience childhood poverty, family structure is increasingly consigning children to what another sociologist, Sara McLanahan, has called "diverging destinies."[24] I should add that the high cost of raising a child in twenty-first-century America does not mitigate the imbalance. It is estimated now to be over $240,000—which factors into the falling birth rate.

Finally, here is the larger picture: two important points about economics at the national level. First, the United States is in a pension crisis. State pensions are underfunded by more than $1 trillion. Several municipalities have already defaulted over pension costs. And some thirty-eight million individual Americans have saved not a dime for retirement. (Moreover, many of those who did manage to put away something for their later years are hardly better off. The median savings of people ten years ahead of their projected retirement is $12,000.[25])

The second point pertains to the national debt which remains a significant problem. How to pay for everything that we think we need? How to pay for everything to which we think we are entitled? How to reverse a trend, escalating entitlements, that in recent years has tended to be relentless? Consider this comparison. In 1960, the total cost of all entitlement programs came to about one-third the federal budget. Everything else, all other government expenses, was covered by the remaining two-thirds. Fifty years later these numbers are reversed. Entitlement programs now consume about two-thirds of our federal budget, while everything else is covered or supposed to be by the remaining one-third. The federal government has become, to put it perfectly, "an insurance company with an army."[26]

Technology

From 2001 to 2011 Eric Schmidt was chief executive officer of Google. In 2013, he along with a colleague, Jared Cohen, wrote a book, *The New Digital Age: Reshaping the Future of People, Nations and Business*. As the title implies, the book assumes that global connectivity will continue its "unprecedented advance" and that communications technologies will "reallocate the concentration of power away from states and institutions and transfer it to individuals." (There it is again, that running theme: power and influence will be more widely distributed.) As a result, leaders will be forced to "rethink their existing operations and adapt their plans for the future, changing how they do things as well as how they present their activities to the public."[27]

Along with *The New Digital Age* came a slew of other prognostication publications, all at about the same time and all touching on technology. Deloitte Consulting, for example, issued a report titled *2013 Technology*

Trends, which identified ten trends grouped into two categories. "Disrupters" are technologies that "can create sustainable positive disruption" in, say, information management and business operations. "Enablers," in contrast, are technologies that already represent an investment of time and effort, but which "warrant another look because of new developments or opportunities." Disrupters could turn out revolutionary; enablers already are evolutionary. Disruptive trends include, as we have seen, the changing role of chief information officers (CIOs), who now, because they manage ever more complex information flows with consequences both inside the organization and out, hold positions of unprecedented power. ("CIOs can lead the move to tomorrow.") Enabling trends are more mundane, such as "If you build it, they will hack it."[28]

While other publications are unable to resist making predictions that are obvious to the point of being ridiculous—*Forbes* opined that 2013 would "be the year of collaboration technology," the year in which "telepresence for globally distributed teams will continue to grow"—the book by Schmidt and Cohen identifies two other trends worth briefly mentioning.[29] First, while the virtual world will not overtake or overhaul the existing world, it will "complicate almost every behavior." (Notice, again, the importance of complex context.) Second, with the spread of connectivity and mobile phones, citizens everywhere "will have more power than at any other time in history."[30] What the authors did not say but could have is that technology is a double-edged sword. Its impact on jobs for example—here is where the economy and technology visibly intersect—is sometimes positive and sometimes negative. In his book *Who Owns the Future?*, Jared Lanier argues that it is precisely technology, the rise of digital networks, that has led inexorably to the hollowed-out middle class. His great example is the difference between Kodak and Instagram. At its height Kodak had 140,000 employees. In contrast, when Instagram was sold to Facebook for $1 billion in 2012, it had in its employ all of thirteen people.[31] MIT professor Erik Brynjolfsson put it this way, "There is no economic law that says technological progress has to benefit everyone. It's entirely possible for the pie to get bigger and some people to get a smaller slice."[32]

Ideology

Our beliefs—spiritual, social, political—are more diffuse and diverse in the present than they were in the past. To start, as we have seen, in the past half century Americans have become more religiously diverse, a trend likely to continue, if only because of immigration from places other than Europe. Moreover, the least religious people are more likely now than they were either to have no religion at all, or to have no meaningful attachment to any particular religion. "A cultural trend has accompanied this demographic trend: Americans have become more accepting of religious diversity and more appreciative of religions other than their own."[33]

At the same time, evangelical and conservative churches have tended to thrive in recent decades, while more liberal Christian denominations have not. In fact, the decline of liberal Protestantism is one of the most striking of recent American trends. Still, a decline in liberal religious institutions is not the same as a decline in liberal religious ideas. In fact, more than half of religiously active people say that their church or denomination "should adjust its traditional beliefs and practices or adopt modern beliefs and practices in light of new circumstances."[34]

This rising level of tolerance is evidenced nearly across the board. Increasing egalitarianism governs black-white relationships. Greater acceptance is accorded different roles for women, as well as different lifestyles, including gay marriages and single-parent households. In addition, although there is growing ambivalence about the role of the federal government in addressing the nation's problems, "middle-of-the-road positions generally outnumber extreme ones."[35]

Counterintuitively, perhaps, while during the thirty-year period 1974 to 2004 the percentage of people who identified themselves as "liberals" held more or less steady, the percentage of people who identified themselves as "conservatives" grew rather more rapidly, especially among southern whites. But, importantly, successful conservative politics has not translated into successful conservative policies. In fact, there has been no "massive or widespread shift in public opinion toward conservative positions," such as opposition to big government or even big spending.

"Movement away from belief in an expanded government role in solving social problems has been mainly toward a more moderate view, not a belief that government should substantially contract."[36] Further, young people seem increasingly to support the idea that government support is a positive, not a negative. "Young people have voted more Democratic since the 2004 election of George W. Bush, and they are much more likely than other groups to support a larger role for government."[37]

Still, as we have seen, there has been substantial decline in confidence in American institutions and in those who lead and manage them. The reasons for the decline are complicated, multiple, everything from systemic shortcomings to new media and old, both tirelessly negative not only about certain specifics but about American society more generally.[38] But there is another trend that relates and is important in its own right, which brings us back to jobs. I refer to the increase in "precarious work"—work that is insecure and uncertain; work in which the employee, not the employer, or for that matter the government, bears most of the burden and carries most of the risks. Precarious work is work that is devoid of benefits and often even of a living wage.[39]

Here's another trend: by 2020, the United States is expected to overtake Saudi Arabia as the world's largest oil producer. And another: young people are favoring living in cities as opposed to living in suburbs. And another: the heyday of the big box retailer is over, with retailers of all sizes increasingly focusing on online shopping, and online shopping itself increasingly dependent on mobile apps. And another: student loan credit conditions are rapidly deteriorating. Delinquencies in almost every other category of personal debt have declined in recent years, but not in student loans, which have gone up, not down.[40] And another: synthetic biology has become so cheap and easy its practitioners are no longer, necessarily, classically trained biologists.[41] And yet another: hot sauce is going mainstream. Hot sauce, believe it or not, is now one of the ten fastest growing industries in the U.S.[42]

Of course, leaders can go nuts contending with trends in, to take some random examples, geo-engineering, performance enhancing drugs, and artificial intelligence. As usual, the amount of information we receive is too much, way, way too much, and too arcane for any single leader to take in—and way, way too much for any single leader effectively to act on. Moreover, many of the most important trends represent challenges so great they are beyond any single individual's capacity even to begin to meet, at least alone. In his book titled *The Future*, former vice president Al Gore looks at "six drivers of global change"—six trends. Let me name just one: "the emergence of rapid unsustainable growth . . . and economic output that is measured and guided by an absurd and distorted set of universally accepted metrics that blinds us to the destructive consequences of the self-deceiving choices we are routinely making."[43] What's a leader to do? How to begin to lead when the "destructive consequences" of our "self-deceiving choices" are so daunting?

I'm reminded of Alan Greenspan, one of the outstanding economists of our time, and former chair of the Federal Reserve. Notwithstanding his previously sterling reputation, it was Greenspan who in good part has been held responsible for the Great Recession. To his credit, Greenspan has since struggled, publicly, with how he and others like him were so wrong, were so woefully unable to foretell the future. In an article titled "Never Saw It Coming," Greenspan admitted how cloudy his crystal ball: "The financial crisis . . . represented an existential crisis for economic forecasting. The conventional method of predicting macroeconomic developments . . . had failed when it was needed most."[44]

What leaders are saddled with then is cognitive dissonance. On the one hand is someone like Greenspan, overwhelmed by a trend he never foresaw. And on the other hand is someone like Gore, intoning that unless we "find better ways to understand the forces shaping our future so that we do not simply surrender to the deterministic outcomes," the "promise of America" will never be "redeemed."[45] Of course, if you're a leader who happens to make ketchup, you should be fine. All *you* need to worry about is the trend to hot sauce.

PART VI   INVERSIONS

22 LEADERS

MY REFRAIN REMAINS THE SAME: leaders are getting weaker. This is not a rule without exceptions. To the contrary—it's a rule with many exceptions. There are many examples in this country, as elsewhere in the world, of powerful leaders and powerless followers. But there is a good case to be made that one of the reasons leaders in twenty-first-century America find it hard to lead is that leadership itself has been compromised, devalued.

As I claim in this book and have done elsewhere, though leaders do not necessarily have less *influence,* in democracies as opposed to autocracies, and in democratic organizations as opposed to autocratic organizations, they do have less *power* than they did and they also have less *authority.* To be sure, the workplace can be a notable exception to this general rule, but by and large leaders are less able than they were even a generation ago to use their titles or the positions they hold as a way of getting other people to do what they want them to do. Whether the leaders are executives or politicians, hospital administrators or military officers, priests or principals, their status means less, which means that their ability to lead has been lessened as well.

We have seen it in the literature on leadership, which has shifted from command and control to teams and empowerment, and from organizational pyramids to flatter or even flattened hierarchies. Similarly, we have seen it in the handful of books that have taken up the larger theme: how patterns of dominance and deference have changed more generally. In *The End of Leadership* this was, as the title implies, my primary point. "Leadership has a long history and a clear trajectory," I wrote. More than anything else it was and is "about the devolution of power—from those up top to those down below."[1] This was also the argument made by Moises Naim, in his similarly titled subsequent volume, *The End of Power*. Like me, Naim found that power is "undergoing a historic and world-changing transformation." And, like me, Naim argued that "big players are increasingly being challenged by newer and smaller ones," and that those who have power are "more constrained in the ways they can use it."[2] More recently, in November 2013, political scientist Ian Bremmer made the same claim. He wrote in *Foreign Affairs*, "One of the most important issues facing the world is the growing vulnerability of political elites. This problem makes effective public and private leadership much more difficult."[3]

This is not, clearly, simply and solely an American phenomenon. While the focus here is on leadership in twenty-first-century America, seasoned observers of power at the international level, Naim and Bremmer included, make similar points. Historian Timothy Garton Ash refers to this as a time in which there is "not a new world order but a new world disorder," in which previous patterns of dominance and deference are upended.[4] Political scientist Joseph Nye points out that world politics is no longer "the sole province of governments"—of people in positions of political leadership. Instead there are new players—individuals, groups, informal networks—all of which "undercut the monopoly of traditional bureaucracy."[5] In democracies, in other words, power is, again, more widely distributed now than it used to be, a trend certain to continue and maybe even to accelerate.

If power has been devolving for centuries—from kings and queens; emperors and empresses; tsars and tsarinas; sultans and sultanas; popes, priests, and priestesses to us, to ordinary people—what we are witnessing now is simply more of the same. Still, there are some moments in time when change is more rapid, more dramatic than at others. We know, for example, that the social and political upheavals of the late 1960s and early 1970s were just such a time—the various rights revolutions testifying to the fervor and fever of the power of the people. It's too early, of course, to know how history will judge the first ten or twenty years of the twenty-first century. What we do know though is this: that there are reasons why, now, leaders are getting weaker and followers stronger. And, what we do know is that the reasons relate to context. Put differently, humankind, human nature, does not change, or, at least, it does not change much. What does change is the circumstance within which people—in this case Americans, leaders and followers—are situated.

The most obvious reasons leaders have been enfeebled are first, changes in culture that entitle and embolden subordinates to demean and diminish their putative superiors, and second, changes in technology that enable ordinary people to obtain information, engage in self-expression, and make interpersonal connections in ways and to degrees that historically are unprecedented. The changes in culture are overarching—they set the stage, if you will, on which leaders and followers play their parts. The changes in technology are specific—they can be identified to illuminate not only why they matter to leader-follower relations but how. Of course, what's of particular interest here are the ways in which culture and technology intersect, interact. More precisely, since the turn of the century technology has been responsible for at least some of the changes in culture.

In *Leadership and Web 2.0*, authors Grady McGonagill and Tina Doerffer explore the impact of the Internet specifically on relations between leaders and followers.[6] In the corporate sector, technology has changed relations between employees and employers, among employees, between companies and their customers or clients, and between companies and their competitors. The social sector in turn is experimenting with new forms of communication and information distribution, and new modes of organization and governance. The same holds true, or rather it should, for government. New and different challenges include enabling new forms of participation; containing the dissemination of secret information; managing threats to legitimate authority when everyone everywhere has a voice; and managing period, as in managing, say, the Affordable Care Act, which as most Americans know by now depends heavily on technology.

In consequence of changes like these have been changes in leadership and management—including increasing the flow of information from the top down, increasing the flow of communication from the bottom up, decentralizing decision making, and reducing if not eliminating impediments to self-organization. Still, it's not easy. It's not easy because what this all adds up to is leadership that is less autocratic and more democratic. Put differently, like power, which is more widely distributed, leadership, unless it reverts to being centralized, to being authoritarian, is more widely shared. Think of Barack Obama, who decided he had better seek the approval of Congress before striking Syria. As president of the United States he could have acted on his own authority as chief executive, and on his own authority as commander in chief. But faced with the prospect of a political firestorm, he did not dare. He was the leader, but he was constrained, or he felt he was constrained, by his would-be followers—members of Congress, and the media, and the American people. (It turned out that the Russians stepped in and offered a deal on eliminating Syria's chemical weapons. This allowed Obama to put the Syrian strike on hold without losing face, more or less.) A more general example is the previously mentioned elevated role of the chief information officer—vis-à-vis the chief executive officer. As the Pew Research Center's Paul Taylor put it in the *Financial Times*, "Just as IT systems have come to pervade almost every aspect of business, so the relationship between the chief information officer and other senior—or C-suite—executives has also shifted."[7] Just think how technologically sophisticated almost any CEO would now have to be in order to be fully independent of subordinates who are more technologically expert.

Changes at the national level are in evidence at the international level as well. In his most recent book, *Presidential Leadership and the Creation of the American Era*, Nye references "the context of American Power in the Twenty-First Century." He points out how the situation abroad mirrors the one at home, quoting from a report by the National

Intelligence Council: "By 2030, no country—whether the U.S., China, or any other large country—will be a hegemonic power." More specifically, there are two major power shifts "to which American leaders will have to adjust. One is power transition among countries, from West to East, and the other is power diffusion from governments to nongovernmental actors, regardless of whether it is East or West."[8]

Nye is writing here about presidential leadership in foreign affairs. But the point pertains more broadly. First, other national leaders are vulnerable to the same dynamic. Even so effective and successful a leader as Germany's Chancellor Angela Merkel cannot respond to, say, Russia's incursion into Crimea without taking into account the German people, who depend heavily on Russia for energy. Second, we are talking here not only about political leaders, but about corporate leaders, educational leaders, military leaders, religious leaders—all are operating in a context in which the U.S. no longer is paramount, and in which actors other than leaders, such as stakeholders and constituents—all followers in my parlance—have greater say, hold more sway.

Having argued that technology has an impact on culture, I should say that sometimes it simply exaggerates and exacerbates it. More precisely, technological trends exaggerate and exacerbate cultural trends in ways that enfeeble leaders further. Here is an example: followers making fun of leaders, which, to be sure, likely they have done forever. Certainly, political satire has existed at least since Aristophanes, who took aim at the elite in ancient Greece; and since Honore Daumier, who caricatured, ridiculed King Louise Philippe in nineteenth-century France; and since George Orwell, who penned the ultimate leader put-down, *Animal Farm*. But now things are different. Now making fun of leaders, teasing them, mocking them, making them the butt of jokes, has become a growth industry. It has gone from being a preserve reserved for a precious few to a mass market phenomenon propelled, again, by changes in both culture and technology. "The internet has made it easier for the masses to join in the fun. Cartoons and lampoons can be posted online, no longer needing a print publication to host them. Social media have helped political sideswipes to spread as contagiously as laughter, and have fostered a 'remix culture' in which internet-users share memes and post spoofs with abandon. The internet has also made it easier for satirists to bypass censors and stay anonymous."[9] Johnny Carson, known for his barbed but gentle jokes about powerful people, has morphed into Jon Stewart, known for his loud, often viciously funny attacks on anyone and everyone who would dare something as offensive as trying to lead. In contrast to Carson, for whom taking jabs at leaders was a sometime pastime, for Stewart it's what he does. It's his full-time job.

Of course this humbling, this pushing people in high places off their putative pedestals, is endemic. We see it all the time, assaults on leaders, public humiliations of leaders, even if they have been for the largest part of their professional lives estimable, even venerable. Some of the most notorious of these leaders previously were famous, such as Joe Paterno, who for decades was revered at Penn State and well beyond for being fabulously successful at coaching football. Nevertheless, not long before his death, he was reviled for being implicated, though indirectly, in a child sex abuse scandal. Others of these leaders were not famous—more precisely they were not famous until they became infamous. I am thinking, for example, of another educational leader, this one a man by the name of Stanley Teitel. For thirteen years Teitel was principal of one of the nation's most prestigious public schools, New York City's Stuyvesant High. Until the end, when he too was ensnared in a scandal not of his own making—some students were discovered to have been cheating—Teitel was credited with being a "superstar principal" of a superstar school.[10] But as soon as there was blood in the water, sharks circled. Not only did Teitel feel obliged to resign shortly after the news broke—one parent, a professor of law at Fordham, called it a "dark day for all those who long for excellence in public education"—a year later he resurfaced as the subject of a prominent piece in the *New York Times* that carried the headline, "Stuyvesant Principal, Now Retired, Mishandled Cheating Case, Report Says."

The report was issued by New York City's Education Department, which found that Teitel had "failed to efficiently and effectively carry out the administrative duties entrusted" to him.[11] Let's say it was true. Let's say that Teitel was on this one admittedly important occasion neither efficient nor effective. Is this sufficient reason to besiege and belittle him so he feels obliged to resign? Is this sufficient reason to one year later post his picture in the paper as if he were a convicted felon? Is this sufficient reason to wipe out an otherwise sterling record of educational accomplishment—of educational leadership? I pose these questions not to prejudge the answers, but rather to point out how hard it is in this day and age to lead. One slip and you're not only down, likely you're out. The rewards of leadership can still be great, material and otherwise. But they are lesser, and the risks are greater. Leading has become a high-wire act that only the most skilled are able to perform successfully over a protracted period of time.

Hard lessons have been learned across the board, by leaders in government, by leaders in business, by leaders everywhere else. Notwithstanding the conventional wisdom, even chief executive officers, America's corporate elite, have had, are having, their wings clipped. Not that we need pity them. They continue to have considerable power, authority, and influence. They continue to receive famously high levels of compensation. (Two extreme examples are founder and CEO of Amazon, Jeff Bezos, and founder and CEO of Facebook, Mark Zuckerberg. In 2013 the value of Bezos's Amazon shares jumped by $12 billion, and the value of Zuckerberg's Facebook shares similarly surged by about $12 billion. That's "billion," with a "b."[12]) And most have managed to avoid significant punishment for whatever they might have done that was wrong.

Still, this is not to say that all chief executive officers are all getting off scot-free. They are not. While such changes as have been made are not exactly earthshaking—for example, golden parachutes are falling out of favor amid investor and regulatory scrutiny of rising executive pay—there has been some tightening of the reins, in particular increased governmental oversight of those at the top in financial services. Tough-minded, long-time observer of the financial markets Floyd Norris writes, for example, "Where once the public, and regulators, took it for granted that big banks were adequately capitalized, now there are newly determined regulators."[13] In other words, it is increasingly expected, by all of the relevant players, that those in charge of banks be regularly monitored and held accountable.

JPMorgan Chase is, as previously noted, a clear case in point. During and just after the financial crisis. the bank and the man who led it, Chairman and Chief Executive Officer Jamie Dimon, seemed models of relative rigor and rectitude. Whether by good luck or good leadership the bank had avoided the worst excesses of the big boom, so Dimon was for a time widely regarded as the most respected man on Wall Street. But just a few years later he was widely regarded as the most beleaguered—his bank's legal woes had become legion. In 2013 alone, JPMorgan spent an additional $4 billion and hired five thousand extra employees—just to clean up its risk and compliance problems.[14] And, in 2013 alone, it made roughly $22 billion in payouts to end lawsuits and investigations tied to issues ranging from misrepresentations on past mortgage bond sales to the so-called "London whale" trading debacle.[15]

Moreover, JPMorgan itself moved to limit Dimon's power, requiring him beginning in 2013 to share it with Lee Raymond, the newly titled "lead independent director." Raymond was given considerable authority, including having the discretion to call a board meeting at any time, guiding the annual performance evaluation of the chairman and chief executive officer, and heading the board's deliberations on who would succeed the incumbent chair and CEO.[16] In fact, because the increased scrutiny and new regulatory environment makes running a bank now a lot less attractive than it used to be, Dimon's close colleague and heir apparent, Michael Cavanagh, suddenly and startlingly announced (in 2014) that he was quitting JPMorgan to take a top job in private equity.

Nor is JPMorgan alone—other major banks, that is, bankers, have had to change their ways as well. Former CEO of Morgan Stanley, John Mack, and his successor, James Gorman, now agree that the bank's "No. 1 client is the government." There are tougher capital rules, regulators prowl the office floors looking for land mines, and "Mr. Gorman phones Washington before making major decisions." By every account Morgan Stanley has changed dramatically, the culture now discouraging rather than encouraging anything resembling excessive risk-taking. As Gorman put it, the firm has "taken risk management to a completely different level so we'd never again have the kind of . . . exposures that got us in trouble."[17] Similarly, Michael Corbat, CEO of Citigroup since 2012, is studiously low key. He keeps his profile low and deliberately declines to give interviews, having apparently concluded that it is both in his own interest and that of the firm he leads for him to be self-effacing as opposed to self-aggrandizing.[18]

There are other indicators as well, all of which suggest that while leading in business might be somewhat less stressful than leading in government, leading in corporate America is more difficult than it used to be, and more dangerous as well.

First, companies themselves have contributed to the increased unease, for example, by obliging more CEOs to share power and by moving somewhat more aggressively to align CEO pay more closely with performance.[19] While so far there is no evidence that this increased monitoring is having a major effect, especially on CEO compensation, what is fair to say is that the astronomically high rates of pay are drawing not only increased public scrutiny but increased public censure. (Oracle's notoriously highly compensated CEO, Larry Ellison, has been singled out as being one of the few corporate titans who seems not to have the slightest compunction about being so extravagantly paid—$78.4 million in 2013 alone.[20])

Second, the number of interested stakeholders has increased, and along with it the number of others, which include new media and old, who are keeping close tabs on the leader's performance. Third, the rate of CEO turnover has increased. In 2013, a study conducted by the consulting firm Booz & Company found the "highest share ever of planned CEO successions."[21] Jeff Immelt, CEO of General Electric (GE), is among those weighing in on the subject, apparently rethinking the length of time anyone should head a company as complicated as GE. His newfangled idea is that a very complex company in a very complex context should not be led by any single chief executive officer for longer than ten to fifteen years.[22] Finally, there is evidence that the pressure on CEOs more generally, especially on those newly minted, has also become greater. As one Booz & Company partner put it, "We are seeing executives face more intense pressure to perform during their first year."[23]

CEOs are being threatened in other ways as well, for instance by activist investors, who have no compunctions about challenging companies that seem to them to be in some way weak. In the old days, CEOs and their typically handpicked boards were left largely alone, free to run their businesses as they saw fit. This held true even when times were tough, when the business was performing poorly. And it held true even if management was doing badly, if individual executives, including those at the top, were evidently not up to the task. But when the *Wall Street Journal* has a front-page headline screaming, "Activist Storms Microsoft Board," you know something's changed. Of course, the real point is not that Microsoft's management was obliged to bend, which it was. (The board ended up pushing out Steve Ballmer, who had led the company some thirteen years, since Bill Gates quit to commit to philanthropy full time.[24]) The real point is that what happened at Microsoft is indicative of a larger trend. Activist investors with large war chests increasingly are taking on companies large and small—including blue chip companies such as Procter & Gamble and Pepsico. Such investors engage in an array of aggressive tactics, for example, using the media or going online to excoriate their targets. These sorts of disruptions, clearly aggressive in intent, rattle corporate boardrooms and businesses, and strike "fear into the hearts and minds of executives across the country."[25]

None of this is to say that this sort of investor activism is, by definition, good or bad. In some circumstances it is one; in other circumstances the other. What I am saying instead is that shareholder activists are contributing to the creation of a new, more threatening corporate climate, with which corporate leaders have no choice but to contend. Of course, chief executive officers themselves are hardly oblivious to the trend. In response to activist attacks, some have already changed their ways. "Instead of pulling up the drawbridge as activists approach, corporate executives and directors more often are engaging, concluding that it is easier and cheaper to negotiate rather than resist and risk a public fight."[26]

All these changes—changes in the context within which leaders lead—raise the question of what it takes in the second decade of the twenty-first century for any single individual to successfully exercise leadership in

America. Today's vast literature on the subject has no shortage of answers to precisely this question. In fact, it's what the leadership industry does— it gives advice, offers counsel, provides information and ideas on how to lead. Political scientist Michael Genovese has compressed the morass of material into what he calls "the central leadership competencies." They are (1) judgment, (2) emotional intelligence, (3) empathy, (4) flexibility and balance, (5) moral courage, (6) self- and world knowledge, (7) communication skills, (8) talent development, (9) articulating a compelling vision, (10) adapting, (11) learning from mistakes, and (12) developing contextual intelligence.[27]

It's a perfectly fine list, clearly. But it does suffer from being ideal rather than real—describing the leader as paragon of virtue. And it does suffer from being other than situation specific. There are, in other words, some circumstances, some contexts, within which the leader would not have to be in the least, say, empathetic, or communicative, or visionary. My own preference then is to keep it simple, really simple. Here is how I would put it. It is apparent that in the second decade of the twenty-first century, leaders' power and authority have been diminished.[28] More precisely, they are diminished in democracies and in relatively democratic (flat) organizations, in which those other than members of the leadership team, followers, that is, are free to do and say more or less what they want when they want. But they are much less diminished in autocracies and hierarchical or autocratic organizations, in which people are not free to do and say more or less what they want when they want, and in which leaders feel free to reward and punish as they see fit. What I am saying, in other words, is that in democratic systems and cultures, such as the U.S., and in organizations that are at least somewhat flat, leaders, because they have less power and authority, are more dependent than they ever were on their capacity to exercise influence.

Let me be clear: exercising influence is not tantamount to abdicating all power and authority. In fact, the evidence suggests that too much reliance on the collective, on teamwork, has disadvantages as well as advantages.[29] But exercising influence is a skill especially suited to leadership in the twenty-first century—especially in contexts within which power and authority are meager. Here is an example: Ben Bernanke, chairman of the Federal Reserve between 2006 and 2014. Bernanke was Fed chair during a particularly dramatic, difficult, and demanding period—when the U.S. was for a time on the brink of financial collapse. So how did Bernanke manage to lead during this crisis, both within the Fed and without? He exercised influence. Though he himself was clearly singularly expert, he chose nevertheless to "manage by consensus." For example, breaking with precedent, he gave his Fed colleagues wide latitude to speak their minds, both at closed-door meetings and in public settings. And he worked hard behind the scenes to find common ground among the eighteen other Fed governors and bank presidents, especially in advance of making major decisions. To be sure, there were downsides to this approach; it's not the most efficient way to do business. In this case it took rather a long time for Fed members to get to the point of being able to decide so that everyone was, more or less, on board. Nor would patience and diligence of this sort suit all leaders in all situations. But by every account, Bernanke's influence-is-all approach built him the "much-needed reservoir of goodwill" that he required to lead both the Fed and the nation at large during a time we were in, and then barely recovering from, a financial crisis.[30]

Here is another example. Soon after employees, including long-time editors and reporters, at the *Washington Post* were stunned, stung by the news that the founder and CEO of Amazon, Jeff Bezos, had bought the paper, he flew to Washington to "chat with employees" about his plans for the company. By the end of Bezos's visit he had, at least for the moment, won the staff over. How did he do it? He provided his rationale for buying the *Post*. He expressed optimism about the paper's future. He appeared aware of the journalistic culture to which most *Post* people were deeply committed. He had breakfast, lunch, and cups of coffee with a range of different players. And, at the end of the day, he met with the entire newsroom for a question-and-answer session that lasted an hour and twenty minutes. Of course, how all this will turn out in the end only time will tell. Bezos is scarcely a sentimentalist, so it's altogether possible if not probable that in time the worm will turn. But his brief effort at exercising influence by being ingratiating worked. Initially, at least, the leader had managed to "charm" those who only recently had become, willy-nilly, his followers.[31] Initially, at least, the leader had managed to avoid the sort of public relations fiasco on which followers now love to feed.

Notice that what Bezos did was not hard. All it took for him to avoid being on the occasion the most hated man in Washington was a little bit, a very little bit, of tender loving care.

23 FOLLOWERS

I WANT TO CLARIFY AGAIN my use of the word *follower*. It's obviously not the perfect word because, as I use it, followers follow most of the time, but not all of the time. In spite of this confusion, I continue to invoke *followers* and *followership* because of the exigencies of the English language. In English, *follower* is the only obvious antonym of *leader*, as *followership* is the only obvious antonym of *leadership*. The words *leader* and *leadership* have no other opposites or counterparts—so *follower* and *followership* will have to do.

Of course, different people use different words to signify the same phenomenon—for example, *stakeholders, constituents, participants, subordinates, employees, group members* or *team members*. I, in any case, use the word *follower* to indicate people with no obvious sources of power, authority, and influence. This is in contrast to the word *leader*, which I use to indicate people with obvious sources of power, authority, influence, or some combination. Of course the words *leader* and *follower* are fungible. Sometimes leaders follow, sometimes followers lead. Moreover, followers change, they become leaders. And leaders change, they become followers. So, for the purpose of this discussion the follower is simply the *other*—the person or persons the leader must somehow engage and include if he or she is to control the action.

We know that over the course of American history the balance of power between leaders and followers has changed—and that it continues to evolve even now. We also know that however ideal the original theory of democracy in America, the original practice of democracy in America was far from it. To this day American blacks are in many of the most important ways not equal to American whites, and American women are in many of the most important ways not equal to American men. Still, the trajectory toward democracy—toward increased political, personal, and professional representation and participation—is obvious. Even since the most recent rights revolutions, in the 1960s and 1970s, patterns of dominance and deference have changed, with relations between leaders and followers different now from what they were before.

Evidence of the still continuing decline in respect for people in positions of authority is everywhere in America. The growing refusal of followers to defer literally or metaphorically to their putative leaders, their putative superiors, is obvious in the classroom; in the community; in the streets; in the arts; in the media; and in corridors of power wherever they are, including, under certain circumstances, in the workplace. Increasingly, leaders are beleaguered; increasingly, followers, others, are emboldened. A perfect example is the profession of medicine, which even in recent years has changed dramatically, partly but by no means only because of the changing technologies. As Michael Specter wrote in a piece in *The New Yorker* about Mehmet Oz, the heart surgeon and host of television's "The Dr. Oz Show," the reasons for Oz's success relate also to changes in our attitudes toward medical professionals, toward nearly all people in positions of authority. "The era of paternalistic medicine, where the doctor knew best and the patient felt lucky to have him, has ended. We don't worship authority figures anymore."[1] And because we don't worship authority figures any more, we turn to a "professional soulmate" like Dr. Oz, who not only performs the role of genial guide for the masses but encourages people to stand up for themselves against the antiquated tyrannies of medical professionals.

Participatory democracy is now everywhere in evidence: everywhere we weigh in, express our preferences, and register our opinions. Power, all the while, has become distributed, disseminated, and diffused, rather like information itself. None of this is to suggest that leaders have no arrows left in their quivers. They do. But, notwithstanding, followers frequently feel free to take on leaders, insult leaders, attack leaders, stand up to leaders, even rise up against them. In part this is in consequence of followers more emboldened; in part this is in consequence of leaders more disrespected and disliked.

Worried about the outrage and backlash after the tragic collapse of a clothing factory in Bangladesh, Western retailers, including the parent company of American brands such as Calvin Klein and Tommy Hilfiger, rushed to endorse a plan in which they agreed to finance significant safety upgrades. Worried about a continuing faculty and student revolt at St. Louis University—protesters had accused the president, Reverend Lawrence Biondi, of creating a campus atmosphere of fear and disrespect—the school's board of trustees pushed him to retire after twenty-five years of service. Worried about losing its audience, A&E, the Arts and Entertainment network, rescinded its suspension of *Duck Dynasty* star Phil Robertson (for making comments that were considered anti-gay) almost immediately after receiving a petition signed within days by more than a quarter million people. Worried about the impact of animal rights activists on customer perceptions and preferences, retailers and fast food outlets changed the way they buy animal products, including eggs and meat. Whole Foods Markets and Chipotle banned their suppliers from using gestation crates; Safeway and Wendy's were lauded by the Humane Society of the United States for their efforts to avoid pork suppliers that abuse animals; and, while it was late to the game, fast food giant McDonald's finally concluded that it had better use its massive leverage to push for better animal gestation conditions.[2] Worried that gay rights activists would spoil the traditionally splendid season-opening night at the Metropolitan Opera (featuring Russian singers in Tchaikovsky's *Eugene Onegin*), General Manager Peter Gelb felt obliged to release an extended statement: "Through the choice of our LGBT (lesbian, gay, bisexual, and transgender) rainbow of artists and staff, the Met has long been at the forefront of championing sexual and social equality within our company. . . . We respect the right of activists to picket our opening night and we realize that we've provided them with a platform to further raise awareness about serious human rights issues abroad. . . . Although Russia may officially be in denial about Tchaikovsky's sexuality, we're not."[3] (Gelb stopped short, however, of dedicating the season opener to the "oppressed gay citizens of Russia.") In another somewhat similar case, once it came out that Mozilla's chief executive officer, Brendan Eich, had some six years earlier donated $1,000 to support a measure to ban same-sex marriage, the negative response from gay rights activists was so swift and so strong that Eich felt obliged to resign. And precisely because they worry that their constituents are getting fed up, lawmakers persist in the ritual of facing them head on. But times have changed. Old-fashioned town hall meetings are threatened with extinction, supplanted instead by free-for-alls, in which everyone with an agenda feels entitled to speak up loud and speak up clear. Immigration advocates, tea party organizers, privacy-rights activists, Obamacare opponents and enthusiasts—these are just some of the citizen-participants using public meetings to lobby for their cause, pressure politicians, drive the news cycle—or claim their fifteen minutes of fame. No wonder lawmakers such as Patrick McHenry, a Republican Congressman from North Carolina, complain that meetings like these increasingly are pointless. They "coarsen the debate" and "take the focus off solutions and onto scoring points."[4]

No sector in American society is exempt from follower contempt for leaders, and no sector in American society is exempt from followers, others, trying to take leaders down. Of course most of the time most leaders stay put, where they are. I am not suggesting that people without power, authority, and influence are able, in general, to upend those with. What I am saying is that ordinary people make things *hard* for leaders, even though leaders do get more handsomely rewarded, and do get to control the action. It's the other sorts of rewards—the intangible ones that American followers have sometimes at least bestowed on American leaders—such as deference, respect, support, admiration, even affection—that are in notably short supply. Leadership has, in other words, become a bit of a blood sport. For not only are followers out to get leaders, so are other leaders, to wit, the heightened nastiness in Washington. In sum, the lack of civility and cordiality more generally—badly exacerbated by the anonymity afforded online—is a component of the context within which we live. In other words, in twenty-first-century America, evidence of communitarianism and civic-mindedness is scant.

There is no need here to repeat any poll numbers. We know, to take an obvious example, that in the second decade of the twenty-first century Congress's approval ratings are in the cellar. What this sort of alienation and distrust leads to, of course, is a whole host of disparagements, ranging from relentless verbal attacks on the governing class by both talking heads and ordinary people to the dissemination of embarrassing information to being ignored or even disdained by the electorate, a majority of whom often could care less. What happened in the 2013 election for mayor of Los Angeles was emblematic. The primary was the most expensive on record. But turnout was the lowest on record for any primary without an incumbent in more than thirty years. Just 21 percent of registered voters bothered to vote. Locals were shocked. Newspapers decried the low numbers as "pathetic," "embarrassing," and "stunning." And one local official declared the morning after that he was "in mourning."[5] (Tellingly, one of the few exceptions to the general rule of low turnout in primaries was in a June 2014 election in Virginia, in which House Republican Leader Eric Cantor was upset by his Tea Party–backed opponent Dave Brat.)

But the turnout in L.A. was hardly shocking. Followers, in this case eligible voters, are punishing their leaders, in this case elected officials, by withholding their blessings. To say that the electorate is alienated and cynical is to put it mildly. Polling places are sparsely populated in every off-year election. The year 2013, however, marked a depressing new low. In city after city, including New York, and in state after state, including New Jersey, turnout either dropped from what it was only four years earlier, or it hit new lows. In fact, in metropolises including Atlanta, Houston, Pittsburgh, and Detroit, the turnout percentage of eligible voters barely broke double digits. This tells us something, something big about relations between leaders and followers in twenty-first-century America. When so many eligible voters don't even bother to exercise their franchise, to make a minimal effort to support any of the candidates, the story is not about what did happen in any given election, but about what did not.[6]

Of course, turnout in elections for president is significantly higher (between 51 and 61 percent) than in other elections, such as midterms (in the high thirties). But even the turnout for presidential elections is considerably lower in the United States than for similar elections in other Western democracies. (Turnout in Great Britain is slightly higher than in the U.S.—at the last election, in 2010, it was 65 percent—and in Germany it is notably higher; over 70 percent of eligible voters vote.) This "disappearance" of the American voter is not new; it's been going on for years. Which raises the question of why, during a period in which levels of literacy, education, and technological development have all increased, did voter turnout decrease? The answers obviously are complex, but near the top of the list, just under our dislike and distrust of the leadership class is, again, that word *culture*, here *civic culture*. Put simply, most of the experts agree that by and large the American people—followers, folks like you and me—have shifted their focus away from political leaders to themselves, and away from larger political issues to smaller quality-of-life issues. The shift is away from the collective and toward the self, away from the political toward the personal, including toward our own individual needs for autonomy and self-expression.[7] (Technology supports the trend—many of us are dedicated to nothing so much as our own devices.) This could, of course, change. If the economy takes another hit, or if income inequity becomes incendiary, or if the dysfunction of the leadership class gets to the point of being downright destructive, the American people could in some way rebel. They, we, could become, again, deeply engaged in consequence of our becoming not merely alienated, but angry.[8]

Though the conventional wisdom is that corporate leaders are exempt altogether from being hit, the conventional wisdom is, as we have seen, incorrect. The truth is that just like leaders in government, leaders in business are vulnerable to attack by both individuals and institutions, including government watchdogs acting more aggressively against corporate malfeasance than they did before the fiscal crisis. Though these are not the game changers that many would like to see—it's still rare for individuals personally to be held to account—to say that new laws such as the Dodd-Frank Act and the Consumer Protection Act have no effect whatsoever, no impact whatsoever, is simply wrong. The Dodd-Frank Act alone contains more than ninety provisions that give the Securities and Exchange Commission (SEC) considerable discretionary rulemaking authority. This means, among other things, that the SEC now asks companies to reveal not only the compensation of their chief executives but also how much more their chief executives are being paid than their average employee. Moreover, the SEC is also no longer willing to tolerate settlements allowing defendants to "neither admit nor deny" wrongdoing. Instead it is insisting, certainly in some cases, that any settlement include an admission of individual as well as institutional wrongdoing.

We have seen that JPMorgan Chase's CEO, Jamie Dimon, was a poster boy turned whipping boy. As a result of his travails, Dimon himself admitted that "adjusting to the new regulatory environment will require an enormous amount of time, effort and resources. We fully intend to follow the letter and spirit of every rule and requirement."[9] But of course Dimon was hardly alone. For instance, New York State's top prosecutor filed a lawsuit against Wells Fargo, accusing the bank of flouting the terms of a multi-billion-dollar settlement aimed at staunching foreclosure abuses. And years after the worst of the mortgage mania was over, lawyers for the Justice Department took Countrywide Financial, a unit of Bank of America, to court, charging that it had misrepresented the quality of mortgages it sold to Fannie Mae and Freddie Mac (the taxpayer-owned mortgage giants). Lawsuits like these do not fundamentally change the balance of power between leaders and led, or between rich and poor. But they provide some evidence that both the federal government and the judiciary have not been entirely lax about going after big banks and those who lead and manage them. In a growing number of cases, judges, like government regulators, are "losing patience with the banks." Many are doing what they can to hold them accountable, which, as Gretchen Morgenson wrote in the *New York Times*, "may not seem like a lot, but it is progress."[10]

Of course, the heads of big banks are hardly the only corporate leaders obliged to protect themselves against whoever is the other.

The other, however defined, has halved the average CEO tenure, from about ten years in the 1990s to about five a decade or two later. In fact, about 80 percent of CEOs of S&P 500 companies are out of office before retirement.[11] Seems no one is exempt anymore—at the least from being publicly criticized. The aforementioned Larry Ellison, Oracle's famously rich and powerful CEO, finally came under shareholder attack for his long years of excessively high pay. Facebook's Mark Zuckerberg was subjected to angry questions by shareholders at the company's first ever annual meeting (2013). And not only was Microsoft's CEO Steve Ballmer pushed out by his increasingly restless board, no less a deity than Chairman Bill Gates was nudged, if so far only very gently, to step down. Three of Microsoft's top twenty investors lobbied the board to press Gates to quit his position, suggesting that his time had come and gone, and that his deep dedication to philanthropy did not suit his still dominant role at the company he years earlier had founded. Along somewhat similar lines Microsoft finally bowed to pressure and abolished its controversial policy of "stack ranking," a system of reviewing employees that required superiors to grade their subordinates against one another, and to rank them on a scale from one to five.

Of course, activist investors also contribute to the growing awareness that corporate leaders are more susceptible than they were to attack from outside. As a result, those in charge are obliged to play not only offense but defense. As one close observer put it, "People are starting to realize that no one is safe. Companies are thinking through their vulnerabilities."[12] When high-flying activist investor Daniel Loeb took on Sotheby's, the venerable art auction house, he went public with a statement aimed directly at the chief executive officer: "Sotheby's malaise is a result of a lack of leadership and a strategic vision at its highest levels." Loeb went on to embarrass Sotheby's top managers more generally, charging that they led too extravagant a lifestyle, all at the company's expense, feasting on organic delicacies and fine wines "at a cost to shareholders of multiple hundreds of thousands of dollars."[13] Loeb's attack was, not incidentally, successful. Within months Sotheby's agreed to, among other things, return $450 million to shareholders though a dividend and share buyback, and separate its agency and financial services units.[14]

To be clear, a wealthy investor such as Loeb is not a "follower" in the usual sense of this word. In the context of his assault on Sotheby's, he is bereft of authority but not, or not necessarily, of power and influence. He is, however, the other, the type of outsider who in this day and age must be brought along, in this instance if Sotheby's leadership team is to be left in peace. The phenomenon of someone like Loeb is not, as we know by now, altogether new. Rather it is emblematic of the rising numbers of outsider raiders, and the many efforts by many people in many places publicly to humiliate leaders, personally and professionally. What I am pointing to, in other words, is the diminishment of whoever is on top by one or another other, ready, willing, and able to mount a serious challenge and sometimes even a serious threat.

Even institutions historically relatively impervious to criticism—such as the American military and the Catholic Church—have been changed by the changing times. The change in the Church—the result of attacks on those up top by those down below—is self-evident. Similarly, the military's top leadership cadre has proven newly vulnerable not only to personal humiliation—exhibit A: David Petraeus and, similarly, his close associate, General John Allen, who retired from the military in consequence of being ensnared in scandal (though he was cleared of any wrongdoing)—but also to public criticism of its professional performance.

Military historian Max Boot charges that even as America's military finds itself increasingly entangled in guerilla wars, its "ignorance" of this sort of struggle "runs deep."[15] Similarly, in his tellingly titled book, *Bleeding Talent: How the U.S. Military Mismanages Great Leaders and Why It's Time for a Revolution*, veteran Tim Kane claims that while our armed services are good at attracting and training leaders, "in terms of managing talent, the U.S. military is doing everything wrong."[16] Finally, in his scathing look at top brass, long-time reporter and observer of the American military Thomas Ricks concludes that by almost every measure the soldiers and marines who went into Iraq and Afghanistan "were grossly unprepared for their missions, and that the officers who led them were often negligent." Ricks argues that so long as the military "cares more about not embarrassing generals than it does about taking care of soldiers," it is unlikely to do what it should. It is unlikely to conduct "a soul-searching review of its performance in Iraq and Afghanistan."[17] (Recently there have been signs that the military is listening to some of its critics. In 2013, two high-ranking Marine generals were, in effect, fired for failing to "take adequate force protection measures," and for not exercising the "level of judgment expected of general officers."[18] And in 2014, ten officers resigned or were relieved of their command at Malmstrom Air Force Base, following investigations into cheating and morale problems among missile launch crews.)

Evidence supporting the overarching argument—that leaders generally are being weakened and followers generally strengthened—includes web-based initiatives such as Kickstarter, the high-profile website dedicated to crowdfunding anyone and everyone who happens to have a great idea. Kickstarter avoids, sidesteps, and even competes with traditional venture capitalists and angel investors. Put differently, by now we all know that given the new technologies, not only a select few but the ordinary many are perfectly capable of performing functions such as funding enterprising entrepreneurs, collecting the word's knowledge (Wikipedia has rendered the *Encyclopedia Britannica* virtually obsolete), reporting breaking stories faster than traditional news-gathering organizations, and just generally shaking up the establishment and establishment practices. Again, some of this is generational. The young, the so-called millennials (born roughly 1980 to 2000), more than the old are new types of followers, men and women with no obvious resources but with a new set of demands: for transparency, autonomy, and inclusiveness.

Pertinent to this argument is the newfound power of the consumer to make or break a product. In the old days, consumers had to rely on their own experience, or on what the company told them, usually in advertisements, about whatever it was they wanted to buy. Now things are different. Reams of research are available to nearly every American about nearly every product. As *New Yorker* writer James Surowiecki points out, what's really weakened the power of brands is the Internet. It gives "ordinary people easy access to expert reviews, user reviews and detailed product data," which is why 80 percent of consumers now look at online reviews before they make a major purchase. The trend is, of course, further accelerated by social media, which can turn a "dud product" into "a laughingstock in a matter of hours."[19]

Also pertinent to the argument about the increased impact of the follower is obviously someone like Edward Snowden, an ordinary man or, more precisely, a man without obvious power, authority, or influence, who created great change. Until he became famous for being infamous, a notorious leaker, nobody had ever heard of Snowden. He was not, in any case, by any definition, a leader. But by revealing large amounts of previously secret intelligence data, he became a person of immeasurable power and influence, a person who, literally, changed the conversation on privacy versus security not only at home but abroad. Leaders as conventionally defined—including the president of the United States, members of Congress, heads of various agencies such as the Central Intelligence Agency and the National Security Agency—found that they were forced to bend to the man from nowhere, to Edward Joseph Snowden. (Snowden was, not incidentally, aided and abetted by several others of similar ilk. One such was renegade journalist Glenn Greenwald, who is similarly determined to push back against the post–9/11 "surveillance state" and similarly intent on using his newfound notoriety to reinvigorate journalism though "an aggressive and adversarial position to political and corporate power."[20])

Notwithstanding all this follower power is, simultaneously, a glaringly evident *follower paradox*. All sorts of leaders are being targeted by all sorts of followers—but followers themselves by and large are acting alone, not in concert. They are disorganized and atomized, not organized and aggregated. We know for example that in the 1950s one-third of American workers belonged to a union. Today that number is down to 11.3 percent. The reasons why are well documented—globalization, technology, the growth of the service sector, and tougher anti-union policies and politics. Still, the fact remains that "organized labor" has become nearly an oxymoron. Similarly, the "crisis of confidence" in government is close to cliche—just 17 percent of Americans say that they have confidence in the federal government, the figure for Congress we know is way worse, and while trust in the American president is higher, it is notably lower than it was just a decade ago.[21] But so far at least, the American people have been unable to group in ways that could significantly change or at least shake up the system.

To be clear here, we—we the American people—have not been inert. We did elect Barack Obama (it was Hillary Clinton who in 2008 was the candidate of the Democratic establishment). And we did start the Tea Party. But every effort to start a third major party—there have been several over the years—has failed and failed miserably. Similarly, workers and the mainstream middle class have not coalesced or effectively joined forces. And while chief executive officers make relatively easy targets, much more elusive are members of corporate boards, who ultimately are responsible for how companies are run. Shareholder efforts to remove directors in uncontested elections have rarely succeeded, or even come close. In 2012, 86 percent of directors received 90 percent or more of the vote—testimony not to shareholder satisfaction, but to shareholder inattention, disorganization, and alienation—to feelings of helplessness.

There are some exceptions to this general rule, which, counterintuitively, support the larger point. Fast food and restaurant workers have started occasionally to organize, at, for example, McDonald's and Capital Grille, to protest to get a living wage. The Freelancers Union, one of the nation's fasted growing labor organizations, now with some two hundred thousand members, is trying with some success to tap into the large number of freelancers and other independent workers to secure for their members some collective benefits. Similarly, there are so-called worker centers springing up here and there, one of the new types of worker advocacy groups that, though they hardly constitute a major threat, drive American businesses to distraction.[22] There is as well a fresh push to raise the minimum wage—though this is mainly because leaders, specifically Democrats, both in the White House and the Congress, finally detected an acceptable peg on which they could hang their political hats. And, to their credit, Tea Partiers, who of course came out of nowhere only rather recently, have been remarkably well organized, highly disciplined, and ideologically consistent. In fact, it is precisely this internal cohesion that has made them much more effective than their relatively small numbers would seem otherwise to suggest.[23]

But, again, these are the exceptions. In general the follower paradox—the paradox between the emboldened follower on the one hand and the ineffectual follower on the other—explains in part why we are where we are in the second decade of the twenty-first century. Emboldened followers make it hard for leaders to lead. Ineffectual followers make it easy to see why leaders usually remain in place, no matter how evidently inadequate. No wonder collective problems remain impervious to collective solutions.

24 OUTSIDERS

THIS BOOK IS ABOUT LEADERSHIP in America—about leadership in the American context. To this general rule there is one exception—this section. *Outsiders* pertains not to the context that constitutes the United States of America but to the context within which the United States of America itself is situated. This is not, obviously, irrelevant. It is impossible to be any kind of leader in twenty-first-century America without being aware of the world beyond: of the international system; of globalization; of competition from abroad, whether in business or education or any other field of human endeavor; of threats from abroad, whether political, economic, military, or terrorist; of opportunities abroad, personal and professional, individual and institutional; and of changes taking place in U.S. foreign policy that impinge in some way on U.S. domestic policy.

Not long ago America was perceived not only at home but abroad as being invulnerable and impermeable. Once the world order made the transition from bipolar—when the United States and the Soviet Union each dominated large swaths of the earth's surface—to unipolar, the U.S. stood alone. The collapse of communism and the end of the Cold War meant the last decade of the twentieth century was one in which the defining feature of world politics was "the enormous power and pervasive influence of the United States."[1] Of course, in some parts of the world American supremacy was regarded with animosity, if not downright antipathy. But in many other parts of the world it was welcome (if only tacitly), and at home in any case, it was widely thought something to be proud of, a state of affairs that while in some ways was burdensome, was nevertheless preferable to any other. This is not to say that Americans perceived themselves imperialists, astride the world like a colossus; quite the contrary. Rather, it is to say that Americans considered their democracy a model of reasonably good governance, and that they, we, were content to conceive of ourselves as immune to outside harm.

What a difference a decade makes. Not long after what turned out a brief moment in time, a decade during which the peerless power and influence of the United States were universally acknowledged, this self-same nation seems, if not exactly under siege, then beleaguered. Some of this is simply mind-set—it's not as if the U.S. has morphed from strongman to weakling in the blink of an historical eye. Still, the world sees the United States differently than it did just a decade and a half ago, and we see ourselves differently as well. Whereas only recently it was the United States of America that led in international relations, now the United States of America seems reluctant to get out front. In fact, if the U.S. leads at all, it likely as not, certainly during the presidency of President Barack Obama, "leads from behind." It leaves, to bring in another phrase from the Obama administration, no more than a "light footprint." Similarly, whereas only recently the U.S. was the single economic superpower, now competition comes from every direction, most obviously but of course by no means exclusively from China.

Polls confirm the impression. For the first time, in surveys dating back almost forty years, a majority of Americans believe that the United States is playing a less important and powerful role as world leader than it did a decade ago. An even larger majority believes that the U.S. is losing respect worldwide.[2] Equally relevant are our policy preferences. In part because many of us are under personal, professional, and financial stress; in part because many of us believe that the U.S. is weaker than it was, both politically and militarily; and in part because for the better part of his presidency Obama himself has emphasized domestic over foreign policy, a majority of Americans now say that their country is doing *too much*—not too little!—to help solve the world's problems.[3]

Some of the reasons for America's diminished role in the world are internal, wounds that are self-inflicted. Washington's internecine dysfunction and intermittent paralysis, as well as high government debt, the financial crisis, failing schools, and decaying infrastructure—all and more contribute to the sense that the U.S. is a nation in decline. Other reasons are, however, external, located in an international system over which the United States sometimes has some control, but other times has little or even no control.

This decline in confidence is the result of American defeats or, if you prefer, disappointments in, for example, Iraq, a war that (among its many other costs) claimed more than four thousand American lives. Experiences like these, including, notably, also the war in Afghanistan, have led to America's growing reluctance to intervene in struggles far from home, even when such intervention is, in the main, humanitarian. (The U.S. and for that matter the rest of the world have watched impotently while over a hundred and fifty thousand people have died in the war in Syria, and while over two million refugees have continued to testify to the world's worst such crisis in a generation.) The decline in confidence is also comparative. Simple statistics confirm that the U.S. is faring less well now than it did in comparison with other countries, in areas such as health, basic (as opposed to advanced) education, and ecosystem sustainability. In a major new ranking of livability in 132 countries, the United States placed no higher than a "sobering 16th place."[4] (These figures reflect, among other things, the aforementioned "rise of the rest," the rise of countries with rates of growth until recently thought impossible.[5]) Finally, the decline in America's self-confidence is a reflection of our obvious vulnerability to attack, notably by terrorists. I can only repeat: the events of September 11, 2001, shattered our sense of self. They ended in an instant what political columnist Charles Krauthammer has called America's "holiday from history"—that ten-year period of relative peace and prosperity immediately preceding, during which America was the sole superpower.

This change in America's place in the world order (or disorder) raises the question of human agency, in particular the role of key players ranging from Osama bin Laden to Barack Obama. What role, in other words, did human agency play in our transition from here to there, from the halcyon last decade of the twentieth century to the troubled second decade of the twenty-first? Political scientist John Ikenberry described the U.S. at the turn of the century as follows: "By the 1990s, [the] American-led order was at a zenith. Ideological and geopolitical rivals to American leadership had disappeared. The United States stood at the center of it all as the unipolar power."[6] But by the 2000s "the American-led order" was "troubled." Only a decade after America was at its "zenith," it was mired in international conflict and controversy.

So, again, what accounts for the decline? The reasons of course are complex, but let's be clear. Virtually none of the experts lets leaders and, in some cases, followers entirely off the hook. These would include among others bin Laden and Mohamed Atta (one of the September 11 attackers) at the one extreme, and at the other (from an American perspective), Bill Clinton, George W. Bush, and Obama.[7] Not even Clinton, who presided over the "zenith" of American-led hegemony, escapes blame for what happened. About him former national security advisor Zbigniew Brzezinski writes, "Complacent determinism, personal shortcomings, and rising domestic political obstacles overcame his good intentions. It was an inconclusive and vulnerable legacy that Clinton bequeathed in 2001 to his doctrinally antithetical successor."[8] Brzezinski was even more critical of that successor. "Because of Bush's self-righteously unilateral conduct of U.S. foreign policy after 9/11, the evocative symbol of America in the eyes of much of the world ceased to be the Statue of Liberty and instead became the Guantanamo prison camp."[9] The truth is that George W. Bush has been assailed from many sides. More than any other recent president, he is faulted for conducting what is still generally judged a failed foreign policy.[10]

Bush was enabled in his conduct of international relations by the events of 9/11, which gave him enormous leeway, especially in his first term, to make foreign policy decisions, including military decisions, more or less as he saw fit. But, according to his countless subsequent critics, Bush fell seriously short. First, he and key members of his administration overestimated the impact of American military power. They envisioned the United States as having hard power, military might, so awesome "it no longer needed to make compromises or accommodations . . . with any other nations or groups or countries."[11] Second, he and key members of his administration overestimated their store of soft power. For example, contrary to the administration's expectations, in the run-up to the war the Americans were unable to persuade either the Russians or the Turks to cooperate. Third were other misunderstandings or un-understandings, such as the failure to appreciate what it would take not only to accomplish regime change in Iraq but then, in its immediate aftermath, to build a new nation, one that was at least somewhat democratic and somewhat secure. Finally, there was the matter of style. Bush was so unpopular a foreign policy president not only because of what he did, but also because of how he did it. At home he was seen as deaf to military and foreign policy experts who disagreed with him, again, especially in his first term. And abroad "he saw little except palaces and conference rooms. His trips involved almost no effort to demonstrate respect and appreciation for the country and culture he was visiting."[12]

Nor has Obama been spared bad marks for his performance in foreign policy. *The Economist* (a centrist British publication) said this in December 2013: "Barack Obama has pulled back in the Middle East. . . . He has also done little to bring the new emerging giants . . . into the global system. This betrays both a lack of ambition and an ignorance of history. . . . Unless America behaves as a leader and guarantor of the world order, it will be inviting regional powers to test their strength by bullying their neighboring counties."[13]

In retrospect this seems prescient. For once Russia seized Crimea during Obama's sixth year in office, unsettling if not upending what was assumed since the end of the Cold War to be a stable Europe, the incumbent president came in for special censure. While most Americans, including among the leadership class, understand perfectly well that America can no longer easily dominate the international order, many Americans, including among the leadership class, do wonder if President Obama's distinctly deliberative, even cautious conduct of foreign policy has encouraged (at least some of) our adversaries to test us. This impression was exacerbated once Iraq again imploded, many Republicans certainly blaming Obama for having pulled all American troops out of the country.

Maybe it goes with the territory, with being president of the United States at this particular moment in time. Or maybe the international system has become so complex, it's simply impossible easily, gracefully to manage America's foreign affairs. Or maybe other countries, even those that are far smaller and less powerful, are less deferential than they used to be. Or maybe our three most recent presidents were just not competent in their conduct of American foreign policy. In the event, if Bush is seen by many as having overreached, Obama is seen by many as having underreached, as being too reluctant to use American power, too disinclined to employ American diplomacy, too reliant on others to take the lead, too timorous and too vague to translate his sometimes soaring rhetoric into a coherent plan of action.[14] The point is this: whatever the context within which America is situated, it is widely assumed that this context is shaped to some degree, some of the time, by human agency, by leaders and, yes, absolutely, also by followers. It is shaped by men and women who, sometimes alone, sometimes in concert, in one or another way play a part in world politics. Always the most visible of these, and sometimes the most powerful, is the president of the United States.

However, more important than any single individual, much more important, is the international system itself. The context within which the United States is situated has changed dramatically, even in the past ten, twenty years. In the old days, which were not so long ago, from about 1965 to 1990, the world was dominated by a small number of countries that for the purpose of this discussion I call national leaders. These national leaders were the United States; the Soviet Union; countries in Western Europe including Britain, France, and West Germany; and Japan. Then the international system made a transition—from bipolar to unipolar. And then, ten, fifteen years after that, it made another transition, to where we are now. Now the world is dominated not by a single national leader or even by a few national leaders. Instead it is leaderless. It is neither bipolar nor unipolar—it is nonpolar. It is "influenced by dozens of states and other entities possessing and exercising military, economic, diplomatic, and cultural power—power that is diffused."[15]

This is a view now so widely held it is almost commonplace. So let's be clear what exactly it consists of. First and foremost has been an astonishing increase in the number of national and transnational, or multinational, actors who matter. Similarly, there has been an astonishing change in the nature of these actors, who include but are by no means limited to the nation-states to which historically we have been accustomed. Some national leaders are nation-states with which we have long been familiar, namely the United States, members (some, by no means all) of the European Union, Russia, and Japan. Others are newcomers, notably China and India, Australia, and, arguably, Brazil. In addition are regional powers, for example, in Latin America, Chile, Argentina, Venezuela, and Mexico; in Africa, Nigeria and South Africa; in the Middle East, Egypt, Iran, Israel, and Saudi Arabia; in Asia, Pakistan, Indonesia, and South Korea; and in Europe, along with the familiar ones, Poland and Turkey.

Moreover, added now to nation-states are many other sorts of transnational, multinational actors. They include global organizations such as the United Nations, the World Bank, and the International Monetary Fund; regional organizations such as the European Union, the Organization of American States, and the African Union; and functional organizations such as OPEC, NATO, the World Health Organization, and the International Energy Agency. Further, there are transnational corporations, large multinationals such as JPMorgan Chase, ExxonMobil, Apple, and Caterpillar. And there are more, other international actors, including global media outlets such as the BBC, CNN, and Al-Jazeera; militias such as Hezbollah and Hamas; political parties; religious organizations; terrorist groups such as Al Qaeda, ISIS, and Boko Haram; international nongovernmental organizations such as Greenpeace and the Gates Foundation; large, even mass groups of activists; and also individual activists and hacktivists, including types such as Julian Assange and Edward Snowden. As President of the Council on Foreign Relations Richard Haass has pointed out, none of this is to say that all these players possess either the same kinds of power, authority, and influence, or equal amounts thereof. Rather, it is to indicate how many actors and how many different sorts of actors now participate in the international system—now potentially have an impact on world affairs.[16]

The trajectory of history is the single best explanation for this shift in the international system. Indeed, what has happened at the international level simply reflects what has happened at the national level. Put directly, whatever the role of individuals in accounting for America's recent decline, the more powerful explanation for where we are now lies elsewhere. It lies in the course of history itself, which over the past several hundred years has tended more toward being democratic. It has evolved in ways that tend to diffuse power at both the national and international levels, not to concentrate it.

Of course, changing technologies play a part in these changing patterns of dominance and deference as well. Joseph Nye has, again, written especially persuasively about the impact of technology on world affairs, his main point by now familiar: power, authority, and influence are not what they used to be. "The diffusion of power in the cyberdomain is represented by the vast number of actors therein and the relative reduction of power differentials among them. . . . What is distinctive about power in the cyberdomain is not that governments are out of the picture . . . but that different actors possess different power resources and that the gap between state and nonstate actors is narrowing in many instances."[17] No nation, not even those with impressive arsenals of hard power, such as the United States, is immune to the changing times. They too "find themselves sharing the stage with new actors."[18]

This diffusion of power in world affairs manifests itself politically, economically, and culturally.[19] Notwithstanding Russian president Vladimir Putin's notion of resurrecting the Soviet empire, the fall of the Berlin Wall was a turning point. The demise of the Soviet Union and the collapse of communism resulted in a sea change in international relations, and in the world order. Triggered by repressed political aspirations, depressed economic conditions, and growing dissent, the downfall of the Soviet Union signaled what has been described as a "global political awakening," an awakening that was "socially massive, politically radicalizing, and geographically universal."[20] Evidence of this awakening, this increasing political participation, this increasing democratization, can be seen in a single simple measure: the numbers of countries considered "free" versus "not free." In 1972 only forty-four countries were ranked free. By 1992 this number had climbed to seventy-five. In 2013 it was eighty-eight.[21]

Again, what this means so far as governance is concerned is that the power and influence of leaders have been demeaned and diminished nearly everywhere, and that the power and influence of followers, of ordinary people, have been expanded and enhanced nearly everywhere. (This does not, of course, apply, or apply as much, to governments that are repressive.) The voice of people worldwide, all sorts of people, good people and bad people, is far louder and more clamorous now than it was even a generation ago—which is not to say that this is a good thing or a bad thing. The jury is out on whether people power is more disruptive—or even, sometimes, destructive—than constructive. It is simply to say that leading now is harder in foreign affairs as in domestic affairs. America's chief diplomat, the president, has to be mindful not only of leaders in other countries, but of followers in other countries. Whatever our policies toward, say, Russia or Canada, Brazil or Bangladesh, they can no longer be divorced entirely from considerations of public opinion, of the popular will, both at home and abroad. *New York Times* columnist David Brooks refers to this new state of affairs as "global affairs with the head chopped off." Political leaders, he writes, are "not at the forefront of history; real power is in the swarm."[22]

The implications of this worldwide awakening are in evidence not only politically but also economically. Once communism was, in effect, dead and gone, the only viable alternative was capitalism or at least a variation thereof. Moreover, once globalization kicked in, money and goods began to float more freely, which in turn implied the benefits of free trade and good economic governance. "Governments from

Vietnam to Columbia realized they couldn't afford to miss out on the global race to prosperity," which successively encouraged foreign investment and created new jobs.[23] Now we have reached a point at which there is greater international cooperation on economic issues than on political ones. This cooperation covers trade, monetary policy, investment, development, and financial regulation.[24] No wonder foreign policy expert Michael Mandelbaum came to conclude that economic issues have "replaced matters of war and peace as the major focus of national leaders because economic matters came to have greater effects on the countries they led."[25]

Of course, economic relations are at least as competitive as they are cooperative. Still, the overarching point is not about the nature of these economic relationships but about the proliferation of them, about how many more players and pieces in the puzzle there are now than even in the recent past. Participants are American and foreign, public and private and nonprofit, institutional and individual—all of them contributing yet again to the diffusion of power, authority, and influence. In the old days states controlled the action. Now, for many different reasons including the many different *market* actors, states find it difficult even to control the markets themselves.

Finally, there is the cultural component—authority ain't what it used to be. Leaders generally are deprived of the deference that only recently was theirs and so, specifically, are national leaders. As indicated, size no longer matters so much, nor does perceived power, especially military power, especially *American* military power, which in the twenty-first century has turned out so far at least to be relatively useless.[26] Smaller, weaker countries routinely go their own way, independent of others, and they routinely challenge other countries that are larger and stronger, emboldened to do so by precisely the same phenomena that now embolden weaker people everywhere to challenge stronger people everywhere: the spread of democracy, the rhetoric of empowerment, and the practice of participation.[27] This cultural change is of course connected to the other changes—in politics, economics, and technology. There is a symbiotic relationship among them—they feed into each other, leach into each other.

What does it mean to say about the U.S. in the international system that "there is a widespread view that no one elected the United States to its position of privilege"?[28] What does it mean to say about the U.S. in the international system that even the largest and most powerful country in the world has no choice any longer but to share the stage with other actors, every one of which is smaller and less powerful? What does it mean to say about the U.S. in the international system that we are in a "post-hegemonic era" in which "no nation has the capacity to impose its will on others in a substantial or permanent way"?[29] What does it mean to say about the U.S. in the international system that even countries in thrall to the United States are other than deferential? (Egypt, the recipient of billions of dollars in U.S. economic and military aid, defies it nevertheless.[30] The same goes for Israel, and for Pakistan, and for Afghanistan, and for other countries around the world.) And, finally, what does it mean to say about the U.S. in the international system that we live in a time when even the smallest and least developed of countries openly take on the largest and most developed, for example in the area of climate change, where supposedly subordinate nations are challenging supposedly superior ones to help them cope with the effects of global warming? Clearly we are witnessing a change in culture, a change that reflects a decline in the international system of both hierarchy and hegemony.

I want to be careful here. While the United States is not now what it was, it remains in many of the most important ways more powerful than any other single global actor—politically, economically, culturally, technologically, and militarily. Despite a general sense of American foreboding that power is shifting—from Europe to Asia and from the U.S. to China—the U.S. remains singularly strong. In fact, one could plausibly argue that all our hand-wringing about America's deteriorating position in the world is no more than peevishness at being pushed from our previous perch.

Still, it would be a mistake to minimize the challenge to American leaders of trying to lead in a world in which existing institutions are "floundering" and in which the U.S. is only one among many players, nearly all of whom are determined to strut their stuff.[31] Similarly, it would be a mistake to minimize the challenge to American leaders of trying to lead in a world in which followers, ordinary people, "the street," can play as significant, as powerful, a role in world affairs as leaders. It is, as indicated, impossible to be any kind of leader in twenty-first-century America without being aware of the world beyond, of the context within which the United States itself is situated. That this context has grown complex in ways that are as daunting as they are different from what was, is almost to the point of being self-evident.

EPILOGUE   WHAT'S BEEN FOUND?

FINALLY, JOHN BOEHNER had had it. Or, maybe, secretly he had had it a long time ago, but decided finally to let the rest of America know he was sick and tired: sick and tired of contentious conservative advocacy groups; sick and tired of Tea Partiers who were nothing so much as obstructionists; sick and tired of Republicans who were alien to anyone of his centrist sensibilities; and sick and tired of followers, fellow House Republicans, who refused to follow, follow him, the duly elected speaker of the United States House of Representatives. Of right-wing Republicans Boehner finally said one day in December 2013, "They're pushing our members in places where they don't want to be. And frankly, I just think that they've lost all credibility." And, of right-wing Republicans Boehner finally said another day in December 2013, "They are not fighting for conservative principles. They are not fighting for conservative policy. They are fighting to expand their lists, raise more money and grow their organizations. . . . It's ridiculous."[1]

In the beginning of this book I asked whether, if Boehner had had greater contextual expertise—if he had better understood from the start of his speakership the complex context within which he was operating, and the ways in which those who peopled it had changed—he would have been a better, more effective leader. To this question I replied, "I don't honestly know." And I still don't. After all this, after this checklist, after considering context every which way, twenty-four different ways, to be precise, I cannot say with certitude, I cannot prove, that contextual expertise would itself have made the difference, given Boehner the edge that he needed to lead more effectively. But I will claim this. It couldn't hurt!

It couldn't hurt those among us who want to lead wisely and well to make meaning of leadership in America—to have a better, deeper understanding of the United States of America in the second decade of the twenty-first century. This applies not only to practitioners of leadership, to leaders, but also to students of leadership, to leadership novices, even to experts. Why? Because more than ever it is better—better in practice and better in theory—to focus less on the leader and more on the leadership *system*. Again, this system consists of three parts, leaders, followers, and context, each of which is equally important and each of which impinges equally on the other two. Hence this book, which has found and focused on the lost piece. Hence this book, which is not about looking in but about looking out. Hence this book, which is not so much about leaders or for that matter about followers as it is about the context within which they are situated. Not the proximate context, not the immediate group or organization, but the distal one—the larger context that constitutes this particular country at this particular moment in time.[2]

Above all, the context is complex. It is complex because of the connection between the context within which we operate and complexity theory. That is, the leadership system is similar to other complex systems. Though it has only three parts—leaders, followers, and context— they are independent and, simultaneously, interdependent. Each affects, and is affected by, the other two. Or, to put it slightly differently, the person (leader, follower, or both) affects the situation, and the situation affects the person (leader, follower, or both).

The context is complex also because of the checklist per se, because of the many different contextual components and the ways in which each has an impact on leadership and, yes, management. In this sense context is itself a system, consisting here of twenty-four parts. Every part is separate and distinct; at the same time, every part relates to every other part.

Finally, I use the word *complex* to convey something akin to what political scientist Steven Teles has dubbed "Kludgeocracy." Teles was writing about the U.S. government in particular, but his point pertains in general. He argues that the problem with the U.S. government is not what we usually fight about, its size. Rather, the problem is—it's complicated. "Understanding, describing, and addressing this problem of complexity and incoherence is the next great American political challenge. But you cannot come to terms with such a problem until you can properly name it. . . . For lack of a better alternative, the problem of complexity might best be termed the challenge of 'kludgeocracy.'" Why? *Kludge* is an "ill-assorted collection of parts assembled for a particular purpose." This notion and the clumsiness that even the word conveys make the point. Teles compares, for instance, the utter simplicity of the Social Security program with the daunting complexity of 401(k) retirement accounts, IRAs, state-run 529 savings plans for college, and the rest of our "intricate maze of incentivized-savings programs," each of which requires large investments of time and effort to manage effectively. Similarly, he points out that the American tax code is without question the most complicated in the world. And that the American health care system is equally arcane, difficult if not impossible for ordinary people to navigate. (Health insurance is now so complicated that only about 14 percent of beneficiaries can answer simple questions about deductibles and co-pays.)[3]

So the leadership system is complex and the context itself is complex—truths worth carefully contemplating. Each item on the contextual checklist is, in other words, a challenge in and of itself, first to comprehend—say, the importance of the law to leadership in America—and then to bend, to transform the law from something that could hinder into something that could help. No wonder leaders in twenty-first-century America often feel overwhelmed and undervalued. No wonder the leadership industry is thriving—all those coaches and courses, all those self-help books, self-help tapes, self-help exercises, every one intended to shore up leaders leading or trying to in a complex context, leading or trying to in hard times. No wonder the poll numbers are so low—in the first six months of 2014 only about 30 percent of Americans believed their country was headed in the right direction—sobering reminders of followers now chronically dissatisfied, distrustful of leaders independent of where they are located.[4]

The importance of context, of distal context, has been my main theme. But there are in addition several pertinent and powerful subthemes to which I wish to draw attention. In no particular order, the first is technology: the fear of it; the future of it; the relentless stimulation; the abundance, over-abundance, of information. There is so much technology so much of the time, much of it changing so fast that even the best and the brightest leaders find it difficult if not impossible to keep pace and difficult if not impossible to lead, to manage groups and organizations now permeated with and utterly dependent on technology. There are the various sensations: needing it; wanting it; feeling bored, lost, and insecure without it; feeling anxious about being excluded, insufficiently competitive, not of the moment, not completely in control when technology is not constantly at hand, immediately at hand, in hand literally. And, there is too much information coming at us too fast, too much to take in all the time at any given time. Just as we start to process what we know or think we do, there is new information, the latest information, hotter information, information that supersedes in importance that which immediately preceded it.

The second running theme is money: so much concentrated in the hands of so few, so little distributed as equitably in the present as it was in the recent past. Money as the root not of all evil, but of some evil or, at least, of some considerable dysfunction, whether in politics (especially in politics), or in business, or in the media, or even in places where it comes not immediately to mind, as in schools, and in art, and in the air we breathe, and in the soil in which we grow our food. This dysfunction manifests as too much greed, too much poverty, too many mega-rich, too many homeless, too few middle class, too much big business, not enough small business, too much big money in small places (see Washington, D.C.), too many living too well, too many chronically unemployed and underemployed.

In 2013 the nation's economy improved. In fact the U.S. stock market had one of its best years ever, which, however, only exacerbated an already existing sensation confirmed by nearly every statistic that something's off, awry in America. Above all, there is inequity to the point of disequilibrium, inequity that we now know is greater in the U.S. than in any other advanced country because for the past three decades Americans in the lower- and middle-income tiers received lower pay raises than their counterparts in, say, Canada, Britain, or the Netherlands.[5]

This is not to claim that in comparison with other periods in American history this one is singularly trying. In fact, while many of us struggle in the present, many more of us (certainly proportionally) struggled harder in the past, before the New Deal and the War on Poverty created social welfare programs such as Social Security and Medicare. Still, this past truth does not negate the present one, which is that times are hard—and that America itself is "unwinding."

This brings me to the third running theme: America in decline. The winner of the National Book Award for nonfiction in 2013 was George Packer. He won for his book *The Unwinding: An Inner History of the New America*, which begins as follows: "No one can say when the unwinding began—when the coil that held Americans together in its secure and sometimes stifling grip first gave way. . . . [But] if you were born around 1960 or afterward, you have spent your adult life in the vertigo of that unwinding. You watched structures that had been in place before your birth collapse like pillars of salt across the vast visible landscape. . . . [And] when the norms that made the old institutions useful began to unwind, and the leaders abandoned their posts, the Roosevelt Republic that had reigned for almost half a century came undone. The void was filled by the default force in American life, organized money."[6]

In this single poignant paragraph Packer speaks to the zeitgeist. And he touches on what more specifically is ailing us. There is the past—a past evoked as better than the present. There is America disassembling—coming apart, breaking up as the coil that held us together "unwinds." There are institutions in decline, institutions to which not long ago we looked up, such as government and schools, objects now of disappoint-ment, even derision. There is the social contract, "the Roosevelt Repub-lic," that held for fifty years, now frayed to the point of fracture. There is money, again money, always money, this time "organized money" as America's "default force." And, finally, there are leaders who "aban-doned their posts." What does this even mean—"leaders abandoned their posts"? It might mean that good leaders deserted us, left us at the mercy of bad leaders. Or, it might mean that those who today exercise power and authority are not, according to Packer, leaders who can lead. Whatever his intention, it's pointed, sharply critical of America's current leadership class.

If Packer were alone in his view of what is, it would be one thing. But he is not. There is a whole literature on America in decline. And there is a whole literature on America coming apart at the seams—which brings me to the fourth running theme: America, once indivisible, is now di-visive to the point of dysfunction. This divisiveness is most obvious in Washington, where differences of opinion have morphed into irrecon-cilable differences, and where compromise and civility are commodities become scarce. But it is by no means confined to Washington—America is replete with stresses between right and left, old and young, men and women, white people and people of color, gay and straight, big city and small town, advocates for abortion and advocates against, advocates for gun control and advocates against, advocates for liberalizing immigra-tion laws and advocates against, advocates for legalization of marijuana and advocates against, and advocates for development and advocates for protection of the environment, as well as stresses among the differ-ent classes, upper and lower, and the malcontent, dwindling, squeezed, middle.

The fifth running theme is related to the preceding, and for that mat-ter to the succeeding. It is the pressure on leaders that is now nearly relentless, with leaders in all places getting pushed and pulled by others and by events over which they have little or no control. Leaders are pres-sured to behave, lest they be found out, in an age when even the smallest of missteps can lead to embarrassment or even debasement. Leaders are pressured to excel, lest they be shredded 24/7 by talking heads waiting, wanting, apparently needing instant gratification, constant satisfaction. Leaders are pressured to perform—to be constantly competitive, constantly innovative, constantly communicative, constantly at the top of their game, constantly at the service of followers whose level of patience with those in charge has dropped to new, arguably precipitous lows.

The sixth running theme is the relentless sense of danger. Leaders are threatened from within by mistakes or mismanagement or wrongdoing of some sort, either their own or someone else's, and threatened from without, by other leaders, or by followers, or by an emergency or catastrophe, natural or otherwise, or by someone or something neither anticipated nor adequately prepared for. The dangers are domestic, American in origin, and they are foreign, global in origin. And they are on many fronts: personal, political, economic, environmental, military—each a reminder that America's leaders as well as America's place in the world are other than fully secure.

Finally, there is this: the running theme that touches on leaders per se. It is leaders as disappointments. It is members of an entire leadership class diminished in the eyes of their followers, the American people. To be fair, this problem is not parochial, it is global. It transcends leadership in twenty-first-century America, democracy in twenty-first-century America, extending to leadership and democracy nearly everywhere in the world. It is what I talk about when I talk about leaders generally getting weaker and followers generally getting stronger. It is in consequence of changes in culture and technology, and it is evidenced in the decrease in the number of "control cultures" and the increase in the number of democratic cultures—cultures that celebrate individuality, independence, and participation by the many as opposed to only an elite few.[7] It is not, moreover, only a political phenomenon. It pertains to people in nearly all groups and organizations, wherever they are located and whatever their function.[8]

On the face of it, this is a good thing. In theory, we support people participating, registering their preferences, having a voice—online; in the voting booth; in organizations that are flat or, at least, flatter than they would have been as recently as a decade or two ago; and, sometimes, in the streets. But, as we have seen, "participation" in American life and for that matter elsewhere in the world is not quite what it's cracked up to be. Most of us are free to do and say what we want when we want in so far as our political and professional circumstances will reasonably allow. However, the freedom to participate does not translate necessarily into constructive engagement. While in the developing world some people in some places have forced regime change, most have yet to realize their original, democratic, intentions. And while in the developed world, the relatively rich world, people are in all of the obvious ways politically free, they have not by and large, certainly not in the U.S., participated as they ought, for example, by being willing to pay higher taxes for goods and services that they consider rightfully are theirs. Even voter turnout, the most fundamental form of political participation, has declined over the past thirty years, especially in the U.S. and especially in elections apart from those for president. In fact, our disillusionment and distrust run so deep that we are disposed to disengage from discourse altogether. By and large we, we Americans, are uninterested and poorly informed. By and large we do not actively participate in community or even communal life. And by and large we are far more disposed to disparage our leadership class than to seek constructively to better it. We do, mostly, go along—protest has not so far been a hallmark of twenty-first-century American life—but we go along grudgingly, without much evidence of enthusiasm.

Again, some of this is endemic to democracy in the twenty-first century. Everywhere there is what some call a crisis of legitimacy, a crisis of leadership, a fracturing of the social contract that previously bound leaders and led. But at the same time, this crisis must be seen in context, in this case in the context of leadership in America since the beginning of the republic. As we have seen, leadership in this country has always been difficult to exercise. For reasons ranging from our revolutionary heritage to the content of the American Creed to the fractured structure of the American government, the led historically have been recalcitrant, reluctant to follow their leaders unless they felt they had to, most obviously in the workplace, or because they genuinely wanted to.

Given this history and ideology it could be seen as a collective con-venience that for many years most Americans were content (or content enough) to be led by those who predominantly were members of a par-ticular group: white Anglo-Saxon Protestants, WASPs. To be sure, by no means was every white, Anglo-Saxon Protestant a WASP. Rather, the acronym referred to a small, select group, described by Joseph Epstein as "an unofficial but nonetheless genuine ruling class, drawn from what came to be known as the WASP establishment." In other words, WASPs belonged to a particular caste, or lineage, that implied the best schools, the best neighborhoods (mostly on the east coast), the best businesses (workplaces), the best clubs, and the best money—inherited and well invested.

Franklin Roosevelt and George Herbert Walker Bush were the last certifiable WASPs to live in the White House.(In contrast to his father, who was schooled entirely in New England, George W. Bush spent most of his early years attending schools in Texas.) More generally though, male members of the WASP establishment dominated America's lead-ership class until the 1960s—which coincides precisely with when the high esteem in which America's leaders generally were held began grad-ually to wane. One might even be tempted, as Epstein clearly is, to look at WASP leaders with a measure of nostalgia. He argues that they were characterized by "trust, honor, character," that they "had dignity and an impressive sense of social responsibility," and that under WASP hege-mony, "corruption, scandal and incompetence in high places weren't, as now, regular features of public life." Epstein goes further. He claims the meritocracy—I would add the diversity—that replaced the WASP hegemony falls far short. "Thus far in their history, meritocrats, those earnest good students, appear to be about little more than getting on, getting ahead and (above all) getting their own. The WASP leadership, for all that may be said in criticism of it, was better than that."[9]

One does not have to agree wholeheartedly with Epstein to suspect that he is on to something. Like Packer, who wrote "leaders abandoned their posts," his point is stark as it is simple: America now is not what America was then, American leaders now are not what American lead-ers were then. Again, this is not only about political leaders but, as the polls confirm, about leaders across the board, about all sorts of leaders in twenty-first-century America. Epstein writes, for example, about university presidents who "no longer speak to the great issues in education but instead devote themselves to fund raising and public relations, and look to move on to the next, more prestigious university presidency."[10] What has changed? Why this shift? Can it be that people have changed—that people in early twenty-first-century America are a species apart from people in mid-twentieth-century America? Or is it instead as I have argued here: that the context has changed in ways that have an impact on us all—on leaders and followers alike? The context has not changed us, not fundamentally. But since *it* has changed, so have what we think and how we behave.

As the checklist that constitutes this book testifies, there are ways in which context does not change. History remains the same, and what originally was the American ideology still is the American ideology. But in most areas some change, sometimes great change, is inevitable. Here is Peter Drucker, who nearly a decade after his passing is still regarded as perhaps the preeminent guru of leadership and management: "We are at the beginning of a period of extreme flux, of extreme change and great competitive pressure in which traditional ways of doing things, traditional products, traditional processes will be challenged on all sides."[11] What was the year in which Drucker spoke these words? It was 1955. (Drucker was giving a talk to executives at IBM.)

If an expert on leadership as exalted as Drucker stresses so strongly the importance of context, of contextual change, what does this say about the importance of leaders? Have leaders always been less important than we think they are? Are they any less important now than they were? For all our fixations on leaders, for all of our obsessions with leadership, on these key questions the jury is still out. In fact, there is a "school of thought, supported by some evidence," that leaders, particularly in business, "do not have much effect on organizational outcomes." Not many in the leadership industry are willing to admit this, of course, admit that there is empirical evidence "that, at least on its face, suggests top executives have far less effect on organizations than do other factors." What might these "other factors" be? Well, they certainly include context, though as earlier indicated, the context that is referred to in the corporate literature typically is proximate, not distal. Still, since I am making a case for the importance of context—however defined, however extensive or circumscribed—far be it from me to dismiss a line such as this one. "The characteristics of the firm's task environment"— for example, product differentiability, market growth, industry structure—"greatly affect the level of executive discretion and, in turn, how much influence managers have on organizational outcomes."[12] In other words, contexts, proximate *and* distal, matter. They matter a great deal.

I want to be clear: not all leaders are in trouble; hardly. Across the country there is evidence that in many ways America is growing and thriving, and that, notwithstanding hard times, numberless American leaders are both ethical and effective.[13] Moreover, the leadership industry continues to hang in there. Leadership training and development remains a big business; in the U.S. alone it doubled in size in the past fifteen years, developing new tools for leaders to use, ranging from measuring devices to assessment tools to the outsourcing of public functions to private citizens with smartphones.[14] In addition, leaders in twenty-first-century America are making certain adjustments, especially regarding their followers. Leaders in business have come to understand that the shift away from the traditional organizational hierarchy is irrevocable. And they have come to understand that this requires a new kind of leadership, one less focused on power and authority and more focused on influence—influence achieved through, yes, intimacy as well as interactivity and inclusion.[15] (This explains why a leader such as Barack Obama, who inclines to shun interpersonal engagement, is in some ways less effective than those who welcome it.) Similarly, leaders in government have come to understand the power of pressure from those below—"the transformational ability of positive peer pressure"— not, necessarily, only from those up top.[16]

Contextual expertise—especially in areas that are distal as opposed to proximate—has not exactly been at the forefront of what leaders think they need to know.[17] This book then is intended to be no more than, but no less than, a corrective. Which raises this final question: What do we do with what we now know? What lessons, if any, can be learned from the contextual checklist and from the lessons that it teaches—among others about complexity; about technology and money; about the U.S. in decline and divisive to the point sometimes of dysfunction; about pressure and danger; about followers enhanced and leaders diminished; and about the larger global context within which all of us necessarily now are located?

Here are three responses to the preceding questions. First, there is value in knowing the thing itself—the leadership system. In other words, there is value in leaders knowing who they are, in being self-aware. And there is equal value in leaders knowing their followers—who they are, what they think and feel, and what they actually do, and don't do. Finally, there is value, again, *equal* value, in leaders knowing about the contexts, both proximate and distal, within which they operate. I have become, in other words, completely persuaded that leadership education and training that is focused on leaders per se, to the exclusion of everyone and everything else, does a disservice. It deprives leaders of what they need to know. And it deprives us of leaders who are as well-informed and well-rounded as they are self-actualized.[18]

Second, there is value in having some conception of what it takes to lead in twenty-first-century America—what it takes to *overcome the contextual odds*. I will refrain from providing a comprehensive list of traits and characteristics that potentially pertain. It's obvious though that certain traits and characteristics emerge directly from the checklist itself. Some are not new: they appear and reappear in every discussion of what it takes to lead wisely and well, such as integrity and intelligence and, nowadays, emotional intelligence.

There are others, however, other traits and characteristics that are different, less self-evident because they are in consequence of the contextual constraints. I include in this category having a convincing connection to American history and ideology; being a uniter not a divider; being a navigator, willing and able to navigate and negotiate between, among different groups and competing interests; being a delegator and also a talent manager, someone who knows what he or she does not know, cannot know, and so engages the best of the experts; being other-directed rather than inner-directed, someone who is interested in and empathetic with the other, as opposed to being preoccupied primarily with self, especially with self-aggrandizement; being even-tempered and of good temperament, able to cope with the inevitable, considerable pressures and stresses of leading in this place at this time; being resilient and also buoyant, able to adapt to whatever the information or situation, to whomever the actors, anticipated or unanticipated, to rebound with energy and optimism from whatever the defeats or misfortunes, and to convey to others—followers, stakeholders, constituents—a sense of resurgence; being expansive, as in able to pivot in different directions, both at home and abroad, and to peer into the future, not necessarily the far future, but the near future, say one generation hence; and, finally, being civil and curious—the capacity to reach out to win friends and influence people, which is what you need to do to lead in twenty-first-century America.

Third, in a world characterized by complexity and change, there is value in simplicity and stasis. There is enormous appeal in the idea that there are timeless truths about leadership that pertain even in changing times. There is a reason for the recent raft of biographies about America's founders. There is a reason that some of our most seasoned observers look back to a time when America seemed better and leaders seemed better—and it's not nostalgia. Rather, it is that we long for leaders whose primary purpose is our best interest—not theirs. Leadership is not a profession. Nor is it, or it ought not to be, a stepping stone, to, say, money or power or authority or even influence.

Rather, it is a mission. Given the context this book considers, given the United States in the second decade of the twenty-first century, it seems clear that no American leader can genuinely engage American followers unless he or she exemplifies that which has stood the test of time. I refer to American history—and to the best of those who shaped it. And I refer to American ideology—and to the best of those who exemplified it. These remain remarkably, gorgeously, unchanged, even now.

THE AUTHOR

BARBARA KELLERMAN is the James MacGregor Burns Lecturer in Public Leadership at Harvard University's John F. Kennedy School of Government. She was the founding executive director of the Harvard Kennedy School's Center for Public Leadership, and served as research director from 2003 to 2006. She has been ranked by Forbes.com as among "Top 50 Business Thinkers" and by *Leadership Excellence* as one of the top fifteen thought leaders in management and leadership. In 2010, she was given the Wilbur M. McFeeley award by the National Management Association for her pioneering work on leadership and followership.

Kellerman was cofounder of the International Leadership Association, and is author or editor of fourteen previous books: *The End of Leadership*; *Leadership: Essential Selections on Power, Authority, and Influence*; *Followership: How Followers Are Creating Change and Changing Leaders*; *Women and Leadership: The State of Play and Strategies for Change* (with Deborah Rhode); *Bad Leadership: What It Is, How It Happens, Why It Matters*; *Reinventing Leadership: Making the Connection Between Politics and Business*; *The President as World Leader* (with Ryan Barilleaux); *Leadership and Negotiation in the Middle East* (with Jeffrey Z. Rubin); *Political Leadership: A Source Book*; *Women Leaders in American Politics* (with James David Barber); *The Political Presidency: Practice of Leadership*; *Leadership: Multidiscplinary Perspectives*; *All the President's Kin: Their Political Roles*; and *Making Decisions* (with Percy Hill et al.).

The End of Leadership was listed by the *Financial Times* as among the best business books of 2012, and selected by *Choice* as an "Outstanding Academic Title" in 2013. Kellerman has appeared often on media outlets such as CBS, NBC, PBS, CNN, NPR, Reuters, and BBC, and has contributed articles and reviews to the *New York Times*, the *Washington Post*, the *Boston Globe*, the *Los Angeles Times*, and the *Harvard Business Review*. She serves on the advisory boards of *Leadership*, the AAUW project on Women and Leadership, and the Brookings Institution Leadership Initiative, among others.

Kellerman blogs regularly at barbarakellerman.com.

NOTES

Prologue

1. For a scathing piece on the explosion of "How-To" or "Self Help" books, see Boris Kachka, "The Power of Positive Publishing," *New York*, January 2013, 14–21. "Today," Kachka writes, "there are at least 45,000 specimens in print of the optimize-everything cult we now call 'self-help.'" He continues, "These days self-help is unembarrassed, out of the bedside drawer and up on the coffee table, wholly transformed from a disreputable publishing category to a category killer" (p. 26).

2. Barbara Kellerman, *The End of Leadership* (New York: HarperCollins, 2012), p. xii.

3. The terms were originally coined by David Riesman, Nathan Glazer, and Reuel Denny in *The Lonely Crowd: A Study of the Changing American Character* (New Haven, CT: Yale University Press, 1963).

4. Ronald Heifetz, Alexander Grashow, and Marty Linsky, *The Practice of Adaptive Leadership* (Cambridge, MA: Harvard Business School Press, 2009), p. 49.

5. Michael Useem, "The Leadership Template," in Scott Snook, Nitin Nohria, and Rakesh Khurana (eds.), *The Handbook for Teaching Leadership: Knowing, Doing, and Being* (Thousand Oaks, CA: Sage, 2012). Also see Deborah Ancona's chapter, titled "Sensemaking: Framing and Acting in the Unknown." It stresses the importance of providing leaders with a "better grasp of what is going on in their environments." But again, the environment to which the author alludes is, to use my word, proximate. For example, leaders are advised to "combine financial data with trips to the shop floor," where, among other things, they should "listen to employees as well as customers" (p. 8).

6. The Catholic hierarchy has endured the most obvious crisis of confidence, triggered initially by the sexual abuse scandal in the Boston archdiocese in 2001. The American military has also been demeaned, particularly beginning in 2012. The abrupt resignation of military hero and CIA director General David Petraeus (following a sexual scandal) did not help. But, as several recent books testify, the problems of leadership and management in the American military go deeper. See, for example, Tim Kane, *Bleeding Talent: How the US Military Mismanages Great Leaders and Why It's Time for a Revolution* (New York: Palgrave Macmillan, 2012).

7. Figures are from Fareed Zakaria, "Can America Be Fixed?" *Foreign Affairs*, January/February 2013, p. 23.

8. This does not, however, mean that I have excluded context from my considerations. See, for example, *Bad Leadership: What It Is, Why It Happens, How It Matters*

(Cambridge, MA: Harvard Business School Press, 2004). In *Bad Leadership* I take a three-dimensional approach that foreshadows my more recent thinking on leadership across the board.

9. Lee Ross and Richard Nisbett, *The Person and the Situation: Perspectives on Social Psychology* (London: Pinter & Martin, 2011), p. 4.

10. The term *contextual intelligence*—as opposed to *contextual expertise*—has been around for several years. Robert Sternberg argued that contextual intelligence is the all-important equivalent of "street smarts"—the capacity to select a favorable environment, to modify it as necessary, and to adapt. Anthony Mayo and Nitin Nohria described contextual intelligence as the ability to understand the environment and to capitalize on it. And Joseph Nye defined it as an "intuitive diagnostic skill that helps . . . align tactics with objectives to create smart strategies in varying situations." See Sternberg's article, "The Theory of Successful Intelligence," *Interamerican Journal of Psychology*, 2005, Vol. 39, pp. 189–202. Also see Mayo and Nohria, *In Their Time: The Greatest Business Leaders of the Twentieth Century* (Cambridge, MA: Harvard Business School Press, 2005) and Joseph Nye, *The Powers to Lead* (New York: Oxford University Press, 2008), especially p. 87.

11. See barbarakellerman.com.

12. Barack Obama, on the other hand, was nearly new to Washington when he became president. Moreover, he had never held any sort of executive position before becoming chief executive. One can certainly make the argument that Obama would have been a more effective a leader had he better understood how Washington functioned (or not) early in the twenty-first century.

13. For an excellent discussion of Boehner's dilemma, see Elizabeth Drew, "Are Republicans Beyond Saving?," *New York Review*, March 21, 2013. Drew describes Boehner as a "deal-maker of the old school whose idea of being a legislator is to work out legislative solutions."

14. Atul Gawande, *The Checklist Manifesto: How to Get Things Right* (New York: Henry Holt, 2009), p. 186.

15. Office for Civil Rights, U.S. Department of Education, "Questions and Answers on the ADA Amendments Act of 2008 for Students with Disabilities Attending Public Elementary and Secondary Schools" (Washington, DC: U.S. Department of Education, n.d.).

Chapter 1. History

1. Howard Zinn, *A People's History of the United States* (New York: HarperPerennial, 2003), Chapter 3.

2. Gordon Wood, *The Radicalism of the American Revolution* (New York: Vintage, 1991), p. 110.

3. Edmund Morgan, *American Slavery, American Freedom* (New York: Norton, 1975), p. 4.

4. Morgan, *American Slavery, American Freedom*, pp. 369, 373. For an outstanding history of colonial America, see Morgan, passim.

5. Thomas Paine, *Common Sense* (New York: Penguin, 1969 [1776]).

6. Edmund Morgan, *Inventing the People: the Rise of Popular Sovereignty in England and America* (New York: Norton, 1988), p. 267.

7. Quoted in Gordon Wood, *The Creation of the American Republic 1776–1787* (Chapel Hill: University of North Carolina Press, 1969), p. 133. Wood's book is a classic treatise on the period between the American revolution and the ratification of the Constitution.

8. James MacGregor Burns, *The American Experiment: The Vineyard of Liberty* (New York: Knopf, 1981), pp. 60 and 61.

9. See, for example, Jeffrey Toobin, "Our Broken Constitution," *The New Yorker*, December 9, 2013. Toobin writes that increasingly the question is asked, "whether the pervasive dysfunction in Washington is in spite of the Constitution or because of it."

10. I recognize the point is debatable. I, however, would argue that when powerless Americans number a critical mass that is angry enough and organized enough to persist in an effort to create change, they have, in time, a reasonable chance of accomplishing just that.

11. Wood, *Radicalism of the American Revolution*, p. 95.

12. Bernard Bailyn, *The Ideological Origins of the American Revolution*, (Cambridge, MA: Harvard University Press, 1967), p. 304.

13. Barbara Kellerman, *The Political Presidency: Practice of Leadership from Kennedy Through Reagan* (New York: Oxford University Press, 2004).

14. Samuel Mitchell, quoted in Wood, *Radicalism of the American Revolution*, p. 308.

15. Alexis de Tocqueville, *Democracy in America* (New York: Doubleday/Anchor, 1969), p. 430.

16. James Morone, *The Democratic Wish: Popular Participation and the Limits of American Government* (New York: Basic Books, 1990), p. 15.

17. Zinn's book epitomizes this attitude, this approach to American history.

18. Morone, *Democratic Wish*, p. 15. For more on different interpretations of original American intentions, see Morone, pp. 15ff.

19. For a great, one-volume history of the Civil War, see James McPherson, *Battle Cry of Freedom: The Civil War Era* (New York: Oxford University Press, 1988).

20. Philip Foner (ed.), *Fredrick Douglass, Selected Speeches and Writings* (Chicago: Chicago Review Press, 2000), p. 446.

21. Given the theme of this book—the importance of context—I particularly recommend Bruce Levine, *The Fall of the House of Dixie* (New York: Random House, 2013). For an excellent review of Levine's volume, see Edward Kosner, "Uprooting the Plantations," *Wall Street Journal*, January 19–20, 2013.

22. For more on how change in America is created—significant change—see Morone's section on the "Dynamics of the Democratic Wish," pp. 9ff. and passim.

23. Martin Luther King, "Letter from Birmingham Jail," August 1963, available at http://www.uscrossier.org/pullias/wp-content/uploads/2012/06/king.pdf. King was not himself, however, by nature a grassroots organizer. In contrast to some of those with whom he worked closely, such as Robert Moses, King believed that leadership came from the pulpit, not the pew.

24. *Inaugural Address by President Barack Obama*, Office of the Press Secretary, The White House, January 21, 2013, available at http://www.whitehouse.gov/the-press-office/2013/01/21/inaugural-address-president-barack-obama.

25. Steven Pinker, *The Better Angels of Our Nature: Why Violence Has Declined* (New York: Viking, 2011), p. 476.

26. Marital law in the U.S. is determined by the individual states, not the federal government. However, the ban on gay marriage that persists in the large majority of American states is vulnerable to legal challenges that have reached the Supreme Court.

27. I write "or at least has not always been" because, as I argue in *The End of Leadership* (New York: HarperCollins, 2012), nearly everywhere now leaders are weaker and followers stronger. In this very, very important way, other nations resemble the U.S. much more now than they did, say, a hundred or even fifty years ago.

28. In *The End of Leadership*, I distinguish more fully among power, authority, and influence. See p. xxi.

29. For more on differences in national culture as they relate to leadership and management, see the work of Geert Hofstede and The Hofstede Centre. For example, in contrast to people in other countries, Americans are highly individualistic.

30. The quote is from Lincoln's *Second Annual Message*, December 1, 1862, available at http://www.presidency.ucsb.edu/ws/?pid=29503.

Chapter 2. Ideology

1. Edmund Morgan, *Inventing the People: The Rise of Popular Sovereignty in England and America* (New York: Norton, 1988), p. 13. See the short introduction to Part One, "Origins," pp. 13–15.

2. Bernard Bailyn, *The Ideological Origins of the American Revolution* (Cambridge, MA: Harvard University Press, 1967), p. 27.

3. Gordon Wood, *The Radicalism of the American Revolution* (New York: Vintage, 1991), p. 95.

4. Bailyn, *Ideological Origins*, p. 56.

5. For further excellent discussion on this, see Richard Hofstadter's classic, *The American Political Tradition* (New York: Random House Vintage, 1948).

6. For more on the powers of, and limits on, the American president, see Clinton Rossiter's classic text, *The American Presidency* (New York: Harcourt Brace, 1956). Also see Peter Baker, "For Obama Presidency, Lyndon Johnson Looms Large," *New York Times*, April 8, 2014.

7. Barbara Kellerman, *Leadership: Essential Selections on Power, Authority, and Influence* (New York: McGraw-Hill, 2012), pp. 55–56.

8. John Stuart Mill, *On Liberty* (n.c.: Dover Publications, 2002 [1859]),excerpt in Kellerman, Leadership, p. 71).

9. This section, which references the American Creed, is based on Samuel Huntington, *American Politics: The Promise of Disharmony* (Cambridge, MA: Harvard University Press, 1981).

10. Huntington, *American Politics*, p. 14 and passim.

11. Some of the components of the American Creed have a counter-narrative, such as, for example, individualism, which some political philosophers counter by taking a more communitarian approach. Still, the Creed as described by Huntington is a good place to start any serious consideration of the ideology that was the foundation of the American experiment.

12. This original preference persists, even in a time in which government is part of peoples' lives in ways the founders could never have anticipated. In fact, the proper role of government in the lives of ordinary people underlies the great twenty-first-century debate between right and left.

13. Huntington, *American Politics*, p. 33.

14. Quoted in Barbara Kellerman, *Leadership: Essential Selection on Power, Authority, and Influence* (New York: McGraw-Hill, 2010), pp. 93, 94.

15. Douglas McGregor, *The Human Side of Enterprise* (New York: McGraw-Hill, 1960).

16. Peter F. Drucker, Quotes online, www.goodreads.com/quotes/167298.

17. Daniel Goleman, Richard Boyatzis, and Annie McKee, *Primal Leadership: Realizing the Power of Emotional Intelligence* (Cambridge, MA: Harvard Business School Press, 2002), p. 69.

18. Ken Blanchard Companies, "Take a Combination Approach to Become a 'Best Boss,'" *Ignite!* Newsletter, February 2013, available at http://www.kenblanchard.com/Leading-Research/Ignite-Newsletter/February-2013.

19. This theme is explicitly explored by John Kane and Haig Patapan in *The Democratic Leader: How Democracy Defines, Empowers, and Limits Its Leaders* (New York: Oxford University Press, 2012). See p. 12 and passim.

20. For more on the relationship between the decline of American self-confidence, in both business and government, and the concomitant rise of the leadership industry, see Barbara Kellerman, *Reinventing Leadership: Making the Connection Between Politics and Business* (Albany: State University of New York Press, 1999).

21. Morgan, *Inventing the People*, pp. 305–6.

Chapter 3. Religion

1. Timothy Beal, *Religion in America: A Very Short Introduction* (New York; Oxford University Press, 2008), p. 64.

2. Frank Lambert, *Religion in American Politics: A Short History* (Princeton, NJ: Princeton University Press, 2008), p. 11.

3. Irving Berlin's patriotic song, "God Bless America," written in 1918 and revised in 1938, became iconic for good reason.

4. Kenneth D. Wald and Allison Calhoun-Brown, *Religion and Politics in the United States* (Lanham, MD: Rowman & Littlefield, 2011), p. 28.

5. "Partisan Polarization Surges in Bush, Obama Years," Section 6, "Religion and Social Values," Pew Research Center for the People & the Press, June 4, 2012, available at http://www.people-press.org/2012/06/04/partisan-polarization-surges-in-bush-obama-years/.

6. Wald and Calhoun-Brown, *Religion and Politics*, p. 77.

7. An allusion to the words of Jesus, from Matthew, which were "Judge not, that ye not be judged."

8. Abraham Lincoln, *Second Inaugural Address*, March 4, 1865, available at http://www.bartleby.com/124/pres32.html.

9. Lambert, *Religion in American Politics*, p. 161.

10. Martin Luther King, "Letter from Birmingham Jail," August 1963, available at http://www.uscrossier.org/pullias/wp-content/uploads/2012/06/king.pdf.

11. Samuel Huntington, *American Politics: The Promise of Disharmony* (Harvard University Press, 1981), pp. 14, 15.

12. Quotes in this paragraph are from Wald and Calhoun-Brown, *Religion and Politics*, pp. 358, 359.

13. William Q. Judge, *The Leader's Shadow: Exploring and Developing Executive Character* (Thousand Oaks, CA: Sage, 1999).

14. Richard L. Zweigenhaft and G. William Domhoff, *The New CEOs: Women, African American, Latino, and Asian American Leaders of Fortune 500 Companies* (Lanham, MD: Rowman & Littlefield, 2011), p. 81.

15. Diana Eck, "Faith and Interfaith in the New America," in Harold Rabinowitz and Greg Tobin (eds.), *Religion in America: A Comprehensive Guide to Faith, History, and Tradition* (New York: Sterling, 2011), p. 15.

16. "'Nones' on the Rise," Pew Research Religion & Public Life Project, October 9, 2012, available at http://www.pewforum.org/2012/10/09/nones-on-the-rise/.

17. Pew Research Religion & Public Life Project, "Religious Landscape Survey," April 6, 2014.

18. All the figures in this paragraph are from "'Nones' on the Rise."

19. Pew Research Religion & Public Life, "Religious Landscape Survey," April 6, 2014.

20. Robert D. Putnam and David E. Campbell, *American Grace: How Religion Divides and Unites Us* (New York: Simon & Schuster, 2010), pp. 3 and 501.

21. "'Nones' on the Rise."

22. Introduction to a report on a survey of the American Catholic community. See Dan Merica, "Survey: U.S. Catholics Going to Church Less Frequently," CNN.com, October 25, 2011.

23. *New York Times*/CBS News Poll, March 5, 2013, available at www.nytimes/com/2013/03/06/us/poll.

24. Ashley Parker, "As the Obamas Celebrate Christmas, Rituals of Faith Become Less Visible," *New York Times*, December 29, 2013.

25. Christopher Hitchens, *God Is Not Great: How Religion Poisons Everything* (New York: Twelve, Hachette Book Group, 2007).

Chapter 4. Politics

1. Evan Osnos, "Chemical Valley," *The New Yorker*, April 7, 2014.

2. Stein Ringen, *Nation of Devils: Democratic Leadership and the Problem of Obedience* (New Haven, CT: Yale University Press, 2013), p. 8.

3. "Trust in Government Near Record Low, But Most Federal Agencies Are Viewed Favorably," Pew Research Center for the People & the Press, October 18, 2013, available at http://www.people-press.org/2013/10/18/trust-in-government-nears-record-low-but -most-federal-agencies-are-viewed-favorably.

4. "One in Four Americans Satisfied with Direction of U.S.," *Gallup Politics*, January 13, 2014, available at http://www.gallup.com/poll/166823/one-four-americans-satisfied -direction.aspx.

5. Jack Citrin, "Political Culture," in Peter H. Schuck and James Q. Wilson (eds.), *Understanding America: The Anatomy of an Exceptional Nation* (New York: Public Affairs, 2008), p. 177.

6. James C. Scott has written of these "hidden transcripts" in his book *Domination and the Art of Resistance: Hidden Transcripts* (New Haven, CT: Yale University Press, 1990).

7. "Partisan Polarization Surges in Bush, Obama Years," Pew Research, Center for the People & the Press, June 4, 2012, available at http://www.people-press.org/2012/ 06/04/partisan-polarization-surges-in-bush-obama-years/.

8. Christopher Ellis and James Stimson, *Ideology in America* (New York: Cambridge University Press, 2012. This paragraph is based on pp. 1–5.

9. For my analysis of the Tea Party as it particularly pertains to leadership and followership, see *The End of Leadership* (New York: HarperCollins, 2012), pp. 108ff.

10. As the title of their book suggests, this particular argument is made most expansively and forcefully by Thomas Mann and Norman Orenstein, *It's Even Worse Than It Looks: How the American Constitutional System Collided with the New Politics of Extremism* (New York: Basic Books, 2012).

11. Fareed Zakaria, "Will He Fight or Compromise?", *Time*, February 18, 2013.

12. See, for example, his article written with Geoffrey Canada and Keven Warsh, "Generational Theft Needs to Be Arrested," *Wall Street Journal*, February 14, 2013.

13. David Brooks, "Another Fiscal Flop," *New York Times*, December 31, 2013.

14. See, for example, Bruce Katz and Jennifer Bradley, *The Metropolitan Revolution: How Cities and Metros Are Fixing Our Broken Politics and Fragile Economy* (Washington, DC: The Brookings Institution, 2013.)

15. Quoted in Thomas Friedman, "It's Lose-Lose vs. Win-Win-Win-Win-Win," *New York Times*, March 16, 2013.

Chapter 5. Economics

1. "Weak field" is Richard A. Posner's term in *The Crisis of Capitalist Democracy* (Cambridge, MA: Harvard University Press, 2010), p. 305.

2. Richard Hofstadter, *The American Political Tradition* (New York: Vintage, 1973), p. xxxvi.

3. Jerry Z. Muller, "Capitalism and Inequality," *Foreign Affairs*, March/April 2013, p. 31.

4. For further analysis, see Max Weber, *The Protestant Ethic and the Spirit of Capitalism with Other Writings on the Rise of the West*, trans. Stephen Kalberg (New York: Oxford University Press, 2009).

5. Gordon Wood, *The Radicalism of the American Revolution* (New York: Vintage, 1991), p. 312.

6. Wood, *Radicalism of the American Revolution*, p. 313.

7. Unless otherwise indicated, all quotes in this paragraph are from James McPherson, *Battle Cry of Freedom: The Civil War Era* (New York: Oxford University Press, 1988), p. 6.

8. The quotes in this paragraph are from James MacGregor Burns, *The American Experiment: The Workshop of Democracy* (New York: Knopf, 1985), pp. 74, 79.

9. Michael Zakim and Gary J. Kornblith (eds.), *Capitalism Takes Command: The Social Transformation of Nineteenth Century America* (Chicago: University of Chicago Press, 2012), p. 508.

10. Fareed Zakaria, "Can America Be Fixed? The New Crisis of Democracy," *Foreign Affairs*, January/February 2013, pp. 29, 30. This paragraph and the two preceding ones borrow from the article.

11. Deborah Hargreaves, "Can We Close the Pay Gap?" *New York Times*, March 30, 2014.

12. Joseph Stiglitz, "Inequality Is Holding Back the Recovery," *New York Times*, January 19, 2013.

13. Zachary Goldfarb, "Study: U.S. Poverty Rate Decreased Over Past Half-Century Thanks to Safety-Net Programs," *Washington Post*, December 9, 2013.

14. Thomas Piketty, *Capital in the Twenty-First Century*, trans. Arthur Goldhammer (Cambridge, MA: Belknap Press, 2014).

15. Jill Lepore, "Long Division," *The New Yorker*, December 2, 2013.

16. Owens is quoted in Catherine Rampell, "Job Growth Steady, but Unemployment Rises to 7.9%," *New York Times*, February 1, 2013.

17. Glenn Hubbard, "Where Have All the Workers Gone?" *Wall Street Journal*, April 5–6, 2014.

18. Rampell, "Job Growth Steady," including quote from Owens.

19. Alan Blinder, *After the Music Stopped: The Financial Crisis, the Response, and the Work Ahead* (New York: Penguin, 2013). Both quotes in this paragraph are on p. 8. Since Blinder's book, former Secretary of the Treasury Timothy Geithner has come out with his own book, which does try to explain what happened leading up to, during, and immediately after the financial crisis. The book, *Stress Test: Reflections on Financial Crises* (Crown, 2014) has been generally well received.

20. See Blinder on "the backlash," *After the Music Stopped*, Chapter 13, pp. 343ff.

21. *USA Today/Gallup Poll*, July 23, 2012, available at https://www.google.com/?source=search_app#q=USA+Today/July+Gallup+Poll+Romney+would+do+better+job+of+handling+the+Nation's+economy&spell=1.

22. Floyd Norris, "A Dire Economic Forecast Based on New Assumptions," *New York Times*, February 28, 2014.

23. Some of the ideas in the preceding paragraphs are based on an unpublished paper by John Kane, "Leadership Judgment in Economic Affairs." The paper was prepared for a symposium on democratic leadership that was held at Yale University in 2013.

24. Posner, *Crisis of Capitalist Democracy*, p. 387.

Chapter 6. Institutions

1. Seymour Martin Lipset and William Schneider, "The Decline of Confidence in American Institutions," *Political Science Quarterly*, Vol. 98, No. 3, Fall 1983.

2. Lipset and Schneider, "Decline of Confidence," p. 380.

3. Catherine Rampell, "Losing Faith in American Institutions," *New York Times*, June 21, 2012.

4. Lipset and Schneider, "Decline of Confidence," p. 401.

5. Howard Gardner, "Can There Be Societal Trustees in America Today?" *Educause*, n.d., available at https://net.educause.edu/ir/library/pdf/ffp0504s.pdf.

6. Center for Public Leadership, *National Leadership Index 2012—A National Study of Confidence in Leadership* (Cambridge, MA: Harvard Kennedy School, 2012), p. 10.

7. Center for Public Leadership, *National Leadership Index*, p. 1.

8. Jeffrey M. Jones, "Confidence in U.S. Public Schools at New Low," *Gallup Politics*, June 20, 2012.

9. See results from the 2012 Program for International Student Assessment, which is administered every three years by the Organization for Economic Cooperation and Development. The exam is given in sixty-five countries and locales, representing 80 percent of the world's economy. See, for example, Stephanie Banchero, "U.S. High-School Students Slip in Global Rankings," *Wall Street Journal*, December 3, 2013, available at http://online.wsj.com/news/articles/SB10001424052702304579404579234511824563116.

10. The figures compare Gallup polls from 2001 to 2011. See Ron Fournier and Sophie Quinton, "In Nothing We Trust," *National Journal*, April 19, 2012, available at http://www.nationaljournal.com/features/restoration-calls/in-nothing-we-trust-20120419.

11. Andrew Sullivan is quoted by John Heilpern in "Out to Lunch," *Vanity Fair*, May 2013.

12. Quoted by Fournier and Quinton, "In Nothing We Trust."

13. Stein Ringen, *Nation of Devils: Democratic Leadership and the Problem of Obedience* (New Haven, CT: Yale University Press, 2013), p. 8.

14. Lucas Kawa, "America's Infrastructure Ranks 25th in the World," *Business Insider*, January 16, 2013.

15. Jennifer Steinhauer, "A Day of Friction Notable Even for a Fractious Congress," *New York Times*, July 13, 2013.

16. Gates's memoir is *Duty: Memoirs of a Secretary at War* (New York: Knopf, 2014). The quote is from Mark Thompson, "Gates vs. Congress Is the Real War," Time.com. Thompson adds, "*What if he's [Gates] right?*"

17. This paragraph is based on the concluding section of a book titled *A Republic Divided* (The Annenberg Democracy Project, New York: Oxford University Press, 2007). See page 235. Also see, in the same volume, the chapter by Ronnie Janoff-Bulman and Michael Parker, "Moral Basis of Public Distrust," pp. 7–23.

18. Anthony Romano, "How Dumb Are We?" *Newsweek*, March 20, 2011.

19. Rod Kramer and Todd Pittinsky (eds.), *Restoring Trust in Organizations and Leaders: Enduring Challenges and Emerging Questions* (New York: Oxford University Press, 2012), p. 1.

20. This particular discussion, on restoring trust after the global financial crisis, is based on Nicole Gillespie, Robert Hurley, Graham Dietz, and Reinhard Bachmann, "Restoring Institutional Trust After the Global Financial Crisis: A Systemic Approach" in Kramer and Pittinsky, *Restoring Trust*, pp. 185–215.

21. Margaret Rundle, Carrie James, Katie Davis, Jennifer O. Ryan, John M. Francis, and Howard Gardner, "My Trust Needs to Be Earned, or I Don't Give It," in Kramer and Pittinsky, *Restoring Trust*, pp. 31.

22. Katie Davis, Jennifer O. Ryan, Carrie James, Margaret Rundle, and Howard Gardner, "I'll Pay Attention When I'm Older," in Kramer and Pittinsky, *Restoring Trust*, p. 62.

Chapter 7. Organizations

1. Matthew Shaer, "The Boss Stops Here," *New York Magazine*, June 24–July 1, 2013, p. 28. Shaer is quoting Nikil Saval, *Cubed: A Secret History of the Workplace* (New York: Doubleday, 2014.)

2. Columbia Business School professor Adam Galinsky, quoted in Shaer, "The Boss Stops Here."

3. I use *he* here because when Weber wrote, leaders were thought men, not women.

4. *Max Weber: The Theory of Social and Economic Organization*, ed. Talcott Parsons (New York: Free Press, 1947). My comments here are based on Parsons's Introduction.

5. Robert Michels, *Political Parties* (New York: Free Press, 1962), p. 71.

6. Sydney Finkelstein, Donald Hambrick, and Albert Cannella, *Strategic Leadership: Theory and Research on Executives, Top Management Teams, and Boards* (New York: Oxford University Press, 2009), p. 8.

7. For a complete discussion, see Christine Mallin, *Corporate Governance* (New York: Oxford University Press, 2010). The quote in this paragraph is on p. 166.

8. Raghunan Rajan and Julie Wulf, "The Flattening of the Firm: Evidence from Panel Data on the Changing Nature of Corporate Hierarchies," report prepared for the National Bureau of Economic Research, 2003.

9. Julie Wulf, "The Flattened Firm—Not as Advertised," *Harvard Business School: Working Knowledge*, May 10, 2012.

10. Shaer, "The Boss Stops Here," p. 29.

11. Jeremy Faludi, "Flattening Hierarchies in Business," *Worldchanging*, December 22, 2005.

12. Ori Brafman and Rod Beckstrom, *The Starfish and the Spider: The Unstoppable Power of Leaderless Organizations* (New York: Penguin, 2006).

13. Rachel Emma Silverman, "Who's the Boss? There Isn't One," *Wall Street Journal*, June 9, 2012.

14. See Shaer, "The Boss Stops Here," for a fuller description of how Menlo Innovations works day to day.

15. Finkelstein, Hambrick, and Cannella, *Strategic Leadership*, p. 123.

16. Maria Guadalupe, Hongyi Li, and Julie Wulf, "Who Lives in the C-Suite? Organizational Structure and the Division of Labor in Top Management," *Harvard Business School: Working Knowledge*, January 25, 2012.

17. Amy Edmondson, *Teaming: How Organizations Learn, Innovate, and Compete in the Knowledge Economy* (San Francisco: Jossey-Bass, 2012), p. 2.

Chapter 8. Law

1. Lawrence M. Friedman, *Law in America: A Short History* (New York: Modern Library, 2002); and Lawrence M. Friedman, "The Legal System," in Peter H. Schuck and James Q. Wilson (eds.), *Understanding America: The Anatomy of an Exceptional Nation* (New York: Public Affairs, 2008).

2. Friedman, "The Legal System," p. 68.

3. Friedman, *Law in America*, p. 152.

4. Friedman, "The Legal System," pp. 74, 75.

5. Friedman, *Law in America*, p. 168.

6. Niall Ferguson, "How America Lost Its Way," *Wall Street Journal*, June 8–9, 2013.

7. Thomas F. Burke, *Lawyers, Lawsuits, and Legal Rights: The Battle Over Litigation in American Society* (Berkeley: University of California Press, 2002), p. 4.

8. Investopedia, available at http://www.investopedia.com/terms/c/compliance-officer.asp, accessed May 9, 2014.

9. "How to Comply with the Americans with Disabilities Act: A Guide for Restaurants and Other Food Service Employers," January 19, 2011, published online by the Equal Employment Opportunity Commission and available at http://www.eeoc.gov/facts/restaurant_guide.html. OSHA, the Occupational Safety and Health Administration, has been similarly charged since the 1970s with ensuring "safe and healthful working conditions for working men and women by setting and enforcing standards and by providing training, outreach, education, and assistance" (United States Department of Labor, OSHA, available at https://www.osha.gov/about.html). It reflects another law that, however well-intentioned, resulted in a blizzard of bureaucratic regulation.

10. "Understanding the Americans with Disabilities Act Amendments Act and Section 504 of the Rehabilitation Act," Parent Advocacy Brief, published by the National Center for Learning Disabilities, 2009, available at http://www.ncld.org/images/stories/Publications/AdvocacyBriefs/UnderstandingADAAA-Section504/Understanding-ADAAA-Section504.pdf.

11. Philip K. Howard, *Life Without Lawyers: Restoring Responsibility in America* (New York: Norton, 2009), p. 98.

12. Philip Howard, *The Rule of Nobody: Saving America from Dead Laws and Broken Government* (New York: Norton, 2014.

13. Howard, *Life Without Lawyers*, p. 63.

14. "FDA Reviewing Diabetes Drugs Due to Pancreatic Disease Risk," CBS News, March 14, 2013.

15. See, for example, the debate in *Harvard Law Review*, on the one side an article by Mitchell Polinsky and Steven Shavell, "The Uneasy Case for Product Liability" (n.d. 2010, available at http://cdn.harvardlawreview.org/wp-content/uploads/pdfs/polinsky_shavell.pdf), and on the other side a response by John Goldberg and Benjamin Zipursky, "The Easy Case for Products Liability Law: A Response to Professors Polinsky

and Shavell" (March 24/April 26, 2010, available at http://papers.ssrn.com/sol3/papers .cfm?abstract_id=1577653).

16. For more on this, see Ben Protess, "Wall Street Is Bracing for the Dodd-Frank Rules to Kick In," *New York Times*, December 12, 2012.

17. Quoted in Peter Lattman and Ben Protess, "SAC Capital Agrees to Plead Guilty to Insider Trading," *New York Times*, November 4, 2013.

18. Dana Cimilluca and Jean Eaglesham, "Documents May Boost Civil Suits," *Wall Street Journal*, December 20, 2012.

19. An excellent article on this particular hearing is by Gretchen Morgenson, "JPMorgan's Follies, for All to See," *New York Times*, March 17, 2013.

20. "Year of the Lawyer," *The Economist*, January 5, 2013.

21. Jessica Silver-Greenberg and Ben Protess, "JPMorgan Chase Faces a Full-Court Press of Federal Investigations, *New York Times*, March 27, 2013.

22. Rana Foroohar, "The Money Cop," *Time*, December 24, 2012.

23. Holder is quoted in Andrew Ross Sorkin, "Realities Behind Prosecuting Big Banks," *New York Times*, March 12, 2013.

24. The 906-page Affordable Care Act (Obamacare) did not, for example, even deal with the issue of medical liability reform. This was in spite of the fact that physicians overwhelmingly, understandably, practice defensive medicine to protect themselves against legal liability. And this was in spite of the fact that in 2008 in Massachusetts alone an estimated $281 million was spent in unnecessary physician costs and more than $1 billion in excessive hospital costs—all to shield against costly litigation. Anthony Youn, "Health Care Act's Glaring Omission: Liability Reform," *CNNHealth*, October 5, 2012.

Chapter 9. Business

1. An exception to this general rule is Rakesh Khurana, *From Higher Aims to Hired Hands: The Social Transformation of American Business Schools and the Unfulfilled Promise of Management as a Profession* (Princeton, NJ: Princeton University Press, 2007). Khuran's is an excellent look at the theory and practice of pedagogy on leadership and management—and at the politics in which this theory as well as this practice is embedded.

2. James Hoopes, *Corporate Dreams: Big Business in American Democracy from the Great Depression to the Great Recession* (New Brunswick, NJ: Rutgers University Press, 2011), p. 2.

3. Mark Mizruchi, *The Fracturing of the American Corporate Elite* (Cambridge, MA: Harvard University Press, 2013), pp. 4–11.

4. Hoopes, *Corporate Dreams*, p. 24.

5. Hoopes, *Corporate Dreams*, pp. 25, 26.

6. All quotes in this paragraph are from Gordon Wood, *The Radicalism of the American Revolution* (New York: Vintage, 1991), pp. 325, 326.

7. Wood, *Radicalism of the American Revolution*, p. 322.

8. Mizruchi, *Fracturing of the American Corporate Elite*, p. 46.

9. The quotes and information in this paragraph are from Schumpeter, *The Economist*, March 2, 2013.

10. Rana Foroohar, "The Myth of Financial Reform," *Time*, September 23, 2013.

11. Judge Jed Rakoff among others has raised serious questions about why the federal government did not do much more to prosecute prominent people responsible for the financial crisis. See "The Financial Crisis: Why Have No High Level Executives Been Prosecuted?" *New York Review*, January 9, 2014.

12. Hoopes, *Corporate Dreams*, pp. 196, 197.

13. Gretchen Morgenson, "That Unstoppable Climb in C.E.O. Pay," *New York Times*, June 30, 2013.

14. Kim Phillips-Fein and Julian Zelizer, "Epilogue," in Kim Phillips-Fein and Julian Zelizer (eds.), *What's Good for Business: Business and American Politics Since World War II* (New York: Oxford University Press, 2012), p. 249. This paragraph is based on information provided on this page.

15. Charles Ferguson, *Predator Nation: Corporate Criminals, Political Corruption, and the Hijacking of America* (New York: Crown Business, 2012).

16. David Rothkopf, *Power, Inc.: The Epic Rivalry Between Big Business and Government—and the Reckoning That Lies Ahead* (New York: Farrar, Straus and Giroux, 2012), p. 19.

17. Dan McCrum, "Boom Year for Activist Investors," *Financial Times*, December 24, 2012. Also see Steven Davidoff, "In Shareholder Fights, Activists Aim at Bigger Targets, *New York Times*, April 17, 2013.

18. Quoted in Rana Foroohar, "The Original Wolf of Wall Street," *Time*, December 16, 2013.

19. Gregg Feinstein, quoted in David Gelles, "Boardrooms Rethink Tactics to Defang Activist Investors," *New York Times*, November 12, 2013.

20. Joann Lublin, "More CEOs Sharing Control at the Top," *Wall Street Journal*, June 7, 2012.

21. Ram Charan, Dennis Carey, Michael Useem, *Boards That Lead: When to Take Charge, When to Partner, and When to Get Out of the Way* (Boston: Harvard Business Review Press, 2014).

22. Barbara Kellerman, *The End of Leadership* (New York: HarperCollins, 2012).

23. Moises Naim, *The End of Power: From Boardrooms to Battlefields and Churches to States, Why Being in Charge Isn't What It Used to Be* (New York: Basic Books, 2013), p. 163.

24. Spencer Stuart, "2013: A Year of CEO Changes," *Wall Street Journal*, January 2, 2014.

25. The Miles Group, "10 Key Challenges for CEOs in 2013," available at http://miles-group.com/article/10-key-challenges-ceos-2013.

26. Thomas Donohue, "State of American Business," speech delivered on January 10, 2013, Washington D.C.

27. Michael Porter, Jay Lorsch, and Nitin Nohria, "Seven Surprises for New CEOs," in Michael Porter (ed.), *On Competition: Updated and Expanded Edition* (Cambridge, MA: Harvard Business Review Book, 2008), p. 507.

28. Porter, Lorsch,and Nohria, "Seven Surprises," pp. 507ff.

29. "Glass Half Empty," *The Economist*, January 21, 2012.

30. Jesse Eisinger, "In Shareholder Say-On-Pay Votes, Whispers, Not Shouts," *New York Times*, June 27, 2013.

31. The figure is according to the American Society for Training and Development. In Mike Myatt, "The #1 Reason Leadership Development Programs Fail," *Forbes.com*, December 19, 2012. available at http://www.forbes.com/sites/mikemyatt/2012/12/19/the-1-reason-leadership-development-fails.

32. This is according to a study conducted by PriceWaterhouseCooper. See Taffy Brodesser-Akner, "The Merchant of Just Be Happy," *New York Times*, December 29, 2013.

33. This is not just an American phenomenon. "The 'labour share' of national income has been falling across much of the world since the 1980s." See "Labour Pains," *The Economist*, November 2, 2013.

34. Eduardo Porter, "Stubborn Skills Gap in America's Work Force," *New York Times*, October 9, 2013.

35. Jay Lorsch, *The Future of Boards: Meeting the Governance Challenges of the Twenty-First Century* (Boston: Harvard Business Review Press, 2012), p. 8.

36. Mizruchi, *Fracturing of the American Corporate Elite*, p. 267. Some corporate leaders have tried to get other corporate leaders to play more prominent parts in taking on government dysfunction. One such CEO has been Honeywell's David Cote. See, for example, Russ Choma, "Unhappy with Dissident Republicans, Honeywell Could Make Them Feel Pain," *OpenSecretsblog*, December 10, 2013.

Chapter 10. Technology

1. Don Tapscott quotes himself from 1998 in his later book, *Grown Up Digital: How the Net Generation Is Changing Your World* (New York: McGraw-Hill, 2009), p. 2. *Grown Up Digital* is his sequel to *Growing Up Digital*, which appeared a decade earlier.

2. Sue Halpern, "Are We Puppets in a Wired World?" *The New York Review*, November 7, 2013.

3. Thomas Friedman, "If I Had a Hammer," *New York Times*, January 11, 2014, available at http://www.nytimes.com/2014/01/12/opinion/sunday/friedman-if-i-had-a-hammer.html?_r=0. Friedman is quoting Erik Brynjolfsson, who with Andrew McAfee is the author of *The Second Machine Age: Work, Progress and Prosperity in a Time of Brilliant Technologies* (New York: Norton, 2014).

4. Stephen Pritchard, "Risk of Information Overload That Threatens Business Growth," *Financial Times*, November 7, 2012. "Rise of Big Data."

5. Andrew McAfee, "What Every CEO Needs to Know About the Cloud," *Harvard Business Review*, November, 2011.

6. Kenneth Cukier and Viktor Mayer-Schoenberger, "The Rise of Big Data: How It's Changing the Way We Think About the World," *Foreign Affairs*, May/June 2013.

7. James Glanz, "Is Big Data an Economic Big Dud?" *New York Times*, August 18, 2013.

8. Steve Lohr, "Sizing Up Big Data: Broadening Beyond the Internet," *New York Times*, June 20, 2013.

9. Cukier and Mayer-Schoenberger, "Rise of Big Data."

10. Cukier and Mayer-Schoenberger, "Rise of Big Data," p. 39.

11. Glanz, "Is Big Data an Economic Big Dud?"

12. Erik Brynjolfsson, director of the MIT Center for Digital Business, quoted in Lohr, "Sizing Up Big Data."

13. "The Power of Information: Why the World Needs Anonymous," *Online Post by Anonrelations Team*, January 18, 2013.

14. Quoted in Michael Scherer, "Number Two: Edward Snowden, the Dark Prophet," *Time*, December 23, 2013.

15. Halpern, "Are We Puppets?"

16. Halpern, "Are We Puppets?"

17. George Anders, "Inside Amazon's Idea Machine: How Bezos Decodes Customers," *Forbes*, April 4, 2012.

18. Adrian Wooldridge, "The Coming Tech-lash," *The Economist*, November 18, 2013.

19. Nathan Heller, ""Naked Launch," *The New Yorker*, November 25, 2013.

20. Stewart Patrick, "The Unruled World: The Case for Good Enough Global Governance," *Foreign Affairs*, January-February 2014, p. 72.

21. Tom Standage, "At Your Service," *The Economist*, November 18, 2013.

22. Brynjolfsson and McAfee, *The Second Machine Age*, pp. 11 and 34.

23. Honor Mahony, "EU Faces a Lost Generation of Almost 8 Million Young People," *EU Observer*, July 9, 2012.

24. For a cogent, if somewhat dismal assessment of the link between "tech leaps" and "job losses," and the consequences thereof, see Eduardo Porter, "Tech Leaps, Job Losses and Rising Inequality," *New York Times*, April 16, 2014.

25. Philip Elliott, "Youth Unemployment: 15 Percent of American Youth Out of School and Work, Study Finds," *Huffington Post*, October 21, 2013.

26. Douglas Belkin, "Former Yale President Will Lead Coursera," *Wall Street Journal*, March 25, 2014.

27. The quotes in this paragraph are taken from the websites for Udacity, at https://www.udacity.com/us, and edX, at https://www.edx.org.

28. See, for example, Nathan Heller, "Laptop U," *The New Yorker*, May 20, 2013. I might add that two of the Harvard Business School's leading lights, professors Michael Porter and Clayton Christensen, disagree on how the Business School should proceed. Christensen argues that it should "disrupt" its existing business by going online in a big way. Porter recommends a more conservative approach. See Jerry Useem, "Business School, Disrupted," *New York Times*, June 1, 2014.

29. Faisal Hoque, *The Power of Convergence: Linking Business Strategies and Technology Decisions to Create Sustainable Success* (New York: American Management Association, 2011), p. 4.

30. Charline Li and Josh Bernoff, *Groundswell: Winning in a World Transformed by Social Technologies* (Boston: Harvard Business Review Press, 2011) p. 9.

31. See Erik Qualman, *Socialnomics: How Social Media Transforms the Way we Live and Do Business* (Hoboken, NJ: John Wiley & Sons, 2011). Qualman is widely known for using the word *revolution* to describe the transformational change of technology.

32. "Surfing a Digital Wave, or Drowning," *The Economist*, December 7, 2013.

33. Eric Schmidt and Jared Cohen, "A Trip to the Digital Dark Side," *Wall Street Journal*, April 20–21, 2013. The article is adapted from their book *The New Digital Age: Reshaping the Future of People, Nations and Business* (New York: Knopf, 2013).

34. John Negroponte, Samuel Palmisano, and Adam Segal, "Defending an Open, Global, Secure, and Resilient Internet," Council on Foreign Relations, 2013. This is not even to speak of a range of other foreign policy threats related to changing technology, such as, for example, "rapid advances in biotechnology" and "uncoordinated efforts at geoengineering." See Patrick, "The Unruled World."

35. John Seabrook, "Network Insecurity," *The New Yorker*, May 20, 2013.

36. Manuel Castells, *Networks of Outrage and Hope: Social Movements in the Internet Age* (Malden, MA: Polity Press, 2012), p. 1.

37. Thomas Friedman, "The Rise of Popularism," *New York Times*, June 24, 2012.

38. "Everything Is Connected," *The Economist*, January 5, 2013.

39. See particularly *The End of Leadership* (New York: HarperCollins, 2012).

40. Groysberg and Slind, *Talk, Inc.*, p. 7.

41. Charlotte Clarke, "Generations to Come Will Learn Quickly," *Financial Times*, November 7, 2012.

42. Paul Taylor, "Relationships in the C-Suite Set to Change," *Financial Times*, November 7, 2012.

Chapter 11. Media

1. S. Robert Lichter, "The Media," in Peter S. Schuck and James Q. Wilson (eds.), *Understanding America: The Anatomy of an Exceptional Nation* (New York: Public Affairs, 2008), p. 183.

2. Lichter, "The Media," p. 186.

3. Lichter points out that more recent scholarship on the war in Vietnam suggests that the effect of television on public opinion was not so much the result of pictures transmitted as in the impression conveyed that the war might be in vain ("The Media," p. 195).

4. For more on this perspective, see John Nichols and Robert McChesney, *Dollarocracy: How the Money-and-Media Election Complex Is Destroying America* (New York: Nation Books, 2013), passim.

5. Frank Bruni, "Who Needs Reporters?" *New York Times*, June 2, 2013.

6. Recent evidence suggests that this might change, at least slightly, for the better. Print stars, some of them iconoclasts, such as Glenn Greenwald and Matt Taibbi, and also Ezra Klein, have all recently quit old media to start up their own new media enterprises, while the head of the Pew Research Center, Alan Murray, notes "there's been a spate of hiring in the digital world." See Murray, "Seven Reasons for Optimism About the News Business," *Wall Street Journal*, March 26, 2014.

7. Murray, "Seven Reasons for Optimism."

8. Alex S. Jones, *Losing the News: The Future of the News That Feeds Democracy* (New York: Oxford University Press, 2009), p. 4.

9. Thomas Patterson, *Informing the News: The Need for Knowledge-Based Journalism* (New York: Vintage, 2013).

10. Matthew Yglesias, "The Glory Days of American Journalism," *Pew State of the Media*, March 19, 2013.

11. Pew Research Center's Project for Excellence in Journalism, *The State of the News Media 2013: An Annual Report on American Journalism*, March 13, 2013.

12. Jones, *Losing the News*, pp. 5, 6.

13. Frank Rich, "Inky Tears," *New York*, April 15, 2013.

14. To see the series, go to nytimes.com/walmartabroad.

15. To see the series, go to nytimes.com/economy.

16. To see the series, go to nytimes.com/chinas-secret-fortunes.

17. Investigative journalism survives at the *Times* not only at the national and international levels, but at the state and local levels as well. See, for example, Sam Dolnick, "Halfway Houses Prove Lucrative to Those at Top," *New York Times*, December 30, 2012, and William Glaberson, "Waiting Years for Day in Court," April 14, 2013.

18. Matthew Hindman, *The Myth of Digital Democracy* (Princeton, NJ: Princeton University Press, 2009), p. 133. As its title implies, Hindman's book is to a large degree about this overarching point.

19. Manuel Castells, *Communication Power* (New York: Oxford University Press, 2009), p. 55.

20. The only thing he had done up to this point that drew national attention was to deliver a speech at the 2004 Democratic National Convention that was generally judged outstanding.

21. Castells, *Communication Power*, p. 390.

22. "How the Presidential Candidates Use the Web and Social Media," *Pew Project for Excellence in Journalism*, August 15, 2012.

23. For more on all this, see Barbara Kellerman, *The End of Leadership* (New York: HarperCollins, 2012), Chapter 5, "The American Experience."

24. See Kellerman, *The End of Leadership*, passim.

25. This paragraph is based on, and the quotes therein are taken from, Henry Jenkins, Sam Ford, and Joshua Green, *Spreadable Media: Creating Value and Meaning in a Networked Culture* (New York: New York University Press, 2013), pp. 23–25.

26. For details on the Steubenville rape case, check out the Internet, which provides ample documentation of how the new media environment can affect not only big national stories but also small ones, heretofore considered no more than local. I should also note that the *New York Times* played its part by carrying a significant story on the case at a propitious moment.

27. This paragraph is based partly on Jenkins, Ford, and Green, *Spreadable Media*, p. 297.

28. For a full discussion of this particular issue, see Jonathan Ladd, *Why Americans Hate the Media and How It Matters* (Princeton, NJ: Princeton University Press, 2012).

29. Nichols and McChesney, *Dollarocracy*, p. 196.

30. Jones, *Losing the News*, p. 26.

31. *National Leadership Index 2012: A National Study of Confidence in Leadership*, Center for Public Leadership, Harvard Kennedy School, Harvard University.

32. Rich, "Inky Tears."

Chapter 12. Money

1. John Eligon, "Koch Group Has Ambitions in Small Races," *New York Times*, November 3, 2013.

2. Jeff Connaughton, quoted by Frank Rich, "The Stench of the Potomac," *New York*, August 12, 2013.

3. Both Presidents Obama and Bush are quoted in Eduardo Porter, "In Public Education, Edge Still Goes to Rich," *New York Times*, November 6, 2013.

4. Porter, "In Public Education." The following paragraphs are based on Porter's piece, which contains more related information.

5. For a detailed discussion about all this, from a liberal perspective, see Bruce Baker and Sean Corcoran, "The Stealth Inequities of School Funding," Center for American Progress, September 2012.

6. See the quote by education expert Andreas Schleicher, in Porter, "In Public Education."

7. Yi Wu, "Privatize Schools, Why It's Crony Capitalism at Its Worst," *Policymic.com articles.*

8. Sarah Reckhow, *Follow the Money: How Foundation Dollars Change Public School Politics* (New York: Oxford University Press, 2013), p. 141.

9. Robert Lipsyte, another preeminent sportswriter, said this of Zirin. The quote is on the jacket of Zirin's book, *Game Over: How Politics Has Turned the Sports World Upside Down* (New York: New Press, 2013).

10. Zirin, *Game Over*, p. 26.

11. This paragraph is based on Gregg Easterbrook, "How the NFL Fleeces Taxpayers," *The Atlantic*, September 18, 2013. Also see Easterbrook's book *The King of Sports: Football's Impact on America* (New York: Thomas Dunne, 2013).

12. Gregg Doyel, "Time to Pay College Football Players," CBS Sports.com, September 25, 2013.

13. George Will, "NCAA Football: The College Money Tree," Newsmax.com, September 19, 2013. Will is citing figures provided by Easterbrook in *The King of Sports*.

14. Joe Nocera, "Let's Start Paying College Athletes," *New York Times*, December 30, 2011.

15. Nelson Schwartz and Steve Eder, "College Athletes Aim to Put a Price on 'Priceless,'" *New York Times*, March 28, 2014.

16. The quote in this paragraph is from Ken Belson, "N.F.L. Agrees to Settle Concussion Suit for $765 million," *New York Times*, August 29, 2013. The paragraph is based on Belson's account.

17. Belson, "N.F.L. Agrees to Settle Concussion Suit."

18. Ken Belson, "Many Ex-Players May Be Ineligible for Payment in N.F.L. Concussion Settlement," *New York Times*, October 17, 2013.

19. Mark Fainaru-Wada and Steve Fainaru *League of Denial* (New York: Crown Archetype, 2013). A public television show based on the book was aired on PBS's *Frontline*.

20. A note on money in American medicine, from an article by Steven Brill, "Bitter Pill: Why Medical Bills Are Killing Us," *Time*, February 20, 2013. On the MD Anderson Cancer Center in Houston, Brill writes, "Although it is officially a nonprofit unit of the University of Texas, MD Anderson has revenue that exceeds the cost of the world-class care it provides by so much that its operating profit for the fiscal year 2010 . . . was $531 million. That's a profit margin of 26% on revenue of $2.05 billion, an astounding result for such a service-intensive enterprise." Not incidentally, in 2012, the president of MD Anderson had a total compensation of $1,845,000.

21. "Leaders: The Unsteady States of America," *The Economist*, July 27, 2013.

22. If our elected officials were fully honest, economically honest, they would, for example, tell the American people that they need to retire later, that they should support increased immigration in order to expand the number of people who work, that we should borrow less from abroad, and that we should stop cannibalizing the young in favor of the old and middle-aged. See, for example, Stephen King, "When Wealth Disappears," *New York Times*, October 6, 2013.

23. Adriel Bettelheim and Jay Hunter, "50 Richest Members of Congress: The Wealth Keeps Growing," *Roll Call*, September 13, 2013.

24. Eric Lipton, "For Freshman in the House, Seats of Plenty," *New York Times*, August 11, 2013.

25. Michael Waldman, "Preface," in Monica Youn (ed.), *Money, Politics, and the Constitution: Beyond Citizens United* (New York: Century Foundation, 2011), p. xi.

26. Lawrence Lessig, *Republic Lost: How Money Corrupts Congress—and a Plan to Stop It* (New York: Twelve, 2011), p. 91.

27. Quoted in John Nichols and Robert McChesney, *Dollarocracy: How the Money-and-Media Election Complex Is Destroying America* (New York: Nation Books, 2013), p. 3.

28. Monica Youn, "Introduction," in Youn, *Money, Politics, and the Constitution*, p. 2.

29. Adam Liptak, "Supreme Court Strikes Down Overall Political Donation Cap," *New York Times*, April 2, 2014.

30. James Bennet, "The New Price of American Politics," *The Atlantic*, September, 19, 2012.

31. S. V. Date, "Crossroads GPS Reports a Single Donation of $22.5 Million in 2012," November 19, 2013, available at http://www.npr.org/blogs/itsallpolitics/2013/11/18/246030728/crossroads-gps-reports-22-5-million-single-donation-in-2012.

32. Nichols and McChesney, *Dollarocracy*, p. 37.

33. Sheila Krumholz of the Center for Responsive Politics, quoted in Nichols and McChesney, *Dollarocracy*, p. 43. Also see Jacob Hacker and Paul Pierson, *Winner-Take-All Politics: How Washington Made the Rich Richer—and Turned Its Back on the Middle Class* (New York: Simon & Schuster, 2010).

34. Lessig, *Republic Lost*, p. 168.

35. Quoted in Maureen Dowd, "Money, Money, Money, Money, MONEY," *New York Times*, August 18, 2013.

36. Rich, "The Stench of the Potomac."

37. Vivian Giang, "The 15 Highest Paid CEOs in America," *Business Insider*, October, 26, 2013.

38. Giang, "15 Highest Paid CEOs."

39. Theo Francis and Joann Lublin, "Pay Check: A Few CEOs Dominate Ranking," *Wall Street Journal*, May 28, 2014.

40. Eduardo Porter, "Inequality in America: The Data Is Sobering," *New York Times*, July 30, 2013. Porter compares the performance of the U.S. to other countries in the Organization for Economic Cooperation and Development. So, for example, within the organization, only in Turkey, Mexico, and Poland do more children live in poor homes.

41. Lessig, *Republic Lost*, p. 1.

42. For more on high rollers in the fine arts, see Nick Paumgarten, "Dealer's Hand," *The New Yorker*, December 2, 2013.

43. Andrew Rice, "The Gavel Drops at Sotheby's," *New York*, March 10–23, 2014.

44. For more on this argument, see Chrystia Freeland, *Plutocrats: The Rise of the New Global Super-Rich and the Fall of Everyone Else* (New York: Penguin, 2012), pp. xiiff.

Chapter 13. Innovation

1. Frederick Hess, "America Is Still the Most Innovative Country in the World," *The Atlantic*, November 14, 2011.

2. Christopher Mims, "Why Isn't America Innovating Like It Used To?" *MIT Technology Review*, August 5, 2011.

3. Eamonn Fingleton, "America the Innovative?" *New York Times*, March 30, 2013.

4. Fareed Zakaria, "The Future of Innovation: Can America Keep Pace?" *Time*, June 5, 2011.

5. Arianna Huffington, "When It Comes to Innovation, Is America Becoming a Third World Power?" *Huffington Post*, March 29, 2010.

6. The phrase is taken from a report by the National Economic Council, Council of Economic Advisers, and the office of Science and Technology Policy, titled "A Strategy for American Innovation: Securing Our Economic Growth and Prosperity," February 2011.

7. Michael Greenstone and Adam Looney, "A Dozen Economic Facts About Innovation," Brookings Institution, Washington, D.C., August 2011.

8. National Economic Council, Council for Economic Advisers, and Office of Science and Technology Policy, "A Strategy for American Innovation," Washington, DC: The White House, February, 2011.

9. U.S. Department of Commerce in consultation with the National Economic Council, "The Competitiveness and Innovative Capacity of the United States," Washington, D.C., January 2012.

10. Erika Fitzpatrick, "Innovation America: A Final Report," The National Governors Association, July, 2007.

11. Gigi Georges, Tim Glynn-Burke, and Andrea MacGrath, "Improving the Local Landscape for Innovation: Part 3: Assessment and Implementation," Ash Center for Democratic Governance and Innovation, Harvard Kennedy School, Cambridge, Mass., November 2013, p. 1.

12. Georges, Glynn-Burke, and MacGrath, "Improving the Local Landscape," pp. 8ff.

13. Drew Boyd and Jacob Goldenberg, "Think Inside the Box," *Wall Street Journal*, June 15–16, 2013. The article is based on a book by Boyd and Goldenberg, *Inside the Box: A Proven System of Creativity for Breakthrough Results* (New York: Simon & Schuster, 2013).

14. See, for example, Scott D. Anthony, *The Little Black Book of Innovation: How It Works, How to Do It* (Boston: Harvard Business Review Press, 2012).

15. Boyd and Goldenberg, "Think Inside the Box."

16. On this particular question, see, for example, Henry C. Lucas Jr., *The Search for Survival: Lessons from Disruptive Technologies* (Santa Barbara, CA: Praeger, 2012).

17. Clayton Christensen, *The Innovator's Dilemma: When New Technologies Cause Great Firms to Fail* (Boston: Harvard Business Review Press, 1997; revised edition, New York: HarperBusiness, 2011). By now Christensen has expanded his research to include also nonprofit areas, especially education. See Clayton Christensen, Michael Horn, and Curtis Johnson, *Disrupting Class: How Disruptive Innovation Will Change the Way the World Learns* (New York: McGraw-Hill, 2011).

18. Brian Abbott, "The Innovator's Dilemma: Is Apple a Sustainer or Disrupter?" seekingalpha.com, January 1, 2013.

19. This paragraph is based on the first chapter of Christensen, *The Innovator's Dilemma*.

20. Clayton Christensen, with Michael Raynor, *The Innovator's Solution: Creating and Sustaining Successful Growth* (Cambridge, MA: Harvard Business School Press, 2003).

21. Christensen and Raynor, *The Innovator's Solution*, p. 267.

22. Larry Downes and Paul Nunes, "Big-Bang Disruption," *Harvard Business Review*, March, 2013, and Downes and Nunes, *Big Bang Disruption: Strategy in the Age of Devastating Innovation* (New York: Portfolio, 2014).

23. Quoted by Mike Masnick, "Is the 'Innovator's Dilemma' About to Get Disrupted by 'Big Bang' Disruption?" *Techdirt*, March 8, 2013.

24. Steven Strauss, "Managing Innovation," *Huffington Post*, June 3, 2012.

25. Gary Hamel, *What Matters Now: How to Win in a World of Relentless Change, Ferocious Competition, and Unstoppable Innovation* (San Francisco: Jossey-Bass, 2012), p. 42.

26. Ben Casselman, "Risk-Averse Culture Infects U.S. Workers, Entrepreneurs," *Wall Street Journal*, June 3, 2013.

27. The quote is from Amazon's Jeff Bezos. See Scott Anthony, "Your Innovation Problem Really Is a Leadership Problem," *HBR Blog Network*, February 13, 2013.

Chapter 14. Competition

1. Michael Porter, *On Competition* (Boston: Harvard Business Review Press, 2008), p. xi. This book is an "updated and expanded edition" of his earlier books on the same subject.

2. It has been pointed out that later-Porter is more open to the possibility of collaboration and cooperation than earlier-Porter. See Robert Huggins and Hiro Izushi (eds.), *Competition, Competitive Advantage, and Clusters* (New York: Oxford University Press, 2011), pp. 13ff. and passim.

3. Porter, *On Competition*, p. 63.

4. Porter, *On Competition*, p. 97.

5. Huggins and Izushi, *Competition*, p. 2.

6. Porter, *On Competition*, Chapter 15, written with Jay Lorsch and Nitin Nohria, pp. 507ff. For more on Porter, also see Joan Magretta, *Understanding Michael Porter: The Essential Guide to Competition and Strategy* (Boston: Harvard Business Review Press, 2012).

7. Michael Porter, *The Competitive Advantage of Nations* (New York: Free Press, 1990).

8. The quote from Crawford is from her NPR appearance on "Fresh Air," February 2014, available at http://www.npr.org/blogs/alltechconsidered/2014/02/06/272480919/when-it-comes-to-high-speed-internet-u-s-falling-way-behind. For more on Crawford's competitive cautions, see her book *Captive Audience: The Telecom Industry and Monopoly Power in the Gilded Age* (New Haven, CT: Yale University Press, 2014).

9. Fareed Zakaria, *The Post-American World: Release 2.0* (New York: Norton, 2008), p. 4.

10. Michael Porter, Jan Rivkin, and Rosabeth Moss Kanter, *Competitiveness at a Crossroads*, Harvard Business School Survey on Competitiveness, February 2013, p. 1, available at http://www.hbs.edu/competitiveness/pdf/competitiveness-at-a-crossroads.pdf.

11. Porter, Rivkin, and Kanter, *Competitiveness*, Page 17.

12. Klaus Schwab, *The Global Competitiveness Report, 2012–2013*, World Economic Forum, n.d., available at http://reports.weforum.org/global-competitiveness-report-2012-2013/#.

13. Xi Xiaonian, "U.S. Competitiveness and the Chinese Challenge," *Harvard Business Review*, March 2012.

14. Steve Denning, "The Surprising Reasons Why America Lost Its Ability to Compete," *Forbes*, February 2013; Jay Alcie, "What's Killing America's Global Competitiveness?" *The Fiscal Times*, September 2012; Ansuya Harjani, "U.S. Slips Down the Tanks of Global Competitiveness," CNBC, September 2012; "U.S. Productivity Growth Lags Behind That of Foreign Competitors," *US News*, August 2012.

15. Zakaria, *Post-American World*, pp. 100ff.

16. Ian Bremmer and Evan Feigenbaum, "Watch Out for Rising U.S.-China Competition," *HBR Blog Network*, August 1, 2011.

17. Charles Kupchan, *No One's World: The West, the Rising Rest, and the Coming Global Turn* (New York: Oxford University Press, 2012), p. 99.

18. The quote in this paragraph and some of the ideas therein are from Steven Weber and Bruce Jentleson, *The End of Arrogance: America in the Global Competition of Ideas*, Cambridge, MA: Harvard University Press, 2010, p. 11.

19. Joel Klein and Condoleeza Rice, "U.S. Education Reform and National Security," Council on Foreign Relations, March 2012. As has been noted elsewhere in this book, more recent figures confirm all of the earlier findings. In other words, so far at least the downward trajectory continues.

20. The report was issued by the Program on Education Policy and Governance at Harvard. It was cited in "U.S. Students Still Lag Behind Foreign Peers, Schools Make Little Progress in Improving Achievement," *Huffington Post*, July 23, 2012.

21. Klein and Rice, "U.S. Education Reform."

Chapter 15. Class

1. Ward McAllister, quoted by James MacGregor Burns, *The Workshop of Democracy* (New York: Knopf, 1985), p. 117.

2. Burns, *Workshop*, pp. 140, 141.

3. Burns, Workshop, pp. 145 and 147.

4. Jeff Faux, *The Servant Economy: Where America's Elite Is Sending the Middle Class* (Hoboken, NJ: John Wiley & Sons, 2012), p. 24.

5. Burns, *Workshop*, p. 57.

6. Faux, *Servant Economy*, p. 34.

7. Faux, *Servant Economy*, p. 43.

8. Faux, *Servant Economy*, p. 44.

9. Faux, *Servant Economy*, p. 48.

10. Annie Lowrey, "Recession Worsened Wealth Gap for Races," *New York Times*, April 29, 2013.

11. Both the quote by Mitt Romney and the discussion over what exactly constitutes the middle class have been widely discussed. See, for example, Dylan Matthews, "What is The Middle Class," Wonkblog, *Washington Post*, September 16, 2012.

12. Pew Research Social and Demographic Trends, "The Lost Decade of the Middle Class," August 22, 2012, available at http://www.pewsocialtrends.org/2012/08/22/the-lost-decade-of-the-middle-class.

13. See, for example, Catherine Rampbell, "Student Loan Debt Rising, and Often Not Being Paid Back," *New York Times*, November, 27, 2013.

14. Pew Research Social & Demographic Trends, "The Lost Decade of the Middle Class."

15. Carol Morelo, "Census: Middle Class Shrinks to an All-time Low," washington post.com, September 9, 2012.

16. D'Vera Cohn, "Middle-Income Economics and Middle Class Attitudes," *Pew Research Social & Demographic Trends*, August 22, 2012. Also see Eduardo Porter, "America's Sinking Middle Class," *New York Times*, September 19, 2013. Porter notes that one of the reasons the middle class is feeling squeezed is because of steeply rising costs in, for example, health care and college education. He also points out that whereas people in other developed nations work less as they get richer, Americans work about as much as they did a quarter century ago.

17. This quote and the one immediately preceding are from Annie Lowrey, "50 Years Later, War on Poverty a Mixed Bag," *New York Times*, January 5, 2014.

18. D'Vera Cohn, "The Middle Class Shrinks and Income Segregation Rises," *Pew Research Social & Demographic Trends*, August 2, 2012.

19. Uri Dadush, Kemal Dervis, Sarah Puritz Milsom, and Bennett Stancil, *Inequality in American: Facts, Trends, and International Perspectives* (Washington, DC: Brookings Institution Press, 2012), pp. 11, 12.

20. For a commentary on inequality made by Joseph Stiglitz in 2013, see "The Great Divide: Inequality Is Holding Back the Recovery," *New York Times*, January 19, 2013.

21. Bonnie Kavoussi, "Average Student Loan Debt for Borrowers Under Age 30 Is Nearly $21,000, Study Finds," *Huffington Post*, July 17, 2012.

22. Katz is quoted in Edward Luce, *Time to Start Thinking: America in the Age of Descent* (New York: Atlantic Monthly Press, 2012), p. 44.

23. Dadush, Dervis, Milsom, and Stancil, *Inequality in America*, p. 20. There is some dispute about whether the odds of moving up the economic ladder have declined over time. See the discussion of this in David Leonhardt, "Upward Mobility Has Not Declined, Study Says," *New York Times*, January 23, 2014.

24. Paul Taylor and others, "The Lost Decade of the Middle Class," *Pew Research Social & Demographic Data*, August 22, 2012.

25. Center for Public Leadership, *National Leadership Index: A National Study of Confidence in Leadership*, 2012.

26. Theda Skocpol, "America Disconnected," in James Lardner and David A. Smith (eds.), *Inequality Matters: The Growing Economic Divide in America and Its Poisonous Consequences* (New York: New Press, 2005), p. 178.

Chapter 16. Culture

1. I am grateful to Professor Thomas Wren for this definition, as I am for his helpful comments on an early draft of the manuscript.

2. Robert D. Putnam and David E. Campbell, *American Grace: How Religion Divides and Unites Us* (New York: Simon & Schuster, 2012), p. 92.

3. Martha Bayles, "Popular Culture," in Peter H. Schuck and James Q. Wilson, *Understanding America: The Anatomy of an Exceptional Nation* (New York: Public Affairs, 2008), p. 237.

4. Putnam and Campbell, *American Grace*, p. 92.

5. Sidney Ahlstrom, quoted in Putnam and Campbell, *American Grace*, p. 92.

6. Barbara Kellerman, *The End of Leadership* (New York: HarperCollins, 2012), p. 26.

7. Anthony Castellano, "David Petraeus Apologies for Affair in First Speech Since Resignation from CIA," *ABC News*, March 27, 2013.

8. See my article on this increasingly common phenomenon in the April 2006 issue of *Harvard Business Review*, titled "When Should a Leader Apologize and When Not?"

9. The apology was published on January 13, 2014. It was contained in an open letter from Steinhafel, which was published in newspapers all across the country.

10. Lee Siegel addresses the coarseness of America's popular culture in "America the Vulgar," *Wall Street Journal*, December 7–8, 2013.

11. Kellerman, *The End of Leadership*, p. 34.

12. Paul Cantor, *The Invisible Hand in Popular Culture: Liberty vs. Authority in American Film and TV* (Lexington: University Press of Kentucky, 2012), p. xi.

13. Cantor, *Invisible Hand*, p. xi. For more on American culture as exemplified by Westerns, see Chapter 1, "The Western and Western Drama."

14. David Brooks, "What Our Words Tell Us," *New York Times*, May 20, 2013.

15. Philip Slater, *The Pursuit of Loneliness: American Culture at the Breaking Point* (Boston: Houghton Mifflin, 1971).

16. Robert Putnam, *Bowling Alone: The Collapse and Revival of American Community* (New York: Simon & Schuster, 2001).

17. Eric Klinenberg, *Going Solo: The Extraordinary Rise and Surprising Appeal of Living Alone* (New York: Penguin, 2013).

18. See, for example, Jacqueline Olds and Richard Schwartz, *The Lonely American: Drifting Apart in the Twenty-First Century* (Boston: Beacon Press, 2009); and Sherry Turkle, *Alone Together: Why We Expect More from Technology and Less from Each Other* (New York: Basic Books, 2011).

19. Quoted in Bill George, *Authentic Leadership: Rediscovering the Secrets to Creating Lasting Value* (San Francisco: Jossey-Bass, 2003), p. 45.

20. Terry Price, "Behind the Curtain of Leadership," *Richmond Magazine*, January 28, 2009. Again, thanks to Thomas Wren for pointing me to Professor Price's work in this area.

21. Lane Crothers, *Globalization and American Popular Culure* (Lanham, MD: Rowman & Littlefield, 2013), p. 112.

22. Mike Marqusee, "The Politics of Bob Dylan," *Red Pepper*, quoted in "Protest Songs in the United States," Wikipedia, available at http://en.wikipedia.org/wiki/Protest_songs_in_the_United_States. This and the preceding paragraph are based on this Wiki entry.

Chapter 17. Divisions

1. Jeremy Pope, Samuel Abram, and Morris P. Fiorina, *Culture War? The Myth of a Polarized America* (London: Pearson Longman, 2005). The quotes in this paragraph are on p. ix and p. 66. I should perhaps point to the fact that the book is nearly a decade old.

2. *Still a House Divided* (Princeton, NJ: Princeton University Press, 2011); *It's Even Worse Than It Looks* (New York: Basic Books, 2012); *The Great Divergence* (New York: Bloomsbury, 2012); *Hopelessly Divided* (Lanham, MD: Rowman & Littlefield, 2012); and *Our Divided Political Heart* (New York: Bloomsbury, 2012).

3. Miles Corak, "Who's Your Daddy?" *New York Times*, July 21, 2013. The article is an extended examination on the decreasing opportunities for upward mobility in America, even in comparison with other, similar countries, such as Canada.

4. Joseph Stiglitz, *The Price of Inequality* (New York: Norton, 2012), pp. 25 and 118ff.

5. Noah, *Great Divergence*, pp. 1 and 144ff. (Chapter 9, titled "Rise of the Stinking Rich.")

6. Peter Eavis, "Invasion of the Supersalaries," *New York Times*, April 13, 2014.

7. Noah, *Great Divergence*, p. 166.

8. Thomas Piketty, *Capital in the Twenty-First Century*, trans. Arthur Goldhammer (Cambridge, MA: Belknap Press, 2014).

9. Mann and Ornstein, *It's Even Worse Than It Looks*, p. 45.

10. There have been times when partisan rigidity seems somewhat less, when generally right-wing ideologues such as Senator John McCain seem more interested in compromise than conflict. Still, such times have in recent years been few and far between.

11. Schoen, *Hopelessly Divided*, p. 148.

12. For an excellent explication of the Tea Party phenomenon, see Theda Skocpol and Vanessa Williamson, *The Tea Party and the Remaking of Republican Conservatism* (New York: Oxford University Press, 2012). They describe the Tea Party's rise to success as "stunning" on p. 6.

13. Marc Caputo, "Poll Shows Vast Racial Divide Between Blacks and Whites Over Trayvon, Zimmerman, Justice System," *Miami Herald* blog, July 22, 2013.

14. The White House, "Remarks by the President on Trayvon Martin," July 19, 2013.

15. King and Smith, *Still a House Divided*, p. 13. One could go on. Here, for example, is just one startling additional statistic: the median household income for black people is approximately $33,000; the median household income for white people is approximately $57,000 (Pew Research Center, "Four Takeaways from Tuesday's Census Income and Poverty Release," September 18, 2013, available at http://www.pewresearch.org/fact-tank/2013/09/18/four-takeaways-from-tuesdays-census-income-and-poverty-release).

16. Hanna Rosin, *The End of Men and the Rise of Women* (New York: Penguin, 2012), pp. 149ff. and pp. 117ff.

17. Christina Huffington, "Women and Equal Pay: Wage Gap Still Intact, Study Shows," *Huffington Post*, April 9, 2013.

18. Gerald Seib, "Sexes Are Divided on Hot-Button Issues," *Wall Street Journal*, December 18, 2013.

19. Meredith Whitney, *Fate of the States: The New Geography of American Prosperity* (New York: Penguin, 2013), p. 163ff.

20. David Leonhardt, "Geography Seen as Barrier to Climbing Class Ladder," *New York Times*, July 22, 2013.

21. Enrico Moretti, *The New Geography of Jobs* (Boston: Houghton Mifflin Harcourt, 2012), p. 3.

22. Dante Chinni, "The Next America: America Divided," *National Journal*, May 29, 2013.

23. Emily Badger, "5 Maps That Show How Divided America Really Is," *The Atlantic Cities*, June 7, 2013.

24. "A Decade Later, Iraq War Divides the Public," *Pew Research Center for the People & the Press*, March 18, 2013, available at http://www.people-press.org/2013/03/18/a-decade-later-iraq-war-divides-the-public/.

25. Marjorie Connelly, "Support for Gay Marriage Growing, but U.S. Remains Divided," *New York Times*, December 7, 2012.

26. Lawrence Hurley, "Views on Gay Marriage Still Divided After Court Ruling," Reuters/Ipsos Poll, June 28, 2013, available at http://articles.chicagotribune.com/2013-06-28/news/sns-rt-us-usa-court-gaymarriage-20130627_1_gay-marriage-reuters-ipsos-marriage-act. Also see "Public Divided Over Same-Sex Marriage Rulings," *Pew Re-*

search Center for People & the Press, July 1, 2013, available at http://www.people-press
.org/2013/07/01/public-divided-over-same-sex-marriage-rulings/. For more on this history of this issue in the U.S., see, for example, Michael Klarman, *From the Closet to
the Altar: Courts, Backlash, and the Struggle for Same-Sex Marriage* (New York: Oxford
University Press, 2013.

27. Ronald Brownstein, "Red, Divided and Blue Fly this Independence Day," *National Journal*, July 5, 2013.

28. "Gun Control: Key Data Points from Pew Research," *Pew Research Center*, July
27, 2013, available at http://www.pewresearch.org/key-data-points/gun-control-key-data
-points-from-pew-research/.

29. Lexington, "America's Gun Divide," *The Economist*, March 29, 2013.

30. "Partisans Divided About Level of U.S. Support for Israel," *Pew Research Center*, March 5, 2013, available at http://www.pewresearch.org/daily-number/partisans
-divided-about-level-of-u-s-support-for-israel/.

31. "'Borders First' a Dividing Line in Immigration Debate," *Pew Research Center for
People & the Press*, June 23, 2013, available at http://www.people-press.org/2013/06/23/
borders-first-a-dividing-line-in-immigration-debate/.

32. Drew DeSilver, "As Supreme Court Defers Affirmative Action Ruling, Deep Divides Persist," *Pew Research Center*, June 24, 2013, available at http://www.pewresearch
.org/fact-tank/2013/06/24/as-supreme-court-defers-affirmative-action-ruling-deep-
divides-persist/.

33. Bob Cohn, "The Divided States of America, in 25 Charts," *The Atlantic*, June 28, 2013.

Chapter 18. Interests

1. Quoted in Jeffrey M. Berry and Clyde Wilcox, *The Interest Group Society* (New
York: Pearson, 2007), p. 3.

2. Anthony J. Nownes, *Interest Groups in American Politics: Pressure and Power*
(New York: Routledge, 2013).

3. Nownes, *Interest Groups*, p. 90.

4. Berry and Wilcox, *Interest Group Society*, p. 6.

5. Allan J. Cigler and Burdett A. Loomis, eds., *Interest Group Politics* (Washington,
DC: CQ Press, 2007).

6. Nownes argues that the two main explanations for the proliferation of interest
groups are societal change (the point I make here) and also government growth. See
Interest Groups, pp. 33ff.

7. Nownes, *Interest Groups*, p. 24.

8. Frank R. Baumgartner, Jeffrey M. Berry, Marie Hojnacki, David C. Kimball, Beth
L. Leech, *Lobbying and Policy Change: Who Wins, Who Loses, and Why* (Chicago: University of Chicago Press, 2009), p. 111.

9. Adapted from Nownes, *Interest Groups*, p. 95.

10. Nownes, *Interest Groups*, p. 189.

11. Robert Kaiser writes, "Not surprisingly, a congressman or senator who first
made friends with his colleagues as a peer had a big advantage over mere mortals if he

returned to the House or Senate as a lobbyist trying to introduce his clients to important people and persuade those important people to pass legislative provisions for the
clients' benefit." In *So Damn Much Money: The Triumph of Lobbying and the Corrosion
of American Government* (New York: Knopf, 2009), p. 252.

12. Berry and Wilcox, *Interest Group Society*, p. 170.

13. Mark Leibovich, *This Town: Two Parties and a Funeral—Plus Plenty of Valet Parking!—in America's Gilded Capital* (New York: Blue Rider Press, 2013). Leibovich's book is
an excoriating, and witty, look at Washington's degraded money culture. The quote was
singled out by Christopher Buckley, in his review ("A Confederacy of Lunches") of Leibovich's book for *The New York Times Book Review*, July 28, 2013.

14. OpenSecrets.org Center for Responsive Politics, "Influence and Lobbying: Microsoft," n.d., available at https://www.opensecrets.org/orgs/summary.php?id=D000000115.

15. Todd Shields, Stephanie Green, and Laura Litvan, "Time Warner Cable Deal
Sets Comcast's D.C. Lobbying Machine in Motion," *BloombergBusinessweek*, March 6,
2014.

16. My discussion of the Citizens United case is based on various chapters in Paul
S. Herrnson, Chrisopher J. Deering, and Clyde Wilcox (eds.), *Interest Groups Unleashed*
(Thousand Oaks, CA: Sage, 2013).

17. Herrnson, Deering, and Wilcox, *Interest Groups Unleashed*, "Introduction," p. 2.

18. Michael M. Franz, "Past as Prologue: The Electoral Influence of Corporations"
in Herrnson, Deering, and Wilcox, *Interest Groups Unleashed*, p. 123. This paragraph and
the one before is based on Franz.

19. Edward Luce, *Time to Start Thinking: America in the Age of Descent* (New York:
Atlantic Monthly Press, 2012), p. 215.

20. Buckley, "A Confederacy of Lunches."

21. Luce, *Time to Start Thinking*, p. 222.

22. The following figure is somewhat dated, but still instructive. In 2007 customers
spent nearly $3 billion to lobby the federal government. But even then this was "a frac-
tion of the real amount spent to try to influence decisions in Congress and the executive
branch." Kaiser, *So Damn Much Money*, p. 340.

23. Nownes, *Interest Groups*, pp. 255, 256.

24. Kaiser, *So Damn Much Money*, p. 345.

Chapter 19. Environment

1. All this ominousness was underscored yet again in a 2014 report by the prestigious United Nations group the International Panel on Climate Change. See, for example, Justin Gillis, "Panel's Warning on Climate Risk: Worst Is Yet to Come," *New York
Times*, March 31, 2014.

2. John Dryzek, Richard Norgaard, and David Schlosberg (eds.), *Oxford Handbook
of Climate Change and Society* (New York: Oxford University Press, 2011), p. 3.

3. For the role, for example, of religious leaders in environmental issues, see Laurel
Kearns, "The Role of Religions in Activism," in Dryzek, Norgaard, and Schlosberg, *Oxford Handbook*, pp. 416ff.

4. The phrase is from Brian Stone Jr., *The City and the Coming Climate: Climate Change in Places We Live* (New York: Cambridge University Press, 2012).

5. Will Steffan, "A Truly Complex and Diabolical Policy Problem," in Dryzek, Norgaard, and Schlosberg, *Oxford Handbook*, p. 21.

6. Steffan, "Truly Complex," p. 22.

7. For more on this see Stewart Patrick, "The Unruled World: The Case of Good Enough Global Governance," *Foreign Affairs*, January-February, 2014.

8. Much of this paragraph was based on information contained in Steffan, "Truly Complex," pp. 22–32.

9. For a discussion geared to those who are interested in climate change but not specialists in it, see Andrew Guzman, *Overheated: The Human Costs of Climate Change* (New York; Oxford University Press, 2013), Chapter 2, pp. 19–53.

10. Bruce Drake, "Most Americans Believe Climate Change Is Real, but Fewer See It as a Threat," Pew Research Center, June 27, 2013, available at http://www.pewresearch .org/fact-tank/2013/06/27/most-americans-believe-climate-change-is-real-but-fewer-see-it-as-a-threat/.

11. This paragraph was based on Dale Jamieson, "The Nature of the Problem," and Riley Dunlap and Aaron McCright, "Organized Climate Change Denial," in Dryzek, Norgaard, and Schlosberg, *Oxford Handbook*, pp. 38 and 144, respectively.

12. Ryan Lizza, "The President and the Pipeline," *The New Yorker*, September 16, 2013.

13. This paragraph draws from Thomas Friedman and Michael Mandelbaum, *That Used to Be Us: How America Fell Behind in the World It Invented and How We Can Come Back* (New York: Farrar, Straus and Giroux, 2011), pp. 200–203.

14. Coral Davenport, "Political Rifts Slow U.S. Effort on Climate Laws," *New York Times*, April 15, 2014.

15. Stone, *The City and the Coming Climate*, p. 14.

16. Stone, *The City and the Coming Climate*, p. 160.

17. William Holt, "Bloomberg Unveils Initiative to Protect New York City from Climate Change," *Yahoo News*, June 11, 2013. The dollar estimate of damage incurred comes from a different source: Meg Crawford and Stephen Seidel, "Weathering the Storm: Building Business Resilience to Climate Change," Center for Climate and Energy Solutions, 2013, cited in the Foreword, p. v.

18. Center for Climate and Energy Solutions, "About the Center for the Environment and the Economy," n.d., available at http://www.c2es.org/about.

19. This paragraph is based on Crawford and Seidel, "Weathering the Storm." See both the Foreword, written by Eileen Claussen and Alexandra Liftman, and the Executive Summary.

20. Crawford and Seidel, "Weathering the Storm," p. x.

21. Coral Davenport, "Industry Awakens to Threat of Climate Change," *New York Times*, January 24, 2014.

22. For a specific recommendation, see, for example, Jerry Patchell and Roger Hayter, "How Big Business Can Save the Climate," *Foreign Affairs*, September/October 2013.

23. Dave Grossman (lead author), "GEO-5 for Business: Impacts of a Changing Environment on the Corporate Sector," United Nations Environment Programme, 2013.

24. David Gardiner & Associates, "Power Forward: Why the World's Largest Companies are Investing in Renewable Energy," Ceres, n.d., available at http://www.ceres .org/resources/reports/power-forward-why-the-world2019s-largest-companies-are- investing-in-renewable-energy.

25. See, for example, Andrew Winston, "The Era of Corporate Silence on Climate Policy Is Ending," *HBR Blog Network*, July 17, 2013, available at http://blogs.hbr.org/2013/07/ the-era-of-corporate-silence-0/; and Andrew Winston, "10 Sustainable Business Stories Too Important to Miss," *HBR Blog Network*, December 17, 2012, available at http://blogs. hbr.org/2013/12/2013-in-sustainability-the-year-business-got-off-the-sidelines/.

26. More information on the Clinton Climate Initiative is available on the Clinton Foundation website at http://www.clintonfoundation.org/our-work/clinton-climate -initiative.

27. Andrew Buzman, *Overheated: The Human Cost of Climate Change* (New York: Oxford University Press, 2013), p. 14.

28. Michael Levi, *The Power Surge: Energy, Opportunity, and the Battle for America's Future* (New York: Oxford University Press, 2013), p. 209.

29. William Nordhaus, *The Climate Casino: Risk, Uncertainty, and Economics for a Warming World* (New Haven, CT: Yale University Press, 2013).

30. Paul Krugman, "Gambling with Civilization," *New York Review*, November 7, 2013. Krugman's piece is a review of and discussion of Nordhaus's book.

Chapter 20. Risks

1. Nassim Taleb, Daniel Goldstein, and Mark Spitznagel, "The Six Mistakes Executives Make in Risk Management, *Harvard Business Review*, October 2009.

2. Justin Gillis, "By 2047, Coldest Years May Be Warmer Than Hottest in the Past, Scientists Say," *New York Times*, October 9, 2013.

3. Robert Kaplan and Anette Mikes, "Managing Risks: A New Framework," *Harvard Business Review*, June, 2012.

4. Though the events of 9/11 were a shock to the national system, in fact they were not a "bolt from the blue." For more on how risk associated with damage to the World Trade Center was widely dismissed as unlikely ever to be realized, see Scott Gabriel Knowles, *The Disaster Experts: Mastering Risk in Modern America* (Philadelphia: University of Pennsylania Press, 2011), pp. 6ff.

5. Knowles, *Disaster Experts*, pp. 165, 166.

6. Thomas Mockaitis, "Terrorism, Insurgency, and Organized Crime," in Paul Shemella (ed.), *Fighting Back: What Governments Can Do About Terrorism* (Stanford, CA: Stanford University Press, 2011), p. 17.

7. Thomas Coleman, *A Practical Guide to Risk Management* (New York: CFA Institute, 2011).

8. James Petroni, "Risk Assessment," in Shemella, *Fighting Back*, pp. 117ff.

9. Paul Shemella, "Tools and Strategies for Combating Terrorism," in Shemella, *Fighting Back*, p. 195.

10. See, for example, Kevin McGrath, *Confronting Al Quaeda: New Strategies to Combat Terrorism* (Annapolis, MD: Naval Institute Press, 2011).

11. John Seabrook, "Network Insecurity," *The New Yorker*, May 20, 2013.

12. Paul Rosenzweig, *Cyber Warfare: How Conflicts in Cyberspace Are Challenging America and Changing the World* (Santa Barbara, CA: Praeger, 2013), pp. 3, 4.

13. Ronald Daniels, Donald Kettl, and Howard Kunreuther, *On Risk and Disaster: Lessons from Hurricane Katrina* (Philadelphia: University of Pennsylvania Press, 2006), p. 1.

14. Daniels, Kettl, and Kunreuther, *On Risk and Disaster*, p. 5.

15. Ronald Daniels, Donald Kettl, Howard Kunreuther, "Introduction," in Daniels, Kettl, and Kunreuther, *On Risk and Disaster*, p. 8.

16. Robert Meyer, "Why We Under-Prepare for Hazards," in Daniels, Kettl, and Kunreuther, *On Risk and Disaster*, p. 169.

17. "A Nation of Hazards" is the title of Chapter 6 in Knowles, *Disaster Experts*.

18. Joseph Bower, Herman Leonard, and Lynn Paine, *Capitalism at Risk: Rethinking the Role of Business* (Boston: Harvard Business Review Press, 2011), p. 21.

19. For a brief, readable overview of Gordon's theory, see Benjamin Wallace-Wells, "The Blip," *Time*, July 29–August 5, 2013.

20. This paragraph draws on Raghuram Rajan, *Fault Lines: How Hidden Fractures Still Threaten the World Economy* (Princeton, NJ: Princeton University Press, 2011); see especially pp. 119 and 152.

21. Bower, Leonard, and Paine, *Capitalism at Risk*, p. 110.

22. James Barth, Gerard Caprio Jr., and Ross Levine, *Guardians of Finance: Making Regulators Work for Us* (Cambridge, MA: MIT Press, 2012). The term *guardians of finance* is from the book, and the quote is on p. 3.

23. Barth, Caprio, and Levine, *Guardians of Finance*, p. 3.

24. Barth, Caprio, and Levine, *Guardians of Finance*, p. 213.

25. Barth, Caprio, and Levine propose the idea of a "sentinel," an entirely new institution intended to "improve the system for selecting, interpreting, implementing, and adapting regulations" (*Guardians of Finance*, p. 215). It's an interesting idea—but it is not one that is likely to be realized in the short term.

26. See, for example, the thoughtful discussion in Rajan, *Fault Lines*, pp. 154ff.

27. Herman Leonard and Arnold Howitt, "Boston Marathon Bombing Response," *Crisis/Response*, Vol. 8, No. 4, available at http://www.hks.harvard.edu/var/ezp_site/storage/fckeditor/file/pdfs/centers-programs/programs/crisis-leadership/Leonard%20and%20Howitt_Boston%20Marathon%20Bombing%20Response%20CRJ%20Vol%208%20Issue%204%20June%202013.pdf.

28. Authors Torben Andersen and Peter Schroder put it well. They write, "The major risk management problems seem to arise when the environmental context evolves, and sometimes quite abruptly, in entirely new and unexpected directions, where the records of past events no longer serve as a viable basis for predictions about the future." *Strategic Risk Management Practice: How to Deal Effectively with Major Corporate Exposures* (New York: Cambridge University Press, 2010), pp. 225, 226.

Chapter 21. Trends

1. Mary Parker Follett, "The Essentials of Leadership," in Barbara Kellerman, *Leadership: Essential Selections on Power, Authority, and Influence* (New York: McGraw-Hill, 2010). "The Essentials of Leadership" was written in 1933.

2. *Global Trends 2030: Alternative Worlds*, is, as indicated in the text, a publication of the National Intelligence Council. It was released in December 2012. The quotes are on p. i.

3. These quotes are from the introduction to *Global Trends 2030*, which was written by Christopher Kojm.

4. Barbara Kellerman, *The End of Leadership* (New York: HarperCollins, 2012). I discuss at length leaders getting weaker and followers, in many ways, getting stronger.

5. All quotes in this paragraph and the one immediately above are from *Global Trends 2030*, pp. iii–xi.

6. Daniel Franklin with John Andrews (eds.), *Megachange: The World in 2050* (Hoboken, NJ: John Wiley & Sons, 2012), p. xi.

7. Franklin and Andrews, *Megachange*, p. 264.

8. James Surowiecki, "Punditonomics," *The New Yorker*, April 7, 2014.

9. Paul Taylor, *The Next America: Boomers, Millennials, and the Looming Generational Showdown* (New York: Public Affairs, 2014). Taylor's book is a repository of information on where Americans recently were, and where they are likely to be next. Note that although statistics on trends might differ slightly from one source to the next, the projected trajectories are virtually always the same.

10. Laura Shrestha and Elayne Heisler, *The Changing Demographic Profile of the United States*, Congressional Research Service, 2011, p. 18.

11. Cheryl Russell, *Demographics of the U.S.: Trends and Projections* (Amityville, NY: New Strategist, 2012), p. 165.

12. Linda Jacobsen and others, "America's Aging Population," *Population Reference Bureau*, Vol. 66, No. 1. 2011.

13. Shrestha and Heisler, *Changing Demographic Profile*, p. 25.

14. Shrestha and Heisler, *Changing Demographic Profile*, pp. 18ff.

15. Kay Hymowitz and others, "The New Unmarried Moms," *Wall Street Journal*, March 16–17, 2013.

16. Lauren Sandler, "None Is Enough," *Time*, August 12, 2013. "A Pew Research report showed that childlessness has risen across all racial and ethnic groups, adding up to about 1 in 5 American women who end their childbearing years maternity-free, compared with 1 in 10 in the 1970s." The quote is from Jonathan Last, "America's Baby Bust," *Wall Street Journal*, February 2–3, 2013.

17. Annie Lowrey, "Inertia Nation," *New York Times Magazine*, December 15, 2013.

18. Catherine Rampell, "U.S. Women on the Rise as Family Breadwinner," *New York Times*, May 29, 2013.

19. The information in this section is from Russell, *Demographics*, passim, unless otherwise noted.

20. Andrew Cherlin, quoted in Natalie Angier, "Families," *New York Times*, November 26, 2013.

21. Uri Dadush, Kemal Dervis, Sarah P. Milsom, and Bennett Stancil, *Inequality in America: Facts, Trends, and International Perspectives* (Washington, DC: Brookings Institution Press, 2012), p. 15.

22. Dadush, Dervis, Milsom, and Stancil, *Inequality in America*, pp. 25–38.

23. The quote in this paragraph is from, and the paragraph more generally is based on, Jerry Z. Muller, "Capitalism and Inequality: What the Right and the Left Get Wrong," *Foreign Affairs*, March/April 2013, p. 38. See also Mark Peters and David Wessel, "More Men in Their Prime Are Out of Work and at Home," *Wall Street Journal*, February 6, 2014.

24. The quotes in this paragraph and the information it contains are from Jason DeParle, "Two Classes, Divided by 'I Do,'" *New York Times*, July 14, 2012. Also see Binyamin Applebaum, "As Men Lose Economic Ground, Clues Are Seen in Changing Families," *New York Times*, March 21, 2013.

25. Amelia Granger, "When You Haven't Saved Enough for Retirement," *Huffington Post*, May 18, 2013; and Rodney Brooks, "Haven't Saved Enough for Retirement? What to Do?" *USA Today*, July 1, 2013.

26. The quote is from Ezra Klein. It and the information in this paragraph are from Fareed Zakaria, "Can America Be Fixed? The New Crisis of Democracy," *Foreign Affairs*, January/February 2013, p. 31.

27. Eric Schmidt and Jared Cohen, *The New Digital Age: Reshaping the Future of People, Nations and Business* (New York: Knopf, 2013), p. 8.

28. Deloitte Consulting, *2013 Technology Trends*, n.d., Executive Summary, "At a Glance."

29. Meghan Biro, "5 Trends Defining the World of Work and Leadership in 2013," *Forbes*, December 16, 2012.

30. Schmidt and Cohen, *New Digital Age*, pp. 253ff.

31. Jared Lanier, *Who Owns the Future?* (New York: Simon & Schuster, 2013). For a synopsis of Lanier's argument, see Joe Nocera, "Will Digital Networks Ruin Us?" *New York Times*, January 7, 2014.

32. Quoted in Thomas Friedman, "It's P.Q. and C.Q. as Much as I.Q.," *New York Times*, January 30, 2013. For more on Brynjolfsson's argument, see his book with Andrew McAfee, *Race Against the Machine: How the Digital Revolution Is Accelerating Innovation, Driving Productivity, and Irreversibly Transforming Employment and the Economy* (n.c.: Digital Frontier Press, 2012). Essentially, they argue that not only are advances in technology not opening up employment opportunities, they are encroaching on skills that used to belong to humans alone.

33. Mark Chaves, *American Religion: Contemporary Trends* (Princeton, NJ: Princeton University Press, 2011), p. 26.

34. Chaves, *American Religion*, p. 92.

35. Peter Marsden (ed.), *Social Trends in American Life: Findings from the General Social Survey Since 1972* (Princeton, NJ: Princeton University Press, 2012), p. 13.

36. Jeff Manza and others, "Public Opinion in the 'Age of Reagan'—Political Trends 1972–2006," in Marsden, *Social Trends in American Life*, p. 138.

37. Sheryl Gay Stolberg, "A Growing Trend: Young, Liberal and Open to Big Government," *New York Times*, February 11, 2013.

38. Tom Smith, "Trends in Confidence in Institutions, 1973–2006," in Marsden, *Social Trends in American Life*, pp. 177ff.

39. Arne Kalleberg and Peter Marsden, "Labor Force Insecurity and U.S. Work Attitudes, 1970s–2006," in Marsden, *Social Trends in American Life*, pp. 315ff.

40. "The US 20: Twenty Big Trends That Will Dominate America's Future," available at http://www.businessinsider.com/the-us-20-2012.

41. Laurie Garrett, "Biology's Brave New World: The Promise and Perils of the Synbio Revolution," *Foreign Affairs*, November/December 2013.

42. "The Biggest Trends in Business for 2013," available at www.entrepreneur.com/article/printthis/224977.html.

43. Al Gore, *The Future: Six Drivers of Global Change* (New York: Random House, 2013), p. xiv.

44. Alan Greenspan, "Never Saw It Coming: Why the Financial Crisis Took Economists by Surprise," *Foreign Affairs*, November/December, 2013, available at http://www.foreignaffairs.com/articles/140161/alan-greenspan/never-saw-it-coming.

45. Jeff Goodell, "Gore's Grim Prophesy," *Rolling Stone*, February 28, 2013.

Chapter 22. Leaders

1. Barbara Kellerman, *The End of Leadership* (New York: HarperCollins, 2012), p. 3.

2. Moises Naim, *The End of Power: From Boardrooms to Battlefields and Churches to States, Why Being in Charge Isn't What It Used to Be* (New York: Basic Books, 2013), p. 1.

3. Ian Bremmer, "Lost Legitimacy: Why Governing Is Harder Than Ever," *Foreign Affairs*, November 18, 2013.

4. Quoted by Carne Ross in *The Leaderless Revolution: How Ordinary People Will Take Power and Change Politics in the Twenty-First Century* (New York: Penguin, 2011), p. 7.

5. Joseph Nye, *The Future of Power* (New York: Public Affairs, 2011), p. 116.

6. Grady McGonagill and Tina Doerffer, *Leadership and Web 2.0: The Leadership Implications of the Evolving Web* (Brussels: Bertelsmann Stiftung, 2011). This paragraph is based in part on Chapter 3.

7. Paul Taylor, "Relationships in the C-Suite Set to Change," *Financial Times*, November 7, 2012.

8. Joseph Nye, *Presidential Leadership and the Creation of the American Era* (Princeton, NJ: Princeton University Press, 2013), p. 152.

9. "The Satirical Verses," *The Economist*, August 31, 2013.

10. Thane Rosenbaum, "Stuyvesant's Stanley Teitel Resigns?", *Huffington Post*, August 6, 2012. The "dark day" quote just below is also from Rosenbaum.

11. Al Baker, "Stuyvesant Principal, Now Retired, Mishandled Cheating Case, Report Says," *New York Times*, August 31, 2012.

12. Gregory Zuckerman, "Top Executives Scored Big in '13 Rally," *Wall Street Journal*, January 4, 2014.

13. Floyd Norris, "The Perils When Megabanks Lose Focus," *New York Times*, September 6. 2013.

14. Monica Langley and Dan Fitzpatrick, "Embattled J.P. Morgan Bulks Up Oversight," *Wall Street Journal*, September 12, 2013.

15. Dan Fitzpatrick, "J.P. Morgan Settles Its Madoff Tab," *Wall Street Journal*, January 8, 2014.

16. Dan Fitzpatrick and Joann Lublin, "J.P. Morgan Juices Up Director's Job," *Wall Street Journal*, September 10, 2013.

17. The quotes in this paragraph are from Aaron Lucchetti and Julie Steinberg, "Life on Wall Street Grows Less Risky," *Wall Street Journal*, September 10, 2013.

18. Susanne Craig and Jessica Silver-Greenberg, "Quiet Boss at Citigroup Setting Tone for Wall Street," *New York Times*, December 2, 2013.

19. Scott Thurm, "CEO Pay More Closely Matches Firms' Results," *Wall Street Journal*, September 12, 2013.

20. David Streitfeld, "Still No. 1, and Doing What He Wants," *New York Times*, April 13, 2014.

21. Marketwired, "Booz & Company Chief Executive Study Finds Steep Rise in Planned CEO Turnovers as Companies Take Active Control of Their CEO Succession Planning," April 16, 2013, available at http://www.marketwired.com/press-release/booz -company-chief-executive-study-finds-steep-rise-planned-ceo-turnovers-as-companies -1779057.htm.

22. Joann Lublin, Ted Mann, Kate Linebaugh, "GE Rethinking the 20-Year Chief," *Wall Street Journal*, April 15, 2014.

23. Strategy&, "The Heat Is (Back) On: CEO Turnover Rate Rises to Pre-Recession Levels, Finds Booz & Company Annual Global CEO Succession Study," May, 24, 2012, available at http://www.strategyand.pwc.com/global/home/press/article/50560531.

24. For a detailed accounting of what happened, see Monica Langley, "Impatient Board Speeds Ballmer's Exit, *Wall Street Journal*, November 16–17, 2013.

25. Joseph Perella and Peter Weinberg, "Powerful, Disruptive Shareholders," *New York Times*, April 9, 2014.

26. David Benoit, "Companies, Activists Declare Truce in Boardroom Battles," *Wall Street Journal*, December 10, 2013.

27. Michael Genovese, draft copy of *Building Tomorrow's Leaders Today: On Becoming a Polymath Leader* (New York: Routledge, 2013).

28. In *The End of Leadership*, I define *power* as A's capacity to get B to do whatever A wants, whatever B's preference. And I define *authority* as A's capacity to get B to do whatever A wants, on the basis of A's position, or status, or rank. And I define *influence* as A's capacity to get B to go along with what A wants and intends, of B's own volition. See p. xxvi.

29. For a brief summary of this argument, see Schumpeter, "Montessori Management," *The Economist*, September 7, 2013.

30. The quotes in this paragraph are from Jon Hilsenrath, "Next Fed Chief's Big Test: Quelling the Dissent," *Wall Street Journal*, August 19, 2013.

31. This paragraph is based on Christine Haughney and Michael Shear, "Bezos Is a Hit in a *Washington Post* Newsroom Visit," *New York Times*, September 5, 2013.

Chapter 23. Followers

1. Michael Specter, "The Operator," *The New Yorker*, February 4, 2013.

2. Fights for the rights of animals have been exceedingly important since the mid-1970s. While the fight is far from over, the animal rights movement, a follower movement if ever there was one, has made enormous strides in recent years. To take just a single example, the Nonhuman Rights Project is trying to use the law to gain rights for chimpanzees in captivity. To this end it has filed a classic writ of habeas corpus, in particular for Tommy, a chimp in Gloversville, New York.

3. Statement released by Metropolitan Opera general manager Peter Gelb on September 22, 2013.

4. Janet Hook, "Town-Hall Dramas Use Activists' Scripts," *Wall Street Journal*, August 21, 2013.

5. Jennifer Medina, "Los Angeles Frets After Low Turnout to Elect Mayor," *New York Times*, March 9, 2013.

6. George Packer, "Mixed Results," *The New Yorker*, November 18, 2013.

7. There is a large political science literature on the vanishing or disappearing voter, and also on the reasons why. For a brief but solid synopsis of this complicated issue, see Luca Ferrini, "Why Is Turnout at Elections Declining Across the World?" E-International Relations Students, September 27, 2012, available at http://www.e-ir.info/2012/09/27/why-is-turnout-at-elections-declining-across-the-democratic-world.

8. For an excellent discussion of the big impact of low voter turnout in midterm elections, see Elizabeth Drew, "The Stranglehold on Our Politics," *New York Review*, September 26, 2013.

9. Jill Treanor, "JP Morgan Chase Hires 3,000 New Staff in Its Compliance Department," *The Guardian*, September 17, 2013.

10. Gretchen Morgenson, "Why Judges Are Scowling at Banks," *New York Times*, September 29, 2013.

11. The figures in this sentence and the one immediately preceding are from Moises Naim, *The End of Power: From Boardrooms to Battlefields and Churches to States, Why Being in Charge Isn't What It Used to Be* (New York: Basic Books, 2013), p. 163.

12. Alex Khutorsky, quoted in Emily Chasan and Maxwell Murphy, "Activist Investors Go Big," *Wall Street Journal*, October 1, 2013.

13. Alexandra Stevenson, "An Art-Collecting Investor Is Pressing for a Shake-Up at Sotheby's," *New York Times*, October 3, 2013.

14. Alexandra Stevenson and Michael J. de la Merced, "Pressured by Investors, Sotheby's Takes Steps," *New York Times*, January 29, 2014.

15. Max Boot, "The Guerrilla Myth," *Wall Street Journal*, January 19–20, 2013. For elaboration of Boot's argument, see his book *Invisible Armies: An Epic History of Guerilla Warfare from Ancient Times to the Present* (New York: Liveright, 2013).

16. Tim Kane, *Bleeding Talent: How the U.S. Military Mismanages Great Leaders and Why It's Time for a Revolution (New York:* Palgrave Macmillan, 2012). The quote is taken from a review of the book by Fred Andrews, "The Military Machine as a Management Wreck," *New York Times,* January 6, 2013.

17. The "grossly unprepared" quote is from a review of Thomas Ricks's book by Dexter Filkins, "General Principles," *The New Yorker,* December 17, 2012. The Ricks quote is on page 446 of his book *The Generals: American Military Command from World War II to Today* (New York: Penguin, 2012).

18. The two men who were forced into retirement were Maj. Gen. Charles M. Gurganus and Maj. Gen. Gregg Sturdevant. See, for example, David Cloud, "2 Marine Generals Told to Retire Over Breach of Base in Afghanistan," *Los Angeles Times,* September 30, 2013.

19. James Surowiecki, "Twilight of the Brands," *The New Yorker,* February 17 and 24, 2014.

20. Greenwald is quoted in Roger Cohen, "A Journalist with a Mission," *New York Times,* November 1, 2013.

21. This set of numbers is from Gerald Seib, "The People's Choice: Distrust," *Wall Street Journal,* June 20–21, 2013.

22. Steven Greenhouse, "Advocates for Workers Raise the Ire of Business," *New York Times,* January 17, 2013.

23. For an excellent short comment on this, see Sam Tanenhaus, "The Benefits of Intransigence," *New York Times,* October 6, 2013.

Chapter 24. Outsiders

1. Michael Mandelbaum, *The Case for Goliath: How America Acts as the World's Government in the Twenty-First Century* (New York: Public Affairs, 2005), p. xv.

2. "Public Sees U.S. Power Declining as Support for Global Engagement Slips," Pew Research Center for People & the Press, December 3, 2013.

3. David Brooks, "The Leaderless Doctrine," *New York Times,* March 11, 2014.

4. Nicholas Kristof, "We're Not No. 1! We're Not #1!" *New York Times,* April 3, 2014. The ranking to which Kristof refers is the Social Progress Index, which was spearheaded by Michael Porter.

5. The phrase, "the rise of the rest," is Fareed Zakaria's. See *The Post-American World: Release 2.0* (New York: Norton, 2011), p. 2 and passim.

6. John Ikenberry, *Liberal Leviathan: The Origins, Crisis, and Transformation of the American World Order* (Princeton, NJ: Princeton University Press, 2011), p. 3.

7. I have described Mohamed Atta as a "Diehard" follower. For more on this, see *Followership: How Followers Are Creating Change and Changing Leaders* (Boston: Harvard Business School Press, 2008), Chapter 8.

8. Zbigniew Brzezinski, *Second Chance: Three Presidents and the Crisis of American Superpower* (New York: Basic Books, 2007), p. 133.

9. Brzezinski, *Second Chance,* p. 185.

10. Our opinions of Bush do, however, grow less harsh with time. As has been the case with other American presidents, we tend to become less critical of them as they recede into history.

11. James Mann, quoted in Andrew Bacevich, *The New American Militarism: How Americans Are Seduced by War* (New York: Oxford University Press, 2005), p. 203.

12. Zakaria, *Post-American World*, p. 249.

13. *The Economist*, "Look Back with Angst," December 21, 2013.

14. For a harsh but reasoned critique of American foreign policy during President Obama's first term, see Vali Nasr, *The Dispensable Nation: American Foreign Policy in Retreat* (New York: Doubleday, 2013). For a more sympathetic commentary on Obama as foreign policy leader, see "America's Foreign Policy: Special Report," *The Economist*, November 23, 2013.

15. Richard Haass, *Foreign Policy Begins at Home: The Case for Putting America's House in Order* (New York: Basic Books, 2013), p. 15.

16. This paragraph and the one immediately preceding are based on Haass, *Foreign Policy Begins at Home*, pp. 15, 16. Also see Zakaria, *Post-American World*, p. 5ff.

17. Joseph Nye, *The Future of Power* (New York: Public Affairs, 2011), p. 132.

18. Nye, *Future of Power*, p. 121.

19. These coincide in part with Zakaria, *Post-American World*, p. 22.

20. The quote is from Zbigniew Brezinski. It is in my book *The End of Leadership* (New York: HarperCollins, 2012), in which I discuss the impact of the collapse of communism on the changing dynamics between leaders and followers (pp. 19ff.).

21. Freedom House, "Freedom in the World 2014," n.d., available at http://freedomhouse .org/report/freedom-world/freedom-world-2014#.U1F4cfldX7w.

22. Brooks, "The Leaderless Doctrine."

23. Zakaria, *Post-American World*, p. 27.

24. Haass, *Foreign Policy Begins at Home*, p. 53.

25. Mandelbaum is quoted by Tod Linberg in "An Elite Guide to Globalizaton," *Wall Street Journal*, April 3, 2014. Linberg's piece is a review of Mandelbaum's book *The Road to Global Prosperity* (New York: Simon & Schuster, 2014).

26. For more on "the decaying power of large armies," see Moises Naim, *The End of Power: From Boardrooms to Battlefields and Churches to States, Why Being in Charge Isn't What It Used to Be* (New York: Basic Books, 2013), pp. 107ff.

27. Kellerman, *The End of Leadership*, pp. 25ff.

28. Ikenberry, *Liberal Leviathan*, p. 10.

29. Zbigniew Brzezinski, quoted in Naim, *End of Power*, p. 131.

30. Naim, *End of Power*, p. 131.

31. Stewart Patrick, "The Unruled World: The Case for Good Enough Global Governance," *Foreign Affairs*, January-February 2014. The word *floundering* is on page 67.

Epilogue

1. Carl Hulse, "Boehner's Jabs at Activist Right Show G.O.P. Shift," *New York Times*, December 14, 2013.

2. Again, while some number of leadership theorists look at proximate context, very few look at distal context. In fact, overwhelmingly the leadership literature ignores distal

context altogether, as if it were either irrelevant or unimportant. Two exceptions to this general rule are two political scientists (maybe no accident), Archie Brown and Joseph Nye. See Brown's *The Myth of the Strong Leader: Political Leadership in the Modern Age* (New York: Basic Books, 2014), especially Chapter 1, "Putting Leaders in Context." Also see Nye's *The Future of Power* (New York: Public Affairs, 2011), especially pp. xviiff.

3. This paragraph is based on, and the quotes are taken from, Steven Teles, "Kludgeocracy in America," *National Affairs*, No. 17, Fall 2013.

4. David Leonhardt and Kevin Quealy "The American Middle Class Is No Longer the World's Richest," *New York Times*, April 22, 2014.

5. Leonhardt and Quealy, "The American Middle Class."

6. George Packer, *The Unwinding: An Inner History of the New America* (New York: Farrar, Straus and Giroux, 2013), p. 3.

7. The term *control culture* is Phillip Slater's. See his book *The Chrysalis Effect: The Metamorphosis of Global Culture* (Eastbourne, UK: Sussex, 2008).

8. To repeat a point I made elsewhere, the only way to stamp out this push toward individual independence is to suppress it, to oppress it.

9. All quotes in this paragraph and the one preceding are from Joseph Epstein, "The Late, Great American WASP," *Wall Street Journal*, December 21–22, 2013.

10. Epstein, "The Late, Great American WASP."

11. Quoted in R. S. Traub, "Managing Complexity—Invitation to Join the Conversation," *Drucker Society Europe Blog*, February 28, 2013.

12. All quotes in this paragraph are from Sidney Finkelstein, Donald Hambrick, and Albert Cannella Jr. *Strategic Leadership: Theory and Research on Executives, Top Management Teams, and Boards* (New York: Oxford University Press, 2009), pp. 16, 20, and 27.

13. See, for example, Bruce Katz and Jennifer Bradley, *The Metropolitan Revolution: How Cities and Metros Are Fixing Our Broken Politics and Fragile Economy* (Washington, DC: Brookings Institution Press, 2013). The book describes how in some cases local and state leaders are successfully tackling problems that Washington will not, or cannot, seem to solve.

14. I have been critical of the leadership industry, especially in *The End of Leadership* (New York: HarperCollins, 2012). For a recent article that, like me, takes the industry to task for not generally evaluating its offerings, see Robert Kaiser and Gordy Curphy, "Leadership Development: The Failure of an Industry and the Opportunity for Consulting Psychologists," *Consulting Psychology Journal: Practice and Research*, American Psychological Association, 2013.

15. See, for example, Boris Groysberg and Michael Slind, *Talk, Inc.: How Trusted Leaders Use Conversation to Power Their Organizations* (Boston: Harvard Business Review Press, 2012). They describe a "new source of organizational power," which they call "organizational conversation" (page 2).

16. Tina Rosenberg, *Join the Club: How Peer Pressure Can Transform the World* (New York: Norton, 2011), p. 349. Rosenberg refers to this sort of people power as the "social cure."

17. This seems to be changing, albeit slowly. A conference held in Vienna in 2013, in fact to honor Drucker's work, focused on how managing complexity was now the corporate leader's single most important task. See Schumpeter, "It's Complicated," *The Economist*, November 23, 2013.

18. I am impressed by the argument that Thomas Patterson makes on behalf of "knowledge-based journalism." His claim is blissfully simple: journalists who know more about the subjects they cover will be, surprise, better journalists. See *Informing the News: The Need for Knowledge-Based Journalism* (New York: Vintage, 2013).

INDEX

A&E network, 272
AARP, 210–11
Abortion, 199, 202, 207
ADA, *see* Americans with Disabilities Act
Adelson, Sheldon, 151
Advocacy groups, 186, 212–14. *See also* Interest groups; Lobbying
Affirmative action, 208
Affordable Care Act, *see* Patient Protection and Affordable Care Act
Afghanistan war, 139, 278–79, 285
African Americans: affirmative action opinions, 208; churches, 41, 43; civil rights movement, 21, 42–43, 94, 131, 197; incomes, 204, 336n15; inequality, 271; lynchings, 196; poor, 183; protest songs, 196–97; slavery, 14–15, 19–20, 22, 25; wealth, 181. *See also* Racial groups
Aging of Americans, 247. *See also* Generations; Retirement savings; Social Security
Allen, John, 278
Al Qaeda, 53
Amazon, 124, 131, 263
American Airlines, 194–95
American Creed, 29–30, 302. *See also* Ideology
American Dream, 76, 78, 183–84, 186, 248–49
American Revolution, 13–15, 16, 24, 26, 29, 39
Americans for Prosperity, 142–43
Americans with Disabilities Act (ADA), 8, 94, 97–98
Animals: pets, 194; rights, 21, 272, 346n2

Anonymous, 123, 140
Apple Computer, 124, 134
Armour, Phillip, 178
Art market, 153
Assange, Julian, 102, 123, 138–39, 289–90
Atta, Mohamed, 286, 347n7
Auburn University, 147
Authority: anti-authority attitudes, 17–18, 22, 54, 79; challenging, 188, 189; decline, 257–68, 273–74, 291, 292, 301; definition, 345n28; loss of respect for, 188–89, 190, 261–62, 271, 292; of political leaders, 23, 92, 273–74, 291; of presidents, 260; rational-legal, 84–85, 88, 91; tension with individual liberty, 191–93, 198; types, 84. *See also* Influence; Power
Autocracies, 267

Bacon, Nathaniel, 14
Bacon's Rebellion, 14
Bailyn, Bernard, *The Ideological Origins of the American Revolution*, 26
Ballmer, Steve, 266, 277
Bank of America, 276
Banks, *see* Financial sector
Beckstrom, Rod, 89–90
Bernanke, Ben, 71, 268
Bernstein, Carl, 134
Berry, Jeffrey M., 214
Bezos, Jeff, 124, 131, 263, 268–69
Bharara, Preet, 101
Bible, 42. *See also* Religion
Biden, Joe, 73
Big data, 122–23, 124
Bin Laden, Osama, 286

Biondi, Lawrence, 272

Birth rates, 247, 249, 342n16

BlackRock, 102

Black swan events, 234, 243, 245

Blanchard, Ken, 34

Blinder, Alan, 69–70

Bloggers, 135–36, 140

Bloomberg, Michael, 50, 228–29

Boards of directors, corporate, 87, 112, 205, 264, 266, 281

Boehner, John, 4–5, 138, 295–96

Boot, Max, 278

Booz & Company, 265

Boston Consulting Group, 155

Boston Marathon bombing, 243

Boston Tea Party, 14

Boyd, Drew, 159

Brafman, Ori, 89–90

Brat, Dave, 150, 274

Braunstein, Douglas, 102

Bremmer, Ian, 258

Britain: abolition of slavery, 22; American colonies, 13, 14–15, 17, 39; industrialization, 63; voter turnouts, 275

Brookings Institution, 156, 183

Brooks, David, 59, 291

Brynjolfsson, Erik, 125, 251

Brzezinski, Zbigniew, 286

Buffett, Warren, 63

Bureaucracies, 85, 93, 149. *See also* Organizations

Burns, James McGregor, 178

Bush, George H. W., 227, 303

Bush, George W., 70, 132, 139, 143, 286–87

Businesses: activist investors, 266, 277–78; boards of directors, 87, 112, 205, 264, 266, 281; capital, 106; communication with customers, 139–40; competition, 164–67; complex, 115; compliance officers, 96–98, 101; corporate culture, 33; corporate governance, 87, 111, 112; data breaches, 189–90; energy supplies, 229, 231; failures, 108; government and, 107–8, 109–10, 242–43; information collected, 123, 124; innovation, 158–62; large, 106, 115; lawyers, 95; lobbying, 214–15, 216, 218; multinational, 289; political spend-ing, 150, 214–15, 338n22; role in America, 105–8. *See also* Employees; Organizations

Business leaders: advice for, 166; challenges, 113, 115, 263–66, 273, 275–77; climate change and, 225, 229–32; constraints, 23, 111–13, 275–77; corruption and fraud, 108, 109, 134; in early twentieth century, 64; effectiveness, 304–5; financial crisis and, 70, 71, 72, 108–9; in financial sector, 100, 102, 103–4, 110, 111, 263–65, 276; fired, 112, 265, 277; followers, 30–34, 86–87, 114–15, 305; genders, 45, 205; global competitive-ness and, 169; influence exercised, 305; innovation pressures, 158–59, 160–61, 162; Internet millionaires, 124, 131, 263; law and, 96–98, 99–104; mistakes, 234; new media and, 139–40; politics and, 115, 324n36; power, 87, 90, 106, 110–12, 113–15, 263, 264, 265; public views of, 92, 108–9, 110–11, 112; religious affiliations, 44–45; shareholder criticism, 277–78; teams, 90–92; technological change and, 119–22, 127, 129, 259, 260; training and development, 114, 305; trust in, 108–9; unbalanced lives, 194–95. *See also* Chief Executive Officers; Management

Business leadership: command and control style, 30–31, 32, 84, 106; compared to political leadership, 30–31, 33, 34; com-plex contexts, 115, 305; democratic, 34, 267; organizational theory, 86–88; soci-ety and, 105, 106, 115; stakeholders and, 33, 87, 113, 230, 265, 266, 277–78. *See also* Organizations

C2ES, *see* Center for Climate and Energy Solutions

California: inequality, 206; wildfires, 240–41

Campbell, David E., 47

Cantor, Eric, 150, 274

Cantor, Paul, 191, 192

Capitalism: alternative systems, 171; com-plexity, 71, 72; definition, 63; democracy and, 73; government regulations, 179, 180; history in United States, 63–69, 105–7, 179; industrial, 105–7; inequality in, 63, 64–65, 67–68, 153, 201; property rights, 62–63, 107; Protestant values and, 63; risks, 241; spread, 291–92. *See also* Economic system

Carnegie, Andrew, 178

Carson, Johnny, 262

Carson, Rachel, *Silent Spring*, 223

Carter, Jimmy, 52, 195, 227

Castells, Manuel, 128

Caste system, *see* Class

Catholic Church, 47, 48, 53–54, 179, 278, 311n6. *See also* Christianity

Cavanagh, Michael, 264

CCI, *see* Clinton Climate Initiative

Census Bureau, U.S., 182

Center for Climate and Energy Solutions (C2ES), 229, 230

Center for Economic Opportunity (CEO), New York City, 157

Center for Public Leadership, 76, 141

CEO, *see* Center for Economic Opportunity

CEOs, *see* Chief Executive Officers

Change, *see* Context; Cultural change; Technological change

Charter schools, 145

Checklists, 1, 6–9, 10, 305–6

Cherlin, Andrew, 249

Chesapeake Energy, 111

Chief Executive Officers (CEOs): challenges, 111–13, 166; direct reports, 88–89, 91; mistakes, 109; power, 87, 110, 114–15, 263, 264; turnover, 265, 277. *See also* Business leaders

Chief Executive Officers (CEOs), compensation: clawbacks, 103; compared to employees, 67, 152; disclosure, 276; high levels, 109, 110, 114, 152, 201, 263, 265, 277; linked to performance, 265; median, 201; public scrutiny, 265; shareholder criticism, 277

Chief information officers (CIOs), 129, 251, 260

Children: birth rates, 247, 249, 342n16; costs of raising, 249; poor, 109, 183, 249. *See also* Education

China: carbon dioxide emissions, 225; competition with, 170–71; cyber espionage, 128; economic growth, 170; innovation,

155, 171; Internet controls, 136; manufacturing, 134; political leaders, 171

Christensen, Clayton, 159–61

Christian Coalition, 213–14

Christianity: Catholic Church, 47, 48, 53–54, 179, 278, 311n6; civil rights movement and, 42–43; Evangelical, 41, 252; liberal, 252; in United States, 40. *See also* Protestants; Religion

Christie, Chris, 102

Churchill, Winston, 16–17

CIOs, *see* Chief information officers

Cisco, 122

Cities: climate change impact, 228–29; compared to rural areas, 206; economic growth, 206; income inequality, 205–6; innovation in, 157; poverty, 178; tenements, 178; voter turnouts, 274

Citigroup, 103, 162, 265

Citizens United v. Federal Election Commission, 150–51, 215

Civic culture, 275

Civic participation, 185–86, 194, 275, 302

Civil rights movement, 21, 42–43, 94, 131, 197. *See also* King, Martin Luther, Jr.

Civil War, 19–20, 42

Class: conflicts, 179; as context for leadership, 181–86; definition, 177; of founders, 18; hierarchies, 17, 64–65; mobility, 179, 184, 200–201, 205–6, 249; politics and, 185–86; upper, 64, 177–78, 181, 182, 183, 184, 186, 201; White Anglo-Saxon Protestants (WASPs), 303; working classes, 178–79, 180–81, 182, 183. *See also* Inequality; Middle class

Climate change: addressing, 224–25, 227–28, 231; business leaders and, 225, 229–32; complexity, 224, 225; politicization, 225–28, 231–32; potential impact, 223, 228–29, 235, 245; public opinion on, 226; risks, 55, 224, 228–29, 230–31, 232

Clinton, Bill, 55, 152, 190–91, 231, 286

Clinton, Hillary, 132, 137, 281

Clinton Climate Initiative (CCI), 231

Coaches, 262

Coca-Cola, 162, 231

Cohen, Jared, 250, 251

Cold War, 237, 288; end of, 283–84, 290–91

Collaboration, *see* Teams

Colonial America, 13, 14–15, 17, 39. *See also* American Revolution

Comcast, 131, 215

Commerce Department, U.S., 156

Communism, 179, 290–91

Compensation, *see* Chief Executive Officers, compensation; Incomes; Wages

Competition: in business, 164–67; context, 163–64, 165, 166–73; in education, 171–72; global, 79, 154, 155, 163–64, 166–73, 284, 285; of ideas, 171; strategic analysis, 164–65

"Competitiveness at a Crossroads," 168–69

Complexity: business leadership and, 115, 305; contextual, 91, 296–98; of federal government, 297; of financial sector, 69–70; of health insurance, 297; of problems, 59–60, 67–71, 72, 73; risks and, 234; of systems, 296; technological, 121–23, 251, 298

Compliance officers, 96–98, 101

Congress: business regulation, 107; comity, 57; criticism of, 80; elections, 71, 218, 275; extremists and, 56–58; female members, 205; financial crisis and, 70–71; former members as lobbyists, 152; hearings, 102; House of Representatives, 4–5, 71, 295–96; lobbyists and, 152, 212–19; polarization, 68, 79–80; public views of, 51, 78, 274, 281; re-elections of incumbents, 218; Senate, 57–58; wealth of members, 150

Congressional Budget Office, 73

Conservatives: billionaires, 142–43; gun control policies, 207–8; increased number, 252; polarization, 68, 79–80; religious beliefs, 41, 47; in Republican Party, 41, 202, 295; views of government roles, 56, 109–10, 202–3, 252–53. *See also* Tea Party

Constitution, U.S., 15–16, 26–27, 30, 93

Constitutional Convention, 16

Consumers: online product reviews, 279–80; preferences, 190; spending on positional goods, 248

Context: change in, 259–62, 266–67, 273–74, 304; checklist, 1, 10; of competition, 163–64, 165, 166–73; complexity, 91, 296–98; contemporary, 9–10; distal, 1, 4, 296; economic, 72–73; human agency and, 288; legal, 7–8, 98–99; proximate, 2–3, 4, 305; as system, 296–97. *See also* International context; Politics

Contextual expertise: checklist, 6–9, 10, 305–6; importance, 3–6, 7–8, 165, 295–96, 305–6; of political leaders, 295–96

Contextual intelligence, 4, 312n10

Control culture, 301

Cook, Tim, 134

Corbat, Michael, 265

Corporate governance, 87, 111, 112

Corporate leaders, *see* Business leaders; Chief Executive Officers; Management

Corporations, *see* Businesses

Corruption, 108, 109, 134

Council for Economic Advisers, 156

Council on Foreign Relations, 172

Countrywide Financial, 276

Coursera, 126

Courts, *see* Law; Supreme Court

Crandall, Robert, 194–95

Crawford, Susan, 167

Creativity, 159

Crime: cyber-, 128, 238–39; financial, 276; rates, 247. *See also* Law

Crossroads GPS, 151

Cukier, Kenneth, 123

Cultural change: coarsening, 190–91; leader-follower relations and, 54, 259, 273–75, 292, 301; legacy of 1960s, 187–89, 191–92; in political culture, 54, 273–75, 301; technological change and, 120, 124, 259, 261–62, 279

Culture: civic, 275; corporate, 33; heterogeneity, 195; leadership and, 188–98, 259; meaning, 187; national, 23, 195–96; of 1960s, 21, 187–88, 191–92, 197; popular, 192–93, 195–96, 197–98. *See also* Political culture

Culture wars, 188, 195, 200

Curry, Aaron, 148

Cyberattacks, 128, 238–39

Dangers, *see* Risks; Threats
De Blasio, Bill, 50, 73, 229
Declaration of Independence, 25, 29, 62
Deloitte Consulting, 250
Democracy: American ideology, 30, 34–35; capitalism and, 73; followers, 92, 271–72; inequality in, 271; innovation and, 155; interest groups and, 210, 215–19; leadership in, 16–17, 185–86, 267; Locke's influence, 28; media role, 135; participatory, 271–72, 273; power distribution, 258, 271–72; in private business, 34, 89–90, 92, 301–2; Protestant values and, 44; spread, 34, 290, 291, 301–2. *See also* Elections
Democracy in America (Tocqueville), 18, 23
Democratic Party: economic policies, 66, 68; environmental policies, 226; membership, 55–56; presidential candidates, 137, 281; religious beliefs of voters, 41; voters, 59, 71, 253. *See also* Liberals; Obama, Barack; Political parties
Demographics: birth rates, 247, 249, 342n16; divisions, 203–6; life expectancies, 79, 247; trends, 245, 247–48. *See also* Generations
Deregulation, *see* Regulations
Detroit, bankruptcy, 149, 249–50
Dimon, Jamie, 103, 111, 264, 276
Disabilities, individuals with, 97–98. *See also* Americans with Disabilities Act
Discrimination, employment, 97–98. *See also* Rights revolutions
Diversity: meritocracy, 303; in organizations, 209; racial and ethnic, 247; religious, 40, 41–42, 45, 47, 252. *See also* Gender; Racial groups
Divisions: demographic, 203–6; economic, 200–201; general, 200–206, 300; geographic, 205–6; ideological, 56–58, 79–80, 202–3, 207–9, 300; leadership and, 200, 209; political, 68, 79–80, 199, 202–3; religious, 43, 47; specific, 207–9, 300; in United States, 199–200, 300. *See also* Class; Inequality
Dodd-Frank Act (Wall Street Reform and Consumer Protection Act), 101, 109, 114, 275–76

Doerffer, Tina, 259
Donohue, Thomas, 113
Douglass, Frederick, 19–20
Downes, Larry, 161
Druckenmiller, Stanley, 58–59
Drucker, Peter, 32, 88, 304
Duck Dynasty, 272
Dylan, Bob, 197

East India Company, 14, 106
Eavis, Peter, 201
Eck, Diana, 45
Economic growth: in China, 170; in future, 241–42; innovation and, 106, 156–57; recovery from Great Recession, 71, 110; technological change and, 64, 125; in United States, 65, 66, 180–81, 241–42, 299
Economic Mobility Project, 184
Economic policies: context, 72–73; fiscal, 58–59, 60, 66, 250; New Deal, 65–66, 94, 107, 179; politics and, 66, 67, 68. *See also* Regulations
Economic system: complex problems, 67–71, 72, 73; globalization, 66, 69, 73, 291–92; individual leaders, 65–66, 69, 70, 71, 72–73; politics and, 71–72; problems, 298–99; public understanding of, 62; risks, 241–43; trends, 248–50, 254, 299. *See also* Capitalism
Economist, 245–46, 287
Edmondson, Amy, 92
Education: attainment, 248; charter schools, 145; competition in, 171–72; higher, 180, 184, 204, 248, 272, 304; importance, 143–44; innovation in, 158; laws, 7–8, 98–99, 143; massive open online courses, 126–27; privatization, 145; public funding, 143–45; quality, 79, 145–46, 172; reforms, 145; school safety, 237; standardized test scores, 77, 172; student loans, 184, 253; students with disabilities, 98; of women, 204, 248, 249
Educational leaders: innovation pressures, 158; legal context, 7–8, 98–99; loss of respect for, 262–63; online learning and,

126–27; public views of, 77, 146, 185, 262–63; university presidents, 272, 304

EdX, 126

Eich, Brendan, 111, 273

Elections: campaign contributions, 72, 110, 150–52, 216; congressional, 71, 218, 275; costs, 151; local, 142–43, 274; presidential, 41, 56, 275, 281; turnout, 80, 151–52, 274–75, 302. *See also* Political parties; Politics

Ellison, Larry, 124, 152, 265, 277

Emotional intelligence, 23, 34, 267, 306

Employees: authority, 85; in decentralized organizations, 89–90; of fast-food restaurants, 281; global competition and, 114–15; jobs lost to automation, 125–26; reviews, 277. *See also* Followers; Management; Unions

Employment: discrimination in, 97–98; insecurity, 253; rates, 51; technological change and, 68, 251; of women, 204, 248. *See also* Unemployment

The End of Leadership (Kellerman), 112, 129, 258

Energy, sustainable supplies, 58, 229, 231

Enlightenment, 21, 26, 28

Enron, 108

Entitlement programs, 20, 59, 68, 250. *See also* Social Security

Environmental groups, 224

Environmental problems: awareness, 223; leadership and, 224–32; politicization, 225–28; regulations, 58; wildfires, 240–41. *See also* Climate change

Environmental Protection Agency (EPA), 226–27

Epstein, Joseph, 303–4

Equal Employment Opportunity Commission, 97

Equality: American ideology, 29; in corporate cultures, 33; ideals, 19, 25; increases, 252; Protestant values, 44. *See also* Inequality

Establishment, WASP, 303

Europe: Enlightenment, 21, 26, 28; inequality, 17

Expertise, *see* Contextual expertise

Experts, 189, 190, 238, 239

Explanatory journalism, 133–34

ExxonMobil, 124

Facebook, 121, 124, 131, 136, 251, 263, 277. *See also* Social media

Factions, *see* Interest groups

Families, 247, 249, 252. *See also* Children

Faux, Jeff, 180

Federal government: agencies, 94, 97, 103; budget deficits, 66; complexity, 297; constitutional powers, 16; economic role, 65–66, 73, 94, 107; education funding, 144; effectiveness, 51; financial crisis and, 70–71; growth, 93; leaked documents, 102, 123, 139, 280; lobbyists and, 212–19, 338n22; separation of powers, 16, 26; Social Security, 94, 179, 211, 297, 299; spending and debt, 58–59, 60, 66, 250; trust in, 51–52, 80, 281; welfare programs, 20. *See also* Congress; Presidents; Regulations; Supreme Court

Federal Reserve system, 71, 73, 268

Feingold, Russ, 151

Ferguson, Charles, 111

Films, Westerns, 192, 193

Financial crises, risks, 241–43

Financial crisis (2008): causes, 69–71; criminal prosecutions, 100, 276; effects, 108–9, 111; failure to predict, 234, 254; political responses, 70, 111; public reactions, 71–72, 81–82, 108–9. *See also* Great Recession

Financial sector: complexity, 69–70; criminal prosecutions, 276; growth, 109; leaders, 100, 102, 103–4, 110, 111, 263–65, 276; LIBOR rate-setting scandal, 103; regulations, 70–71, 100–102, 103, 109–10, 242, 263, 264, 275–76; risk management, 264–65; risks, 102–3, 242; "too big to fail" banks, 104; trust in, 81–82, 108–9, 111

Finkelstein, Sydney, 87

Fiorina, Morris, 199

Firms, *see* Businesses

Fiscal policy, 58–59, 60, 66, 250. *See also* Taxes

Flattened hierarchies, 33, 88–89, 189, 267, 268–69, 301–2

Follett, Mary Parker, 31, 244
Follower paradox, 280–82
Followers: balance of power, 129, 271; of business leaders, 30–34, 86–87, 114–15, 305; contempt for leaders, 273–74, 301; independence, 18, 22, 49, 302; leadership industry view of, 2–3; liberties, 25, 27–30; opinions, 190; power, 17, 20, 267–68, 279–82, 291, 301; respect for authority, 188–89, 190, 262, 271, 292; risk management roles, 238; satire of leaders, 261–62; self-interest, 18; strengthened, 257–62, 267–68, 271–74; tension with leaders, 191–93; trade-offs, 28; use of word, 270. *See also* Employees; Political followers
Forbes, 251
Ford, Gerald, 52, 227
Forecasting, *see* Trends
Foreign policy: of Bush, 286–87; challenges, 291; divisions, 207, 208; economic issues, 292; of Obama, 284–85, 287–88; presidential authority, 260–61. *See also* International context
Founders, 13, 16, 18, 26, 29, 39–40, 307
Francis, Pope, 48
Freedom: American ideology, 29; contradiction with slavery, 14–15; of followers, 20, 25, 27–30; religious, 39–40, 41–42; of speech, 215; tension with authority, 191–93, 198
Freelancers Union, 281
Friedman, Lawrence M., 93, 95
Friedman, Thomas, 128, 227
Fries, Michael, 152

Gallup polls, 51, 77
Gardner, Howard, 76
Garton Ash, Timothy, 258
Gates, Bill, 66, 145, 266, 277
Gates, Robert, 80
Gawande, Atul, *The Checklist Manifesto*, 6–7
Gay rights, 20–21, 272–73. *See also* Same-sex marriage
GE, *see* General Electric
Geithner, Timothy, 71
Gelb, Peter, 272–73

Gender: economic relations, 249; income inequality, 204–5, 248, 249; inequality, 271; in politics, 205. *See also* Women
General Electric (GE), 265
Generations: divisions in 1960s, 188; equity, 247; incomes, 182; technological change and, 119–20, 129; younger, 82–83, 182, 253, 279
Genovese, Michael, 267
Gensler, Gary, 103
Geographic divisions, 205–6
Gingrich, Newt, 151, 202
Glass-Steagall Act, 70, 101
Global competition, 79, 152–53, 154, 155, 163–64, 166–73, 284, 285
Globalization: business leadership and, 114–15; economic effects, 66, 69, 73, 291–92; political leadership and, 55
Global warming, *see* Climate change
Goldenberg, Jacob, 159
Goleman, Daniel, 34
Google, 131, 250
Gordon, Robert, 241
Gore, Al, 228, 254
Gorman, James, 264–65
Governments: basic services, 50; distrust of, 3, 50–52, 71–72, 80, 281; education funding, 144; employee pensions, 149–50; ideological conflict over roles, 56, 109–10, 202–3, 252–53; information collected, 123–24; innovation, 157; private sector and, 107–8, 109–10, 242–43; risk management, 237–38, 239–40. *See also* Federal government; Law; Regulations
Great Depression, 20, 65–66, 107. *See also* New Deal
Great Recession, 69–72, 100, 109, 110, 182, 185, 254. *See also* Financial crisis (2008)
Great Society, 180
Greenhouse gases, 225, 231. *See also* Climate change
Greenspan, Alan, 71, 254
Greenwald, Glenn, 280
Groups, *see* Advocacy groups; Interest groups; Membership groups
Gun control issues, 58, 190, 207–8

Haass, Richard, 290

Halpern, Sue, 123

Hamel, Gary, 162

Hamilton County, Ohio, 146

Hansen, Laura, 78

Harvard Business Review, 170, 235

Harvard Business Review Blog Network, 231

Harvard Business School, 113, 168

Harvard Kennedy School: Ash Center for Democratic Governance and Innovation, 157–58; Center for Public Leadership, 76, 141

Harvard University, massive open online courses, 126

Hayek, Friedrich, 66, 68

Health care: authority of physicians, 271; medical liability, 322n24; money in, 329n20

Health insurance, 297. *See also* Medicare; Patient Protection and Affordable Care Act

Hierarchies: class, 17, 64–65; flattened, 33, 88–89, 189, 267, 268–69, 301–2; in organizations, 84–86, 87–89, 90, 267

Higher education, 180, 184, 204, 248, 272, 304. *See also* Education

Hill, Joe, 196

Hispanics, 181, 183, 204, 208, 247

History: change from below, 17, 20, 21; public ignorance, 81; trends, 290; of United States, 13–24, 302, 307

Hitchens, Christopher, 49

Hobbes, Thomas, *Leviathan*, 27–28

Hofstadter, Richard, 63

Holder, Eric, 104

Holiday, Billie, 196

Homeland Security, Department of, 238

House of Representatives: elections, 71; Republican members, 71, 295; speaker, 4–5, 295–96

Housing, 178, 194, 276

Howard, Philip K., 99

Hubbard, Glenn, 69

Huffington Post, 184

Human capital, 88. *See also* Education

Humane Society of the United States, 272

Huntington, Samuel, 29, 30, 44

Hurricane Katrina, 239–40

Hurricane Sandy, 228–29

IBM, 155

Icahn, Carl, 111

Ideology: American, 25–31, 34–35, 307; anti-government, 30, 56–57, 71–72; centrist, 199, 252–53; divisions, 56–58, 79–80, 202–3, 207–9, 300; extremism, 56–57; trends, 252–53

Iger, Robert, 111

Ikenberry, John, 286

Immelt, Jeff, 265

Immigration, 45, 58, 208

Immigration and Nationalities Act of 1965, 45

Income inequality: education and, 144; by gender, 204–5, 248, 249; generational, 182; geographic, 205–6; history, 177–78; increases, 67–68, 109, 181, 182–84, 200–201, 248; by race, 204, 336n15; in United States, 152–53, 299. *See also* Class; Inequality

Incomes: growth, 180; median, 180, 182, 336n15; of middle class, 180, 181–82; of women, 248; of working classes, 180–81, 182. *See also* Chief Executive Officers, compensation; Wages

Independence: of followers, 18, 22, 49, 302; of media, 130

Individualism: American ideology, 29–30; increases, 193–94, 275; in language, 193; Protestant, 44; tension with authority, 191–93, 194

Inequality: in capitalist systems, 63, 64–65, 67–68, 153, 201; in education funding, 144–46; in Europe, 17; gender, 271; growth, 181; political, 17; racial, 271; of slaves, 14–15; socioeconomic, 17, 18–19, 64–65, 67–68, 109, 299. *See also* Class; Equality; Income inequality

Influence: of business leaders, 305; definition, 345n28; exercising, 267–69; of political leaders, 23

Information revolution, 119–20. *See also* Big data; Technological change

Information Technology and Innovation Foundation, 155

Innovation: in business, 158–62; competition with other countries, 154, 155, 171; concerns about, 154–58; economic growth and, 106, 156–57; in education, 158; in local government, 157; military, 158; in past, 154; patents, 155; risk and, 160–61, 162. *See also* Technological change

Instagram, 111, 140, 251

Institutions: decline seen, 74, 299–300; definition, 74; leaders, 75–78; power, 53–54; trust in, 74–80, 81–83, 253

Insurance: health, 297; product liability, 100. *See also* Patient Protection and Affordable Care Act

Interest groups: *Citizens United* decision, 150–51, 215; concerns about, 215–17, 218; corporate, 110; definition, 210, 211; evolution, 210, 211–12; increased number, 211–12, 219; leadership and, 212–19; lobbying, 211, 212–19; political activities, 210–11, 212–19; power, 210, 211, 212, 214, 215–17, 219, 258; websites, 213–14

Internal Revenue Service, 75

International context: actors, 289–90, 293; change in U.S. position, 283–89, 293–94; competition, 154, 155, 163–64, 166–73, 284, 285; economic, 291–92; national power, 288–89; power diffusion, 288–91, 292–94; technological change and, 290. *See also* Foreign policy; Globalization

Internet: bloggers, 135–36, 140; cloud computing, 122; crowdfunding sites, 279; cyberattacks, 128, 238–39; data breaches, 189–90; disclosure of leaked documents, 102, 123, 138–39, 280; growth, 121; interest group websites, 213–14; massive open online courses, 126–27; political satire, 261–62; power diffusion and, 290; product reviews, 279–80; shopping, 253; social and political mobilization, 128–29, 136, 137–38; social media, 53, 136, 140, 194, 259, 261–62, 280; as toolset, 166; tracking users, 123; younger generation and, 119

Investigatory journalism, 132–35

Investors, 111, 266, 277–78, 279

Iran, 136, 139

Iraq war, 132, 139, 207, 278–79, 285, 287, 288

Iron law of oligarchy, 85, 88

Iron triangle, 213

Israel, 208

J.C. Penney, 234

Jefferson, Thomas, 14

Jews, 41, 42, 45. *See also* Judeo-Christian tradition

Jobs, *see* Employment

Johnson, Lyndon B., 52, 180, 183

Johnson, Ron, 234

Jones, Alex S., 132–33

Journalists, 132–35. *See also* Media

JPMorgan Chase, 102–3, 111, 264, 276

Judeo-Christian tradition, 41, 42–43, 44, 45, 48, 179. *See also* Christianity; Jews; Religion

Judicial system, *see* Law

Justice Department, U.S., 101, 134, 276

Kaiser, Robert, 218

Kane, Tim, 278

Katz, Lawrence, 184

Ken Blanchard Companies, 34

Kennedy, John F., 47, 52, 191, 195

Kennedy, Robert F., 52, 195

Keynes, John Maynard, 66, 68

Keystone Pipeline, 227

Kickstarter, 279

King, Desmond, 199–200, 204

King, Martin Luther, Jr.: assassination, 52; "I Have a Dream" speech, 46; "Letter from Birmingham Jail," 20, 43; as preacher, 43; view of leadership, 313n23

Klinenberg, Eric, 194

"Kludgeocracy," 297

Knowledge-based journalism, 133–34, 350n18

Knowledge workers, 88

Knowles, Scott Gabriel, 237

Koch, Charles and David, 142–43

Kodak, 251

Krauthammer, Charles, 285
Kupchan, Charles, 171

Labor force, skills, 114–15. *See also*
    Employees; Employment
Labor laws, 179
Labor unions, *see* Unions
Lambert, Frank, 43
Language, individualistic, 193
Lanier, Jared, 251
Law: corporate, 95; in education, 7–8,
    98–99, 143; evolution, 93–95; harmful
    effects, 99, 100; labor, 179; leadership
    and, 95–104; litigation costs, 102–3; liti-
    gious culture, 7, 96–97, 99, 101–3; medi-
    cal liability, 322n24; product liability,
    99–100; reforms, 104; tax code, 94, 297.
    See also Supreme Court
Lawyers, 95, 96, 101, 102–3
Leaders: apologies, 189–90; influence,
    267–69, 305; isolation, 194–95; loss of
    power and authority, 257–68, 273–74,
    291, 292, 301; military, 158, 189, 278–79,
    311n6, 347n18; mistakes, 234, 262–63,
    300; pressures on, 300–301, 305; public
    confidence levels, 3, 75–80, 83, 141, 301;
    religious, 43–44, 311n6, 313n23; traits and
    characteristics, 306–7; WASP establish-
    ment, 303. *See also* Business leaders;
    Educational leaders; Political leaders
Leadership: competencies, 267; constraints,
    25, 26–27, 28, 29, 30; current challenges,
    9–10; as mission, 307; opportunities,
    185–86; shared, 260; as system, 2, 296,
    306; use of word, 35; weakening, 257–68,
    301, 303–5. *See also* Context
Leadership crisis, 35, 77, 185, 302
Leadership industry: advice, 267; books,
    114; coaching, 114; criticism of, 1, 2–3,
    306; fixation on leaders, 2, 33, 306;
    growth, 120, 297–98; perceived crisis, 35;
    risk management, 235–36; soft skills, 23,
    34; training and development, 114, 305;
    view of followers, 2–3
Legal system, *see* Law; Lawyers
Le Roy, Michael, 148
Lessig, Lawrence, 150

Leviathan (Hobbes), 27–28
Levin, Carl, 102
Levin, Rick, 126
Lewinsky, Monica, 131, 190–91
Liberals: gun control policies, 207–8;
    number of, 252; polarization, 68, 79–80;
    religion and, 41, 44, 47, 252; support of
    financial regulation, 109; views of gov-
    ernment roles, 56, 67, 202–3, 252–53. *See
    also* Democratic Party
Liberty, *see* Freedom
Life expectancies, 79, 247
Lincoln, Abraham, 19, 20, 24, 30, 40–41, 42
Liu, John, 103
Lobbying: by businesses, 214–15; expenses,
    214, 215, 217, 338n22; by former members
    of Congress, 152; by interest groups, 211,
    212–19; restrictions, 217; techniques,
    213–14
Locke, John, 26, 28, 62
Loeb, Daniel, 277–78
Loneliness, 193–94
Los Angeles, mayoral election, 274
Luce, Edward, 217

Mack, John, 264
Madison, James, 15–16, 26, 107, 210
Major League Baseball, 146
Management: levels, 86, 88–89; scholarship,
    31–34; styles, 32; teams, 90–92; top-down,
    84, 106. *See also* Business leaders; Chief
    Executive Officers
Mandelbaum, Michael, 227, 292
Mann, Thomas, 200, 202
Manning, Bradley/Chelsea, 102, 139
Manufacturing automation, 125–26
Many hands, problem of, 70
Manziel, Johnny, 147
Marriages: ages, 194; economic benefits,
    249; trends, 247. *See also* Same-sex
    marriage
Martin, Trayvon, 203
Marx, Karl, 179
Massachusetts Institute of Technology
    (MIT), 126
Massive open online courses (MOOCs),
    126–27

Mayer-Schoenberger, Viktor, 123
McAfee, Andrew, 125
McCain, John, 41, 336n10
McConnell, Mitch, 80
McGonagill, Grady, 259
McGregor, Douglas, 32, 86–87
McHenry, Patrick, 273
McLanahan, Sara, 249
MD Anderson Cancer Center, 329n20
Media: adversarial journalism, 280;
    broadcast, 131, 289; business leaders
    and, 139–40; change in, 80, 131, 132–33,
    135–41; conglomerates, 80, 131; financial
    crisis and, 71, 72; global, 289; history in
    United States, 130–31; independence,
    130; investigatory journalism, 132–35;
    knowledge-based journalism, 133–34,
    350n18; leaders, 141; new, 54, 131, 135–41,
    326n6; political leadership and, 54–55,
    131, 132, 133, 135, 274; public participa-
    tion, 140, 141; role in democracies, 135;
    technological change, 54–55, 131; trust in,
    78, 141; watchdog role, 130, 132. *See also*
    Social media
Medical liability law, 322n24
Medicare, 59, 180, 211
Medicine, *see* Health care
Membership groups, 185–86, 194, 211. *See
    also* Interest groups
Menlo Innovations, 90
Menlo Park, California, 206
Meritocracy, 303
Merkel, Angela, 261
Metropolitan Opera, 272–73
Mexico, Walmart corruption, 134
Meyer, Robert, 240
Michels, Robert, 85, 88
Microsoft, 214–15, 266, 277
Middle class: growth, 64, 178, 179–80; hol-
    lowed-out, 201, 251; incomes, 180, 181–82;
    jobs lost to automation, 125–26; political
    power, 281; shrinking, 67; size, 182. *See
    also* Class
Miles Group, 113
Military leaders, 158, 189, 278–79, 311n6,
    347n18
Military power, 287, 292

Mill, John Stuart, *On Liberty*, 28–30
MIT, *see* Massachusetts Institute of
    Technology
Money: campaign contributions, 72, 110,
    150–52, 216; dysfunctional distribution,
    298–99; in education, 143–45; in health
    care, 329n20; in politics, 142–43, 149–52,
    214–17, 298; power and, 142–43, 153; in
    sports, 146–49. *See also* Economic sys-
    tem; Incomes
MOOCs, *see* Massive open online courses
Moonves, Leslie, 152
Morgan, Edmund, 14, 35
Morgan Stanley, 264–65
Morgenson, Gretchen, 276
Mozilla, 111, 273
Music: popular, 196, 197–98; protest songs,
    196–97

Naim, Moises, 112, 258
National Basketball Association (NBA), 146
National cultures, 23, 195–96
National Football League (NFL), 146, 147–48
National Governors Association, 156–57
National Intelligence Council, 245, 260–61
National Labor Relations Board, 147
National Leadership Index, 76–77
Nation-states: global competition, 163–64,
    166–73, 284, 285; leadership of interna-
    tional system, 288–89; relative power,
    260–61, 292–93. *See also* Foreign policy;
    International context
Native American religions, 39
Natural disasters, 223, 228–29, 239–41
NBA, *see* National Basketball Association
Net Generation, 119–20, 129
New Deal, 65–66, 94, 107, 179
New Orleans, Hurricane Katrina, 239–40
Newspapers, 132–35, 141. *See also* Media
Newsweek, 81
New York, 90
New York City: Center for Economic
    Opportunity, 157; educational leaders,
    262–63; Hurricane Sandy, 228–29; may-
    ors, 50, 228–29; tenements, 178
New York Times, 114, 132, 134, 142–43, 262,
    327n26

NFL, *see* National Football League
9/11 terrorist attacks, 53, 234, 236–37, 285–87
Nixon, Richard M., 52, 195, 227
Noah, Timothy, 200, 201
Nocera, Joe, 147
No Child Left Behind Act, 143
Nooyi, Indra, 45
Nordhaus, William, 232
Norris, Floyd, 73, 263
North Royalton (Ohio) City School
    District, 98
Nunes, Paul, 161
Nye, Joseph, 258, 260–61, 290

Obama, Barack: accomplishments, 51;
    Afghanistan war and, 139; approval rat-
    ings, 51, 72; climate change policies, 226;
    economic experience, 73; on education,
    143; on equal rights, 20–21; failings, 6,
    305, 312n12; family, 195; financial cri-
    sis and, 70, 72; foreign policy, 284–85,
    287–88; presidential campaigns, 41,
    136–37, 151–52, 216–17, 281; relations with
    Congress, 57, 260; religious groups and,
    40; on Trayvon Martin case, 203
Obamacare, *see* Patient Protection and
    Affordable Care Act
Occupy Movement, 73, 110, 181, 183, 197
Oklahoma, University of, 146–47
Online learning, 126–27
Oracle, 124, 265, 277
Organizations: authority in, 84–85; change
    in, 88–92; complex contexts, 91; decen-
    tralized, 89–90; diversity in, 209; flat-
    tened hierarchies, 33, 88–89, 189, 267,
    268–69, 301–2; hierarchical, 84–86,
    87–89, 90, 267; iron law of oligarchy, 85,
    88; large, 84; leaderless, 89–90; leaders,
    85, 86, 90–91; political context, 92. *See
    also* Management
Organized labor, *see* Unions
Ornstein, Norman, 200, 202
Outsiders, 283. *See also* International context
Owens, Christine, 69
*Oxford Handbook of Climate Change and
    Society*, 224
Oz, Mehmet, 271

Packer, George, 299–300, 303
PACs, *see* Political action committees
Paine, Thomas, *Common Sense*, 15
Patents, 155
Paterno, Joe, 262
Patient Protection and Affordable Care Act
    (Obamacare), 51, 260, 322n24
Patterson, Thomas, 133
Paulson, Henry, 71
Pensions, 101–2, 149–50, 249–50. *See also*
    Retirement savings; Social Security
PepsiCo., 45, 266
Petraeus, David, 189, 278
Pew Research Center, 46, 47, 51, 133, 182,
    246, 260
Piketty, Thomas, 68, 201
Pinker, Steven, 21
Polarization, political, 68, 79–80, 199, 202–
    3. *See also* Divisions; Ideology
Political action committees (PACs), 216
Political culture: anti-authority attitudes,
    17–18, 22, 54, 79; change in, 54, 273–75,
    301; civility, 57, 274; democratic, 301
Political followers: activists, 273; alienation,
    51, 55–56, 274–75; apathy, 80, 151–52, 274–
    75, 302; blame shared by, 58–59; centrists,
    199, 252–53; civic participation, 185–86,
    194, 275, 302; criticism of leaders, 54, 298;
    in democracies, 271–72; engagement, 275,
    302; grassroots mobilization, 56, 137–38,
    140; ignorance, 80–81, 302; polarization,
    202; power, 53, 271–72, 291, 294, 305;
    social media use, 53, 128–29, 136; town
    hall meetings, 273; turnout for elections,
    80, 151–52, 274–75, 302. *See also* Ideology;
    Public opinion; Resistance and rebellion
Political leaders: assassinations, 52–53;
    challenges, 23, 258, 273–74; comity, 57;
    constraints, 35, 261; contextual exper-
    tise, 295–96; in democracies, 16–17, 18,
    258, 261; disconnect from public, 58,
    190; distrust of, 185, 274, 302; failures,
    4–6, 61, 300; financial crisis and, 103;
    fundraising, 72, 110, 150–52, 216; interest
    groups and, 212–19; isolation, 195; loss of
    power and authority, 92, 258, 273–74, 291;
    media coverage, 131, 132, 133, 135; public

views of, 50–52, 61, 78, 79–80, 274; risk management, 237–38; scandals, 102, 131, 190–91; self-interest, 67; technological change and, 127–29. *See also* Democracy; Presidents

Political parties: decline, 55–56; dominance of major, 281; extremists, 5, 56–57, 58, 79–80, 199. *See also* Democratic Party; Republican Party

Politics: climate change issue, 225–28, 231–32; complex problems, 59–60; compromises, 199, 208–9, 227; dysfunctional system, 57–58, 60–61, 67, 80, 300; endogenous problems, 55–60; exogenous problems, 52–55; gender gap, 205; globalization and, 55; media coverage, 131, 132; money in, 142–43, 149–52, 214–17, 298; online mobilization, 128–29, 136, 137–38; polarization, 68, 79–80, 199, 202–3; public ignorance, 80–81, 302; public opinion, 207–9; religion and, 40, 41, 42–44, 47–48; satire, 261–62. *See also* Congress; Ideology; Interest groups

Popular culture: exports, 195–96; films, 192, 193; heroes, 192–93; music, 196, 197–98

Population, *see* Demographics

Populism, 56–57, 138, 202

Porter, Eduardo, 143–44

Porter, Michael, 164–67

Poverty: children in, 109, 183, 249; education and, 144; increases, 67, 109, 248; persistence, 183, 184; in United States, 64; urban, 178; war on, 180, 183. *See also* Inequality

Power: of business leaders, 87, 90, 106, 110–12, 113–15, 263, 264, 265; decline, 257–68, 273–74, 291, 292, 301; definition, 345n28; in democracies, 258, 271–72; devolution, 258–61; distribution, 250, 258, 271–72, 288–91, 292–94; fear of, 26; of followers, 17, 20, 129, 267–68, 271, 279–82, 291, 301; of institutions, 53–54; of interest groups, 210, 211, 212, 214, 215–17, 219, 258; in international context, 260–61, 283–91, 292–94; military, 287, 292; money and, 142–43, 153; of political followers, 53, 271–72, 291, 294, 305; of political leaders,

23, 92, 258, 273–74, 291; soft, 196, 287. *See also* Authority

Precarious work, 253

Predictions, *see* Trends

Presidents: authority, 260; constitutional powers, 27; economic advisers, 73; effectiveness, 52, 72, 73; elections, 41, 56, 275, 281; families, 195; former, 152; inaugural address themes, 42; isolation, 195; limits on power, 26–27, 260; privacy, 191; public views of, 51, 72, 78, 281; relations with Congress, 57; religion and, 40–42. *See also* Foreign policy; Obama, Barack

Press, *see* Media; Newspapers

Privacy, 123–24, 191, 193–94

Private property, *see* Property rights

Private sector, *see* Businesses

Privatization, in education, 145

Product liability law, 99–100

Property rights, 62–63, 107

Property taxes, 144

Protestant ethic, 63

Protestants: African American churches, 41, 43; civil rights movement and, 42–43; Evangelical, 41, 252; liberal, 41, 252; Puritans, 39; in United States, 40, 41, 47; values, 44, 63, 179; WASPs, 303. *See also* Christianity

Protests: Occupy Movement, 73, 110, 181, 183, 197; against Vietnam War, 21, 197. *See also* Civil rights movement

Protest songs, 196–97

Public administration, 87. *See also* Governments

Public confidence, *see* Trust

Public opinion: on business leaders, 92, 108–9, 110–11, 112; on climate change, 226; on Congress, 51, 78, 274, 281; divisions, 207–9, 252; on educational leaders, 77, 146, 185, 262–63; on political leaders, 50–52, 61, 78, 79–80, 274; in politics, 58, 190, 207–9; on presidents, 51, 72, 78, 281; on U.S. decline, 51; on U.S. power, 284–85

Public schools, *see* Education

Puritans, 39

Putin, Vladimir, 290

Putnam, Robert D., 47, 194

Quakers, 41–42

Racial groups: affirmative action, 208; diversity, 247; divisions, 203–4; economic inequality, 204, 336n15; improved relations, 252; inequality, 271; WASPs, 303; wealth differences, 181. *See also* African Americans
Railroads, 84, 106
Rating agencies, 101
Rational-legal authority, 84–85, 88, 91
Raymond, Lee, 264
Reagan, Ronald, 40–41, 52, 66, 195, 227
Recessions, *see* Great Recession
Reckhow, Sarah, 145
Regulations: compliance officers, 96–98; environmental, 58; financial services, 70–71, 100–102, 103, 109–10, 242, 263, 264, 275–76; growth, 94, 107, 179; product safety, 100
Rehabilitation Act, Section 504, 98
Reid, Harry, 80
Religion: definition, 40; diversity, 40, 41–42, 45, 47, 252; divisions, 43, 47; freedom of, 39–40, 41–42; importance in America, 40–41, 44, 45–47; Judaism, 41, 42, 45; Judeo-Christian tradition, 41, 42–43, 44, 45, 48, 179; leadership and, 43–46, 47, 48–49, 311n6, 313n23; major traditions, 41; Native American, 39; organized, 47, 77; politics and, 40, 41, 42–44, 47–48; separation of church and state, 39–40; social reform movements, 179; unaffiliated individuals, 41, 46–49, 252. *See also* Christianity
Republican Party: divisions, 295; economic policies, 59, 66, 68; environmental policies, 226, 227–28; House members, 71, 295; membership, 55–56; religious beliefs of voters, 41; voters, 59, 71. *See also* Conservatives; Political parties; Tea Party
Resistance and rebellion: anti-authority attitudes, 17–18, 22, 54; in colonial America, 14, 17; in developing countries, 302. *See also* American Revolution; Protests
Retirement savings, 250, 297. *See also* Pensions

Revolutionary War, *see* American Revolution
Rich, Frank, 134, 141
Ricks, Thomas, 278–79
Ridley, Matt, 246
Rights: of animals, 21, 272, 346n2; individual, 19, 27–30, 34–35; litigious culture and, 99; property, 62–63, 107; Protestant values, 44; of women, 20, 21. *See also* Democracy; Freedom
Rights revolutions: cultural change, 138; effects, 21, 34–35, 88, 212, 259, 271; gay rights, 20–21, 272–73; legal changes, 94, 99; ongoing, 187. *See also* Civil rights movement; Same-sex marriage
Riis, Jacob, 178
Ringen, Stein, 50–51, 79
Risks: black swan events, 234, 243, 245; climate change, 55, 224, 228–29, 230–31, 232; complexity and, 234; external, 234–35, 236–43; of financial crises, 241–43; general, 235; in innovation, 160–61, 162; internal, 233–34; legal, 102–3; managing, 233, 235–36, 237–41, 242–43; natural disasters, 239–41; proliferation, 301; specific, 235; terrorism, 236–39, 285–86
Robertson, Phil, 272
Robeson, Paul, 196–97
Robots, 125–26
Rockefeller, John D., 178
Romney, Mitt, 47, 72, 137, 181–82
Roosevelt, Franklin Delano, 20, 65–66, 94, 107, 179, 191, 303
Rothko, Mark, 153
Rothkopf, David, 111
Rove, Karl, 151
Rule of law, 30, 93. *See also* Law
Rural areas, 206
Russia, 260, 261, 273, 287. *See also* Soviet Union

SAC Capital Advisors, 101
St. Louis University, 272
Same-sex marriage, 22, 187, 205, 207, 252, 273, 314n26. *See also* Gay rights
Satire, political, 261–62
Savings, retirement, 250, 297

Scandals: corporate, 108; financial, 103; military, 278; political, 102, 131, 190–91

Schmidt, Eric, 250, 251

Schneiderman, Eric, 103

Schools, *see* Education

Science, synthetic biology, 253. *See also* Climate change

Seabright, Jeffrey, 231

SEC, *see* Securities and Exchange Commission

Secularization, 46–49

Securities and Exchange Commission (SEC), 94, 101, 103, 134, 276

Seib, Gerald, 61

Self-interest: checks on, 26; economic, 63, 111; of political leaders, 67

Senate, supermajorities, 57–58. *See also* Congress

September 11 terrorist attacks, 53, 234, 236–37, 285–87

Service industries, automation, 125, 126

Shays' Rebellion, 15

Shemella, Paul, 238

Sherman Antitrust Act, 94, 107

Shultz, George, 227

Silicon Valley, 206

Simpson-Bowles plan, 60

Skocpol, Theda, 185–86

Slater, Philip, 193–94

Slavery, 14–15, 19–20, 22, 25

Smith, Rogers, 199–200, 204

Snowden, Edward, 102, 123, 139, 280, 290

Social class, *see* Class

Social contract, 28, 179, 300, 302

Socialism, 179, 196

Social media, 53, 128–29, 136, 140, 194, 259, 261–62, 280. *See also* Facebook

Social Security, 94, 179, 211, 297, 299

Societal trustees, 76

Sotheby's, 277–78

Southern Christian Leadership Conference, 43

Soviet Union, dissolution, 290–91. *See also* Cold War; Russia

Special interests, *see* Interest groups

Specter, Michael, 271

Spencer Stuart, 112

Sports, money in, 146–49

Stakeholders, 33, 87, 113, 230, 265, 266, 277–78. *See also* Investors

Standard & Poor's, 101

Steinhafel, Gregg, 189–90

Steubenville (Ohio) rape case, 140, 327n26

Stewart, Jon, 262

Stiglitz, Joseph, 183, 201

Stock market crash, 65

Strategic analysis, 164–65

Student loans, 184, 253

Sullivan, Andrew, 78

Summers, Lawrence, 234

Supreme Court, 150–51, 215

Surowiecki, James, 279–80

Syria, 260, 285

Taleb, Nassim, 234, 235

Tapscott, Don, 119, 120

Target, 189–90

Taxes: complexity, 297; income, 94; liberal and conservative views, 202–3; property, 144

Taylor, Paul, 246, 260

Teams, 32, 33, 89, 90–92

Tea Party (political movement): antigovernment ideology, 56, 72; Boehner and, 5, 295; cohesion, 282; effectiveness, 56–57, 282; emergence, 5, 56, 72, 73, 137–38, 202, 203; immigration policies, 208; members, 138, 281; power, 203

Tea Party, Boston, 14

Technological change: automation, 125–26; big data, 122–23, 124; complexity, 121–23, 251, 298; cultural change and, 120, 124, 259, 261–62, 279; disruptive, 159–62; economic growth and, 64, 125; employment and, 68, 251; in future, 250–51; generational differences, 119–20, 129; incremental, 159; information revolution, 119–20; leadership and, 53–54, 119–29, 250–51, 259–60, 298; news media, 54–55, 131; organizations and, 88; power diffusion and, 290; speed, 121, 124, 127, 161–62; as threat, 124, 159–60, 161–62. *See also* Internet

Teitel, Stanley, 262–63

Teles, Steven, 297

Terrorism: 9/11 attacks, 53, 234, 236–37, 285–87; Boston Marathon bombing, 243; cyber-, 238–39; definition, 237; groups, 289; risks, 236–39, 285–86

Tetlock, Philip, 246

Texas A&M University, 147

Theory X and Theory Y, 32, 86–87

Threats: leadership and, 301; technological change as, 124, 159–60, 161–62. *See also* Risks

Time Warner, 131, 215

Tisch, Laurence, 45

Tocqueville, Alexis de, *Democracy in America*, 18, 23

Tomblin, Earl Ray, 50

Trade unions, *see* Unions

Trends: demographic, 245, 247–48; economic, 248–50, 254, 299; ideological, 252–53; implications for leaders, 253–54; mega-, 245; predicting future, 244–46, 254; technological, 250–51

Truman, Harry, 152, 195

Trust and distrust: in business leaders, 108–9; in financial sector, 81–82, 108–9, 111; in governments, 3, 50–52, 71–72, 80, 281; in institutions, 74–80, 81–83, 253; in leaders, 185; in media, 78, 141; in political leaders, 185, 274, 302; repairing trust, 81–82

Twitter, 121, 128, 131, 136, 140

Udacity, 126

Unemployment, 51, 68–69, 109, 115, 125, 126, 242. *See also* Employment

Unions: collective bargaining, 94; college sports, 147; declining membership, 69, 114, 280–81; of freelancers, 281; influence, 179; legal protections, 179; pension funds, 101–2; political spending, 150; pro sports, 146; public-sector, 149. *See also* Interest groups

United States: Civil War, 19–20, 42; Constitution, 15–16, 26–27, 30, 93; decline seen, 51, 60, 156, 241–42, 284–86, 298, 299–300; divisions, 199–200, 300; economic growth, 65, 66, 180–81, 299; economic stagnation, 152–53, 241–42; foreign policy, 207, 208, 260–61, 284–85, 286–88, 291, 292; founding myths, 13; history, 13–24, 302, 307; ideology, 25–31, 34–35, 307; military power, 287, 292; power in international context, 283–88, 293–94; unique characteristics, 17, 22; WASP establishment, 303. *See also* Federal government

U.S. Chamber of Commerce, 216

Useem, Michael, 2–3

Valve Corporation, 90

Vietnam War, 21, 131, 197, 326n3

Violence, gun, 207–8, 237. *See also* Terrorism

Visalia, California, 206

Volcker Rule, 101

Voters, *see* Elections; Political followers

Wages: living, 281; minimum, 281–82; in nineteenth century, 178; stagnation, 115, 152, 180–81. *See also* Incomes

Wall Street, *see* Financial sector; Stock market crash

Wall Street Journal, 90, 102, 123, 266

Wall Street Reform and Consumer Protection (Dodd-Frank) Act, 101, 109, 114, 275–76

Walmart, 134

Walt Disney Co., 111

Washington, *see* Congress; Political culture

Washington, George, 13, 14, 16, 40–42

Washington Post, 268–69

WASPs, *see* White Anglo-Saxon Protestants

Wealth, *see* Class; Inequality; Money

Weber, Max, 63, 84–85, 88

Websites, *see* Internet

Wells Fargo, 276

Wen Jiabao, 134

"We Shall Overcome," 197

White Anglo-Saxon Protestants (WASPs), 303

Whites, *see* Racial groups

WikiLeaks, 138–39. *See also* Assange, Julian

Wilcox, Clyde, 214
Wildfires, 240–41
Wilson, Woodrow, 191
Women: business leaders, 45, 205; childless, 342n16; education, 204, 248, 249; employment, 204, 248; equal rights, 20, 21; incomes, 248, 249; skills, 249. *See also* Gender
Wood, Gordon, 106–7
Woodward, Bob, 134
Work, *see* Employment
Work ethic, 63, 64

Working classes, 178–79, 180–81, 182, 183. *See also* Class; Poverty
World Economic Forum, "The Global Competitiveness Report," 169–70

Yosemite National Park, 240–41

Zakaria, Fareed, 167–68
Zimmerman, George, 203
Zirin, Dave, 146
ZTE, 155
Zuckerberg, Mark, 124, 145, 263, 277